P9-BAT-682

THE
CONFESSIONS
OF
AL CAPONE

BOOKS BY LOREN D. ESTLEMAN

Kill Zone

Roses Are Dead

Any Man's Death

Motor City Blue

Angel Eyes

The Midnight Man

The Glass Highway

Sugartown

Every Brilliant Eye

Lady Yesterday

Downriver

Silent Thunder

Sweet Women Lie

Never Street

The Witchfinder

The Hours of the Virgin

A Smile on the Face of the Tiger

City of Widows*

The High Rocks*

Billy Gashade*

Stamping Ground*

Aces & Eights*

Journey of the Dead*

Jitterbug*

Thunder City*

The Rocky Mountain Moving Picture
    Association*

The Master Executioner*

Black Powder, White Smoke*

White Desert*

Sinister Heights

Something Borrowed, Something Black*

Port Hazard*

Poison Blonde*

Retro*

Little Black Dress*

Nicotine Kiss*

The Undertaker's Wife*

The Adventures of Johnny Vermillion*

American Detective*

Gas City*

Frames*

The Branch and the Scaffold*

Alone*

The Book of Murdock*

Roy & Lillie: A Love Story*

The Left-Handed Dollar*

Infernal Angels*

Burning Midnight*

Alive!*

The Confessions of Al Capone*

*A Forge Book

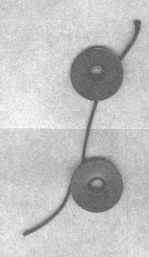

THE
CONFESSIONS
OF
AL CAPONE

Loren D. Estleman

A Tom Doherty Associates Book

New York

This is a work of fiction. All of the characters, organizations, and events portrayed in this novel are either products of the author's imagination or are used fictitiously.

THE CONFESSIONS OF AL CAPONE

Edited by James Frenkel

A Forge Book
Published by Tom Doherty Associates, LLC
175 Fifth Avenue
New York, NY 10010

www.tor-forge.com

Forge® is a registered trademark of Tom Doherty Associates, LLC.

Library of Congress Cataloging-in-Publication Data

Estleman, Loren D.
    The Confessions of Al Capone / Loren D. Estleman.—First edition.
      p. cm.
    "A Tom Doherty Associates book."
    ISBN 978-0-7653-3119-9 (hardcover)
    ISBN 978-1-4299-4325-3 (e-book)
    1. Capone, Al, 1899–1947—Fiction.   2. Criminals—Illinois—Chicago—Fiction.
3. Gangsters—Illinois—Chicago—Fiction.   4. Biographical fiction.   I. Title.
    PS3555.S84C66   2013
    813'.54—dc23
                                           2012043861

Forge books may be purchased for educational, business, or promotional use. For information on bulk purchases, please contact Macmillan Corporate and Premium Sales Department at 1-800-221-7945 extension 5442 or write specialmarkets@macmillan.com.

First Edition: June 2013

Printed in the United States of America

0 9 8 7 6 5 4 3 2 1

This book is lovingly dedicated to the memory of my parents,
Leauvett and Louise Estleman. Most of what I know
about the times in this book, they told me.

ACKNOWLEDGMENTS

Thanks to Carl W. Thompson, a friend and divinity scholar, and knowledgeable colleagues in the writers' group in Beverly Hills, Michigan, for their counsel on Catholicism. Any mistakes that occur in that area are mine.

Nobody's on the legit.

—*Alphonse Capone*

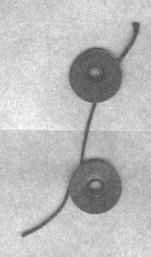

1944

AN ELEPHANT IN THE ICE BOX

ONE

AN INVITATION TO THE DIRECTOR'S OFFICE ALWAYS MEANT TERMINATION. Even a man without faith could depend on that.

It was waiting for him on his desk, in a large brown interoffice envelope tied with red string, neatly typed in elite characters on the same undersize stationery the Director had used to congratulate the men who killed Dillinger:

Peter Vasco
Division Four
Records and Communications

Dear Mr. Vasco:

The Director would appreciate your presence at the SOG at 1400 hours this date.

    (signed)
    Helen W. Gandy

Gandy was the Director's executive assistant: "Hoover's secretary" to the unindoctrinated. She'd sat outside his door since his appointment to the General Investigation Division in 1919, and had processed every decision he'd made from the start, including converting to the military timetable after Pearl Harbor. SOG stood for Seat of Government. In early days this had referred to headquarters' location in the District, but more recently it had become shorthand for the Director's own office, and by extension the Director himself.

To compare the Bureau to a beehive was a cliché, but clichés are nothing if not accurate. At the center was the queen—a career-destroying description if overheard, given the rumors that circulated among the Director's enemies on the Hill. The field agents were the scouts swarming outside, while the drones inside worked around the clock to maintain the hive. Vasco was the drone of drones, assigned to proofread non-classified instructions to Special Agents in Charge and the odd innocuous press release for errors of spelling and grammar. The aptitude test he'd taken when he applied for employment had shown a high degree of stenographic ability; with no background in law or accountancy he'd hardly hoped for a field position, but it was dreary, tedious work, with the added inducement of a reprimand in his file if a single participle continued to dangle once it left his desk. The smallest blunder festered throughout the system and had to be cauterized at the source.

Evidently a proper noun had escaped capitalization or, worse, a live document had been swept into the wastebasket with the day's litter and sent directly to the incinerator where obsolete secrets were interred in the ashes. Vasco wasn't incompetent on the job, merely indifferent to it. That hadn't always been the case, but after nearly a year shackled to the same tin desk in a room filled with them, his hopes for advancement had died—pounded flat by the incessant artillery barrage of booming drawers and typewriters thundering on metal stands. He suspected that on some subconscious level he'd realized that consistency and reliability counted against change rather than for it, and had sabotaged himself deliberately.

Shrink talk. Swallow two opiates with water and say three Hail Marys. The Director had no use for either, and these days neither did he.

Whatever the nature of the dereliction, it was beneath the attention of a man concerned with keeping Fifth Column spies out of the War Department; but the Director had been known to take interest in petty personnel matters. He'd fired a veteran inspector for reporting in from sixteen hours of surveillance with his shirttail hanging outside his vest. Vasco's own supervisor had forgotten to wear the regulation fedora in a press photo and forfeited his chance to head up the Detroit office.

The morning dragged past on flat tires. He ate a sack lunch, an egg salad sandwich provided by ration stamps he'd been hoarding, but it might as well have been boiled pulp for all he tasted it. At quarter to two he walked up the aisle between rows of desks, a condemned man resigned to his fate. His colleagues discovered a sudden fascination with their little correction marks as he passed. They all knew about the envelope. For an organization dedicated to national security—it had practically coined the phrase—the Bureau was the whisperingest place outside the community rooms across America where mothers and daughters turned peach pits into weapons-grade cyanide.

Stepping off the elevator on the fifth floor, he followed a beige hallway carpeted in navy—Justice Department colors—and lined with diversions. Inside brushed-aluminum frames Hoover shook hands with presidents and movie stars, squinted through a tommy gun sight, and walked his cairn terrier, G-Boy, beside the Potomac. Arsenals bequeathed by various bandit gangs shared glass cases with heroic G-man movie posters, pieces of exploded hand grenades, a replica of the Justice building assembled from popsicle sticks, and bulletproof vests hemorrhaging steel wool out of vicious holes torn in the fabric. The Black Museum, senior agents called the display. A small library of books in shiny jackets arranged face out bore Hoover's name as either the author or the contributor of a foreword. Ghostwritten, every one, but doubtless the galley proofs had passed across his desk and then those of Vasco's superiors in Records and Communications, to eliminate heresies and stray commas. John Dillinger's morgue session had a case to itself, including bits of federal lead dug from his corpse and the infamous shot of the bank robber's storied twelve-inch erection skewing the line of the sheet covering him. The visitor searched in vain for the actual member preserved in a jar of alcohol. Another myth shattered: but at the Bureau there was no shortage of legends even in wartime. They issued forth like bombers from an assembly line and took flight immediately.

Despite all the sniping from inside and outside the hive, and perhaps partly because of it, Vasco's admiration for the Director bordered on worship. (Patton's men, it was said, smirked at the general's jodhpurs and pearl-handled pistols, but would follow him into hell.) A twenty-four-year-old U.S. attorney with little experience, Hoover had taken charge of a government agency created for the sole purpose of political patronage, turned out the rascals by guile and force, and within a few years transformed it into the most efficient police department in the world. Vasco was fourteen when Hoover made international headlines by singlehandedly arresting Alvin Karpis, Public Enemy Number One, after Karpis had boasted publicly that he would kill Hoover for the slaying of his outlaw friends the Barkers in Florida. A newspaper photo of the Director leading the murderer-kidnapper in manacles into the Federal Building in St. Paul had gone up on the wall in Vasco's bedroom between Jesus and the Pope.

He hesitated before the door to the reception room. He'd never met the man who'd hired him, had seen him in person only from a distance, presenting badges to graduates of the training course during the turning-out ceremony. This was his first time on the executive floor. Opening the door was like taking the Eucharist; there was no going back. He wiped his palm on his trousers and twisted the knob.

Miss Gandy—as it was with Hoover, there was no spouse in her life, but dirty-minded rumors withered in the monastic atmosphere that hung over this Vatican—sat behind an ordinary desk in command of extraordinary equipment: intercom, black bulbous telephone with rows of buttons lit up like a movie marquee, a Dictaphone player, an Electromatic Typewriter the size of a radio-phonograph on a stout table placed perpendicular to the desk. She was chugging away at the last. At her back, a larger table supported a similar machine linked to a Teletype, waiting to receive and decode ciphers from the White House and Pentagon. Vasco recognized this arrangement from the March of Time, dozens of Siamese-twin machines chuckling in a big room in an undisclosed location, but hadn't thought he'd ever find himself in the presence of one. It was an imposing sight, and incongruous in view of the unprepossessing figure in charge.

If Helen Gandy had ever been photographed, Vasco had missed the result. She took no visible role in official functions. Yet another legend insisted that she had a private apartment in the building and hadn't ventured outside since the Coolidge Administration, preferring to serve her master day and night in the holy war against criminal rats, the Nazi-American Bund, and Eleanor Roosevelt. In the dense mist of such speculation, Vasco forgave himself the mental picture of a sour-faced spinster in black bombazine, lace-ruffled to the throat, spectacles constricting the blue veins in her nose. Any one of the sisters of St. Francis could have served as the model.

What he saw, when she swiveled to face him, was a pleasant-faced redhead in her midforties with freckles on her cheeks, wearing a pale green blazer lightly padded in the shoulders, jet buttons in her ears, and a necklace of the same polished coal stones around her neck. She smiled at him with slightly crooked teeth.

"Mr. Vasco? Most punctual. I'm Helen Gandy. The Director asked me to show you in the moment you arrived."

"Thank you." Traumatic thought: What if he'd been thirty seconds late? Could a man be fired twice?

She rose, smoothed her skirt, and led him to a paneled door with a knob engraved with the FBI seal. He caught himself glancing at bare muscular calves—nylon was for making parachutes—tendons stretched by platform heels, and averted his eyes in a rush of facial heat. It was like lusting after his den mother. He felt like scourging himself.

Here was Xanadu, the stately dome: if not of pleasure, then at least of imperial splendor. The walls were paneled and polished, and plush navy carpeting cloaked the floor with the ubiquitous seal embroidered in gold in the center and mounted in relief on the back wall. The room was vast, but it was in proportion to the desk, which ought to have been called something else because it did not belong in the same category as Vasco's tin station. A massy gold eagle stood sentinel with wings half-spread astride matching ink receptacles on the near edge. Gold-fringed flags of the United States and the District of Columbia flanked the desk in brass stands rubbed to a high yellow shine. Images of the place Vasco had seen in dim picture palaces before the main feature didn't do it justice. A brief glimpse of the Seat of Government in person seemed sufficient to snuff out any felonious conspiracy at the start.

"Not here, Mr. Vasco. The Director wishes to see you in his office."

He had stopped before the great desk, and in his reverie had failed to note that Miss Gandy had continued past it to another paneled door half-hidden behind a swag of blue-and-beige bunting. Belatedly he realized that the fabulous room was just for show, reserved for press conferences and photo sessions with famous faces: a deception, but more in the line of a magician's trick cabinet than a movie set. The fifth floor was a place of sliding panels, secret passageways, and strangers' eyes peering out through holes cut in paintings. Far from being disillusioned, he was charmed by the sorcery.

Beyond the last door the magic evaporated.

Vasco disliked square rooms. They reminded him of wooden packing crates—intriguing at first glance, but which once the straw was removed contained homely hymnals, Bible stories Bowdlerized for the consumption of children, blobby pewter candlesticks, and plaster saints with bored expressions that passed for piety. Nothing wondrous ever came from a crate. This one was twelve-by-twelve and might have been used by an insurance adjuster. Banks of olive-green filing cabinets stood like gym lockers against the side walls and a community of grubby file folders in stacks made city blocks on a plain wooden table. A green-shaded banker's lamp on the table and a single overhead globe created an island of light in an ocean of murk. National Geographic maps of the European and Pacific theaters of war were pinned to a wall beneath portraits of Washington, Lincoln, President Roosevelt, and for some reason Davy Crockett.

A small man with a big head sat in an upholstered chair behind the table, engrossed in the contents of a folder flayed open before him. He was built like a bantamweight boxer running to fat, with coarse hair brushed straight back from a bulging forehead and eyes that stuck out like white rubber door bumpers beneath heavy black brows. His nose was blunt, his cheeks jowly; "bulldog" was the popular description, "porcine" common among detractors. Vasco, whose own face had been compared to a rodent's, was less judgmental. He thought the Director heroically ugly and appropriately intimidating, like a boar in the forest. J. Edgar Hoover should look like nothing else.

"Peter Vasco, sir."

"Thank you, Miss Gandy."

She drew the door shut as she retired, sealing them in silence.

For most of a minute—if minutes were generations—Hoover continued to study the sheets before him, reading one page to the bottom, turning it over, and starting on the next as if he were alone. Vasco remained standing. He tried not to look at the carpeted platform that raised the table and its owner six inches from the floor. He'd heard that the stool the Director stood on during the turning-out ceremony was a litmus test for new special agents: one glance at his feet and the man went away empty-handed and out of a job. The effort of not looking down made his eyes want to water, and he found no comfort in the realization that the folder on the table contained his own personnel file.

Suddenly it smacked shut. He felt the full heat of Hoover's hard-boiled-egg gaze, white all around the irises.

"Sit down, please."

Four chairs covered in soft leather faced the table. The one he chose was less comfortable than it looked, the legs too short by inches so that he felt as if he were sitting in a tub. From that position the Director towered above him on his platform.

The one-sided staring contest continued a few more seconds. Vasco scratched an eyebrow, giving himself the chance to blink. The hot gaze shifted to a pudgy hand brushing the folder.

"You've been with the Bureau ten months and have yet to take a sick day. Why?"

He blinked again, openly. "I haven't been sick, sir."

"I hope that's true. Some people believe reporting to work ill is evidence of dedication, paying no mind to the half-dozen people who are forced to stay home the next week because of all the plague germs they left lying about. Are you under the impression you're indispensable?"

"No, sir."

"Because there is only one person this organization cannot possibly do without."

Inspiration seized him. "Miss Gandy."

Hoover stared. Vasco was sure he'd outsmarted himself. The obvious answer was not always the right one, but it was politic.

"We begin well," the Director said then, and Vasco resumed breathing. "Most people would say it's myself, and hope to curry favor. Nothing is so insincere as flattery, especially when it's addressed to a superior."

He felt a little less ill at ease. Hoover's speech was rapid-fire, a verbal strafing delivered in a nasal tone Vasco associated with radio announcers heard on tinny receivers. The words seemed to come a thousand to the minute, like rounds from the Model 1928 Thompson (familiarity with the Manual of Arms was required of all employees, in the field and at home). A man wanted to duck rather than respond; but he had remembered the Director stating the invaluability of Helen Gandy's services for the record when he'd added "executive" to her title, and the memory had surfaced during the onslaught. He still couldn't guess the reason he'd been summoned, but he'd begun to believe that it wasn't his dismissal.

"You're Sicilian?"

"Calabrese, sir. Irish on my mother's side." That was safe enough. A man couldn't help his ancestry. "I was born in Chicago." He couldn't remember if a birth certificate had been necessary for employment. Almost everything else had.

Hoover twisted around in his chair. He seemed to be searching for Calabria on the war map. It was peppered with red-white-and-blue flag pins. Mussolini had been captured once, then freed by the German Army; Vasco hoped he hadn't unpacked.

"You're still a practicing Catholic?" Hoover turned back, adjusting the padding in one shoulder. His double-breasted suits were tailored to correct deficiencies.

"Practicing? No, sir."

"Question of faith?"

"I have no questions."

"Atheist?" The heavy brows drew together.

"No, sir. I just stopped asking."

"Is that why you quit the seminary?"

"I failed. Many are called . . ."

"No judgments, understand. I have Roman Catholics in the field. Good men. None of them studied for the priesthood, which is why I asked to see you. One of the reasons. How much do you remember from your training?"

Only every novena, the names of all the saints, where the good vintage was kept so it wouldn't get mixed up with the swill they served for the sacrament. He practically farted in Latin. "A fair amount."

"We'll arrange a refresher course."

"A refresher course?"

"Are you still in contact with your father?"

He sat a little straighter, and he had not been slouching.

"I got a card last Christmas."

"No scenes in public, I hope."

"Our differences are private. With all due respect," he added. So it *was* possible to forget who he was talking to when that subject came up.

Hoover smiled. He had excellent teeth; Vasco suspected extensive orthodontia in early adulthood. They gleamed like new appliances against the Director's swarthy skin.

"There's no need for secrecy. Did you think, just because you applied for a low-clearance position, your background wouldn't be checked? Paul Anthony Vasco had a wife and a child to feed and clothe, a roof to provide. That was difficult enough for an unskilled laborer during the Depression, and harder still for a recent immigrant in a city crawling with them. He drove a beer truck when beer was illegal and performed odd jobs for the Capone organization. I've been called a puritan and a martinet, but I'd be worse than that if I held a man's bad choices against him after all this time. Worse yet if I visited the sins of the father upon the son. You wouldn't be working here if I did."

"We haven't spoken since before I joined the seminary. He thought the decision was a joke."

"Your dropping out would only support that opinion, in his eyes. I understand."

"No, sir, I'm afraid you don't."

Hoover's smile was a thing of the past—dead, petrified, and buried in dust. But Vasco was committed and stumbled on.

"My father *liked* his work. He had a decent job driving a cab in Cicero, but one day a thug hailed him, threw a pistol into the backseat with some cash, and told him to step on it. He did, just as a policeman came running up with his gun out and ordered the thug to throw up his hands. That night the same thug came to our apartment, took back his pistol, and gave my father a hundred-dollar bill from a roll he carried in his pocket. He also gave him a business card and said to look him up if he ever got tired of pushing a hack. My father quit the company the next day."

"What was on the card?" The Director seemed to have forgotten his pique.

"Al Brown, Antique Dealer. I'm sure I don't have to tell you who Al Brown was, sir."

"Al Capone. That must have been early in his career. He dropped the alias when he got big."

"The gun had been used to murder a man named Howard," Vasco said. "My father said the barrel was still hot. I don't want to know anything about those odd jobs."

"No one would blame you. Nothing is worse than betrayal. However." Hoover dragged another folder off a nearby heap. The file was much thicker than the one that contained Peter Vasco's life and secured with a piece of dirty cord.

He slipped the knot and spread it open. His fingers were pink and immaculate, like a baby's.

"This wind wasn't so ill it failed to blow some good. Your flirtation with the spiritual life wasn't enough to take you out of Division Four. If it weren't for your father's indiscretions I wouldn't have been able to use you at all." He drew out a newspaper clipping and placed it on Vasco's side of the table.

Vasco had to climb out of his chair to see it. It was brown and brittle and had a five-year-old date scribbled in red ink in one of the margins. He saw a picture he'd seen before, of a broad flat face photographed close up under a white Borsalino hat with the brim turned up rakishly on one side, and a headline:

CAPONE LEAVES ALCATRAZ

TWO

"I THOUGHT THE BUREAU CLOSED THE CAPONE FILE YEARS AGO."

"Treasury did. Violation of the Volstead Act was their jurisdiction, but they couldn't even nail him for that. We know of three murders he committed personally, on top of the legions he conspired in; that was Chicago's baby, but the police there were so crooked they didn't even pretend to try. They put up some squawk when we didn't bring them in on the Dillinger kill. If we had, he might still be in business."

Vasco read the article without learning anything he didn't already know; in fact, he knew more than was written. Capone was released from federal prison after serving seven years of an eleven-year sentence for income tax evasion. Good behavior and poor health were given as the reasons, but the precise nature of his illness couldn't be detailed in a family newspaper.

"Syphilis," said Hoover, as if he'd asked. "God punishes where man cannot or will not. I'd have seen he went to the chair, but I suppose a vice-related contagion is more poetic. The wages of sin, etcetera, if you'll pardon the blasphemy."

Vasco chose not to point out that, yes, Virginia, there was venereal disease in the Bible. He avoided religious discussions, the more so when the other person knew he'd studied for the clergy. He didn't like the way people walked on eggs around him when they found out. Even the Director wasn't immune. Vasco asked what Capone had done to bring him under Bureau jurisdiction at last.

"He's too far gone to work a jigsaw puzzle, much less knock over a bank. It's a wasting condition, body and mind, and he's in the third stage. His medical record is in the file. You'll want to read it, but we have Frank Nitti, his closest associate, to thank for the best and clearest diagnosis: 'Al's as nutty as a fruitcake.'"

"If that's true, I don't understand why he's under investigation."

"He isn't. His friends are, Nitti and Al's brothers Ralph and Matt and that blob Guzik. After Prohibition was repealed the boys in Chicago turned to narcotics and labor racketeering, and of course they were always up to their eyes in gambling and prostitution. At the moment our chief concern is their activities in the black market. Every tire and pound of butter those rats smuggle past the OPA helps to cripple the war effort. Imagine what it would mean if we succeeded in dangling just one of them by the neck for treason."

Vasco had not failed to note the *we*. "But if Capone—"

"No. He isn't involved in that. Not that he wouldn't feed at the trough if his accomplices could trust him to keep his mouth shut. In the stage he's in he's inclined to babble, and if it weren't for who he is his friends would have measured him for a cement overcoat long before this, to protect their own skins. But we can't count on their nostalgia forever. That's why we have to work fast, before

Capone gets the same treatment he dished out to so many others during the beer wars."

We. There it was again, the brotherly collective pronoun, but he'd decided to lay off asking questions for a while. He had the bizarre feeling the Director had rehearsed this conversation, just as he prepared for his oral reports to Congress when the budget needed hiking. Too many interruptions might force him to go back and start all over again, and that would be unpleasant for them both.

"We *know* what they're up to," Hoover said. "We always have, just like all Chicago. The challenge isn't even to prove it in court, but to make the proof stick. Even when some ambitious assistant D.A. manages to land a witness who can't be bribed or scared silent, the judge throws out the case or the jury votes for acquittal on any number of phony technicalities because they've been bought off by the defendant's friends. Bootleg profits and public apathy gave those characters the opportunity to create an iron-clad system of corruption unique since pagan times. In that town, it isn't just possible to get away with murder, nor even probable; it's a one-hundred-percent certainty."

He had to ask. "What about a change of venue?"

"The Capone mob's pockets are deep enough to include the people who make that decision. In any case it's not a sure thing. Three years after Treasury got Scarface Al, they tried the same thing with Dutch Schultz in New York. The trial was moved to a hick town upstate. Schultz went up there a week before it convened, spread money around like suntan oil, and was found not guilty on all counts. Building up a federal case takes time. The less time these hoodlums have to poison the jury pool and soften up the district judges, the better. We need to keep them busy defending themselves against local charges so they don't have the chance. But they won't remain distracted as long as they can swat those charges away in early innings. What's required is an absolutely unimpeachable witness; one who can't be threatened or bought, and whose testimony can't be ignored, because his very name is synonymous with crime in the twentieth century."

Vasco had begun to see where the conversation was heading. He still didn't know why he was part of it, but he returned to his chair without asking. Standing in front of the platform brought his eyes on a level with the Director's, and he sensed that was a source of irritation. Hoover's pupils had shrunken to pinpricks, and if anything his speech was faster. Tiny flecks of spittle flew like sparks from an emery wheel.

"Capone knows literally where all the bodies are buried," he went on in more measured tones. "He put them on the spot, and he can name his accomplices and provide details that no slippery criminal attorney can twist into something else, that no court can ignore. His evidence will be reported on every front page in the country and shove the war news below the fold. Winchell, the ham, will eat it up. It's been five years since he helped nab Lepke and he still acts like he strapped him in the hot seat and threw the switch." No love was lost between the radio gossip columnist and the FBI man, although they used each other. "It's the chance for every ward heeler in public office to advance himself on the legit, by convicting every last hoodlum in Chicago. Then it'll be our turn."

"If they put Capone on the stand, what's to prevent the defense from having his testimony disallowed on the grounds of mental incompetence?"

Hoover tapped a rounded fingernail on the open folder. "According to his medical file, his dementia is progressive, not regressive. That means his memory of the distant past is more reliable than of events much more recent. He could tell you, for instance, what Johnny Torrio wrote on the card he sent with flowers to Big Jim Colosimo's funeral in 1920, but he couldn't remember what he ate for breakfast this morning, or for that matter if he even had breakfast. Any sampling of doctors can establish that in court. But Capone will never appear on the stand.

"This case will be years in preparation. He isn't expected to live that long. If he did, his former associates would see he never made it as far as the Illinois state line, even if they have to pump some maniac full of dope and send him in guns blazing, the way they did when they killed Cermak in '33, and to hell with it if he never makes away, as long as he does the job. We can't take that chance."

This was a revelation to Vasco. The FBI had gone on record saying that Mayor Cermak of Chicago was an innocent bystander, slain by bullets intended for President-elect Roosevelt, who was riding beside him in an open car in Miami, Florida. Hoover himself had turned aside speculation that the corrupt city official had been marked for a very public murder after he'd welshed on certain promises he'd made to Caponeites. The shooter, an Immigrant Italian bricklayer named Zangara, had been arrested by the Secret Service, labeled an anarchist, and executed after a brief trial. Vasco felt the sinking sensation that he'd been let in—inadvertently, it appeared, almost casually—on a state secret that would make it impossible for him to leave that room without agreeing to some concession. It was like seeing one's own kidnapper removing his mask, because he wouldn't be around to identify him later. Worrying about getting fired was beginning to seem like the good old days.

Hoover retrieved the old newspaper clipping and began tidying the file with a spinsterish attention to detail. A fusty puff reached Vasco's nostrils as the folder was closed, a smell of old ledgers moldering in an uninsulated storage room.

"The evidence will be presented in the form of a deposition, with a signed affidavit attesting to its accuracy and the circumstances under which it was obtained. Assembling it will take months, possibly years, if Capone holds out that long. Unfortunately, what the Lord giveth He also taketh away, because while it destroys inhibitions, tertiary syphilis also brings on episodes of severe paranoia. I'm informed by agents with the surveillance team that the sight of a strange automobile parked near Capone's Florida estate is sufficient to trigger an anxiety attack; complaints to the local authorities have forced our field men to use commercial vans advertising businesses well known in the area, swimming pool services and kosher foods delivery; many of the neighbors are wealthy Jews, retired and otherwise. Jolson rents there in the winter.

"It's a big house on an island, but only three people reside there full-time: Capone, his wife, and his son. His sister-in-law and her husband visit, and the two Negro servants don't stay over. The only others allowed inside are his brothers. Ralph is fiercely protective of Al. He's running Chicago now and doesn't get down often, but he employs bodyguards to patrol the grounds in shifts and sit in automobiles outside the gate and cruise the neighborhood on an irregular schedule. The toll man on the causeway has a direct telephone line to the house, in case a carload of assassins tries to cross over. The bodyguards are licensed private detectives, legally permitted to carry firearms, so in theory we can't touch them and neither can the Miami Police, although they take them downtown from time to time to show them who's boss. We hope to put a stop to that. It agitates the household and makes it that much harder to penetrate."

Penetrate, Vasco thought. Like a Communist cell or a nest of enemy saboteurs.

Hoover rattled on, like Miss Gandy at her typewriter. "Convince Ralph, you convince Al. But Ralph is suspicious by nature, and the wars with the O'Donnells and O'Banion did nothing to restore his faith in the brotherhood of man."

These names from the past—Nitti, Guzik, Torrio, O'Donnell, O'Banion—sent a caterpillar scampering up his spine. They brought back old nightmares, meals eaten in tense silence, the boards creaking under the linoleum while his mother paced back and forth in her uneven tread, waiting for his father to come home from some unexplained errand in the dead of night, or for the landlady to call her to the telephone downstairs and hear bad news from a stranger. The names had sprawled across extra early-bird editions of the *Tribune* and *Herald-Examiner,* and shuddered the glass tubes in the Philco in the parlor, misspelled often, mispronounced frequently, but accompanied usually by words never heard in normal conversation: *slain, bludgeon, massacre.* It had taken Peter Vasco months to connect the surnames to the diminutives Paul Vasco slung around when he drank: Frank, Jake, Johnny, Spike, Deanie. By then his mother was drinking too.

None of them came to the apartment. That night the man who called himself Al Brown showed up to redeem his pistol for cash was the only time he ever visited. Peter assumed they all looked like the lower primates in editorial cartoons, beetle-browed trolls in cloth caps with stubble cross-hatching their chins. It had been a shock when Dion O'Banion's photograph appeared with an account of his assassination, his round face and long upper lip resembling the young choirmaster's at St. Francis. Torrio might have been any philanthropic captain of industry the day shotguns shattered his jaw. All family acquaintances.

Once again, Hoover appeared to have read his mind. "Your father's connection to the Capone gang is the Bureau's best hope of infiltrating that society. Those people respect four things only: money, violence, religion, loyalty. They can never have enough of the first two, and it doesn't matter to them that no self-respecting priest will grant them burial in consecrated earth, for all their solid bronze caskets and hundred-thousand-dollar floral displays; they baptize their children in church, give them first communion, send their families to Mass and sometimes attend themselves. Hymie Weiss was gunned down on the steps of Holy Name Cathedral on his way to confession, right across from the florist's shop where O'Banion bled out among the roses and horse manure. When they're not slaughtering rivals or suborning juries, you can find them in some shadowy booth fiddling with their beads and begging forgiveness for their crimes against America. I pleaded with Homer Cummings to let me install wire recorders there, but he said it was a Treasury matter. If I'd been with Treasury and gone to Andrew Mellon, he'd have said it was Justice. They were both afraid of the Supreme Court. This filth thinks it can fix God the way it fixed city hall."

It occurred to him that the Director spoke in present tense, as if the days of gangster funerals, corpses bleeding in gutters, and smoky speakeasies where naked girls bathed in bathtubs foaming with French-Canadian champagne weren't as obsolete as crystal sets. He wasn't grandstanding, Vasco was certain; this wasn't just fire-breathing for the yokels. Hoover believed every word. For him, a case unclosed by the Bureau was a war unwon. When the guns went silent there would be no treaties or conditions, only a single victor standing in a scorched field. In spite of himself—his part in the battle was emerging from the fog, and it frightened him nearly out of his senses—he felt his blood beginning to glow. Such was the power of Hoover's gravitational pull.

Vasco scarcely heard the peck at the door. Hoover yelped an invitation and Helen Gandy came in carrying a sheet with perforated edges, torn from a roll of Teletype paper.

"You said to bring this in right away."

"Yes. Thank you."

She cast the young man a reassuring smile on her way out. He wondered just how deeply she was in her employer's confidence.

Hoover read the text swiftly and set it aside. "As I was saying. Loyalty is a lesser coin of their realm—they expect it without necessarily giving it in return, and reward it, after all their baser needs are gratified. Your father performed his duties for the Capones consistently and giving satisfaction for ten years, then opened a bar in Cicero after Repeal, probably with financial assistance from his former superiors. That's assumption without evidence, but the relative ease with which he procured a license from the Illinois State Liquor Control Commission, when federal law barred former bootleggers from eligibility, suggests political influence. They were protecting their investment."

He felt the need to defend his flesh and blood. "He said he'd saved up."

"Unlikely. The bills for your mother's medical treatment and her funeral expenses would have strained the budget of someone much higher up in the organization. The rent alone would have been beyond his means, not counting the day-to-day graft every legitimate merchant in Cook County must pay to remain in business."

The Director's casual dismissal of his mother's illness and death—the central tragedy in Vasco's life—shocked him into silence.

His own file was back open. "Three years ago, Paul Vasco sold his interest in the bar to Rocco Fischetti, a Capone cousin—honestly, this shapes up to be the most incestuous gang of cutthroats since the Borgias—and retired to Florida to operate a charter-boat service in Fort Lauderdale. Everyone in the Chicago underworld seems to migrate to the Gold Coast eventually. The wind off Lake Michigan in January gets to be too much if they survive long enough for their skin to wrinkle."

"Sir, my father was hardly an underworld character."

"Granted, he didn't wear silk shirts or keep a mistress. How far do you think the men who did would have gotten if not for the thousands of supernumeraries they paid to run errands for them?

"I've said I don't condemn him," Hoover continued. "No one took taxis to bread lines and there weren't any defense plants to put him to work." He frowned. He was repeating himself, and he might have suspected that he wasn't as convincing when he sympathized with the plight of the working man as when he was sermonizing against the criminal cancer infecting society. "The situation pleases me, as a matter of fact. All our attempts to place agents inside the gang were failures, and we couldn't turn anyone already there because the penalty of discovery trumped anything we could offer. But the son of a loyal soldier has the advantage of tradition. Peter, do you consider yourself a man of courage?"

The use of his first name struck him as clumsy, an adjective he would never have thought to apply to a man who had outmaneuvered political infighters from both sides of the aisle through five administrations. He proceeded cautiously, anticipating a trap. "I like to think so. Then again, I've never been tested. I tried to join the army, but I was rejected on the grounds that I provide an essential service as an employee of the FBI."

"I saw to it you were rejected. Normally the deferment is restricted to special agents and my personal staff. But your background is unique in the Bureau. It's the reason I expedited your assignment to Records and Communications, where I could keep an eye on you, and it's the reason this country can't afford to waste you on some beach; Miami Beach excepted." Perfect teeth flickered, acknowledging the slightness of his joke. "I asked if you're courageous because I don't believe in sending a man into harm's way without satisfying myself he's aware of the risk."

Hoover, the master magician, exhibited his legerdemain, shuffling the folders on the table once again so that the hefty Capone file was back on top. Vasco pictured the Director alone in that homely room night after night, repositioning his cardboard army like a general pushing toy tanks around a map table.

"On St. Valentine's Day, 1929, seven men died in a commercial garage on North Clark Street in Chicago." He wet his thumb and paged through the tattered sheaf of pink carbons, yellow flimsies, crumbling clippings, densely typed reports, and letters written in smudged pencil and blotchy ink. "'In a hail of bullets' is the journalists' hackneyed phrase. Forgive me if I insult your intelligence with a nursery tale everyone knows, but to presume knowledge is to encourage ignorance. That Al Capone was behind the massacre there is no doubt, despite the appalling lack of evidence needed to indict.

"We know also, within an acceptable margin of doubt, that two of his favorite shooters, John Scalise and Albert Anselmi, were directly involved. The gang had absolute faith in their allegiance based on past performance, and Capone himself refused to turn them over to Hymie Weiss over an old offense in the interest of restoring the peace: 'I wouldn't do that to a yellow dog,' I believe, was Capone's response. But the wheel of gangdom turns perpetually, as do the gangsters' coats. Scalise and Anselmi were accused of conspiring against their boss with his enemies. Capone threw a banquet in their honor at an Indiana roadhouse, raised toasts to their health, and then demonstrated for their benefit how his good friend, Babe Ruth, hit home runs. He started things off with a baseball bat and left the rest to hired guns. Ah. I knew it was here somewhere. These prewar files are in deplorable condition." He snatched up an eight-by-ten sheet and paid Vasco the compliment of rising from behind the table and walking around to hold out the item.

Vasco stood to accept it. Hoover had the smallest feet he'd ever seen on a grown man, neatly encased in black wingtips laced so tightly the tongues didn't show, polished to a high gloss like onyx. He thought, disloyally, of a doll, or of a small boy carrying the ring at a wedding.

The grainy black-and-white photograph, reproduced on coarse police stock, drove all personal remonstrances from his head. He'd begun to fidget when the names Scalise and Anselmi came up; his father had attended that banquet as a guest, invited by a shylock to whom he owed money, and although Paul Vasco had been laconic about the details, even deep in drink as he was, his son had gathered that the fate of the guests of honor had served as a lesson to those who failed to live up to their obligations. The pictures Peter had seen in tabloids had been unsettling enough—too much so to appear even in the sensational Hearst press—but this one would have shut down the yellowest bosoms-and-blood sheet under the laws of decency. It was for official use only.

The murdered men lay naked on gurneys in a bare room, hairy specimens of Sicilian manhood with large, flaccid genitals and puckered holes in their chests (*il cuore,* the heart), temples (*il cervello,* the brain), and throats (*la gola,* the center of speech—a customary precaution in case they survived long enough to name their assailants). A little finger was missing; a defensive wound, proof that at least one of them had been alive after the beating. All four arms were bruised and probably broken. But the worst injuries were the blows to the skulls. They looked like empty goatskin bags. An orbit had been crushed, spilling the eye.

"Thank you." Vasco returned the photo with the slow elaborate gesture of a drunkard trying to pass for sober.

"Are you all right? Do you need a stimulant?"

"Please."

The Director disapproved. His face was as transparent as a baby's: arranged into upright *V*'s, pleasure; *V*'s inverted, the opposite. But Vasco was beyond caring. His head felt as light as the goatskin bags.

A switch snapped on the intercom on the table, a twin of the sleek walnut instrument on Helen Gandy's desk. Within three minutes, two inches of Kentucky rye materialized in a glass as heavy as a paperweight. Miss Gandy glided out with no smile his way. A more intimate connection with the man she worked for could not be imagined.

"Better?" Hoover sounded impatient.

"Yes. Thank you." He was seated again, the warmth of the spirits climbing up from the floor of his stomach to turn his ears pink. His father's taste for the stuff had made him numb to its pleasures.

"I sometimes forget what impact these things have on the layman. Most people encounter death only after the mortician has done his wonders with wax and paint."

"It isn't that. I knew those fellows. They came to my fifth birthday party. They brought a wooden rocking horse signed by Tom Mix." Scalise and Anselmi had not been the kind that attracted banner headlines. Their gruesome deaths alone had made them worth the outlay in paper and ink. He remembered their loud neckties and immigrant haircuts, their halting command of English; attempts at the *th* in "birthday" had made Peter giggle, and grown men present to hoot and put them in headlocks. He had not connected the men to their names until that moment. Photos of their corpses released to the press had shown them with sheets drawn to their chins, their features foreshortened.

"That's understandable," Hoover said. "Jesse James read to his children from the Bible, and Capone himself set up free soup kitchens in the depth of the Depression. These hooligans will stop at nothing to win over the illiterate. Your rocking-horse heroes poured seventy slugs into a Chicago Police car in 1925, killing two officers before they had a chance to return fire. The murderers pleaded self-defense and were acquitted." His eyes lingered on the photograph. Then he returned to his chair. "Are you prepared to accept the assignment, knowing how these people reward those who plot against them?"

"I don't know what the assignment is, sir. I understand I'm to join the household, but I don't think just being Paul Vasco's son will get me in the door."

"Nor do I. But Capone's a superstitious peasant, despite his modern methods, the automobile and the machine gun. Medical reports confirm his fear of death and eternity. In Alcatraz he spent nearly as much time in the chapel as at the mangle in the laundry. Like all the rest he thinks he can fix God.

"You'll be retrained by a priest. The Bureau will arrange the necessary documents and references to show you completed your novitiate at St. Francis Catholic Church in Cicero, Illinois. The records of your expulsion will be destroyed. It so happens the parish is in need of a new community center, and the diocese has promised to cooperate in return for a donation to the building fund. All we need now is agreement from you."

Vasco opened his mouth to ask a question. But the Director picked up the Teletype Miss Gandy had brought earlier.

"Paul Vasco just secured a loan from the Everglade State Bank of Miami, Florida, to buy the charter boat he's been leasing for three years. He doesn't know it, but the Bureau is now his business partner. You'll visit him. Friendly relations must be established."

"Sir, I—"

"Ralph keeps tabs on all his brother's confederates, current and former. If he suspects you're estranged, the operation will fail. I understand it's distasteful, but your country requires it."

"I suppose if it's necessary—"

"It is, I said. Do you object to posing as a priest on moral grounds?"

"No." Fearing he'd answered too quickly, he shook his head. "No, sir, I don't."

The Director pursed his lips; a distressing effect, more blowfish than feral hog. "If you're afraid of the consequences of discovery, there's no shame in it. These men are savages. You'll return to your duties and no one will know what took place in this office."

He remembered the picture of J. Edgar Hoover with Alvin Karpis in handcuffs. "I'm not afraid."

"You accept the assignment."

It wasn't a question, but he said, "Yes."

"Splendid. As far as anyone is concerned, you're a man of the cloth, and thanks to Paul Vasco you're practically family. Al Capone is looking for a father confessor, to hear his sins and pray him through Purgatory. There's no reason it shouldn't be one of ours, because either way he's going to hell."

Hoover traded the Teletype for another sheet and wrote on it with a fat fountain pen. "This is a directive reassigning you from Division Four to Division Five: National Security." He stood and held out his hand. "Congratulations, Special Agent Vasco."

THREE

IT WAS A BEAUTIFUL SPRING DAY ON THE MALL. THE MONUMENTS LOOKED like soap sculptures in the sun. The marine guards posted in front were as motionless as cribbage pegs in their white gloves, rifles at parade rest. Men from other branches of the service leaned on fountains and sat on the steps of the Lincoln Memorial smoking, some with crutches beside them. Nurses, office workers, tourists, and couriers with briefcases bustled about. A portable radio mentioned Monte Cassino. It was four o'clock Eastern War time, and a long way from dark.

A great change had taken place since Vasco had walked through the place that morning on his way to work. Then, he had avoided eye contact with the military men and women, ashamed of his obvious good health and lack of a uniform while others his age and younger were fighting and dressing wounds on foreign shores throughout the world. They could not know that his attempt at self-recruitment had failed under the Essential Services clause of the Selective Service Act: but in his heart he knew that any four-f clerk or war wife could sit at his desk polishing the Bureau's image while he trained for combat. Now he strolled past the soldiers and sailors on leave and the marines on duty with his spine straight. He was preparing to fight the war at home.

And he had already made a sacrifice. He'd given up his fifth birthday party, one of the few happy memories of his childhood.

He had no idea what had become of that rocking horse, built by hand from sturdy pine by some Old World craftsman, brightly painted, with the cowboy star's name written on the neck in simple script that even a small boy could read. Lost, no doubt, in some move; the Vascos had changed addresses several times as their fortunes slid up and down the turbulent scale. He'd outgrown it by then, so it didn't matter. What did was that two men he didn't know ("Uncle John" and "Uncle Albert" barely resonated, mysterious relatives entering and leaving their kitchen and parlor as frequently as they did) had thought enough of his father to bring his only child so grand a gift.

When he was older, he'd assumed the two were like Paul Vasco, worker ants toiling at the base of the heap: the Outfit, as the press called it after Capone went to prison and peace descended—as of course it had to, with him out of commission and most of the O'Banion gang in the ground. Public outrage and private crusades had had little to do with ending the violence. It had swept through the city like influenza, sparing some, striking down many, and run its course once the last susceptible party had fallen. Now he knew that the two funny foreign men who'd stumbled over "Happy birthday" had been both virus and victim. He would never again think of that day without seeing two pale naked bodies stretched out like hogs that had been stunned, then slaughtered.

THE CONFESSIONS OF AL CAPONE

The St. Valentine's Day Massacre was too monumental a thing to have been the work of two men operating under the direction of a third. It was more on the order of a natural disaster. To a boy staring at a front page, seven corpses sprawled on a poured floor might as well have littered a beach in Singapore, hurled there by a typhoon, mindlessly and without malice. Shotguns and Thompsons had done the damage: So what? They were machines, hardly less sentient than the anonymous fingers on the triggers.

It was names that made the difference. Scalise and Anselmi and Capone, who as everyone knew was answering routine questions by the Dade County, Florida, district attorney while bullets were chugging into James Clark, Albert Weinshank, Adam Heyer, Frank and Pete Gusenberg, a quack optometrist named Schwimmer, and John May, a mechanic; who to Peter Vasco's thinking was the only one with a legitimate excuse for hanging around a garage. George "Bugs" Moran, O'Banion's heir and the principal target, was absent also, lingering over a cup of coffee in a drugstore up the street. The Outfit's track record in missing the whole point of a mission almost matched the law's.

He wondered if that mistake had helped to erode Capone's faith in the loyalty of his two favorite killers. He wondered, too, if he himself was a "man of courage," to borrow Hoover's radio-drama rhetoric. He pictured himself with his arms pinioned to a chair, watching the slow approach of the bull-shouldered vice lord patting his palm with a Louisville Slugger, the long scar on his cheek flaring white against a face engorged with rage. Such exertion would be beyond him now, if his medical information could be trusted, but Brother Ralph was healthy enough, and in any case all his old associates had rallied around him in defeat as they had at the height of his brutal reign.

Vasco's blood pressure dropped at the thought. But then he supposed it was no worse than riding a landing craft through heavy seas toward a fortified beachhead. Either event would be the test of a man.

Florida.

The place came up nearly as often as Chicago when Capone's name was mentioned. He fled to its refuge whenever the city on the lake failed to smile upon him; when he tired of riding his custom Cadillac tank a distance he could have walked in five minutes and crossing hotel lobbies inside a scrum of bodyguards just to buy a newspaper; when the city fathers decided to throw a bone the reformers' way and issue a warrant for his arrest. Legend said a secret passageway led from his office in the Lexington Hotel to an alley where the armored sedan waited to whisk him to Union Station whenever uninvited visitors entered the reception room.

Even when, after the massacre, Miami wouldn't have him, the place remained his good luck charm. He remembered Hialeah and a Philadelphia detective he'd befriended there, who arranged to jail him in coal country for the crime of carrying a concealed weapon until cooler heads prevailed and Moran withdrew the five-figure bounty he'd put on Capone's head. (The chief turnkey placed an armchair and a Turkish rug in his private cell.) Federal agents gave him a cross-country lift to his Palm Island estate after he was discharged from Alcatraz. Asked by a fresh reporter if he intended to go after any of his old enemies, he'd said the only thing he wanted to kill was fish. It was all there in the file in Vasco's moleskin briefcase, next to his Thermos.

Florida was a sanctuary, and he'd agreed to violate it.

It was like being asked to ambush Hitler at Berchtesgaden, only better. *Der Fuehrer* had done nothing to him personally, but Al Capone had taken his mother from him, his respect for his father, and now his fifth birthday.

HE DIDN'T LIKE THE PRIEST WHO'D BEEN SELECTED TO REACQUAINT HIM with the ceremonies of the Church. The feeling was mutual, although on Father McGonigle's part it was more a matter of general policy than personal distaste.

He lived a streetcar ride away from the marble halls of government, in a Negro neighborhood where boys barely old enough to walk pitched pennies against the curb and overweight women sat on stoops fanning themselves with paper fronds advertising a local funeral parlor. Youths in zoot suits and peg-top trousers smoked cigarettes on street corners and everyone stopped what he was doing to look when a white man got off at that stop, holding a scrap of paper with an address written on it; but they lost interest when he started up the steps of a row house near the end of the block. Pennies resumed jingling, fans fell back into their halfhearted rhythm. Shrill nasal voices argued over the day's number.

McGonigle wore his gray hair long, and although he had on a clerical collar with a rusty black short-sleeved shirt, he kept pulling at it with a finger as if he wasn't used to wearing it. After Vasco declined an offer to pour him a glass from a bottle of Green Spot whisky, he didn't ask again, although he helped himself several times.

Under its influence he waxed autobiographical, but not nostalgic. He'd been suspended by the archbishop from a pastorship in Maryland for lecturing the Vatican from the pulpit about the persecution of the Jews in Nazi-occupied Europe.

Plainly he didn't believe the story he'd been told by someone with the General Intelligence Division, that Vasco was an actor researching a small but important role in a defense documentary. (For McGonigle's benefit he was "Philip Viterelli," to derail possible inquiries from Florida and Chicago.) "Bing Crosby made a better-looking priest than you, and he didn't sell me, either." Just as plainly, he didn't care, because a cashier's check had been delivered to his address by special messenger an hour before his protégé arrived, drawn on the account of a business front maintained by the Bureau.

"You could call yourself O'Reilly and it'd stick just as tight," McGonigle said, observing him from beneath paper-thin lids watermarked with blue veins. "The District's rotten with mongrels. Half the tar babies in this neighborhood could sue for a piece of the Thomas Jefferson estate. I'm the only purebred for eleven blocks. County Cork, both sides, clear back to William the Bloody Conqueror."

"Is it a problem?"

"Not as long as the check clears. I just want it on the record this Mick ain't so far gone in drink he can't tell a ginzo from a potato-eater."

Vasco hoped the transparency didn't extend to the credentials Hoover's people had furnished to fool Ralph Capone.

"My mother came to this country from County Sligo, if it's any of your business." A pinch of truth never hurt when a lie needed seasoning. He'd learned that much at his father's knee.

"Shanty Irish, the lot. I might've guessed."

"I'd have thought a man who risked so much to speak up for the Jews would be more tolerant."

"And what's being tolerant to do with crying out against injustice, I ask you? Hook noses and greedy mitts offend me as much as the next fellow, but wholesale slaughter's not the answer. That man that calls himself Pius behaves as if the kike that comes around offering to sharpen all the knives in my kitchen pounded the nails into Jesus personal. He'd speak up bloody quick if Mussolini wasn't an Eye-tie and it was his people taking the gas pipe."

"Father, I'm just here for the Canons."

"Right." He dashed the liquor around in his glass, then knocked it back like a cowboy in a movie; Vasco had a flash of Tom Mix and a rocking horse, lost along with so much else. The glass slammed down on a mission oak table hard enough to crack a vessel made of finer material. "Let's start with what you *don't* know, and see just how much heathen we need to burn out."

The first session was humiliating.

It amounted to a grade-school catechism, and he was mortified by how much he'd forgotten. He was like a graduate mathematician stumped by two-plus-two. McGonigle's inebriated self-satisfaction at every stumble put him right back in the corner of Brother Dismas' classroom at St. Francis—the one nearest the barrel stove, and by ham-handed metaphor nearest the Lake of Fire—for confusing Isaiah with Ezekiel. When he was dismissed after three hours, the sadistic gleam in the priest's eye promised no respite the next time.

Vasco returned to his furnished room on Sixteenth Street, amazed in spite of his exhaustion to find it unchanged from that morning. He'd left it a government clerk and had returned a special agent of the FBI. He'd met J. Edgar Hoover and been chosen by him to perform a service vital to national security. (Not precisely vital, perhaps, but more distinctly connected than splicing split infinitives.) From that adrenaline-charged moment, the day had drained him of energy and self-worth. He dragged his limbs up two flights of stairs, the briefcase hanging heavy on one side, and fell back against the door. If he'd had the strength, he'd have hauled the chest of drawers across it to keep the world out.

Most nights he cooked supper, read, listened to the war news, and went to bed at ten. Tonight his brain was too stale to focus on anything but the basics. He ate the second half of his egg-salad sandwich from the icebox and fell onto the mattress at half past eight. Dreams disturbed his rest, but the next morning all he could remember was Seamus McGonigle coming at him with a baseball bat.

THE ORDEAL WAS JUST AS BAD THE NEXT FEW DAYS—HIS TUTOR SEEMED DE-termined to reduce him to Protestant—but when his studies moved beyond the basic tenets of the Church into theosophy, Vasco had the opportunity to demon-strate his grasp of those metaphysical questions that had kept him in the semi-nary long after his zealotry faded. The insults and sarcasm fell off precipitously. He'd forgotten the joy of the challenge, and McGonigle was a gifted adversary when they differed over interpretation. Vasco admired his scholarship without disliking him any less.

When the priest broke to drink and ruminate, Vasco learned that in his youth McGonigle had run guns to the rebels in Northern Ireland, but having been drawn more by the thrill of adventure than devotion to Home Rule, he'd quit when it became routine. For a time he'd courted a young woman in Belfast, but that ended when she took the veil.

"We were related by blood," he said. "I like to think that was the reason, but in any case I was relieved when it happened. Beautiful women can be boring, have you noticed?"

"Is that when you got the Call?"

"Oh, I was already wearing the collar. You might say I was a priest without portfolio."

He continued before the shock set in. "A friend who'd emigrated for his health—he had a king's order of execution upon his head—cabled me with an offer to leave the politics behind and run whisky to the States. Scotch, it shames me to confess; the Sons of Erin lacked the criminal enterprise of our neighbors to the North and of our cousins over here. The money was good, and I'd rather be shot at for it than just for fun, but when my friend took one in the belly and I brought him to hospital I made the mistake of hanging around to see what be-came of him. Two blokes with blue chins arrested me in the waiting room: nine months in the Baltimore jail."

Vasco began to see how McGonigle had come to Hoover's attention. He won-dered how long the Bureau had been tracking him. "What happened to your friend?"

"He got better. He's a judge now. Well, I was always one for a brawl, and when I got out I hadn't a shilling, so I accepted two dollars to go five rounds with a fel-low who called himself Paddy Ryan, though he was as Irish as a plate of lasagna. I dropped him in the second round. I'd found a career, I thought. Then a bruiser named Sailor Maccabee laid me out flatter than unleavened bread thirty sec-onds after the bell. I was still snatching at invisible butterflies three weeks later."

"Then what?"

He grinned for the first time, showing a row of lower teeth dyed amber. "Hell, after bootlegging and prizefighting, what else was there? Saints Mary and Joseph needed an assistant pastor, and with rum boats steaming in and out of the harbor regular as the tide, the committee wasn't asking questions it didn't want to hear the answers to. It was steady work in unsteady times."

"That's all it meant?"

"It was fourteen years ago, and six months is as much of an investment as I put into anything before that, not counting the hoosegow. Judge for yourself."

"Others have already judged."

"This?" He swept a hand around the room cluttered with open books and empty bottles. "The *Church* is responsible for this. God's the only commitment I ever made past payday. How about you?"

He remembered what he was about. "I'm just an actor preparing for a part."

McGonigle poured. "Bit of advice, Phil, my lad. Take the Civil Service exam and you'll never go hungry."

MORNINGS WERE THE ONLY TIME HE HAD TO STUDY THE FBI FILE ON AL-phonse Capone. His sessions with the priest left him too wrung out to concentrate at night, and McGonigle wasn't available the next day until he'd slept off the previous lesson.

Over his ration of coffee, which he stretched out with burnt chicory, he looked at Scarface Al's earliest arrest photo at age eighteen, round-faced and balding even then, booked for beating a man half to death in a dockside saloon in Brooklyn, New York (charges dropped); a candid shot taken at Comiskey Park, getting a baseball signed for his son by Babe Ruth; a relaxed pose on the steps of the Federal Building in Chicago, smiling with one hand in his suit pocket and his hat at its jaunty angle; the infamous "Public Enemy Number One" mug that had run again with the article announcing his release from prison; finally, the gangster in retirement, fishing in a striped bathrobe off Palm Island, Florida.

He was arguably the most photographed felon in U.S. history. Billy the Kid had posed only once, Jesse James a handful of times, and a roll of Kodak film had been sufficient for John Dillinger. John Wilkes Booth looked like Clark Gable in some lithographs, in others like a deranged Mark Twain. Everyone old enough to remember Black Friday knew Al Capone's face as well as Charles Lindbergh's, and better than the president's.

Vasco thought that if he cut the images to a uniform size and arranged them into a child's flip-book, he could provide a moving-picture account of the rise and fall of America's Crime King, from his squalid origins in the slums to his palace of debauchery at age twenty-five to his decline into imprisonment and madness in his forties. It was a cautionary tale for all would-be transgressors.

The medical reports were frightening enough without illustration: penile discharge, skin eruptions, genital warts, periods of rage and panic. Then there was his arrest file, with its description of the facial disfigurement that had given him the nickname he detested: "oblique scar of 4" across cheek 2" in front left ear—vertical scar 2¹/₂" under left ear on neck"; retaliation for an indiscreet remark made to a woman in a Brooklyn nightclub, courtesy of her brother. Vasco could only guess at the vengeance that Capone Ascendant had exacted for this Mark of Cain. The record was silent where it should be explicit.

But the sheer volume of material that had been collected would take days to digest; weeks even, with his afternoons and evenings pledged to his spiritual re-education. Someone with a blunt pencil had scribbled in the margins and on the backs of the parcel-brown pages of the *Institution Rules & Regulations* manual for residents of Alcatraz, providing a semilegible account of Prisoner #85's day-to-day life for a number of weeks; apparently, Hoover's people had either planted an undercover man in Capone's cell block or recruited an inmate to observe and report upon him with a promise of favors. It was clear that Capone had continued to be of interest to the Bureau long after the rest of the world had turned to other diversions: Depression, labor unrest, the war.

What to do with the fat folder when Vasco went out posed a challenge. His landlord, whose son had gone down aboard the *Arizona,* considered him a shirker, and certain items left out of order indicated that his room had been searched from time to time for evidence of subversive activity. At length he settled on wrapping it in an undershirt and getting on a chair to push it to the end of his reach inside the ventilation duct; he had six inches on the landlord, and the old man's rheumatism argued against such exertion even in the interest of protecting the Home Front. After replacing the screen he carefully smeared the screws with grimy dust. It made him feel like Secret Agent X-9.

At the end of two weeks, Father Seamus McGonigle—IRA retired, former pugilist, ex-convict—marked his place in St. Thomas More with a book of ration stamps and fingered the burst blood vessels on his nose. It had been broken and reset at least once.

"Who'd you study with, boyo? Dollars to dog shit I've heard of him. I've been shuttled so many places I know the King of the Hoboes by his Christian name. You're no novice. You've had training, and it took. The training, I mean. You can teach a monkey to dance but it don't make him Fred Astaire."

"The first day you said I was unteachable."

"The first day I was as drunk as the Wedding at Cana, as who wouldn't be with an open bar. You expected me to swallow that crock-a-shit story you came in with, which didn't improve my disposition. 'Philip Viterelli,' my Aunt Katy's ass. I called you Phil three times that night and you didn't look up once. Whoever sent you must've been in one hell of a hurry."

He held back panic, but a palm shot up before he could frame a response.

"Hold your fire for the enemy. In the first place I don't care damn-all, and in the second place who'd listen if I did? I'm a pope's fart away from a mission in Greenland. It just might have saved us some effort in this our season of trial if you'd told me up front you'd worn the surplice. We could've dispensed with the first communion horseshit no one remembers anyway and cut straight to the prime rib."

"I never said I had no religious education. You assumed I knew nothing."

"I'm saying it still. You know all the verses right enough, and not to spill soup on the vestments, which is more than I can say for a certain archbishop. It don't matter to me if you sat at the feet of the Fisherman himself, though I'm curious as to why you wasted your time since it's as clear as Galilee you don't believe any of it."

"I believe in God. I hold sacred the teachings of Jesus Christ, our Lord and Savior."

McGonigle skinned back his upper lip and blew a Bronx cheer.

Vasco rose, his face burning. "I won't sit here and be called an atheist."

"Stand, then. If you're worried the disguise won't hold up, don't. I know a cardinal with a wife and three brawling boys in Albany. No one expects you to fall for your own pitch, only that you don't forget the words. As for me, I make it a practice not to stand between a man and his own damnation."

"I doubt that. I don't think you're a believer any more than you think I am."

"I'd not bet any red points on it, if I were you." He lifted his glass. "Here's to the Father, the Son, and the Holy Ghost. And your immortal soul, while I'm about it." He drained it. "Leave my sight now, and don't come back. I just drank up the last of my tutorial."

FOUR

HE HADN'T RIDDEN A TRAIN SINCE BEFORE THE WAR. THE CHANGES THAT had taken place in the years between made him feel like an old-timer of thirty. By now, the coal-burner that had carried him from Chicago to Washington, D.C., was probably part of a submarine or troop transport, or demoted to switch-engine duty in some rail yard. The diesel-electric locomotive pulling this impossibly long line of cars south wore a shiny aluminum skin and looked like a flashlight. It made no noise except when its horn blew. Would his children, he wondered, know what he meant when he said *choo-choo*?

The bartender in the club car was colored, with polished-looking skin and the best-kept hands Vasco had ever encountered in his sex; Hoover's were manicured, but the Director spoiled the effect by biting his nails. "Beverage, sir? I'm sorry I can't serve spirits for another ten minutes. We're passing through a dry county."

That explained the fact they had the car to themselves. "Ginger ale is fine."

The bartender opened a bottle of Canada Dry from the refrigerator and poured. He paused when the glass was half full.

"To the top, sir?"

"Yes."

He filled it. "Some gentlemen carry a flask. I guess the old days aren't so old."

Vasco smiled. He'd been feeling positively antique. "Did you tend bar during Prohibition?"

"Tended it, varnished it, swept around it, and helped a coupla gen'lemans out into de alley." His sunny grin flickered; he'd forgotten his Pullman grammar in the moment. "I was single then, and wicked in my ways. I guess I'd be six feet under now if not for my Cassie."

"Shot in the dark: Chicago South Side?"

"No, *sir. De*-troit. Chicago got the press, but Detroit's where it got its liquor. Those days, if you drank, it either came across the river from Windsor or you mixed it up in a tub. Did you ever hear of the Purple Gang?"

"They ran whiskey for Capone." Should he have played dumb? The time he'd spent studying the rituals of the Church might better have gone into learning undercover etiquette. Maybe the Director considered naivete an asset in the field: but it was a minefield.

"To, not for: that's an important distinction. Detroit fellows, every one. Hired their guns to him, too. It was Purples killed those gentlemen on St. Valentine's Day."

"I heard it was—someone else." Feigning ignorance felt proper here.

"Oh, Scarface Al used a couple of local boys to slap on the final coat, as we say, but it was Killer Burke and the Keywell brothers wearing the uniform of

Chicago's Finest that day, to throw off witnesses. Well, the gang's all in jail now, or dead. But you know who's out? The Big Fellow himself. Capone. If you're riding through to Miami, you might just see him."

"I wouldn't know him if I did. I was ten years old when they put him away."

"A railroad job, sir, with all due respect to the industry I work for. Are you aware of the number of people who have served time in maximum security for failure to pay their income taxes in the thirty-one years since the law was ratified?"

"Not offhand."

"Just one, sir. Alphonse Capone. I'm not saying he wasn't guilty, but do you think he'd have spent a day behind bars if his name was Mahoney?"

Vasco drank ginger ale. He'd almost forgotten it; the bubbles were flattening out. "You make him sound like a martyr. You just said he hired the Purple Gang to commit murder."

"I did, and he should've hung for it, or done a stretch for selling liquor when it was illegal, as I surely would if I sold you a gin-and-tonic in the next three minutes. If you want to punish a man for something he did, you ought not to punish him for something else, and throw the book at him for the other thing. That's just my opinion," he said, grinning suddenly; shambling. "Where else can a man blow off but in a bar?"

"He couldn't even do that for thirteen years."

"Not legally, no, sir. But I seen me some blowin' off when the law said no; I did indeed. What time you got, sir, if you don't mind my asking'? My old pocket winder needs cleaning."

He looked at his strap watch. "I have three-eighteen." He'd stopped himself shy of giving it in military time; he pledged to spend the long ride purging himself of Bureauese.

"What's two minutes?" With sudden energy, the bartender rang a brass bell hanging above the bar. "What'll it be, sir? I'll be sure and pour it slow."

"Kentucky rye." It had calmed him in Hoover's office. No other kind of alcohol sprang to mind.

The man behind the bar set down a pony glass and filled it with Old Overholt. "Not many asking for it these days. Folks got suspicious of American brands when they started spiking 'em with wood alcohol and fusel oil. If it sounded imported they lapped it up, even when it came from a car radiator with iodine to taste. These days it's Scotch, Scotch, Scotch. Can't keep it in stock."

"What's your preference?"

"Soda pop, sir, same as you. I made that promise to Cassie on our wedding day. A man's nothing if he don't keep his promises."

That soured the taste of the whiskey, but it was too sweet for him anyway. He still couldn't see what people saw in it, why wars had been fought over it. Passengers were entering the car. He had the bizarre feeling they'd been hovering on the platform outside, listening for the magic bell. The bartender left him to take orders. Scotch did seem to be the variety of choice. Vasco let his drink stand unfinished and left money on the bar, including a tip that wasn't so generous he'd be remembered later.

Back in his compartment, he spread out the Capone file on the bench opposite and selected a ragged sheaf of pink onionskin containing an incident report by the Cook County, Illinois, Sheriff's Department dated April 28, 1926. A bullet-mangled body had been discovered in a ditch beside a country road a few miles south of Chicago. All means of identification had been removed, but another report filed later that day, rescued from the disorderly pile of material, identified the victim as William Harold McSwiggin, a young assistant state's attorney; Jake Lingle, a reporter with the *Chicago Tribune,* signed a statement to that effect.

A bundle of crumbling newspaper clippings harvested over succeeding weeks provided more details. Two more bodies surfaced in woods and a puddle of brackish water, O'Donnell Gang members ambushed in front of a Cicero roadhouse by an armed motorcade. McSwiggin was believed at first to have been an innocent bystander cut down while investigating the O'Donnells from inside. The blame fell heavily on Capone: His men were swept up by the paddy wagonload for interrogation, and he himself surrendered to authorities in the Federal Building to give a statement accounting for his whereabouts on the night of the assault. A Grand Jury was summoned. A second was announced days before its term ran out at the end of a month. There would be six in all.

A weary Capone finally told reporters: "Of course I didn't kill him. Why should I? I liked the kid. Only the day before, he was up to my place and when he went home I gave him a bottle of Scotch for his old man."

The "old man," a detective sergeant and thirty-year veteran of the Chicago Police Department, said, "Those bullets weren't meant for my boy." The innocent-bystander theory had become official policy.

Then it began to unravel. Capone made a second appearance in the Federal Building: Vasco looked again at a man obviously harried, but smiling for the benefit of the photographer on the front steps, one hand in the trousers pocket of a beautiful suit. I PAID MCSWIGGIN, ran the headline.

"I paid him plenty," he was quoted in the article, "and I got what I was paying for."

By October, the state attorney's name had slipped from page one and begun its migration to two paragraphs in the Contests section. The press had many other fish to fry.

That spring and summer, the battle for the streets seemed to have escalated from trench warfare to full mobilization. Three cars had been involved in the attack on the O'Donnells. Less than five months later, ten seven-passenger sedans cruised past the Hawthorne Inn on Cicero's Twenty-Second Street, where Capone was dining in the ground-floor restaurant with Frankie Rio, one of his bodyguards, and poured at least a thousand rounds into the building, by police estimate; the walls and fixtures were so torn apart there was no telling how much had been sprayed from shotguns and how much from Thompsons. Thirty-five cars parked on the street were clobbered with holes and four people hit, none of them Capone or Rio, who pulled his employer to the floor and piled on top of him at the sound of the first report. The savagery had become commonplace, but Vasco was shaken by the incompetence and casual disregard for collateral victims. A shard of glass pierced the eye of a woman seated in a parked car. Capone paid for her medical treatment.

According to Lingle of the *Tribune,* it was the Big Fellow's first personal experience with mechanized weaponry. "That's the gun," he said. "It's got it over a sawed-off shotgun like the shotgun has it over an automatic. The trouble is they're hard to get."

Not so hard, it seemed, that exactly three weeks later they didn't chatter from upper-floor windows across State Street from Holy Name Cathedral in Chicago, killing Hymie Weiss and a companion and wounding two others. Police reports and newspapers agreed that it cleared up any mystery as to who had bankrolled the siege on the Hawthorne Inn. A photo in the *Herald-Examiner* showed the cornerstone of the church chewed up by bullets, leaving the chiseled inscription to read: EVERY KNEE SHOULD   HEAVEN AND   EARTH. Vasco made note of it to look up later.

More morgue pictures, McSwiggin quartered on an autopsy table, his intestines draining in a sink. "Red" Duffy, one of his criminal companions, had been dumped in a puddle by his friends while still alive. He'd died with his lips skinned back from his teeth like an angry dog's. According to the report, a coroner's assistant had been obliged to break his fingers in order to open his fist, but he wasn't clutching any telltale buttons or incriminating messages, à la Edgar Wallace. Hymie Weiss was uncircumcised.

Cook County, Vasco learned, tattooed ID codes on big toes in case the tags slipped off. If you died violently or without a physician in attendance, you went to your reward marked for all eternity. It should have furnished a subject for conversation in Limbo. He'd always pictured the place as a huge waiting room with magazines on tables and the doctor running late. The work would have been stacked up that year.

There was balance in the file. Capone's highly publicized efforts to feed the unfortunate during hard times was documented; a photostat of an invoice, stamped PAID and signed by Jacob Guzik, his financial officer, listed six pages of utensils, canned goods, and fresh produce to supply the soup kitchens he'd established throughout Chicago, totaling more than twenty-five hundred dollars. Men and women dressed in their shabby best were photographed lining up outside one of the locations, months before the Salvation Army and the federal government came on board. Guzik had signed the hospital bill for Anna Freeman, the woman injured in front of the Hawthorne: a whopping five thousand. Capone's own signature appeared nowhere. A cagey man, even in his philanthropy.

Young Peter Vasco hadn't been aware of the turbulent events at the time. It would be another year before uncles John and Albert gave him a rocking horse. He assumed his mother had taken charge of keeping him uninformed. His father was seldom home, going out before Peter got up and returning hours after he'd gone to bed.

Rio, the man who'd saved Capone's life in the restaurant, appeared in a photo with his eyes rolled to one side as if looking for a way out. He slicked his hair like Valentino, but his upper lip was badly out of line, as if it had been torn by a bullet or a razor and stitched by an amateur. Vasco vaguely recalled a man with a funny lip sharing a jug of brown homemade wine with his father at the kitchen table. It was late; the boy had gotten up for a drink of water and come upon them in their shirtsleeves. He remembered the red suspenders the stranger wore with a tie that matched, and the way the conversation stopped when he'd entered the room in his nightshirt.

He shook his head. A lot of men had bad lips back then, cratered by smallpox or split by a fall on a loading dock. He didn't even know when the meeting had taken place. It didn't mean Frankie Rio had been in his home or that it had anything to do with "Terrible 26," as the delirious press called it. An acquaintance with Scalise and Anselmi was too close to Capone for comfort, but his personal bodyguard? Paul Vasco drove a beer truck, played fetch for spear-handlers on the fringe of the Outfit. ("Performed odd jobs," Hoover had said; and who would know if not J. Edgar Hoover?) The boys could be clumsy, but they knew better than to engage menials for important work.

He'd spent too many hours with that file. It was warping his imagination. He was like the hypochondriac who read impenetrable medical journals and concluded he suffered from beriberi.

Time to part with that folder filled with ancient horrors, wars no one cared who'd lost and won. He indulged himself once more only, mining the desiccating heap of paper to excavate the record on Jake Lingle, the *Tribune* journalist who always seemed to be around when a John Doe in the morgue needed a name and Al Capone had something to say worth putting out on the AP wire.

He had no trouble finding it. That was the telling thing.

THE TRAIN STOPPED IN RALEIGH TO EXCHANGE PASSENGERS. HE GOT OFF, bought packing material at a Piggly Wiggly, and sent the Capone file by special delivery to Washington, using the address of a paper-and-pen supply company with direct ties to the Bureau, as instructed. What he hadn't read was an omission less dangerous than if he were caught in possession, and in any case the man he'd been assigned to befriend and betray had far more to offer, and at first hand; assuming his brains hadn't broken down into a pile of debris worse than his file.

North Carolina was hot and sodden, at a time when the District had not yet accepted a spring season unclouded by icy rain or even a snow shower; climatologists predicted a modern Ice Age, touched off by promiscuous plosive activity in Northern Europe. The conditioned air from the compressors in the day coach evaporated the sweat from his body and chilled him—if not to the bone, then at least to the flesh beneath the skin. He thought fondly of the warming properties of Kentucky rye, but vetoed a return to the club car so soon, in case the bartender fixed him too well in his memory.

Possibly it was an unnecessary precaution. He'd begun to suspect that his background was less valuable to undercover work than his general lack of color; but then since adolescence he'd been determined not to become "a character," as Paul Vasco referred to the plug-uglies who drifted in and out of their apartment, gnawing on toothpicks and adjusting their genitals as if they were capsules of nitroglycerine that might detonate if not allowed to swing free. He was perfectly satisfied of the stability of his own in the sling of his BVDs. The habits of a lifetime provided their own camouflage. His only adult relationship had ended when he was informed that an entire pair of socks need not be thrown out when one had a hole in it and every other pair in the drawer was the same color and style. The door had slammed in the middle of a dissertation on the wisdom of rotating tires.

"Dear God, I'm a stuffed shirt," he breathed aloud.

"Huh." The woman seated across the aisle, cloche-hatted and knitting a gray scarf suitable for sending to a soldier in the Aleutians, chuckled aloud and stepped up the operation, as if that were the source of amusement.

He returned to his compartment and rang for the porter to make his berth. Left alone he stripped to those marvelous BVDs and factory-matched socks and climbed in. The slight sway of the car put him into a deep sleep, interrupted only twice, when the train made another passenger stop and when it lurched and shuddered with the coupling and uncoupling of cars.

In the morning he put on his robe, washed and shaved in a cramped but spotless lavatory, and went back to the compartment to open his valise. In a little while he looked at himself in the full-length mirror on the compartment door. He wore a sixty-dollar gray suit over a black dickey and white clerical collar, all supplied by the FBI wardrobe department; really just a large walk-in closet supervised by a fussy Special Intelligence officer, but stocked with an impressive variety of uniforms and business attire, formal wear, and ragtag garments appropriate to stevedores, taxi drivers, and handymen. An elevator operator or street sweep would not have come away from that room unprepared. In that light, the Director's fascination with movie stars seemed less a symptom of public vanity and more a matter of free exchange. Washington and Hollywood shared a dependence on putty noses and padded suits; likely a barter system existed, trading professional consultation on Bureau-related films for access to studio tailors and seamstresses.

The train got into Fort Lauderdale at noon. He'd boarded it a civil servant, part of the drab fabric of the wartime bureaucracy, and left it a soldier in the service of God, which was invisibility of another kind. People he encountered in the crowd smiled politely or touched their hats and looked straight through him.

Very quickly he wondered how priests in that part of the world kept their collars fresh. He'd brought changes, but it seemed he might go through them all the first day. If the weather experts were right about the cooling of the earth, the news hadn't reached Florida. Deceptively mild, the air, creaking with gulls and smelling faintly of fish and diesel oil, grew heavy as he walked along the platform and broke him into a sweat.

"Father, can I take your bag?"

He blinked at the colored porter with his handcart—the first person to call him Father—and shook his head. "No, thank you; my son. Could you direct me to the local branch of the Everglade State Bank?"

It was the porter's turn to hesitate. Vasco considered explaining the vagaries connected with Mammon and the Church, but thought it better to blend with the scenery. When the directions were forthcoming he thanked the man again and walked to the streetcar stop in front of the station.

When he got off, the breeze through the open windows had refreshed him. He went through a heavy leaded-glass door into a marble lobby and felt the air-conditioning brush the back of his neck.

The bank was a prime example of post-Dillinger architecture. Behind the tellers' cages the vault door was sealed tight, and the cages themselves were enclosed in ribs of glistening rock maple and bulletproof glass. A Hispanic guard stood in an ostentatious spot with his thumbs hooked inside his Sam Browne belt, the checked handle of a big revolver leaning out from his hip. A challenging pair of hickory-colored eyes watched the man dressed as a priest carrying a large valise up to the writing bench.

Vasco dipped a pen, filled out a withdrawal slip, and walked to the tellers' cages, waving the ink dry as he went. A plump young woman with a pretty face smiled at him through the bars, called him Father, and asked what she could do for him. A tiny silver crucifix winked at him from the hollow of her throat. He smiled back and slid the slip under the glass.

Budgeting and Accounting had wired the equivalent of a Division Four clerk's annual salary in his name to Everglade's main office in Miami, to draw on for expenses. This was the same bank that had approved Paul Anthony Vasco's application for a loan, and with good reason. It was an open secret in Washington—open to everyone, it seemed, but holders of ephemeral national office—that the Bureau had bought up a number of failed banks and other businesses during the Depression, and used them to direct funds to various operations around the country and as fronts to prevent paper trails from leading to the FBI. It was doubtful that the ordinary employees of these institutions knew who they were really working for, but Vasco watched closely as she read the slip. Nothing but friendliness showed on her face when she asked for identification, and still when she handed back his brand new Florida driver's license with a picture of him wearing a collar. She excused herself to check his balance.

In her absence he glanced toward the guard, but the man had lost interest when a tommy gun failed to materialize from the big suitcase and switched his attention to a middle-aged man coming in the door in baggy shorts and a Panama hat, anchors on his shirt.

"Sorry to keep you waiting, Father. We just got notice of the account from Miami this morning." The teller counted out two hundred dollars from her drawer. "Are you new to Florida?"

"Yes. My father lives here in town and I've been transferred to Our Lady of Redemption in Miami."

Her smile grew brilliant, exposing braces. "That's my aunt's church! I guess I'll see you there next visit."

"I guess you will." He smiled back, and held the expression for the guard's benefit until he was outside. He hoped Hoover knew what he was doing; and felt a twinge of guilt for doubting him.

Either Southern hospitality was everything it was cracked up to be, or ecclesiastical garb sweetened hearts soured by the heat. The first person on the street he asked for directions to a respectable hotel, a large-hipped woman in a thin cotton sundress carrying a grocery sack, glanced from his lifted hat to his collar, then down to his valise, and told him how to get to the Sea Breeze Motor Court on Atlantic. A quart of ice cream had sweated through the sack and dripped down the side of her dress, turning it transparent and showing her girdle.

The Sea Breeze was a shotgun arrangement of rooms in a pink stucco building with a scripted neon sign identifying the office at one end. The office smelled of disinfectant and chewing gum and the female clerk nursed a short soggy cigarette stub smoldering in her face. But his room was clean, with the damp of the ocean apparent, if not the ocean itself; it was across the street, behind a row of shops selling bathing suits and tackle. Four pale blue ribbons stirred feebly in front of a window-mounted air conditioner to show it was doing its job.

He opened a window to help out. He turned on a radio, but getting only static on all stations snapped it off and unpacked the Bible that had traveled with him all the way from Cicero and sat on the bed to search for the verse that had been all but shot away along with Hymie Weiss in front of Holy Name. He found it in St. Paul's Epistle to the Philippians (2:10):

> That at the name of Jesus every knee should bow, of things in heaven and
> things in earth, and things under the earth . . .

Vasco had made all the necessary appearances for one day. He put away the book, changed into gabardine slacks and a rayon sports shirt, and went out to walk on the beach, leaving the uniform behind.

Afternoon sunlight scalloped the waves, drawing a strong shoreward wind that riffled his hair and drove away the heat. A flock of sailboats glided around as aimlessly as butterflies far out, but few motor craft with gasoline rationing in place. A man in a white Civil Service helmet stood on the end of a pier with binoculars, scanning the horizon for U-boats. Despite these things it was difficult to believe that men were spilling and shedding buckets of blood on just the other side of the Atlantic.

He looked at the horizon, too, but not for enemy submarines. God, he believed, was not to be found in the sky, but at the junction of heaven and earth. In that murky violet line was Paradise Everlasting; Hell, too, because at the end of his time in the seminary he had come to the conclusion that God and the Devil were one and the same, and that was why he'd left. He believed it still, and now he had entered that place that was always within sight and forever beyond reach.

"Forgive me," he said into the wind.

HE ROSE EARLY, WITH DEWY DROPLETS MAKING TRACKS IN THE BRINE ON the windows and before the heat could come rolling in against the tide. In a fresh dickey, with his summer-weight suit falling lightly on his shoulders, he breakfasted on powdered eggs and ersatz bacon in a diner that opened at dawn to serve fishermen. Most of the anglers had come and gone, but local types and a smattering of tourists drank Postum, a coffee substitute, and looked at the ocean through a row of windows with a roll of black oilskin mounted above it to serve as blackout curtains during air raid drills. The waitress who refilled his cup, a tall bony woman in a teal uniform, said that the ban on pleasure driving had knocked a hole in the tourist trade worse than the Maginot Line.

He replied sympathetically, but made little effort to sound sincere. The morning was going to be unpleasant enough, and he wanted to get all he could out of these last few contemplative moments. The waitress, apparently thinking him distracted by reflections of a religious nature, withdrew without belaboring her subject. Later he felt guilty and left a generous tip.

The address Hoover had given him for Sunrise Charters was burned into the lintel of a shack built of the same planking material as the pier it shared with a competitor. It had a slant metal roof with a recent coat of white paint to deflect the sun and retard rust, but orange spots had already burst through it like boils in the salt air.

He had a flash of hope, inspired by the name of the enterprise, that the owner had sailed with a customer, but the small motor launch tied up to the pier told him procrastination wasn't an option. MAUREEN was painted in professional lettering on the fantail: his mother's name. He stood on the dock with his fists balled in his pockets, waiting for the anger to fade.

Friendly relations must be established.

He took a deep breath, let it out, fanned the heat from his face with his hat;

walked up to the door and knocked on it before he had a chance to change his mind.

It opened on brass hinges. But verdigris had managed to do what rust could not. They squeaked like startled rats. A man blinked at him from the doorway, naked but for a pair of dirty shorts with cargo pockets, a can of beer in his hand.

"Well, if it ain't the little sky pilot," he said.

"Hello, Dad."

FIVE

"Come ahead in, since you're here. Don't track in no fish scales on the Persian rug." His father turned and retreated inside, not so much leading his visitor as walking away from him.

People who'd seen them together never guessed they were related. Paul Vasco was short, stooped from too many years sitting in driver's seats not designed for the human spine, and scrawnier than Peter remembered; a man could cut a finger on his shoulder blades. His son was taller by a head and had to watch his weight. He had his mother's face and fair coloring, while his father's belonged on an Indian-head penny.

The rug was a straw mat, faded to the same shade of khaki as the plank floor. There was a kerosene lantern on a nail, a writing table and chair, a tin ice chest, and a sprung rattan chair with a firm cushion for Paul's back. An army cot was the only other furniture.

"You live here?"

"Sleep it off here sometimes. I got arrangements with a lady in town. That shock you?"

"I've heard too many confessions to shock easily."

"It ain't no confession." He lowered himself into the rattan, squirmed around until he got the cushion right, and crossed his bare ankles. The sun had bleached his close-cropped hair white and burned his body dark as red oak. He looked older than fifty, but his arms were strung with sinew, his eyes as bright as a bird's. The soles of his feet looked like ox hide. It occurred to Peter he'd never seen him with his shoes off before. "You want a beer?" He gestured toward the ice chest with the can in his hand.

Thirty years since he left Calabria and he hadn't altered the accent, except to seal it with a hard Chicago overlay.

"It's early for me."

"Breakfast of champions, like it says on the Wheaties box." He swigged from the can. "Sit yourself down. Or you more comfortable on your knees?"

"You used to kneel in church."

"I didn't do it for no living. When'd you get out?"

"You make it sound like I was in prison."

"Prisoners don't got a choice."

Peter drew the chair out from the table and sat, bracing his hands on his thighs. "I was ordained two years ago. I stayed to serve at St. Francis, but now they're sending me to Miami."

"Blessed Sacrament?"

"Our Lady of Redemption."

"I took the choir director from Sacrament out after marlin coupla times. Swears like-a the police sergeant." His enunciation came and went when he drank; this wasn't his first of the day. Peter wondered what he did with the empties. "How come you didn't join the army and be a chaplain?"

"You might not think so, but civilians need spiritual counseling just as much as soldiers."

"Also you don't get shot at."

Were you ever? he wanted to ask. But that wasn't the point of the visit.

"Cubans," Paul said.

"What?"

"Miami's crawling with 'em, that's why there's two Catholic churches. Otherwise there'd be a temple on every corner and kosher in every restaurant. Jolson comes down in December and stays till February, what you think of that? The Jazz Singer himself."

"Do you think he'd convert?"

The joke failed. He didn't remember his father's eyes being so steady and bright; maybe it was the deep sunburn. "I figured it had to be work brought you when I seen what you was wearing. You wouldn't come here just to see the old man."

"I didn't have to come at all."

"How'd you find me, anyway?"

"You wrote me at the seminary."

"I didn't think you got any of my letters. You never answered."

"I'm sorry. That's one of the reasons I came, to apologize. And forgive."

"I don't need no apologies and you can stick the other thing up your ass. What psalm's that from, Padre?"

He felt the blood engorging his face. Probably the old man thought he was offended by the language. What right did *he* have to be bitter? Peter touched the gold crucifix on the chain around his neck. It was a gift from his mother. Her serenity touched him back.

"Christ, it's hot already." Paul rolled the can of beer across his forehead. "A man misplaces his manners. Lower that thing."

He got up to pull the cord that secured the wicker shade over the window facing the sun. The beer can cleared the sill just before the shade came down, missing him by inches, rolled on wood, and landed on water with a splat. "Get me another one while you're up. That one was warm as piss."

That solved the mystery of the missing empties. He fished a fresh can of Pfeiffer's out of the chipped ice in the chest. Paul took it and punched two triangular holes in the top with an opener he took from a cargo pocket. "You're gonna like Florida, especially when the rest of the country's freezing its nuts off. Come July you'll swear you're in hell. What you do, you can't stand it no more, you come up here. I'll take you out on the boat. It's like taking a cold shower, only wetter."

"Is business that slow?"

"It's this pleasure-driving ban, but they're gonna lift it because they can't enforce it any better than they done Prohibition. Diesel's a bitch to get hold of on account of rationing. But I got connections."

"Still?" He sat down, keeping his voice neutral.

Paul heard something anyway. "What, you never hoarded stamps so you could stuff yourself on roast beef one day out of the month? They say it's wrong, but everybody does it."

"I was just saying I didn't know you knew anyone with the black market."

"Let me tell you, I was in line at the OPA, I heard a sailor tell the clerk his air base in Alaska had so much fuel they dumped it out on the runway and set it on fire to melt the ice. We need it more than they do. The way I see it I ain't doing nothing no worse than what I done back in Chicago."

There it was, right in his lap. *Lead us not into*— "What *did* you do back in Chicago, Dad?"

"I drove trucks, son. I gave some fellows a lift when they needed it. I loaded and unloaded crates. Sometimes I stood outside a place and gave a whistle when I seen someone coming. You knew all that."

Peter stared, but the face had gone as immobile as the Indian's on the penny. He never had been able to read him when that happened, and it was worse with the shade breaking him up into horizontal bars of twilight. Maybe after another beer; but that wasn't why he was here.

"Anyway, this war can't last forever. That's what I told the man at the bank. He thought about it for a week, then saw I was right. It didn't look at the start like I'd ever own that boat, just go on paying rent on it till I was all dried up and blind like my uncle Umberto in Strongoli. But I'd've made a hell of a fine senator a coupla thousand years ago. Your old man could have talked Pontius Pilate into giving Jesus the key to the treasury."

"That's good, Dad. You always had the gift of gab." Even if he hadn't been sworn to silence, he'd never have been able to bring himself to tell him it was J. Edgar Hoover's miracle and not his. No matter what else had passed between them, he couldn't take that away.

Paul beamed and lifted his beer. "Any day now, our boys will land in Europe and go through them Huns like salt through a hired girl. The Japs are already on the run. We'll have peace by Christmas, and then I'll be up to my neck in tourists and fuel for old *Maureen*. Did I tell you I named her after your mother, God rest her soul?"

"I guess she earned that much at least."

Once again he'd misjudged his father's ear. The can remained at half-mast. "What does that mean, Pietro?" He only called him that when he told him to fetch the strop.

"I didn't come here to rake up the past."

"Then you should not have brought a rake. You said you had something you wanted to forgive, so spit it out."

He retreated onto less dangerous ground. "Do you remember what you said when I told you I'd been accepted at St. Francis?"

"I don't remember what I said two minutes ago. I never learned anything listening to myself."

"You said, 'Son, there's no sense giving up on fucking girls your whole life. You won't always look like something that just crawled out of a sewer pipe.'"

"Well, you don't. You don't look like me, either, but nobody'd mistake you for a rat no more. I almost didn't know you at first." He swallowed beer, burped. "Maybe lay off the potatoes. Dames like a flat belly." He slapped his. It made a sound Peter found vaguely obscene.

"I'm a priest, Dad. You don't get to be one if you aren't meant for it."

"Bullshit. You think I was meant to push a hack?"

"That was a job. This is a calling."

"There's-a no difference. Don't forget, I was an altar boy in the Old Country. Also I was the bocci champion of the neighborhood."

"I don't see what those two things have to do with each other." He wondered if his father's mind was wandering.

"You're lucky, then, because if I wasn't fast on my feet I'd've got the Holy Spirit rammed up my ass. You think Father Angelino got the Call to do what he done to the boys that wasn't?"

"I didn't expect your blessing, but I didn't deserve to be insulted."

"A man don't like to see his son throw his life away. I hoped you'd find that out for yourself, but that won't happen now. You were what, eighteen?"

"Nineteen. Three years older than you when you came through Ellis Island."

"You know what they done to me there?"

"What?" He regretted asking. He was afraid he would say they'd rammed the American way up his ass.

"Took away who I was, that's what. Paolo Antonio Bascano was my name when the boat put in, but the man in the processing center was in too much of a hurry to write it down right." A bony shoulder lifted, fell. "Life is an accident. When there is a Call it's usually a wrong number."

"This one wasn't."

"Well, then." His father made the sign of the cross, blessing him with the beer can.

It made him absurdly happy, and he chided himself for it. "What about you? Wrong number or lucky accident?"

"So it is confession you're after."

"Can't a son ask his dad if he's happy?"

"It'd be easier if you'd take off that choker."

Peter reached behind his neck and unbuttoned the collar. He put it and the dickey on the writing table, next to a tin cigar box that might have been the same one Paul Vasco had kept his fares in back in Cicero.

His father looked surprised. "Them things can't be too comfortable down here."

"Cross to bear." He smiled briefly, surprising himself. "I asked you a question."

"I want you to meet Sharon."

He wasn't prepared for that, but he doubted he'd get away with changing the subject again. "That's the lady you have an arrangement with?"

"I shouldn't have put it like that, but I wasn't expecting you. We help each other make ends meet. She gives me a place to stay, and a woman deserves butter and eggs now and then."

"So it's convenient." Paul seemed determined to flaunt his black market connections; but Peter was just as determined not to appear curious. If it came up again—and he was sure it would—he'd use it to get what he came for.

"Well, it's a little more than that. She has her widow's pension, apart from what she makes working in the shipyard, but you can't curl up with no paycheck. I'm not trying to shock you now. Seeing your Adam's apple makes things different. Her husband died at Midway."

"How *old* is she?"

"She says thirty, and she could pass for it. She takes care of herself. I may be an old drunk, but I never robbed no cradle. Your grandmother wasn't born yet when my father buried his first wife."

"What's she like?"

"You can judge for yourself. She gets off her shift at four."

"I'll take a rain check. I'm leaving on the four-fifteen to Miami. Father Kyril's expecting me."

"Fuck kind of name's Kyril?"

His father had become profane. Maybe he always had been, with his cronies, but had held back around his wife and child.

"Russian, I think."

"Don't turn bolshevik. Bad enough you wear a dress Sundays."

"Is it serious?"

"Damn right it is. FDR should never have crawled into bed with that *moffetta* Stalin."

"You know what I mean."

"Me and Sharon? Well, we smile a lot, so I guess the answer's no."

"I'm happy for you, Dad. Mom wouldn't want you to be alone."

"That's the second time you did that."

"Did what?"

"That thing with your mouth when your mother came up, like you had a mouthful of boiled turnip. It's a good thing nobody can see you in the booth. What's wrong?"

He wasn't strong enough to retreat a second time. Maybe if he'd had training. "You were away a lot. It wasn't easy taking care of me with her leg in a brace."

"She never told you that."

"You think I couldn't figure it out?"

"There was bills to pay, boy. I couldn't go to work and stay home both."

"The cab company paid you a decent wage."

"And after I turned it all over to the doctors, what then?"

"That was later. She wasn't in the hospital then."

"Where you think she was when you was in school?"

"What do you mean?"

"I asked you a question." Throwing it back at him.

"Home, scrubbing floors and shaking out the rug."

"She was at Sisters of Mercy Hospital, getting treated for polio."

"That was over before I was born. It made it hard for her to get around, which is why she could've used your help. She didn't need treatment until her heart failed."

"She needed therapy. Hot and cold compresses. Vitamin shots to keep up her strength. All that costs money, son, more than a man could make just driving people around. And all down the drain, because she died anyway."

He felt himself pale. "The death certificate said nothing about polio."

"It weakens the heart."

"I don't believe you."

"All the same it does. It stopped once when she was giving birth. They had to pound on her chest to start it back up. She wasn't supposed to have children, but she didn't tell me that till after we brought you home.

"Wherever I was, Chicago or Cicero, whatever I was doing, whoever I was with, I left him to go back to the apartment, pick her up, and bring her back home after her treatment. I bet you Maureen Vasco's the only patient ever got a ride to Sisters of Mercy in a beer truck."

"I didn't know. I never even guessed."

"We timed it so you were in school. No little kid should have to worry if his mother's gonna be around to see him graduate."

He was suddenly, perversely glad she hadn't seen him fail. He would never have been able to fool her as he had his father. She'd have stared at him with those eyes like blue-green lagoons until he broke down and confessed.

"That's why you came home so late and left so early. You had to make up for the time you took off."

"Sure. The Outfit's like any other job when it comes to punching the clock."

He shut his eyes tight. Breathing hurt; he had a furniture clamp on his chest. He should have felt the opposite. A burden he'd been carrying all his adult life had vanished. But it had done its damage. He opened his eyes. He could see his father better now in the dimness. "Why didn't you tell me? It's been five years."

"I'm Italian. Your wife dies, you blubber a lot, you don't shave, you pray her over to the other side, you go home, and don't talk about her for a while. Then your son comes down with a bad case of Jesus. There didn't seem no point."

Sea noises broke in on silence. Paul set his can on the floor and got up with a gentle yelp of familiar pain. "Time to scuttle the old bladder. Buy me lunch. I'll say you shooed me back into the fold and you can charge it to the pope."

"Is there someplace quiet?" He had more questions to ask that couldn't be shouted over chatter and colliding crockery. He reached for his collar.

"Place we're going, you'll think you're in Pharaoh's tomb."

Paul Vasco had a gift for saying the wrong thing at the right time. It lifted the weight from his son's chest.

Peter waited outside a public lavatory while his father relieved himself. It sounded like a gushing fireplug. He came out wiping his hands on his shirt, pale yellow with half-sleeves and flap pockets. Dirty white deck shoes covered his feet and a fisherman's cap with a long bill cast his face in shadow.

They walked to a twelve-story beachfront hotel. "Bubble job," his father explained. "Owner shot himself when he couldn't unload it. Then when real estate turned around a syndicate bought it and renovated. Now they soak big shots in munitions sixty-five bucks a night to stay in the suites. 'The Warbucks Wigwam,' we call it."

Peter checked his valise with a bellhop in the lobby. The dining room was modern Havana, with cedar wainscoting, potted palms, bowl fixtures suspended from chains, and all kinds of exotic flowers exploding on the wallpaper. The maitre d', a smooth Cuban in a white drill suit, frowned slightly at Paul Vasco in his beachcomber's costume, but Peter's collar secured them a corner booth upholstered in red leatherette.

"The monkey suit comes in handy." Paul took off his cap and ran a thick palm over his Fuller Brush haircut. "Most days I'd have to dress up like Carmen Miranda just to get in the door."

"They probably think you're a charity case."

"Look who made a joke."

"I guess you missed the one about Al Jolson."

"Your heart's got to be in it to make it funny."

He'd surprised himself at how easily it had come out. Was it that simple? A moment of excruciating pain followed by instant recovery? He doubted it. These things probably came in waves. They were all extensions of grief.

It was early. The place was less than a third full, and they were waited on quickly, by a younger Cuban who filled in his pencil moustache with eyeliner. Peter ordered the sea bass, Paul a steak, blood rare. "I can eat fish anytime I drop a line," he said. "Nobody can do what Sharon does with day-old bread crumbs."

Peter didn't want to talk about Sharon. He sensed he was about to start mourning his mother all over again. "Back home, I'd never have pictured you owning a boat."

"Shows how much you know. All the Bascanos lived on the water. My grandfather had webbed feet. But I'm not the fisherman he was. You ever read Hemingway?"

"There's a fisherman." He'd never seen his father with a book in his hands, not even a hymnal in church.

Paul snorted. "He fishes like Boris Karloff dances ballroom. I took him out once."

"Ernest Hemingway?"

"Don't act so surprised. Hang around Florida long enough you'll hear him if you don't see him, he's that loud. He signed up as a war correspondent and put his boat in mothballs, but then the trip was delayed a week, so he picked me out of the book to kill time. He's a big fucker, bigger'n you, and fumble-ass clumsy. When you ain't tripping over his big feet he's tripping over them himself.

"He comes on board carrying this big canvas zip bag. I figured he had a coupla six-packs in there, but out he hauls a fucking tommy gun. To shoot sharks, he said."

"Did he shoot any?"

"If it swam he shot at it, but the dolphins and Gertrude Ederle didn't have nothing to worry about. Son, he couldn't hit the ocean. I told him a tommy pulls to the left and up, so you got to hold it sideways against your hip and put that failing to your advantage; you know, sweep to the side. He tried it and shot the hell out of my beer cooler."

Peter laughed, loud enough to turn heads. He wondered if he'd laughed in years.

"Funny to you, maybe," his father said. "Beer was easier to come by when it was against the law. He was the worst shot I ever saw, and the second worst fisherman. He must be just about the best writer in the world or he'd've starved to death by now."

Peter stopped laughing. "Where'd you learn how to operate a machine gun?"

"Who do I look like, Edward G. Robinson? You can't drive and shoot at the same time. You'll miss what you want to hit and hit what you want to miss; a telephone pole, say, or a cop. Like I said, I never learned nothing listening to myself. Jack McGurn liked to talk, and he knew what he was talking about, guns and dames. They didn't call him Machine Gun Jack for nothing."

"He was a Capone lieutenant, wasn't he?"

"That's newspaper talk. The Outfit didn't hand out military commissions. But, yeah, they was tight, him and Mr. Capone. Word in the pool hall was he plotted out that Clark Street business."

He couldn't get away from the St. Valentine's Day Massacre, for some reason. "I thought you only associated with hangers-on."

"Associated?" Paul Vasco's grasp of English was slipping—conveniently, his son thought.

"Worked with."

"Worked? Shit. I told you I gave some fellows a lift time to time. Jack had this souped-up Auburn was always breaking down. I guess he liked the way I handled a Mack in traffic. He asked for me whenever his car was in the shop, and he always paid."

He felt the pressure again on his chest. He shifted in his seat. "Dad, about Capone."

His father wasn't paying attention. "It's about time. I could eat a horse."

The waiter had returned, balancing their plates on a shimmering tray.

"What's this? I asked for a steak." Three slices of meat the size and thickness of half-dollars shared Paul's plate with a scoop of mashed potatoes and greenery. They were deep maroon and looked like sliced beets.

"Medallions of beef, sir."

"What's-a matter, you run out of red points? I wouldn't bait a hook with one-a these. Any self-respecting fish would swim right past it."

"I'm sorry, sir. That's our standard serving." He placed the sea bass in front of Peter. His father looked over at it.

"I threw back bigger."

"Sir?"

"Please, Dad."

He shrugged. "Medallions, you said? It's still steak, right?"

"Yes, sir."

"Okay. You better bring me a Schlitz. This won't hold me till I get out the door. This war," he said when they were alone. "I bet they're using frozen T-bones for home plate on that air base in Alaska."

The waiter brought a smaller tray containing a tall foaming glass and a brown bottle. Paul took a long slurpy draught and swallowed loudly. "You believe I never drank beer back when I was hauling it around? I couldn't wait to get back home to that wine Mrs. Terrazzini made in the basement."

Peter couldn't remember which landlady Mrs. Terrazzini was, but he remembered two men sitting at a kitchen table with a jug between them.

"Dad, did you know Frankie Rio?"

His father's head was bent over his plate. He forked beef into his mouth and chewed. "It don't ring a bell. There was a shitload of Frankies around in the old days."

"He wore a lot of grease in his hair and had a bad lip."

"The grease ain't no clue neither. There was more sheiks around than Frankies. You couldn't find a jar of Vaseline in Woolworth's. Bad lip? Nope." He washed down a mouthful with beer.

"He was Al Capone's bodyguard."

"Closest I ever got to Mr. Capone was that time in the cab and in the apartment when he came for his gun. He stopped running his own errands after he took over. Didn't hang around the working stiffs like Henry Ford."

"What about the roadhouse in Indiana?"

He slid the knife and fork into his plate and sat back with his napkin tucked in his shirt. His eyes were bright. "Who told you about that?"

"It was a small apartment. I heard you and Mom talking. You'd been drinking Mrs. Terrazzini's wine."

"Not wine. All the wine in Cicero wasn't strong enough that night. It ain't lunch conversation, son."

"You witnessed two murders."

"I never did. Whatever happened to them poor bastards happened after the party broke up."

"But you saw them beaten."

"I still do. You don't forget a thing like that."

"It was an object lesson. You owed the Outfit money."

"I got a bum steer on the World Series. Somebody told me it was fixed like in 1919. I ain't so much as dropped a nickel on the slots since."

"Capone must have trusted you not to go to the police or you'd be dead too."

"You been to Wrigley Field. You seen what a wood bat does to a ball when it clears the fence. You know what it does to a man's head?"

He did, but he couldn't tell him he'd seen a picture. "It would scare anyone, but frightened people talk to the police sometimes, even in Chicago. Capone knew you well enough to know you wouldn't talk." It was a long shot, not much more than a wild guess; but hypotheticals were lost on the immigrant mind.

"I didn't talk when he threw that pistol in my backseat."

"That's because he paid you. He didn't pay everyone at that banquet to keep his mouth shut."

"I needed the job."

"That wouldn't be enough for Capone."

"Why should I talk? Them two didn't mean shit to me."

"Then why did you invite them to my birthday party?"

Paul's face darkened beneath the sunburn. "You was five. You wouldn't remember if Mary Pickford was there."

The constriction worsened. He drew as deep a breath as he could, but it only increased the pressure. He expelled it. "How did you know I was five? I didn't say which birthday it was."

His father didn't move, didn't blink. He was something stamped in copper. Then a pale tongue-tip emerged and slid along lips chipped and cracked by sun and wind. When it finished they looked as dry as ever. "What is it you want, Pietro?"

"I want to know about you and John Scalise and Albert Anselmi."

"But what do you *want*?"

He'd been working toward it all morning, but now that it was here he wished he could change the subject again. Then again, he wished many things that would never be.

"I want you to introduce me to Al Capone."

SIX

THE NOISE LEVEL HAD INCREASED, ALTHOUGH IT WOULD NEVER BE MIS-taken for the din of a burger palace or corner tavern. The lunch trade had arrived: women in bright silk and men in pastel sport coats and foulards, their eyes making a reverse-raccoon effect where dark glasses had left the skin pale. The rest of their faces were tanned a uniform caramel.

The scent of money wafted from them; not quite the deep pungency of unlimited wealth—that would come with winter, when hotel rates and slip fees were at their highest—but a scent that Peter Vasco would never know at firsthand. An unseen piano spread a light strain under the sliding of chairs and rustle of fine linen: "Brazil," which was close enough to the tropical atmosphere to pass. No one had yet written a song called "Cuba." That gangsters' haven would require brass accompaniment. That island ninety miles off Key West would be the source of the black market in that region.

Peter looked at his sea bass, giving his father a few moments to collect himself. It was flaky and moist and melted on his tongue. He wondered how many of his contemporaries were eating K rations at that moment and chasing them with water from a canteen.

"I told you I only saw him a coupla times," Paul said finally. "Why you want to meet him anyway? Get his autograph, trade two of 'em for one of MacArthur's?"

He'd rehearsed the speech in his head a hundred times, in Washington and on the train and last night in bed while waiting for sleep. Now that the time had come to give it, it struck him as artificial and hollow, a tour guide's spiel the thousandth time around. He drank water from a tall crystal glass with a lemon wedge perched on the rim and put down his fork.

"I'm guilty of the sin of pride," he said. "If I can save Al Capone from eternal damnation, I can become a bishop before I'm thirty. I want to be his confessor."

Utensils tinkled around them, the piano fluttered (". . . where hearts are entertaining still . . .")

Paul Vasco laughed then, drawing stares from other tables. Peter could count on the fingers of one hand the times he'd heard his father laugh, really laugh, and keep free the thumb: once while dancing with his mother to a Paul Whiteman record on their second-hand Victrola; two or three times when he was drunk, which didn't really count; another time when he'd given his small son a bright penny, explaining that it was fresh from the mint, and Peter had licked it to see if he could taste the mint.

But those were happy occasions. The laughter had not had a cynical edge.

"I never knew the Church was so much like the rackets," he said, dabbing at his eyes with a corner of his napkin. "Climb right over another man to get to the top."

Peter wasn't offended. He'd seen things similarly and it had contributed to his neglect of his studies. He said, "It's like every other job when it comes to punching the clock."

Having his own words thrown back at him offended Paul, and that was a surprise. His mouth turned down. "You seriously see him stretched out on some cloud eating grapes from an angel's mitt?"

"He's dying, they say. In that situation a man starts thinking about things of the spirit."

"You know how many times they came after him with guns? They even tried to poison him once. If he didn't go all Christ back then, he ain't about to now just 'cause he caught a cold in his pants." He pushed aside his glass and drank straight from the bottle. "Anyway, you're half his age. A sinner likes his Hail Marys from someone that's sinned himself a coupla hundred times."

"When Capone was my age, he was already running Chicago with Johnny Torrio."

"Did your homework, did you?"

He wasn't unstrung by this. "Anyone who reads the Sunday supplements is an expert on the subject."

His father held the bottle by thumb and forefinger, drumming the rest of his fingers on the neck. "Scalise and Ansclmi got here about the same time I did. They was mixed up in some vendetta or other back in Marsala and shipped out with just what was on their backs. They never bothered to learn the language so good. Your mother didn't want me talking Italian around the house; she wanted you to grow up a hundred-percent American. It was good to have a coupla fellows I could talk with in the language of the Old Country."

"They were the ones you whistled to when you saw someone coming?"

"No, that was strictly cloth-cap work. They didn't bend their suits busting into places and hijacking. They followed me in a Cadillac. This stuff was gold." He waggled the beer bottle. "Anybody can cook alky on a kitchen stove, but breweries was an investment. You needed a warehouse, a crew, trucks, protection. They made sure the beer got to where it was going and that the delivery was accepted. Some-a them saloon keepers had short memories. Albert and Johnny helped them remember who they was buying from.

"They was like Mutt and Jeff in the funnies. Johnny was built like a fireplug, close to the ground and about as easy to knock down. Albert was a beanpole. When a barman wanted to fight, he'd hold him off with one arm, let him swing at the air, while Johnny busted up the place."

"You went in with them?"

"Seen it through the window coupla times. They was all crooks, son. They knew what they got themselves into. And it wasn't just them. I felt an itch one night, like I wasn't alone on the street. Looked down the block and seen a Chicago

Police captain sitting in a sedan under the light on the corner, watching Albert and Johnny kick the shit out of a barman. I could see the bars shining on his shoulders plain as day. He just sat there, and pulled out just before we did."

"Did anyone ever try to hijack you?"

"Two O'Donnells went to block me in once. I wheeled around them before they got set. I didn't have an escort that night; it was just after Polack Weiss went after Mr. Capone with a whole army in Cicero and every man was needed. Tommy O'Donnell pulled a U-turn and put the hammer down. But I outran him."

"What was he driving?"

His father's smile was proud and shy at the same time, like a child's when the nuns gave him a prize. "Packard Eight. Put me behind the wheel of a Mack or a White with a full load, point me downhill, and I'll outrun Barney Oldfield. Wasn't long after that I met Jack McGurn. Word gets around fast."

"Was he at my party?"

"Nobody from work was except Scalise and Anselmi, and they just dropped in lugging that rocking chair up four flights of stairs. I guess I'd bragged on my boy a little. Two things Sicilians can't resist are children and money, but not always in that order. I don't mind telling you your mother wasn't keen on them just showing up like that. You might've heard us talking about it that night."

He didn't remember. His parents often had loud differences of opinion, his mother in her mile-a-minute brogue, his father breaking into Italian when his English was inadequate. These sessions were an annoyance, disturbing sleep, but raised no alarm. The buildings they'd lived in all had thin walls and the details of domestic disturbances were well known to all the residents. No one ever separated or divorced. People whispered about husbands strangling wives and wives stabbing husbands; strangers all, the survivors photographed by reporters sitting on benches in police stations looking like stunned cows. Black eyes and broken dishes were as bad as things usually got in their circle. A Mrs. Benedetti had made her point by commandeering Mr. Benedetti's Franklin and driving it down the steps of a cellar club on Twenty-First Street. She'd never operated a motor vehicle before. It was a conversational topic for weeks.

Paul and Maureen Vasco never raised a hand to each other, but they sure could yell. A boy got used to covering his head with a pillow to get his rest. The next morning everything would be fine.

Peter didn't really believe that story about outracing a high-powered automobile with a lubberly truck. It was just the kind of tall tale a father made up to impress a son he knew was drifting away from him. It was sad and a little pathetic, but things changed and a man couldn't stop them. What concerned him more was he didn't believe that Paul had known John Scalise and Albert Anselmi only from his beer route. Assassins were specialists. They didn't moonlight, guarding shipments and strong-arming reluctant customers. He'd learned that much from studying the Capone file.

Who was Paul Anthony Vasco, and how had he come to be friends with cold-blooded killers?

"Coffee, gentlemen?" The waiter cleared their dishes onto his tray. Peter jumped; the young Cuban moved soundlessly on gum soles.

"Another Schlitz for me," said his father. "I seen them teeny cups you use. They can make a pot of Chock Full o' Nuts last for the duration," he told Peter.

"Coffee'd be nice, thanks."

The cup could have belonged to a child's tea set. The waiter poured slowly from his silver carafe, looking a little nervous at the charade. Peter had noticed that serving containers had been shrinking, to fool the eye into seeing life as normal. If the war went on long enough, everyone would be eating from the head of a pin.

"Flea couldn't drown in it." Paul drank from a fresh beer glass.

"What about it, Dad? Will you introduce me?"

"If you'd *read* them Sunday supplements, you'd know his house is protected like a U.S. convoy. If we was to drive up to the gate they'd shoot me second."

"Why second?"

"You're the bigger target."

"I didn't say not to call first."

"Sure. Just look him up under 'Gangsters.'"

"Why not 'Al Brown, Antique Dealer'?"

Paul swallowed, nodded, looked across at the lunch crowd piling up in the entrance. "Appears I do talk too much when I'm drinking. You were too young to remember that."

"There must be someone you can call. You said you had connections."

"I only said it so you wouldn't think I'm just a harbor rat."

"I don't believe you."

"Why should I call? It's been four Father's Days since I got so much as a card."

"That was a mistake. But you should have told me about Mom."

Paul raised his glass from the table, but he didn't drink. "You know that painter, Norman Rockwell?"

"Not personally."

"Nobody knows everybody else, like you think I know Al Capone. I was asking, you know the stuff he paints, all that warm family shit?"

"I've seen *The Saturday Evening Post*."

"My theory is he's an orphan."

Peter sipped coffee. It was as weak as expected.

"This means a lot to you?"

Peter looked at his father, still looking off into the void. "It does."

"You're at Blessed Sacrament, you said?"

"Our Lady of Redemption."

"Right, the other one. Stick by the phone. I ain't leaving no messages with no altar boy."

"Thanks, Dad."

"I ain't promising nothing. No, that ain't true. Nothing's just what I *am* promising. Last time I talked with anybody from the old days, we was friends with Germany and Japan."

Peter didn't know what to say to that. He didn't try. He clicked his cup in his saucer and smiled.

"So. If you'd never left the Old Country, my name would be Pietro Bascano."

"Be a different person, though. Back in Strongoli we didn't know no Irish girls."

It was getting on toward train time. Peter paid the bill, tipping 10 percent. His father watched him return the rest of the money to his wallet. "I didn't know the Lord's work paid overtime."

"Travel expenses. I have to account for every penny."

"I was just kidding about the pope. My treat next time; not here, though. There's a spaghetti joint six blocks away serves meatballs a-size-a oranges. Ralph Capone's got a half interest, so red points are no problem."

"Did you ever meet Ralph?" Hoover had said Al's brother kept track of old acquaintances.

"Not to talk to. There was six brothers in Chicago, all of 'em big as the Board of Trade. You couldn't hardly tell one from another on the street. Brooklyn wops breed like guinea pigs. *Guinea* pigs, get it?"

He said he got it.

There was a streetcar stop on the corner. Paul told him where to transfer to the train station and shook his hand. They weren't at the hugging stage. Peter doubted they ever would be. But then as late as that morning he hadn't thought they'd get to the point where they shook hands.

"The interurbans ain't air-conditioned," Paul said. "You want to spruce up before you meet the boss. Father Cyril, you said?"

"Kyril. With a *K*."

"Sure he ain't a bolshevik?"

"Doesn't go with the job."

His father held up an index finger. His eyes were as bright as sun on steel. "You ever drop something?"

Peter waited.

"Make sure he's out of the room before you bend over to pick it up."

"I don't think Norman Rockwell has a painting for that."

The streetcar braked with a shrill squeal. An elderly couple got off, a matched set with shirttails outside their shorts, cocoa straw hats, blue-tinted glasses, and sandals; the man completed his ensemble with calf-length black socks. They were burned as dark as palm bark and wore cameras on straps around their necks.

Paul Vasco laughed in delayed reaction to his son's joke; and now Peter had one for all the fingers of one hand. He hoisted his valise aboard and plunked a token into the slot. He looked out the window, but his father had turned and started back toward the docks in his stoop-shouldered crouch.

OUR LADY OF REDEMPTION WAS BUILT ON THE SAME GOTHIC DESIGN AS Blessed Sacrament Cathedral, whose steeple Peter Vasco had spotted from the train, but much smaller, as if it were a neighborhood branch of the faith. Parti-colored birds he'd seen in Chicago and the District only when summer was in full swing perched on buttresses preening themselves for the northern migration. Their waste formed stalactites that were difficult to distinguish from the elaborate stonework, but apart from their presence the place might have belonged to any medieval village still standing in bombed-out Europe.

A novice wearing what must have been the only face in southern Florida untouched by the sun apologized, saying the pastor was engaged at present. He took his valise and led him across a courtyard paved with limestone and more splatter to the rectory. This was yet a smaller reproduction of the same building. Vasco was left in an eight-by-ten room with an iron bed, a pitcher and basin on a washstand with a cracked marble top, and a narrow wardrobe scaly from too many coats of inexpensive varnish with no sanding in between. A barred window looked out on a spiked iron fence. It was a mixed neighborhood, Cuban and colored, and the security precautions had obviously been installed to protect churchmen from the parish.

He stripped to the waist, filled the basin, and washed his face and under his arms with cold water and a cake of yellow soap. After drying off, he put on a clean shirt and fresh dickey and inspected himself for respectability in the tiny shaving mirror. He had a full face and his hair was beginning to thin. Had he inherited nothing from his father, other than his sense of irony?

He was peeling a thread of lint from his suit coat when the novice returned. "Father Kyril can see you now."

The room the young man took him to, at the end of a tapestry runner in a dusty-smelling hallway, was twice as large, but hardly less cramped. It doubled as storage for cartons of pamphlets and stationery. A chunky desk with a leather top claimed much of the remaining space, leaving little traveling room for the chair in front and the chair in back. Battered books with Roman and Cyrillic titles crowded a pair of glazed cases and there was about the place a moldy odor of old brandy, stale cigars, and melted wax. That last was universal, a feature of rectories everywhere. He wondered if the Vatican furnished pump sprayers filled with the scent.

"Father Vasco. Sergei Kyril. Welcome to Redemption."

The man was all right angles in black broadcloth, a square hole punched by a railroad conductor. From hips to shoulders to the top of his head the lines of his body didn't vary by so much as a degree from the desk he stood behind. His collar was a chalk-white slash to tell the killer where to cut his throat.

"Thank you." Would no one on this assignment smile when he met him?

But when they sat down, the pastor was courteous. "You're young. That's not surprising. Everyone between twenty-five and fifty is in the military. The archdiocese is recalling men from retirement to take up the slack. A ninety-year-old priest in Tampa offered to horsewhip a boy for confessing to the sin of masturbation. He's back home now, bullying his roses."

Vasco said nothing. He couldn't tell if Kyril was amused. His speech had a burring rumble one heard in Balkan neighborhoods, where laughter was rationed like sugar.

"My instructions are specific. You're to live here and come and go as you like. I'm to assign no duties. I won't ask why. Monsignor Donahue at Blessed Sacrament and Bishop O'Meara in Chicago belonged to the same class at the seminary, which is a bond only God can break."

"It's a Home Front project." Vasco repeated what he'd been told to say. "Civilian morale—"

"Not interested. Under normal circumstances I'd register a protest, but it so happens I'm awaiting my orders from the Corps of Chaplains. Nothing here has relevance when you've been promised a commission on an aircraft carrier."

"Congratulations, Father."

"Don't press your luck." Kyril opened a drawer and placed a key on the desk. "It seems we're a transportation service as well as a hotel. Brother Thomas will show you where the Ford is kept. I assume you'll furnish fuel. We'd use it more often if we could turn water into gasoline."

"Thank you." A drop of sweat trickled down under his collar. Kyril's blue-gray gaze followed it. He plucked at his own. It made a strumming sound.

"Celluloid. Our laundry bills are high enough as it is."

"Yes, Father."

"That reminds me. Your father called. When he asked if I'd read *The Communist Manifesto* I was inclined to believe him."

"I'm sorry."

"Mine butchered peasants in the service of the Czar. You're to call him at this number." He tore a sheet off a pad, put it next to the key, and rose. "I'll give you a few minutes. This is the only telephone."

Vasco stood and thanked him again. Kyril went out, cassock rustling, and drew the door shut behind him. Vasco lifted the heavy black receiver and dialed the operator.

A woman answered in Fort Lauderdale; the famous Sharon. When he identified himself she said, "Sec." A moment later his father came on. "You got a business card?"

"Yes." The same printer the Bureau used for its fugitive circulars had provided him with a hundred cards bearing his name and new title and the number at Our Lady of Redemption.

"Give it to the guard in front. He might tell you come back later and he might tell you get lost. Do what he says either way."

"Thanks, Dad."

"Don't thank the old man for asking somebody not to shoot his son on sight. That goes with the territory."

"I appreciate it anyway." *Who* had he asked? He envied Sergei Kyril his apathy.

"Your boss sounds like a cossack."

"I think his father was one."

"Tell him about yours?"

"Did you have to ask him if he's a communist?"

"You rather I asked if he diddles boys?"

"I'll call you later, Dad."

BROTHER THOMAS, THE PALE NOVICE, UNLATCHED THE DOORS OF A LARGE toolshed on the church lot and dragged them open. Inside was a Model T opera coupe, a tin telephone booth balanced on a chassis that looked as if it would bend in half when Vasco stepped on the running board. He used a notched stick to check the tank for gas, then replaced the seat cushion and worked the crank, something he hadn't done since Cicero. He was rusty, but the Ford was not. The motor made two false starts and chucked into life.

Hoover's people had given him plenty of stamps, but rather than draw attention to himself at the station he asked for two gallons only, and picked up a complimentary map of the Miami area. He had the address memorized: 93 Palm Avenue.

The directions were easy: a left, a right, another left.

He drove east toward open sky, then south, with nothing outside his window but ocean and gulls and watercraft and bell buoys ducking and bobbing like shadow boxers. The sun westering behind hotels under construction cast purple fingers that followed the tide out to sea, reaching for the sinister violent line of the horizon. He saw no sunbathers, no one splashing in the surf. The war had whittled away at all that.

He turned left onto the County Causeway. The toll man—Hoover said he was a public employee in Capone's pocket, the latest in a long line—made change from his quarter without expression and raised the gate. In his rearview mirror, Vasco saw him on the telephone inside his booth. He'd have been told to report when a man came through wearing a clerical collar.

His grip tightened on the wooden hoop of the steering wheel. He wasn't in the war room any longer, pushing toy tanks across a hypothetical battlefield. He'd passed into enemy territory, and the enemy was watching.

He drove over empty air and Biscayne Bay, bumped over a metal grid, and was on Palm Island, an oblong built by man from excavated swamp, rusted automobiles, and crushed houses, with tons of sand added for presentation. It felt hardly more substantial than the thin strip of reinforced concrete that led to it from the mainland.

Nothing identified the estate, only a solid block wall that permitted no view of the habitation behind it and a spiked iron gate buttressed by heavy oaken portals, like a Spanish redoubt or a prison in the Mediterranean. He hadn't been looking for a homely rural mailbox with CAPONE stenciled on it, but on the other hand he hadn't expected the occupant to have stripped it of its street number to turn away uncertain assassins. Idling in the outside lane in front, he peered through the window until the ghosts of two numerals came into focus, a shade darker than the surrounding concrete, hammered by sun and blasted by salt: 93. Raised figures of brass or copper, recently pried away. Surveillance reports had recorded a descent into paranoia.

Well, he'd wanted a challenge.

He pulled as far as he could into the drive, set the parking brake, got out, and crunched through crushed limestone to a metal box containing a telephone, like a policeman's call box. He was connected the instant he lifted the receiver.

"Yes?"

That surprised him. The tone was almost polite. He'd anticipated a surly "Yeah?", a gutter accent.

"Paul Vasco's son, here to pay his respects to Mr. Capone." At the last moment he'd chosen family over church.

"Wait there, please."

The sun slipped perceptibly in the interval. A puff of Atlantic air touched the back of one ear like a damp breath.

There was a sliding sound and a clack. A Judas window had opened in the left portal, but the face behind it was blurred by steel mesh. He felt himself scrutinized. The panel shuttled back into place. A bolt slid and banged, the portal pivoted inward, and a man in a blue serge suit unlocked the iron gate on that side and opened it just wide enough for Vasco to pass through. The man clanged it shut behind him, sealing the visitor between himself and the gate.

Vasco had a card ready and handed it to him. The man glanced at it, then slid it into a handkerchief pocket. "I have to check you for weapons." He sounded apologetic.

"I was told just to leave my card."

"It will just take a minute."

Bewildered, he held his arms out while a pair of hands slid down his sides, patted his coat, grazed his groin, and continued down to his ankles inside and outside each leg. When the man squatted, something heavy in a reinforced inside breast pocket tugged his coat away from his chest, but his tailoring prevented anything from showing when he straightened. Vasco's hat was lifted from his head, a finger slid inside the leather sweatband and followed it all the way around. The man handed him the hat and stepped back. He was a few years older than Vasco, with wavy chestnut hair neatly barbered and freckles all over, even on his eyelids. His accent was American Midwest. This would be one of the licensed private detectives Hoover had mentioned, legally permitted by the State of Florida to carry a firearm.

"Thank you. You can drive up to the house." He pulled the iron gate back open.

Climbing onto the driver's seat, Vasco had a panicky urge to reverse directions and drive back to Our Lady of Redemption. He'd prepared himself for a courtesy call, not a face-to-face meeting with the ogre, not the first day. But he shifted into low gear, let out the clutch, and crept forward past a gatehouse as large as all the apartments his family had crowded into put together.

The main house stood in a grove of royal palms, two pink stucco stories of Moorish design with a green tile roof. All his life, it seemed, he'd heard stories of the gangster's exotic Xanadu, a palace of Sodom, but it seemed modest compared to many he'd seen on the drive there. Was this the scene of all those wild revels, women squealing and men discharging Thompsons from balconies, that had disturbed President Herbert Hoover's sleep as a guest at the J. C. Penney estate, and resolved him to demand Capone's destruction? To begin with, there were no balconies.

A mosaic walk led to the front door. He pressed a coral button. Stately chimes reverberated deep inside the house.

He expected another bodyguard, more brutish, as must be the case the closer he got to the center. A pretty colored girl opened the door. She wore black-and-white maid's livery with a lace cap over hair that reminded him of delicately carved mahogany. Her eyes were large and tawny in a face the golden shade of cognac.

She dropped into a light curtsy. "Please come in, Father. Mrs. Capone is expecting you."

"*Mrs.* Capone?"

"The first time people visit the house, she prefers to speak with them before they meet Mr. Capone."

She had a pleasant Deep Southern accent, not at all the brassy twang he'd overheard among Negroes in the District and on Chicago's South Side, which he'd always suspected was exaggerated for Caucasian ears. She took his hat and hung it on a hall tree and he followed her across an entryway dim to his eyes, still adjusting from the sunlight, through a wide doorway into a large living room lit by table lamps. Chairs and davenports built for a race of giants invited one and all to sink into their chintz-covered depths. The focal point, above a huge ceramic hearth that could not have hosted many fires in that climate, was an oil painting in a gilt frame, easily seven feet tall, of a stocky, round-faced man with a pensive expression, resting one hand on the shoulder of a boy of about twelve. Vasco recognized Al Capone and assumed the boy was his son; he'd seen only one picture of a lad eagerly watching Babe Ruth sign a baseball, and he'd been nine or ten.

"Mrs. Capone will be down shortly. Would you like iced tea or lemonade?"

An ironic selection. "Neither, thank you."

She nodded and left, skirts rustling against bare brown legs; no curtsy this time. Vasco attributed all such subtleties to Mae Coughlin Capone—like his mother, the Irish helpmeet of an Italian. ("It ain't that they like dark meat so much as you have to kneecap a Mick to get him to the altar before he's forty," his father had told him once when he was drunk.)

A number of irregular shapes littered the red stone mantel among what appeared to be family photographs in silver frames. He stepped closer to examine them. Elephants of varying sizes and attitudes, quite finely carved from ivory. He reached to pick one up.

"How can you tell there's an elephant in the icebox?"

The voice—masculine, middle-register—wasn't loud, but it jolted him so hard he nearly swept the mantel clear. He turned, his heart thundering, to face a bulky purple outline against the low red sun shining through a window in line with the doorway at its back.

The answer came before he could respond. "You can see his footprints in the provolone, that's how! Har-har!"

Vasco force-fed a smile to his face and before he knew what he was doing grasped the hand that had murdered dozens.

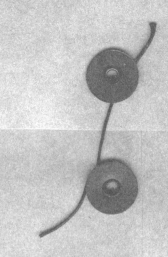

1944

THINGS UNDER THE EARTH

SEVEN

"I'M A SUCKER FOR ELEPHANTS," AL CAPONE SAID. "THEY'RE ALL OVER THE house. I used to keep these ones on my desk back in Chicago. They're good luck, and they never forget. Those are two of the things that took me to the top."

The first impression Vasco had, as the master of the house stepped farther into the room away from the glare behind him, was that he had beautiful lips. Chiefly it was the curve of the upper that gave them beauty; the lower was thick and meaty, but the sharply defined dimple beneath his nose acted as a sculptor's chisel, creating a scrolling effect, like the shape of a violin.

The rest of him was much as he'd appeared in photographs: a two-hundred-plus-pounder just under six feet tall, with the sloping shoulders of a saloon bouncer and a bullet head mounted directly on the torso. The neckless look was accentuated by a yellow silk scarf knotted Noël Coward fashion at his throat, printed with red-and-white dice. Over it he wore a coral sport shirt and over that a brown mohair smoking jacket tied with a sash, the initials AC embroidered in gold thread two inches below the breast pocket. Yellow flannels and oxblood loafers with tassels put the finishing touches on the picture of the country squire at home.

Vasco's second impression was that the medical reports were wrong. Capone had lost weight in prison, and his well-known affinity for swimming daily in his pool had shaped what was left into muscle. He looked fit enough to go back to Brooklyn and hurl drunks and belligerents into the street. The gray eyes under the heavy brows were clear, the brows appearing even darker than they were against the talcum dusting his face; a cosmetic attempt, the visitor assumed, to conceal the scars scoring his left cheek. Flecks of it clung like dandruff to the collar of his jacket. He was nearly bald now, but there was no gray in the hair that remained, cut close to the skull.

"Jim Colosimo gave me my first one, that big one on the end. It's genuine elephant ivory, from the tusk. It was a welcoming present when I came out from New York, and it brought me luck right away, so I started a collection. But this one here's my favorite."

He reached past Vasco and took down a carving one-third the size of the ornate one he'd pointed out first, fashioned far more crudely from coarser material with a dull white finish, probably soapstone. Vasco hadn't noticed it among the others.

"George Kelly gave it to me," he said, holding it out in front of him in both hands. "Took him three months to make it. 'Course, he spent a month of that time in solitary, where they don't let you have tools."

"*Machine Gun* Kelly? The bank robber?"

"*Pop*-gun, we called him. He couldn't pull the trigger on a mouse. He's the

only man in the history of Alcatraz asked to be sent there. His wife was convicted of kidnapping, and when he found out inmates couldn't receive visits
from convicted felons he couldn't wait to go. He was more afraid of her than he
was of J. Edgar Hoover."

Vasco felt himself go pale, but the other man appeared more interested in the
childlike carving than in his visitor's face. The very name on those graceful—
cruelly graceful—lips chilled him. Was he being played with, like a guest at one
of Capone's ghastly banquets? He was suddenly sure the Big Fellow knew all.

Capone returned the object to its place. "I liked Georgie. I wouldn't hire him
to carry my bags, never mind a rod, but he was good company. He told me that
elephant joke. Dentyne?" He produced a brightly wrapped square from the
pocket of his smoking jacket and held it out.

Vasco detested chewing gum, but he thanked him and took it. Accepting his
host's hospitality was an important first step. He unwrapped it and watched Capone strip the foil off another piece for himself. He had powerful hands with
blunt fingers and neatly pared nails. A diamond the size of a lemon drop sparkled on his left pinky. Agents of the Bureau of Internal Revenue must have
missed it when they put him away for tax evasion.

Capone chewed fastidiously, keeping the wad out of sight as he spoke. He
seemed to have some social graces, as well as a good grasp of grammar. His speech
betrayed none of his New York borough origins, and not even the flat Chicago
dialect. Mob legend said Johnny Torrio, his early sponsor, had spent a lot of money
grooming his protégé for polite society.

"Doc Phillips says I have to give up cigars. I don't miss booze, but personally
I think a stogie looks better in an ashtray than a glob of wet rubber. Don't go
looking for dignity when your health's shot to hell."

"You don't seem infirm. Quite the opposite."

The man's grin was wide. It was perfectly scaled to his broad face. "I'm going
to beat this rap, Padre. I hope you're patient if you're here to give me Last Rites."

The Director had cautioned him not to rush things. ("Let him think confession is his idea. He's not used to taking suggestions from anyone.")

"I'm not here on Church business. My father asked me to look you up. You
gave him a job when he needed one and he never forgot it."

"I never forgot what he did for me. I didn't have the juice then to beat a beef
with the gun still smoking in my paw."

He felt himself reeling. That Capone had just casually confessed to murder—
had he?—was unsettling enough. That he would so readily remember the circumstances of a relatively minor event in a sanguinary life, after twenty years,
astonished him and fed his darkest suspicions. Paul Vasco's infinitesimal role in
the Chicago underworld should have banished him from memory. If it *was* infinitesimal; that was the sticking point.

A stubby finger shook in Vasco's face. "Take a lesson from the elephant: Never
forget. That bum Joe Howard roughed up my pal Jake Guzik and got what he had

coming: four slugs in the kisser fired by a person or persons unknown. That's what the coroner said, and who am I to argue with a servant of the people?"

"I'll remember."

The grin slammed back on, a thousand-candlepower lamp in a dark alley. The hand flattened, patted Vasco's cheek. He shrank from it, but only inside. Capone's breath was cinammony from the gum. "Your old man's proud, I bet. Mine wanted me to be a priest. I had six brothers, so he didn't have to worry about the name carrying on. He gave up on Jimmy and Ralph, but he had hope for me right up to the day I smacked my sixth-grade teacher and ran away from school."

"I think Dad's getting used to the idea." He'd resolved to respond candidly whenever the truth didn't conflict with his mission. The fewer lies he told, the easier they were to keep track of.

"Well, it's different with just one kid. We're put on this earth to be a disappointment to our parents. My brother Jimmy let us all down when he took off with the circus and became a policeman."

How did he know Vasco was an only child?

A woman came in. "Snorky, I thought you were resting."

It may have been that he was thinking of family just then, but her light brogue reminded him immediately of his mother—right down to the note of mild alarm—and she might have resembled her physically had Maureen Vasco lived into middle age. She was an attractive blonde with a heart-shaped face and blue eyes the size of half-dollars. He'd seen only one photograph of Mae Capone, who much unlike her husband had covered her features with the collar of a mink coat when the shutter clicked, but there was something about the way a woman entered a room that announced she was the mistress of the house. She wore a sky-blue cotton dress with a full skirt that came to her knees and woven leather sandals on her pedicured feet. Her waist was the least bit thick, but she was evenly tanned and looked younger than she was. Vasco had read that Mae was two years older than Al.

"You know I can't sleep when it's light out. Pipe that, will you?" Capone told Vasco. "Sunup used to be bedtime for me. I entertained the head of the crime commission in my pajamas at noon. Now I'm down with the chickens and up with the rooster."

"Will you introduce me to your friend?" she asked.

"This is little Petey Vasco. Last time I saw him he was in a high chair. His old man was the best driver in the Outfit."

Shaken by yet another demonstration of Capone's memory, Vasco took her outstretched hand. It was cool to the touch. "I'm serving at Our Lady of Redemption. I stopped by to pay my respects."

"That's very thoughtful. Snorky, you should be in bed. It'll be dark by the time you're ready."

"I thought I'd take a swim first." Irritation crept into his tone. He sounded like a rebellious child.

"In the dark?"

"The pool's forty by sixty. I think I can find it."

"First thing in the morning."

Capone's face clouded. Vasco braced for one of his infamous rages. Instead the man turned and shook his hand. His grip was looser than before. "Bring the old man sometime. I don't get much chance to talk about the old days."

Mae kissed Al on his unscarred cheek. "I'll send up your supper later. Pretend it's breakfast in bed."

He left the room, shuffling a little; exhaustion seemed to have set in all at once. Most of the energy present left with him nonetheless.

The sugar substitute in Vasco's gum had lost its flavor. Lacking a place to dispose of it he swallowed.

Mae smiled at him. "Won't you sit down?"

"I should be getting back to Redemption."

"I know Father Kyril. He can manage without you a few minutes longer."

This was authority speaking, in a pleasant voice with the brush of Old Erin, and it chilled him head to foot. Kyril was suspicious of him already.

He sat on the end of a massive davenport. It was surprisingly firm. More surprisingly still, his hostess chose the adjoining cushion. Their knees nearly touched when she turned his way. At that moment the pretty maid entered.

"Iced tea, please, Rose. Would you like some?" Mae looked at her guest.

"Thank you." His mouth was dry, and the lump of latex lay on the floor of his stomach like an ejected shell.

When they were alone, her voice dropped to a murmur. "We have to be quiet. Al's hearing is excellent. When we used to throw parties, he'd hear someone say his name in a group across a roomful of people and go over to eavesdrop. Are you with the Treasury Department?"

The question caught him so far off guard he was glad she hadn't asked if he was with Justice. His reaction might have told her the truth. "No."

"If you are, then you know this house is in my name. The mortgage is paid through the generosity of Al's old friends in Chicago. Nothing here belongs to him, not even his clothes. You saw his ring?"

"It's hard to miss."

"It's paste. He gave the original to his brother for safekeeping when he was sentenced and Ralph disposed of the stone and had it replaced with an imitation. Al doesn't know that, so if he tells you it's worth fifty thousand dollars and you run to your superiors with the information, you'll only embarrass yourself."

"Mrs. Capone, my superiors are all prelates of the Catholic Church."

"What seminary did you attend?"

"St. Francis, in Cicero."

"A call came in concerning your father. He lives in Fort Lauderdale?"

"Yes, ma'am. He owns Sunrise Charters."

"You gave the guard at the gate a card. Do you have another?"

He got one from his wallet. She slid it into a pocket of her skirt without look-ing at it. "I'll see Ralph gets the information. It's best if you don't come back un-less you're invited."

"Is that what Mr. Capone wants?"

"Thank you, Rose." She removed a tall glass from the tray the maid had car-ried in, handed it to Vasco, and took the other for herself. Rose withdrew. "Mr. Capone is an invalid. He doesn't make decisions. How do you like Florida so far?" She sipped. Her eyes were blue steel above the rim of the glass.

"I like it. I understand it gets very hot in summer."

"It's a pressure cooker. We can't turn on the air conditioner, because Al might get a chill. Nothing gets done around here in July. We used to fly down to Bimini, where the trade winds are pleasant, but now he gets agitated as soon as the plane leaves the ground. Anyway, we can't afford it. Did you know government accoun-tants estimated Al earned more than three million dollars in 1929?"

"I never dreamed." Actually he'd seen copies of Treasury investigator Frank Wilson's memos and knew the amount to the penny.

"What became of it all, I ask you? Albert had to leave Notre Dame because we couldn't pay his tuition."

That would be Sonny, their only child, who in fact had dropped out when his classmates learned his real name. He'd registered under 'Al Brown,' his father's favorite alias. Vasco envied Mae her effortless obfuscation. He sampled his iced tea, discovered it was sweetened with real sugar. He made conversation. "Do you ever get back to Chicago?"

"Al won't fly, and he tires too easily for train travel. But there's nothing for us there. His mother lives in the house on Prairie, and she visits us every winter. If we did go back, detectives and federal agents would follow us everywhere we went. There's always at least one stationed outside this house. You'd think they'd have better things to do with a war on."

You married him. Aloud he said, "I'm sorry."

They sipped in silence for a while. A foghorn croaked out in the bay. The tem-perature had dropped noticeably with the onset of evening. He hoped the Model T's headlights were equal to the fog.

"I wish we'd stayed in Brooklyn."

He waited politely, but she seemed to have completed her thought.

"Speedboats buzz the dock all the time," she said. "They throw Al into a panic. We never know if it's federal men or curiosity seekers or someone coming to murder him."

"Why that? He's retired."

"Some people never forget."

"Like the elephant."

She smiled. The expression seemed genuine, and genuinely sad. "Al and his elephants. I bought four of them in bronze when we moved in here, to make him feel at home. I sold them at auction along with his boats and most of the furniture when he was away. No one was helping out then. They were afraid to spend a penny in case Washington decided to go after them just like Al. A fat lot of luck they brought us, those elephants. I wasn't sorry to see them go.

"Back in Chicago I couldn't go shopping in Marshall Field's without a car in front of me and a car behind, and someone to check out the store before I went inside. Al hired a bodyguard to look after Albert on the playground. A little boy, can you imagine? He was afraid he'd be kidnapped and tortured. He posted men to keep strange cars from parking within four square blocks of his hotel. The *president* doesn't do that. Once when we were on vacation in Wisconsin, he had our driver stop while he watched a family eating supper in a house with all the windows open and the shades up. He said he'd give anything to be able to do that. I never wanted him to be a barber like his father, but if he'd kept that night-club job in Brooklyn, our lives would have been different."

He refrained from pointing out that Capone had fled west to avoid a murder indictment. It was possible to overstudy for an assignment.

She looked at him quickly—almost guiltily—and he had the odd feeling that for a moment she'd forgotten her suspicions of him. Was it that simple? A white collar and an honest face? Had he an honest face? He'd always thought it heavy and bland. "Are you finished with your tea?" she asked.

He hadn't thought about it after that first sip. "It's sweeter than I'm used to."

"Al likes it that way. We traded gasoline stamps to my sister for her sugar rations. We seldom go out driving. So many strange cars fall in behind us we practically have to apply for a parade permit." She set down her glass and smoothed her skirt. "I'll have Brownie show you to the door."

"Brownie?"

"Our handyman. He's also the cook."

"Please don't bother. I know the way."

But Rose had returned, and Mae asked her to send Brownie in. She never rang a bell or seemed to operate any other kind of summoning device, but the girl always appeared just when she was needed. She had even brought him his hat.

They were standing when the biggest Negro Vasco had ever seen came in, ducking to clear the doorway in his white chef's toque. He wore a knee-length apron over a twill shirt rolled up past massive forearms and old dress trousers two inches too short—hand-me-downs, perhaps, from the master of the house. His feet were the size of swim fins in scuffed brown oxfords. Strips of scar-tissue pulled his eyes into Oriental slits.

"Brownie came with the house," Mae said. "He'd wrestle an alligator to protect Al, and he'd win."

Vasco got the message. "My father would do the same. I'm not sure he'd win, but the gator would know it'd been in a fight." He smiled at her. "I hope you'll invite me back."

"Please say hello to Father Kyril." She gave him a cool hand.

She had not once called him Father.

The hand Brownie used on the front doorknob was missing its third and fourth fingers, the stumps healed over hard and shiny. He caught Vasco looking at them. "Prison cafeteria." They were as many words as he ever spoke to him at one time.

The headlights were barely adequate in the smoky mist, the heater less so. It made his feet sweat without clearing the windshield of condensation, and the vacuum wipers struggled against the moisture accumulating outside. After the guard closed the gate behind him he drove all the way back to Our Lady of Redemption with his head stuck out the window to see where he was going.

Snorky.

Transcripts of statements in Capone's file had contained several references to him by that nickname. It meant elegant, or nattily dressed, and from 1924 on, the mug from the eastern slums had improved the fortunes of tailors and jewelers throughout Cook County and, later, Florida, with his extravagant tastes in clothing and accessories. A Panama hat cost a hundred dollars, a dozen shirts made to his order twenty-five dollars apiece. His diamond ring alone would have bought six houses for the working class. But the evolving language had given the name a humorous note, suggesting a buffoon. People too young to remember the lawless days might snicker when they heard it. It had been a badge of privilege to be allowed to address him so, like belonging to an exclusive club. The membership had fallen off through jail, death, and indifference. Mae Capone was probably the only one left who called Al Snorky, and however patronizingly she behaved toward him in his dependency, no such taint attached to the name. Vasco wondered if this woman so sheltered by her husband, whom the press had dismissed as a drab appendage to the most colorful figure of the young century, in fact held the key to his chest of secrets.

A block from the church, Vasco pulled into a diagonal space a few doors down from a Rexall Drugs, switched off the ignition, and watched his side mirror for a few minutes, reaching out twice to clear moisture from the glass with the heel of his hand. He'd been warned to look out for followers, but he decided the visibility was too poor to risk running into their quarry from behind; no cars came along in either direction while he was waiting.

The air in the drugstore was a pungent mix of quinine, carbolic, eucalyptus, ginger, and malt, with a faint sting of turpentine. A radio on a back shelf played Les Brown. The soda fountain was deserted and Vasco had the place to himself and the skeletal bespectacled pharmacist grinding a prescription by hand on his elevated platform; the man glanced up when the copper bell jangled above the door, then lost interest when the customer entered the telephone booth and shut himself inside.

He placed a collect call to a number he'd memorized. Since it had to be rerouted, he listened to various vaguely marine noises for two minutes, as if the line ran underwater, then came alert when he recognized Helen Gandy's voice. She never left the office ahead of her employer, and Hoover rarely went home to the house he shared with his mother until well past dark. She listened to Vasco's identification number and put him through. No names were exchanged.

Hoover's greeting was brusque. "Your instructions were to report by mail except in an emergency."

"I think this is one. It can't wait. Mrs. Brown knows Kyril." Capone himself had provided the code name they'd agreed to use.

"You've made contact?" The Director may or may not have been surprised. His words ran together no matter what the subject.

"Briefly. At this point she may be more dangerous than Brown. Kyril, too. I'm concerned what will happen when they compare notes."

"Our intelligence is she attends Mass at Blessed Sacrament."

"I'm reporting what she said."

"I'll have Cicero call him, say there was a miscommunication. Do you have reservations about sitting in the booth?"

He was being asked to hear confessions. The suggestion violated every tenet of the Church. "Not as long as I'm allowed to respect the seal."

"I'm not interested in knowing how many times little Tommy Tucker skipped school to see Gene Autry. Do you trust Kyril to keep his suspicions to himself?"

"If he believes I'm serving the parish. Right now he's more interested in a naval commission than what's going on at Redemption."

"You were right to call." It sounded grudging. "How did things go with your father?"

"Better than expected. He got me into the house."

"Indeed." Just then the line crackled; he couldn't tell if it was an expression of curiosity or a confirmation of fact. Vasco wondered if he'd inadvertently spilled information about his father's status the Director hadn't known. At the same time he couldn't help thinking Hoover knew more about it than he pretended. For a spy, Vasco seemed to know less about what was going on than anyone, including the people he was spying on.

"Is there anything else?"

He shook himself out of his thoughts. "Nothing that can't wait for the postman."

"Very well. Carry on."

When he left the booth, the Shadow was taunting a nest of Japanese collaborators. The pharmacist yawned and switched off the radio.

Vasco discovered that the car didn't want to start when it was warm. The lights in the drugstore went out just as he was considering going back inside to escape the clammy air. He waited a few more minutes, blowing into his hands, then tried again. He couldn't believe he'd thought fireplaces were useless in Miami. After one encouraging chuck-a-luck, the crank failed to produce any more compression from the cylinders. He turned up his coat collar, stuck his hands in his pockets, and walked the rest of the way to the church. He hoped it wasn't a tow-away zone.

EIGHT

"You wanted to see me, Father?"

"Brother Thomas—*woof!*—tells me the Ford—*woof!*—isn't in its shed. Do you know—*woof!*—where it is?"

They were in the bell tower, which seemed to serve the same storage purposes as the pastor's study in the rectory. More boxes and piles of broken chairs and candlesticks surrounded the bay where the great bronze bell hung motionless, as well as bundles of newspapers evidently intended for a scrap drive. A soiled pallet occupied the remaining space, forcing Vasco to stand on the top step of the staircase he'd just climbed. Father Kyril lay on his back on the pallet, pushing a pair of barbells toward the top of the steeple, lowering it to his chest, then pushing again. The noise he made when he pushed sounded like a bored German shepherd. Vasco had seen the identical black spherical weights in a Mickey Mouse cartoon, but that was where the resemblance ended. The priest was heavily muscled in a gray sweatshirt, boxing trunks, and high lace-up shoes.

Vasco reported what had happened. "I couldn't find either of you to tell you last night. I assumed you'd both gone to bed."

"At present—*woof!*—Thomas has made other sleeping arrangements. You're—*woof!*—in his quarters. Space is at a premium—*woof!*—as you may have noticed." He lowered the dumbbells onto a pair of props welded together from galvanized pipe. "It would be different if Redemption had a basement. You won't find one in southern Florida." Snatching a towel he'd had draped over the oaken railing around the bay, he mopped sweat from his face, neck, arms, and legs. "I'm training myself to rise and retire early. There is no Midnight Mass in the South Pacific."

"I don't want my presence here to inconvenience anyone."

"Thomas is a novice. In old Russia he wouldn't *have* a bed." He got to his feet and slung the towel around his neck. He was a solid square slab younger than his years. "The Ford is temperamental. Fortunately, the local police know the car and look the other way. Don't procrastinate, however. Scrap iron doesn't last long these days."

"Yes, sir."

Kyril's gaze probed at him. "It was a strange hour to visit a drugstore for a man sworn to chastity."

He was ready. "I stopped in to call my father. I didn't want to impose on you for the use of the telephone."

"When I spoke to him, I got the impression you weren't that close."

"We haven't been. But we're trying."

"Try not to be too disappointed when it doesn't work as well as it does in the movies. The Fifth Commandment says nothing about his honoring you back."

"Thank you, Father."

He waited a beat, then turned to go downstairs.

"It seems a mistake was made."

He turned back. His heart pulsed in his throat.

"St. Francis called this morning. The church in Cicero, not the man; I'd have mentioned that before I brought up the subject of the automobile. It seems you *are* to perform a service for Our Lady of Redemption. Does that distress you?"

"No, sir. Quite the opposite." Which was as true as truth could be. His heart slipped back into his chest.

"I doubt that, but I'll hear your confession later. First I need you to take your place on the other side of the screen. The sinners of this parish will find you alert and ready every afternoon between two and four P.M., beginning today. Two priests, no waiting."

"Yes, sir."

"Stop calling me sir. I don't have my bars yet."

"Yes, Father."

A gust of sea air brushed the bell, making it hum in the conversational lull.

"The *car,* Father Vasco. By this time next week it could be flying over Berlin."

"What if it still won't start?"

"Since you were able to get up those stairs without throwing out your back or suffering a coronary, I think the answer's obvious."

No pushing was necessary, as it turned out.

A little boy who belonged in an *Our Gang* comedy, complete with knickerbockers and a corduroy cap with its bill twisted sideways, sat on the bottom step of a flight of stairs leading to a doctor's office next to the drugstore, eating a sandwich and watching him insert the crank. When it didn't engage on the first try he said, "Pray, Reverend."

But it started on the second, abruptly enough to break his wrist if he hadn't remembered to put his thumb on the same side of the handle with the rest of his fingers. A puff of black smoke the size of a softball exploded from the tailpipe and the motor settled into a staccato idle like an undercranked machine gun. The boy raised his fists over his head like a football referee, a pickle disk sliding out from between slices of bread and hitting the sidewalk with a smack.

"How about a ride, Reverend?"

He smiled, absurdly proud of himself. "How about a bite of your sandwich?"

"Ma says I shouldn't share food with strangers." The boy brought it down and clutched it to his chest.

"Are you Catholic?"

"Lutheran, Ma says."

"The pope says I shouldn't give rides to Protestants."

But the smell of mustard and liverwurst reminded him he hadn't eaten since lunch yesterday with his father, and he left the motor running while he went into the drugstore and bought two hamburger sandwiches and a Coke at the soda fountain. The boy was gone when he came out carrying the bottle and greasy sack, but Vasco wasn't alone. A policeman stood with one foot propped up on the Model T's front bumper, writing on a pad braced on his knee. He wore whipcord breeches, stovepipe boots, and a leather windbreaker, goggles perched on the peak of his cap. His partner sat in the sidecar of a city motorcycle burbling alongside the automobile, holding his chalked parking-enforcement stick at parade rest.

"I'm sorry, Officer," Vasco said. "It wouldn't start last night."

"I'm ticketing you for leaving it running unattended. A pint of gas wasted is a pilot down behind enemy lines." The man with the pad put his foot back on the pavement, tore off the top sheet, and held it out. "Also there's car thieves here like everywhere else. We got enough to handle with half the force overseas without you giving 'em a leg up."

He took the ticket. "I wasn't thinking."

"You're new, ain't you?"

"I just got in yesterday."

"If you pay that before five, you can save the collection plate another fifty cents." He gave him directions to police headquarters.

"Thank you, Officer . . ." He couldn't read the signature.

"Horowitz."

Likely not a parishioner. "Did you ever happen to meet Al Capone?"

Officer Horowitz had started to pull his goggles down over his eyes. He stopped halfway. "I been asked that question before, but not by a priest. I'd've thought you gave up on him years ago."

"The Church never gives up."

"Tourists neither. They ask about him a couple times a week during the season. You'd think some of 'em would want to see the aquarium." He settled the goggles astride his nose. "I saw him once in that big car he rides around in, after he got out. He didn't look like so much. Sergeant Fowler's the one you want to talk to. He's with Bunco, down at headquarters."

"Did he spend much time with Capone?"

"He put the cuffs on him three times. There ain't another cop in the country can say that."

Horowitz straddled the motorcycle, put it in gear, and the pair putted away down the street. At the end of the block they stopped and the officer in the sidecar leaned out with his stick and marked an X on the rear tire of a car parked on the corner.

Vasco drove to police headquarters, a stone building with POLICE lettered in black on lighted glass globes the size of bowling balls flanking the steps to the entrance, and parked in the first civilian space he found next to a black-and-white sedan with police markings and chrome spotlights mounted on both sides. He cut the motor so it could begin cooling and ate his sandwiches behind the wheel, sipping Coke through a straw between bites. The sea air increased his appetite and the late-morning sun felt pleasantly warm slanting through the window on the passenger's side. A seagull pecked at a wad of gum stuck to the sidewalk, found it petrified, and circled around it searching for another angle of attack. It made him think of Capone and his Dentyne. Scarface Al, the Gum-Chewing King of Crime.

He got out, committed his trash to a green-painted receptacle shaped like a public mailbox, and climbed the stairs to the entrance, where a freestanding sign on a pedestal directed him where to pay his fine. In an oak-and-marble lobby smelling of cigarettes he waited in line, then handed his ticket between the bars of a cage to a girl in bangs and a shoulder-length bob, who clucked humorously over the offense scribbled in the blank. "Shame on you, Father."

"I told the officer I wasn't thinking."

"That wouldn't cut any mustard with Dave Horowitz. He has two brothers in the service. Fifty cents, please."

He slid a half-dollar between the bars. She tore loose the original sheet, used a heavy-duty stamp on the carbon, and poked the copy out at him. He asked her where he could find Bunco.

She raised her eyebrows. "Second floor."

He took the elevator, which was handy. The tobacco fug was even stronger in the car, which shuddered all during the ascent. He promised himself to use the stairs whenever possible until wartime restrictions on replacement parts were lifted.

Doors with pebbled glass panels lined a corridor painted green above the wainscoting. Some were identified by the names of departments, others only by numbers lettered on the glass. He came to one marked BUNCO SQUAD and entered.

It was a large room with a high ceiling, lit entirely by the sun coming through the east windows. A memo taped to the wall above the light switches reminded employees to avoid illuminating the overhead globes during the hours of daylight.

His first impression was that the room had been shut down for the duration. Rows of scratched yellow-oak desks stood with their chairs unoccupied, the typewriters on perpendicular stands covered with rubber shrouds. Then he heard keys striking paper and, shielding his eyes against the strong sunlight, observed a man seated in shirtsleeves and suspenders with his back to the windows, typing with two fingers. A thread of smoke coming from a cigarette parked on the edge of his desk hung motionless in a question mark above his head, but he himself betrayed no curiosity toward the visitor or even that he was aware of him.

A hinge squeaked. Vasco turned his head and saw a man holding the knob of an open door to an enclosure whose glass walls fell two feet short of the ceiling. The man had rimless glasses balanced on the end of his nose and a sheet of paper in his other hand, but he was dressed for the street, in a pinstripe suit with his bow tie neatly knotted, a felt hat on the back of his head. He was looking at Vasco.

"Lost?"

"I'm looking for a Sergeant Fowler."

"We only have one of those. If you're here for his soul, you're fifteen years late. He lost it in the Crash."

"An Officer Horowitz gave me his name."

"We only have one of those too, for which I'm profoundly grateful. I'm Fowler." He stepped aside from the door, holding it open. Vasco went in past him.

The cubicle was as crowded as Sergei Kyril's study, but far less orderly in appearance. Dog-eared green file folders made mounds on desk and floor, increasing in bulk as they climbed the glass walls in open rebellion against the laws of physics. A speaker on a metal utility rack also heaped with folders crackled indecipherable dialogue between radio-car patrolmen and a bored dispatcher, and an old-fashioned gallows telephone leaned at a Krazy Kat angle atop one of the stacks on the desk.

Sergeant Fowler hung his hat on the telephone and sat, his chair creaking like a flock of excited gulls. He put aside the paper. "Maid's day off. The consensus among the brass is there's no place in time of war for paper-hangers, dollar-bill splitters, pyramid schemers, pigeon-droppers, and well-heeled, cash-strapped Texas oilmen in need of short-term loans on surefire investments, which is why most of this squad is out looking for Tokyo Rose; what's left of them in this hemisphere, anyway. Did you know all you need is a surplus navy uniform and a freckled face to sell hundreds of dollars' worth of subscriptions to magazines that folded under Herbert Hoover? But who am I, a lowly sergeant, to upset the grand plan? This isn't even my office. The lieutenant who belongs to it is busy infiltrating the Dade County chapter of the Nazi-American Bund. His name's O'Malley. What do you think his chances are?"

Vasco saw no answer for these rhetorical questions. Fowler, gray at the temples and meticulously shaven, struck him as a cross between the vice president of a bank and one of the bunco steerers he'd warned him against. He had a high-flown grasp of language that suggested the latter, and when he took off his glasses the bank executive went out the window. When Vasco introduced himself he said, "What church?"

"Redemption, but I'd rather you didn't bother my pastor. My reason for being here is personal. I'm not filing a complaint."

Fowler had his hat off the telephone and the earpiece in hand. "Well, I need a reference. That collar just makes a man in my line suspicious."

"I was ordained at St. Francis Catholic Church in Cicero, Illinois."

The sergeant gave the information to the switchboard operator. While he was waiting for the call to go through he said, "We nailed a character dressed like a rabbi last month for raffling the same Cadillac all the way down the coast. He stole it in New Jersey and just sort of ran out of U.S. here in town. The beard

was genuine. Who's this?" he said into the mouthpiece. "Brother, I'm Estes Fowler
with the Miami Police. Florida, where else?" He rolled his eyes at Vasco. "I'm
talking with a fellow says his name is Father Peter Vasco, with Our Lady of Redemption here, friendly visit. Says he's from your neck of the woods. I'm checking his credentials. Sure, I'll hang on."

A minute went by, during which Fowler twirled his hat by its crown around
his fist. He said, "Yes? Okay, thanks." He hung up and replaced his hat. "What's
on your mind, Father?"

He hesitated. He hoped he wasn't making a mistake. Capone's healthy appearance had made him question the surveillance reports, and he wanted to
know more about the gang chief in Florida. He expected Capone's people to find
out he'd been asking questions; a show of reluctance on Vasco's part to become
involved would lend support to his story. But there was no guarantee it would be
taken that way.

"My father knew Al Capone slightly, many years ago. I went to Capone's
house last night to give him his regards. Is that all right?"

"It's jake with me, but I'm not the one you should be asking. Those feds
stacked up around his place think he's planning to smuggle Mussolini into the
country by way of Key West."

"That's not really why I'm here. I may be invited back, but before I accept I
want to make sure Capone isn't in any trouble with the authorities. I don't want
to embarrass the Church."

"What's your father's name?"

"Is that necessary? He's never been in trouble himself."

Fowler waved it off with a hand wearing an elk's-tooth ring. "I guess Horowitz told you Capone and I have a history."

"He said you arrested him three times."

"That wasn't hard. He was as easy to track as a parade float. He made the society page every time he came down and trailed C-notes all the way down Seventh
Avenue."

"What laws did he break?"

"I think he went fishing on an expired license, but he paid the fine and gave
the game warden a box of cigars for his trouble. It was before he went to the joint.
There was one conviction on his record, in Philadelphia, for carrying a concealed
weapon, which he never did here. Nothing stuck because there wasn't anything
to stick. Vagrancy? He had on a pearl stickpin you could shoot marbles with and
a roll in his pocket as big as a coconut. Disorderly conduct? He made Emily Post
look like Ma Barker. I think the last time we picked him up was for being Al Capone, which of course was the reason all along. We had a director of public safety
who wanted to be governor. He thought he could make it by taking the one citizen he could count on obeying all the local laws and running him out of town."

"I suppose having him here was bad for tourism."

"I don't know about that, but real estate agents loved him. After the land bubble burst in '26, you couldn't give away lots on Ocean Beach. Then Capone pumped a hundred grand into that house on Palm Island and property values shot up all the way to Jacksonville. That twerp McCreary threatened to arrest Capone's *mother* if she showed her face here. In the end even the reformers wouldn't touch it. By the time he was through, Al had the better chance of being elected."

"How about now?"

Fowler leaned an ear toward the crackling speaker, but it was just a traffic accident. "The four-f punks give us more trouble than Capone ever did, them getting drunk and picking fights with airmen on leave every Saturday night. Now and then the boys in Rackets get bored and pull in his bodyguards, but they're back on the job with their guns in their pockets before the paperwork finishes processing. Last year an FBI agent got arrested by mistake and J. Edgar Hoover himself called the chief to bawl him out."

Hoover seemed to be a subject of conversation nearly as often as Capone. "There was only one bodyguard on duty last night."

"Only one you *saw*. He's got himself a regular fortress there, with Biscayne Bay for a moat. One of the reasons I asked to be transferred to Bunco was so I wouldn't have to go down there every time some busybody do-gooder had a conniption fit because he saw *Little Caesar* too many times. The last straw was when Dade County deputies brought me along for backup while they padlocked the house. Capone's own house. If he'd been home, he'd have been within his rights to shoot them for criminal trespass, but Director McCreary would've eaten that up. He'd have leveled the place."

"I never thought I'd hear an officer of the law defend Al Capone."

"He should've fried for McSwiggin, which was the same as killing a cop. Only he didn't, so the rest is chickenshit. Sorry, Father."

"I've heard the word. I wasn't born a priest. Since his record here is clean, I'm guessing you won't object if I visit him again."

"Not me, but if I were you I'd cash in all my stamps and bring Brownie a great big hunk of prime rib. You don't want to get on the wrong side of him."

He remembered the Negro cook. "He told me he lost his fingers in a prison cafeteria."

"More like misplaced. For the record, he was part of the civilian kitchen staff, not a convict. That was in Raiford. A trustie dishwasher went berserk with an ice crusher and Brownie cut his head half off his shoulders with a cleaver: it was a case of scissors breaks rock. He overlooked the fact he had his other hand on the trustie's throat at the time."

"Self-defense?"

"Uh-uh. It was his assistant the guy went after, another civilian. Brownie didn't even like the assistant, said he was a screw-off who made more work for him. He likes Capone: he's as loyal to him as a big old dog. Think what he'd do if he thought you were going to hurt him."

The radio speaker crackled in the brief silence. "I'll remember."

"Then, of course, there's the Outfit, which is forming quite the colony down here since Capone drew all the lightning for them. Come to think of it, you'd better cash in all your friends' stamps while you're at it."

He tried not to dwell on that part. "I heard Capone was sick. He doesn't look it or act it."

"Syph comes and goes. We get cases sometimes, illegals mostly, who can't afford or won't trust a doctor to give them penicillin; they think it's poison. Cool as ice when we book them, then when we put them in the cells upstairs they try to bend the bars with their skulls."

"Is it that common? I never heard of the disease until Capone got it."

"Wait till the boys come back home. It'll make Spanish influenza look like chicken pox."

"Thank the Lord for modern drugs."

"They came along too late for Capone, though I hear he's being treated to slow down the rot. One day it'll be friendly Uncle Al, the man with the free soup kitchens. Next day he'll think you're Bugs Moran and drag you into that giant pool of his and hold your head under until you learn to play the harp."

He had what he'd come for. "Thank you, Sergeant. You've been very helpful."

"We're pretty friendly down here when no one's running for office. It isn't Cicero." Fowler put on his hat, squaring the brim across his brow, and now the bank vice president was back. "On that same friendly note, I wouldn't worry about embarrassing the Church by dropping in on Capone. The last time we picked him up, back in '31, he was having cocktails with a cardinal."

THE FUSSY LITTLE WARDROBE MAN AT THE BUREAU HAD CONSULTED HIS books of sketches and missed nothing.

Vasco put on the soutane, whose black hem reached his insteps, and over it the knee-length chasuble, kissed the stole, and draped it around his neck, crossing the ends on his chest. He felt a sting of shame, as if he were naked in public; but when he observed the result, turning the small square mirror this way and that to see himself head to foot, he felt somehow more comfortable with what he regarded as a mortal sin, as if taking care to look the part represented respect.

That, at least, was the case he would try to make to the angel in charge of perdition.

He left his borrowed quarters and, vestments rustling, crossed the courtyard and entered Our Lady of Redemption, genuflecting inside. A smattering of people sat in pews and he looked at none of them directly, a nod to the anonymous nature of confession for those who were waiting.

The atmosphere in the confessional mingled darkness with dust and furniture polish and aftershave lotion. Vasco, who at St. Francis had done his part to remove dust and apply polish, was under no illusion that priests spent their time

between confessions meditating on pious subjects. He'd caught old Father Mc-
Closkey snoring there on several occasions, and had found various items of
reading material left behind, including an illustrated brochure from a nudist
camp. They used flashlights, like little boys reading Nick Carter under the covers. He'd comforted himself by assuming they put aside such distractions when
someone was actually unburdening himself on the other side of the partition.

Father Kyril, not the sort of man to conceal his behavior or make excuses for
it, had installed a ceiling bulb with a chain switch, under which he studied the
U.S. Navy manual of arms. Vasco found the slender volume bound in grubby
leatherette lying open-side down on a cushion covered in striped ticking and
picked it up to examine it. Most of the page-corners were turned down and numerous passages underlined in ink.

He'd just taken his seat when someone entered the booth and sat down on
the other side. He slid aside the panel, revealing a face shadowed by the screen.
"Bless me, Father, for I have sinned. It's been six weeks since my last confession."

It was a woman, and for his first sinner he'd drawn a subject more absorbing
than any book. She'd spent much of those six weeks violating her marital vows
with a succession of men, most recently within the hour; he detected a faint
residue of sweat and semen that confirmed the admission. When she began to
go into detail, he interrupted to ask if she intended to stop being unfaithful.

She hesitated. "You haven't *met* Harold, have you?"

He told her to say ten Hail Marys.

"Ten!"

"One for each transgression."

"You're stricter than Father Kyril."

Oddly, this pleased him. If he couldn't be genuine, he could at least be a
stickler.

He did a thriving trade for most of two hours. A man had made change from
the collection plate: two Hail Marys. A girl had talked back to her mother: three
Hail Marys. A young woman had gone to see *Bataan* and had had impure
thoughts about Robert Taylor: one Our Father.

"That's all? I thought lust was bigger than that."

"Actors are chosen to create temptation. The greater sin is Hollywood's."

He felt wrung out at the end. Two hours in the booth was like eight hours
digging ditches, only without the sense of self-satisfaction that came of honest
labor. He no longer feared damnation, as that was everyone's fate thanks to the
God-Devil, but he was mortified to have swindled the devout out of the absolution they had every right to expect. He wanted to tell them that redemption was
for this world.

After three days he felt the same. He learned of minor indiscretions, shocking indecencies, infractions that sounded like inventions; lonely people desperate
for human contact, even separated by a screen. He heard petty crimes described
in such detail he suspected the penitents were secretly proud of having gotten

away with them: a decade of the Rosary for that deadly sin. He was an ecclesiastical vending machine, dispensing penance like candy and cigarettes. He wondered if the church would run out of candles.

Some sessions were slow, and these were the most exhausting of all. Thanks to Kyril's reading preferences, he learned how to dismantle and reassemble a bolt-action carbine in under five minutes, assuming he was as good with his hands as he was with his imagination. (He wasn't.)

When not in the booth he tried to stay close to Redemption, in case an invitation came from Palm Island. But he refrained from asking if there were any calls for him lest he create suspicion. Father Kyril, he knew, was dubious. Brother Thomas was harder to read. He went about his menial duties with broom and taper and polishing rag with little conversation and, it seemed, great devotion. Novices often whistled during chores, but he didn't even hum, not even a solemn hymn. Attempts to draw him out with polite personal questions were unrewarding, although the responses were respectful. At the end of three days, Vasco knew he was twenty years old and that he'd been born in Ohio.

Vasco made an effort to be useful. He made his own bed, took Kyril's advice and bought a half-dozen celluloid collars from a uniform store to save on laundry, drove the Model T to a garage for a tune-up so it would start when the motor was warm. To avoid draining the church of its provisions he ate his meals in the drugstore and at inexpensive lunch counters (gaining, no doubt, a reputation for aloofness, but avoiding awkward exchanges at table). He considered offering his assistance at Sunday Mass, but rejected the idea in fear of being invited to officiate. He knew the rituals but had never put them into practice before a congregation.

The owner of the garage where he took the Ford, a small wiry Italian who reminded him of his father, had a bleeding heart in a frame on the wall of his greasy office. He said the tune-up was on the house, but Vasco kept insisting and he finally accepted five dollars. It was bad enough he was cheating the Catholic community of its trust.

"That left front tire's balder than me," the garage man said. "I got one out back I can let you have, and FDR don't have to know about it. Not many tin lizzies around no more. I'd hate to see it rot."

"Another time, and I'll pay you for it. I have to get back to church."

"I wouldn't wait too long. You don't want to get a flat in the middle of a blackout."

Two o'clock found him back in the booth:

"Bless me, Father, for I have sinned. . . ."

"Bless me . . ."

"It's been two weeks since my last confession. . . ."

"Bless me . . ."

"It's been three days . . ."

"Ten minutes . . ." (A compulsive liar fresh from Kyril's booth, looking for a second opinion.)

"Bless me, Father . . ."

"Bless me . . ."

That fourth day was slow. He almost nodded off once, and chided himself for judging Father McCloskey too harshly. He shifted his weight onto his feet to improve circulation just as the curtain rings on the other side slid this way, then that, and the floor bent beneath a heavy tread. The penitent sat with the wheezy grunt of a man seriously overweight.

Vasco slid open the panel. He heard heavy breathing, but no words. Some people required more patience than others; they were out of the habit, their sin was embarrassing or too great in their eyes to find instant expression. With his elbow on the padded rest and his hand to his brow—the classic confessor's pose—he risked a sideways glance at the screen. The face in artificial twilight was enormous, as big and round as a medicine ball. If Vasco hadn't been sitting there all week he'd have thought the screen had magnifying qualities.

More silence.

"My son?"

A throat cleared, a long liquid gurgling like a drain coming unclogged. Loose particles seemed to rattle in the voice that followed. "The name's Ralph Capone. My friends call me Bottles. How they hanging, Father?"

NINE

VASCO'S HAND WENT TO THE CRUCIFIX HIS MOTHER HAD GIVEN HIM; AN AU-
tomatic reaction lately when shock came his way. He drew courage from it, and
from his surroundings. The Church of Rome was older than Prohibition, older
than the Black Hand, and its traditions went deeper than the rules of vendetta.

"I'm pleased to meet you, Mr. Capone, but I'm afraid this isn't the place and
time."

"Bottles. I figured that, but I didn't want to take a chance on missing you. The
pasty-faced kid sweeping the floor told me where to find you."

Ralph Capone's accent was as broad and solid as the Brooklyn Bridge. Unlike his brother, he hadn't had the advantage of Johnny Torrio's crash course in
drawing-room deportment. Al's senior by six years, he'd be about fifty, but his
phlegmy voice and shortness of breath belonged to a man a decade older.

"I'm free in ten minutes."

"I'll be the one wearing a carnation." The bench on the other side of the partition made a sighing noise, like a horse made when a heavy rider stepped down.
Curtain rings rattled and then the entire booth seemed twice as large.

It was a long ten minutes. No one came to replace Ralph, and Vasco was left
to contemplate the futility of regular hours and a rigid schedule. It made for better thoughts than wondering what was in store for him when he stepped out. If
just one link failed in the long and delicate chain of credentials the Bureau had
forged to put him across as a priest in good standing with the diocese of Cicero,
Illinois—a place not exactly known for its loyalty to any faction that might be
outbid by another—well, history had shown that sacred places gave no sanctuary from the Outfit. *That at the name of Jesus every knee should bow, of things in
heaven, and things in earth, and things under the earth*; a legend all but obliter-
ated by bullets on the front steps of Holy Name Cathedral, along with Hymie
Weiss.

Ralph, he found when at last he emerged, was a man without irony; a very
real carnation had burst like a huge popcorn kernel from one lapel. He stood
near the big front doors in a cocoa-brown double-breasted suit that made him
resemble a stout chest of drawers with a white hat set on top. Next to him stood
a man not as broad, but broad, dressed all in gray; a shadow enveloped in shadows. In Cicero the deep gorge of his suit coat would have meant easy access to a
shoulder holster. There was no reason it meant otherwise in Miami.

"I don't know how you stand it," Ralph said as Vasco approached. "I try to
stay out of tight places ever since Frank and Pete Gusenberg gunned Jack Mc-
Gurn in a telephone booth at the McCormick Hotel. He pissed through a tube
for six months."

"My room's not much less tight, I'm afraid."

"I got a can outside. We can talk there."

"A can?"

"A bus. A heap. A jalop. How long you been in this country, you don't know English?"

"I'm not exactly dressed for outdoors."

"You look swell, like the angel on top of the tree. This here's Frankie."

The other man stepped out of the shadows and shook Vasco's hand with his left, as if there was something wrong with the other. One of Dion O'Banion's killers had grasped his gun hand while the others pumped bullets into him. The lesson had not been lost. "Hiya."

The face under the gray felt brim was heavier now, older, the chin less blue with the graying of the beard beneath the skin; but time alone couldn't straighten that crooked upper lip.

Frankie Rio. Al Capone's personal bodyguard. Survivor of the attack on the Hawthorne Inn. The man he'd seen helping his father empty a jug of Mrs. Terrazzini's homemade wine in the kitchen of their apartment.

He felt the armor of the Church melting away from his body. He was a little boy in a nightshirt standing on a cold linoleum floor staring at a pair of suddenly silent men seated at the table staring back.

Rio's face showed no recognition. Vasco took comfort from that. He himself had changed, of course, and the encounter had lasted seconds; but if the name Vasco didn't ring bells, Rio's relationship with his father couldn't have amounted to much.

Then again, career mobsters weren't in the habit of tipping off others to what they were thinking.

It was a rare cloudy day, with a stiff breeze blowing from the southeast. It was early for hurricanes, but one couldn't help but think about them when the weather changed abruptly. In 1928, a savage storm had torn through the area, killing twenty-five hundred people, doing millions of dollars' worth of damage, and putting fifty thousand residents out of their blasted homes. Farmers were still plowing up bodies when Capone went to prison.

Ralph plodded down the front steps, his toes turned out like a duck's; a ponderous man, heavy on his feet, a blimp filled with suet instead of hydrogen. Not one of those bouncy fat men you saw in vaudeville. Rio preceded him by a step, leading with his left shoulder like a boxer. Vasco seemed to remember he'd fought professionally under an Irish name. Or was that Jack McGurn? Cramming for a test always carried the danger of forgetting much of what you'd learned.

The car, straddling two spaces parallel to the curb, was a 1942 Lincoln, the last model before the auto manufacturers in Detroit retooled to make B-24 bombers and Liberty ships. It was long and rounded and the sky-blue finish, many coats deep, reminded him of Mae Capone's eyes. All the chrome was painted over, the headlights too, in flat black with narrow slits for the light to get out. The vehicle had been parked strategically, preventing other cars from boxing it in without advertising deadly intent.

"I keep it down here," Ralph said. "Rentals are all shit since the war and Al needs the wheels. Fucking feds took everything he had and Mae had to sell the rest to keep the house. She and Ma don't get along so good, so the house in Chicago was out. Damn shame, them blackout headlights. You can't see two feet in front of the car. Like the krauts and Japs got enough planes left between 'em to drop a bomb on one crummy Ford."

He looked like his brother, only heavier and softer, with eyes that seemed to make direct contact only when he was looking at Vasco out of the corners. His hat had to have been custom-made; few haberdashers would have one his size in stock. It was a Panama, worn the way Al wore his in photographs, the brim flipped up on one side and down on the other, in Al's case to place a shadow on the side where the scars were. He had a ruby stickpin in his striped tie and a ring just like Al's on his left little finger. Vasco assumed that this time the diamond was real. It occurred to him fleetingly that Ralph may not have disposed of the infamous sparkler after all, as he'd told Mae. A thief was a thief, in burlap or silk.

"Let's go for a ride."

He felt himself pale. Ralph noticed and laughed. His laugh sounded like a dog panting; no, a broken bellows; no, steam sputtering from a loose safety valve; no, a dog panting. He'd been right the first time. "Not that kind of a ride, Padre. You been listening to *Gang Busters* when it shoulda been the Shrine of the Little Flower."

Heat came into his cheeks. White to red, a human chameleon. "This is Danny Coughlin, Mae's brother. We coulda used him behind the wheel in Chicago."

He shook the hand of a smiling middle-aged Irishman with the beginnings of a double chin, standing by the open door to the backseat. He wore plain blue serge like a chauffeur's uniform but no cap. Vasco had seen more hatless heads outdoors in Florida than in all his life. "How are you liking Miami, Father?" His brogue was more pronounced than his sister's.

"Very much." Although it was starting to look like Cicero.

"Danny manages business for the Bartenders and Waiters Union when he ain't driving. You ask me in the old days I'd let a Mick count my money, I'da coldcocked you for cracking wise."

"Not me, though, greaseball." Danny's smile remained sunny.

Ralph panted; roughhouse teasing was nothing new to a man with many brothers. "Not you, neither," he told Vasco. "Not dressed up like Pat O'Brien. What was that picture, Danny, he played a priest?"

"Pretty much all of 'em."

"Danny'd know. Al's got him one of them pull-down screens in the living room, projector behind a panel just like a fairy Hollywood producer. They get all the latest down there, even before the theaters in Miami."

"I've a friend through the Projectionists Union," Danny said. "Fella whose job's to pick up the reels at one theater and drop 'em off at the next. On the way he stops by Palm Island. You like religious pictures, Father?"

"Westerns, actually." He found himself smiling. Danny's attitude was contagious.

The other man's smile got wider, if that was possible. "We're screening *Buffalo Bill* tonight. Joel McCrea. Maureen O'Hara, but don't tell Winnie. She's visiting her mother, and she's the jealous type. You should come down."

"Let's don't get ahead of ourselves." Ralph's thick voice held an impatient edge for the first time. Danny's smile went away. "Well, let's not stand out here waiting for a gull to fly over and shit on us." Ralph tipped a flipper-size palm toward the backseat.

The interior was tan glove leather, soft as meringue. Vasco sank into it. He could straighten his legs without scuffing the back of the front seat. Ralph got in beside him, the springs squeaking on his side. Danny slid under the wheel, Rio took shotgun. Vasco wondered at what point a metaphor became literal.

Ralph told Danny to drive alongside the ocean. "There was still snow on the ground when I left Chicago," he said. "The lake don't get that blue till Mother's Day."

The motor started with almost no noise at all, just a pleasant vibrating massage Vasco felt in his buttocks and in the soles of his feet. Danny spun the wheel between thumb and forefinger and they swung out into shift-change traffic and turned east. The mayor of Miami turned on all the green lights for him. Paul Vasco had been that kind of driver as well.

With the bay on their right they powered north on Highway One. The water was choppy and not as blue as when the sun shone, but bluer than Lake Michigan that time of year. Sailboats, a seaplane floating on an updraft, its pontoons reminding him of Brownie's feet in their giant Oxfords. He wondered if he had stamps enough to swing that prime rib Sergeant Fowler had recommended. But then he wouldn't need it if he failed whatever test Ralph had in mind.

It started right off the bang: No "pencils up," no countdown by the clock. "Cicero, huh?"

"Born and raised. Well, born in Chicago. My father said he didn't want me delivered by an abortionist."

"Smart man. I wouldn't trust no Cicero doctor except maybe to pull a slug out of my fanny. They're good at that, through practice. I own a coupla joints there, but I wouldn't want to slip in one and hit my head. When's the last time you went to Umberto's on Second, ate a mess of fried clams?"

"Five years, anyway. That's when it burned down. It was on Twenty-Second, not Second, just down from the Hawthorne Inn."

Ralph was lighting a cigarette, watching him out of one of those eye-corners. He shook out the match, coughed smoke, a stuttering blast as from a tommy gun, dropped the match into a nickel tray with a hinged lid in his elbow rest. "Kerosene bomb. Insurance job. One of them Molotov cocktails didn't have a name till the krauts tried to take Stalingrad."

"Leningrad." Not that it mattered. He wasn't being quizzed about the Russian campaign.

"Grad this, grad that. You don't get nowhere in this life till you learn good English. My old man was Michelangelo with scissors and a cutthroat razor, but he never did learn how to put together six words in American, and he died with only a suit with two pairs of pants and his white smock. We buried him in 1920, know why?"

Death by heart failure in a pool hall down the street from the family apartment. "I imagine it was because he was dead."

Ralph shared his brother's affinity for bad jokes, but not his laugh. One of Al's "har-hars" was worth ten of Ralph's leaky bursts of steam. He didn't like Ralph.

But then of course he didn't like Al either. Focus.

"You're hep for a psalm-seller, I'll tell the world. Not like old Father Ahearn. 'Father A-Hole,' we called him. He ever tell you about the time my boy Ralphie hollowed out a votive candle and stuck a cherry bomb down inside?"

"I never met a Father Ahearn. Was he at St. Francis?"

Ralph took a drag that burned the cigarette all the way down to where *Melachrino* was printed on it in Arabic-looking letters and mashed it out in the tray. Vasco had never seen a man smoke a cigarette in less than a minute. Gray smoke kept coming out of his mouth and nostrils long after the point at which he thought a pair of human lungs could hold it. He could think of no argument to justify setting fire to something and sucking on it. "You're right, I got mixed up. Ahearn was in Brooklyn, and it was our brother Mimi planted that cherry bomb. A lot's happened in a little time. You know, it was just four years between the papers spelling Al's name right and the day they put him away for skimming off Uncle Sam? Things sure moved fast after the country went dry."

Vasco drew a deep breath and let it out, coughing a little smoke from Ralph's exhaust. He cranked down his window without asking permission. He didn't have to beg leave of thugs. He wasn't his father. "Mr. Capone—"

"Bottles. I got that name on account of I was the chief distributor of bottled water in Chicago. Surprised? City up to its fanny in bootleg beer, I'm selling God's own bounty? But ask yourself, whaddaya order to take the sting out of a slug of needle beer? Or you're a saloonkeeper, you want to turn a case of Old Log Cabin into five and cut down on overhead? Not that pisswater they pump from Lake Michigan, where fish fuck and everyone on down from Big Bill Thompson to Molly the Meter Maid flushes their toilet. Bottles Capone, that's who you come to. Nectar straight from the pure springs of Maine, or maybe Montana. One of them *M* states. See, I cornered the market not just on boozers, but on teetotalers as well. Al said I was a genius. Coming from a genius, that's like being asked to ride tailgunner for Lindbergh. Bottles, that's me." He jerked both thumbs toward his well-padded chest like Jimmy Cagney.

"Bottles. Why don't you just ask me what you want to know, and I'll answer as truthfully as I can."

Ralph lit another cigarette, coughing again and spraying sparks, which he swept off his coat with a panicky gesture that suggested a closetful of expensive suits pockmarked with holes. Then he turned his head and met Vasco's gaze square on for the first time. "That sonofabitch Hitler. May his soul rot in hell. Thank God for him." Belatedly he took note of the company and crossed himself awkwardly. He was out of practice.

"Why do you say that?" The confessional had been a good idea, even if it had been arranged for a different reason. It had increased Vasco's capacity to suspend judgment.

"He took the heat off Al, that's why. Until that goosestepping, sauerbraten-eating, house-painting son of a pretzel-twisting pimp came along, Al Capone, my brother Snorky, was the by-God Antichrist." No sign of the cross this time. "They tried to hang everything on him from the Chicago fire to Leopold and Loeb. Every harness bull on the street thought he could run him in on no charge at all, him without a single conviction or even an indictment, till that business in Philly. When they arrested him here in Miami on nothing at all, they took his cash and jewelry and threw 'em in the toilet. In the shitter. I ask you, what kind of person don't respect diamonds and greenbacks?"

Incorruptible public servants.

"Bolsheviks, that's who. Bolsheviks and Nazis and them little monkey-faced Japs what rubbed out Pearl Harbor. And for what? Cutting the dust from the throat of some street-sweeping schnook on South Clark with the same hootch drank by the judge what sent him to jail for lugging a pint around in his pocket? So excuse me, *Father*, if I don't buy that get-up you got on as any more than sweat from Christ's left nut. The Bible says a man's got to stand up for his brother when he can't stand up for himself. Take that to federal fucking court and see how far you get."

"Actually, Cain says in Genesis, 'Am I my brother's keeper?' "

But Ralph wasn't listening. "I done most of three years in Leavenworth and on McNeill's Island on a tax rap. That was just practice for Al. I'd do three times that to keep this country that ought to be putting up Hitler's ass what they're putting up Al's from chiseling him out of what life he's got left. *Hai capito?*"

"*Capisco.*" He had to admit Ralph made a good case. Mob mouthpieces had been making good cases for years without coming close to the truth.

"All right. Just so's we're clear."

The radio was playing softly in the front seat. A baseball game, with simulated cheers and sound effects to suggest the action was being broadcast live. Dizzy Dean's drawling play-by-play had a soporific effect as the conversation lulled.

There were fewer sails now, and those that were visible were tacking shoreward. Raindrops spattered the windshield and made crooked tracks in the slipstream. Danny turned on the wipers. Vasco rolled up his window. Unseen lightning crackled on the radio speaker. A flat gust of wind slapped the side of the car, but the Lincoln was heavy and solid and held the road like a brick. The sky was low and dirty. The water had turned a gunmetal shade. Interesting how easily "gunmetal" came to mind in that company. In leaner days Ralph had worn brass knuckles and swung a blackjack during the Cicero takeover and on the streets of Chicago in the Pineapple Primary of 1928, when Outfit grenades hurled into polling places did the campaigning for favored candidates for office. Now those big meaty hands, broken several times and healed over shiny white, busied themselves lighting a fresh cigarette off the butt of the last.

"I put in a call to St. Francis before I left Chicago," he said. "That stuck-up pastor wouldn't come to the phone, but some flunky said you made the grade in the seminary there and got transferred here. I talked face-to-face with your pastor while you was in the booth. Not exactly the curious type. He didn't even ask who I was."

"His mind's on other things." He looked out at the rising waves, seeking calm. He felt like a schoolboy waiting for his parents to come back from a meeting with his teacher; and his academic record was rocky.

"He says you're working out so far. I ain't just sure what that means. I guess you didn't set fire to the place."

Vasco said nothing. There was always another shoe.

"I dropped by your old man's boat dock on the way down. I was in his bar once after Repeal, but I think it was after he sold it to my cousin Rocco, so maybe we didn't meet. I could be wrong; come hard times we had a hundred people a day looking for work, and like I said I was in charge of water, not beer. Anyway I missed him again. The boat was gone. Must of had a customer."

"He'll be disappointed. He could've told you about the time he went out on the water with Hemingway."

"Fuck's Hemingway? Never mind. I ain't interested." He popped open the gold case with his initials engraved on the lid (the Capones slapped their brand on everything), but he was out of cigarettes. He snapped it shut, cracked his window, and poked his stub out into the current of air. "Frankie, gimme a nail."

Rio reached inside his coat and turned in his seat to pass a cellophane-wrapped pack over the back.

Ralph snorted. "Camels. Know why they call 'em that?"

Rio said it with Ralph: "'Cause they cure the tobacco in camel shit.' Hey, sor-*ry*. There's a war on, you know? We don't all have your connections."

"Go boil your head, you Sicilian son of a bitch." Ralph snatched the pack out of his hand, speared one between his thick lips—they lacked his brother's Rubenesque curve—and jammed the rest into an inside pocket. Danny chuckled and turned up the volume on the ball game. The 4-F first baseman for Cincinnati whiffed an easy fly.

Vasco watched Ralph light up, marveling at the democracy that appeared to exist between gangland general and lowly GI, the casual insults and name-calling.

In movies the henchmen always called their superiors boss and scrambled to carry out orders.

"I couldn't get a line on your father's crib. He sure don't sleep in that shitty shack."

"He has a lady friend."

"Where's she live? I'll drop in on the way back."

"He didn't tell me." He spoke before he thought. Ralph turned his giant head, the Camel smoldering in the corner of his mouth. It bobbed up and down when he spoke.

"You don't get along? My Ralphie and me don't see eye-to-eye all the time, but I'd take a bullet for him."

This impression was precisely what Hoover had told him to avoid. He saw all the progress he'd made slipping away.

"We lost touch for a while when I was studying. Now he thinks I'll disapprove of him because he's living in sin. I'm hoping to convince him he's my father no matter what and I love him."

"Huh."

The Lincoln rolled on, the tires squishing now as the rain stepped up its pace. Danny put the wipers on high. They whumped and swished. The ball game was mostly static; they were driving out of range of the signal. He switched off the radio, and now there was just the sound of the wipers swamping.

"Al told me he told you our old man wanted him to be a priest in the worst way. They didn't talk for a long time. Me, I wanted to be a Rough Rider, only that war finished when I was five. He tried to get me to enlist when the boys went to France, but I cured myself of the soldier bug long before then. Jimmy run off when he was sixteen. We never did hear from him till he showed up at my fishing cabin in Wisconsin not long after Al got out of the pen, with a crock-a-shit story about being a two-gun sheriff out West."

"We're put on this earth to be a disappointment to our parents."

Ralph smiled for the first time, not a third as widely as Danny, or nearly half as widely as his brother. A purse-lipped expression and brief, as if he was afraid it might stick. "You got that from Al. He's all the time saying it. Sonny was a handful when he was a kid. Turned out all right, though. Mae saw to that. She thinks you're okay."

This was news. He'd thought her cool, distant, suspicious.

"Here's the thing." The fat man twisted in the seat, propping an elbow on the deep ledge under the back window and resting a massive thigh on the cushion. His trousers cuff rode up, exposing a dark blue silk sock with a white clock and a hint of garter. "She says you can come for cocktails tomorrow. Four o'clock, out by the pool. I said hold on, I ain't through checking him out. She says go ahead, check him out, just don't forget to invite him. Women."

"I'll have to ask Father Kyril. I'm supposed to be in the booth from two to four."

"I already asked. He says he'll cover for you."

"Did he know who the invitation was from?"

"Mr. and Mrs. Brown, of Miami Beach."

The Capones got a lot of mileage out of the nom de guerre. Hoover had been misinformed when he said Al hadn't used it since early days. "May I ask how *Mr.* Brown feels?"

"It's his idea. Al's the trusting type, always was. I spent most of my time way back when, protecting him from his friends. Mae thought maybe he'd forget in a day or two, but he kept saying. When he gets his mitts onto a notion you have to bust his fingers before he'll let go."

Vasco thought of "Red" Duffy, killed along with Assistant State's Attorney Bill McSwiggin, and how a morgue attendant had to break his fingers in order to open his fist. *He should've fried for McSwiggin,* Sergeant Fowler had said, meaning Capone. Was it a deliberate reference? If Ralph thought Vasco would recognize it, he was in trouble. Baseball bats and pistols. He asked Ralph if he'd be there.

"I go home tomorrow. Cleaners and Dyers are electing a new president next week." He rested his cheek on his hand. The weight of something in his inside breast pocket—not the pack of Camels—pulled his coat out of line. "I ain't figured you out yet, but I will. Meantime you don't say boo to Al with Mae not in the room. If she steps out to tinkle and he sneezes and you say 'Gesundheit,' I want to hear about it. I'll hear anyway, but if it don't come from you"—he raised his voice—"Danny, what's that song, Roy Rogers sings it, something about a empty saddle?"

"Gene Autry. 'Empty Saddles in the Old Corral.'" He sang it. He had a beautiful tenor voice, high and pure. It made the heart ache."

"That's it. There'll be one more empty saddle in the old corral at Our Lady of Redemption. Turn us around, Danny. We don't need to see Georgia today."

"That's more than three hundred miles."

"Listen to Christopher Columbus. Make with the wheel."

They turned around on the rutted dirt lot of a half-finished hotel and headed back down the two-lane blacktop. Ralph faced forward again, took another drag on his cigarette, and squashed it in the tray. "Camel shit." He illustrated it with a long jet of smoke. Vasco touched his crucifix. The magic seemed to be wearing off. Their tires bumped over streetcar tracks and the rain stopped as abruptly as if for a red light. The pavement was dry. Vasco would never understand how the universe worked, how something as natural as rain observed jurisdictions as rigidly as a Cook County ward heeler. Danny, who'd tugged on his lights when the sky darkened, pushed in the switch, shutting them off. Somewhere west of Seventh Avenue the sun pried at a crack in the overcast.

Ralph said, "Danny's dropping me and Frankie off at the Ponce. I got a meeting. He'll take you back to church."

"Thanks, Mr. Capone."

"Bottles."

He knew he'd never be able to bring himself to call him that.

A four-foot wall covered with pink seashells held a plaque reading PONCE DE LEON HOTEL. They coasted through the open gate and the Irishman behind the wheel drew the brake in front of a set of revolving doors belonging to a Moroccan palace with balconies railed in curlicue wrought iron. A doorman dressed like a conquistador, in crested helmet and striped balloon pantaloons, beat Danny to the door on Ralph's side. Before he got out, Ralph reached over and took Vasco's leg above the knee in a steel grip. "*Andate con Dio,* Padre." His pursed smile flickered. Then both vanished. Vasco felt the pressure in his leg a moment longer.

Frankie Rio, outside the car, leaned back in to thrust his left hand at the passenger. He grinned through his badly joined lip. "Tell your old man Frankie said hello."

TEN

"Twenty-three!"

"One moment, please."

"Do I have all day?"

Vasco didn't answer. In the five minutes he'd been in the shop, no one had come in to claim the next number hanging on the peg.

It was a small block building with a flat roof, G. RUBENSTEIN & SON FINE MEATS painted across its width. The forgotten carcass of the NRA blue eagle curled and faded on a cardboard placard in the front window.

The little man behind the counter shrugged and folded skinny red arms across the bib of his blood-flecked apron. He wore a paper hat and a fat yellow pencil behind one Dumbo ear. Whether he was the father or the son depended on how long the place had been in business.

Behind the glass, thick and distorted to make the cuts of meat look bigger, with pink bulbs installed to make them look more fresh, tiny picket signs advertised prices and points needed to satisfy the government that the customer wasn't cheating some soldier out of a square meal. If that customer had stamps and the points added up, he ate steak. If, as was more often the case, they didn't, he went home with hamburger or less. Vasco, gummed sheets clutched in hand, compared numbers like a man with a sweepstakes ticket. So far no winner.

A pound of prime rib was twelve points. Three pounds minimum were needed to impress Brownie, with three Capones to feed, but not even J. Edgar Hoover had the connections to put thirty-six points in the hands of an untried field agent.

Lamb chops were nine points per pound. Better, but some people didn't like lamb—something about the smell when it was cooking—and a lot of them happened to be Italian. Wiser to avoid embarrassment altogether.

Seven for hamburger. He pictured himself standing on the doorstep at 93 Palm Island holding a dripping sack of ground meat. Given the master of the house's background they might mistake it for someone's head.

"Father, I been on my feet since six in the ayem. My daughter-in-law's home sick and my son's in the merchant marines. I'm sorry as anything about Jesus, but that wasn't my call. Please pick something so I can take my break."

Ham was seven. He straightened. "Three pounds of ham, please."

RUBENSTEIN, A STICKLER, LOOKED AT THE NUMBER VASCO GAVE HIM, THEN hung it on the peg and slid open the glass on his side. He weighed one of the smaller hams on his big white scale and turned to place it in the gliding stainless-steel bed of his slicer. "Run a little under. Over, more points. You want it exact, I'm not the butcher for you."

He said that would be fine. Food vendors were all just a little bit hostile since rationing. A few minutes later he put his purchase, wrapped snugly in shiny white paper and placed in a brown sack, on the floor of the Model T and worked the crank. It started on the first turn, with the motor still warm.

That reminded him of the garage owner who'd supervised the tune-up and what he'd said about the left front tire. The tread was worn smooth, but the cord wasn't showing. The spare mounted on the back of the car looked sound, a little weather-checked. It made a solid sound when he slapped it, like an unripe melon. He didn't want to be late. If he got back before dark he'd see about buying that new tire.

Father Kyril had excused him for the day. He looked up from his notes on Sunday Mass and said, "It's always when you have to be someplace that someone plops himself down in the booth two minutes before you have to leave and says it's been fifteen years since his last confession."

"Thank you, Father."

"You're becoming a regular country preacher, invited home for fried chicken. Just remember to load up on mashed potatoes. It's Friday."

Ralph Capone had made an understatement when he said Kyril wasn't the curious type. Pastor and church were barely in the same latitude.

It was one of those days the Chamber of Commerce chose to take the post-card picture. Everything was pink and blue and sea green. Women in spaghetti straps and picture hats strolled the sidewalks holding the hands of children in sailor suits. A leathery old man dressed like a bird watcher, in khakis and a dimpled campaign hat, prowled the shoreline poking at the sand with something that looked like a minesweeper. Long-legged birds scampered around him in and out of the tide, more concerned with crabs than explosions. Vasco kept to the edge of the pavement to make room for bright-colored open-top roadsters to pass carrying girls and young men waiting for their orders. You wouldn't know there was a war on if you weren't being reminded constantly by posters selling liberty bonds and the radio selling blood drives and headlines on newsstands selling the names of medieval walled cities, current for the first time since crossbows.

The toll man on the causeway, burned dark as a cherry under his postman's cap, silver at the temples, took his dime and frowned down at something from the window of the booth. "Father, you got a flat."

He opened his door and leaned out, aware as he did so that the car was list-ing several degrees toward the left front corner, a queasy sensation with the ocean at his elbow. That tire lay on its rim with black rubber pooled around it like melted wax. "I didn't hear it blow."

"Sometimes they just sit down and don't get back up, like a sick old man. How's your spare?"

He smiled. "Would you believe I checked it twenty minutes ago?"

But the toll man wasn't amused. "Another year this whole country'll be up on blocks. Try and pull 'er over up ahead." He worked the controls inside the booth. The striped barricade lifted on squeaking pulleys.

The tire slap-slapped as he crept forward. Steering to the side was like pulling himself up a rope hand over hand, but he got the car out of the traffic lane, killed the motor, and stepped down. As he unlatched the battered tin toolbox attached to the running board, he had the horrible feeling there would be no jack inside. He'd inspected the spare, but it hadn't occurred to him to make sure he had the equipment he needed to make the change.

He crossed himself. It was there, a stout screw glistening with brown grease lying in a jumble of crescents, wooden-handled screwdrivers, pliers, greasy rags, and a mallet. There was even a vulcanizing kit complete with air pump and rubber patches, but when he went to move the can of adhesive to get to the jack handle, it was stuck fast to the bottom of the toolbox. He had to use both hands to tear the handle loose and barked his knuckles on the base of the pump.

"You okay, Father?"

He sucked his knuckles, looking sheepishly at the toll man standing next to him. An old cavalry revolver with a saddle ring sagged in a flap holster on his hip. "I'm a little rusty."

The toll man took the jack handle from him. "My first car was a Ford. Brass radiator, sport red. That's before Henry found out black's cheaper. It went through tires like my nephew went through diapers. Stand back, please, and give me room."

Before Vasco could protest, he had the jack under the front axle and the tire off the ground. Loosening the bolts that held the rim on the wheel he said, "Going back out to see Al?"

There was no reason to be surprised, except by his candor. He was the Capones' first line of defense whenever anyone drove out to the island, and he'd have been told to expect Vasco both times. "Yes. Do you know him very well?"

"I been on the job a long time. Saw him when he first came out to look at the house. He tried to tip me five bucks, but I said I couldn't accept gratuities. He grinned wide as a barn door, leaned over from the back of this big black Cadillac he was riding in then and shook my hand. 'That's the first time anybody ever refused to take something from me.' See, I didn't know who he was until that moment."

"Were you afraid?"

"Scared sh—" He remembered his audience. The rim came free. "Afraid? Sure. When he came back the other way I expected guns blazin', like in *City Streets*. But he just sat back while his driver paid the toll. Next time, he had somebody with him in the car. He pointed to me, said, 'There's the man wouldn't take a fin from Al Capone. He'll never get to be mayor being honest.' I bet I heard him say the same thing a dozen times after, even when the other person in the car heard it before." He got up, carried the damaged tire around to the back, took down the spare, and rolled it up to the front, smacking it with the heel of his hand like a boy driving a hoop with a stick.

"That's an interesting—"

"Not long after, my brother-in-law lost his job. He was out of work a year. I don't know how Al found out, but Miami was a small town then, word got around. His car comes up, I put out my hand for the toll—it was a nickel then—he reaches up from the backseat again and shoves a fistful of bills into it, closes my fingers around 'em. His hands look soft, but let me tell you, they could squeeze juice out of a cue ball. 'Tell your brother-in-law I'm renting his garage. I'm thinking of getting back in the furniture business and I'll need the storage. Forty bucks a month, there's two months in advance. He can go on parking in it till I need it.'" He fitted the rim of the spare to the wheel and threaded the lugs onto the bolts, talking the whole time.

"My sister was plenty scared. She reads all the detective magazines, thinks she knows all about the Capone mob, how it works. She's sure he'll fill the place with liquor or guns, maybe even a couple dozen stiffs. You know what he put in there, that garage?"

"Furniture?"

"Nothing, that's what. He never even saw the place. But come the first of every month somebody shows up at the booth with forty bucks cash, right up to the day Al went to the pen. He never figured to put anything there. It was just his way of helping out without it looked like charity. Public Enemy, my foot. John D. Rockefeller never did nothing for the working man but hand out his stinking dimes, and they called *him* a philanthropist." He tightened each lug with a savage jerk of the wrench. It would take a powder charge to get them loose. Vasco shook his head. Was there anyone outside Washington who didn't think Al Capone's head belonged on Mt. Rushmore? Even policemen thought he got the short end, him with his hands bathed in blood to the elbows.

"There you go, Father. I'd see about a new spare right away. You were lucky you didn't blow out on South Beach. It ain't the same place since the air depot and the defense plants. Payrolls bring in trash."

He returned the tools to the box. Vasco started to thank him, but the toll man cocked his head and hurried back into the booth. He heard rumbling then and saw a green panel truck slowing for the turn. The name of a pool-cleaning service was lettered on the side. Hoover had said something about concealing surveillance crews in pool-cleaning and kosher food delivery trucks. Curious, Vasco strolled alongside it, just another tourist stretching his legs in the sea air.

Just as he reached the rear of the truck, one of the doors in back popped open. Smoke rolled out. He thought it was on fire. Then a curl of vapor touched his face with the sting of dry ice. A cigarette butt sailed out of the back, nearly grazing his shoulder before it struck the ground almost at his feet. For an instant he locked gazes with the smoker before he pulled the door shut. The man stood in a half-crouch, raising himself from his seat on one of a dozen or more card-board packing cases. He wore a red-and-black-checked mackinaw over bib over-alls and a matching hunting cap pulled low on his swarthy forehead. One hand held a sawed-off pump shotgun across his thighs. The truck contained no pool maintenance equipment and the man bore no resemblance to the clean-cut types Hoover selected to place in the field. Neither legitimate service nor under-cover work explained the presence of dry ice. The gate lifted, the light truck shifted into gear, and Vasco was alone once again with the toll man, who smiled at him crookedly through his window. "Meat. Steaks, chops, short ribs. Grain-fed Black Angus, not them broke-down milk cows stuffed with grass you get in stores, when you got the points. Sweetmeats, that's Al's favorite. Calf's stomach. They're early this month, but I hear he's throwing a wingding. Guess you'd know all about that." His smile became a smirk. So now Vasco was part of the circle, along with the cardinal who drank with Scarface.

"Black market?"

"I don't ask, Father. My job's just to see the toll gets paid."

He thanked the man for his help and reached into the Ford to turn on the ignition. He spotted the sack on the floor, made a swift decision, and carried it back to the booth.

"It's a ham," he said. "Not much point in giving it to the Capones' cook now. Maybe you can share it with your sister and brother-in-law."

"My brother-in-law's missing in action in Germany." He made no move to take the sack.

"I'm sorry."

"I can't accept gratuities."

"Not for doing your job, which like you said was to see the toll gets paid. Can't a man show his appreciation to a fellow Christian who helped him out?"

The man considered. His brain appeared to work slowly, conditioned as it was to accepting bills and coins and making change, not decisions. Vasco began to feel conspicuous standing out in the open holding a bag of meat. He inserted a gentle prod. "It'd be a sin to let it spoil, especially now."

The toll man nodded abruptly and took the sack. "Thank you kindly, Father. Betty'll appreciate it, with a fifteen-year-old to feed. Mind if I tell her it came from a minister instead of a priest? She belongs to the Eastern Star."

"Tell her whatever you like." He hesitated. "I'd like to pray for your brother-in-law. May I ask his name?"

Shorter period of consideration. "Fred Norris, Airman First Class. He was—is—a tail gunner on a B-17. That's the duty Clark Gable volunteered for, after Carole Lombard was killed in that plane crash. Most movie stars, they do USC, or clerical work stateside; the War Department tries to keep 'em alive. But you know what they say about tail gunners? Pilot lands at an airfield, says, 'Gimme five hundred gallons and a new tail gunner.' Gable? He wants to commit suicide. So I ask you, what's a husband and father want with that duty? Sure, pray for him, but pray for Fred, Junior, while you're at it. Them recruiters don't look too hard at what they write under Date of Birth."

"My father thinks the war will be over by Christmas."

"That's what they said about Prohibition back in 1920."

"I'll pray for them both."

"Beg pardon, Father, and not to speak ill of absent parties, but Fred always was a pain in the ass. That's the job description for in-laws. I'd never tell Betty, but you made the right choice in life."

He started the car. Not much had changed since Chicago, despite the evidence of Repeal and economic recovery and world war. The man guarding a shipment of contraband animal flesh might have received his training riding in the back of a beer truck.

This time the freckle-faced guard at the gate didn't pat him down for weapons. He smiled, adding cordiality to politeness, and swung both portals wide. Vasco parked behind a string of sport roadsters and sedans trimmed with gleaming nickel in the turnaround before the front door. The sun felt hot on his back when he got out; a liveried chauffeur scrubbed at fresh gull-splatter on a fender with a chamois cloth, taking care not to touch the blistering metal with bare hands. Music was playing somewhere: a sprightly prewar dance tune arranged for a small combo. There was no sign of the green panel truck, but an arrow pegged in the driveway directed deliveries around the side of the house.

Brownie, the houseman, opened the door to the bell. He'd traded his apron for a white dinner jacket, black bow tie crooked and looking like the propeller screw on a battleship against his broad brown throat. The raised scar of an old scalp wound showed through his coiled graying hair. At sight of his scowl, Vasco regretted showing up empty-handed, even knowing how pathetic a three-pound ham would look among glistening slabs of fresh beef. But the big man stepped aside to let him enter and held out a hand—the one with all its fingers—for his hat. Another pair of Al's castoff trousers swung clear of his insteps.

Vasco drifted toward the sound of voices and music. The living room was a dazzle of sunlight, the drapes drawn aside from glass-door walls fronting on a blue pool that he thought at first was the bay. To have heard about the size of the pool, bigger than many houses, wasn't the same as seeing it.

"How, chief! You missed a corker last night."

He blinked, not recognizing Danny Coughlin at first without his blue serge. Mae's brother, the Capones' driver, weaved out of a cluster of guests chattering by the fireplace, wearing a loud print shirt with the tail outside gray gabardine slacks. He clutched a glass tumbler half-filled with amber liquid and ice cubes in one fist. His big Irish face was red and his eyes lacked focus, the blue irises swimming in scarlet. His other hand seized Vasco's. All the male family members seemed to have practiced shaking hands with a stone hammer.

Belatedly, Vasco remembered Danny's invitation to watch *Buffalo Bill* in the living-room theater. "I'm sorry I couldn't make it. I'll be sure and go see it on your recommendation."

"Gangster picture tonight." A stage whisper, delivered in his ear with a gust of bourbon breath. "Al says they help take his mind off business."

He didn't know how to respond. His experiences with his father had taught him that people in a drunken condition were difficult to carry on conversations with. He was rescued by Rose the maid, who suddenly appeared between them offering an etched silver tray containing hors d'oeuvres. As he was carefully selecting a morsel of broccoli and cheese from among shrimp puffs and things wrapped in bacon (it *was* Friday, as Father Kyril had pointed out), Danny drifted outside by way of the sliding doors. Vasco placed his choice on a paper napkin and thanked Rose, who smiled and dipped a knee. She looked crisp in black-and-white and smelled faintly of lemon-scented soap, much to his approval. He disliked perfumes and colognes.

After she left to serve others, he felt marooned. The guests, some in cocktail attire, others dressed more casually in sports shirts and jackets and sundresses, stood in groups talking, sipping from glasses shaped like funnels and silos, and munching on ladyfingers and tiny triangular sandwiches, engrossed in their private galaxies. The preponderance of tans suggested year-around residents and vacationers who took bungalows by the season; wealthy people and people of social influence, if not political, as in earlier days; souvenir hunters in search of anecdotes, not the vote in the sixty-sixth ward. As two women passed him presumably bound for the powder room, he overheard part of their conversation:

"A *machine gun,* can you believe it? Covered by a towel. She actually sat on it in the cabana. Of course, that was before."

"Sylvia said there was an Indian chest in the master bedroom filled with cash: nothing smaller than hundred-dollar bills in stacks. She went up there looking for a"—whispered word, probably *tampon*—"I'm sure the government has it all now."

Gray hair and crow's-feet abounded; one old lady in raw silk and pearls leaned on a cane with a rubber foot. He was the only person in the room under forty, not counting the maid. He'd have felt ostracized by his youth if he thought anyone was paying attention to the man in the clerical collar trying to keep crumbs off his coat.

He went outside, where the flat surface of the water hammered blue back at the sky, bright as burnished steel. The pool was a rectangular slot in an acre of mosaic that looked as if the island had been built around it. More guests stood and reclined in chaises on its apron. Here were swimsuits, robes, puddles spreading where people dripped. A woman whose figure was not yet matronly posed in a white sharkskin suit and bathing cap on the end of a diving board, bounced twice, and executed a respectable swan into the water. The ripples struggled to reach the other end and patted the concrete gently. A man with a potbelly left his cigarette burning in his mouth to applaud.

Behind a portable bar, a short dark Cuban in a dinner jacket chugged a cock-tail shaker to the beat of a four-piece band playing nearby ("Never saw the sun/ shining so bright . . ."). A brief line waited in front of the bar. Danny Coughlin was part of it.

Brownie cruised up carrying a tray full of drinks. Vasco declined, but took advantage of the tray to discard his napkin. The houseman moved on, silent in his tread.

Vasco had begun to wonder if host and hostess were absent when Mae Ca-pone detached herself from a group gathered under a squat palm and came his way, towing a man in a cream-colored shirt and tan flannels by the arm. She wore a white tennis dress that left her mottled shoulders bare. With no clouds to interrupt reflection, her eyes looked as deep blue as her brother's. She was a very attractive middle-aged woman and must have been a startling beauty at twenty.

"I'm glad you could come, Father. I was beginning to think you'd had second thoughts about the company."

He took her hand. It seemed to maintain the same cool temperature indoors and out. He noticed she'd addressed him as Father for the first time. "I wish I had a more original excuse, but I had a flat on the bridge. The toll man changed it for me."

"Third one I heard about today! In six months we'll all be on foot. Dear Henry," she said. "I suppose he told you that story about turning down Al's tip."

He said he did. He kept the other story to himself. There was something sin-ister about it. How many other garages had Capone rented, and how many had he actually used, and for what purpose?

"The poor man can't have much to talk about. The world's turned so many times, and there he is still in his booth."

"Well, I'm glad he was there today."

"What's the matter, they don't teach you to fix flats at the seminary?"

He shifted his attention to the young man at Mae's side, who had spoken. He was tall and well-built, heavy-faced, with beautiful lips Vasco had seen before on someone else. His broad smile drew the sting from his words.

"Sonny, that's no way to talk to a priest."

"Sorry, Father." But the grin remained in place.

"Father Peter Vasco, Albert Capone. I apologize for my son's manners. I promised him I'd find someone his age to talk to, but I didn't tell him the rest."

"No reason to apologize. For what it's worth, Henry beat me to the jack." He found Sonny's handshake normal and brief, a refreshing change. A wire led from a button in his left ear to an object that resembled an electric-blanket con-trol clipped to his pocket. He was partially deaf, the result of mastoid surgery to correct a defect Capone's doctors attributed to his syphilis, contracted in a Brooklyn brothel before Sonny was conceived. How odd to meet a man whose prehistory he knew so well.

"I saw a picture of you with Babe Ruth."

Mae's face stiffened, and he knew he'd taken a bad chance. "I wish he'd never gone to that game. My boy's face in the crime section with the trunk murderers and rapists."

"It made me a hero at school. I don't think the Bambino minded the publicity, either."

"I was eight years old the first time I saw it. I envied you. . . ." Once again he drew from the armory of truth. He hadn't known at the time who the smiling, scar-faced man was in the picture, but he'd wanted to be the boy.

Al Capone's son shrugged. "It was okay. My real interest was football." His smile turned bitter; he'd played during his brief time at Notre Dame, an unwelcome memory. "Dad says your dad worked for him in Chicago."

Mae touched his arm, sparing Vasco the effort of framing a diplomatic answer. "See if you can get your uncle Danny to slow down his drinking. I think he forgot he's driving Rose home tonight."

"I'll see if I can find a brick to hit him with. I don't know how to stop him otherwise. It was good to meet you, Father."

"Please call me Peter. Under the right circumstances we might have been at school together." He shook Sonny's hand again.

"I wish we had."

When he left, Mae said, "A normal childhood, that's the only thing we couldn't afford to give him. You can do everything right for your children and it can still turn out wrong."

"He seems to have his feet on the ground." It seemed a priestly thing to say.

"His father spoiled him. He adores Sonny. But you're right. He's a mechanic's apprentice at the air depot in Miami, contributing to the effort. His deafness is an advantage there. You couldn't imagine a noisier place. And he's a good husband and father." She put her arm in his and led him away from the pool. "The last thing I wanted you two to talk about was old times. Young people should live in the present."

"The present is a frightening place."

"You weren't around for the past."

Capone's bodyguards were easier to spot with a crowd in place; they were the only ones wandering around without a drink or a snack. When a private plane circled overhead, turning into the wind with engines groaning to land in Miami Beach, Vasco saw the undersides of half a dozen jaws.

"You have a beautiful home."

"Al's proud of it. He built the cabana and that ridiculous pool and hired an army to do the landscaping. It belonged to a brewer who rarely came down. An old associate. The place was a jungle."

The palm trees were spaced widely apart like columns, with no shrubbery to provide cover for intruders

. . . a regular fortress, Lieutenant Fowler had said, *with Biscayne Bay for a moat.*

"You've made many friends here."

"Well, we can always count on those men in hot heavy jackets. Some of the others are friends. The rest are here to pet the giraffe."

He puzzled over that.

"Al will be happy to see you. He's talked about practically nothing else all week."

At a round glass table sheltered under a broad umbrella, the master of the house sat playing cards with a group of male guests. His striped terry robe hung open over a black one-piece swimsuit stretched taut across his barrel torso and his square solid feet were stuck in black suede slippers with dragons on the toes. A thick cigar with a red-and-gold band smoldered in the corner of his mouth, distorting his face on that side. Vasco thought of every Edward G. Robinson movie he had ever seen, with the addition of a pair of gold-rimmed glasses on the end of the Capone nose. They appeared in none of the dozens of photographs he'd studied. A vain man, Al, who powdered his face to cover the scars.

"Snorky, is that the same cigar you were smoking twenty minutes ago?" Mae's eyes went to a white ceramic ashtray the size of a dinner plate on the table, littered with ash in heaps and hollow cylinders. Embossed letters around the rim identified it as the property of the Lexington Hotel. What was petty theft in a career founded on murder?

He looked up at her, startled. His hair, what was left of it, was slicked back and dripping down his neck. He'd had a swim. "Well, sure. A good corona takes an hour. You're in a hurry to finish, get yourself a box of Dutch Masters." He spread his cards faceup on the table. "Gin."

One of the other players, white-haired with curdled skin, cleared his throat delicately. "Al, it's pinochle, not rummy."

"Oh, right." He picked up the cards and started rearranging them. Another player folded.

"Snorky, look who's here," Mae said.

He looked at her again over the tops of the glasses, then at Vasco. The gray eyes looked murky. He took the cigar out of his mouth and smiled. "Afternoon, Your Reverence. How's that new roof holding up?"

"It's not Bishop Fantonetti, dear. It's Peter Vasco. You remember, Paul Vasco's son from Cicero."

The grin flickered, then brightened. Capone laid the cigar in the tray and reached up to crush Vasco's fingers. His palm was clammy. "Hiya."

The player who'd thrown in his hand got up to offer his seat. Vasco accepted, grateful to be relieved of the burden of standing. It was clear Capone had no idea who he was. He'd joined the game too late. Al's mind was gone.

ELEVEN

THE WHITE-HAIRED MAN WITH THE MEALY COMPLEXION—HE TURNED OUT to be the president of the Dade County Board of Realtors—dealt the next hand. Vasco held up a palm when he turned his direction. "I don't know how to play."

"Does it matter?" muttered the other.

Mae's eyes darkened. When the realtor saw them, like twin shotgun muzzles, he looked down quickly at the deck in his hand. But Capone was lost in his cards and didn't seem to be listening.

The fourth party at the table spoke up. "I'm up for gin rummy."

"I don't know how to play that either."

The man's mouth hung open. He was pudgy-faced with buck teeth and looked like a beaver gulping oxygen. Apart from Vasco he appeared to be the youngest person present. He looked remotely familiar, like someone seen in a photograph. "Good Lord, Father, were you raised in a monastery?"

"Parker, mind your manners," Mae said. Vasco had sized her up as the den mother of Palm Island, correcting the behavior of sons, brothers, and men of tender years.

"I *am* sorry;" and he sounded as if he was. "It's just that I grew up here. If you don't learn to swim and play cards, you might as well walk into the ocean."

Mae laughed, a girlish sound coming from the iron matriarch. "Parker's a native Floridian. He went to school with dolphins. His father's a former mayor of Miami."

"Parker Henderson." He stuck out a plump hand without a torn cuticle in sight.

"Peter Vasco." He grasped it. He expected to qualify for a term in office by day's end, all this pressing of flesh. He knew who the man was now. Parker Henderson managed the Ponce de Leon Hotel, where Ralph Capone had had a meeting and where Al had stayed locally until he moved into his house. Henderson had been instrumental in that transaction, and several others. His picture had found its way into the FBI file along with a transcript of his testimony as a reluctant witness for the prosecution during Capone's trial for tax evasion. He and Reinhart Schwimmer would have understood each other, the spoiled child of wealth and politics and the hapless optometrist slain on St. Valentine's Day, a victim of his extracurricular interests. They shared a boy's fascination with gangsters, drawing a vicarious thrill from associating with them, as Capone had when rubbing elbows with baseball players and movie stars. In Henderson's case, the infatuation had led him into willing service as a bagman for the Outfit, taking delivery on shipments of cash on his idol's behalf and putting it through channels, buying ordnance and corrupting public servants. He'd done his part, however unwittingly, in arming the assassins in the garage on North Clark Street.

"We gonna play cards or patty-cake?" Capone barked. It was the first sign of impatience Vasco had seen from him, a mild taste of his tantrums in the board-room at the Hawthorne Inn and the roadhouse in Indiana where Scalise and Anselmi had left their brains.

The realtor, an irritable sort also, said, "Well, we can't play gin or pinochle without a fourth. Even poker would just be pushing the same money around till you wouldn't know Abe Lincoln from Wendell Willkie."

"I can play poker," Vasco said.

Even Mae looked shocked. Capone alone went on sorting the cards in his hand like a fey decorator comparing paint chips.

"I learned from the Jesuits," Vasco said, "when the pastor at St. Francis was out." A general collapse of curiosity ensued, from all but Henderson, the poster child for Unitarianism. What was it about Jesuits? They were the Jews of the Church.

"Poker's the berries with me," Capone said. "I need to get even. I dropped a quarter-million smackers just the other night."

The realtor gathered in the cards and shuffled, Henderson watching him with the same exaggerated attention to detail. It was plain to all but the host that quarter-million-dollar pots were relics of a past long dead.

"A box of matches, please, Rose. We're not casting lots for the clothing of Christ." The maid, who had materialized to replace the nearly empty pitcher of lemonade on the table with a fresh one, curtsied to Mae and withdrew.

It was an interesting game of chance, and one not likely to be duplicated: a gang lord, a hotelier, a real-estate salesman, and a false priest, with the gang lord's wife looking on to make sure no old secrets came out in her husband's confusion; Vasco detected Ralph's influence in the last. But he was less inter-ested in game strategy than in studying Parker Henderson. He could not fathom the thinking of a respectable citizen who voluntarily kept company with the underworld. He himself had spent most of his life fleeing the very thing the other sought.

"Full house. Read 'em and weep, boys." Capone spread his cards on the table.

The realtor belched into a fist. Vasco caught the acrid odor of a peptic ulcer.

"Al, you've got two pair. That's a ten of clubs, not a jack. I've got three sixes." He showed him his hand.

Capone's face flushed a deep shade of—mauve? magenta?

Vasco's mother would have known. She could pick out a curtain color that matched the dishes in a box she hadn't opened in two weeks, since the last move. Capone caught the eye of a bodyguard walking past, trying to look like a guest. "Hit this guy, willya?" He pointed at the white-haired man, whose face turned a color that matched the cottage cheese of his complexion.

The bodyguard's tongue made a bulge in one cheek.

Mae intervened. "Snorky, you're playing for matchsticks."

"You're right. He ain't worth a bullet. Beat it," he told the bodyguard, who looked at Mae. She made a little motion of her head and he coasted away. There was a new boss in charge.

"George, I'm dying to hear about the place next door. You swore to me you'd let me know when it came on the market. I *want* that home chapel." Mae scooped the realtor out of his seat with a touch of the shoulder and twined her arm inside his, drawing him toward the house. By the time they reached the corner of the pool his color was returning.

"How do you like that guy?" Capone picked up the deck and shuffled. "In the old days he'd've had eels crawling out of his eyes down by Coral Gables."

Henderson produced a folded handkerchief from inside his seersucker coat and sponged his forehead.

Vasco began to have hope. If Capone's regression allowed him to make the kind of threat in the open that he'd been accustomed to making in the past in private, he could be careless about other secrets as well.

At that moment Vasco picked up the cards he'd been dealt and discovered he was more than halfway to a straight. He immediately threw away two key cards and asked for two more from the deck.

While Capone was studying his hand, Vasco glanced around and saw Mae and the realtor near the bar, the white-haired man gulping from a tall glass and massaging the base of his sternum with his other hand. Liquor was hard on an ulcer, but not as hard as having one's life threatened. Sonny Capone joined them. Mae said something to him, pointing toward the table. He nodded and started that way. The second shift was clocking in. There would be no wheedling anything out of Snorky whenever one of them was around.

Sonny sat in. He played quietly and bet conservatively, as if the matchsticks were dollars, but he was an inept bluffer, easily read. Capone, on the other hand, was a sphinx. His file said he was Homerically unlucky at the track, dropping millions at Hialeah and Charlestown, but Vasco could see that when skill and intelligence were required he was as lethal in the parlor as he had been on the streets of Chicago. His early mistake wasn't repeated. He won steadily, losing only when he folded before a hand that proved unbeatable afterward. Here was the Scarface of old.

But the man who had tried to have another player killed for correcting his play; that was the old Scarface, too.

Vasco played patiently and well. In Cicero he'd taken quickly to the game and usually left the table with pocket money, but he was careful to lose to Capone lest his anger flare up again. He wasn't afraid that one of his threats would actually be carried out, but he didn't want to alienate the man he was there to befriend.

Sick or not, however, Capone was no simpleton. Losing constantly invited doubt. It made Vasco want to sigh. Poker was complicated enough without adding diplomacy.

On the fifth hand he beat Capone's pair of eights with three deuces. Capone's face darkened and he thought he'd made a horrible mistake. But Capone merely ground his teeth on his cigar stub and said, "A man can't lose when he's playing partners with God."

Henderson chuckled nervously. Capone glared at him. There was a beat during which pinheads of sweat glittered along the hotel manager's hairline. Then Capone yanked out the cigar and laughed.

It was a boy's laugh, uninhibited and irresistibly contagious. It spread as far as the group gathered on the other side of the vast pool, who laughed without knowing what the joke was. Henderson joined in, reaching for his handkerchief.

"Had you going there, Park," Sonny said, dragging in the cards. "You, too, Father. Dad's a comic."

"Peter," he reminded him.

Capone replaced his cigar, which had gone out. Henderson scratched the wheel on a pigskin-and-platinum lighter and relit it for him. It was a glimpse into the past, and into the nature of their relationship. "You boys bring your old dads next time," Capone said. "We'll have a father-and-son tournament, show you sprouts there's still lead in our pencils."

They played a few more hands with the sun hanging low and turning the surface of the pool a coppery shade of pink. The guests began to thin out. Capone sat back as they filed past the table in a reception line, shaking hands and mouthing pleasantries learned at Johnny Torrio's knee a quarter-century ago. Old friends got the two-handed shake; Vasco paid special attention to them, but couldn't place their faces with pictures in the FBI file. He supposed Florida had furnished an entirely different set of companions from the Chicago crowd. Henderson rose. Capone paid him the compliment of rising himself to grasp his hand. Evidently he harbored no ill feelings for the other's testimony at his trial. The man was a conundrum, threatening violence for no reason at all while forgiving old grievances that had shattered his life. His medical report had listed mercurial mood swings among the symptoms of his disease, but Vasco suspected they were part of his nature. It was the difference between stroke-induced lameness and a congenital limp; and it had played no small role in his fall from grace.

If grace was the proper term. It rang of blasphemy.

When he stood to say good-bye, Capone locked his hand in an unbreakable grip. "Stick around, Padre. We're showing a movie later. Mae hates crime pictures, and come this time of day Danny's too far gone to appreciate 'em. I don't like watching alone."

"What about Sonny?" He looked at him.

"I run the projector," Sonny said. "It runs hot. It's a choice of paying attention to the story or keeping the house from burning down around our ears."

"There's grub in it." Capone was smiling, but there was a pleading quality behind his eyes. His dip had washed the talcum off his face, exposing the deep curving trench on his cheek.

"I'd enjoy that," Vasco said. "Thank you."

Mae came up. He couldn't tell how she took the news when Capone told her. She was a harder puzzle to solve. She smiled at Vasco, then put a hand on her husband's arm. "You should rest before dinner."

He nodded, seeming to deflate suddenly, as he had at the end of their first meeting. He started toward the house, slippers scraping the tiles, Sonny close at his elbow.

"I'll understand if you'd rather I left," Vasco told Mae when they were out of earshot. "You've been entertaining all afternoon."

"I wouldn't hear of it. You're invited. Actually, I'm glad you were. I have a big favor to ask." White teeth bit her lower lip, a unique sign of indecision on her part. "My brother has a problem. He knew I was counting on him to drive Rose home after the party, but he's up in the guest room snoring like a stevedore. Sonny has poor night vision, part of his condition. She doesn't live very far away. Do you suppose—"

"I'd be happy to drive her, but why not Brownie?"

"He doesn't go home until after he serves dinner, and he lives north of Miami. Rose has been here since early morning getting things ready. It wouldn't be fair to make her wait, or to ask Brownie to drive four miles out of his way, with gas rationing. It's a terrible imposition."

"Not at all."

"Thank you, Father. Dinner will be ready when you get back."

"Peter."

She shook her head. "I attend Mass at Blessed Sacrament four times a week. I go to confession there, and sometimes at Redemption when I can't be away from the house long, because it's closer. I could never address a priest by his Christian name."

He smiled understanding, but his mind was racing. If Mae Capone confessed to Sergei Kyril, the odds were he knew who Mr. and Mrs. Brown were. For a man who was supposed to be working undercover, Vasco had never felt so transparent.

ROSE WORE A LIGHT TAN CLOTH COAT OVER HER UNIFORM AND A TAUPE felt beret pinned to her hair at a jaunty angle Vasco found surprising in someone so seemingly quiet. She smiled shyly when he opened the front door for her and again when he took her white-gloved hand to help her up onto the seat. She slid over into the passenger's side and folded her hands on a shiny black patent-leather purse in her lap.

She gave him directions to a part of town that was mixed Cuban and Negro—a place of small houses, many in need of paint, but in good repair, the lawns clipped. Larger, older places stood among them, turn-of-the-century relics with signs in the windows offering rooms to let.

"The Capones seem to be good people to work for," he said, hand-signaling a turn.

"They've been very kind to me."

"Brownie seems dedicated." He knew that was an understatement, but it wasn't the houseman he wanted to talk about.

"He's not as mean as he looks."

"He couldn't possibly be."

It was a gamble that paid off. She made a sound of amusement, too low for a giggle, not dry enough to be called a chuckle. "He made me comfortable my first day. I was afraid to leave the kitchen. My mother said I'd be butchered in my sleep. I said, 'But I won't be sleeping there.' She said, 'Well, then, they going to get you when you're awake. It's open season on us all the time.' You know, a Negro candidate in the Chicago elections was murdered just 'cause he was black."

He knew the incident from the file. Octavius Granady, an attorney, ran for sanitary trustee in the twentieth ward and was torn apart by shotgun slugs moments after the polls closed.

They'd chased him in an automobile and surrounded his car after he crashed into a tree. Fish in a barrel. His opponent was Boss Morris Eller, a Capone man. Seven arrests, including four police officers, all acquitted.

"I think it had to do with more than just his being colored." He wasn't comfortable with *black*. It seemed to be an inside thing.

She smiled in profile, with a bitter shake of the head. She had a fine nose, high forehead, small round chin. He liked her melodic accent, the lemon scent that clung to her after a long day of hard work in the Florida heat. "Brownie told me they never kill civilians, only gangsters and politicians, and anyway Mrs. Capone would protect me, and if she didn't, he surely would. I've been happy there. Mr. Danny's funny when he drinks." She turned his way suddenly, flushing under the caramel. "I shouldn't have said that."

He touched his collar. "I've had practice keeping secrets."

She smiled again, no bitterness this time, and faced front.

"I imagine finding good help is more complicated for them," he ventured. "People are always listening."

But she said nothing. He couldn't afford to press it. "Is this your street?"

"That big house there on the right."

It was one of the older buildings converted into rooming houses. It had been painted fairly recently, before the war, in Victorian colors, faded now to pastels. A thickset black woman in a long skirt was sweeping the front porch, a man's old fedora on her head with the brim pulled down all around. She stopped to watch as a priest alighted and helped his passenger down.

"Thank you, Reverend," Rose said.

"Father's the usual form of address." He felt the stiffness of the words.

"I only called my own father that, and he's passed."

He watched her climb the steps to the porch. The thickset woman resumed sweeping.

Remarkable young woman. Remarkable household.

"You're in for a treat, Padre," Capone said. "Brownie cooks good Italian for a shine. I smell a Sicilian in the woodpile on the old plantation."

The houseman set out the main course, his face chiseled from stone. Vasco would have been hard-pressed to win a hand of poker against him, Mae, and Al.

He felt self-conscious in his gray business suit. Capone, looking rested from his nap, eyes clearest gray, wore a tuxedo with glistening satin lapels over an immaculate white shirt with black studs and a black tie knotted flawlessly, possibly by Mae. She had on a gray satin off-the-shoulder dress and a string of matched pearls. Dressing for dinner seemed to present a tangible link to the days of old. Caruso sang *Pagliacci* on an unseen phonograph. Changing records appeared to be one of Brownie's many responsibilities.

The pasta was superb, obviously hand-rolled and topped with a delicate tomato bisque sauce that had not come from a jar. Vasco didn't share his father's passion for all-Italian, all the time—he suspected it was the Irish in him—but he ate with energy and didn't hesitate to accept seconds when they were offered. All he'd had to eat since breakfast was a piece of broccoli in a crust of cheese. Trust Mae, the devout Catholic, to make sure that Friday's meal contained no red meat.

Sonny was present, manipulating his fork bottom-side up in the accepted European fashion, and Danny Coughlin, looking bloated and hungover with his starched collar slicing into his sunburned neck. He poked at his plate and made short work of the first carafe of red wine. The wine in Capone's glass looked pale, diluted from an identical carafe filled with mineral water.

"You like opera, Padre?" Capone sat back with his napkin tucked inside the *v* of his coat—a peasant despite all training—trailing his fingers in the air to the melody from the phonograph.

"The music. I have trouble following the libretto. My mother insisted on English only at home."

"Irish girls, prettiest on the planet. Name one contribution the Irish made to music."

"'Danny Boy.'" Mae smiled at Danny, who wasn't paying attention, involved as he was in rearranging the pasta in front of him to appear as if he'd eaten more than a small portion.

"Name another one."

"'When Irish Eyes are Smiling.' 'Londonderry Air.' 'Who Threw the Overalls—'"

"I said one." Capone scowled, and the party lapsed into silence, broken only by Caruso and metal clinking crockery. Vasco was only partly aware of the tension. How could Capone remember his mother was Irish? Their meeting had been brief, no longer than it had taken to exchange a roll of bills for his pistol. So many years ago.

"Patsy Lolordo loved grand opera," Capone said suddenly. "He taught me to love it. He had *Carmen* playing in his place on North Avenue when that *assassino* Joe Aiello—"

Sonny pushed away his plate. "Mother, may I be excused? That old Bell and Howell takes some coaxing."

"Don't you want any dessert?"

"Ruth says I'm getting fat." He patted his stomach.

"All right. More wine, Father?"

"I'd better slow down. It wouldn't do for Miami's newest man of the cloth to be arrested for driving under the influence."

He was happy to be allowed some part in diverting his host from a dangerous conversation. He had confidence now that Capone could be drawn out by a canny practice of patience rather than by applying pressure. *Pasquale Lolordo, slain in his own home with his wife in the next room, on orders of Bugs Moran, in violation of all the rules of Mafia etiquette regarding murder, to weaken Capone's hold on the Sicilian order: January 8, 1929, thirty-seven days before St. Valentine's Day.* Put a nickel in the Vasco vending machine, get absolution or a lesson in mob history, complete with names and dates.

Dessert was orange ice, the oranges fresh-squeezed from local groves. Capone ate greedily; his guest thought it wouldn't be long before he was back up to his preincarceration weight. He finished ahead of the others, plucked free his napkin, and wiped his palms, immaculate like his shirtfront, the nails rounded and buffed. (Did Mae submit a record of expenses to Jake Guzik, mob accountant? So much for barbering and manicure, cigars, pasta, wine, entertainment? The Bureau of Internal Revenue would insist on receipts.) "This is the life, Padre. A night at the pictures without sitting through a crummy newsreel and somebody's brat squalling in the back row. Ever see *Scarface*?"

Was it that night's selection, or some kind of test? For once Vasco could answer truthfully. He avoided gangster movies as assiduously as he avoided gangsters; until recently, that was. He shook his head.

"Malarkey. I sent some boys out to California to find out if they were making a picture about me without my permission. A man's got rights, even if the world thinks he's public property. The guy that wrote it was no fool, a Chicago boy; he said it wasn't about me. He didn't even know he wasn't lying through his teeth. This guy, this actor—Mooney?" He looked to Danny, who was galvanized suddenly.

"Muni. Paul Muni. Jew pretending to be a guinea. Not worth your time, Al."

"Like I didn't know already." He twisted his mouth. "'Allo, Louie,' what's that, 'Allo'? I was born in Brooklyn, not Naples, for chrissake."

"Al," Mae said.

"Sorry. For Pete's sake. I'm as American as Charles Lindbergh."

He lost focus. "You know, I offered to help rescue his baby boy. All I asked for was a little fresh air while I got on the horn, called in a couple of markers, maybe a year or so off my sentence. He turned me down cold, and his boy wound up in some hole in the ground. Charley Luciano, he put his crew to work on the New York docks, protecting this country from Nazi spies, and the government's letting him rot in Sing Sing. My pal Lucky. Fuck this country." He flapped a hand. "What's the show tonight, Danny?"

"*All Through the Night.* Bunch of gangsters fighting Nazi spies."

"Aw, shit."

Mae excused herself and stood. Vasco rose politely after her. "I'll let you boys enjoy your show. I have letters to write, starting with Muriel."

Muriel, Mae's sister, and her husband, Louis Clark, lived at the Palm Island estate part-time. During the winter season the household might include them, Danny and his wife, Winifred, Sonny and his family when they left their own Florida home to join him, Capone's brothers and their wives and children, their sister Mafalda, and Teresa Capone, their mother. The size of the house seemed far less palatial when one considered how many people were sleeping under its roof at any given time.

Brownie poured coffee from a silver carafe into white-and-gold china cups and the three men carried them into the living room, balancing them on their saucers. Sonny was busy threading a reel of film from a large open flat can through the mechanism of a motion-picture projector bolted to a metal table that rolled out from behind a panel in the wall opposite the fireplace. The whole affair was as big and bulky as an icebox and when he flipped the switch, a cooling fan inside the machine clattered to life and whirred loudly. Walking past to take his seat on the great davenport, Vasco felt the wind of the fan and also the heat of the lightbulb that projected the images onto a screen that pulled down from the ceiling in front of the portrait of Al and Sonny. Considering the volatile nature of the celluloid that passed within inches of the bulb, Sonny had not exaggerated the fire hazard.

The sun was long gone, and with the drapes closed over the glass doors, the beam from the projector was the only light when Sonny turned off the ceiling fixture. Capone was chewing Sen-Sen tonight; Vasco recognized the flat slim box he poured into his palm and smelled licorice. The powerful Capone jaws worked with an abrasive noise like worn gears. His molars must have been ground down to stumps after many years of such abuse.

The movie, an action-comedy, was puerile, unconvincing, and enormously entertaining, as two rival racketeering gangs battled each other and the police on an urban back lot, then joined forces to defeat Fifth Column saboteurs peopled by the usual studio cast of foreign subversives. The heroic crooks were named Gloves and Sunshine and Starchie and Spats. When Sonny turned the lights back on to reverse the film, Danny Coughlin was snoring with his head tipped back over the top of his overstuffed chair and his coffee cold and untouched on the end table beside him.

"Malarkey," Capone said again; Mae's Irish upbringing had had its effect on her mate. "If Johnny couldn't get the gangs to work together when there were millions to be made, whaddaya think this mug Bogart's chances were? And those names are a crockashit. Reporters make 'em up to sell papers. Anybody called my pal Jake Guzik 'Greasy Thumb' to his face, I'd've shot him in the head."

Which was precisely what had happened, and how, by a route so twisted no one could have predicted it, Peter Vasco had come to share a sofa with Al Capone. He glanced over his shoulder at Sonny, engrossed in the action of the projector. He couldn't believe he wasn't aware of his father's conversation.

"I give this Bogart points for balls. His old man was a doctor, Winnie says. She reads all the movie magazines." Winnie would be Winifred, Danny's wife, away on a visit. "If the old man was as tough as Doc Phillips, I can see where he got it. I could've used all three of 'em when that crazy Polack came at me in the Hawthorne along with the whole North Side."

Vasco figured it out then. In order to increase his concentration for fire control, Sonny had turned off his hearing aid so the soundtrack on the film wouldn't distract him. He'd forgotten to turn it back on after the movie finished. Vasco's heart began to beat with a slow, steady rhythm. It was a fallacy that the pulse quickened with excitement. That, or he was some kind of freak.

"If I knew what was waiting for me, Padre, I'd've listened to my old man and gone into your line, or maybe learned to cut hair."

Vasco sensed that this was prelude to a personal memoir.

An inactive hearing aid. An ill-timed binge. He couldn't believe his luck. For this one moment in eternity, God had turned His Devil's side away.

He sat perfectly still, afraid to move or speak and risk interrupting Capone's train of thought. He would make notes later.

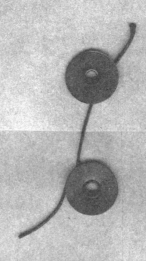

THE CONFESSIONS OF AL CAPONE

1899–1920

Compiled from Transcripts
by Special Agent P. Vasco Division 5 FBI File #44/763

TWELVE

DEANIE O'BANION SAID IF ALL THE MUGS WHO SAID THEY WERE ALTAR BOYS crowded into Holy Name at the same time, the walls would bust. He had his own old robe, white with a mothy black collar, in a big glass frame in the flower shop. His wife Viola set it up on an easel at his funeral. I bet he stole it. The point is none of us was born in the rackets. It was a brand new business and we made up the rules as we went. Deanie broke the rules he helped write and he went to hell for it. Not that we aren't all of us going to hell. The trick is to get your innings in first.

I was the fourth of nine, in Brooklyn, 1899, a last-century boy: "After the Ball" was playing on the Edison in the parlor. If you believe these characters who say I was born in Italy because no real American would ever do what I did, I'm there right now, deported, ducking Yankee bombs with that bald-headed ginzo Mussolini. You're just dreaming I'm here in sunny Florida. The only one of us who didn't come into this world a U.S. citizen was Jimmy, and he became a cowboy.

I'm no Italian. I buy my suits from Marshall Field's and from Sewell Brothers here in Miami and I had boxes at Comiskey Park and Wrigley Field all the years I lived in Chicago. Baseball's my game. I don't know how to play bocci, but I can tell you there's no balk to third base.

When I had a car custom made, Jake said I should get a Rolls Royce or a Duesenberg, but I went to Detroit. I wanted a Lincoln, but Henry Ford wouldn't have anything to do with it. He refused to even meet with me. So I went to General Motors and had them build me a Cadillac from the ground up: special heavy-duty frame, truck springs, steel plates in the doors. You wanted to get in and wire a pineapple to go off under my ass, you had to know the combination to the door lock. The engineers used transmission gears to crank the windows up and down because they were bulletproof, an inch and a half thick, and heavier than a son of a bitch. It wound up weighing seven tons and cost me twenty grand. In those days you could buy four houses for less. I didn't care. The economy can always use a boost and it gave people a lift when they saw me rolling down Michigan Avenue and Lake Shore Drive. "There goes Al," they said.

But to get back to Brooklyn. Father Garofalo baptized me in the basement of St. Michael and St. Edward on St. Edward's Street. I got my catechism in the same basement. It smelled like potatoes and pee. When I think about it, I spent a lot of time in basements when I was young. I learned to shoot pool there good and I popped bottles with a revolver underground in the Adonis Social Club on Flushing. My ears ring when I think about it. I know I'm part mole. For years I did all my moving around at night and slept till noon.

I was pretty good at school at first, though you won't hear that from anybody but me. If I'd stayed at P.S. 7, I might've become a bookkeeper with a big company. I was always good at figures, especially when there was a dollar sign in front of them. And I've always been interested in history. I read a book about Napoleon when I was locked up in Philly, too late to profit from his mistakes. But in sixth grade they moved me to P.S. 133, big ugly building looked like a jail and that's how they ran it. My teacher slapped me for talking back and I pasted one on her, knocked her ass over teakettle into the potbelly stove. I swear I didn't mean to hit her that hard. I was fourteen then and didn't know my own strength.

Anyway the stovepipe came apart and dumped soot all over her. It got a big laugh. Not from the principal, though. He beat the shit out of me and punctured my eardrum. I didn't see any point in going back after that.

I got a hiding from my old man, too, when he found out. He was as good with a strop as he was with a razor. Once when a census taker came around asking my mother how many children she had before they were married, my father excused himself and came back with his razor. The census taker left, and when a policeman came around, the old man told him what had happened. The cop said—speaking Italian—"Gabriel, don't threaten no census takers no more," and left. See, the Black Hand had forced my old man to put a telephone line in his barbershop to take bets, and the cop didn't want to have to run him in and give up the five bucks a week he got for looking the other way. That's how it was then. It's probably fifty bucks now.

After that I didn't stay home much, not that I ever did. Jimmy was gone, my brother Frank was moving furniture, and Ralph was out selling artichokes for Ciro Terranova, the Artichoke King, he was called, because he had a corner on the market, which he hung onto with strong-arm men like Ralph; but even after my sister Rosalia died before she was one, there were still five of us crowded in a three-room apartment that smelled like pee. Every place smelled like pee then, except the saloons, so that was another good reason for not staying home.

I liked to have fun. Who doesn't: There was no radio, and if you had a nickel for the movies you hoped it was a western, because if there wasn't a lot of riding and shooting you had to read title cards to know what was going on. I wanted to read, I'd go to the library. How it worked, you gave the man at the door your money and you'd go in and sit down on a folding chair and there would be a lady up front playing piano along with what was happening up on the screen. She'd play slow when people were just talking on title cards and fast when something exciting was going on, so you'd listen at the door and if she was playing fast you went in and if she was playing slow you didn't. I learned this in 1909 when I was ten, before I could read the sandwich board out front that said what the movie was. Broncho Billy Anderson never wasted time talking on title cards.

But you couldn't always be at the movies. They didn't run late or on Sundays, and nickels didn't fall off the backs of wagons like pieces of coal. Or dresses, like in the garment district in Manhattan; I got that from Charley Luciano, who had

Jew friends across the river. These days, you've got Boy Scouts, the YMCA, gymnasiums where kids can play basketball or whale on each other in a ring, with gloves and leather helmets so they don't come away silly. Not then, not there. I joined a gang.

Partly it was for protection, because if you didn't belong to one you were fair game for all of them, and believe me, there isn't a thing happens to a man in prison doesn't happen to a boy on the street without someone to stand behind him. But mostly it was from not having anything better to do. Sure, there was work: I clerked a candy store on Fifth Avenue, set pins in a bowling alley—"being an angel in Polack heaven," we called it—cut paper in a bindery, which let me tell you dries your hands and makes them crack and bleed. I see a Cuban cane-cutter on the street here, bandages on his hands, I tell Danny pull over, I give him a twenty.

Being in a gang, it's like having a family that looks after you but doesn't smack you with a paddle when you don't know where Serbia is and don't give a shit what the Bulgarians are up to there. And the basements where you shoot pool and craps don't smell like pee. Rat shit sometimes; but rats don't stink as bad as people.

If they ever make a movie about the Five Points Gang, they can throw away the slow sheets. That asshole Dutch Schultz told me the punks down there are still singing songs about it, like Robin Hood and his Merry Men. Trust a kike to shine up to your good side. You say he's dead? Fuck him, and good riddance to bad rubbish; but even a clock that's busted is right twice a day, Johnny told me. The pope gave me a medal, I wouldn't be prouder than saying I belonged to Five Points. We'd march up the street banging on washboards and tubs, diddy-dum, diddy-dum-dum, diddy-dum-durn-dum, singing, "We're the boys of Navy Street, and touch us if you *dare*." Top of the lungs, every cobblestone and wooden spoon hitting the boards and tubs on "dare." Then we'd beat the shit out of the Irish gangs, or they'd beat the shit out of us. It depended on who had the numbers that day. This went on till the police whistles blew, then we'd scatter like cockroaches when the light goes on. Not one of us was ever collared after any of those affairs. The Irish cops were too fat and drunk to chase us far and the dago cops were too smart to try. So we had plenty of time to dish it out and eat it up. By the time I was eighteen I had enough bloody noses to last a lifetime. I think of those days, I can taste the blood and snot. I'm not kidding. It's like I just got popped.

Four years from school to my first rackets job. To a kid that's forever, but it seems now like a lot happened fast. I made friends, got arrested, lost my cherry. And I met Johnny Torrio. Cherry first. That's more important than you'll ever know, Padre. A man's life falls into two parts: before he got his tie straightened and after. Her name was Constanzia, but hookers are like hotels, reaching for the moon from the toilet. You ever see a hotel sign says The Royal Arms, don't go in, because those arms have got needle tracks. I had Constanzia in a brass bed in the back room of the Harvard Inn on Coney Island. I think it lasted three minutes, but that may be the golden glow of middle age obscuring the true facts. I remember thinking, if this is what it's about, why all the hollering? But then I couldn't wait to go again. Food's like that, booze too. To hell with heartburn and puking. Anyway they tell me, Doc Phillips and the quacks in Alcatraz, that's probably when I picked up the bug. Wouldn't you know it? One bang and I'm doomed. I'm Norma Shearer.

It was through Charley Luciano I hooked up with Constanzia. I don't hold it against him. You can't stay mad at Charley, even when he's slipping you the knife. In those days we figured if a dame took care of her teeth she was clean everywhere, so the first thing we did, we looked at her teeth, like Jimmy says you do when you're shopping for a horse. But you don't fuck horses unless you're one of those crazy Genna brothers. They'd fuck anything and shoot it in the head after. Charley ran Five Points. He was older than me by a couple of years, had some killings under his belt when I met him: pimps, rats, nobody you'd miss. Impressing women was never a problem for him. His trouble was they impressed him back. He had a droopy lid like he was winking all the time and was always combing his hair, even when we were squatting in some alley waiting for the beat cop to walk past before we broke a lock. Combing his hair and talking about some dame he was meeting after the score. Lucky, they call him now. There's a story going around that he got that name after some mugs took him for a ride, sliced him up with razors, and left him for dead on Staten Island, and he survived. Benny Siegel swore it was true, but they don't call him Bugsy on account of his bad temper, like we did Moran in Chicago; he's as looney as they say I am sometimes, had this scheme to personally put Hitler on the spot or something like that, right in the middle of a war. Nobody ever came back from a ride, not even Charley, unless it was women took him. He might be able to talk himself out of that deal. His name's Luciano. It don't take a genius to come up with how the newspapers arrived at Lucky.

Those names. Scarface. Three Fingers. Dingbat. The Enforcer. All malarkey. Those reporters get all their ideas from *Dick Tracy*. They was to start calling Churchill Fats and Roosevelt Gimpy, they'd be drafted in a week.

Right from the start Charley's weakness was women. He couldn't take a whore to bed without he had to fall in love first. The reason he never married, there was always another hooker around to fall in love with before he finished falling out of love with the last. It didn't surprise me when he went to the joint finally on a white slavery rap. Sure, he was framed, but Charley wasn't the first mug to furnish the frame. There's talk of deporting him back to Sicily when the war's finished, place he left when he was in diapers. If I were him I'd tell those boys he's got prowling the waterfront hunting for Nazis to take their time.

The first time I laid eyes on Johnny Torrio, I knew he was quality. Charley introduced us in Johnny's office at Fourth and Union. Johnny used to run the Five Pointers, which was how they knew each other. He was a natty little guy dressed like a banker, wore a Homburg like Woodrow Wilson. Always smiling, twinkle in the eye. He had some gray hairs even then. I was looking for a job, and Charley thought I'd make a good bouncer down by the Navy Yard where Johnny had a place.

"Those sailors are a rough bunch," Johnny said, looking me over. He was an Old Country wop, but he left when he was little, so you wouldn't know he wasn't Brooklyn born from the way he talked. "He's a big fellow, but how do I know he won't fold up first time someone clips him?" Johnny was the first one to call me the Big Fellow. It stuck.

"You don't know Al. He grew up in the Yard. When he was ten he called out a recruit twice his size."

"How'd it turn out?"

"His corporal broke it up," I said. "Big break for him." Johnny nodded, smiling and twinkling. Then he hit me right on the button.

Point of the chin, where it rattles your brains. I hardly saw him move. I took a couple steps back and almost tripped over this contraption on a stand, thing with wax cylinders and like a telephone receiver, you talked into it and a machine recorded your words. I'd never seen anything like it.

I got sore and charged him, but Charley stuck out a hand and I ran into it. "Easy, Al," he says. "Johnny didn't get to be Johnny buying no pig in a poke."

Johnny blew on his knuckles. "Okay, Charley. He doesn't fold. I don't need a boy just now, but tell your friend the big fellow to give Frankie Yale my name. That Harvard Inn of his goes through bouncers like a dose of clap."

Which if I were a superstitious person I'd wish I paid more attention.

"Thank you, Mr. Torrio," I said. "I hope I can return the favor."

Nothing could take that smile off his face, not even shotguns, as it turned out. "I look forward to it," he said.

Out in the hall, Charley threw me up against a wall. No one else I ever knew had the guts to do that. "What're you doing?" he said. "Man does you a favor, you threaten to knock his block off?"

I said, "He sucker-punched me."

"You know who gets sucker-punched?"

"Suckers." What else could I say, backed into a corner?

"You had your guard up, you'd be working for Johnny instead of that *puzzo* Yale."

But Frankie Yale never played me false all the time I worked for him. That came later. I don't know what Charley's beef with him was. He was another old Five Pointer I'd heard plenty about. They said he had a dozen notches on his belt by the time he was twenty. Some said eight, some ten. When everyone agrees it's more than five, you can bet it's more than one. That was a few years before I caught up with him, and I hadn't heard where he'd slowed down in the widow-making racket. Later he got fat, but in those days he looked like the Arrow Collar man. Georgie Raft reminded me of him a little, and Georgie went into the movies.

Frankie had a finger in everything: milk, ice, the laundry business, if you picked up and delivered, he took his cut. He ran protection for the Black Hand, gambling and liquor in the Harvard Inn (Yale, Harvard, get it? Humor was different then, not wise-ass like now), and had a string of girls in back, which was how I met Constanzia. For a while he sold cigars with his picture on the box, but he gave it up when he overheard a guy on the El tell another guy you don't smoke a Frankie Yale, you flush it. I think he really thought he had a good product till that moment. He didn't smoke himself, and he could make a tumbler of whiskey last all night.

Frankie was the quietest man I ever knew, even quieter than Johnny, and a lot more dangerous. He had this low way of speaking that made everybody lean in to hear what he was saying. You saw him sitting at a table, people crowded around him close, you thought he must've been talking about something important, when he might've just been saying it looked like rain. Anyway I heard it got him close enough to one chiseler to cut his throat.

That job was a low point in my life. The place was lousy with bouncers, so Frankie put me to work out front. He dressed me up like a carnival barker, swear to god, in a striped coat and straw boater. I'd spot a fellow passing by looked like he had dough, I'd walk alongside him and say quiet, like it was a secret, "They got some nice-looking girls inside, buddy, whaddaya say?" I was a pimp was what I was. It still shames me to say it. But I needed the job. I was getting married.

I met Mae in a cellar club on Carroll Street; another basement. You ought to have seen her then. Skin like skim milk and she had the longest legs I ever saw on a girl. She was a salesgirl in a department store, lived with her parents in a class Irish neighborhood. Good Catholics.

Her real name's Mary, but she looked like Mae West, who was playing at the Shubert Theater then, so everybody called her Mae. What she saw in me God knows. I was eighteen, good with my dukes or a pool cue, but put a teacup in my hand and you can guess the rest. I couldn't turn around or fart in that teensy parlor in her parents' house on Third Place without knocking something over. I had pimples, for chrissake. And I had these scars.

There's more lies told about me than Mata Hari, and most of them are about where the scars came from. I spread a few of them myself. I told Jake Lingle I got them fighting in France, but the closest I ever got to there was a truckload of champagne bottled in Montreal. I even read where a barber cut me with his razor when I asked for a haircut only a member of the Mafia was allowed to have. Back then I never heard the word Mafia. We just called it the Black Hand. Most of those boys cut their own hair, and it showed.

A lot of people think I'm vain of my good looks and that's why I turn that side of my face away from cameras. I know I'm no Jack Barrymore. In my old neighborhood, you turned rat, they cut you so everybody knew. Well, I never turned rat on anybody, but I'm not proud of how I got these.

Drink's to blame. When Frankie was short-handed inside, I got to change out of my pimp clothes and fill in at the bar or at the door. One of those nights in comes this scrawny little guinea, Frank Galluccio, drunk, with a beautiful girl on his arm. She looked like Louise Brooks, I'm not exaggerating. Fantastic figure. So naturally I kept finding reasons to pass their table while I'm serving drinks and clearing away glasses. I wasn't as bombed as Galluch, as we called him, but one reason I never made bartending my profession is I always liked what I was pouring as much as my customers. So I had a little bit of a bag on or I wouldn't have said what I said. I leaned over the table. I thought I was being quiet, but they told me it was loud enough to carry to the next party over. You always think you're goddamn Vernon Castle when you're looped. "Honey," I said, "you got a nice ass, and I mean that as a compliment."

Turns out the dame is Lena, Galluch's sister, which as you know is a very big deal with Italians. Everybody's sister is the Virgin Mary. He's on his feet in a flash, yelling at me to apologize. Others heard what I'd said, so he's got to play it big. But others heard what he said, so I'm better off keeping it small. So I'm saying take it easy, pal, I didn't mean nothing; smiling, you know. "This is no fucking joke, mister," he says, and now I'm in it. Bar full of people sees me back down from a runt, I won't get a job bouncing baby showers. So I make my move.

Here's a free lesson, Padre, you ever decide to ditch that collar and work in a saloon. You only throw punches as a last resort. That's a good way to get glass hands, break one every time you knock on a door, because jaws are harder than fists. Ask Samson. What you do, you get him in a bear hug, and if he's smaller than you squeeze till he stops wiggling and if he's your size or bigger, hang on till help comes from the bar or the door with a pool cue or a blackjack. That's what I had in mind for Galluch, the old squeeze. Snap a rib or two.

But little guys are fast, and for a drunk he had good reflexes. He must've practiced the move in front of a mirror, which is a sound idea if you've got a sister pretty as Lena.

The knife seems to open up by itself as it's coming out of his pocket. Swish! He opens up my cheek like slicing the casing on a sausage. Swish-swish! On the jaw and on the neck; two inches higher and I'd be short one ear. Hurt? Not at first. It was like when you nick yourself shaving and you watch in the mirror to see if you broke the skin and then the blood comes. It came plenty. I'm bleeding like a stuck pig, sure my throat's cut, and Galluch, who's a drunk but no fool, gathers up his sister and takes it on the ankles. I think he left his hat.

Thirty-two stitches they took in my face over at Coney Island Hospital, where they had plenty of experience patching up knife wounds but no sense of aesthetics. They didn't close them tight enough and they healed over white. When I go out I still dust my face with Johnson & Johnson's, which I suppose makes me look like a clown but it's better they think that than ask how I got slashed up. For a long time I was madder at the doctors than I was at Galluch.

Not that I didn't want him in the ground. My face was burning on one side, covered with gauze, I had pills for the pain, but they weren't nearly as good as the morphine they pumped into me at the hospital. My face throbbed and I was dopey from the pills and sore at the world, but mostly at myself. Well, you can't fight the world—I couldn't even fight the U.S.—and I wasn't about to commit suicide over a bonehead mistake, but I spread word around Brooklyn I was looking for Frank Galluccio.

Next thing I know I'm talking with Frankie Yale and Charley Luciano at the Harvard Inn, their invitation, and who walks in but the man I'm looking for. I jump up, dumping over my chair, but just like that Frankie's got my arms pinned from behind and Charley's looking at me that same way he did when he had me up against the wall outside Johnny Torrio's office. "This is a sit-down," he said, "so sit."

Frankie let go and I sat. You don't argue with them two when they got their backs up.

"You, too," Charley tells Galluch, who is also not a man to saw off his legs when he might need them to run on later. He sits, too, and he's so pale you can see right through him. He had no more idea I was going to be there than I did him.

Frankie uncorked a jug of chianti in a basket and we drank and listened to Charley. This vendetta shit is for the Old World, bad for business here in the land of opportunity. The decision has come down that I am to apologize for insulting Galluch's sister and he is to apologize for overreacting to an unintended slight. This, Charley said, is direct from Joe Masseria, who in those days ran all the rackets in New York clear up to Albany, where the governor asked the president to hang on while he took a call from Masseria—"Joe the Boss," he was called. Now that I see how the cow ate the cabbage I got up and stuck my hand out to Galluch in friendship. He took it, the blood coming back into his cheeks as he did, partly I think out of relief that his pretty sister Lena wouldn't be attending his funeral anytime soon and partly out of shame for having disfigured me so badly when all he wanted to do was kill me.

Charley hugged me, hugged Galluch; so did Frankie. Peace was restored that day, and I have never broken it between me and the man who made me Scarface. Every time business took me back to New York after I relocated to Chicago, I looked up Frank Galluccio and paid him a C-note a week to serve as my bodyguard. Who better to protect me than the only man who ever got close enough to carve me up and lived to tell about it?

Mae didn't see the scars when she looked at me. She still doesn't, and I thank God every day I went to that cellar place on Carroll that night instead of going to shoot pool, which was what Little Augie Carfano wanted me to do. He was Frankie's bodyguard, mean little shit: shot rats in the spine and laughed when they crawled along on their front legs. A man's nothing without a woman who can't see his scars. I sure traded up from Little Augie.

We took our vows at St. Mary Star of the Sea, spitting distance from the docks, December 30, 1919, Father James J. Delaney presiding; I remember he had gin blossoms on his nose. Mae's whole family was there, though I can't say they all approved of the union: I was a greaseball booze-slinger, the scars on my face still bloodred, and like I said they was lace-curtain Irish; the master of the house took a walk around the block when he had to pass wind. (My old man the barber leaned over on one cheek at Christmas dinner and let fly.) But you know Mae. Getting her to do a thing's a simple matter of telling her not to. She ran that house same way she runs this one. There's no appeal from a blond head, blue eyes, and a blowtop. If she ran the North Side, Chicago'd be a different place.

She gave me Sonny. If she never gave me anything else, that would be plenty. He's the hope of the family. He's got my smarts and Mae's sense of what's right and wrong, and there's no stopping a man with those qualities. I dealt him a rotten hand, whoring around before Mae came along and passing down the bug, but he's playing it and I've never heard a word of complaint.

After the wedding, things changed for me. Johnny Torrio was getting ready to leave for Chicago, where his uncle, Diamond Jim Colosimo, needed a young man with ideas to manage the rackets, and he was throwing himself a going-away party in the restaurant below his office. I was never so surprised to get an invitation in my life. I was a settled man now, with family responsibilities, a kid on the way, and word that I'd played ball with Charley and Frankie over the Galluch business had gotten back to Johnny. He knew now I wasn't the same hothead who tried to tag him for clipping me on the chin all those months before.

You never saw such a party. Beer and champagne in tubs of ice, quarter cigars, girls, a shine band playing that monkey music they brought up from New Orleans. I never cared for it myself. King Terranova dropped in for a few minutes, and Frankie was there, and Charley and his friend Frank Costello and their Jewish friends Benny Siegel and Meyer Lansky and Lepke. Joe the Boss and Arnie Rothstein, the man who crooked the World Series, couldn't make it, but Joe sent a big floral horseshoe with a sash that said "Good Luck, Johnny," and Rothstein sent a basket of meats and cheeses and fifty-year-old brandy that must've set him back a couple of C's. There were Five Pointers all over the place. Even Dinny Heehan paid his respects. He ran the Irish mob in Brooklyn, what called itself the White Hand, which was a thumb to the nose of the Black Hand, but what the hell, there was a truce in force. He didn't look happy to be there, and he wasn't drinking. When a Mick don't have a glass in his hand at a party, you know he's expecting trouble.

I don't think I truly appreciated how big Johnny had become till this leprechaun shows up in a derby and chinchilla coat and I recognize Jimmy Hines from Tammany Hall, whose picture was in the paper. Jimmy the Gent didn't go to just any party. He was too busy electing the mayor and governor. So that explains Dinny Meehan. He couldn't afford to stay away with Hines there.

Right then I knew something big was in the wind. That was New York reaching out to shake hands with Chicago. The rackets weren't just local affairs anymore. They were branching out across the country, and Johnny had been appointed ambassador.

When he saw me he hugged me, right there in front of everybody. He'd had good reports about my work from Frankie, and like I said he knew I'd learned how to sit down and talk peace for the good of the Outfit. He made a lot of trips back home after that, organizing connections, and he always came by to visit Mae and me at home. He stood godfather to Sonny and sent him a five-hundred-dollar bond every birthday till Johnny threw in with that sheeny prick Dutch Schultz and I tore them all up. But that was years later. Johnny was as much my godfather as Sonny's and my guardian angel.

He liked my ideas, like setting up a legitimate front to keep the reform crowd from asking embarrassing questions, some easy thing to maintain, like a second-hand furniture store. This was the beginning of Al Brown, Antique Dealer. It wouldn't fool a baby, but it wasn't busting the law in their face, so there wasn't any public show of disrespect, which when you come down to it is the only thing they really care about, the church committees and politicians. Johnny said I had too good a head on my shoulders to make thirty-five bucks a week slugging drunks.

Sometimes, I have to admit, I lost that head. In the fall of 1919 I was drinking in a harbor saloon when this character Artie Finnegan comes in. I didn't know him. Short, squat, face like a cheese. He sees me and starts cussing me out, greasy nigger wop this, greasy nigger wop that, stinking up the place. I'm thinking, what's your problem, Paddy, you got piles or what? Stranger minding his own business, you want to start something over nothing? That's kid stuff. After Five Points I never in my life went looking for a fight. In Chicago I never hit back but that they hit me first. Well, he keeps on, and now he's dragging my family into it, my mother, my father, my wife if I've got one, bastards and whores, all of them. He's dotting *i*'s, crossing *t*'s. He didn't come here to lift a pint and sing "Danny Boy."

I beat the Irish clean out of him. My hands still ache when I think about it. They had to drag me off him. Now he's on the floor leaking blood from every-where, even his ears. I think, well, there you are, you cocksucker, you wanted to dance, now you're dead. I really thought he was.

I wasn't worried about the cops. I'd been pulled in before over a couple of scraps and questioning, roughed around, turned loose with the charges dropped, and when the doctors said they figured they could put Artie Finnegan back to-gether after all, minus a few pieces, I knew the cops wouldn't waste their time looking for an eyewitness that wouldn't say Finnegan slipped on a puddle of beer and fell down a couple dozen times. It was the White Handers I was concerned about. Finnegan was one, and Dinny Meehan didn't like his boys being abused any more than Frankie Yale did his. Dinny sicced Wild Bill Lovett on me.

Lovett put the fear of God on the waterfront. He wasn't any bigger than little Frank Galluccio, and he had these big cow eyes and teensy ears that poked out like an elf's. But he'd kill you as soon as shake your hand. He'd fought abroad with the 77th Regiment and been awarded the Distinguished Service Cross for valor under fire. He carried his old service .45 everywhere and never packed a bodyguard, not even after Frankie put Meehan on the spot months later and Wild Bill took over the White Hand. He walked alone.

A lot can change in a short time. A year earlier I'd have waited for him, or more likely gone out looking for him myself with the rod I used to pop bottles in the basement of the Adonis Social Club. But I had a family now. If anything was to happen to me, Mae and Sonny would be on their own. I went to Frankie for advice. He shook his head. Even Joe the Boss couldn't get me out of this jam. There's no sitting down with the Irish. What he did, he called Johnny in Chicago. Johnny said he could use an extra man who wasn't a mug and sent first-class tickets for me, Mae, and Sonny. Lovett could go on turning over every rock in Brooklyn looking for the scar-faced punk who beat up Artie Finnegan. What's a White Hander's time worth, anyway?

So we got on the train at Grand Central Station, and on January 17, 1920, I celebrated my twenty-first birthday with Johnny at Colosimo's Cafe in Chicago. That same day, the Volstead Act kicked in and the whole country went on the wagon. Who says God doesn't appreciate a joke?

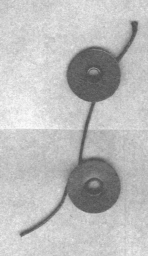

1944

CORNED BEEF AND CRIBBAGE

THIRTEEN

THERE WAS A LITTLE SILENCE WHILE SONNY FINISHED SEALING THE FILM reels in their cans before Vasco realized Capone was asleep. His wing collar was sprung, the tie hanging loose on either side like two black socks, and the overhead light poured shadows into the lines of fatigue on his face, Frank Galluccio's handiwork on the side he hid from the world. He'd always looked older than he was—people who thought they knew his story were shocked when told he was barely thirty at the time of the St. Valentine's Day Massacre—and now at forty-five with the vital spark dormant he could pass for a man ten years older. Illness and mortal sin had taken its toll.

Danny Coughlin awoke with a snort—startled, perhaps, by the silence—looked around quickly, lurched to his feet, and left the room, describing an arc when a straight line would have done. Vasco doubted he'd noticed he wasn't alone in the room, or that he'd remember anything of the evening the next day.

With the table lamps extinguished and the rest of the room in darkness, the davenport Vasco shared with Capone might have been the bench in a confessional. It might have helped him to open up. Hoover had said he was predisposed to seek forgiveness for decades of depravity. *Decades of depravity*; that was a phrase that would appeal to the Director, whose every utterance rang with the Old Testament thunder of a *March of Time* announcer reporting on the Battle of Britain. His man in Miami would have to stop arranging his thoughts along those lines if he were to assimilate himself into Capone's society.

But what, ultimately, had Capone revealed that wasn't already public knowledge, or was of any practical use?

His pimp's tale had sounded sufficiently shame-faced, but it would hardly galvanize the authorities to action even if he were the target; and it must not be forgotten that it was his friends the Justice Department was after, not him. The Galluccio incident was illuminating, something the younger Snorky would never have admitted to, but it was nothing more than a sordid story garnished with gore. Frankie Yale was dead, the victim of Capone killers after their association soured. It was the first tommy gun murder in New York; as innovators went, Al Capone was to gang killing what Louis Armstrong was to jazz. In any case there was no prosecuting a dead man for a dozen or so murders his former employee had attributed to him. Artie Finnegan, if he still lived, couldn't press charges against Capone for brutal assault so long after the statute of limitations had expired, and it was a rap scarcely worth pursuing considering his slaughterhouse career.

He'd even fudged the facts of Sonny's birth. That event took place twenty-six days before Al and Mae were wed, a matter of public record; were gangsters so reticent about childbirth out of wedlock? Assuming Capone himself chose not to shirk his responsibility (he was many, many, many things, but a moral coward was not one of them), the delay suggested severe antipathy to the marriage on the part of Mae's parents. Ordinarily, a father willing to preserve a young woman's honor received encouragement—and a swift ceremony. In turn, Capone's glossing over the facts suggested eagerness to spare his wife's reputation.

Interestingly, there was a crime involved in their very application for a certificate of marriage: in order to avoid embarrassment, Mary Coughlin, twenty-two, had sliced one year off her age, and Alphonse Capone, twenty, had added one to his, bringing them even. It was a mild fraud, and certainly not uncommon, but it bemused Vasco to learn that Al could not enter even into the holy union without breaking the law.

So far as the record was concerned, that document appeared to be the very last thing that carried his signature. Apart from it, one could argue that the most photographed and quoted felon in history had never existed. It would have been the slickest public disappearing act ever, if only his legitimate friends hadn't caved in to authority.

Capone had also overlooked at least one murder.

He was questioned in the shooting death of the big winner in a crap game sponsored by Frankie Yale; one of those "scraps" he'd mentioned in passing. Police accused him of demanding the money from the man at gunpoint, then putting a bullet in his belly when he balked. No witnesses came forward to confirm the details, but shortly after the case was filed as an unsolved homicide, Capone was promoted from street pimp to bartender.

In that context, Yale's intervention on his behalf after the Galluccio indiscretion made perfect sense. Capone delivered the money to Yale, and Yale never failed to reward loyalty. Whatever his motives, chivalry or self-defense, Capone remained Machiavellian even in his extremity. He appeared to let his hair down while buttoning himself up tight. No wonder he was so good at poker.

"Father? I mean, Peter?"

He looked up at Sonny, who was standing in front of the davenport. The young man looked worried. Evidently he'd discovered he'd neglected to turn his hearing aid back up after finishing the movie.

Vasco put a finger to his lips. He felt like a damn fool playing a priest on stage. "Your father's asleep. Can I help put him to bed?"

"I can manage. I've done it before. Did he fall asleep during the picture?"

"No, he saw it all the way through. I can't say the same for your uncle."

"Did you talk about the movie?"

"Yes."

"May I ask what else you talked about?" Sonny colored. "I'm sorry to pry, but Dad rattles on sometimes. Mother"—he stopped, started again—"*I* didn't want you to go home with the wrong impression."

It was late. His defenses were down, and like a man mildly drunk he needed to slow down his reflexes to avoid catastrophe. But he'd anticipated the interrogation. He'd considered letting Sonny think Capone had been sleeping all this time, but if Capone remembered and their stories didn't match, even the little bit of progress Vasco had made would be lost. He'd be barred from the house.

The challenge was to tell neither the whole truth nor an outright lie.

"He told me how he got his scars. I didn't ask. Something in the movie must have put him on the subject."

Sonny smiled. It was so strange to see that expression, those lips, on another's face. "Did he tell you that story about fighting with the Lost Battalion in France?"

"No. He said it happened in a place called the Harvard Inn."

The smile faltered. "He never tells anyone that story outside the family. What's your secret, Pete?"

So it was Pete now. He couldn't tell if he was being mocked, but it seemed time to crack the whip.

"I'd prefer it if you called me Peter. Pete was the name of a man who went to jail for exposing himself to the sisters of St. Francis in Cicero." Pete and his Peter, ran the chant in the street.

"Peter." He didn't repeat the question. He waited for the answer.

"I'm a priest. People sometimes feel compelled to tell me things, knowing they won't be passed on."

"You just told me what he told you."

"No. You asked what we talked about. That's not the same as pressing for details. That request I would have refused."

"High-wire act, is it?"

"You have no idea."

"I'd like one."

He suppressed a sigh. Sonny was three years his senior, but in many ways he was an obstinate child. It might have been the disease in his blood, the debt he'd inherited from his father's profligate youth, or it might have been his sheltered upbringing. In either case it required patience.

"I keep confidences, Sonny. It's part of my work, but I inherited the ability from my father. I still know very little about the time he worked for yours. I'm not his confessor."

"But you're Dad's."

"I'm not."

"Yet you tell me you're honoring the seal of the confessional."

"I'm honoring something told me in private by a friend."

"Are you friends?"

"I hope so. You'll have to ask your father."

Sonny looked at Capone, breathing evenly with his mouth open slightly and a dot of spittle glittering in one corner. He ran a hand through his hair. It was receding in front and he'd trained the forelock to tumble forward and cover the loss, a Napoleonic effect. "Mother won't be happy to hear I let you two talk alone.

Uncle Ralph says we have to be careful when strangers are around. Dad gets confused sometimes and forgets who he's talking to."

"I saw that this afternoon. If it's any help, tonight he called me Padre two or three times. He was quite lucid. He talked about his family and how he met your mother and some people he knew in Brooklyn. Nothing I couldn't have read about in *Liberty* or *Collier's.*" Which was true. Even the scarring story had probably appeared somewhere, offered as a choice among tall tales.

Sonny sat in an upholstered chair turned toward the davenport, a Louis XIV replica that seemed to reflect Mae's personality more than the oversize pieces; possibly a remnant of the furnishings she'd been forced to sell while Capone was in prison. He loosened his collar and tie. He was dressed formally, like his father, but his coat and vest were cut more sportily in the collegiate fashion. "Did he say anything about when I was born?" His tone was transparently casual. The man simply could not bluff.

"I can't see any harm in talking about that. Your father's very proud of you. He said you and your mother made him a settled man, a solid citizen. He couldn't imagine his life without you." A safe falsehood. By his own testimony, he'd either have been slain by Wild Bill Lovett or added another murder to his rosary. But Capone would not be likely to contradict Vasco's version.

"I doubt that. If anything, Dad's imagination is too vivid. He hallucinates sometimes. The doctors say it's part of his condition. It's one of the reasons he has to be watched. People don't always know when he's talking about things that really happened or about some dream he had. It's hard sometimes. Mother has the Church for comfort, but when she's at Mass or confession it's up to me. Uncle Danny's no help after the sun goes under the yardarm. I'm in the middle, with Dad to take care of here and Ruth and the kids at home. Sometimes I'm not sure if I've started my own family or am still living with my parents. A man needs to grow up, you know?"

He realized he was listening with his elbow propped on the upholstered arm at his side and a finger touching his temple, as he did in the booth at Redemption. He hadn't anticipated becoming Sonny's confessor. "Your mother says you're working for the war at the air depot. That must bring some fulfillment."

"I'd rather be in Europe or the Pacific. This thing." He tapped the hearing aid clipped to his lapel. "I tried all the services. I couldn't even get clerical work."

He wondered if Sonny was aware of the connection between his affliction and his father's syphilis, if there was resentment there. He hadn't seen anything about hallucinations in Capone's medical record. That might have been an invention to prevent an outsider like Vasco from assigning importance to anything that slipped out.

"If it means anything, I know how you feel. I tried to enlist myself, but all the branches had all the chaplains they needed."

That was a gamble, if Ralph had any sources in the War Department. Unlikely, considering Ralph's own history with the federal government. But he *had* been turned down by the military, and the fact that he empathized with Sonny's frustration was an advantage he felt he couldn't afford to ignore. He reminded himself to run it past Hoover for possible damage control.

Sonny smiled boyishly. He sat slumped forward with his wrists resting on his knees, hands dangling between them. He was a handsome young man of the rumpled-gigolo type. In two years he'd be overweight and bald beyond conceal-ment, but at that moment in time Vasco could see something of Al's appeal to twenty-year-old Mae Coughlin. He'd portrayed himself as an oaf during that courtship, but personal accounts in his file said he was quiet-mannered in youth (when he had his rage and drinking under control) and a graceful dancer.

Capone stirred suddenly, shifted positions, and lapsed back into uncon-sciousness. It was as if he overheard thoughts about him the way Mae said he heard people discussing him aloud despite distance and ambient noise. Keen instincts had played at least as large a part in surviving numerous assassination attempts as guns. Larger; Dion O'Banion had died with three revolvers on his person, all unfired. Sonny glanced at his father, then fished a pack of Camels from his inside breast pocket and offered it to Vasco.

"Thank you, but I don't smoke."

He tapped one loose, drew it out with his lips, and used a heavy brass lighter shaped like an elephant from the coffee table to ignite it. Tawdry thing, that lighter, in a world of silk and gold and full-grain leather, with lead showing dull where the thin plate had worn through, an item from a secondhand shop. It smacked of Al, the inveterate collector; anything elephants. How Mae must have loathed it. But she wouldn't get rid of it while he lived. "I think I only took up the habit to annoy my uncle," Sonny said.

"Danny?"

"God, no." He crossed himself for taking the Lord's name in vain. "You can't blast the smile off Danny's face with dynamite, drunk or sober. I mean Uncle Ralph. He smokes a fancy Egyptian brand. They smell like scorched rags and burn twice as fast as American."

He remembered the smell, from the Lincoln. It had clung to his clothes after-ward. How quickly Ralph went through them.

"What he says about Camels—"

Vasco finished. "They call them that because they cure the tobacco in camel shit."

The sun broke out on Albert Capone's face when he grinned. It was no won-der everyone called him Sonny.

"I never heard a priest say shit before."

"I'll have to confess it. But I'd be misquoting your uncle if I said *spit*."

"It wouldn't sound like him. Ralph's a good man, don't get me wrong. He shamed Dad's old cronies in Chicago into coming through for Mother when they were afraid to let go of a buck because the government might trace it. He called them ungrateful sons of bitches and got them to see where they'd be without

Dad, which was nowhere. But he's always complaining about something, Uncle Ralph: The country's going to hell, kids have no respect, that communist cock-sucker Roosevelt. He sucks all the energy out of a room just by walking into it. The only way to have any fun when he's around is to push him so hard he starts stuttering. Lighting up a Camel works every time." He drew on the cigarette and sat back, blowing smoke out his nostrils. "I guess I have something to confess myself. Does honoring your mother and father apply to uncles?"

"My pastor says it doesn't even apply to sons. The Golden Rule would seem to cover your situation. My policy is to confess when there's any doubt at all. What's a Hail Mary or two compared to eternity? Better safe than sorry."

"There's a policy to salvation?"

"It's all based on good and bad investments, like banking. St. Peter keeps the ledger."

"Sometimes you don't even sound like a priest."

He didn't respond. There was something about the company that made him relax his guard, let leak his disillusionment with Holy Mother Church. He'd worried first about Al, then Ralph, then Mae, now Sonny, who was most danger-ous of all because Vasco was beginning to like him. Capones, the lot, each with a unique advantage. He ought to have that tattooed inside his eyelids.

"Forgive me, Father. I didn't mean to offend." He didn't remind him to call him Peter. He needed the reaffirmation.

"I wasn't offended. We do a lot of business with the laity, construction firms and automobile dealerships. Schools and hospitals don't build themselves, and a diocese takes in too much territory to cover on foot. The early Christians did it unshod. Today it's in a Pontiac. Sometimes I forget I'm talking to a parishioner." That was a splinter of truth that threatened little. A real-estate developer in Ci-cero had let it be known the pastor at St. Francis could sell building plots under Lake Michigan. Only pious idiots believed spirituality fed on itself.

"What did you and Ralph talk about besides camel shit, or is that asking you to violate a confidence?"

"If you do, I won't hold it against you. I just won't answer. But we said noth-ing I can't repeat. He advised me to report to him anything that passed between your father and me whenever your mother wasn't present. I'm sure he meant you as well."

"Don't be so sure. He thinks I'm still ten years old. He has his heart set on Ralph, Junior, taking over someday. Ralphie's idea of a square meal is a six-pack and sleeping pills. I'd be grateful if you kept that between us."

"Of course. No seal doesn't make me a gossip." So now Sonny had entered the fold. He had the beginnings of a cult. "He said if I failed there'd be one more empty saddle in the old corral."

"He said that?"

"Word for word." He crossed himself at the heart.

"Danny must've been there."

"It was in Ralph's car. He was driving."

"Danny loves his westerns. I don't apologize for my family, Peter."

"I like westerns."

"I think you know what I mean."

"No one should have to." A bald lie. Vasco had been apologizing for his father all his life. What was he doing now, if not that? The sins of the fathers.

"Ralph doesn't make empty threats," Sonny said, "but he's a fair man. He won't back someone into a corner if he can leave him a way out. It would be different if you heard it from Frank Nitti. He's the muscle in the Outfit. I only met him once, when I was a boy. I had nightmares for a week; Mother blamed Dad for taking me to see *The Phantom of the Opera*. But Lon Chaney's eyes were never as cold as Nitti's, like black stones. In Chicago they said when he gave you a warning, it was already too late.

"I'm not telling tales out of school," Sonny added. "I wasn't part of that world. But you hear things even when you're deaf."

He'd heard some of the same things. The file was light on information about Nitti: "The Enforcer," the newspapers tagged him. Undoubtedly he had his own file, but there seemed to be pieces missing from the record as opposed to what Vasco had been given on Capone's other close associates.

There had been something in the papers, after Capone was sent up, a botched attempt to arrest Nitti in his offices or an attack on his life; the reports were confusing. He'd been badly wounded. Vasco wondered if the Miami library had old Chicago newspapers on file. He didn't want to bother Hoover with questions he might be able to find the answers to himself.

He realized suddenly that he and Sonny Capone had had the same childhood. No bodyguards had accompanied Vasco to the playground and he owned no signed baseballs, but they had both been sequestered from their fathers' worlds by order of their mothers. Al's only son could no more tell him what had taken place in the Hawthorne Inn or in Capone's Chicago headquarters in the Lexington Hotel than he could tell Sonny what Paul Vasco had been doing all those days and nights when he said he drove a beer truck. They'd grown up in the Judas calm of the eye of the hurricane, unaware of the death and destruction surrounding it. And he sensed that Sonny sensed it as well.

"I wouldn't want to waste your uncle's time with what we talked about tonight," Vasco said.

"I don't think there's anything to tell."

A conspiracy of innocents. Vasco allowed himself a smile. It was impossible not to indulge oneself in the presence of Sonny's. At least Vasco had been allowed to grow up.

"So how was the movie?"

"Good. A little fantastic. Your father thought it was a lot of hooey."

"It's a good thing Ralph wasn't there. Gangster pictures really set him off. He thinks they're all about Dad."

"Most of them are," Mae said.

Vasco had failed to feel her presence. She was standing in the doorway clutching a blue satin dressing gown closed at the throat. She wasn't wearing makeup and her blond hair was twisted into a plait on one shoulder. The satin clung. She had a good figure for a woman her age; for a woman of any age. The slight spreading of the waist did not look at all matronly on her. Sonny put out his cigarette and stood. Vasco rose also.

"Wallace Beery played him once," she said. "Wallace Beery, who played Long John Silver. Danny could tell you about all the others. Jake Guzik wanted your father to sue them all, but he said he never wanted to see the inside of another courtroom as long as he lived. The settlement would have supported us for years with no help from Chicago. What are you boys doing still up?"

Vasco flushed, as if he'd been caught thinking unfilial thoughts about his own mother. (*Mother?! Sonny is* not *your brother.*) He looked at his strap watch. It was past midnight. He wondered how much of the conversation she had overheard. "I'm terribly sorry. I didn't realize it was so late." Was there a local curfew? With his luck, he'd be stopped by Officer Horowitz, who had already ticketed him once for leaving his motor running.

Sonny said, "It was my fault. I asked Peter about the movie."

"We need a new projector. You ought to be able to let it run on its own and enjoy the show with everyone else. It's the father I'm concerned about." She looked at him. "I hope you don't have early devotions."

Her eyes were clear of sleep. There was just no telling what she was thinking at any time. People who went to confession on a regular basis seldom opened themselves up outside the booth.

He turned aside the implied question. Better she didn't know how light his duties were. "I'm often up late studying the breviary. I seem to get along best on four or five hours' sleep."

"I'm an insomniac, too. All those nights not knowing if Al was coming home."

"That sounded melodramatic." Sonny seemed ill at ease. He, too, was wondering what she'd heard.

"Albert, he had an armor plate installed in the back of his desk chair. But that wasn't what I meant. I never knew when he was coming back to the house on Prairie or staying at the hotel. You'd think I'd be used to sleeping alone by now."

That was it. *Cree-crump.* The sound of Maureen Vasco pacing back and forth in her leg brace, listening for Paul at the door. Two Irish girls married to the Italian underworld. Peter wished all his disturbing associations were so easily explained.

Sonny yawned, stretching until something cracked. "I'm an eight-hour man myself, and I've got a tail assembly to rebuild tomorrow. Is it all right if I make up the davenport for Dad? When he's this far under it's like hauling a two-hundred-pound sack of cement up the stairs."

"You weren't raised to be disrespectful. I want you to come with me to Blessed Sacrament tomorrow. You'll tell Monsignor Donahue you broke the Fifth Commandment."

"Yes, Mother."

She moved silently across the carpet on blue mules and bent to stroke Capone's fringe of hair. He was breathing fitfully now. What did Al Capone dream about? Mae drew the silk handkerchief from his outside breast pocket and wiped away the tiny pool of spittle that had formed in the corner of his mouth.

"I'll take care of him. You go to bed."

"Are you sure?"

"I've been putting your father to bed for twenty-five years. Let's not have any planes falling out of the sky because you didn't get your beauty sleep."

"I'll see Peter out. Brownie went home hours ago."

She smiled and held out her hand. "Thank you again for Rose, Father."

"It was my pleasure. She's a charming girl."

"Charming, yes. And quiet."

An odd thing to say. Or perhaps not so.

"Thank you for a wonderful evening."

"I'm sorry about my brother. It's the curse of Erin."

"I like Danny."

"Everybody likes Danny except Danny. Don't let that smile fool you." She was still holding his hand. She laid her other atop it. "There you are, Father, part of the family. Once in, never out. Don't say you weren't warned."

An even odder thing to say.

Sonny shook his hand at the front door. "Ruth and I are entertaining the family at my place St. Patrick's Day; I'm half Irish, you know, and it's the only day of the year Mother gets to cook. You'll think you died and went to Mick heaven. Next Friday. Please say you'll come."

"Should you ask your mother?"

He stopped smiling. "It's my house."

"I'll have to run it past Father Kyril."

"He won't refuse to let you go. It's a holy day. Even the pope says it's okay to eat corned beef when it falls on Friday."

"I'll need directions."

"Just drop by here about five o'clock. You can ride with Mother and Dad in the Lincoln. She'll be bringing covered dishes, so if you can't stand the smell of cabbage you can always follow. Everyone else does."

When Vasco drove out the gate, a delivery van with Hebrew letters on the side panel was parked across the street. He shook his head. Hoover's people ought to have known that Jews who ate kosher didn't answer their doors after sundown Friday.

FOURTEEN

"How was your outing, Father?"

The pastor's voice almost made him trip over his feet. Vasco had entered Our Lady of Redemption moving fast, dipped and crossed, and hurried up the aisle heading toward the rectory to report. He wasn't late, it was hours before he was expected in the booth, but asking out of his only responsibility the day before made him anxious. He needed to make a show of dedication, especially since he had to make the same request next Friday.

Mass was over, and officiates usually retired soon after to collect themselves and prepare for the larger Mass the next day. Vasco had passed Father Kyril without seeing him, seated on his spine in a pew near the aisle with his feet braced against the high curving back of the pew in front and a book spread open on his thighs. He was in short sleeves and wore the same scuffed black high-top shoes he wore when he lifted weights.

"I'm sorry, Father. I didn't see you."

"I often dry-dock here following the service. There's something restful about a church when it's empty, like a theater after a performance. A working building in repose between shifts. A man can purge his mind. Sometimes I envy Brother Thomas, without a thought in his head except to empty the sweeper from time to time."

Thomas was working a wooden Bissell along the runner in front of the altar rail. The rollers squeaked on the backstroke and rumbled when he pushed. The room's acoustics were excellent; a young hooligan carving his initials in the back pew could have been heard at the pulpit, the gnawing of the knife as loud as a beaver felling a pine. But Thomas went on working regardless of what he'd heard.

The book Kyril was reading belonged in a weight class with the Gutenberg Bible. Its leaves were thin—there must have been three thousand of them in that gray cloth binding with MIAMI PUBLIC LIBRARY stamped across the page ends—and contained intricately drafted cross sections of fighting vessels, supports Xed throughout the hulls, the split guns like celery stalks. How much did an ocean-going chaplain need to know about hatches, double bottoms, the mechanical mysteries of torpedo tubes?

"I asked about your visit." His eyes behind gold-rimmed spectacles remained on the text. The glasses reminded Vasco of Capone's when he played cards. There was a kind of muted power in studying things through strong lenses, like an admiral observing the enemy through field glasses from the bridge. Kyril would appreciate the nautical imagery.

"It was very pleasant. People in Florida seem much more relaxed than in other places." Banal and obvious. The man must think him a fool, who thought him one as well.

"A little too much sometimes. They splash in the same ocean that's stained with blood just three thousand miles away without seeming to give it any thought. That isn't a metaphor. During the invasion of Sicily the surf was a pink froth."

No "I'm told" or "I read"; a statement of fact, as if he'd witnessed it personally. The evidence of things unseen.

"I'm sure they're as concerned about the war as everyone else." But it struck him that the two Capone men were the only ones at the party who had mentioned the thing that saturated most conversations, and then only in relation to their own lives. Al had referred to Lucky Luciano's men patrolling New York harbor and Sonny had lamented his failure to enlist. Most of the guests had come to warm themselves in the glow of 1929. This was an epiphany. He knew now the secret of Capone's strange appeal. The lion had been caged and released, his claws pulled and his fangs blunted, and even the most timid of men and women could stroke his coarse coat and feel the pounding of his heart. Savage creatures prowled and preyed in the jungles of the night, but this one was tame, the stories of old attacks quaint and thrilling. Vasco finally understood what Mae had meant about petting the giraffe. It had been her choice of animals that had stumped him.

"I'm sure you're right," Kyril said, "and that the people here aren't as apathetic as they seem. It's just that I have difficulty concentrating on anything *but* the war." He closed the book with a boom that reverberated in the nave. Brother Thomas looked up, then returned to his sweeping. The rollers rumbled and squeaked. "I suppose you think I'm neglecting this parish." The pastor was looking at Vasco, the glasses folded in one hand.

"Certainly not, Father. You have other things to think about, but I've never seen a church better maintained."

"The credit for that belongs to Thomas and his Murphy's Oil Soap. I know what people say about me. I'm not as remote as they think. I am of the opinion that most of their souls will keep until I get back. Meanwhile young men are dying by the thousands outside a state of grace."

"Yes, sir."

"Contrary to anything you might have heard, there are entirely too many atheists in foxholes."

"Yes, sir."

"If I were a tailor, I'd feel more useful making uniforms than First Communion suits. If I had any mechanical aptitude, I'd rather change the oil in a jeep than tinker with a Stutz Bearcat."

"Yes, sir." He wondered if Kyril was that far out of touch or testing him. He chose silence. A young man only pretending to be raised to the cloth might succumb to the temptation to correct him.

"And don't call me sir."

"Yes, Father."

"You haven't been to confession, Father."

He'd been dreading that subject. "No, Father."

"Perhaps you've been to Blessed Sacrament. Many priests feel it awkward to confess to their own pastors."

"No, Father, I haven't been to confession at Blessed Sacrament either."

The carpet sweeper squeaked and rumbled.

"Well, it's not required. But not confessing sets a bad example. Promise me you'll consider it."

"I'll pray over it."

"Any nitwit can pray. I once met a woman at a Catholic fund-raiser who said she'd taught her cocker spaniel to sit up with its paws together and whimper the first line of the Lord's Prayer. Pray over it if it brings you comfort, but think about it."

"Yes, sir. Father."

"Now get some sleep. You wouldn't be the first priest to nod off in the booth, but it would be the last time for you at Redemption."

Kyril must have seen his light on. He'd been up for hours after he got back from Palm Island, writing down everything Capone had told him about his early life. When he realized he'd slept through Mass, he rose, read and corrected his notes, and went out to post them to Hoover by way of the paper-and-pen supply company, insuring the package for a hundred dollars. He doubted it was worth it except to a crime enthusiast. There was no place to hide the material in his room where Brother Thomas wouldn't find it with his relentless cleaning. The library was a short walk from the post office, but it was closed on Saturday. The lowdown on Frank Nitti would have to wait.

"I was familiarizing myself with the breviary. I'm sorry I failed to attend this morning."

"Save it for confession. The breviary story too."

"Yes, Father."

Kyril nodded jerkily and opened his book. He paused with his spectacles half unfolded. "How is the reconciliation coming along?"

"Reconciliation? Oh, you mean with my father. I'm afraid I haven't pursued it."

"Mondays are slow here after the Sunday hangovers and Saturday infidelities. I'll handle the booth. If you have no plans, why don't you go up and visit him then? That isn't an order. A priest without portfolio would hardly obey it."

"Thank you, Father. I'll think about it."

"You're learning." He put on his glasses and returned to the diagrams. Vasco started to take his leave.

"Is it true Mr. and Mrs. Brown's swimming pool is larger than the YMCA's?"

*　*　*

He didn't miss a step, an accomplishment he assigned to exhaustion and slow reflexes. He'd been expecting something of the sort ever since Mae had said that she sometimes confessed at Redemption, but Kyril was a master of shrewd timing. Vasco turned back to find him reading his book.

"It's a monster," he said. "Father, I never intended to deceive you, but I should have been more forthcoming. I was afraid you'd disapprove of the relationship."

"Mary Capone is an exceptional woman, and I've heard very good things about Albert. Alphonse has paid his debt to society. His debt to his Savior is another matter, but I understand he attends Mass at Blessed Sacrament from time to time, so there is a ray of hope. Monsignor Donahue has yet to hear him confess."

"I have no expectations, Father. It all began when I went there to pay my respects on behalf of my father, who worked for him a long time ago."

"I thought I detected a Chicago tough on the telephone that first day."

"Not exactly. He spent all his time behind the wheel of a truck."

"Certainly not all. It wasn't a union shop. Advice, Father?" He looked at Vasco over the tops of his glasses.

"Always, Father."

"Doubtful. It's a dubious gift. Your father's love or Al Capone's immortal soul. Choose between them. Either one will take you the rest of your life and break your heart in the end."

"Thank you, Father."

"I'd like you to assist me at tomorrow's Mass."

"Anything." The thought terrified.

"Nothing taxing. I want you to hand me the chalice."

"That's all?"

"That, and stand up front throughout the ceremony in the glory of your vestments and impress the heathen."

"There are heathens in the congregation?"

Kyril's lips twisted at the corners, a purely hydraulic operation. "Many of them are heathens six days a week."

"I'd be honored."

"Make sure your chasuble is cleaned and pressed. I want it to dazzle."

He heard himself snoring lightly, waking him up. If not for that he'd have said he hadn't slept at all. It gave him no rest. Kyril vexed him. He did not know the man well enough to speculate on ulterior motives. In his heart of hearts he was sure he could spend years in his company and know him no better. (Not likely, if the pastor was called up by the navy. But who would succeed him?) Perhaps his request was to provide busywork for a priest with too much mysterious time on his hands. Or it might be a trap. How well had Father McGonigle's lessons taken? Tonight Vasco would retire early and actually study the breviary before exhaustion took him.

He found no seafaring material left behind in the booth. Kyril was hearing confessions in the booth on the opposite side of the pulpit. A new feature had been added to this one: "Fr. Vasco," hand-printed in vaguely Cyrillic letters on a strip of white cardboard slid into the two grooves intended for a nameplate on the frame between the two sets of curtains. Some parishioners preferred to shop their confessors based on past exposure, choosing leniency or severity, depending upon their attitude toward absolution. Branding was as important in faith as it was in the supermarket.

He fought sleep, a capricious thing that refused to acknowledge appropriateness of place and circumstance. He yawned as quietly as he could into his palm during a man's confession to impure acts; which meant, of course, either adultery or unnatural sex. The semantics of the Church were sheltering. He'd heard rumors at St. Francis of priests who insisted on details. What use they made of them he spent as little time speculating on as possible. Sheltering himself.

Strange how it seemed women were more straightforward about their baser sins than men. But then he'd been in harness only long enough to hear a small sampling. A Rosary for this impure act, whichever it was.

"Bless me, Father, for I have sinned. It's been two days since my last confession."

Sleep left him in a twinkling, a synaptic click. A woman's voice, framed by a light brogue. Low-register and warm. A warm voice, a cool hand. Mae Capone commanded every situation with those two formidable weapons.

Ecclesiastical etiquette was silent regarding the screen. Did one look directly at the face behind it, or avert one's eyes entirely in the service of anonymity? He compromised, using a sidelong glance under the shield of the hand at his temple. He felt like a little boy trying to steal a glimpse through a bedroom window. She wore a veil attached to the brim of a dark felt hat that reminded him of rotogravures of sophisticated young women in riding habit. A double obstruction, the veil and the mesh. He recognized the rounded face, the paleness of blue eyes.

What sin worthy of confessing could she have committed in two days? She would have been too busy all day Friday, preparing for a party and hosting it. But then there wasn't one in the book that couldn't be polished off in less than a day. He was more concerned with why she had chosen him. He kept silent.

"I was sharp with my serving girl."

"Rose?" It slipped out. Would he be a better priest if he'd gone about it legitimately, graduation and ordainment? It seemed to be a character issue, not one of bases touched. She showed no surprise. He'd forgotten about the nameplate.

"Yes. I didn't sleep well last night and I was impatient with her this morning. I called her a stupid girl."

"What had she done?"

"Must I answer? It was a small mistake. The best of us make them, and she's the best girl I ever had."

"It's not important. Is there anything else?"

"I humiliated my son in front of one of his friends."

"What did you do?"

"You were there, Father. You must remember."

She had scolded Sonny for comparing his father to a sack of cement. Vasco lowered his hand and faced her; to continue the subterfuge was ludicrous. "Did he tell you he was humiliated?"

"He never would. He's a respectful young man. He wouldn't have said what he had if he weren't tired. Anyway it wasn't that bad. Just a joke, although one in bad taste. His father would have laughed if he'd heard it."

He was relieved. He'd feared she'd come to beard him in his den. And he was elated. "Do you consider me his friend?"

"Don't you?"

"Nothing would please me more than to be considered a friend to you all, Rose included."

"Rose keeps her own counsel. But Sonny likes you, and you must know Al was taken with you from the first."

"And you?"

She hesitated. "This may not be the place for this conversation."

End of subject. And telling. Or not. The woman was the Siegfried Line. "Of course you regret your acts."

"I do."

"For the injury to your son, five Hail Marys."

"And for Rose?" A stickler, Mary Coughlin Capone. She really thought he might forget. Not one to smuggle expiation through a warp in the confessor's memory. Al's opposite.

"Do something kind for Rose every day for a week."

"Something kind? That doesn't sound very spiritual."

"It is the definition of it, regardless of language. Consider the Good Samaritan."

"Can't you be more specific?"

"I could, but it wouldn't be as if it came from you." He blessed her with the Sign and the absolution, which he delivered in Latin but always thought in English: "God the Father of mercies through the death and resurrection of His Son . . ."

"Amen," she repeated after him, signing in response. Silence spread. Into the gap he offered, "Is there any other service I can perform?" He sounded to himself like a salesclerk behind a counter. *Will there be anything else?*

"I'd like to know what you and Al talked about last night."

In the house on Palm Island the question would have set a maelstrom going in his head. The confessional was his home court, however fraudulently he had come to occupy it. He had merely to dismiss her with a polite phrase. She had supplied it herself: *This may not be the place for this conversation.* But he had said something along the same lines to Ralph Capone, which had led to a change of venue to a place where he'd had no authority, the Capone limousine. He decided to be truthful.

To bear false witness on her side of the booth was damnation; what circle of hell awaited one who had lied on *his* side? He expelled the breath he'd been holding.

"He did most of the talking. He spoke of early days in Brooklyn. His child-hood, mistakes he'd made in his youth, your marriage, Sonny's birth. He fell asleep after he came to your leaving for Chicago."

"My God." The cross, swift as Frank Galluccio's disfiguring blade: *Why that connection?* He thought at first she was concerned with birth out of wedlock, but she disavowed him of that. "Father, you mustn't attach too much importance to everything Al says. He doesn't always know what's real."

This apparently was the story the Capones had worked out, probably at Ralph's direction. Short of gagging Al or locking him in his room, there was no way to guarantee he wouldn't blurt out something that would lead to complications. So they'd agreed to dismiss everything he said in advance as the ramblings of a sick mind. Best course for Vasco was to go along with the policy.

"Sonny said the same thing. In any case, Brooklyn was so long ago. The world has other things to worry about."

"You young people think anything that happened before the miracle of your birth has no meaning. Twenty years is nothing. Stalin had Trotsky killed in Mexico twenty years after they broke. Halfway around the world wasn't far enough to run even after twenty years."

Vasco let this lesson in history pass without comment. Russia held no inter-est for him. Lenin takes the Czar for a ride, Stalin muscles in on Trotsky, Trotsky goes on the lam and is bumped off south of the border. Vasco had seen it all be-fore in Chicago.

"I don't repeat private conversations, in or out of the confessional."

"I believe you," she said after a moment. "Al's been chipper all day. Even Dr. Phillips noticed; he mentioned it this morning when he came by to give him his shot. His blood pressure was normal for the first time in weeks."

"Maybe the shots are working."

"Phillips says they can't reverse the damage at this stage, only slow down the progression. But he said there was no reason to renew Al's prescription for anti-depression tablets because he hasn't used up the last batch. I didn't tell him about last night, but he said whatever we've been doing, we should keep it up. Al's a different person since you showed up. Sometimes it's like having him back the way he was." Her voice broke on the last word.

"He seemed to be enjoying himself. I thought it was the movie."

"I doubt he remembers anything about it. You should have seen his face when Sonny told us he invited you to his house on St. Patrick's Day. Father, I'm beginning to think you're the medicine he needs."

"He's probably just happy to be telling his stories to someone who hasn't heard them all a hundred times."

"You don't understand. He never talks about Brooklyn. I only know how he got his scars because it was the talk of the whole town, even on Third Place where I lived with my parents. When Sonny was old enough to start asking awkward questions, I took him aside and told him. Al always said it was shrapnel in France. I don't know what he said to that woman that night and I don't want to know. That wasn't the man I've been with all these years.

"Those scars were one of the reasons my parents opposed our marriage. It's one thing to hear things against a person, something else when you can see the truth on his face. You're the only one he ever told, Father. The only one. Do you know what that means?"

"I honestly don't." He'd been asking himself the same question for fourteen hours.

"He trusts you. It's as simple and as complicated as that. In his world, trust is worth more than hard cash. When you come down to it, that's as sacred as it gets in his world."

"Mrs. Capone, I have the impression you're asking for something, but I don't know what it is."

"Just your loyalty. The sun and the moon. It's the only thing Al respects outside the family. You can't know how precious it is if you haven't lived the life he's lived. That I've lived." She raised a pair of hands in white cotton gloves and folded the veil back over the brim of her hat. Her eyes were turquoise in the dimness of the booth. He saw now the delicate webwork around her eyes; each tiny fissure a day waiting to hear Capone's key in the door of the house on Prairie Avenue. "Ralph must never know what passes between you."

"I promise you he won't hear it from me."

"Nor from me, and certainly not from Sonny. He always was a secretive child, and now he's a man who keeps secrets. I suppose his upbringing is to blame. I worked so hard to protect him I never realized he was aware of what I was doing and learned from my example. I didn't even know he'd dropped out of Notre Dame until he didn't go back to finish the semester."

The conspiracy was widening. It really did seem to be turning into some sort of cult: the Church of the Buttoned Lip.

"You know why, of course," she said.

He thought at first she was still talking about Sonny and how he had grown to be a man who kept secrets; in other words, a Capone. But she had returned to the earlier subject. "Because if Ralph found out I wasn't reporting to him he'd kill me."

"I don't know if Ralph ever killed anyone. I don't know if Al ever did. But I know. Anyway, what's the difference between doing it yourself and having it done? I mean in the eyes of the Lord, not the law, which parses itself out by pleas and degrees. If, for instance, I thought you were sharing Al's stories outside the family, I'd be just as damned if I took the matter to some of the people who still come to the house as if I pulled the trigger myself. I couldn't cop a plea."

He stared at the smoky face behind the screen. "Mrs. Capone, are you threatening a priest in the House of God?"

"Father, if I thought you would do anything to hurt Al, I'd kill you even if it was in the lap of the Holy Mother Virgin.

"Now I have something to confess next time, haven't I?"

And she crossed herself.

SUNDAY MASS WAS THE ONE THAT COUNTED.

You could miss the weekday services without inviting disapproval from any but the most hidebound priest. People had jobs, and employers didn't place as much store in the disposition of the souls of the people who worked for them as in daily time sheets. But miss Sunday and you had better be prepared to confess Monday.

Vasco had no intention of missing, although he'd hoped to be allowed to attend as just another member of the congregation and not as a participant. Transcribing Capone's memoirs at the expense of sleeping during the customary hours had kept him from his duties. He couldn't help thinking he was being punished for the lapse by being compelled to take an active part. If passing Father Kyril the chalice like a boy handing his father a wrench in the garage of the family home could be considered active. And he still suspected a trap. He repeated to himself the office of the breviary as he dressed. He almost forgot to kiss the stole before draping it around his neck.

Every pew was taken, but he was too distracted to pay close attention to the parishioners at first. There was a boys' choir, containing some dark faces—he remembered what his father had said about the preponderance of Cubans in Miami, hence the presence of two Catholic churches. Kyril appeared to be a progressive in the matter of integration, and a shrewd judge of vocal talent. The boys were quite good. The organ, on the other hand, a middle-size Wurlitzer, had leaky pipes. They whooshed like a broken bellows and the notes lacked resonance. The player was an elderly woman with a dowager's hump in a flower-print dress and silver-framed bifocals that she let dangle from a chain around her neck when she wasn't playing. Kyril had said he'd rescued her from retirement ten years after the Olympia Theater on East Flagler stopped showing silent movies. Either her glasses weren't strong enough or her skills were failing in her old age, because she missed some chords, putting out of step the extraordinary ministers during their march up the aisle.

"Bless you, and welcome." The pastor, resplendent indeed in his silks and brocade and heavy gold cross, was not a man to overgild an affair already ponderously ornate with a flowery greeting. Vasco's mind wandered during the Penitential Rite, a hundred or more voices untrained in oratory droning the collective sins of the *Confiteor* ("I confess to almighty God, and to you, my brothers and sisters, that I have sinned through my own fault . . ."), which had always been a long way from his favorite part of the ceremony. Standing behind the pulpit two steps upstage of Kyril and two steps to his left—not a position required by ritual, but the one he found the least uncomfortable—with his head bowed and his hands clasped, he felt the weight of his vestments in a room without air-cooling in a southern climate in a church packed with people, each putting out ninety-eight-point-six degrees of body heat, some undoubtedly more; deep rat-tling lung-coughs and noses braying into handkerchiefs punctuated the quieter moments, as they did everywhere else throughout the year. He hoped, when the time came to perform his function, that the chalice, a moderately hefty-looking one of silver, wouldn't slip from his sweaty palms, sending the Blood of Christ splattering on all the Catholic finery within range.

Gloria, Trinity, the reading from the lectionary, by Kyril, a fat deacon in a tropical-weight tan double-breasted suit, and a lector with a bad toupee that looked like a rasher of bacon. The lector broke at awkward places in the text to breathe noisily through his mouth. He was one of the stricken, pumping out more than their share of heat. Vasco wished they'd stayed home in bed and con-fessed afterward, and wondered if he should confess *that*.

Of course he should. But then he had worse things to confess that he could not.

Came the Eucharist. Surreptitiously he wiped his palms on his soutane as the collection basket made its rounds. His cue was approaching like the express train from Jerusalem.

Choir and congregation chanted the *Sanctus,* all the Holies and Hosannas. Then the worshippers knelt for the Eucharist Prayer, which Kyril delivered in Latin in a strong baritone, speaking of the Last Supper. The fat deacon poured sacramental wine from a silver pitcher into the chalice, sprinkled it with water, and lifted the chalice for Vasco to take. He had evidently been instructed by Kyril not to offer it directly to him. Vasco accepted it in both hands. He wished churches provided towels and talcum like bowling alleys. A rogue chalice was worse than a runaway bowling ball.

The deacon let go. The heavy vessel remained steady. He'd dodged that bul-let. He turned and presented it to Kyril. The pastor hesitated, hands at his sides. Vasco was certain this was the springing of the trap. Now that he had him hold-ing the bag in public, Kyril expected him to finish the blessing that would trans-form the wine into the Blood of Christ, the wafers on the altar into the Body of Christ; and compromise the trusting souls who had come forward to kneel on the rail and take into themselves the corpus of the Savior; although Kyril didn't know that part. Or did he? Would he risk becoming an accessory to heresy just to punish a heretic?

The answer seemed to be no. After what seemed like five minutes but was more likely two seconds, Kyril accepted the chalice and held it up for all to see. "This is the cup of My blood, the blood of the new and everlasting covenant. . . ."

In his relief, Vasco turned his attention to the pews; more dark faces there. Redemption seemed to be the church of choice for immigrants from the Carib-bean. He thought, however uncharitably, that this may have helped press Mae Capone's decision to worship at Blessed Sacrament. The Irish were the Cubans of their day and had selected the next group down to ostracize.

But he may have been hasty in this conclusion, because in the third row left he spotted the Family Capone: Al himself, yawning into a fist wearing the fabulous fake diamond ring, draped in a fine dark suit with a bright yellow tie, a pearl-gray fedora resting on his lap; Mae in a violet dress with an ivory jabot at her throat and a hat that might have been the same one she'd worn to confession, with a bowl-shaped crown and a veil pinned above the brim; Sonny in an Ivy League suit with what looked like a fraternity pin in his lapel, a hat similar to his father's placed in the identical position on his lap; Danny Coughlin in his serge, the eternal smile tattooed on his face. Mae was the ringleader, that much was certain. The mob boss.

FIFTEEN

A SEAGULL FLUTTERED BLACK-TIPPED GRAY WINGS, DODGING THE PURPLE sphere that struck the boardwalk near its toes and bounced, a projectile the size and shape of a musket ball. The bird stopped six inches away, scrutinized the alien object with first one eye, then the other, cocked its head, and hopped forward to pluck it up.

The gull exploded, replaced by a tuft of feathers attached to a pair of yellow feet. No blood: it seemed to have been vaporized by the blast. The sphere remained untouched where it had landed.

"Blueberries. Filthy fuckers can't get their fill. Up in New England they flock fifty miles inland at berry-picking time. I guess they're like an imported delicacy here."

Paul Anthony Vasco broke his pistol, basically a hollow pipe mounted on a straight handle with black grips and a trigger in a big loop, took a paper shell with a brass receiver from a cargo pocket, inserted it in the pipe, and snapped the action shut. From another pocket he fished a fresh blueberry—he carried them loose, and his shorts on that side were stained purple clear to the hem—and flipped it with an overhand twist toward a gull that had just landed a little farther away. He took careful aim, steadying his hand on the weathered salt-stained two-by-four railing in front of him, and squeezed the trigger. The pistol made a small, sharp crack, and a load of shot, each pellet no larger than mullet seed, rattled and skittered on the boardwalk. He'd missed. The bird snatched up its prize and took to the air.

Peter Vasco was mildly horrified. The birds could be annoying in their numbers, only reluctantly opening a path when he strode on the beach and even on a sidewalk downtown, and their creaking cries sounded like someone pulling rusty nails from siding, but the destruction seemed to him a kind of sin, magnified by the fact that it was Paul who supplied the bait. When he'd produced the weapon from his waistband, his son had assumed it was an air pistol and that he intended to take target practice on seashells and discarded Dixie cups.

Paul spat. "Out of range. Must-a woke up the patron saint of birds with that first shot."

Peter watched him extract the smoking shell, drop it into yet another pocket, and replace it with a fresh one. "Dad, why?"

"First week I was here, the harbor patrol towed in a small skiff with a corpse in it. Local fisherman. Coroner said he had a stroke, but I don't see how he had enough to work with to say that. He figured the poor son of a bitch was still alive when the gulls started on him. They couldn't even wait for him to cool off." He flicked another blueberry and took aim, but the berry struck the bird it was intended for, startling it into flight. "Aw, hell."

"Did you know him?"

"Who?"

"The fisherman."

"No. I said it was my first week. What's that got to do with nothing?"

Paul could turn a conversation in a circle better than anyone his son had ever met. They'd had a late lunch in the small Italian restaurant Paul said Ralph Capone had an interest in, a place with red-and-white-checked tablecloths and empty green Chianti jugs hanging in baskets from the ceiling, noisy and boisterous, jabbering diners and fat waiters and waitresses shipping cargos of crockery through narrow twisting channels like battlewagons maneuvering in the bay. Paul joked with their waitress in English and Italian, twisted spaghetti onto his fork with winch-like precision, and washed it down with the wine he called dago red. The meatballs nearly measured up to his description ("size-a cantaloupes"); great reddish-brown mounds poking out of the pasta like earthworks in tall grass blown over by the wind. There was no opportunity for serious talk in all that din. Paul talked Peter into meeting Sharon when she came home from work in the shipyard. After his father paid the check with a wad of fishy-smelling bills, leaving a quarter tip, the two went out to walk off the sluggish effects of a very heavy lunch.

The wind was brisk, tipping the waves with white foam. It blew tantalizing glimpses of a woman's slender thighs under the dirndl she had wrapped around a green-and-white-striped bathing suit, walking on the boardwalk. She let it flap, concentrating on holding a wide-brimmed straw hat on her head. Peter wondered if indulging in the temptations of the flesh compounded the sin of a man posing as chaste.

"Think she needs spiritual counseling?" His father turned to lean his back against the railing and remove the live shell from the chamber. He grinned wickedly. The man missed nothing.

He didn't rise to the bait. "I've never seen a pistol like that before. I thought it was an air gun when you took it out."

"It used to be. I had it rechambered to fire a .410 shotgun shell. It meant installing a firing pin, too, and it cost more than the whole thing was worth. It's almost forty years old. I wanted it to still look like a kid's air pistol in case a cop pulled me over in the truck. They was all on the payroll, but you never knew when one of 'em might decide to up the ante. Gun rap's tough to beat if you don't provide what they are calling now an essential service." He pronounced *essential* with slow precision in his Calibrisian accent.

"You carried it in Chicago?"

"Sure. I wasn't-a peddling ice cream."

"Did you ever have to shoot anyone?"

"I like that you said 'have to.' That's an improvement over our last talk." He snapped shut the action and returned the pistol to his shorts, dropping his shirttail over the handle. The shirt was the same pale yellow one he'd put on during

Peter's last visit, or one just like it; same shorts, same old deck shoes, a little dirtier than before. Either it was his daily work uniform or he just didn't have any other clothes. Back in Cicero he'd had a suit for church, dungarees for work, and alternated between two shirts during the week. "I never shot no one, but that don't mean anyone's life was spared. The shells are full of birdshot, with a half-load of powder. That's enough to blow a bird to hell but it just stings a man and raises welts, maybe enough to keep him occupied while I run for the hills. I like to live, but I try to keep the Sixth."

"Where'd you get it?"

"Sporting goods store on West Diversey, run by a guy named von Frantzius; fat little kraut with a lisp. I think he batted left. I bet he moved a ton and a half of ordnance to the North and South Side in four years. Made himself a nice little bundle Valentine's Day week."

"You knew some nice people."

"What can I say? It was Chicago."

"Everyone talks about Chicago like it's a foreign country."

"It isn't, though. It's one hundred percent American."

A seagull stuck out its feet and landed on the railing, not six feet away from where Paul was leaning. Peter stiffened, but his father only looked at the bird briefly and without interest, then returned his gaze to the string of arcades and saltwater taffy shops facing the ocean. Apparently, in Paul Vasco's war on avian scavengers, the railing represented Switzerland.

"So how you like Miami?"

"I like it. People are friendly and Father Kyril's a good man."

"He know what you're up to?"

Peter turned around and took up his father's pose, his back to the water with his elbows resting on the railing. He reminded himself that "up to" meant the plan to spare Al Capone from the Pit. "He guessed it. I'm not to get my hopes too high."

"I thought all you biscuit-pushers thought everybody can be saved."

"Everyone can. Some cases are a little more complicated."

"What did you think of Mr. Capone?" Not, "Did you have any luck?" Instead a question based on certainty that he'd succeeded in making contact. Paul Vasco and Sergei Kyril shared an abiding faith in their impressions. A common truck driver, connected and convinced of it.

"Damn it, Dad, how can you be so sure a call from you would get me past the gate?"

"I'm not, but you haven't brought up the subject since you got off the train. You was so hot to trot last time, you didn't get in, you'd-a been all over me to give you the name of somebody who could *get* you in. You always was a rat terrier when you got your teeth in something."

"And you always have an answer."

"Always tell the truth and you always will." He rubbed his stomach, pooched out a little from the pasta. A man could trace the progress of digestion through that tubular body like a pig through a python. "That sauce gave me indigestion. What say you buy me a beer on the Vatican and put out the fire?"

A lunch wagon was parked at the end of the little Coney Island, with an opening in the side and a counter that disappeared behind a canvas flap when it closed. An Eskimo painted on one side of the opening and a red devil with a pitchfork painted on the other both pointed to a sign above advertising cold beer and hot dogs. A smell of sauerkraut and molten grease lived deep inside the wagon.

The proprietor, a beefy man in a spattered BVD undershirt and a paper hat, a mermaid tattooed on one forearm, took Peter's money, opened two bottles of Goebel's from a zinc tub filled with ice, and set them on the counter. Beads of moisture prickled on the brown glass and vapor drifted out of the necks. They walked from there to a small oval park with picnic tables and a swing set and slide. It was Monday, a school day, and the equipment was deserted.

Seated opposite his son at one of the picnic tables, Paul clinked bottles. "I know what you get when you consecrate a cup of wine. What do you get from a bottle of beer?"

"A loud belch." He swigged. He'd never cared for the beverage, personal connotations aside, but it was Arctic cold and a sinful pleasure with the sun beating down on the crown of his hat.

"You loosened up some. I always heard Mr. Capone could put a guest at ease or scare him out of his pants with just a look."

"Well, I still have my pants."

"What happened?"

"Not much. I gave him your regards the first night, talked with his wife, and went home. They invited me back for a party Friday afternoon, where I met their son and we played cards. Mrs. Capone asked me to drive her maid home. I did that and came back and watched a movie with Capone in his living room."

Paul paused with his bottle halfway to his lips, then drank. "Sounds like you got in tight."

"Thanks to you. The collar wouldn't have been enough. He's entertained cardinals."

"He remembers me, huh."

"He also remembers how you met, and that you were married to an Irish girl, just like him."

"I'll be damned."

He wanted to press the point, but he sensed that Paul's defenses were going up. "I met Ralph, too."

"Bottles? Here in Florida?"

"In the confessional at Our Lady of Redemption."

"No shit. How long did that take?"

"He didn't come to confess. We went for a ride—not that kind, the other kind—and we went over the rules. The family's afraid Capone will slip up and say something he shouldn't. It's part of his illness. Danny Coughlin did the driving."

"Who's he?"

"Capone's brother-in-law. He runs errands when he's not running a union."

"I don't know him. You already know more about Mr. Capone and his family than I ever did."

"Ralph said if I didn't watch my step I'd be killed."

"Sounds like good advice, but I wouldn't lose much sleep over anything Bottles says. In Chicago they said he was all noise."

"What did they say about Frank Nitti?"

"He mention Nitti?"

"Capone's son did, at the house. According to him, Nitti's more than just noise."

"Jesus. You work fast."

"What do you know about Nitti?"

"I never laid eyes on him. I know Jack McGurn crossed himself every time his name came up. McGurn, that mowed guys down with machine guns and ate a big plate of spaghetti after. They say it was Nitti had McGurn killed in that bowling alley in '36, so maybe crossing himself was a good idea. It was February 14, can you believe it? They stuck a funny valentine in his hand after they plugged him. I think you better go find somebody else to save."

"Frankie Rio was there, too, with Ralph. He sends his regards."

Paul took a pull of beer. His hand was as brown as the bottle. He said nothing.

"You told me last time you didn't know who Frankie Rio was."

"I had a buck for every Frankie I—"

"I said he was Al Capone's personal bodyguard. Now he's Ralph's. I told you about his funny lip. He hasn't forgotten you."

"Maybe he heard about me from Jack. He had a high opinion of me behind the wheel."

"I saw you drinking wine with Rio in the kitchen of our apartment when I was little. I remembered the lip. I wasn't sure it was him until he shook my hand last week and said, 'Tell your old man Frankie said hello.'"

Paul rubbed his stomach. "I gotta cut down on the red sauce. I think I'm getting-a ulcer."

"What about it, Dad? Don't tell me you knew Rio the same way you knew John Scalise and Albert Anselmi. There wasn't room in that truck cab for four."

"Next time you see a movie with your pal Mr. Capone, make sure it's a war picture. Bodyguards don't spend all their time sitting in lobbies reading the papers. They got lives like everybody else. We saw each other in a speak coupla times. I bragged on Mrs. Terrazzini's wine and he said he never had a glass of homemade didn't taste like Flit. It was a case of defending my landlady's good name."

"You expect me to believe that?"

"You don't, I got another." He finished his beer in one long gurgle, then shifted his grip to the neck and sent the bottle cartwheeling through the air toward a trash barrel with CITY OF FT. LAUDERDALE stenciled on it. It struck the inside of the barrel and shattered. "The only time you look me up is when you want something. 'Tell me about Scalise and Anselmi.' 'Introduce me to Al Capone.' 'What about you and Frankie Rio?' What do I look like, a fucking Quiz Kid?" He got up and strode away in his stooping gait. Peter considered letting him go. He left his beer half-finished and went after him. "You invited me to meet Sharon."

"I'm uninviting you. You'd probably stick a flashlight in her face and ask her who killed McSwiggin."

"I'm sorry. There are just a lot of things I don't understand."

"Get used to it. Nobody's Einstein but Einstein."

His legs were nearly twice as long as his father's, but he had to scramble to keep up. "No more questions, I promise."

"That's like a seagull promising not to eat anything can't raise a hand to shoo it away."

"I swear."

Paul stopped so abruptly his son had to backpedal to face him. He was breathing hard, sweating. Paul noticed. "You're getting fat, boy. I told you lay off the potatoes."

He was right. Rich food on Palm Island, a daily diet of drugstore hamburgers, and now the big meal in the Italian restaurant had put him seriously out of shape. He had no mall to walk across twice a day. Cranking the Model T was the only exercise he got. "Father Kyril lifts weights. I'll ask if I can borrow his dumbbells."

"That gym stuff's for rich people that don't work. Come out with me on the boat sometime. I'll keep you so busy you'll look like Johnny Weissmuller in a day."

"I'd like that. Not the Tarzan part; going out with you on the boat."

Paul took off his long-billed cap, flicked a single drop of sweat from his hairline, and put the cap back on, angling it over one eye like a Chicago tough. "You swear no more questions, you said. Swear on what?"

"On my honor as a priest of the Roman Catholic Church."

SHARON WASN'T AT ALL WHAT HE EXPECTED.

She lived on one side of a duplex in an older neighborhood, far enough from the ocean to make the rents and mortgages affordable to the largely working-class people who lived there. A taxicab was parked in the driveway next door and during the short walk from the streetcar stop the Vascos passed a number of men and women carrying lunch pails; shifts were changing throughout the Eastern Time Zone. Paul let them in with his own key, and the first thing Peter noticed inside was a mezuzah attached to the doorpost.

"She's Jewish?" In his surprise he spoke without thinking.

His father grinned. "I guess Italian girls don't want nothing to do with me."

A woman came trotting up a narrow hallway next to the staircase. She wore a red bandanna-print blouse tucked into a gray wool skirt, flat-heeled shoes, and a necklace made of metal trinkets that matched the charm bracelet on her left wrist. She made a sound like Christmas bells as she walked. She was plump and large-breasted, shorter than Paul by an inch, and wore her black hair in a shoulder-length bob. Peter could not picture a woman more different from his tall, slim, blond mother.

She kissed Paul on the cheek, leaving a red print. "You're early. I just put in the roast."

"Take it out. We ate late."

She kept smiling, showing a gum line. Paul's women made allowances for his brusque ways. "So this is Peter. Gosh, you don't look anything like your father."

"He was born out of luck."

Before Peter could say anything, she went up on her toes and kissed his cheek. He reminded himself to wipe off the incriminating evidence before he went back out in public.

"I'm pleased to meet you, Mrs.—"

"Baumgartner; but that's the last time I want to hear it tonight."

"Sharon it is, then."

"Such a polite boy. He must have been raised by his mother."

She took his hat from his hand and hung it on a peg next to Paul's fishing cap. Then she inserted herself between father and son and steered them away from the door with an arm around each of their waists.

The living room was small, with doilies everywhere and a gypsy shawl draped at an angle on a towering Westinghouse radio cabinet, one glittery tassel hanging in front of the dial. There was a bookcase, last week's *Life* on a coffee table with Sharon Baumgartner's name and address mimeographed on the subscription label, and on top of the bookcase a sepia photograph in a standing wood frame of a man in the white cap and uniform of a chief petty officer in the U.S. Navy. A triangular frame on the wall behind the radio contained an American flag folded with only the blue field showing.

"Oliver," she said, noting the track of his gaze. "He fell off the *Yorktown* when the Japs hit it."

"I'm very sorry."

"I'm not," said Paul.

His son stared at him. He was still standing close to Sharon with his arm around her waist now. "Well, I can't stand here and cry no crocodile tears."

"I'm cried out." Her smile hadn't changed. "He was a career man. We were married twelve years and I doubt we were together a year in all that time. Not much chance for children, which was what I wanted."

"Don't look at me. I already done my damage in that department."

"I'd say you did just fine the first time out. Anyway, I've got my hands full taking care of *you*."

Peter did some quick arithmetic. Allowing for the nearly two years that had passed since the Battle of Midway—would this war never end? Christmases piled up like casualty counts, reported by UPI like the stock market tally from week to week—she'd have been sixteen when they married, if she was thirty now as Paul claimed she'd told him. He seemed to think she was older. Peter agreed. He'd been afraid his father had turned into one of those old goats who preyed on leggy young widows. No, he hadn't expected Mrs. Oliver Baumgartner, with her hard *g*'s and tinkling jewelry that screamed Queens, New York. He liked her. Such things you didn't analyze, just accepted them as the evidence of things unseen.

Came the inevitable offer of refreshment. It was Mass all over again: the *Confiteor*, the reading from the lectionary, the Prayer of the Eucharist: Iced tea would be wonderful, thanks. Iced tea and lemonade were the sacramental wine of the Florida laity. Beer for Paul. Sharon tinkled away, to return in moments with a bottle of Schlitz and cloudy brown liquid in a tall glass with ice cubes floating on top. Peter had never cared for tea in any form; it tasted like an idea only half-developed for hospitality's sake. But he drank it like holy water offered to a sinner beyond redemption. "So how did you two meet?" It rang as hollowly as the prayer of absolution; indulgence for the crime against faith, a plea to a lesser offense. An impossible request in the eyes of Mae Capone, mother confessor to the Florida branch of the Outfit.

"Supermarket," they said in unison; Sharon laughed brightly and squeezed Paul's hand, cuddling closer. They were sitting together on a mohair love seat facing Peter's overstuffed chair.

"A-and-P," Paul said. "I got one of them damn carts with a bum wheel, almost threw out my hip every time I turned a corner. I guess I wasn't quiet on the subject."

"I heard him cussing above the PA." She made her voice gruff. "'Ladies and gentlemen, we're having a special on Campbell's tomato soup, twelve cents a— sonofabitch!' I started to laugh. He made this mean face, which made me laugh harder. Then he started in."

"Coupla hyenas howling by the Cream o' Wheat. It's a damn miracle they didn't throw us out and ban us from the whole chain."

"He said if it was a wheel on his old truck he'd know what to do, but they didn't give him a spare. Well, my father drove a vegetable truck in New York. He taught me to drive at the wheel of that truck. I was too short to reach the pedals, so he tied wooden blocks to them. That big steering wheel, it was mounted on top of the column, it took me around with it on every turn, with Papa laughing himself into a coughing fit and reaching out to steady it and put a foot on a pedal when mine slipped off. I had a brother, but he was at medical school, busing tables nights to pay his tuition. Papa needed me as a backup driver in case he got too sick to wrestle with that old White. He had TB."

"Whites take muscle," Paul said. "I wake up some nights with that bee sting you get between the shoulder blades when you put in ten hours, that chain drive rattling in my ears like dragging a rosary through your teeth."

"So right away we had something in common. Pair of gear mashers."

Paul laughed out loud at the supermarket story, sobering when she mentioned her father's illness.

"Is your father still living?"

"He died. Mama sold the truck and we moved here. She had a touch of the TB, too, and my brother recommended a warm climate. It cured her. She's in Tampa, working the switchboard in a hotel."

"Old bat's got no use for me."

"She's got nothing against you except she thinks you're too old for me. I told her, 'Mama, he comes home every day.' You can't maintain a marriage on V-Mail." She took Paul's beer from his hand, sipped, and gave it back, an intimate gesture unlike any his son had ever witnessed between his parents. He felt a strange resentment, and chided himself for it.

"Are you liking Florida, Peter?"

"It takes getting used to. There's still snow on the ground in Cicero."

"It gets old. You can't appreciate summer when there's no winter."

"Speak for yourself," Paul said. "You never had to start a cold engine at four ayem when it's six below. I heated up a teakettle to pour hot water into the radiator and it froze on the way downstairs."

"Where is your brother now?" Peter asked.

"Army Medical Corps. The Aleutians, can you believe it? He's got nothing *but* winter. Last letter I got, he asked me to seal up some sunshine in an Ovaltine jar and send it to him air mail. He said he had to thaw out a bottle of iodine to treat a cut."

He simply could not hold onto a grudge in her cheerful presence. His mother had been a serious woman, if not grave, with flashes of unexpected sardonic humor at what had seemed inappropriate moments but in retrospect he remembered those moments were invariably brightened by what she'd said, after the initial shock wore off. Two half-orphans, Peter and Sharon.

"Can you stay for supper, Peter? I hope it's okay that I call you Peter . . . I'm older than you and *Father* just seems wrong."

"I could eat again." Paul seldom paid attention to conversations in which he wasn't involved. "It's always the skinny guys that win pie-eating contests."

Peter ignored the comment. "We're practically family," he told Sharon.

"See, I told you for a sky pilot he flies close to the ground."

"I think he's sweet. I wish I'd known Maureen. They must have been very alike. You know, Peter, our religions aren't so different. Jews confess, too, at Yom Kippur. The only difference is we do it in public: Everyone stands up in Temple and shouts after the rabbi, 'I have been adulterous,' and so on and so on, whether or not they ever were. We share the sins of all the worshippers. Only"—she leaned forward a little, her black eyebrows assuming the upward-slashing angle of incendiary rockets—"you can always tell who committed the sin under examination, because they're the loudest."

Peter laughed. Twice in one sitting. Sharon Baumgartner, he decided, was good for what ailed him.

SIXTEEN

Supper was brisket—what else?—with heaps of lima beans swimming in butter, boiled potatoes and beef gravy so deeply brown it qualified as black, cottage cheese, strong coffee, and a roasted peach in wine sauce for dessert. Peter had no great head for figures, and the beginning of the meal had not contributed to his ability to total the number of ration points it all represented without a paper and pencil to hand. Paul's black market connections were sterling.

They dined in the kitchen, larger than the living room, with an old-fashioned gas stove that required pumping up a contraption on the side to fuel the burners and oven, a white-enamel sink with zinc drain boards, and a square refrigerator squatting on cast iron bowlegs with compressor coils on top that wheezed and clicked like an old man with a sinus infection. An oilcloth with a windowpane pattern covered the table and they sat in chairs made of shiny aluminum tubes and molded yellow plastic. A sunny room, even after dark. The radio in the living room played a steady program of dance music interrupted occasionally by news of the war. American planes were outfighting the Luftwaffe nearly two to one. It sounded like a sports score.

"I gotta off-load." Paul snatched the napkin from his collar and left the room.

"He's good for ten minutes. There's a stack of *Field and Streams* in there as high as your knee." Sharon rattled crimson nails against her coffee cup, thick porcelain with a green stripe around the rim. "I'm sorry the brisket was overdone. I had to crank up the oven or we'd starve till midnight."

"It was perfect. The first homemade meal I've had in years." His coffee was strong without being bitter; genuine ground, no adulteration. "Why Dad?"

She seemed prepared for the question. She couldn't know he was skirting a promise based on a damnable falsehood. "He's faithful. Oliver; well, a girl in every port, like the song. I'm guessing, naturally. A man needs what he needs. Women are stronger when it comes to such things. I don't blame him. But I don't have to make excuses for Paul. I guess this isn't proper table conversation with a priest."

"Sometimes I think this collar is a stop sign. I hope we can pretend it's just an article of clothing."

She set her cup in its saucer. He thought if the table were more narrow she'd take both his hands in hers. Her face was spade-shaped, pointed at the chin, with streaks of rouge on her cheeks that accentuated the sharpness of the bones. Her eyes were a smoky shade to which he couldn't quite assign a color; black was too severe, gray too far on the other side. Semitic seemed to cover it, with all the Old Testament mysteries that entailed. "Your father is a better man than you know."

For a long moment, the girl singer on the radio seemed to pause overlong between the chorus and the bridge ("Every time we say good-bye, I die a little . . ."); then the woodwinds chirruped and everything was as it had been before, the wheeze and click of the refrigerator, the sizzle of the electric clock plugged into the outlet above the range, the brisket settling into the cooling grease in its clay-ware pot like an old man lowering himself into a tub of scalding water. Peter hadn't realized how much he'd missed the prosaic chords of the domestic life until that moment. Was there a Sharon out there for him? He thought of Mae Capone, loyal beyond all reason; even Helen Gandy, J. Edgar Hoover's disciple in the war against All Things Harmful to Law and Order. For some reason he thought of Rose, the Capones' maid, and resisted the impulse to cross himself. Powerful stuff, that sugary kosher wine in its square bottle; the Jews made no ceremony of it, but it was all caught up in religion just the same, a kind of tran-substantiation from cold calculating sobriety to a mellowness of spirit and the power to arrive at observations without benefit of logic. *Your father is a better man than you know*; such things came from this.

She excavated a pack of Parliaments from the mysterious regions of her blouse and lit one from a book of matches from the same source. The cover bore the name of a hotel in silver on red lacquer. Florida, or what little he'd seen of it, had more hotels than Chicago had churches. A state of transients, Florida. Mae Capone had identified Parker Henderson as a native in the same tones she might have used to refer to a duck-billed platypus or some other genetic freak.

Sharon returned the items to her blouse without offering him a cigarette. "Paul says you have no vices." She made it sound like a disappointment.

"I have my own set. They're not exclusive from the job."

"I like the way you talk. You must've had a good education. They say the Purple Gang enrolled their children in Catholic schools because they did a bet-ter job than public school. Even Jewish gangsters are more broad-minded than most people."

The bartender who had served him ginger ale and then rye in the club car aboard the train from the District had mentioned the Purple Gang. What was it about mob legend that transcended talk of war, global war? Nostalgia for a har-rowing body count now reduced to a trifle by mass slaughter? He pushed away his wineglass, a pressed goblet masquerading as cut crystal. The past was not less counterfeit.

"I don't think Paul ever got over your decision to become a priest. He had his heart set on grandchildren."

"He told you that?"

"He did and he didn't. He talks all around the things he really cares about. You have to piece it together from what he didn't say. He thinks he let you down as a father, all that time away working while you were growing up. The day you started school, he was lugging barrels of malt from a ferry on Lake Michigan to his truck. He didn't say it like he regretted anything, but a woman knows. He wanted another shot."

"I always thought he was just cynical about the Church."

"You don't have my insight. I miscarried in '33. It was a boy. Not a day goes by I don't think, he'd be in fifth grade now, he'd be studying for his bar mitzvah, I'd be teaching him how to do the box step for his first school dance. Sappy stuff. You have all these memories of things that never happened."

"I'm truly sorry."

Her shoulders lifted and dropped, a world of communication. She filled her mouth with smoke and let it spill out. She was a puffer, not an inhaler. His mother had smoked Paul's L&M's that same way, usually while wearing a gully in the linoleum waiting for him to come home; a pack-a-year habit. Paul had said she burned more than she smoked. It occurred to him then he hadn't seen his father light a cigarette in Florida. Beer, pasta, Sharon, and the Atlantic seemed to have eliminated the need.

"I did all my crying at the time," she said, "like when Oliver lost his sea legs and went over the side. He was a good swimmer, but they say the ocean was on fire, from all the oil. What's the point? I'm sorry if I made you feel bad. Paul's proud of you. The priesthood is a profession, and he came from a long line of men who couldn't scrub the fish stink out of their hands if they worked at it from Passover to Rosh Hashanah. I'm translating. I don't know much about the Catholic faith."

"I thought I'd failed him. I just didn't know how."

"That's a son's job. You can't live your father's life and yours too."

Children are put on this earth to disappoint their parents.

Had everyone been let in on that secret but him? "You're a thoughtful woman, Sharon. You're wasted in the shipyard."

"It's honest work. No, it's better than that. I'm a soldier with a drill press instead of a deck gun."

"Also a poet."

She laughed, coughed smoke, sipped wine to settle the spasm. He wondered with a touch of alarm if she'd inherited her family plague. But smokers lived with congestion. "I sent political verses to *The Masses* when I was sixteen. All I got was the poems back, but someone kept a record. I had to sign a loyalty oath before they'd let me poke holes in steel plate, like if I went a quarter-inch off on purpose, a destroyer would sink in the China Sea. Stalin's our ally, but I think some people are getting ready for the next war." She paused to peel a shred of tobacco from a scarlet lip. "Bolshevism's bullshit, though. You grow out of it if you've got brains."

He hadn't heard her curse before; it was the wine. The word sounded more innocent coming from her than from Paul. He wondered how much she knew of his past. Obviously she was aware of it, from the story about unloading barrels of malt. But Peter wouldn't ask. However tainted the vow he'd made on the basis of his monstrous imposture, he was determined to honor it. There would be no pressing questions this night.

The toilet flushed, roaring like heavy surf. A faucet ran, the two-fingered pass of a man who made the simplest obeisance toward hygiene, and Paul rejoined them. "My ear's burning. You two been telling tales out of school?" There was a troubled note in the banter. The father did not trust the son, nor the woman of his companionship.

Sharon blew a plume of smoke at the blue fluorescent ring in the ceiling. "You might as well know it now. I'm running off with your son the priest. We're going to Boca and raise a litter of monks and nuns."

"Well, they have to come from someplace. You got a train to catch."

"Paul!" She tapped an eighth of an inch of ash into her plate of congealed grease.

"What? He's got a boss, same as all of us. Except me. I only answer to time and tide."

"Another poet," Sharon said. "Can you see how we found each other?"

"It would be tragedy otherwise." Peter rose. "Thank you for a wonderful evening. He's in good hands."

"You don't know the half of it." Mogen David glittered in Paul's bright eyes.

"Paul, for gosh sake. Peter isn't one of your buddies down at the Crab Castle."

Astonishingly, Paul's weathered face smoothed out into a mask of contrition. "Sorry, Pietro. Sharon. That hebe wine's full of the devil."

"We don't malign the grape of Israel in this house," Sharon said. "It may not be the Blood of Christ, but you can't blame it for making you stupid. That's an accident of birth."

"All's I know is I never got into no trouble over a jug of dago red. You know your way back to the streetcar?" He stuck out his hand.

Peter took it. "Thanks, Dad. I'll be very disappointed if you let Sharon slip through your fingers."

"Yeah. Well, one thing you can count on in this life is disappointment."

A curious valedictory. He would never figure out his father the way he feared his father would figure out him.

Sharon insisted on wrapping a survival package of brisket and beans in waxed paper for his sustenance; she seemed to think Christians lived on stale bread and water collected from the walls of catacombs. She kissed him again, Paul shook his hand a second time, and he struck off for the streetcar stop drinking in great lungfuls of Fort Lauderdale air to combat the effects of heavy food and wine and someone else's smoke. He'd offered to drive Paul there from the waterfront in the Ford, but his father had said he'd finished with all that; he preferred to depend on strangers to get him around. Peter would never understand him. But he felt he knew Sharon after just one evening as if he'd known her all his life. Was God erecting obstacles or opening gates? More and more he was convinced He had invented the devil, horns, tail, and all, just to furnish Himself with an ironclad alibi.

He put his package of food in the rectory icebox with a note inviting Kyril and Thomas to help themselves, and slept in his monk's cell without dreaming. He had used up all his dreams in fear and speculation. But sleep brought no rest. He wondered, in the semiopaque isinglass vision of reality, if Purgatory took place on earth, in installments, like the layaway plan for a deluxe Philco radio or a Hotpoint range.

THE NEXT MORNING HE WAITED IN FRONT OF THE MIAMI BRANCH OF THE Everglade State Bank while an employee in a three-piece suit unlocked the door. The inside differed from the branch in Fort Lauderdale. Dillinger had not been expected to raid this far south—even the core of the Barker Gang had been on vacation when federal agents shot them to pieces in Ocklawaha—and the tellers' cages were faced in ordinary glass, with the massive round door of the vault standing wide open behind the counter, a fifty-pound sack of pennies acting as a doorstop, and not an armed guard in sight. A pretty blond teller who plucked her eyebrows like Marlene Dietrich's took his withdrawal slip and counted out a hundred in twenties and tens for operating expenses. The cost of living was significantly higher there than in Washington.

The library was open when he got there, a large room with yellow-oak tables and bookcases and card catalogues, steel-shelved stacks in back, reading carrels, and the day's newspapers hung on wooden racks like drying laundry. A male librarian with a clubfoot that had kept him out of the military hobbled into a back room and returned carrying three huge elephant-folio volumes bound in sturdy black cloth; Vasco had not been sure of the date Frank Nitti had been shot in his office at Capone's old Lexington Hotel headquarters, only that the incident had taken place after Capone went to prison in May 1932 and before Mayor Cermak of Chicago was slain in Miami in February 1933, in what had been widely reported as an attempt on the life of President-Elect Franklin Delano Roosevelt, with whom he was exchanging words.

Cermak had given the order to arrest Nitti—or to kill him while "resisting arrest," if one liked his theories cloak-and-dagger—and the boys who gathered in pool halls and barbershops to share their street wisdom said the mayor was the target all along and that Nitti or Capone or both had staged the affair to demonstrate to the world that when the Outfit hung a price on your head it would be paid regardless of how public the venue or how high-placed the company.

It had seemed far-fetched to Vasco. Why give so important an assignment to a blithering anarchist who could barely string ten words together in English, when clearly it called for a professional? Hoover had stressed the point in press conferences. But Hoover himself had blithely endorsed the conspiracy angle in conversation with Vasco, as if that were the official account known to all. Then again, Cermak's murder was a Secret Service black eye, and the Director of the FBI was never coy about his resentment that rival government intelligence agencies were permitted to exist. Embarrassing one of them by rumor and innuendo was more insidiously effective than a public statement that couldn't be proved.

One never knew how much was bureaucratic infighting and how much was genuine intelligence. Hoover had taken the Director's job vowing to keep politics out of the Bureau, but had exempted himself. But he wasn't corrupt or a killer, which satisfied Vasco's sense of right and wrong.

Still, he hoped if he earned full-time status as a special agent, his assignment would take him far from Washington.

The bound newspapers were as large as plat books, and piled up three months at a time from hefty dailies. The Miami Public Library had no more storage space than anywhere else in a state without basements, so had concentrated on local papers like *The Miami Herald*, with *The Chicago Tribune*—Jake Lingle's old sheet—the only exception, to accommodate all the side-of-the-mouth Chicagoans who had flocked South after the authorities abandoned their desperate attempt to discourage Capone from taking permanent residence.

Vasco unshipped the stack of atlas-size books from the crippled librarian's extended forearms and frowned at the reading carrels, awkward places to open huge flat books with privacy partitions in the way. "Do you have anything I could spread them out on?"

The librarian shrugged, brushing dust off his worsted sleeves. "The floor."

"Whatever happened to library tables?"

"We stand up the out-of-town phone books on those. This isn't Texas, mister. You'd cry to see the size of the offices."

No "Father," nor even "Reverend"; the man had either failed to notice his collar through the thick lenses of his spectacles or disdained the Church of Rome and all its titles and customs.

Vasco thanked him and carried the volumes to what he hoped was an untrafficked area between stacks, went back for a chair to hang his hat and coat on, and sat Indian fashion on the floor in his shirtsleeves, spreading out the book like a little boy settling down to read the funny papers.

He began with May 1932, skimming the fading headlines and turning the brittle yellowing leaves carefully to avoid tearing them; but moving as rapidly as he could through society and sports and entertainment sections and past grocery and department store and automobile advertisements ("The New Essexes Are In!"), knowing that the near-fatal shooting of Capone's head muscleman was front-page material. In this way he made steady progress, but it required resisting the temptation to stop and study photos and text devoted to unrelated gang violence: bodies stretched out on the tile floors of barbershops and across varnished oak bowling lanes, spilling out the open doors of automobiles clobbered with holes, wallowing facedown in puddles in ditches, rolled into gutters, staring marble-eyed on white enamel tables in the Cook County Morgue; tailored vests rucked up to expose silk shirttails, glittering patent-leather shoes showing pale scuffed soles, naked torsos stripped of all emblems of status; gardens of

hats, forests of hats, they never seemed to stay on, just fell off in the first orgas-
mic arch of death and lit on the edges of their brims, rolled, and came to rest
against curbs and steam radiators and the bases of primitive jukeboxes. The city
and county property rooms must have been stocked with more hats than the
haberdashery department at Marshall Field's, and each one another dead man.

Tillie the Toiler, Jiqqs and Maggie, Dick Tracy, Thimble Theater, all the funnies
in black-and-buff and on Sunday in four colors. Radio columns, fashion columns,
humor columns bearing Will Rogers' baggy smile in a photo the size of a thumbnail. Rotogravures in a full blossom of lace dresses, picture hats, and movie stars
beaming beside custom-made convertibles. Help Wanted classifieds, giving way
to Situations Wanted as the Depression took hold. Shots of men and women
standing in long outdoor queues, a man selling pencils, residential neighborhoods
transformed overnight into commercial laundering districts; shirts, stockings,
and union suits hanging from transverse clotheslines like flags at the League of
Nations. The usual novelty shot of a boy frying an egg on a blistering sidewalk
followed by the man-on-the-street shot of a fellow in earflaps and a mackinaw,
shoveling snow off a sidewalk. The summer of 1933 and the winter of 1933–4
had been the hottest and coldest on record. Hard economic times hadn't been
enough for God's sinister side.

There was nothing in the first book, just the usual local mayhem, domestic
disasters, and thugs smashing shop windows in Berlin, with some human interest about Capone's first days in the federal penitentiary in Atlanta; he played
tennis and had coddled eggs for breakfast. The Drys were speculating that FDR's
promise to repeal the Eighteenth Amendment was typical election-year grandstanding and would come to nothing. The Wets said the Drys were probably
right and that Prohibition was here to stay like it or not; and of course they did
not. It was the only thing the two groups had agreed upon in fourteen years.
Vasco reflected that this kind of reading carried all the suspense of watching
newsreel footage of a baseball game he'd attended to the finish.

Before opening the second volume, July through September, he got up to
work the kinks from his legs and back and gingerly pluck the handkerchief from
the inside pocket of his suit coat on the back of the chair. His fingers were
stained black to the first knuckles, there was a smudge on his right shirt cuff
(what, exactly, was the composition of newspaper printers' ink, that in twelve
years it had not yet completely dried?), and dusty grains of decaying newsprint
adhered to the sweat on the heels of his hands like sand from a wet beach. Vigor-
ously though he scrubbed, the handkerchief seemed only to grind the black
deeper into his pores and under his nails while staining the linen as black as his
fingers. Nothing he'd seen in the movies or read in sensational serializations
had compared undercover work to sweeping chimneys.

The clubfooted librarian gave him the key to the men's room, dangling a
brass tag with PROPERTY OF THE MIAMI PUBLIC LIBRARY engraved on it, and in the
small echoing room with a narrow window cranked open on elbow hinges he

made headway in the white porcelain sink with liquid disinfecting soap from a dispenser. In the mirror he saw more traces of ink on his forehead where he had swept away perspiration. He attended to that as well, wiped his hands on the roller towel, and went out to return the key.

"Any progress?" The librarian was stamping the library's name on the page-ends of a stack of books on his small oak desk. It was his first attempt at small talk; evidently Vasco's dedication had elevated his status somewhat.

"Hard to tell. I thought working in a library was a white-collar job."

He smiled a constipated, tight-lipped smile and touched his detachable collar. "Celluloid."

Vasco smiled back and tapped his. "Mine too."

"Well, good luck."

The second volume was identically unrewarding. With only two hours left until confession, he decided to put off any more ablutions until he'd finished with the third. The presidential race was heating up. Herbert Hoover insisted the economy was fundamentally sound and would begin to improve by the end of the next quarter. *The Tribune,* a Democratic paper, ran pictures taken from the wire of hobo jungles in city parks across the country; "Hoovervilles," someone had dubbed them. Roosevelt promised to stimulate recovery and addressed the Anti-Saloon League with a pledge to regulate the liquor business heavily once Prohibition was lifted. A cartoon showed Hoover's trademark homburg floating on a field of quicksand with THE GREAT DEPRESSION spidering across its oily black surface. The American Communist Party held rallies in parks and high school gymnasiums. Henry Ford called them anarchists and reinforced security at his automobile plant in Dearborn, Michigan. Al Capone ate tuna casserole and made shoes for his fellow inmates in the prison shop.

Vasco turned the page and Frank Nitti's name leapt out at him.

It was a one-column piece six paragraphs long, not much more than filler when compared to Capone's attention in the press. A head-and-shoulders shot showed a fussily dressed Italian with hair parted left of center and a smudge of moustache, who looked like the floorwalker in a department store. NITTI FREED, ran the headline.

The FBI file had mentioned that both Nitti and Ralph Capone had served time in Leavenworth for income tax evasion: test cases before going after Al. Ralph had alluded to it, but Vasco hadn't seen his name in the editions he'd read. Bottles' day-to-day routine behind bars obviously didn't sell newspapers the way his brother's did. It went some way toward explaining his chronic belligerence; or perhaps not. He was like Sonny Capone, only in Ralph's case he was trapped between his responsibility to Al and Outfit business, and he lacked the irony to smile about it.

Nitti's name and likeness appeared sporadically thereafter as he assumed his duties as Al's surrogate in Ralph's absence, but it was mostly speculation on the part of reporters. Nitti didn't treat the press to fine liquor and rich food and twenty-five-cent cigars, didn't furnish colorful quotes for the bulldog edition, and (on the evidence of fewer grisly photographs and diagrams of murder scenes with Maltese crosses where the bodies had landed), didn't write his name large in machine-gun bullets. Gangland had turned a new page in its playbook.

But then the face of the enemy had changed, too. The North Siders were on the run after February 1929, and with Capone neutralized the authorities were picking off the survivors on both sides with warrants, not weapons. The scarecrow figure of George E. Q. Johnson, the federal investigator who had nailed Scarface Al with his own ledgers, and Prohibition agent Eliot Ness's receding chin and center-parted hair appeared in place of blue jowls and loud neckties, and to ambush such men the traditional way would have brought down the wrath of Washington with all its might. Peace on the streets didn't mean the Enforcer had ceased to enforce, merely that he had channeled his malicious energy in quieter directions: better lawyers, more careful accountants, discreet bribery. No more pineapples or thick envelopes tossed contemptuously into the backseats of official cars, only generous campaign contributions with no cameras present, "anonymous" gifts to the Police Widows' and Orphans' Fund, a handsome cabinet radio-phonograph stocked with all the latest records for the wife of a member of the crime commission. Chicago was still Chicago, even with its boss villain cobbling shoes in Atlanta.

But the old ways weren't entirely dead, even in city hall. Like so many searches, Vasco's took him nearly to the end of his resources before it paid off. He should have started there and worked his way backward.

On Monday, December 19, 1932, the *Tribune*'s printers broke out headline type rarely used since Capone's conviction to spell out Nitti's name in letters the size of Vasco's thumb. Two sergeants with the plainclothes division of the Chicago Police Department, Harry Lang and Harry Miller, burst into Nitti's office towing two uniformed officers they'd recruited on the street, flashed their gold sunburst badges, and at the top of their lungs informed the occupant that he was under arrest by order of Anton Cermak, who had succeeded Capone's handpicked man, William Hale "Big Bill" Thompson, as mayor of Chicago in 1931. That much was reported clearly enough, but what happened next was a jumble.

The account given by a police spokesman said that Nitti drew a revolver and fired. Detective Sergeant Lang was wounded in the arm, but managed to return fire, hitting Nitti three times. Doctors at Chicago General Hospital confirmed rumors that Nitti lay near death and had been given Last Rites by a priest. Nothing Vasco had ever read, in newspapers or in files, contained a single other incident in which a racketeer of Nitti's standing had tried to shoot his way out of a jam with the law. They drew lawyers and fired writs. That paragraph smelled of something other than stale ink and dry rot.

He turned to the next edition. Against all predictions, Nitti rallied, and began the glacial process of recovery from gunshot wounds delivered at close range to the chest, neck, and back near the spinal column, all fired by Detective Sergeant Lang; Maltese crosses marked the entry wounds on an accompanying

anatomical diagram, like corpses in the garage on Clark Street. Lang's statement, corroborated by Detective Sergeant Miller, reported that he'd shot Nitti
first in the neck and chest, then in the back with his finger convulsing on the
trigger after the second impact spun him around.

Pages turned rapidly now. A full-length advertisement for gentlemen's camel's hair overcoats and ladies' astrakhan hats tore three-quarters across in a diagonal with a shrill rip that must have made the clubfooted librarian lift his head
from his book-stamping. Vasco kept going without pausing.

He stopped at the Christmas Eve edition.

A bylined article under a howling headline contained the sworn statement of
Officer Christopher Callaghan, one of the uniformed patrolmen Lang and
Miller had drafted into action, that Sergeant Lang had shot Nitti first in the back
after Nitti raised his hands and turned around, then in the neck and chest when
he swung around to face him. As Nitti collapsed, Lang inflicted himself with a
flesh wound to back up his claim of self-defense.

Vasco read to the end of the year, but the rest was rehash: charges and coun-
tercharges, denials, sputtering outrage from Ted Newberry, Mayor Cermak's
general factotum, first at Officer Callaghan, then at sergeants Lang and Miller,
whom he had selected for the duty, and the inevitable rash of editorials signed by
the city editor, the managing editor, and Colonel McCormick, the publisher, followed by letters from readers calling for a clean sweep from the commissioner's
office on down to the cop on the corner. Undoubtedly it had had the newsboys
crying themselves hoarse, but as for information it was useless.

Twenty minutes to confession. It would take more than Sharon Baumgartner's leftover brisket to smooth this one over with Father Kyril. Vasco apologized to the librarian at his desk and asked if he could see one more volume.

"The *Tribune*?"

"No, *The Miami Herald*. January through March 1933."

THAT NIGHT, PETER VASCO DREAMED; NOT OF SERGEI KYRIL'S WEARY RESIGNED
acceptance of the excuse he'd invented for reporting to his booth half an hour
late, but of hats: supple Panamas, sturdy bowlers, straw skimmers, shaggy bor-
salinos, smart snapbrims, silk toppers, and Tyroleans with feathers in the bands,
rolling around and around on the edges of their brims, bisecting one another's
path in graceful swooping balletic circles, then tilting one by one, falling on
their crowns and wobbling and vibrating to a stop like hubcaps and dead men.

SEVENTEEN

AL CAPONE WAS IN A FOUL MOOD.

A nearly physical thing, that mood, traveling in a white-hot arc and scarring a fine day like a knife slashing through cheek flesh. When Danny Coughlin offered him a steadying hand on the porch steps, he slapped it away and barreled down them, only the top of his yellow crown showing as he made for the sky-blue Lincoln parked in front of the house on Palm Island.

The car was in showroom condition, its enameled fenders like molded mirrors, with only the bottom third of the spotless rear whitewalls showing under the skirts, everything streamlined and bullet-shaped, like a toy spaceship that wound with a key and rolled across the floor. Capone, wound up also, wore a suit the claret shade of sacramental wine, a pale yellow tie on a lemon-colored shirt, and yellow spats buttoned over the tops of black patent-leather shoes. The ensemble suggested Easter more than St. Patrick's Day, but then he'd never been inconspicuous in matters of dress. The reporters from all over the world who had covered his tax trial had filled more columns with his aggressive color combinations than with the fantastic figures unspooling from the witness stand (telephone bills in 1929, $3,141.40; rug for the house on Prairie Avenue, $3,500; twenty-three suits and three topcoats purchased from Marshall Field's in 1927 and 1928, $3,715; meals, entertainment, and valet service at the Metropole and Lexington hotels during that same period, $12,000–$15,000 a week).

He carried a cane with a tapering ebony shaft, a silver tip, and a carved ivory handle, undoubtedly elephant ivory. A swell cane, Vasco thought, coasting up the driveway; very Boul' Mich', as they used to say in Chicago; but a cane just the same. However sportily he hooked it in the crook of his arm, he could lean on it if he had to, and that was the story on what had happened to Scarface Al Brown.

Vasco coasted the Model T to a stop behind the Lincoln and set the brake. Capone was turned away from him and paid no attention to the ratcheting sound or the tockity-tock of the motor at idle. (In earlier days, cracking one's gum would have sent him diving to the pavement.) Having beaten his brother-in-law to the car by three steps, he was glaring at him impatiently, waiting for him to open the door to the rear passenger's seat.

"No green?"

Capone jumped and swung around, his face flushing the color of his suit under its frosting of powder, then returning to its normal swarthy shade as he recognized Vasco. He smiled the same distracted smile he'd given to photographers on the steps of the federal courthouse and showed him a roll of greenbacks from his pocket. It was the size of an artichoke, with the corners of the bills curling around the thick rubber band that bound it. For the first time, Vasco fully understood why some people called cash lettuce.

Danny reached the ground. "Al, you shouldn't take those steps like a kid. I'd have all kinds of people to answer to if you broke your neck."

"Don't be a cunt. Where the hell's Mae? It's her fucking holiday, for chrissake. It was Columbus Day I wouldn't keep her waiting."

He sounded like Ralph, the chronically irritated. This must have been what he was like when he worked himself up to a poisonous rage over the latest O'Donnell atrocity or when Eliot Ness paraded his own confiscated beer trucks past his offices in the Lexington. That the rage was impotent now did nothing to stem it; Vasco imagined it only made things worse.

"She's packing up dinner. She'll be along in a minute." Danny smiled at Vasco. "Happy St. Paddy's, Father. I don't guess them Cubans held you at Redemption with shillelaghs this day." He was clear-eyed in crisp serge, hatless. His curls were coppery in the late-morning sun. Vasco marveled over how a man could drink so heavily, presumably every night, and face the day as bright as his hair.

"Father Kyril has things in hand. Seeing you there Sunday was a nice surprise. I'm sorry you couldn't stay to visit." They'd left right after the service; much to his relief. Vasco, the Capones, and Kyril all in the same place were enough on its own to disturb a man's day of rest without awkward conversation at the door.

"Al got ants in his pants."

"I can't sit still no more in a public place." Capone was calm; a curtain seemed to have dropped on his anxiety. He wore his pale yellow hat in the standard Snorky fashion, the brim turned up on one side and down on the other, casting his scars in shadow.

"*Don Giovanni* came to town last month. I sent Danny to reserve a box, had the tux cleaned and pressed, bought a new shirt and studs. Left before the end of the first act. Never thought I'd ever walk out on the opera."

"I never thought I'd walk in on one," Danny said. "They sing when they're stabbed. I don't get it."

"You might if you left that flask home once in a while."

Vasco changed the subject. "It was good to see you there, anyway."

"My idea," Capone said. "I like to watch a man at his work. If I knew all you were going to do was pass the cup, I'd've fired up the boat and went fishing."

No one pointed out that the boat was long gone.

"I was happy to have any part at all. The church wasn't exactly falling apart when I came."

"You look good in a dress, I'll say that. What's she doing, butchering the cow?" He had a diamond-and-platinum watch in his palm, attached to his vest by a heavy chain. The timepiece was as thin as a communion wafer.

"'Tis herself." Danny pointed his chin up the porch steps, leaning heavily on the brogue.

Mae was descending, carrying a large picnic basket made of brown and tan interlaced strips, with bentwood handles. She wore a light green suit whose material rippled in the breeze toward shore and shoes and hat to match, the hat an upended felt basin that protected her fair skin from the sun. The skirt was split at the knee, showing a well-shaped leg sheathed in sheer nylon; no coconut oil and drawn-on seams for the First Lady of the Outfit.

Rose followed her a step behind. The pretty maid was wearing a cream-colored jacket over a white blouse tucked into a brown pleated skirt, all of which complemented toffee skin, with brown-and-white saddle shoes and a broad-brimmed white straw hat with a brown swag band. She carried two purses, a large woven straw bag and a green clutch that obviously belonged to Mae, who carried the picnic basket in both hands. Rose looked very fresh, like the lemon-soap scent Vasco had come to associate with her whenever she appeared, and very young. She smiled shyly when she saw him. He must have made a good impression a week ago when he drove her home.

A much more pungent odor issued from the basket when the wind shifted, one that reminded him of the community hall at St. Francis on other St. Patrick's Days, of garlic and grease and boiled cabbage.

"Jesus." Capone pinched his nose between thumb and forefinger. "What's that, fertilizer?"

"You know very well what it is, Al, and stop taking the Lord's name in vain." Mae was snappy. "Do we have to have this same conversation every year?"

"Well, I ain't riding with that stink. Put it in the trunk."

"I will *not* put food in that dirty trunk."

"That's an insult to Danny. He keeps that car cleaner'n Miami General."

Mae smiled tightly at Vasco. "Good morning, Father. Don't you look nice."

He'd had his suit cleaned and pressed and his hat steamed and blocked. "Thank you. You look wonderful." The last time they'd spoken, she'd threatened his life in the confessional.

"I mean it. That stuff goes in the car, I take a cab."

"Well, we can't ask Brownie. We gave him the day off."

Vasco said, "I'll be happy to take it in the Ford."

"It's top-heavy. I'd hate to have it tip over and ruin Church property." She turned to the maid. "Rose? I'm sorry to ask. You're a guest."

"I don't mind, Missus, if the Reverend's not tired of me riding with him."

"And here I thought we could all go together." Mae exhaled. Her face was shiny despite makeup. She looked like a woman who'd been cooking all morning. "Father, I'm afraid we're the worst kind of Good Samaritan."

He took the basket from her without another word. Rose gave Mae back her purse and Vasco helped the girl aboard the Model T. She set her bag on the floorboards at her feet, took the basket he handed her, and set it on her lap, folding down the handles and resting her hands on top.

"There," Mae said. "Happy, Al?"

"Peachy."

"Let's get this show on the road. We may make it there by Easter." Danny opened the door of the Lincoln for Mae and Al.

When Vasco got in beside Rose, she leaned over quickly, then back. The kiss was over so fast he only felt it as a moist memory on his cheek. He glanced up through the windshield apprehensively, but the Lincoln was already rolling. No one had seen.

"That's for what you said to Mrs. Capone. She's done something nice for me every day this week. That's why I'm invited to dinner."

He'd almost forgotten the penance he'd given Mae. "I'm sure she would have in any case, or she wouldn't have told you what I said. She said you didn't deserve such harsh words."

"I did, though. I knocked Mr. Capone's favorite elephant off the mantel when I was dusting. I broke off the trunk." He wondered if it was the one Diamond Jim Colosimo had given him or the one Machine Gun Kelly had made for him in Alcatraz.

"Anyone can have an accident."

"We're all supposed to keep from upsetting him. He was taking his nap, and Brownie did a good job fixing it with airplane glue, so maybe he won't notice, but I felt bad anyway. I'd've been just as mad."

He let out the clutch and accelerated. Danny was halfway down the driveway, overlooking the fact that Vasco didn't have directions to Sonny's house. "Hail Marys and Acts of Contrition are appropriate for most things, but they don't always address the injured party. That's just common sense. There's no need to thank me."

"Wanted to, though."

The Lincoln waited at the first stop sign while he caught up. Mae must have said something. But he'd been grateful for the distraction of pushing to keep it in sight. That friendly peck lingered longer than Sharon Baumgartner's lipstick.

"I shouldn't have done that, I guess."

"It didn't do any harm, but as I said, it was unnecessary." They were moving again now.

"My mother says things are the way they are and a person shouldn't try to change them. But if nobody ever tries, they'll go on being the way they are forever."

"What did she say to that?"

"I didn't say it, I just think it. She'd smack me if I said it. She'd say it's for my own good. They lynch folks down here for less."

"What does your mother do?"

"She don't do nothing. Doesn't do anything, I mean. She used to clean a doctor's office, but then some drugs went missing from a locked cabinet and now she can't get work. I pay the rent and my uncle Zack sends money when he can. He makes tracer bullets up in Detroit. Detroit," she corrected herself. "I'm taking a correspondence course in grammar. I'll be in service the rest of my life I don't quit talking like a plantation nigger."

"I've never liked that word."

"It helps if you say it before somebody else does."

They turned onto the causeway, tires singing. A fisherman stood on the pedestrian walkway on the other side of the steel rail, casting his line far out over the water, the thin nylon filament catching the sun briefly, a thread of molten silver, before the lure at the end splashed down. He was shirtless in baggy shorts like Paul Vasco wore, but thickset, with hair graying on his brown back and a long-billed cap worn at a rakish tilt. In a general way he resembled Ernest Hemingway, who at last report was in Europe covering the war. Vasco remembered Paul's story about taking the writer out on his boat, Hemingway hurling streams of .45-caliber bullets at sharks. *A tommy pulls to the left and up.* Paul had credited Jack McGurn with this wisdom. If his son didn't believe that story, he had another. In his wildest imaginings he'd never have thought Al Capone would be easier to crack than Paul Vasco.

The sunburned and silver-haired toll man—Mae had said his name was Henry—recognized him and smiled, tipping his head toward the departing Lincoln. "He said it again. I'll never get to be mayor being honest. You get that new spare, Father?"

"Not yet." He held out a dime.

Henry shook his head. "Al paid. You better get that spare. Florida just *looks* like Paradise."

"I will." He pocketed the coin.

"My sister says thanks for the ham."

"Does she still think I'm a minister and not a priest?"

"When it came down to it I couldn't lie. You know what? She didn't care. 'Meat's meat,' that's what she said. I think it wouldn't matter to her if it came from an atheist. She's changed. This war." He shook his head and waved him through. He hadn't lowered the gate behind the Lincoln.

"Didn't look over at me once," Rose said as it descended behind them. "You really gave him a ham?"

"I bought it to give to Brownie, but then the meat express came steaming along headed for the house. I thought Henry would appreciate it more. He changed a tire for me on my way to the party."

"Two things rednecks know how to do is change tires and gripe about a war they're not even fighting in."

The Lincoln turned right, heading north. A window in back opened and part of the Capone profile leaned out under the yellow hat brim. Something small, pale, and shapeless made an arc and landed in weeds. The chewing schedule seemed to be Dentyne during the day, Sen-Sen at night. "What are your plans after you graduate?"

"Graduate? Oh, the correspondence course. They mail a diploma, I don't get to wear a cap and gown. I'm saving up for secretarial school. There should be plenty of openings after the men get back and the women go home."

"You seem to have your life all mapped out."

"It isn't hard. It's type and take dictation or scrub floors or marry some good-for-nothing that stays out all night and then comes home and slaps me around."

She sounded matter-of-fact. He wondered about her childhood—there had been no mention, during this ride or the one before, of a father—and if it was as bad as or worse than his, and if so how she managed not to sound bitter about her choices.

It was a plain saltbox house, not at all palatial even by Hoover's standards of measuring the homes of gangsters and their spawn, in a well-kept residential neighborhood on Tenth Avenue in the city's Northeast section. A shiny red tricycle stood on a lawn shaggy with clippings that smelled as if it had been cut that morning. Vasco eased into the curb and stopped. The Lincoln took up most of the driveway behind a white Nash sedan. He got out and took the basket from Rose before helping her down.

"You're a guest," she protested.

"So are you, don't forget."

Capone was out of the car before Danny had the door open on Mae's side. Vasco thanked him for paying his toll. Capone looked surprised. "Forget it, Padre. I skip dimes across the bay."

Inside there were overlapping greetings and hugs and cooking smells; apparently Mae's monopoly didn't extend to side dishes. A little girl about two years old in a blue dress and matching ribbon in her dark hair took Vasco's hat and carried it away, dragging the brim on the floor. Another girl in a pink jumpsuit stood gripping the bars of a playpen, gravely watching the proceedings. She was a strawberry blonde, what hair she'd managed to grow in her first year, with an enormous forehead.

"Sorry we're late." Capone embraced Sonny and broke off with two slaps on his back. "Your mother thinks she's feeding every Mick in Florida."

"You mean there are others?" His son grinned the Snorky grin. He wore a light cardigan, pleated slacks, loafers, and a green tie on a white shirt with his hearing aid clipped to the pocket. "Hello, Father. Welcome, Rose."

"Thank you, Mr. Albert. Can I help in the kitchen?"

"Certainly not." Mae's voice came from a room down the hall. She'd relieved Vasco of the basket and bustled off.

"Albert, I'll disown you if you let her anywhere near this room."

"Father, this is my wife, Ruth."

He accepted a slender hand belonging to a wiry woman in her early twenties, an authentic redhead freckled even more severely than Danny. Diana Ruth Capone (so she was identified in her father-in-law's file) looked tomboyish with her hair cut short in the style that had begun to take over since women reported to work in defense plants among machinery that reached out and snatched at anything long and loose. She had a firm grip, a tight smile, and cynical eyes. "Albert's told me so much about you. You half-Irish are thick as thieves."

He couldn't tell if there was irony in the statement.

"The Italians have much to answer for," he said. "Where do Irishmen go to marry?"

Her voice slid into a brogue. "Back to Ireland, and it serves them right for waiting till they're thirty." She turned to Mae's brother. "Uncle Dan, we've got a surprise."

"Hello, Daniel."

Danny turned toward the new speaker, standing in the doorway to a small living room off the entry. His smile broke wide; Vasco hadn't thought there was any room for expansion. "Winnie!" He lumbered forward to throw his arms around a tall woman in a mannish-looking blouse and tweed skirt cut for a traveling suit inappropriate to the climate. Winifred Coughlin, Danny's wife, away visiting a relative until today.

"The streetcar dropped her off an hour ago," Ruth said.

"She went right to work in the kitchen. I couldn't stop her."

"I'm married to a man in the restaurant business." Winnie kissed him and pulled back to hold his face with a hand on each cheek. "There wasn't any point going to Palm Island—I knew you'd all be here soon. How much have you been drinking?"

"Not a drop today."

"And not a drop more until sundown. You can celebrate then."

"Aye-aye, sir." The smile flickered.

"Pleased to meet you, Father. I hope you can put up with this zoo." Her handshake was mannish, like her fashion choice and long square jaw; one pump, then release. An athletic type. He could picture her in riding habit on some English green.

"It's refreshing. I come from a small family myself."

"What can I get you to drink, Peter: We have wine, beer, lemonade, and iced tea."

He surprised Sonny by choosing wine. It was all very dizzying and he'd welcome the calming effect.

"This bunch would drive Billy Sunday to drink." Winnie's smile fell short of her eyes.

THE DINING ROOM WAS THE LARGEST ON THE GROUND FLOOR, AND PROBA-bly in the house, but it was barely large enough to contain a table with all its leaves in place and six people seated around it, the little girl in a high chair between her mother and grandmother, who took turns helping her eat and mopping her off. Sonny had dragged the playpen to the door opening onto the entry, where the younger daughter sat with a baby bottle and rubber blocks. Ruth sat to

Vasco's left, with Al and Sonny at either end, Al with his napkin tucked in his collar. Dennis Day sang ballads in his silver tenor on a phonograph in the living room; Sonny got up only once to change records.

"Automatic changer," he told Vasco when he returned to his chair. "Anniversary gift from Mother and Dad. Great tone. I never got all the good out of one before."

Capone said, "Come a long way from a crank-up Victrola. In the old days we had to work at resting. I bet all you do at that air depot is push buttons all day."

"That's right, Dad. I sprain a finger, we don't eat."

He asked Vasco to say grace.

"Thank you, dear Lord, for these Thy blessings which we are about to receive. . . ."

"Amen."

"Sonny, pass the wine."

Mae said, "Al, you still have some in your glass."

"I need to kill the taste of this Irish lasagna."

"Once a year, Al, corned beef and cabbage. I've put up with spaghetti three times a week for twenty-five years."

"Well, you can wash it down with all the wine you want."

"Dr. Phillips—"

"Phillips is full of shit."

The girl in the high chair looked up, cabbage on her bib. "Gamps said shit. Get the Bible."

"The children, Al."

"Yeah. Sorry."

Gamps Capone, apologizing for saying a bad word. Vasco poked at his corned beef, sympathizing. His mother had served it every St. Patrick's Day until she got too ill to cook. He'd never developed a taste for it, although he didn't mind cabbage. Mae had boiled it short of turning it into mush, a blessing. There were boiled potatoes and green beans and biscuits from Ruth's kitchen and, for dessert, pistachio ice cream.

Sonny smiled at Vasco, winked. "Ask me who made the ice cream."

"Who made the ice cream?"

"Sealtest, I think."

"*I* make ice cream!" shouted the little girl in the high chair. The Capone quick burn darkened her features.

"Shush!" Ruth's finger flew to her lips, eyes flashing danger.

"I finished up, but those first three cranks were the hard part," Sonny said, reaching across his wife to chuck the girl under the chin.

Capone said, "Swear to God, I eat one more green thing I'll sprout leaves."

"The Lord's name, Al."

"Mea culpa."

Danny looked longingly at the decanter of red wine and sipped his coffee. Who's up for cribbage?"

It was another game Vasco didn't know how to play, but as the four women cleared the table, Sonny drew a pack of cards and a square pegboard from the top drawer of a small bureau used as a sideboard and volunteered to partner him, teaching him the rules as the game progressed. He kept their score on the board while Danny kept score for himself and Capone, his partner. Capone played with concentration, showing no trace of the confusion he'd shown over pinochle and poker the week before. (Was the penicillin reversing the symptoms of the disease after all? Vasco couldn't credit Mae's theory that his presence in the gangster's life had had any positive effect: that would be the betrayal of all betrayals, second only to Judas'.) When he disapproved of Danny's strategy he cursed softly under his breath, out of earshot of the two-year-old, who had joined her sister in the playpen, rebuilding the world with rubber blocks.

"You miss Chicago, Padre?" He placed two cards in the end of the board nearest Sonny, who was dealing.

He thought, staring at his hand. "I miss the noise, especially at night. I have trouble sleeping when it's quiet." He spoke the truth. The relative peace of the District at end of day, as compared to Chicago and Cicero, all those brawny flexations day and night, steel shrieking against steel, Klaxons braying, had not prepared him for a city that seemed to shut down at sunset, at least in wartime. Redemption was too far from the waterfront for the sound of surf to reach his monk's cell, and in any case that sound was too organic, a half-human exhalation of pent-up breath: and when the streetcars stopped ringing their bells for the evening, the silence thundered.

"Me, too. I hear that damn foghorn, I sit up in a cold sweat. I think I'm back in Alcatraz and just dreamed I was out. I thought Brooklyn was noisy, but Chicago's like one of them artillery bombardments you hear about in Europe: boom, boom, boom, hour after hour, till you think one more boom, you crack to pieces. Then it stops, and then, boy, you crack. Only in Chicago it never does. First time I met Diamond Jim I said—"

"Two for his nibs." Sonny turned up the top card of the deck, the jack of clubs.

"I said, first time I met Diamond Jim—"

Sonny raised his voice. "Your turn, Danny."

"Sure." Danny played a card.

Capone looked up, nodded. He understood he'd strayed into forbidden territory. "It's a good town, Padre. You and I ought to go back for a visit sometime. I'll show you parts of the city you never knew was there."

"It's a long train ride, Dad."

"Doc Phillips says there's no reason I can't travel. I'm getting better all the time."

"A few minutes ago you said Phillips was full of shit."

"Sonny, the girls!" Ruth's voice snapped from the kitchen.

"Sorry, dear."

"Everybody makes sense sometimes, even doctors." Capone laid his hand faceup on the table. "Straight flush."

Danny said, "Cribbage, Al."

Sonny gathered in all the cards. "The Cubs game starts in ten minutes. You like baseball, Peter?"

"I do, but I'm feeling stuffed. I can use some fresh air." Bloated was the word. He was growing fat on Florida.

Capone said, "I'm in. That cabbage stink makes me sick."

"I always thought it tasted better than it smelled." Danny poured contraband wine into his water glass. "I guess I'm a lousy Irishman when you come down to it."

Sonny said, "You and Dad get comfortable on the porch. Danny and I have a bet on the game. Cubs win, I wash the Lincoln for a month."

"What if they lose?" Vasco asked.

"They never lose when I have money on them."

"Sonny's right," Capone said. "He's got the touch, not like his old man. I bet the one horse on the track don't have hoof-and-mouth, it trips and breaks its neck in the stretch."

As they rose, Sonny leaned close and murmured in Vasco's ear. "Keep your voices down. Danny can't be trusted because of booze."

A small screened porch opened off the back of the house, whitewashed wicker chairs with flowered cushions and a weathered rug that had taken on the contours of the planks beneath. A board fence kept the small backyard private from neighbors and there was a beach smell of salt air and mildew, a not-unpleasant change from the stuffy cooking odors inside.

Capone sat and unbuttoned his vest, releasing the first installment on the belly of palmier days, built on oysters and pasta and gallons of wine. He glanced back at the screen door to the house, then slipped a leather case from his inside breast pocket with his initials hand-tooled on it. It looked as if it had been designed to hold a miniature double-barreled shotgun. He pulled it apart in two sections and drew out a cigar. He stuck the cigar in his mouth, put the case back together and returned it to its pocket, and patted the others.

"Got a light, Padre?"

"I don't smoke. I'm sorry."

"Well, they taste almost as good when you chew 'em." He winked, grinning around the obstruction in the corner of his mouth. It pulled his face out of line as if it were sculpted from soft clay. "I knew it was cribbage we were playing. I never liked the game, but it's Danny's favorite, so I figured a way out that wouldn't hurt his feelings. You can get away with plenty when everyone thinks you're bugs. Winnie wears the pants in that family. I feel bad for Danny when she's around. She made him a souse. What do you miss most about Chicago, after the noise?"

"I shouldn't say it after you fed me so well, but I'd have to say the food."

"Yeah?"

"Definitely. Italian, Irish, Polish, kosher, even Chinese. Made *by* Italians, Irish, Polish, Jews, and Chinese. I doubt you could do better even in the countries they came from."

"Tell you something about them Chinks. You can insult them, their wives, their kids, and their ancestors, they won't spit in your food. Lop off your head with a hatchet, but they'll never dishonor the trade." He masticated the end of his cigar. "The food's up there, all right, no doubt about it. You couldn't beat the menu at the Metropole. Steaks thick as manhole covers, you could leave your teeth home and still eat the veal. Only reason I pulled up stakes and moved to the Lex is the Met started going downhill in '28. I stepped on a roach so big one day the Moran gang could've used it to smuggle six sticks of dynamite into my suite."

Vasco felt the low hum of excitement that preceded an extended Capone trip down memory lane; it tingled in the soles of his feet like a motor starting up. "What do you miss most about Chicago?"

Capone took the cigar out of his mouth and glanced again at the door. Then he put back the cigar and winked again. "The girls, Padre. What else?"

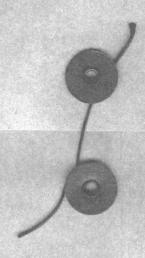

THE CONFESSIONS OF AL CAPONE

January–March 1920

**Compiled from Transcripts
by Special Agent P. Vasco Division 5 FBI File #44/763**

EIGHTEEN

I FELL FOR CHICAGO BANG OFF THE TRAIN. BROOKLYN WAS BIG, BUT IT DIDN'T feel big, all cut up into little countries the way it was: Polacks here, Jews there, Micks over there, even the Italians sorted themselves into Sicilian and Neapolitan and Calabrese neighborhoods and you stuck out like a boil if you weren't from there. Chicago was big. Everything about it was big and fast and loud and it didn't stand still for a second. You could feel the trains rumbling under your feet like you were standing on top of an ocean and then they shot out of the ground and a minute later there they were over your head, racketing along seven stories up and then going into a hairpin turn right in the middle of the shopping district, what they called the Loop, the wheels screeching and spraying sparks that rained down on you like welding arcs, you saw the inside wheels lift right off the rails and the cars leaned out and you always thought they were going to fall off this time but they never did. We could've used one or two of those brass-balled motormen when we went to war with the North Side, but I guess they thought that was too tame.

Every other car on the street was red-topped or yellow or checkered, and I think if I had it to do again I'd go into the taxi business. It was just as crooked as the rackets but none of the men that ran the companies ever went to jail. There always seemed to be an election coming up: You saw gasbags in derbies and toppers waving their arms on platforms in the parks and yelling through megaphones in touring cars with the tops down and somebody's name on a banner on the side. And you saw girls everywhere on the sidewalks wearing clothes you only saw in magazines back East, hats with feathers and dresses they had to wiggle into like socks and strings of pearls you could rope and hog-tie them with if you could only catch up to them, because they broke from the gate like quarter horses. Beautiful girls in powder and paint. Not much up top—titties had went out of style, though I don't know where they went—but nice little asses, you could palm both cheeks in one hand.

The place stunk big too, all that burning coal and the stockyards right there in the middle where most cities put their statues and playgrounds. On a hot day in July it smelled like a buffalo took a bloody dump right under your nose.

Anyway there it was, all those brick warehouses and cattle pens and a thousand miles of railroad track and tall buildings like church steeples jammed in cheek-by-jowl on a lake the size of Florida, and all of it run by a half-dozen smart guys: Deanie O'Banion with his North Side muscle: Mike Merlo, president of the Unione Siciliane, what now they are calling the Mafia; two ward heelers, a little squirt named Kenna they called Hinky Dink and a fat blowhard looked like Major Hoople with a walrus moustache, Bathhouse John Coughlin was his moniker because he started out working in a Turkish bath: Mike da Pike Heitler, a big-time pimp: and Diamond Jim Colosimo. In the prime of life, all of them, and all dead in four years, except Heitler, who lasted ten, and Kenna and Coughlin, who lived to get old. You can't kill a politician with a stick.

Everybody liked Jim, even people who wanted him in the ground. He weighed at least three hundred, but he had teensy feet, so he always looked like he was trying to sneak up on you on tiptoe: back-slapping his way through his cafe, all those tables shoved together, he was like the *Queen Mary* going through the Soo Locks. He slicked his hair and waxed his moustache and wore sack suits and white shirts with elephants on them. First time we met I said, "Mr. Colosimo, I never thought I'd see anybody louder than Chicago." He had a big laugh, big like he was. He said, "Diamond Jim to you, Alphonse." He's the only one ever called me Alphonse outside of my mother and my teachers and Father Garofalo, who baptized me. "You like elephants, Alphonse?" And he gave me my first, hand-carved in Africa from genuine elephant ivory. It's still on my mantel. It brought me more luck than it ever did him. But I'm getting ahead of the story.

Johnny Torrio met us at Union Station, with a teddy bear for Sonny and a bottle of Evening in Paris for Mae, all wrapped up in gold foil and tissue from Marshall Field's, and didn't he look like a million in a camel's hair Chesterfield with a white silk scarf around his neck and a brown homburg. You'd've thought he ran Standard Oil. He leads us out to a limousine parked in a red zone at the curb. Diamond Jim owned two, and this one was imported all the way from England, with the steering wheel on the wrong side and the driver sitting in a sort of cockpit up front, separate from the passengers with nothing to keep the rain off him but his hat. This driver wore a swell uniform with brass buttons and puffy pants and high shiny boots like a lion tamer. When we were rolling Johnny spoke to him through a black tube on a hose he blew into to get his attention. Johnny tipped the redcap a buck for wheeling out our luggage. I gave the guy at Grand Central a quarter. Right then and there I decided to start tipping bills instead of coins, and I never backed off from that decision: ten-spots to hatcheck girls, C-notes to waiters and bartenders; working stiffs. They paid back plenty in friendly service, the best tables, no waiting. It was my first lesson in doing business in Chicago.

What I saw on that drive, busted glass glittering on sidewalks and in gutters; acres of it, street after street, clerks and bartenders with coats on over long aprons sweeping up the pieces and not making much headway. I thought it was window glass. I heard about tornadoes rubbing out jerkwater towns in the Midwest and asked Johnny if they really hit in big cities. He made that dry chuckle of his, like stirring dead leaves. "No, Al, it was Hurricane Andy hit yesterday. Andrew Volstead?" That's when I remembered the Volstead Act went into effect at one minute past midnight that morning. All that glass was from people dropping armloads of bottles from liquor stores and bars, drugstores, getting careless in their hurry to stock the pantry before the whole country went dry from Prohibition.

I said, "What happens when they run out?"

"That's the reason I brought you out here. You think I think you couldn't hold your own against a couple of Micks because you beat up one of their own in Brooklyn?"

I didn't know what he meant. Gosh, was I dumb. But I knew better than to ask, because when Johnny screwed that little smile on his face you knew he'd buttoned up tight. You waited until he decided the time was right.

He had us set up at the Metropole, six-room suite bigger than Mae's parents' house back on Third Place, which I turned into my base of operations after we bought the house on Prairie Avenue. He left us to unpack, then sent back the car to take us to Colosimo's Cafe on South Wabash. Dinner to welcome us to town, the driver said. Mae begged off. She was tired from the trip and Sonny was fussing. "Have a good time, and try not to be too late."

It's night now, and there's a real nut-cutter blasting off the lake with pieces of ice in it. I'm wishing on my way to the car I had a good coat like Johnny's. God put the wind there, I figure, to blow away the stockyard stink, but He could lay off in January. There's a blanket in the backseat and I don't mind saying I wrapped myself up in it like a little old lady. The heater in that secondhand Nash of Sonny's is better than anything we had in those days, limo or otherwise.

We get to the place, which is not in a good area of town, what they called the Levee, where all the Deadly Vices are on display and have been ever since the big fire, but it's all lit up like the Woolworth Building, with COLOSIMO'S spelled out in big copper letters across the front of the ground floor and also in flashing electric bulbs up and down a sign attached to the upper stories. I sprint across the wind and push in through a gold-plated door.

"Surprise!"

I near pissed my pants. The whole joint's in evening duds—men in stiff shirts, women in beaded dresses, with me in my best brown suit, also my only suit—and they're all on their feet, drinks in their hands, shouting surprise and singing, "For He's a Jolly Good Fellow." I was so wound up from the trip and my big opportunity I forgot it was my twenty-first birthday. But Johnny hadn't. He set up the whole thing.

He sticks a glass in my hand, slaps me on the back, asks if I was really surprised. I say, "What do you think?" and show him my rod, which if it hadn't caught in the lining of my coat, the city would've had the first of its splashy funerals four months early.

Johnny's nose went white around the nostrils. The rough stuff made him sick, which in order to understand him you had to understand how he did business. The whole reason Diamond Jim called him out there from New York was he got tired of Black Handers putting the arm on him for protection. He paid them off a couple of times, but when they got to be a nuisance he went to family. Johnny was a blood cousin to Jim, which if you came from the Old Country was as close as a brother, and he had a reputation for settling disputes that couldn't be settled peaceably with a simple demonstration of muscle; just enough to back anybody else off from getting ideas, but not enough to start a war. It's like blowing a whiff of pepper up a drunk's nose to sober him up. Only Johnny always got somebody else to do it, because he himself was allergic to pepper.

The way Johnny told it, he set up a money drop with three of these punks under a railroad bridge at midnight, and when they came out to pick it up, they got four barrels of buckshot instead. It was two boys from Brooklyn behind the shotguns, Joe D'Andrea and Mack Fitzpatrick. Johnny mixed the gangs; he was a pioneer that way. I followed his example when I brought in Jake Guzik to keep the books. You can't beat a Jew when it comes to numbers.

So this night at Jim's he takes me aside and says, "Listen to the advice of an old man: Hire some gorilla to carry your rod for you. That way they might put you in jail, but they'll never hang you." It was good advice, but I couldn't take it. Times were changing. In 1928 my pal Patsy Lolordo caught a slug in the head on account of his bodyguards went for a walk. When push comes to shove the only thing you can depend on is a gun in your hand.

What a night! A band, champagne, mounds of linguini, and piles of pastrami on rye, they had this stage that came up out of the floor on hydraulic lifts with cute little girls in their undies wriggling on top of it to the music. I had Diamond Jim's elephant in my pocket, bringing me luck already, and Johnny made the rounds introducing me. O'Banion impressed me at first. His tux fit him like a second skin—with special pockets, I found out later, sewn in to carry the three guns he never went without—and a fresh carnation from his own shop in his lapel. He had the cleanest hands I ever saw, pink with white nails; they spent a lot of time in potting soil and he washed them six or seven times a day.

Deanie wore a built-up shoe on one foot because that leg was short, but he still limped, so what he did, he picked out a spot and stood there all night and shook hands with everybody who came up, with his left hand in the side pocket of his coat with a piece of artillery in it. They said he killed twenty-five men, maybe fifty tidying up the North Side, let's figure ten, it still don't make him the choir boy he said he used to be, but I say it was that trick of his of standing still and letting the world come to him that got him his reputation as a muckety-muck, a man who held court. Truth to tell he looked like a fairy Irish tenor with that pie face and that cat's smile.

There was gambling upstairs, roulette and craps and poker, with a blackboard to clock the horses when they ran anywhere in the country. Dogs, too; they were popular, probably because racing them was illegal, same as booze. Now they're legit no one plays them but widows living on their dead husbands' pensions here in Miami. Colosimo's had girls, too, but I was on my best behavior as to that, because it was clear to me Mae was in cahoots with Johnny on the surprise party or she'd've wished me a happy birthday sometime that day. Wives keep track of all the occasions. But I dumped a couple of hundred at poker, most I ever lost up to then. I didn't have it. I thought I was in Dutch right off the bat, my first day, but then Diamond Jim dropped a hand like a big pillow on my shoulder and said don't worry, my credit's good. Figuring back over the next ten years, I lost ten million trying to win back that two hundred.

Diamond Jim. Let me tell you, back then, you had a nickname, you had it for a reason, not because some newspaper writer thinks "Dingbat" sells more copies than plain John Oberta. Diamond Jim sparkled like a big fat chandelier: brilliants on all his stubby fingers, stuck in his tie, on his cuffs—Christ, on his belt buckle, which is where I got the idea to have such buckles made for my special friends. Johnny said he even carried them loose in his pockets and played with them like rosary beads. I believe it, though I never got to see it. Jim didn't last that long.

When the poker game broke up, Johnny drifted over and sat across the table from me. He had a glass of club soda. I never saw him drink or smoke or show any other vice. Apart from setting up some murders I guess he could pass through the eye of the needle slick as spit. "Having a good time, Al?"

"Swell, Johnny. Swell place. Jim's a swell guy." I was drinking, can you tell? Hell, I was of age, even if the country wasn't anymore.

"Swell's the word. I just wish he wasn't so comfortable."

"You mean fat?"

"Fat is fine. Fat means you have time to eat and drink because your business is in good hands. It inspires confidence. Get fat, Al. I wish I could. I haven't gained a pound in ten years."

I kept my mouth shut. Pressing Johnny was like blowing your horn at a train crossing. The caboose goes by when it's ready. He lined up the shot glasses the other players had left on the table. He picked up the bottle of Scotch I'd been pouring from, John Haig it was called, a very good mellow whisky, it had a fancy shield on the label. "This is prewar," he said. "Jim's been charging two dollars a bottle. This morning in Baltimore it was going for four. I guess someone missed the fire sale yesterday. Six months from now, once everyone's drunk up what they laid in, it'll be twenty-five, if you can get it." He pulled the cork and filled one of the pony glasses. "Yesterday, at the bar, that was ten cents."

I nodded. Everybody knows you charge more by the ounce.

He filled the next glass halfway. "Ten cents today."

Next glass. He just wet the bottom. "Six months from now."

I saw where he was headed, and it threw me for a loop. I'd never paid more than six-bits for a quart in my life. At this rate I wouldn't be able to wet my whistle for less than a buck.

"Jesus, Johnny."

"Let me finish." Now he hauls over the old-fashioned glass I'd been drinking from, fills it to the top. The bottle gurgles four times. When the glass is brimming he sets down the bottle.

"Six months from now. Fifty bucks." He rams in the cork.

"Nobody could afford that."

"John D. Rockefeller maybe, but he can't drink it on account of that guinea pig's stomach they gave him to replace the one he wore full of holes smashing competitors. What we do, we cut it with water, step on it with fusel oil and mineral spirits, brown sugar so it don't taste like we stirred it up in a piss-pot. Understand, we don't start with liquor near as good as this. Nobody'd appreciate it. Come July, Americans will be paying John Haig prices for Old Underdrawers, and glad to get it." He sat back, smiling that old-maid smile. "It's called the law of supply and demand. I read it in a book."

"That's why you brought me here, to sell booze?" My heart was in my socks. I'd thought he wanted a personal bodyguard, or a bouncer in some ritzy joint that made the Harvard Inn look like Joe's Drink and Spew. A crummy salesman?

"Nothing like that. I've got that all lined out with the Genna brothers, who never take no for an answer. I want you to be my partner."

"Partner in what?" I still wasn't getting it. Johnny worked for Colosimo.

He swept his hand around in a circle, taking in all the gaming tables, the blackboard, the waiters trotting in and out carrying glasses and bottles on trays, towels folded over their arms like at Delmonico's in Manhattan. It sure was a class dive. The bar downstairs was solid mahogany carved all over with flying lions and mermaids, hop-dream stuff.

"The cafe?"

"No, not the cafe." He was losing patience with me.

"Chicago, Al. Chicago. The pearl of the Midwest, and half of it's yours."

THERE WASN'T A THING WRONG WITH JIM COLOSIMO THAT BEING LESS SUCcessful wouldn't cure.

A man's pushing fifty, he looks at how far he's come and how far he's got to go, and if he isn't where he hoped to be back when he was twenty he steps on the gas, and if he's farther than he expected, he shifts into neutral and coasts home. Well, Diamond Jim had come as far as an ignorant dago street sweep could expect to come in this land of opportunity and then some.

At ten he shined shoes and picked pockets. At eighteen he had his own stable of girls, but then he went to jail and when he got out he shoveled horseshit for the sanitation department. Now at forty-nine he owned the gaudiest place in town and collected union dues from every whorehouse in Cook County and even elected himself a mayor. He had a library full of books he never read, a hundred kinds of imported cheese in his basement. Caruso came to see him when he was on tour. Two months after I made Jim's acquaintance, he threw over his wife of twenty years and married a chippie. Money, power, respect, flashy wife, he had it all.

Trouble was that's all he wanted. When Prohibition came, Johnny told him he had to get in on it. Jim had a fantastic inventory already, acres of booze, a wine cellar that went on and on like the catacombs in Rome. But he waved it off. "Johnny, why you wear me out? Things are good. New venture, you never know what's-a gonna happen. This thing, it won't last: six months, a year, drinking's legal again, all you got to show for it's a buncha trucks an' a lot of overhead. Let the punks go broke. I'm-a surprise you come to me with this crazy kid stuff."

That was how Johnny put it, that night in the cafe. "I said he wouldn't have to lift a finger, I'd make the arrangements. He said it was beneath my dignity as his *consiglieri*. I collect from the bagmen, who collect from his whores, liquor's beneath my dignity. I pushed. He forbid me. Forbid me." He shook his head. "Jim's my cousin, he's like my uncle. My father; my old man died in Naples when I was two. Jim's got to go."

We're drinking Diamond Jim's liquor, enjoying his hospitality in his own place, Johnny says he's got to go. That's the way of things: The old bull slows down, it's the young bulls' turn, for the good of the herd. But I can see it's tearing Johnny up inside. He was a sensitive man. I reach under the table and squeeze his knee. "Johnny, *mi padrino,* you don't have to do a thing. I'll take care of everything."

His smile is sad, I know what he's thinking: twenty-one-year-old kid, what's he know about setting guys up for a fall? But he don't say that. What he says, "Okay, Al. So long as it isn't beneath your dignity."

I didn't move right away. Things worked slower then in what I like to call peacetime. Diamond Jim has all the connections; we take him out too soon, we lose them. Johnny's just thirty-eight, for all his talk of being an old man, O'Banion's ten years younger—hell, we was all wet behind the ears, it was a young man's racket—and big political wheels like Hinky Dink and Bathhouse John and even that lunkbrain Big Bill Thompson in the mayor's office won't deal with a bunch of hotheaded squirts liable to put everybody's neck in the noose. They have to be nurtured along first, which is Johnny's department. Meanwhile there's meetings to arrange, logistics to work out, like how you going to get the liquor from where it's at, which is Canada and Mexico, to where it's going? That's my part. Johnny was impressed by the way I listened to reason over the Galluccio affair, when my scars were still raw, and my idea of setting up fronts to simmer down the reform crowd. I'm a visionary.

First thing, I stocked an empty storefront on the ground floor of the Four Deuces Club, a Colosimo crib down the street from the cafe, with used furniture I bought for a song, and had cards printed up saying, A. BROWN, ANTIQUE DEALER. That way none of the neighbors asked questions when we started carrying barrels and crates in through the alley door and stored them in back. I had the same thing painted on the cabs of a couple of army surplus trucks, and now we had us a fleet. Then I made a quick trip back to Brooklyn and struck a deal with Frankie Yale to truck in alky from Canada by way of Buffalo. He's already got the New York market nailed down from his office in the Harvard Inn and looking to expand. While I'm there I discuss with him the Diamond Jim situation. Frankie, he liked to keep his hand in; that was his fatal flaw, he wouldn't delegate the gun stuff, and later when his face was too well-known from his picture on all those boxes of cheap cigars he turned to screwing over his partners just for the boot it gave him. But all that's in the future. He's so grateful to Johnny and me for cutting him in on Chicago he volunteers to do the job himself. That's hunky-dory with me; given the time for planning I always preferred to import talent from out of town, because by the time the bodies cool down to room temperature and the cops start nosing around, the heavy lifters are halfway home aboard the train.

"Just say when, Al," he says in that mushmouth voice I have to lean in close to make out the words. "I'm free all next week."

"Too soon, Frankie. I got a million things to set up, and Johnny's still pouring oil on City Hall. I'll ring you up in a couple of months, invite you to Chicago for a visit. How's that?"

"Smooth, Al. I always said you was too smart to spend the rest of your life roping johns into the inn."

I didn't much care for that, his bringing up my days as a pimp. That was Frankie's way of saying he knew me when and don't get too big for your britches. But I let it slide. I had bigger fish to fry.

While I'm busy playing Henry Ford, reinventing the assembly line for the thirsty customer, Johnny's stroking city hall with gifts and hospitality and sitting down with all the other gang leaders over a big map of Chicago and the suburbs. It was in the back room of the Roamer Inn, a crib in which he owned a part interest, and which was run by Harry Guzik, who introduced me to his brother Jake. Jake balanced the accounts and kept the figures in his head, where no hotshot state's attorney could subpoena them. There was O'Banion, them batshit Genna brothers, Terry Druggan and Frank Lake, who ran the Valley Gang, the oldest around, and Joe Saltis and Frankie McErlane, who imported the first tommy gun to Chicago a few years later. All ambitious boys, tough as underboiled spaghetti. The plan was to carve up the territory so nobody had any beef that would lead to a bloodbath and cut into profits. I sat in on a couple of sessions. With a big black pencil and a lot of palaver, Johnny drew lines between the North and South Sides and along Lake Shore Drive and around the stockyards and wrote a gang leader's name on each section. I shut my yap and paid close attention. It was like watching the U.S. and France and England slicing up Europe after the Kaiser took a powder. The only thing missing was the souvenir fountain pens them high-hats handed out after the signing.

Instead, drinks and cigars and handshakes all around, and a free turn upstairs with one of the girls for those who were so inclined, which I bet is what also happened at Versailles, not that you read of it; it was France, after all. Johnny was a genius. Who else could've gotten Micks to sit down with wops and Polacks and iron out a deal that made everybody happy? I did a lot of reading in stir, about how Attila united all the barbarian tribes that had been putting each other on the spot since Judas was a Cub Scout and shook down the Roman Empire for tribute. That Hun had nothing on Gentleman Johnny Torrio, and Johnny dressed better.

A beautiful thing, that peace treaty. It should be under glass like the Constitution and the Declaration of Independence. I almost cry when I think about it.

It had one tiny crack, which broke it apart in the end. Things would've went different if only somebody had thought to invite the O'Donnells to the table.

I thought if trouble started it would be the Gennas behind it. The Terrible Gennas, they were called, and it wasn't an exaggeration. There were six of them, real Stone Age types, ugly as a dog's ass except for Tony, who I think now must've been adopted. Tony, who was the oldest, wore nice suits and manicured his nails, but the others dressed like circus tents in candy-striped shirts and ties with naked girls painted on them, their mama still cut their hair, slap a bowl on their heads and lop off whatever stuck out. I think they bathed every Easter.

They specialized in blowtorches and fingernail extractions, also the double-cross. If the other party didn't wind up with the shitty end of the stick, they figured they'd been cheated. I begged Johnny to cut them out, but he said we needed them because somehow they'd wangled a government license to distribute industrial alcohol, which they used to make needle beer in their warehouse on West Taylor Street and put into circulation in speakeasies where the clientele didn't much care what they was drinking so long as it wasn't that 3.2 piss was still legal. I didn't argue. I was still at the listening stage, learning as I went like everybody else. But I always thought the Gennas was a disaster waiting to happen, and I've never been wrong about predicting something bad. If I could make a buck betting against bad horses, I'd've had enough to buy off Washington back in '31.

There were only four O'Donnells compared to six Gennas, but to look at their record you'd have sworn there were forty. They stuck up banks, broke strikes, cracked safes, and just for fun lobbed pineapples into polling places on election day; I doubt they cared who won, and I'm damn sure none of them ever stood in line to cast a ballot. Whatever side bid highest for their services, that was the side they threw in with. So they were a force to reckon with, but because Spike, the oldest, was in Joliet for walking out of the Stockyards Savings & Trust with twelve thousand in cash and securities, Johnny figured they were without a leader and that any alliance he made with them was shaky. Meanwhile his brothers were running errands to make ends meet and waiting on a pardon for Spike that nobody thought had a snowball's chance in hell.

But for the moment all the included parties were pleased as pigs in shit. The wonder of it all was that all this was going on right under Diamond Jim's nose and against his express orders, but he was too busy porking his child bride and fingering his diamonds like they was his testicles to notice; which pretty much sums up the general lack of attention to his best interests that had signed his death warrant. The politicians were turning our way, but Johnny was too savvy to jump the gun, as it were, so he let Colosimo simmer in his own fat while he tended to the finer details.

One of which was my dress and deportment.

We was sitting in the cafe, digesting a heap of clams that would go straight to my belly and right on through Johnny, me drinking Chianti, him ginger ale. I'd just handed him a list of the neighborhood speaks that were in line for our first shipment from New York, which had put that prim little smile on his face that if he was Diamond Jim would be a big old smothery bear hug and a cigar big around as your wrist. Suddenly he scoops a roll of C-notes out of his pocket and plunks it down on the table with a splat like old cabbage. "Al, I want you to go to the men's department at Marshall Field's and ask for Sam Levy. Tell him Johnny Torrio sent you and wants him to dress you skin out. On second thought, I'll go with you. People know you're working with me, so it's a personal embarrassment to have you walking around looking like you do."

So I get done over. Levy's a dried-up little Jew with a potbelly, born with his vest unbuttoned and a tape measure dangling around his neck, and by the time he's through with me he knows more about me than my doctor. Johnny's there telling him what's needed special, like a double-stitched pocket for my rod since it's obvious I'm not going to trust it to a flunky like he said I should, and extra room there so it don't stick out like a goiter. Then Levy asks me a question I don't understand. "Dress right or left?" Which is when I found out that the side your cock hangs down on is very important to tailors. I turned red when it's explained.

"Pick one," Johnny tells him. "He'll make the adjustment."

I start off with four suits, two for winter, two for summer, one of each in black for funerals—I got a lot of mileage out of those in just my first five years—a snappy yellow gabardine for ball games and the track and a charcoal with a gay purple pinstripe for business meetings. I threw away my old brown hat and picked out a Panama and a straw boater for after Memorial Day and a pearl-gray borsalino for after Labor Day, and some swell shoes, wingtips and spectators in Italian glove leather. A dozen silk shirts in all colors and a different necktie for each. I came out of the final fitting farting through silk drawers, a new man. To this day I'm down in the dumps, I call up Jack Sewell there on East Flagler and order a new suit for every season.

According to Johnny I am now okay on the outside, but it takes more than a few bolts of cloth to turn a boy from Navy Street into Boul' Mich' material. He loaded me up on library books by Emily Post and whatnot, drilled me on which fork to use with each course, how to introduce people to each other, to ask pardon when I burped, and not to burp. He hired an elocutionist from the University of Chicago to hold a lighted match up to my lips when I said "teapot" and "pretty birdie" until I could do it without blowing out the flame. This same elocutionist, who wears white gloves and travels with throat spray, teaches me also when to say "don't" and "doesn't" and not to drop my g's and to eschew all slang. That's what he said, "eschew." I want to say gesundheit but I know it won't go over so I don't. Most of this took, though when I get tired or careless I forget and take grammar for a one-way ride, and of course you can't do business with mugs like Schemer Drucci and Nails Morton without using the lingo of the trade. But I can talk with reporters and judges and bishops without humiliating myself, and I've got Johnny to thank for that.

Now we've got all the routes set up, the gangs on board, Scarface Al Brown shining like a nugget in a goat's ass, and the politicians so eager for all that graft I'm half-surprised they don't gun Diamond Jim themselves, Johnny says make the call. It's May, Jim's had two months of wedded bliss with his showgirl. He's back a week now from his honeymoon in French Lick, Indiana, where there's a spa, all the swells go there, soak out all the poisons. Get 'em when they're happy, I say. State of grace.

Frankie answers on the first ring, like he's been waiting by the phone since February. "How's chances you passing through my neck of the woods anytime soon?" I say.

"Sure thing, Al. Tomorrow?"

I check the page-a-day calendar on Johnny's desk. May 10, 1920. "Four o'clock."

Johnny watches me hang up. "That's it?"

"That's it."

"All those elocution lessons, fourteen words." He shakes his head. "I knew I made the right decision when I sent you those train tickets."

Which for me is like getting a medal from the pope. The next day Frankie calls the Roamer Inn from Union Station. He knows the time and place, he didn't miss the train. I work the hook and start to dial Diamond Jim at home. Johnny reaches over and breaks the connection. "This is one call I should make."

I push the phone his way, no argument. He wasn't one to stick his head in the sand; he might not push the trigger, but he always gave the go-ahead. Jim's expecting a delivery at the cafe, two truckloads of whiskey for special customers. He never let anyone else officiate in that situation. He prided himself on personal service.

"Four o'clock, Jim. Think you can shake yourself loose from the little woman?"

The Italian hasn't been born that can back off from a challenge like that. The big man's on his way.

He pulls up in front of the main entrance in the same bus I rode in my first day in town, the same chauffeur driving in his uniform. Frankie's running late on account of he didn't figure in the rush hour between shifts at the stockyards. Diamond Jim kills some time in his office discussing the dining room menu with his chef, Caesarino his name is, Jim shipped him in from Italy right out from under the best hotel in Rome. At 4:25 by Diamond Jim's diamond watch, he excuses himself and goes out to the vestibule to wait for his delivery. He sends in his secretary, Frank Camilla, to finish lining out the bill of fare with the chef.

Bang-bang! Caesarino figures it's backfire. Camilla steps out for a look. Jim's on his face on the floor with a bullet hole behind his right ear. Another slug went through the cashier's window and stuck in the plaster wall behind it.

The cops investigated, but of course everyone was where he was supposed to be when Jim went down. Johnny cried when they told him, real tears; I don't think he ever regretted the decision, just that it had to be made. "Jim committed suicide when he took up with that tramp," he'd say.

What a funeral! It was like a block party, if you barricaded off all of Chicago, with the guest of honor riding up front in the procession in a bronze casket cost more than most houses, piled up so high with flowers the pallbearers had to shove it into the hearse with their shoulders, shearing off carnations, lilies, and roses big as bowling balls, the biggest displays with silk ribbons saying FROM JOHNNY and FROM AL; I tell you, if the cops weren't so stupid they'd put all their energy into the names on the splashiest bouquets.

O'Banion outdid himself. If you used any other florist, your name was mud clear from Lake Michigan to Cicero. The procession was as long as the Great Wall of China, with Jim's showy widow leaning on Hinky Dink Kenna in the back of one of his limousines riding behind the hearse and every Cadillac and Lincoln in three states following bumper-to-bumper. It shut down the city for a solid hour.

A Presbyterian minister showed up to pray Jim over; the Catholic bishop stayed home because Jim was divorced. The whoring and gambling didn't count as much as that. Ike Bloom, who ran one of his dance halls, delivered a swell eulogy: "Big Jim never bilked a pal or turned down a good guy and he always kept his mouth shut." When my time comes, I won't complain if somebody can say the same thing about me.

Meanwhile the cops kept digging. A waiter sneaking a smoke outside the cafe said he got a good look at Frankie on his way out and gave them a good description, but by the time the cops hustled him back from Brooklyn the waiter lost his memory. Frankie had to pay his own way home, which shows you what kind of four-flushers cops are.

One thing. Jim's widow told the papers that when he left their big house on Vernon Avenue he had a hundred and fifty grand in cash in his pocket, but when the cops inventoried the corpse they said he had only a few hundred on him. I don't begrudge Frankie a nice bonus, but I doubt he had time to rifle Jim's pockets between when the shots were heard and when Camilla came barreling out to see what the noise was about. Either the secretary got a windfall or the cops found themselves a retirement stake, or the money was never on him and Wifie took it out of the safe at home and told that story so she wouldn't have to pay taxes on it. Dames are resourceful even when they're in mourning.

Anyway, it was chicken feed. Diamond Jim's last garlicky breath gave birth to the biggest golden goose since the Greeks knocked over Troy. From here on out we had nothing to worry about except ourselves.

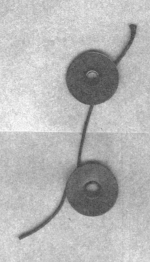

1944

A SEASON OF SECRETS

NINETEEN

Capone seemed inclined to go on, but then the screen door opened against the pressure of its spring and Danny and Sonny came out onto the porch and sat in the remaining wicker chairs. They lit Camels from twin Ralph-agitating packs and Capone leaned over to fire up the cigar he'd been mangling with his teeth from Danny's stainless-steel lighter. Vasco asked how the ball game was going.

Danny shrugged. "They keep breaking in with bulletins. We're bombing the shit out of Berlin. Guess I'll have to wait till tomorrow to collect on our bet."

"Care to put something down on the war?" Sonny smiled.

Capone said, "That's not something you joke about. We got family over there."

"Sorry, Dad."

"The krauts are getting their asses kicked in Russia, too," Danny said. "I said Hitler made a mistake when he turned his back on England. I got no reason to wish any good on John Bull."

"You Micks are just plain sore at the world." Capone blew a series of aromatic smoke rings, each perfectly round.

"Limeys first. Then the world."

They were joined by Mae, Ruth, and Winnie. Vasco got up to offer his seat, but Mae shook her head, wiping her hands on a frilly apron. Winnie stood behind Danny and kneaded his curls with her fingers and Ruth sat on the arm of Sonny's chair, took a puff on his cigarette, and gave it back. It was as domestic a scene as Vasco had ever witnessed. It made him ache for something.

"All those hours of work, it's over in twenty minutes," Ruth said. "Then another hour of washing dishes."

"How long's it take to read Oscar Wilde, and how long did it take him to write it?" Danny purred under Winnie's attention.

"You wouldn't know the answer," she said. "You never read a book in your life."

"Why should I? If it's any good they'll make a movie out of it."

"Where's Rose?" Vasco asked.

Ruth smiled. "Looking after the girls. She insisted. She's a better servant than she ever will be a guest."

"Maybe she'd rather be a mother," Winnie said.

Vasco said, "I should get back to Redemption. Thank you for a wonderful day." He shook hands with Sonny, Danny, and Capone, took the women's in his.

"I'll see you out." Sonny started to rise.

"Please don't. I want to take away the picture of all of you relaxing."

"Leave it to the Irish to declare Sunday in the middle of the week."

"It isn't the middle of the week, Snorky." Mae laid her left hand on top of

Vasco's right. "I want you to know I won't stop doing something kind for Rose every day. Monsignor Donahue would have let me off with a Rosary."

"It's not my place to second-guess his methods, but from what I've seen of Rose, I'm glad."

She smiled. "She's worked her spell on you, I can see."

A strange thing to say to a priest.

Rose was sitting cross-legged on the floor in the entryway, playing jacks with the two-year-old. Her sister lay on her stomach in the playpen, breathing evenly. The little girl squealed. Rose laughed, a musical sound. She saw Vasco and scrambled to her feet. He caught a flash of caramel thigh. "I didn't see you," she said.

"Rose, play with me."

"Hush, child."

He said, "Did you enjoy yourself?"

"I should've helped more."

"That's not what I asked."

She looked up at him, then to the side. Nodded. "Thank you again. It's been a good week."

"It isn't over, Mrs. Capone says. I'll make sure she doesn't forget."

She looked at him again, then went up on her toes and kissed him on the lips.

"BLESS ME, FATHER, FOR I HAVE SINNED. IT'S BEEN FOUR YEARS SINCE MY LAST confession."

"Four years." There was no inflection in Kyril's voice. His face was unreadable behind the screen; but that was normal.

"What is your sin?"

Where to start.

"I have had impure thoughts. I have failed to honor my father. I have lied. I have practiced deceit, by commission as well as by omission. I have violated the sanctity of the Church. I have broken the vow of chastity."

"Would you care to be specific?"

"I allowed a young woman to kiss me."

"That would seem to rule out the second sin. Which of the others applies?"

"Breaking the vow of chastity."

"No, that's restricted to having carnal knowledge. Kissing would imply impure thoughts."

"You're right, of course."

Kyril's vestments rustled, breaking the silence. "My son, I won't press you for details. They're between you and your conscience, and between your conscience and God. Perhaps one day you'll have the courage to discuss them, but if I gave you absolution now, that conversation would only be in the nature of an exchange between colleagues. Do you understand?"

"Yes, Father." No penance, no absolution from the sins that counted most. He was wasting the pastor's time and God's.

"For having impure thoughts, say five Hail Marys and five Our Fathers."

"I will."

"For dishonoring your father, grant him forgiveness."

"How shall I do that?"

"I leave it to you."

An easy out for the confessor. "I'll try."

The prayer of absolution followed. After they crossed themselves, Kyril said, "Do you know golf, Father?"

"I don't play." Was he inviting him out for a round?

"That wasn't the question, but I'll assume you know one or two things about the game. In regard to the other sins you mentioned, we'll call this a mulligan. I hope next time I can give you comfort."

"You're a good man, Father." His eyes swam.

"I'm not even a particularly good priest. I should be out stumping for a new roof instead of sitting around waiting to hear from the War Department. But I appreciate the sentiment. Are you free for supper?"

The dining room was narrow and medieval, with a refectory table that had been cut in half or it would have stuck out into the hallway. (Where was the other half? In the library of some indifferent antiquarian?) The meal, fish stew with leeks to correct the blandness of an ignominious haddock, stewed peaches on the side, was served by Sister Mary Engelbert, a novice from Sisters of the Covenant, a convent Redemption shared with Blessed Sacrament, and the oldest woman Vasco had ever seen who had yet to take the vows, with wisps of gray hair straying out from under the bandanna tied around her head, in a shapeless housedress that was more practical than the habit in the kitchen. Vasco suspected she was a widow who had traded worldly discontent for a life of service; she lacked the bright eyes of fresh devotion and responded to compliments to her cooking with only a distracted nod. She did not dine with them, retreating from the room after clearing the dirty dishes to plunge them into scalding water, on the evidence of her hands, boiled red as lobsters.

The conversation was secular, shop talk being just as tiresome in the clergy as in other professions. Brother Thomas contributed nothing to it, eating in respectful—if not sullen—silence while Kyril displayed an exhaustive knowledge of Russian literature. He appeared capable of separating the genius of Tolstoy's prose from his sympathy with bolsheviks and considered Dostoievski a champion of the Christian faith. ("*Crime and Punishment*," he said. "Also absolution and resurrection.") He thought Gogol a frustrated Cossack, but forgave him that blindness for his grasp of scan and meter. The pastor's face lost its animation only when Vasco asked if he thought the Corps of Chaplains would summon him soon.

"They're overstaffed." Kyril chewed reflectively, his fork pointed at the ceiling. "We'll be invading Europe soon. I expect openings then. I'm caught between ambition for myself and despair for the human carnage. Monsignor Donahue has had an earful from me in confession and is running out of Acts of Contrition."

"Perhaps it's the Lord's will. You're needed here."

"Perhaps so, but I can't help thinking the adulterers of this parish will find balm for their guilt in my absence; possibly from you, Father."

Vasco made the appropriate expression of humility, but he was only half engaged in the conversation. He'd gone straight to confession from Sonny's house, burning with shame, and his long-term memory was busy preserving Al Capone's memoirs of Chicago 1920 in his own words. They had to be committed to paper before they ebbed away.

The material was explosive. Vasco had no idea if Joe D'Andrea and Mack Fitzpatrick, whom Capone had fingered for the ambush slaying of three Black Hand extortionists in a railroad underpass, were still alive, or if they were important enough to attempt to indict on hearsay evidence, but according to Capone's file Johnny Torrio was in good health, a man of respect as one of the early architects of the modern rackets, and his own former lieutenant had linked him to the ambush—and on more direct evidence to the murder of Diamond Jim Colosimo. It was enough to hang Capone, who had set it up; but Capone was neutralized. Torrio was a sitting duck. It was the first solid foothold Vasco had managed to establish in Hoover's campaign to break organized crime and its stranglehold on the black market. Torrio meant a grand jury, subpoenas, and big black headlines, which to the Director were mother's milk. There was an appointment to Special Agent in Charge for Vasco if he played his cards carefully. The trick was to make Hoover aware of his value to the Bureau without threatening to carry away too much of the credit.

The Fargo office would be good, or Denver; some far-flung assignment outside the chill shadow of the Seat of Government.

". . . your father?" Kyril asked.

He blinked at the pastor, watching him above his glass of Chablis. Red wine was readily available for sacramental purposes beyond the reach of the long arm of the OPA, but white was an indulgence. Vasco recognized its significance as a compliment to his presence. He reconnoitered, grasping for the connection.

"I had dinner with him and his lady friend last week. It was pleasant."

"Pleasant is a start. Did you like her?"

"I did. She's Jewish," he added; not knowing why, although it seemed important.

"A noble creed. A good people. They were generous to give us the use of the Old Testament. I don't hold with the popular belief that they betrayed Jesus. In any case, whatever sins they may have committed as a race are more than wiped away by what's happening in Poland. But I'm more curious about your relations with your father. You needn't answer if it makes you uncomfortable."

He sensed that Kyril was backing off, as if he felt he'd come perilously close to Vasco's confession about dishonoring his father. Such things did not stray outside the booth.

"Not at all. Sharon told me he's a better man than I know, and I'm inclined to give the statement the benefit of the doubt. I just wish I knew him better."

Brother Thomas spoke up. "Maybe he should make the effort to know you."

Both of his tablemates stared at him. It was as if a figure on a stained-glass window had addressed one of them.

"What do you mean, Thomas?" Kyril asked.

Thomas's long pale face turned copper. He scraped at the scraps on his plate. "I'm sorry. I shouldn't have said anything."

"But you did, and now you must explain."

"It just seems to me that clothing and feeding a child and giving him shelter are required of parents by Christian and American law, and that they shouldn't expect blind loyalty just for providing them. In order to have it they should themselves be loyal."

"Well, well." Kyril skewered a morsel of fish with his fork. "Perhaps what the Dominicans say is true. Silence leads to wisdom."

HE TRANSCRIBED CAPONE'S NARRATIVE INTO HIS NOTEBOOK, WRITING FE-verishly and without stopping, by the light of the smoking oil lamp that was the only illumination in his room.

How many religious scholars, he wondered, had sat in that same spot, re-cording and interpreting the words of the Lord by greasy light? The comparison was blasphemous, but it kept his mind off Rose.

In the clarity of industry and solitude, he decided she deserved no blame. Some people were more demonstrative in their thanksgiving than others. He hardly thought he represented any kind of attraction, even if the priestly vows held no interest for her. He was more concerned with his own reaction. The mem-ory of her lemon soap lingered in his nostrils, of the soft touch of her lips on his. The blame was his.

The one confession he had been clear on with Kyril was based on a lie. He had not sworn himself to chastity and so he had violated nothing, while violat-ing the law of the confessional by saying he had. In his brief time at Redemption he'd heard admissions he knew were false, but these were made by lonely people craving attention and the presence of another human being in an otherwise empty life. When he'd given them absolution, it had been for that. No such es-cape route existed for him. His hand raced across the page, fleeing before his thoughts. When he was finished he knelt on the floor with his elbows on the bed and his hands clasped, like a child praying before retiring. "Dear God, am I act-ing upon Your will or the devil's? Give me a sign."

Silence.

* * *

IN THE MORNING HE POSTED HIS NOTES TO THE BUREAU THROUGH THE STA-
tionery company and found his way finally back to the commercial garage
where the mechanic who reminded him of his father took two dollars for the
spare tire he'd been hoarding and mounted it on the back of the Model T. A soap
opera sobbed away on a radio in the grimy office as he worked, whistling a dance
tune. A silver star pennant hung in the front window. Vasco hadn't noticed it
before and wondered if the man had lost a son in the fighting since his last visit.
And he wondered if it was possible to whistle one's way through everything.

The days passed seamlessly in a place without seasons. He took most of his
meals at the drugstore counter, but ate at Kyril's table once or twice a week,
where the talk ranged between literature and the arts, popular music (Kyril favored the waltzes of Wayne King; Brother Thomas had no preference and, Vasco
suspected, no ear), and of course the war, which was stalled in the Pacific but
was going badly for the Germans in Russia and Africa. Thomas said little, and
nothing to make anyone pause in his eating. Sister Mary Engelbert brought out
dishes and collected them, a serving machine.

He ran across Sergeant Fowler quite by accident at a fruit stand, hefting an
orange in each hand as if to test the accuracy of the vendor's scale; Vasco was
passing on the street and recognized him at the last moment. The Bunko detective who had given him the lowdown on Capone in Florida looked more than
ever like a distinguished banker in gray gabardine that matched his temples and
a well-brushed fedora. He placed Vasco immediately and smiled. "You're tan-
ning well, Father. Looking less like a ghost. Been sunning yourself by that big
pool?"

"In a manner of speaking. Thank you again for setting my conscience at rest.
The Good Samaritan never worried about His reputation when He saw a soul in
need."

"Well, my booth's always open." He returned the orange to the stack and got
the vendor's attention.

Small world, Vasco thought, walking away. Or perhaps not so small. Had he
been under police observation all this time? He stopped to look at a display of
electric razors in a window. People passed him, no one ducked into a handy
doorway; but he supposed professionals were more subtle than they appeared in
pulp stories. He resumed walking. Capone's paranoia was contagious.

No new invitations came from Palm Island. Vasco wondered if Capone's
porch revelations had been overheard and steps taken to prevent more. Mae's
and Sonny's faith in Vasco's power to bring comfort to the afflicted gangster was
no match for the cloud of secrecy that surrounded their world, that maintained
it. Life in that Moorish house was sealed as tightly as the customs of the Church.
After two weeks he thought of calling, but decided not to. Hoover had warned

him against appearing to take the initiative. It was easy advice to follow, especially since he had no idea how he should behave when he saw Rose.

Kyril asked him to take part in the Easter Mass. He agreed, no fears of entrapment now. He placed the Host on the tongues of the communicants, incensed the Gospel, passing the smoldering pot over the pages to be read, sang the *Alleluia,* managing not to make his voice crack, and read aloud from Matthew. ("His countenance was like lightning, and his raiment white as snow . . .") On this most important of days in the Church calendar, he looked for the Capones among the congregation, but they did not attend. Mae, he thought, would choose to celebrate the Resurrection at Blessed Sacrament, where she was most comfortable, but he couldn't help feeling he'd been cut loose. The thought disturbed him and relieved him. Perhaps silence was the sign he'd prayed for after all. But was the prospect of returning to his tin desk in the Justice Department building God's mercy or Vasco's punishment?

He had never felt so alive as in the past two months. Capone would probably say it was God's idea of a joke and call it malarkey.

Nearing the end of May, and six weeks after St. Patrick's Day dinner, Kyril told him he had a telephone call and excused himself from his study. Vasco recognized Helen Gandy's voice, instructing him to call the secure number from an outside phone. She used no names.

He shut himself in the drugstore booth and dialed the number. Hoover himself answered.

"Where are you calling from?"

He told him.

"Acceptable, but don't make a habit of using any one instrument. This line is safe, so we can speak freely. I'm quite satisfied with your performance so far."

"Thank you, sir."

"I didn't call to scratch you behind the ears. So far you haven't brought us anything worth moving on. We're not officially interested in John Torrio, who's living in retirement in Brooklyn, where he started out. He hasn't had anything to do with the mob in years, except to attend the occasional funeral of a former colleague. If we were to take action against him now, we'd risk tipping our hand to the rats we really want. But you're on the right track. Capone seems to trust you. When do you see him next?"

"I'm not sure. I haven't heard from him or his family in over a month." He was disappointed by the tepid reaction to the Torrio news.

"Surveillance agents report he hasn't left the house in weeks. No one in or out except servants, the immediate family, and Phillips, his doctor. Maybe he's suffered a relapse. As his spiritual counselor, looking in on him would be the natural thing to do."

"Yes, sir. Sir?"

"Yes?"

"Is the Bureau interested in Frank Nitti?"

"Has Capone mentioned him?" The Director's speech became even more rapid when something pricked his interest.

"His son did, in passing. An old memory from childhood, nothing useful for our purposes. I did some research in old newspapers about the attack on Nitti in his office by city detectives in Chicago."

"I remember the incident. The detective who shot Nitti had a personal grudge. He and his partner were fined for assault and allowed to return to active duty. Unarmed man shot three times, a self-inflicted wound to support a self-defense claim, records falsified, they're back in uniform in a matter of weeks. Chicago was and always will be a cesspool."

"The papers said they were sent by Ted Newberry, Mayor Cermak's deputy."

"He might not have known about the detective's history with Nitti."

"A month later, Cermak was gunned down in Miami."

"Everyone knows that. It was an assassination attempt on President Roosevelt. Cermak caught a bullet that was meant for him."

"But, sir, in your office—"

"I'll lead discussions of anything said in this office. The assassin confessed that Roosevelt was his target. He was executed five weeks later, only two weeks after Cermak expired of peritonitis caused by the bullet. Hardly a professional-sounding job, wouldn't you say? What did Sonny Capone say about Nitti?"

"He said he had cold eyes. They gave him nightmares."

"That's all?"

"He said they were like stones."

"Poetic, but as you said, useless."

"He was just a boy at the time. He said he saw him only once and never forgot it."

"For a number of people, the first time was also the last. You didn't mention that conversation in your report."

"I didn't want to waste your time with it. That's why I decided to investigate Nitti myself."

"Reading newspapers is not investigating. Your assignment is Capone, not Nitti."

"Yes, sir."

"If I thought you needed to know more about him than was in Capone's file, I'd have given you his. He's done one stretch for income tax evasion and Treasury is preparing another case against him for the same thing. Al Capone is your resource. He can provide you with more pertinent information than you'll ever get from the press. When you waste your time, you're wasting mine as well. If Capone's condition has taken a turn for the worse, you haven't a minute to waste."

"Yes, sir." The receiver felt hot against his ear. He turned his back on someone waiting to use the booth.

"Nitti's one of those we want to put behind bars, and not just for failing to file a return. Keep your ears open for anything Capone says about him. Linking him to just one of the murders he's suspected of committing would give us the leverage we need to get him to open up about the entire organization, including the black market. Once you separate these rats from their writs and lawyers, they squeal from morning till night."

"Yes, sir."

"Agent Vasco?"

"Yes, sir?"

"Good work. Clyde tried to talk me out of putting you in the field, but as usual my hunch was right."

Clyde Tolson was the deputy director and Hoover's oldest associate after Helen Gandy. Vasco had had no idea he'd been the subject of such high-level discussion. There seemed no point in having told him, apart from Hoover's eagerness to keep him on the job.

"Thank you, sir," he said. But he was speaking into an empty line.

A man in a tweed cap with a cigarette burning in his face swept into the booth as soon as Vasco stepped out. He had a copy of the *Racing Form* rolled up under one arm; Vasco had seen him before in the store, making marks on the handicappers' sheet with a stubby yellow pencil he stuck behind his ear when he used the phone. He'd never seen the man drink from his coffee cup; plainly, ordering it was the cost of taking up space at the counter. Hialeah was only a brief streetcar ride away, with all its color and excitement and fresh air, but the bookies of Miami didn't seem to be hurting for business. Swimming, sunning, and gambling were the local attractions. It was no wonder Capone had been drawn there. Vasco walked back to Redemption. He was beginning to recognize people in the neighborhood, strangers with familiar faces who recognized him in turn. They nodded and smiled and touched their hats. He touched his, wrapped in thought.

The Director had changed stories on the Cermak killing. It confirmed Vasco's suspicion that the conspiracy theory was part of a whispering campaign to discredit the Secret Service as an FBI rival, not to be overheard coming directly from him. Vasco wondered if Hoover had his own line tapped and recorded the conversations. It would explain his reluctance to say anything that could be put on record.

Rubbing out Cermak for orchestrating the attempted murder of Frank Nitti and doing it in the presence of the president of the United States was either brass arrogance or lunacy. The victim's languishing for three weeks afterward supported the official account, that he had accidentally wandered into the line of fire. On the other hand, Cermak's agonizing final days furnished a powerful object lesson for anyone who might have considered finishing the job on Nitti. The papers had reported no further attempts.

Hoover had taken the conversation in a different direction before Vasco could ask him about the other thing he'd learned from his reading session in the library. Ted Newberry, Mayor Cermak's general factotum, the man who had ordered the invasion of Nitti's office (the "hatchet man," as he was referred to by the opposition press), had turned up three weeks later in a roadside ditch in Indiana, shot full of holes. Apparently the Enforcer hadn't considered him prominent enough to wait until he brushed shoulders with a world leader.

The weather was hot and humid. As he climbed the church steps a scrim of perspiration formed on the back of his neck under the celluloid collar. *Come July you'll swear you're in hell,* his father had said; and it was only May.

TWENTY

AFTER A SWEATY, TOSS-TURN NIGHT, PETER VASCO GOT UP RESOLVED TO commit an act of insubordination and compound it by violating national policy in wartime.

It was early and still dark out, but dim light glowing through the stained-glass windows told him Brother Thomas was already at work, sweeping carpets and attacking with a zealot's fervor the daily cobwebs spun by heretical spiders from the crown of thorns behind the altar. Vasco went straight from the rectory to the toolshed and drove off as soon as the Model T sputtered into action. He was not dressed as clergy.

After showering and shaving in the tiny monastic bathroom he shared with Kyril, he'd put on a sport shirt and gray flannels and after a moment's consideration left even his hat behind. He'd seen more bare heads in Florida than anywhere he'd ever been and felt an almost desperate urge not to stand out.

He found a filling station that opened early for fishermen and waited while a man in a dirty yachting cap pulled away from the pump, driving an old Dodge pickup towing a boat with an inboard motor, a bundle of fishing rods sticking out over the stern. The sun was just beginning to stain the empty black sky above the ocean.

The attendant, a man too old for military service, took his stamps and cash, scratching behind his ear with the nozzle in his other hand. "You with the government?"

He'd anticipated that reaction to the number of stamps. "No, I work at home. This is the first time I've had the car out in a month." For some reason he found he could lie with less guilt in civilian clothes.

"Hoarder, huh? Oughtta be ashamed of yourself." The man grinned, his tongue showing through the gap where his front teeth belonged.

He did feel shame, but not for that reason. He was disobeying Hoover's orders, to take back up with Capone as soon as possible, and using gasoline for nonessential travel. A tank or a jeep might be made useless because of this impulsive act. A poster pasted on the station window read IS THIS TRIP NECESSARY?

It was. He was compelled beyond all reason to spend one day as something other than a priest.

A train was out of the question. They didn't begin running for another hour, and he couldn't afford to be seen waiting on a bench dressed as he was. Also, the chance of encountering a regular commuter on board who had seen him around town was too great. How strange that he should feel more as if he were acting undercover as plain Peter Vasco than when he masqueraded as a servant of the Roman Catholic Church.

He turned off a side street onto the coast highway and entered the thickening stream of traffic. The shipyards and defense plants were changing shifts. He crawled along among carloads of workers sharing vehicles, many of them yawning, some of the women applying makeup behind the wheel with the aid of rear-view mirrors. All the windshields bore lettered ration stickers (his was C, the most generous designation, restricted to doctors, ministers, and mail carriers), and a preprinted sign plastered to the rear bumper of a chalky, battered 1939 Plymouth coupe announced that the driver had placed his Cadillac in storage until the boys came home. It was as faded as the glint of optimistic humor that had accompanied its purchase in some novelty store. Pearl Harbor seemed very long ago.

The sun glared harshly through the window on the passenger's side. The Ford didn't have an adjustable visor and he regretted not bringing his hat so he could turn down the brim against the dazzle.

North of the city, the traffic began to thin out and pick up speed. He saw only flashes of water now between clusters of hotels, some still under construction. Hotels in bunches were a new phenomenon in his experience. In Chicago they spaced themselves out, sometimes by only the width of a street, but never stood cheek-to-cheek, as they did here; even in Washington, a city of transient diplomats, reporters, and hat-in-hand governors, visitors tended to segregate themselves by party affiliation and geographic origin, with small parks and heroic statues serving as buffers in between. With so many temporary dwellings arranged so tightly together, the population of coastal Florida waxed and waned according to the inclemency of the weather in the Northeast and Midwest, a census-taker's nightmare. Many of the hotels seemed to have sprung up just since he'd made the trip last. Where did the contractors find the material, with so much of the nation's resources co-opted by the military? Did the black market conduct business with big industry as well as the private consumer, or was big industry funneling money directly to bureaucrats and politicians in return for priority? Hoover had said that Chicago was a cesspool and always had been; but cesspools left undrained had no choice but to spread.

Vasco was getting away from Al Capone just in time. Prolonged exposure to the supreme corruptor was having a corrosive effect on his idealism.

Miami Shores, North Miami, North Miami Beach. What the various city fathers lacked in originality they more than made up for in consistency. He passed housing developments, tracts of homes laid out like games of domino. Some developers were more successful than others in obtaining supplies and labor, based on the projects that were completed as opposed to those where bare wooden frames stood exposed to the elements and grass grew on heaps of turned earth abandoned by the bulldozers. A DeSoto with blackout headlights chugged resignedly between lawns overtaken by feral alfalfa in the absence of sod, towing a banner of ocher-colored dust.

He drove at a steady rate, observing the national forty-mile-per-hour speed limit despite the lingering presence of signs saying he could go faster. (The Model T was incapable of doing more, but he felt sanctimonious nonetheless.) The state police seemed to share the laissez-faire attitude of the highway department in leaving them up; although he was passed frequently by drivers going fifty or better, in the first twelve miles he saw only one car pulled over by a jodhpurred officer on a motorcycle, a wood-paneled station wagon with suitcases lashed to its roof carrier and two children in back. After three years of fighting, the We Can Do It fever had broken, and people were going about their daily business while waiting for it to end. "When the Lights Go on Again (All Over the World)," the singer sang; and the people listening asked, "When?"

A siren sidetracked this train of thought. Flashers mounted on the front fender of a fat-tired motorcycle stuttered in his rearview mirror. His first, irrational thought was that he'd been followed by the same officer who'd ticketed him in Miami for leaving his motor running unattended his first full day at Redemption, but as he decelerated and drifted onto the gravel apron he thought it more likely it was the state patrolman who had stopped the station wagon.

"Is something wrong, Officer?"

"License and registration, please." He was standing at an off angle to Vasco, his leather helmet under his arm, his other gloved hand hanging near the checked butt of the revolver on his hip. He had startling blue eyes in a tanned, square-jawed face crowned by a flattop haircut like Father Kyril wore. In fact he could be the pastor's younger brother. They shared the same expression, equal parts weary and wary; brother officers sworn to uphold different rules of order. Vasco unsnapped the document holder from the steering column and handed it over along with the Florida license showing a picture of him in his clerical collar.

"You're a minister?"

"A priest, with Our Lady of Redemption in Miami." Now that his anonymity had ended, he felt the old rush of shame when he pronounced the lie. But the name of the church was on the registration.

"You have a cracked taillight, Father. You want to get that fixed." His tone had softened slightly.

"I will." He'd noticed the crack the first day, but hadn't thought such things mattered in a world that discouraged unnecessary displays of light.

The officer was still holding the registration and license, pinned to a ticket pad by a leather-encased thumb. "What brings you up from town?"

"I have parish business in Fort Lauderdale."

"That's twenty-five miles from your home base. The trains run all day. Gasoline's precious."

"I had to get an early start. It's a matter of some urgency. Last Rites."

"I'm Presbyterian myself, but I'm pretty sure there are Catholic churches in Lauderdale, each with its own priest."

"This man moved there recently to be near his children and grandchildren. He lived twenty years in Miami. Extreme unction from a stranger—"

"Dressed kind of casually, aren't you?"

"The heat." He fought a stammer. "My vestments and oils are in the compartment on the running board."

"The *tool*box?"

He nodded, struggling to maintain eye contact. The tan line left by the officer's goggles made him feel as if he were being watched closely through field glasses. He was sure the man would ask him to open the toolbox. (Last Rites; children and grandchildren. Where had *that* come from?)

"Well, tools are tools. Sorry to delay you, Father. Don't forget that taillight."

He thanked him and watched in the mirror as the officer strode back to his motorcycle, putting on his helmet and buckling the strap under his chin. Vasco hoped he'd pull out ahead of him and out of his life, but instead after straddling the seat he removed a clipboard from one of his saddlebags and wrote on the top sheet with a fountain pen, glancing once at the watch strapped to his wrist. Vasco could wait no longer without attracting suspicion. He put the Ford in gear and steered back into the driving lane.

As he'd anticipated, the patrolman fell in behind him three minutes later and stayed there despite the fact that Vasco was now driving five miles an hour below the limit, and despite numerous opportunities to pass. Vasco wondered again, as he had when he'd run into Sergeant Fowler on the street in Miami, if the authorities were keeping tabs on him. Would he ever again be in a frame of mind to accept the existence of coincidence?

After half a mile, the officer gunned his motor, swung into the opposite lane, and passed him with a loud blatting that hurt Vasco's ears. The motorcycle swerved back into his lane and sped out of sight.

Vasco drove another five miles before he felt the tension go out of his shoulders. It brought pale comfort. He'd lost that early exhilarating sense of escape. Reality had come crashing back in like high breakers, drenching him from head to foot. The mask did not come off with the collar. In all his life he'd never felt so guilty as when he'd joined the forces of justice.

Fewer hotels now, more open stretches of Atlantic. White-painted marinas with white-painted boats bobbing in their berths, flags stirring on staffs mounted in the sterns. Figures in striped shirts and bare chests polishing brass and scrubbing and sanding decks. Fat women in one-piece bathing suits, clogs on their red-heeled bare feet, sat in chairs made of bentwood and woven strips, sipping Coca-Cola through straws under hats with brims the size of manhole covers, ruffled skirts attached to their suits like mud flaps on moving vans. All the trim waists and perky breasts were in Hollywood (California, not Florida, a community now behind him, indistinguishable from its sun-bleached neighbors), or busy making bomb bay doors out of donated coffeepots and aluminum awnings. He felt a little more comfortable entertaining these carnal observations outside of vestigial uniform, until for some reason he found himself thinking of Rose.

In Fort Lauderdale, he entered a restaurant with a seven-foot marlin mounted above the door, shining blue over white; it looked as if it had been cast from fiberglass. He sat in a leatherette-upholstered booth at a window with an ocean view and ate a plate of fried shrimp. He'd gone without breakfast and cleaned his plate quickly, although he had to summon his waitress back to bring him coffee because the glass of water she'd set down when he arrived brought out the fishy taste. He was still hungry afterward and had apple pie for dessert, an uninspired finish not baked on the premises. The fishermen were all out and the lunch rush wouldn't start for two more hours, and his was one of only three tables occupied, all in a row so the staff wouldn't wear out shoe leather that was difficult to replace. He wondered if things would ever return to normal or stay the way they were from sheer habit, regardless of what happened overseas. He left a tip designed to preserve his invisibility and left.

He turned into the last available parking space at the marina. The federal ban on pleasure driving had been lifted as unenforceable, and tourism had picked up. Steam hissed drowsily from the radiator as from a broken pressure cooker; probably the car had not been driven so far in years. He reminded himself to refill it with water before he left town. He didn't want to have to confess to cracking an engine block belonging to the Church.

The sun, much higher now, assaulted him from above and from the bright-metal surface of the bay. It was like being in a convection oven. How his father had managed to live there all these years without shriveling up like a dried apple was one more of the mysteries that surrounded him. The beer he drank by the gallon must have contained some kind of lubricant.

With business improving, he half expected the old man to be out on the water with a customer. But as he approached the homely headquarters of Sunrise Charters, he saw the boat was in its berth. He was about to knock on the door of the shack when a movement in the water drew his attention back to the boat. Paul Anthony Vasco was standing naked to the waist in water up to his hips, painting over Peter's mother's name on the fantail.

"Dad?"

Paul turned, scowling against the glare. The paintbrush in his right hand paused between the U and R in MAUREEN. After a moment his teeth shone white in his mahogany-colored face.

"Jesus, I almost didn't recognize you. What'd they do, catch you with your mitts in the collection plate?"

"I took the day off. What are you doing?"

"Sprucing up the old tub. Don't let 'em ever tell you the seaman's life is a life of ease." He resumed obliterating the legend.

"Are you going to repaint the name when you're finished?"

"Not exactly. I'm painting a new one on."

"Sharon?" Sudden hatred coursed through him like an electric shock.

"I ain't sure yet. I'm still thinking about it. I mean, if it turns out we're a mistake it ain't as bad as getting rid of a tattoo, but it's bad luck to change the name of a boat even once and I got too much of the Old Country in me to tempt fate more than that. Meanwhile she needs a fresh coat of paint."

"If you're not sure, why not leave Mom's name on it?"

He redipped his brush in the bucket on the pier. "Well, son, your mother never did care for her given name. She got it from an aunt she hated, old bat left what little she had to the Church. Only time she was ever inside it was the day they buried her. Spite. I was drunk when I painted it or I'd-a remembered. I always called your mother 'old girl,' or 'Mommy,' when you was little."

"Her friends must have called her something."

"If they did, I never heard it. They dropped her like a turd when she married a wop."

"She must've made new friends later."

"Ever see any hanging around the apartment?"

He hadn't, only associates of Paul's. His mother was a lonely woman, he realized suddenly; not just in terms of being left alone by his father, but by everyone. Marriage and illness had sequestered her from life.

One long last swipe of the brush and the faint final evidence of the name was gone. It was as if even her memory had been painted away.

Paul tipped the brush into the bucket, braced his palms on the pier, and hoisted himself out of the water. It streamed off his soaked black swimming trunks, which clung to his genitals and sagged in the back, exposing his crack. He replaced the lid on the bucket and pushed it down with the heel of his hand, sealing the brush inside. "I'll finish up tomorrow. I got a late start and it's too fucking hot. I took Sharon out dancing last night, woke up with the sun in my face."

"I'm surprised you have so much time on your hands since they lifted the ban."

"My own damnfool fault. I had an appointment to take someone out this morning and when I didn't show up I guess he took his business down the dock. Hell with it. Less fishing, more drinking. How about a beer?"

"It's still morning."

"We'll drink to the boys in London. It's after five there." He knelt, displaying more of his buttocks, and reeled in a rope he had tied around a piling, hand over hand. His old green ice chest broke the surface. "Who needs Westinghouse when you live next to the world's biggest refrigerator?" With sudden exertion he jerked the chest up onto the pier, opened the lid, and punched two holes in a can of Pfeiffer's with an opener tied with a cord to the handle.

"Death to the enemy." He drank. He stood with his thick-veined feet spread, water dripping off his slat-thin body and streaking his trunks with salt. "How's Mr. Capone?"

"I don't know. I haven't seen him since St. Patrick's Day."

"Your mother never cared for corned beef and cabbage. That's one of the things I loved about her. You piss him off about something?"

"Not that I know of. Maybe he's under the weather."

"Sure you didn't preach at him too much."

"I don't think we've talked about God at all, except in passing."

"How you going to save his soul without His help?"

"I didn't say I was going to. Capone talks, I listen."

He paused in mid-swig, his bright eyes on Peter's. "Talks about what?"

Peter smiled thinly and shook his head.

"Yeah, I forgot." He tipped up the can and swallowed twice. "So what brings you up here? There's lots better things to do on your day off than chew the rag with an old fart like me, even if you are a priest."

"I'm not used to the heat. You said when it got hot I should go out with you on the boat. I should've called you at Sharon's first. If I knew you planned to paint it I wouldn't have come."

"Not even to visit your dear old dad?" Paul's bottom teeth formed a wicked grin.

"I didn't mean that. You'd still be painting if I hadn't interrupted you. I should've called to ask if you were free."

"I'm teasing, Pietro. You're losing what little sense of humor you had hanging around with all them sky pilots." He blew air reeking of hops, swirled the beer in his can. "What-a hell, paint's cheap. Go get your hat and I'll fuel up."

"I left it in Miami."

"Jesus Christ. When God made the sun He left it on its own. It boils the hired help's brains same as everybody's. Let's go in and get you fixed up. Christ Almighty."

"Dad, just for today, can you—?"

"Yeah, yeah." He crossed himself with the hand holding the can. "Just don't preach at me out there or I'll dump you in Davy Jones's locker."

Peter followed him toward the shack. The can gurgled empty and flew out over the edge of the pier.

Inside, his father scooped his fishing cap off its nail and tossed it to him. The leather sweatband was stained with brine and sweat and there was a greasy worn spot the shape of a thumb tip on the end of the long bill. Without warning, Paul stepped out of his trunks and left them in a sodden heap on the floor. Peter had never seen him naked. His buttocks were practically nonexistent, blue-white above and below the tan lines, and when he turned to snatch his khaki shorts off the back of a chair, his son averted his eyes from his plum-colored organs. His dirty yellow shirt hung on the other corner; the sparse furniture in the shack performed double-duty as hangers. When his loins were covered he pulled it on over his head. Fastening and unfastening buttons apparently cut into time reserved for drinking and boating.

Paul's cap was uncomfortably tight and clammy against Peter's forehead. He didn't see another in the place. There wasn't even a nail to hang one up on. "What about your brains? Don't they boil too?"

"Not if you pickle 'em. Oh, I keep an old hat in the boat in case it blows off." He dragged a yellow slicker off a tall square can labeled INFLAMMABLE, picked it up by its handle, and turned toward the door.

"Is it safe to keep that here? You sleep here sometimes."

"It ain't if the krauts strafe the place. I think they're too busy ducking for cover back home."

"My first day here I saw a Civil Defense man watching for submarines."

"Them four-f boys got to have something to do outside air raid drills. Son, right now some grease monkey named Otto's busy in Berlin cannibalizing two wrecked Messerschmitts to make one that works and watching the sky fill with Detroit steel."

"That's almost poetic."

His father actually blushed under his deep burn. "Sharon's rubbing off on me, looks like. Get a move-on. There's storm warnings off the Keys."

"Should we be going out?"

"Sure, but if it makes you feel better, you can bless the boat."

It would and he did, but not as a priest. As Paul stepped aboard carrying the can of diesel fuel, he stood on the pier and quoted a layman's prayer he'd seen hanging above the cash register in a fishermen's restaurant: "Oh, Lord, Thy sea is so great and my boat is so small." He crossed himself and boarded.

It was a twenty-foot cabin cruiser from which the upper part of the cabin had been removed to make room for extra cargo. A hatch had been added and all the passenger comforts stripped from inside. "Rumrunner," Paul explained, screwing the cap back onto the fuel can and lowering the engine hatch. "Guy I used to lease it from bought it at a Coast Guard auction in '34. It had two engines then, forty-horsepower Lycomings, but they was both froze up, so he yanked them out and replaced 'em with a Chrysler sixty. Made more room to store tackle. In its day it could outrun any U.S. cutter, but it still scoots like a greased pig when you drop the hammer down. Shallow draw. All the bullet holes was in the stern, which tells you something." His bottom teeth showed wolfishly at Peter's expression. "Don't worry, he replaced the boards."

"If it was so fast, how'd the Coast Guard end up with it?"

"It capsized during its last run and the legger had to be rescued by the same guys who were chasing him."

Peter laughed. The only times he'd laughed lately were at things his father said.

"The legger fell in love with a Cuban cooch dancer and changed the name of the boat from *The Shamrock* to the *Carmelita*. Told you it's bad luck."

He stopped laughing. "I wish now more than ever you'd kept it the *Maureen*."

"Ten minutes out and it will be again. That paint takes twelve hours to dry. Anyway it wasn't so much luck as poor judgment. Ten cases too many and you turn turtle in the wake of a fish fart."

How far did a man have to travel to escape Prohibition?

Paul clambered back onto the pier and handed the chest of beer down to Peter. Then he cast off and bounded to the deck. For a man of fifty he was as agile as a monkey. A brass-framed swivel chair stood bolted in the stern with a safety harness attached made of leather-reinforced canvas. He slapped the chair as he passed it.

"Marlin," he said; "but it's just for show in these waters. The real monsters run farther down the Gulf Stream. I don't run that far usually. Marlin men head straight down to Miami Beach, on account of the fuel shortage. I can't exactly advertise I don't have any problem with rationing."

"I'm surprised Hemingway didn't go down there when his boat was in dry-dock."

His father registered surprise. He'd had many beers when he'd told the story of the writer and his runaway tommy gun and seemed to have forgotten he'd mentioned it; either that, or he'd made up the whole thing.

"He came with his own supply in the back of a Chevy truck. He's tight with the government in Havana. They get it from the Mafia and give it to him so the president can have his picture taken with the gringo that wrote *To Have and Have Not*. Nobody's on the legit, son, except Sally Rand and her fans. She's got nothing to hide." He grinned and clapped a filthy fedora onto his head. It might have been the one he wore back in Cicero when he left Peter with a neighbor and took his mother into the city to celebrate their anniversary. It had been immaculate then, pearl-gray fur felt with a wide black silk band. Now the band was missing and a piece of the silk lining hung down behind his head like a pigtail.

The pilot house, which was just big enough for them both to stand up in, contained an old-fashioned ship's wheel with rounded pegs like ice-pick handles for gripping and spinning and a two-way radio and gauges built into a dash trimmed with polished teak. When Paul pulled out the choke and switched on the ignition, the motor turned over like a bear waking up from hibernation and settled into a throaty rumble. Peter felt the vibration through the soles of his feet all the way up to his knees. His father pushed in the choke, depressed the throttle, and steered them out toward open water. When they were clear of the harbor he opened it up. The boat skipped over the waves, climbing up one side and plunging down the other. Spray dashed over the bow, cleared the top of the windscreen, and misted in Peter's face, cooling his skin on contact.

Paul became a tour guide, pointing out shoals, leaping fish, other craft. He named the ones he knew, shouting above the roar of the engine. He told stories.

"This guy hires me for the day, swear to God, he shows up lugging five hundred bucks' worth of tackle, fiberglass rods, and hand-carved lures some sharpy unloaded on him in Cleveland. He had on *hip* boots, for chrissake. I said, 'You gonna wade out into the shipping lanes?' We go out, he starts rubbing on hand cream. 'What are you, a fairy?' 'No, I'm a hand model.' 'Fuck's a hand model?' So he tells me. You open a magazine, there's a Lucky Strike advertisement shows the cigarette all peeled open, you can see the fine tobacco, how it's packed.

There's a finger pointing to it, it's his finger, attached to his hand, which if there's a hangnail or a blister or a paper cut, he don't get the job. His hands looked like Marlene Dietrich's.

"His fancy rods are swell for freshwater fish, perch and trout. He coulda left 'em in Cleveland for all the good they are out here, but he's got a hard-on to use 'em and won't rent from me. See, he knows now he's been screwed, so now he's suspicious of anybody else he figures is looking to make a buck; it's always like that, the honest businessman gets the blame for what the crook done ahead of him. Fine. I strap him in the chair, give him a thrill, like he's ever gonna hook something bigger'n one of his dumbshit boots this side of Key Largo. Hang on."

Paul spun the wheel left to describe a wide arc around a navy P.T. boat Peter assumed was out on maneuver. Sailors in combat helmets stood at the rail and a man in a flak jacket braced himself on the handles of a water-cooled machine gun mounted on a swivel.

"Nervous nellies," Paul said when they were well out of the P.T.'s lane. "Think I'm the *Bismarck*. Toss me a beer, son. All this salt's making me thirsty."

Peter surprised him by opening a can for himself as well. They clanked them in a toast. His son found the taste unexpectedly pleasant out there in the sea air. A boy having a beer with his father on a fishing boat.

"Well, the joke's on me, because he ain't in the chair fifteen minutes, he snags something that takes out his line like Seabiscuit, reel's spinning a mile a minute. A ray, maybe. Comes to the end, his seventy-five-dollar rod squirts right out of his hand and over the fantail. All that slippery hand cream, you see. Last we see of it, it's heading straight to Bermuda like a bat out of hell."

Peter choked on his beer. It was his best day in as long as he could remember.

After two hours, the wind came up and the sky turned dirty. Paul wrestled with the wheel as the waves grew steep, the spray now more than mist. Peter felt the beer in his stomach imitate the action of the sea, the rolling of the hull. His father tuned the radio to the Coast Guard band. There was a small-craft warning out all along the coast. They turned back toward land.

Big drops pelted them as they got out and secured the lines, Peter obeying all orders. Paul wanted him to stay until the all-clear, but he said he had to get back to Redemption.

They shook hands. "It's early for hurricane season, but you see any chicken coops bouncing across the road, pull over and find a ditch. Man on his face, it's like scraping off a postage stamp with your thumb, but a box on wheels—"

"I know. The wake from a fish fart. I had a good time, Dad."

"Everything's better with beer."

He sprinted to the car and got thoroughly soaked working the crank. After that, there was no reason to seek cover when he stopped at a station to fill the radiator. Driving back, the vacuum wipers making no dent in the downpour, he shivered while his feet and ankles roasted near the heater, set too close to the floorboards to warm him above his shins. His throat was scratchy. The worst, most miserable colds he'd ever suffered from had started with a sore throat. Then he remembered the story about the hand model at sea and had to pull off the road to avoid losing control of the wheel. Yes, it was his best day in as long as he could remember.

SERGEI KYRIL STEPPED OUT OF HIS STUDY AS VASCO WAS TIPTOEING PAST. The pastor was in his shirtsleeves with his vest buttoned over his dickey.

The sun was just setting, but Vasco had been feeling happily drained by the day, despite his sniffles, and ready to catch up on the sleep he'd lost the night before. Now he felt like an adolescent boy who'd been caught sneaking home after curfew, and in inappropriate clothes. He'd left without notice and had missed confession.

Kyril held up a hand the moment Vasco's mouth opened. "You volunteered to serve. You can ask out whenever you like, although it would be polite to ask. That's not what I wanted to tell you. That woman's been calling all day."

"Woman?" He thought of Rose for no reason at all.

"The one who's called before. She says it's urgent."

Helen Gandy. "Thank you, Father."

"I'd offer you the use of the parish instrument, but you seem to prefer calling from outside."

"It's long distance. I don't want to run up the bill."

"I didn't ask for an explanation. You should change before you go out. Pneumonia is a scourge even in the tropics." He went back inside and shut the door.

Vasco went to his room and resumed his disguise.

The rain had stopped. The street shone as if oiled, littered here and there with broken palm fronds. The druggist was out front removing precautionary tape from his display window.

The man in the tweed cap was in the booth, cigarette bobbing between his lips as he placed his bet. Vasco hovered outside, coughing and sniffing, then dived in as soon as it was vacant. Their roles had reversed. The receiver was still warm when he dialed the Director's office. Helen Gandy put him straight through.

"Is that you?" Hoover rapped. "You sound different."

"I'm coming down with a cold."

"Where have you been?"

He had lied all day. He hadn't the energy to make a new one convincing. Better to tell the truth and take his lashing.

"I—"

"Never mind. Where are you?"

He told him.

"I instructed you last time not to establish a pattern of calling from the same place."

"I was told it was urgent. This is the nearest public phone."

But Hoover had moved on. Most of his conversation was monologue. "You can stop trying to reach Capone. He's gone."

"Dead?" The floor collapsed beneath his feet. Why was that?

"If he were dead I'd have said so. I have no time for polite euphemisms. I mean he's flown the coop. Taken a powder, in his own parlance. Fled Palm Island, possibly Florida, and right out from under the noses of the men I assigned to keep an eye on him."

TWENTY-ONE

"When? How?"

"I intend to find out how, and to discipline the men who let it happen. As to when, I'm narrowing that down. Up until a week ago his wife and son were seen entering and leaving the estate at irregular intervals, but then Mae disappeared. Since Danny Coughlin's wife returned from visiting a sister we assumed he's been staying with her at their home in Miami; that's now confirmed. The fact that Dr. Phillips has been calling frequently suggested that Capone's been ill and in no need of Coughlin's services as his chauffeur.

"At one time we had them all under surveillance, but after December 1941 I reassigned those agents to Alien and Enemy Control. When we lost track of Mae, I directed the Special Agent in Charge in Miami to obtain a warrant to search the house. There wasn't a soul in the place, not even the colored servants. The bodyguard at the gate said he wasn't even aware the house was deserted; he'd been letting the doctor and Sonny in and out every day and said he had no reason to believe they weren't being greeted by someone inside. He was taken to the federal building there, but he stuck to the story, and with no charges to hold him on he was released."

"Did you interview Danny and Sonny?"

"Of course. Danny said Capone had been under the weather, so he was putting the free time to use managing the waiters' and bartenders' union accounts and the two restaurants he owns. He acted surprised to learn his sister and Capone were missing. Sonny refused to answer questions and referred us to Abe Teitelbaum, the family's legal representative. Dr. Phillips told us to talk to his attorney as well. There is no law against visiting an empty house, and since Capone isn't wanted for anything at present, there was no use pursuing the matter." He sounded as if he thought the legislature had failed him personally in not passing such a law. "Needless to say, I have agents watching all of them now, on the chance one will lead us to where Capone is hiding. Did you have any sense at all that something like this was in the works?"

"No, sir. Mrs. Capone told me Capone was in no condition to travel any great distance. He couldn't even sit still at the opera, let alone aboard a train or an automobile."

"Undoubtedly a ruse. We know Mae and Al and Rose, their girl, returned to Palm Island from Sonny's on St. Patrick's Day. They may have been planning this even then. After Capone left, Mae stayed behind a few weeks to keep the surveillance team from suspecting anything, then joined him. Sonny's job at the air depot prevented him from following, but he kept up the pretense until the agents managed, astonishingly, to put two and two together."

Vasco closed his eyes, sympathizing with the agents. He thought it unlikely they'd draw so plush an assignment as Miami for a very long time. How had it been done? With Mae free to move about unobserved, she could have stepped aboard a train anytime, possibly in some disguise as simple as sunglasses and a scarf so ticket agents and porters couldn't identify her from photographs (certainly not from the one Vasco had seen, enveloped to her eyes in a mink collar) and report on her destination; but how did one spirit away a conspicuous person like Al Capone, with experienced men watching him around the clock? Something had been said, weeks and weeks ago, about chartering planes to the Bahamas; but that had been in palmier days, when neither illness nor the law could reach him in his armor-plated Cadillac. Surely a seaplane could not land and take off from his back dock unobserved. A boat seemed more likely, and Cuba its port of call.

Not Cuba. The heat in Florida during the off-season was hard on Capone, and would be worse there. The man had simply vanished.

"Sir, what can I do?"

"Wait for word."

"From you?"

"From Capone. It's all you can do. You're our man inside the family. He trusts you, that much is clear. He told you about four murders no one has ever been able to pin on Johnny Torrio, his old friend and mentor. Stay close to Redemption. Notify me the moment he makes contact."

"I'm not sure he will. He never so much as hinted to me he had anything like this in mind."

"He might not have known about it. Mae's the mastermind in that family. I underestimated her. I should have learned from Ma Barker that you can't deal a woman out of the hand just because she's a woman. This in no way exonerates the agents on the scene," he added quickly. "I don't hire them to sit in the back of a delivery van and read *Dime Detective*."

Sit tight and keep your ears open and your eyes peeled. Was that Helen Gandy's idea of an urgent communication? She had probably been exasperated when she couldn't reach him right away. A regular J. Edgar, Miss Gandy. "You can count on me, sir."

"If I didn't think that, I'd never have taken you out of Division Four." He hung up.

Vasco walked back through dim streetlight shed by low-watt bulbs, a wartime measure to foil enemy aircraft, but a boon to footpads; he hurried past the mouth of an alley with his eyes and ears open. The air reeked of brimstone, a combination of rain on hot concrete and the fear of damnation that dogged him.

What if Capone hadn't left voluntarily? What if he'd been taken for a ride? *His own parlance,* as Hoover had put it, meaning Capone's. Had Danny overheard their conversation on Sonny's porch and reported it to Ralph? It made sense: a middle-aged man, owner of two restaurants and an important position with a union run by the Outfit, reduced to driving his brother-in-law around, his kid sister to Mass and the supermarket, hoping to win favor in Chicago: Ralph was Al's own brother, but family ties could be lethal if Frank Nitti considered Al a liability and suspected Ralph of protecting him. Ralph would protect Ralph. Scalise and Anselmi had been so close to Capone he'd risked prolonging the beer wars by refusing to betray them to a rival in return for peace, but he hadn't hesitated to bludgeon them personally and then hand them over to assassins the moment he detected disloyalty. There was no honor among thieves, not in a world where legitimate contractors bought contraband building materials through Washington.

The more Vasco pondered, the more he was convinced Capone was dead, feeding alligators in the Everglades, and that Vasco had put him there. What sort of Purgatory awaited him, and what chance had he for salvation, if someone like J. Edgar Hoover sat on the tribunal?

He tried, but could not quite convince himself, that his feelings of guilt lay in his betrayal of the Church and of the brotherhood of man. He was strangely sympathetic toward Al Capone in his present state; certainly not for his mortal sins, which piled up day by day like the tiers of hotels under construction in southern Florida, but for his personal charm and his refusal, nearing the end of a life of unspeakable evil, to apologize for it or even to dissemble his darkest crimes against man and God. He was honest about his dishonesty. Who else could claim that? Certainly not Vasco, whose self-flagellation took place in private, and not even in the absolute sanctuary of the confessional.

Pity for the man in his reduced circumstances played a part. He was the same tyrant who had ruled his kingdom with guns and graft, a killer, thief, and philanderer, corruptor of Vasco's father; a monster who'd swaggered among mayors, judges, and cardinals, all of whom accepted his authority without question, and now he couldn't even light a cigar without looking over his shoulder to make sure his wife wasn't watching. When all was said and done, he was human, no more and no less, therefore worthy of compassion. Vasco had never had a friend; although his relationship with Capone would never approach friendship, he was packaging their connection for sale to the highest bidder, and not even for money, but for a numerical step from Division Four to Division Five, a progression that existed nowhere else but the Bureau. Jesus had foresworn earthly kingdoms for agonizing death on the cross; Vasco had traded the closest thing he'd ever had to a friend for a number.

He sat up in bed that night with a pulsing headache, part of it caused by two hours wearing a fisherman's cap too tight for his cranium, and did not know he'd slept until he awoke with a memory of dead men's hats rolling around in gutters, one of them sporting a long bill designed to keep the sun out of the eyes of men at sea.

Over the succeeding days he was surprised that Kyril made no mention of either his dereliction or his return in layman's clothes. The pastor spoke to him politely in his slightly dated Old World fashion and gave no indication that he even remembered the lapse. But no more invitations came Vasco's way to dine with him and Brother Thomas, and on Sunday Mass, Vasco stood with Kyril behind the altar but took no active role in the service because none had been assigned. He knew he was being punished, but it was so subtle he would feel he'd committed an unpardonable breach if he brought it up for discussion. He ate most of his meals at the drugstore counter, read the sacred scriptures to pass the empty hours, and waited for news on the Capone situation. Mornings he walked to a kiosk two blocks over from Redemption where a blind man sold him local and out-of-town newspapers and made change from a contraption on his belt. The war pushed all the other news into the inside pages, but it seemed to Vasco that the mysterious disappearance of Miami's most notorious resident was noteworthy, if only to fill out a column that had run short. No mention was made. Was Hoover's power so great he could drop a cloak of secrecy over the press, sparing embarrassment for himself and the Bureau, or was Capone so much a relic of forgotten days no reporter thought a trip to Palm Island worth the expense of a ration stamp? Vasco pictured the vice lord at thirty, surrounded by newspapermen eating his caviar and drinking his imported liquor, smoking his cigars, and asking him who he liked in the Dempsey fight. CAPONE BACKS THE MANASSA MAULER, the next day's headline would read, and the odds would go through the roof. Now he could be rotting in some roadside ditch and no one had noticed he was gone.

June was like a winepress, flattening the city beneath a solid slab of heat. Nightfall brought no relief; Vasco spent the night of the fifth with the door of his room open to invite any current of air that stirred in the rectory, lying atop the covers in only his undershorts and turning his pillow every five minutes to the cool side. He arose with swollen eyes, dried himself after his shower, and began to sweat again as soon as he hung up the towel. He was buttoning on his collar when the church bell started ringing.

It was too early for Mass. He entered the church and called out to Brother Thomas, who was moving toward the bell tower from the front entrance at an unprecedented trot, carrying a stack of newspapers under one arm. It was Kyril ringing the bell. Thomas stopped, appeared uncertain whether to continue or to acknowledge Vasco's cry. Then he snatched a paper from the stack and held it up, front page out. It was an extra edition with black letters stacked in three lines across the top:

INVASION ON, ALLIES LAND IN FRANCE
AS PLANES AND SHIPS BLAST COAST;
MONTGOMERY LEADS THE ADVANCE

"It was on the radio," Thomas said. "It's started."
"Ask Father Kyril if he wants to arrange a special Mass."

"I already did, and the answer was yes." He left him.

Paul had said the invasion would end the war by Christmas. His son wasn't so sure. A smaller headline said the Germans were putting up fierce resistance. (A smaller one still said American vegetarians had denounced Hitler as a carnivore on the sly.)

The bell stopped. Now he heard horns honking, men shouting, a high trill of feminine laughter ending in a note of drunken hysteria. It was morning. At this rate there wouldn't be a drink to be found in town by sunset.

He held the door of the drugstore for a woman carrying a paper sack with bottles clinking in it and stood in line until the druggist heard his request and raised his eyebrows. He was gaunt, all right angles as if he'd been assembled from an Erector Set; his white lab coat hung on his shoulders as from a wire hanger. "You're in luck, Father. Just one left." He stood a bottle of Old Overholt Kentucky rye whiskey on the counter. "You'd think it was all over but the shouting."

"I'll pray for that until it's true." He handed over cash and stamps, watched the man ring up the sale, and took his change. "Do you have family in the service?"

"No. I'm a widower, no kids. I tried to sign up, but they told me I had a hole in my heart."

"I'm sorry."

"Me, too. I got along just fine not knowing it all my life. Now I think about it every time I go up the ladder for stock. I've been grinding prescriptions for fifteen years, and not one for a hole in the heart." He sacked the bottle and held it out. Vasco took it and thanked him. It was their longest conversation. There was still a line of people waiting, one of them the handicapper in the tweed cap with the *Racing Form* under his arm.

The bell was still silent at Redemption. Father Kyril's study door stood open for ventilation; the heat wave hadn't paused even for D-Day. The pastor sat at his desk with his elbows propped on the blotter and his face in his hands. Vasco hesitated, then knocked on the door frame. Kyril dropped his hands. His gaze went to the sack Vasco was cradling in one arm.

"I take it you've heard the news."

"Brother Thomas told me. Of course, I heard the bell."

"Early exuberance. I wasn't aware you were a drinking man."

"I'm not, as a rule. I thought you might like to celebrate. I'm afraid I didn't pause to wonder if *you* were a drinking man."

"I'm Russian, Father. Ninety percent of my body weight is vodka. That's why I don't keep it in the rectory."

"I should have asked first."

"Come in and shut the door. Thomas is under the impression I'm material for canonization and I haven't the heart to disabuse him of the notion. What's on the menu?"

Vasco pushed the door to and slid the bottle from the sack, showing the label. "I'm afraid it's the only kind I know to ask for. I had a taste of rye aboard the train on my way to Florida."

"It's American, and most appropriate. On several levels; a band of former colonists fought a war with their new Democratic government for the right to manufacture and sell rye without paying a tax on it."

"You shame me with your knowledge of the history of the country where I was born."

"Every native son should be required to take a refresher course for citizenship. Straight up, or with water?" Kyril was standing in front of his water cooler, squat with a white ceramic crock, pulling two pointed paper cups from the dispenser on the wall.

"Mostly water, please."

Bending to the spigot, he filled the first cup to within a half-inch of the rim, twisted the cap off the bottle, breaking the seal, and topped it off. After handing the cup to Vasco he hesitated, then did the same for himself.

"I had a problem in the seminary," he said. "We all did, but a shared problem is a lark, especially when you're young. A rebellion, like they were having in the provinces, before the professionals took charge and started slaughtering priests and stabling their horses in the churches. Stealth was already in our training, because the state religion was Eastern Orthodox, and there were some, Bulgars especially, who'd as soon tar and feather a Catholic as a Turk. We went to extraordinary lengths to conceal our vice from the brothers. Suspending the mash in a cheesecloth sack through the hole in the outhouse took the adventure out of it for me. We made it from rotten potatoes, you see, so covering up the odor was a priority."

"It must've been awful."

"The first taste of sin often is. It takes a certain kind of reckless courage to try it again. I haven't had anything stronger than sacramental wine in more than twenty-five years. Best to start slow. Here's to mercy in victory."

It was a splendid toast, just right. They touched cups and drank. Vasco found the rye much more pleasant in diluted form. The water tasted of iron and limestone—the crock was past due for cleaning—and the combination of minerals and distilled spirits was sweet but not cloying, and warmed his insides in a way he wouldn't have thought he'd welcome, given the day's oppressive heat. But the study's location on the north side of the rectory in the shade of a palm grove provided some relief, even if much of it was illusory; the shades were drawn, plunging the room into artificial twilight and obliterating the vision of a sun burning white in the sky.

They sat on opposite sides of the desk. Kyril stirred his paper cup with a square-nailed finger and sucked on it. "I hope the boys in France take time from the fighting to raid the cellar of a château. I'd hate to think of them drinking the juice of fermented turnips."

"Wouldn't that be stealing?"

"They're killing, too, don't forget. To everything there comes a season, and the Lord has provided thieves with a patron saint all their own. Drink's as important in war as it is in worship. Did you know during the Civil War the Union Army issued a quart of whiskey a day to each soldier in the field?"

"It seems to me that would affect their performance in combat."

"Oh, those Southern boys on the other side could smell out a jug of corn liquor in a pasture covered with cow flop, so it all evened out. The natives up in Georgia dig minié balls out of trees bordering old battlefields, sell them to tourists for souvenirs, and support themselves on the profit. For every human casualty there were a hundred trees riddled with lead. On both sides, from generals on down to buck privates, there wasn't one man in five drawing a sober breath on the day of a major battle. Think how many lives would be spared if the Axis and Allied powers requisitioned rye, Scotch, schnapps, and sake for all their troops. Human lives, that is. The Argonne woods and the Black Forest might never recover."

"If they did all their drinking together, maybe none of them would have to die."

"A pacifist view, and an unpopular one just now, but I think there's merit in it. Unfortunately, the Prince of Peace is in mothballs at present." Kyril wrapped both hands around his cup and lapsed into silence. Outside, a string of firecrackers went off like twigs snapping in a fireplace; apart from that the noise of celebration seemed to be subsiding. The news from Europe was not the beginning of the end, but another beginning, with many more young lives still to be sacrificed, and the hangover was setting in. Kyril himself had not appeared to be in a buoyant mood when Vasco had knocked. Vasco took another sip, which emboldened him. "You're troubled, Father. Are you thinking of those men at Normandy?"

"I think of little else. The bloodshed no doubt is biblical, the horror unimaginable. And I am not there to share in it."

Vasco said nothing. He shouldn't have asked the question. "I tried calling the War Department an hour ago, when I got tired of ringing that blasted bell. I couldn't get through, of course. The switchboards are jammed. Not that it matters. I'd have been told to be patient, just as they've been telling me for months. It may all be over by the time my orders come through. There's something absurd about a military chaplain in peacetime, blessing bones broken in drunken brawls and organizing drives for penicillin to cure the clap. A one-man glee club, cheering for men waiting to ship home and bored half to death."

"Surely there's more to it than that."

"Nothing a first-year seminarian couldn't handle. Brother Thomas would be overqualified."

"I'm sorry to say there is plenty of war left to go around."

"I'm sorry to say that I draw strength from the fact. It makes me sick to my stomach."

The silence that followed was mutually morose.

Kyril brightened suddenly, like a puppet jerking its own strings. "What of you, Father? How are things on Molokai?"

He realized after a moment Kyril was referring to Palm Island. He took a drink and made the kind of decision a man often regretted. "I seem to have misplaced my head leper."

The pastor's immediate response was enigmatic. He got up, carrying his cup—its cone shape prevented it from being set down—walked around behind Vasco, opened the door and looked out, then closed it and shot the bolt, a maneuver from a spy movie. Every portal in the church and rectory secured in this fashion, with heavy cypress shutters that could be bolted in place over the stained-glass windows from inside. Vasco knew nothing of the buildings' vintage, but such precautions seemed designed to protect the occupants from a siege by hostile Seminole Indians. Kyril lifted the bottle from the desk, refilled both cups, the ratio of water to whiskey shifting now, and resumed his seat.

"Nothing spoken of here leaves this room," he said. "An agreement between gentlemen, entirely secular. God has His hands full this day. That door is three inches thick. If Thomas tries to eavesdrop, all he'll get is an earful of splinters."

"Is he so curious?"

"I have no idea, but I don't trust a man who seldom speaks. He takes in more than he gives out. You've lost Capone?"

"Even the authorities have no idea where he is, and he was being watched closely."

"You notified the authorities?"

"They notified me." Vasco drank. The strength of the liquor began to fill his head like a balloon. He had to think around the void. "I'm on a mission, Father. I've been recruited by Washington to monitor the black market. Chicago is a major source, and Al Capone is Chicago." He thought it a plausible distortion of the truth, sustainable by anything he might let slip.

"By monitor you mean investigate."

"I have no experience in detective work. I'm a professional listener, the same as you."

"How is this Church business?"

"Bishop Donahue in Cicero wants a community center. He could spare me, and so he agreed to the trade."

"Not flattering."

"True, nonetheless." At bottom, in the cosmic scheme of things, Donahue would not remember him from his time at St. Francis, and if reminded of him now he would know him only as a bargaining chip.

"You're harsher on yourself than need be. You handle yourself well at Mass."

"Any choir boy could do what I've done, if the Church allowed it."

"Perhaps so, but I've seen bishops who couldn't. You must learn to accept compliments, Father. False humility is nothing more than pride in its most unbecoming form."

"Thank you." Bile rose at the words. He cut it with whiskey.

"What division of the government is responsible for this miraculous community center?"

"The FBI."

"You're a G-man?"

"Hardly that. An informant. A snitch, as they say in melodramatic fiction." He felt a bitter smile twitching at the corners of his lips.

This, too, was close enough to fact that he could tell it without fear of Kyril's pale eyes penetrating to the back of his head. It skirted the worst offenses to the Church; he was certain their "gentlemen's agreement" would collapse in the face of such a revelation, although the seal of the confessional might have survived it. But to confess everything would bring no absolution, because he could not promise to stop. At the same time the pressure was too great to go on as he had, with no one to confide in but the Director, who was all questions and no comfort.

Kyril fingered his cup. He hadn't raised it to his lips since he'd refilled it. "Are you a priest?"

Vasco almost dropped his. The man's perceptions were superhuman. It took all the energy he had not to assume he knew everything already and admit the truth. "Yes, of course. I would never have agreed to sit in confession if I weren't."

No air stirred in the room. A silence so profound hurt his ears like a sudden rise in pressure. Finally Kyril drank, a long draught that caved in the sides of the cup. "Why you, Father? Why not me? I was here already, and I'd had personal contact with Mrs. Capone. Or Monsignor O'Meara at Blessed Sacrament, where she attends Mass several times a week. Miami could use a community center. What are your qualifications?"

"My father drove a beer truck for Capone in Chicago. That tie goes much farther back, and family connections are important to Italians. I was selected specifically on that basis."

"Yes, you mentioned the association. I'd forgotten. I'm glad we're having this talk. I was considering asking the diocese to reassign one of us. Your independence and your mysterious comings and goings had me convinced I was the one under scrutiny."

This surprised him nearly as much as being asked if he was a priest. "Whyever you?"

"The pope is committed to neutrality. Publicly, of course, the Church in America supports the war, but the Vatican distrusts priests who it feels are too—demonstrative. I'm more vulnerable than some, because the case can be made that I'm neglecting my parish while waiting for my assignment to the Corps of

Chaplains. Now that I've said that out loud, I think I've stumbled upon the reason I'm still waiting."

"I assure you you're safe from me." He had a sudden insight. "Have you thought of Brother Thomas?"

"He was my second choice. Do you think Capone suspected you and that's why he fled?"

"My fear is that more drastic measures may have been taken."

"Assassinated by his own people?"

"It has a great deal of precedent. Dementia is a symptom of his disease. I've seen him when he wasn't sure who he was talking to. In criminal circles that's seen as a threat."

"Wicked world." Kyril drained his cup and crumpled it in his fist. He sat holding it at ear level as if he'd forgotten all about it. "Why didn't you come to me earlier?"

"I'm disobeying instructions by telling you now, but the burden was too great. I'm unaccustomed to this work. My own father doesn't know what I'm doing. He thinks I'm out to save Capone's soul."

"Thank you for your trust."

"I'm sorry it took so long. You're a hard man to know. I had to be sure."

Kyril nodded and dropped the crushed cup into the wire wastebasket beside the desk. "Obviously, you're going to be busy. Would you prefer it if I released you from your responsibilities at Redemption?"

"That would draw attention. I have a hunch I'm being watched as well, by Capone's brother, Ralph. And I'd be grateful for the distraction of work. I've been told to be patient, same as you, and wait for word."

"It's worse than perdition, isn't it?"

"I haven't the real thing to compare it with. Can I get back to you?"

The pastor surprised him with a short Slavic bark of a laugh. "I'm happy to hear you're still on board. During today's service I'm announcing a special evening Mass to be held tomorrow night, to pray for our men in combat. I'd like you to lead the congregation in that prayer, and for you to make the selection."

Panic coursed through him like electric shock. He'd never been front and center except when he'd read the Gospel at Easter, and Kyril had chosen the passages. Selecting the text was the next thing to composing a sermon from scratch.

"Surely you should lead, Father."

"I think the parishioners would be more attentive to someone who is the same age as the men he's praying for. Old men talk while young men die. The conduct of war never changes, but that doesn't mean the Church has to follow the example." He pushed the bottle of rye Vasco's way. Vasco left it there.

"I intended it as a gift."

"Lead me not into temptation, Father. I told you I had a problem."

* * *

HE SELECTED PSALM 35; AND IN THE SELECTING UNDERSTOOD WHY KYRIL had insisted that the prayer be pronounced by one of the fighting generation. All of the prayers were in first person. To edit scripture was blasphemous, but for a man clearly too old to serve in the front lines to ask for his own protection would be to defeat its purpose. The congregation was somber, and if anything larger than the turnout at Easter. Men and women, unable to find a seat, stood along the back wall, the line curving around to the sides. He recognized many faces—none of them belonging to the Capone family—and saw many new ones: spillovers, perhaps, from Blessed Sacrament, whose pastor had announced a similar Mass to take place at the same time. Kyril had seemed irritated when he learned of it, although he made no remark. Vasco had sensed tension on the subject of Monsignor O'Meara, based on Kyril's tone whenever he alluded to him.

The air was stifling. Vasco's vestments hung on him with a weight like chainmail, but the hands grasping the edges of the pulpit felt stiff and cold. He was leaning against it to keep from falling. He'd taken the precaution of transcribing the text onto pages from the same notebook he used to record Al Capone's reminiscences, block-printing in large letters, but they swam before his eyes when he tried to focus. He rubbed them and was relieved when his vision cleared.

"'Plead my c—'" His voice caught on a frog in his throat. He made a noise into his fist that sounded embarrassingly like the Chrysler engine on Paul Vasco's boat when he opened up the throttle, and started again. "'Plead my cause, O Lord, with them that strive with me; fight against them that fight against me.

"'Take hold of shield and buckler, and stand up for mine help.

"' Draw out also the spear, and stop the way against them that persecute me: say unto my soul, I am thy salvation.

"'Let them be confounded and put to shame that seek after my soul; let them be turned back and brought to confusion that devise my hurt.

"'Let them be as chaff before the wind; and let the angel of the Lord persecute them.

"'For without cause have they hid for me their net in a pit, which without cause they have digged for my soul.

"'Let destruction come upon him at unawares; and let his net that he hath hid catch himself; into that very destruction let him fall.

"'And my soul shall be joyful in the Lord; it shall rejoice in his salvation.'

"Amen."

At the close of the service, Sergei Kyril placed the Gospel beneath his arm, and as he turned away from the pulpit he grasped Vasco's shoulder briefly and let go.

That evening, Brother Thomas tapped at Vasco's door as he lay studying the breviary, and when told to come in, handed him a Special Delivery letter addressed to him at Our Lady of Redemption.

It was a square blue envelope with a Wisconsin postmark, no return address, block-printed by an androgynous hand. After Thomas left, he opened it and slid out a train ticket and a note, written in turquoise ink in a script he was instantly certain belonged to Mae Capone:

> Mercer, Wis., any day next week. You'll be met.
> Snorky's been asking for you.
> Please don't let us down. We'll make it worth the church's time.
>
> M.
>
> P.S. We're "on the lam," so destroy this note and keep it to yourself.

He reread it. His hands were shaking so badly the first time he'd missed some of the words.

He put the ticket back in the envelope and the envelope in the inside pocket of his suit coat on its hanger. Then he tore the handwritten sheet into tiny pieces and mixed them in with the crumpled notebook pages containing Psalm 35 in the wastebasket.

Why Wisconsin, of all the places on earth?

TWENTY-TWO

CHICAGO THUNDERED UNDER A CANOPY OF SOOT. ITS MILES OF TUBBY BRICK warehouses and skyscrapers like stacked spools of thread wore many coats of it, and chimneys and smokestacks, independent cities themselves, poured fresh black funnel clouds directly into an overcast made entirely of burned coal and animal entrails. If anything, the weather was hotter and more oppressive than in Miami. Laundry hung as motionless as streaks of rust from lines everywhere and the commuter cars racing Vasco's train along the elevated shimmered in waves coming from the pavement seven stories below. Just looking out the window made him break out in a sweat in his air-cooled coach.

He was just a year older than Al Capone when he'd first come to the place, but although it had changed little visibly, he could not match that young man's frame of mind. True, that had been in flinty January, not soppy June, with the Hulk blasting off the surface of Lake Michigan directly from frozen Canada. (Really, how many places had a name for the wind? North Africa had its Sirocco, Southern California its Santa Ana; but they were seasonable and predictable. In Chicago you never knew when it would blow or for how long, or when it would stop while the city festered in filth.) Still, that journey had been charged with escape from the past and hope for the future, and Capone had made it in the company of his new bride and infant son. Vasco was alone, and while he wore the Roman collar there was no escape, and therefore nothing to hope for.

The stop at Dearborn station lasted just long enough for some passengers to step down and others to board. A pair of soldiers in pressed khakis slung their duffels into the overhead rack and sat down in front of Vasco, their overseas caps tilted at the identical jaunty angle. They were younger than he and chatted excitedly about "getting into the show while it's still on." Outside on the platform, a newsboy with the face of an old man was shouting about Cherbourg and rocket attacks on London. A well-dressed couple in their fifties bought a paper and read with their lips moving, the wife over the husband's shoulder. They carried no luggage, probably lived nearby and came down regularly for the latest reports. Every man in the fighting had someone back home hoping not to see his name on a list.

He was glad when the train resumed moving, gladder still as it picked up speed entering the northern suburbs and leaving the brute city behind. Cicero had been particularly painful, his first sight of the St. Francis steeple in four years reminding him of an accusatory finger aimed at heaven. He had asked for a sign and they were all around. A man should think hard before he prayed, look at it from God's point of view.

No one knew he was aboard this train. He had told Kyril only that he was

going away for a while, asked him not to tell anyone who called for him that he'd
left Miami, and said that he would check in from time to time by telephone to
ask if anyone had tried to reach him. Kyril had asked no questions. He would
guess that the word Vasco had been waiting for had come, whether or not
Brother Thomas told him of the Special Delivery letter, but explanations were
unnecessary in a season of secrets. Vasco hadn't called the Director. What little
he'd heard of Wisconsin told him he was headed for a wilderness where strangers stuck out, especially the kind Hoover would send, who brought attention to
themselves by trying so hard to blend in. He hadn't forgotten the kosher delivery
van posted on the street after sundown on the Sabbath. All would be forgiven
once his reports continued; if it wasn't and he was returned to his tin desk or
dismissed, at least he would be free. Apathy had its points.

North of Chicago—not as far north as he might have predicted, but a thousand miles distant in terms of culture—the train chugged past plowed fields,
worked by teams of mules and horses, and increasingly tractors—Farmalls,
John Deeres, Fordsons farting balls of smoke out of straight stacks and dragging
furrows with discs where no plantings had yet occurred. He seemed to be wit-
nessing the tipping point between beast labor and mechanization. Prairie wind
combed acres of graceful wheat and rattled the leaves on stalks of corn. The
crops grew right up to the edges of small towns populated by men, and as often
women, in bib overalls and floppy straw hats, with brief commercial blocks lined
with feed stores and harness shops and general mercantiles, a quaint term banished from big cities; buildings with false fronts, freestanding partitions masquerading as second and third stories, with real windows, blue sky showing
through them on both sides. They looked like western movie sets. Vasco couldn't
see the purpose of the pretense, except to provide shields for villains to hide behind with Winchesters, waiting to ambush Randolph Scott.

He liked westerns, even though he failed to understand the architecture or
why the Indians insisted upon getting themselves shot out of the saddle chasing
stagecoaches instead of shooting the horses in their traces; movies seemed to
operate on a logic all their own, like organized religion. The lawmen were generally incorruptible, with the occasional crooked sheriff dispatched satisfyingly in
the final reel, often at the moment of repentance, and the outlaws died instantly
with bullets in their hearts rather than rotting in prison for nonpayment of
taxes or being elected to high office. Justice was swift and clean and had no need
for coroner's inquests or grand juries or writs of habeas corpus. Perhaps that was
why Danny Coughlin liked westerns as well. In the old West he might have
owned a gambling hall, worn a fancy vest, and been his own best customer at
the bar.

The towns in northern Illinois were named Morton Grove and Wheeling,
Deerfield and Prairie View. They had narrow brick movie houses, not palaces,
but with grand names like The Empress and The Araby, and their rounded mar-
quees advertised westerns and war movies that had played in the cities last

month. Boys on bicycles pedaled the reels in cans from one town to the next for pocket money after school. The train didn't stop at any of these towns. Their stations had been boarded up since the Depression. But they looked prosperous now, with late-model Fords and Chevies parked in diagonals among the pickup trucks with their front wheels turned into the curbs. The government was buying the farmers' crops to feed the troops. All the barns had fresh coats of red paint, even if the farmhouses were weathered gray, with pumps in their backyards supplying the running water.

Pickups bucked along dirt roads, the drivers seated in bulbous cabs with radiator grilles like medieval visors, their beds stacked high with baled alfalfa and sacks of grain and live chickens squawking in slat crates. Vasco watched one stop at a country crossing long enough for its cloud of dust to catch up and powder it with a fresh layer of brown. The crossing was deserted otherwise, but the driver paused obediently before moving on. People abided by the law here.

But that was an unreasonable assumption to make based upon a passing glimpse. Crime recognized no Switzerlands. There would be petty thefts, juvenile delinquencies, drunk driving on Saturday night, and once in a blue moon a farmer would snap under pressure and take an axe to his wife or vice versa. Each community had a constable for a reason. Vasco knew that many of the farmers furnished Washington with faulty livestock counts in order to slaughter pigs and chickens for their own tables without bothering with rationing. But crimes of violence were an anomaly, rare enough to fuel barbershop conversations for months, and chiseling the OPA was a grass-roots rebellion waged against outside interference; entirely American, like bootlegging, penny-ante poker, falsifying tax returns, and the Whiskey Rebellion that Kyril had spoken of so fondly. Resistance to authority was the business of Americans. It was hardwired into them since the Boston Massacre and still thrived in the wartime black market. Vasco realized what J. Edgar Hoover did not, or would not, that to go against it carried no hope of victory or even progress; they might as well try to dig a hole in the surface of Lake Michigan. He felt useless, and yearned more than ever for a well-pressed uniform like the ones worn by the eager young men seated in front of him—bound, as likely as not, for one more visit home on leave before shipping out. They were playing cards now on the armrest that separated them. The game, appropriately enough, was War.

His collar was choking him. He unbuttoned it, slid down as far on his spine as space permitted, and closed his eyes. But sleep missed its cue. In a little while he sat up and looked out, saw tall pines flanking the cinder bed, and knew he was in Wisconsin.

MERCER WAS EIGHT HOURS NORTH OF MILWAUKEE, SOME FORTY MILES southeast of icy Lake Superior, although glimpses he'd seen of water belonging to what turned out to be a mammoth man-made reservoir had fooled him into thinking the town stood on its shore. The station was painted red, like every barn he'd seen in the farm country, but he hadn't seen a tilled field in more than fifty miles, only logging trails and clearings in dense evergreen forests where cabins had been built of the same trees that had been cut down to make room for them, each with a whitewashed iron oil pig to furnish heat. Trucks pulling flatbed trailers with great logs lashed to them whined up a main street as broad as a tennis court, shifting often, their chain drives rattling and clanking like a drawbridge being raised. The street was a dirty orange, a combination of asphalt and iron ore; the entire northern half of the state, it seemed, was built on iron, pierced all over with mines whose towering elevators were visible for miles where they loomed above the tall trees. Tailings were used heavily in all the pavings and foundations, and the ruddy color against the green of the cedars and pines made Vasco think of Christmas.

The climate here enhanced the image. He was glad he'd brought a topcoat. The air smelled of sawdust and iron and chilled his skin. The appeal to the Capones was obvious after the dripping heat of Miami. Vasco felt conspicuous in his city clothes among so many high-laced boots and ear-flapped caps. The fashion palette seemed to be red-and-black buffalo plaid. He stood on the platform with his valise at his feet, out of the way of pedestrian traffic while the greeters and embarkers evaporated and the train blew its ugly-sounding horn and rolled out, leaving behind a flat brown stench of diesel exhaust, like charred nose hairs. Mae's note had said he'd be met, but he wished she'd risked giving him a telephone number or an address to send a telegram so he could let her know when to expect him. Whoever she sent to meet the train daily had missed today, and now he was stranded. Should he step into the Indian souvenir shop across the street and ask where he might find the residence of Al Capone?

That would be the exact wrong note upon which to begin. Small-town people were insular, suspicious of outsiders, and never deviated from first impressions. This he'd learned from reading Sinclair Lewis, which although it had come secondhand, like the lessons he'd learned about theosophy and the inner workings of the Church from Seamus McGonigle, its truths had been acquired through observation and experience. However the locals felt about the gangster living in their midst, seniority alone would direct them to close ranks around him against interlopers, even if the interloper wore the trappings of an ancient faith. That distrust would spread like wildfire because the hearts of natives beat as one, at drugstore counters and in line at the little stone post office and in meetings at the Elks Lodge—a log building with real elk's antlers mounted above the front door—in parlors and over backyard fences. An indiscreet comment inevitably found its way to its subject, and from there back to the source. What intelligence Vasco had managed to gather had come from keeping his mouth shut and his ears open and possessing his soul in patience, and not by promptings on his part. A good spy (let's call it what it is) had all the qualities of an expert confidence man, lying back and allowing the mark to think he was the one calling the shots. All things come to those who—

An automobile horn prevented him from falling into mindless cant. He'd been so wrapped up in rumination he'd failed to notice the green Plymouth station wagon that had pulled abreast of the platform. It might have been there all along, although he knew it had not. He'd simply failed to observe its approach. Some undercover man he was. Its fenders were battered, lacy with rust, and the ubiquitous dust of oxidizing iron had streaked its finish with a pinkish residue like pale lipstick. (He thought suddenly of Rose: Why?) The particles had formed hammocks on the ribs of the varnished wooden panels on the doors. The motor was running, knocking in an uneven, unpredictable rhythm, the product of a loose lifter or of the random quality of gasoline in the provinces, obtained from varying sources according to price and the current attitude toward rationing. Native behavior in regard to edicts from the U.S. capital depended heavily on distance.

The man behind the wheel leaned across the front seat and opened the door on the passenger's side. "Long time no see, Father. Throw your gear in back and hop in."

The smile on Frankie Rio's face, distorted by his imperfectly joined upper lip, was amber, stained by hundreds of generations of Camels like the one burning between his teeth.

He wore a tan shooting jacket with a corduroy patch on the right shoulder over a flannel shirt and dungarees. The square checked butt of a pistol slid back out of sight under his jacket when he straightened up.

Vasco hesitated, then opened the door to the backseat, slung his valise onto its cushions, and got in beside the bodyguard Ralph Capone had inherited from his brother.

Rio seized his hand in a corded, hairy-backed paw, incongruously manicured to perfection, with the trademark diamond ring glittering on the pinky. "I been here every day this week, watching Scandihoovians climbing on and off the train, looking for that collar. I was starting to think you gave Al the bird."

"I came as soon as I could get away." He refused to elaborate. Mobsters were always testing for disloyalty.

Rio let out the clutch and steered a wide path around a farm wagon carrying a contraption that looked like a spider with an iron tractor seat mounted on top. A harrow, possibly; everything Vasco knew of rural life had come from newspaper pictures taken during the Dust Bowl.

"You believe this street? You cross over, you're out of pistol range of the other side. Hicks in the sticks got more space than they know what to do with."

"It's a nice change of scenery."

"Gimme the Loop any day. You fish?"

"My father does. I never saw the point, with a market in every block."

"That's all Ralph and Al do every day. I eat one more fucking fish I'll bust out in scales. I'd kill for a pastrami on rye. How *is* your old man?"

"He's well. I told him you said hello."

"I can't get over him winding up on a boat. He could spin a Packard around on a dime and give you back a nickel."

"I thought he drove a truck."

"Well, he wasn't exactly union."

A nerve jumped in Rio's cheek. Apart from that Vasco would not have known he regretted opening his mouth. On the other hand, it might have been a chronic tic. Rio had gained weight since his photographs, quilting his powerful frame with a layer of fat. He was hatless, and his hair was receding and graying, but not in a dignified way. There were patches all over like pieces of tape. In profile, he left no doubt he was the man Vasco had seen seated across the kitchen table from Paul Vasco in Cicero.

"I saw you once when I was little."

It was a dangerous chance to take, particularly at the start of his stay, and it went directly against everything Hoover had taught him. But he was tired from the long trip and had not expected to be met by Rio. Exhaustion and surprise had made him invulnerable and impatient.

"Yeah?"

"You were drinking homemade wine from a jug with my father. I came in for a drink of water and saw you."

"Sure it was me? It's a long time since you was little."

"I remember your lip."

A hand went automatically to the old injury, the thumb out to rub it smooth, a gesture of long habit. "Everybody asks me about that. I got a story for each one, but I won't lie to a priest. I tripped and split it open on a streetcar track when I was nine. Lost my front teeth. My parents didn't have a pot to piss in: it was either pay a dentist to fix my teeth or pay a doctor to stitch up my lip. My old man flipped a coin and my ma got out her sewing kit. We was living in a five-story walk-up and they said they heard me hollering on the ground floor."

"I wondered what Al Capone's personal bodyguard was doing hanging around with a truck jockey."

"I seen him around. Jack McGurn said he was the nuts behind a wheel. When I heard he retired to Florida, I thought maybe there's hope for me. You get awful tired sitting around hotel lobbies watching people come and go. I don't remember ever drinking with him. There was a shitload of busted lips around then: busted everything. They called Willie White 'Three Fingers' on account of he lost two under a streetcar, and Deanie O'Banion came by that short leg of his falling off one. Streetcars tore up more guys than tommy guns in them days."

"My mistake." He watched a garage roll by, two men with long Nordic skulls in wool caps and mackinaws squatting in front of the glazed bricks drinking Dr

Peppers from a big red cooler with the logo painted on it in white. Rio and Paul Vasco couldn't have gotten their stories straighter if they'd met to compare them. He didn't know whether the man was lying to protect himself or Peter's father.

Outside Mercer the road narrowed, but not by much. It was a logging trail, with chevrons pressed deep into the sandy soil by the tires of big trucks. Rio moved closer to the edge to make room for a mud-plastered Mack coming in the opposite direction carrying more giant logs toward the sawmill in town. If he opened his window, Vasco could put his hand out and touch the pines growing up from the berm. He saw a flash of white among the straight trunks and knew they'd spooked a deer. He'd never seen one in the wild. He couldn't imagine a less promising habitat for the Capone watcher.

"I don't know if Al and Ralph are back yet." Rio rolled down his window to throw out his cigarette stub and lit a fresh one off the dashboard lighter. "They went fishing. You can't walk three miles in any direction without falling in a lake."

"They left you behind?"

"Thank God. Only thing I hate more than eating fish is trying to catch one of the slippery sonsabitches. Up here I'm just an errand boy. A gun punk from the city gets lost in these woods, so unless they piss off some moose, they're both of 'em safe as houses. Things've settled down even in Chicago. Every few months or so some chiseler turns up in a car trunk at Union Station, but that's about it. It ain't like the old days." He blew a jet of smoke in a sigh.

"What do you all do for entertainment besides fish?"

"Not a hell of a lot. Go for walks when Al's up to it, go into town to the picture show or play slots in the Rex, Ralph's joint. The radio in the cabin's swell if you like static. Fucking trees play hell with the reception."

He'd seen the Rex Hotel near the station, a two-story box with false Tudor timbers on the outside. "I suppose Ralph owns most of the town."

"Naw, there's just that and Beaver Lodge and the Redcap at Martha Lake, just to keep from going squirrelly out here among the bugs and birds. Crickets keep you up all night and in the morning the birds are singing their asses off. I don't know how people get any shut-eye up here. I'd rather live next to the elevated." He turned his head to give Vasco his broken grin. "Some night, you don't object, we'll drop by Billy's Bar in the Rex, you'll meet Jake Guzik. He's a hoot."

"*Greasy Thumb* Guzik?" It slipped out before he could think.

"Jesus, don't call him that in front of Al or Ralph. He's just a big tub of blubber, but they stick up for him. People like Jake. He makes 'em laugh. Somebody put a slug in a guy's face back in Cicero just for slapping him around a little." Vasco's temperature dropped suddenly, unrelated to the northern air. That somebody was Capone, the night he ditched the murder weapon in Paul Vasco's taxicab.

"Jake's Ralph's junior partner. He helps out in the kitchen when they're shorthanded, only Ralph don't like it because Jake can't keep his thumb out of the soup when he's waiting table."

At last Vasco knew how Guzik had gotten his nickname. "I didn't realize so many people from the Outfit spend time here."

"You got to go somewhere when the heat's on. The Little Bohemia Lodge ain't far from here. Johnny Dillinger and his boys crawled out of a second-story window when the feds raided the joint in '34. Dumb feds opened up on a bunch of fishermen when they came out the front door, thinking it was them. That kill-crazy punk Baby Face Nelson caught up with a couple of the assholes on the other side of the lake and mowed one down."

"Do you ever go there?"

"Once. It wasn't any fun. Couple that run it ain't spoken to each other in ten years except maybe to say they're out of firewood. The old lady was the one called the feds. All they got for it was all the windows shot out. If they just kept their lips buttoned, the bunch would've finished up their vacation in a day or two and cleared out. Them boys was good tippers. Johnny told me Homer van Meter gave their girl a C-note just for fetching him a pint."

"You *met* Dillinger?"

"Plenty of times. He used to lay low in Al's place on Cranberry Lake when he had it. Johnny always showed up with a different dame. They say he had a dick on him as long as his arm. I can believe it. He had to have something to attract 'em. He was built sort of dumpy and his head came to a point."

This was exclusive information (not the womanizing or the physical description, which were supported by evidence). Nothing in Capone's file linked the Chicago mob with the loosely organized gangs of desperadoes who'd carved a gory swath with machine guns through the banks of the Midwest for a few years during the Depression. The FBI line was that the Outfit considered such open outlawry beneath its notice except when it brought federal pressure upon criminal enterprises everywhere, at which point it offered rewards of its own dead or alive, and issued orders closing every door to bandits on the run. The very thought of an underworld plutocrat like Capone offering harbor to a mad dog like Dillinger challenged the Bureau's entire interpretation of the structure of American crime.

But then Rio had accepted that myth about Dillinger's colossal penis as gospel, and he claimed to have known him personally. An aging street soldier wasn't above trying to exalt his importance by hitching himself to notorious characters, particularly those who were no longer in a position to set the record straight.

They turned off the road into a pair of wheel ruts and wobbled over bumps and potholes while Vasco clutched the dash to keep from colliding with the driver. Pine boughs smacked the windshield and clawed the sides of the Plymouth, then they came over a low rise into a clearing where a one-story log building stood with a peaked roof at either end. Rio circled to a stop in front, with the radiator pointing out, and turned off the ignition. The motor continued knocking for another twenty seconds and died with a wheeze.

Vasco was just opening his door when Rio scrambled out and took his valise from the backseat. A cry made Vasco pause with one foot on the ground. It started low, climbed to a high fluting note, and died away without an echo. A ghost made just the same noise in his darkest imagination, and it sounded as if it were standing next to him.

"What was that?"

"Loon." Rio's nose wrinkled. "Ducks with whistles. If McGurn was still around I'd send him out with his tommy and shut 'em all up for good."

A plain curtain stirred in a window, and a moment later the screen door opened and Mae Capone came out, dressed as he'd never seen her in a black-and-white-checked blouse stuffed into a sturdy wool skirt, penny loafers on her feet. Her hair was tied up in a red bandanna. Her face was freckled all over and she looked much younger than she was. She was smiling broadly.

"Father! I was so afraid you wouldn't come." She wrapped his hand in both of hers, the next thing to an embrace. He noted an oily smell of insect repellent. Mosquitoes feasted on white Irish skin.

"I could hardly return such a generous gift."

"Not for our sake, then?"

He was confused and groped for an answer.

Her laughter was all merry bells. "I'm pulling your leg. Al and Ralph are out drowning worms, but I have a surprise." She wound her arm in his.

He allowed himself to be drawn inside, Rio following with his valise. He wondered if she was referring to Rose, whom Hoover had said had disappeared from Miami as well, along with Brownie. It was frightening, the depth of Mae's perceptions.

Rose was not the surprise. The surprise was as far from Rose as a surprise could possibly get.

The living room belonged to one of the sections with a peaked roof, done entirely in knotty pine and stone, with massive timbers overhead and no ceiling. A fire crackled in a hearth large enough to roast a hog on a spit. Built-in shelves flanked it, packed with leather-bound books in sets that looked as if they were dusted occasionally but read never, and the head of a six-point buck deer gazed out quizzically from the wall to the right of the stone chimney. A bearskin with head attached bared impotent fangs on the plank floor. The furniture was rustic and still wore its bark. Over everything had settled an olfactory mulch of sweet cedar and charred wood and mothballs.

In one of the chairs, seemingly absorbed in a garishly wrapped pulp magazine with an Indian snarling on the cover, sat a large man running to fat, wearing a shirt with pearl snaps, ragged denims, and a broad-brimmed gray Stetson on the back of his head. An ankle in a scuffed leather boot with a hole in the sole rested on the opposite knee. He was white-haired and could pass for a man of seventy, but his ruddy, wind-chapped face might have been responsible for that and not the normal wear-and-tear of years. He went on reading as if he were alone, his jaws working ruminatively at a bulge in his cheek.

"Jim," Mae said, "get your nose out of that book and say hello to our visitor. Father Peter Vasco, this is Vincenzo Capone—Jim—Al's oldest brother. He's a genuine cowboy from Nebraska."

TWENTY-THREE

"How do." Jim Capone turned his head, spat a yellow-brown arc into a Maxwell House can on the floor beside his chair ("Good to the last drop!"), wiped his mouth with the back of a thick-veined hand, and got up, marking his place in the magazine with a finger. Vasco, who was familiar with the family rite of initiation, thrust his fingers deep into the man's calloused palm to maintain blood circulation. The eldest brother favored one eye. A gummy line sealed the other shut over what was obviously an empty socket. "I got out of the church-goin' habit when I run away with the circus."

Vasco had read a sketchy account of Jim's life in his brother's file, which drew heavily from a Sunday feature titled "White Sheep of the Family." He had indeed left Brooklyn in his teens to become a circus roustabout, ridden the rails for a time, visited Central America, and served as a town marshal out West, where he'd slain a bootlegger in a gunfight and earned the nickname "Two-Gun Hart," using the alias he'd adopted when he fled home. An American Legion post in Nebraska had elected him commander on the basis of his service during the Great War.

"Al almost fainted when Jim showed up at Palm Island three years ago," Mae said. "Everyone in the family thought he was dead."

"I ain't much for writin' either."

"The prodigal son," Vasco said. "What brought you back after all those years?"

"Time goes harder on a man where I come from. You start to get on, you think about fambly. They didn't know nothing about me, but I sure knew about Al. I kept a scrapbook till I lost it in the train station in Sioux City."

Vasco nodded politely. Whoever had added Jim to the file had taken pains to correct the popular record. He'd killed the bootlegger during a brawl in a speak-easy, not in his capacity as a peace officer, and been arrested for it, then released when eyewitnesses refused to identify him as the killer; it was the old Capone pattern, running true to form. Friends of the dead man had then ambushed him and beaten him half to death, gouging out his eye in the process. The citizens of Homer, Nebraska, had turned him out of office when they learned he'd been us-ing the keys he was entrusted with to loot a number of the stores on his rounds, and the American Legion had thrown him out when he failed to produce docu-ments to prove he'd ever served in the military. By the time he'd landed on Al and Mae's doorstep, he'd been flat broke, looking for a handout.

The criminal taint ran strong through all seven Capone brothers. It wasn't a matter of environment—Jim had left behind the reeking slums at a young age for the Great American West, maker of heroes—nor was it the fault of their parents. Gabriel had been an honest, hard-working barber who'd wanted one of his sons to enter the priesthood, Teresa the quintessential Old World combination of cook, housekeeper, nursemaid, marital partner, and stern disciplinarian, who still saw fit to counsel her son the public enemy. The world was filled with honest men who'd had far fewer advantages at the start. An accident of birth, this strain of violence and larceny, like a physical deformity: spiritual dwarfism.

Oddly, it seemed to reside most potently in this least notorious of all the Capones. Of the three Vasco had met, Jim was the only one whom he disliked instantly. His body gave off a fetid odor of unwashed flesh marinated in sour mash and personal corruption. He was the one among them who had operated from a position of trust.

"We weren't expecting Jim," Mae said. "Are we ever? He came in on the morning train and hitchhiked out from town."

"Walked mainly." Jim shifted his cud to the other cheek. "Them loggers don't take passengers and I didn't see but two cars the whole way. The one that picked me up didn't seem any too happy about it; the wife, anyway. Reckon she thought I was Jesse James. Pur-dee humiliating, an experienced horseman like myself having to get along by shanks mare. I'd've brung along Old Red, only the clerk wouldn't sell her a ticket. For a horse she's a mite more well-behaved than most of them birds I seen lapping up likker in the club car."

He spoke with a western drawl Vasco supposed he'd picked up from Gary Cooper movies, and with the easy arrogance of a man who had cash in his pocket for the first time in months. Al was the bank he drew on when all the loan officers found pressing business in back the moment he came through the door.

Politeness cost nothing, and Vasco was bound by his alleged vows to reach out to all God's creatures. "I'm pleased you made it. I may live long enough to meet all the Capones."

"Matt's tough to know, and Mimi's in trouble more often than usually. Frank was the best of us, but he got kilt by crooked cops just for trying to elect Al's boys in Cicero. Albert wants to be Al; nothing wrong with that, except a man's not his own man is no man a-tall." Jim's single eye wandered toward the magazine in his hand. Human discourse was evidently not his long suit.

Mae missed nothing. "We'll leave you to your cowboys and Indians. I'm sure the father wants to freshen up."

Jim sat back down and resumed reading as if they'd already left the room. Vasco thought he could follow all the action just by watching the motion of his lips.

"I'm sorry," Mae said, when they were in the long central portion of the building, with doors leading to what were probably private bedrooms. "Jim's been out in country so long he gets on better with horses than people." Her distaste for this particular brother-in-law was tangible.

"He's like a character in a Max Brand novel."

"Please don't tell him that. He's the most preening man I ever met. I thank the Lord he wasn't around when Sonny was little, with his rip-roaring yarns. I wouldn't trust him with the silver, let alone my only son. Is it a sin to detest a man who shares my husband's blood?"

"One can't be judged for his feelings, only for how he acts upon them." That sounded pompous even for a real priest. "Will he be staying long?"

She laughed, surprising him with that silvery tinkle.

"That's the Christian way of asking when he'll leave. Soon, I'm sure. He only shows up when his creditors are barking at his heels. This is your room, Father. I'm afraid it's not the Vatican."

"I'm happy to hear it. I'm used to simple accommodations."

"Well, it's not quite Sing Sing either. Ralph's a bellyacher, but he's a good host. He likes people to be comfortable around him." She opened one of the doors and stood aside for him to pass through.

A double bed on a painted iron frame shared a space twice as large as his room at Redemption with a black-and-red Navajo rug, a bureau with its green paint rubbed down to bare wood on the corners, and a nightstand supporting a filigreed brass lamp that had been converted from oil to electricity, with a faded fringed shade. Green-matted hunting prints hung on the walls and there was a pitcher and bowl on the bureau. Vasco's valise stood at the foot of the bed, which solved the mystery of what had become of Frankie Rio. A window looked out on woods, with a patch of water belonging to a lake turning violet under the setting sun.

"It's perfect," he said. "Very restful."

"You wouldn't say that if it were deer hunting season. Last November, Ralph sent Louie Campagna packing when he brought a machine gun. I'll leave you to freshen up. The bathroom's down the hall on the left."

"However did you do it?"

She paused in the midst of drawing the door shut. A sudden bright Irish grin broke on her face and he saw the resemblance to Danny Coughlin. She tamped it down with a slight effort. "Do what, Father?"

"Escape. You can't park a strange vehicle on a logging trail without attracting attention, so I know there are no FBI men around. How did you slip out from under them?"

"Promise you won't tell?"

He promised, knowing he would.

"The G-men wouldn't hear a rowboat drifting up to the dock in back, or pay attention when a speedboat started roaring out in the bay. A car was waiting in Miami to take Al to a private airstrip. Rose and Brownie and I went along later when we were sure the coast was clear. Ralph set it up, with some advice from Al. Ralph's popular here; he's good for the local economy, and he helped put out a forest fire last summer. He doesn't want his neighbors being bothered with a lot of men in suits asking questions."

"I thought Al couldn't travel."

"He's much better now, thanks to you, but he missed you. We all did."

"All?"

"Al and I, and Rose. You've made quite an impression on her."

"And Brownie?" He was anxious to deflect the conversation.

"Brownie's Brownie. You couldn't make an impression on him with a shovel. It all went off more smoothly than any of us expected; except Al, of course. He's always surprised when something doesn't go according to the grand plan. What do you think, Father? Was it slick or was it slick?"

"It was more than slick. It was Dunkirk. But it seems like a lot of trouble to go to just for a vacation."

"Dr. Phillips ordered it. The heat was getting to Al, and we can't use the air conditioner because he might come down with pneumonia. Phillips even helped out by agreeing to go to the house on Palm Island every day with his bag so Hoover's spies would think Al was sick in bed instead of on the lam." She caressed the phrase with her tongue; it seemed to be a favorite. She'd used it in her letter. "It was medicinal, and the arrangements took time. You probably thought we'd dropped you."

"I was curious. But I'm very grateful for the invitation. I know at last what people mean when they refer to places like this as God's country."

"It is now," she said, and left him, closing the door.

The bathroom was painted country blue, with an old-fashioned gravity toilet with the tank mounted just under the ceiling, a claw foot tub, and a mirror in a tin frame hanging above the sink. He emptied his bladder, pulled the flush chain, and washed up. Back in the room he unpacked, using the bureau drawers, and after a moment's deliberation changed out of his collar into a hunter-green twill shirt he'd bought for the trip and tucked it into pleated khaki flannels secured with a woven-leather belt. The result in the bureau mirror suggested a military uniform. Men's and women's fashions had taken on a decidedly martial air since the beginning of the war: flap pockets and epaulets, overseas caps for women, Eisenhower jackets for men, cut off square at the waist and modified for the Home Front with pale cream-colored sleeves and the rest chocolate brown. His shoes were cordovan loafers, embarrassingly glossy; the untrodden soles were slippery on the Indian rug. He took them off, sat on the bed, and used a pocket knife (the Woodsmaster, complete with two blades, a fork, a spoon, a nail file, and a corkscrew) to score the pale shining leather.

Someone tapped at the door. He put on the shoes and got up to greet Rose.

She stood in the door frame in a plain cotton blouse and tweed skirt; livery was for the city, as Al would have learned from his old tutors. Her hands were folded in front of her and she wore one of those smiles that came on you during solemn moments in church and were as hard to get rid of as a fly in August. Her dimples were deep parentheses bracketing the corners of her mouth. As always, she wore no makeup and looked and smelled as fresh as the woods.

She curtsied. "Mr. Capone and Mr. Ralph are back from fishing. Mrs. Capone asks if you care to join them outside."

"Outside?" It was getting dark.

"It's real nice. Brownie's got the citronella burning, for the bugs."

"Mosquitoes?"

"Big as B-17s. Lake flies, too, up here, but they bite like bedbugs. No-see-ums, they call 'em. Even Eden had its serpent, Reverend."

"Please tell them I'll be down soon."

She started to close the door, paused. "I'm glad you made it. Everybody here's old."

He smiled when the door was between them. In addition to being hard to shoo away, that smile was contagious.

CHINESE-TYPE LANTERNS HUNG FROM ALUMINUM POLES IN A BACKYARD that was all sand and quack grass, shedding tangerine-colored light in an ellipse. Yellow pennants of flame fluttered from round black smudge pots, the kind farmers used to combat frost, that looked like anarchist's bombs, and moths swarmed around the lanterns out of range of the fumes. Every now and then one of them spiraled down to investigate the cylinder of pale blue light suspended from the overhang of the roof, only to incinerate itself in the flash and buzz of an electrical surge, leaving behind a brief brimstone stench of charred wings and exoskeleton. Ralph Capone, sprawled like an upturned toad in his Adirondack chair, never failed to mark the event with a wheezy, "Hah! Fried the bastard!" He interrupted his own conversation to say it.

"Bottles, it's just a moth," Al said after the third time. "It ain't the O'Donnells."

"Ixnay, Al, ixnay." Ralph struck a match off a thumbnail and set fire to one of his Melachrinos. He shook the flame out with a vicious snatch and tossed it into a fire bucket. Vasco had seen fire marshal's warnings posted on buildings and telephone poles since his first pine sighting.

"I know about the O'Donnells," he said. "My father complained about them all the time."

Ralph squinted at him in the dim light. The Capones bore a close resemblance, except Ralph's head was bigger and his lips were more functional and less decorative. He was heavier, too, by at least fifty pounds of pasta and cannolis. "You look more comfortable out of the rig. I never knew they let you fellows go around out of uniform."

Al said, "Leave him be. Even the pope takes off his hat to scratch his head."

"Boys, you're bordering on blasphemy." Mae tried not to sound prim. It was vacation, and they had a guest.

"Mea culpa." Al and Ralph said it together, and crossed themselves in unison.

Vasco said, "Not blasphemy. I'm only a servant of the Lord."

"Well, you don't look like one in that getup," Ralph said. "I don't know what it is you look like, but that ain't it."

So much for making people feel comfortable around him.

The conversation went from there to the day's fishing. It had gone well, and Rose was busy in the kitchen helping Brownie clean a string of walleyes, whatever those might be. When Vasco had joined them, the men rose to shake his hand— all but Frankie Rio, who was back on duty now and not social, and Jim, who had exchanged his pulp magazine for a flask encased in leather with stitching that looked like a canteen in a western movie. It must have held at least a quart, and the sharp smell of the liquid when he tipped it up stung Vasco's eyes. It might have come from the stores of first-pass corn liquor the FBI file had said he'd confiscated from moonshiners on the reservation for his own use. The old reprobate sat with his chins on his chest and metaphorical bubbles floating around his head, like a drunken character in a comic strip. He was as easy to dislike as Al was to like, despite all Vasco and the world knew about Al Capone. Vasco could not understand why Jim mattered, except the teachings he'd almost forgotten until Hoover's memo that had landed on his tin desk had conditioned him to believe that everyone did. Had it been only three months?

Al and Ralph wore identical outfits, fishing vests with batteries of button-down pockets, coarse cotton shirts, trousers of duck canvas, and bucket hats with fishhooks glinting on them. They made Vasco think of Paul Vasco's neophyte fisherman, with his artillery of expensive rods and early convert's faith that one could catch fish with greenbacks for bait. All that was missing were the hip boots. The brothers wore shoes that laced to the ankles, with blue-green algae dried on them like burned-out moss. You couldn't find such gear in the Loop, and not even in Miami, where fishermen's footwear ran toward deck shoes and bare feet. You had to order it from Abercrombie & Fitch, and pay the shipping and handling. The fashion was as far from Chicago gangland as one could get, short of the silver-lame jumpsuits Buck Rogers wore. It was all very surreal, Capone life in northern Wisconsin.

Rose appeared, smelling slightly of fish despite her lemon soap, with a tray piled high with sandwiches and a blue-enamel coffeepot as big as a gasoline can. Everything was big in that company: furniture, fireplaces, even the sandwiches were triple-decked and stapled together with toothpicks. Grilled cheese, the bread toasted by Brownie in an iron skillet with bacon grease left over from breakfast; Vasco, who'd had nothing since egg salad and a glass of milk at noon on the train, ate greedily and drank coffee that had boiled all day but, as always, lacked the bitter wartime intrusion of chicory. He knew he was getting fat on drugstore hamburgers and Cokes, and reminded himself to ask to borrow Kyril's dumbbells. The combination of hot sandwiches and the smell of coffee and pines and lake water was famishing.

A loon fluted out on the lake, saying good-bye to the last rusty traces of sunlight. Tiny bugs popped like corn and made sparks when they hurled themselves against the contraption hanging from the roof. Another bird called in the forest— a whippoorwill, he decided, based on travelogues he'd seen before the main feature. Something heavy crunched brush nearby. He wondered if it was bear country and doubted the firepower under Frankie Rio's arm was equal to six hundred pounds of charging muscle with claws and fangs. It would be an incongruous end for them all to be eaten by a bear. He was a city slicker, he confessed to himself, only without the slick.

Was it slick, or was it slick? Mae had asked, knowing it was slick. No, he was neither slick nor rustic, and felt distinctly out of place dressed like a man of the North Country. But then he felt no less uncomfortable disguised as clergy. It occurred to him that he had not been comfortable in his skin for a very long time.

"Mae tell you how we got shut of the whiskers?"

He was aware suddenly that Al was looking at him, the whites of his eyes glistening in lantern light; that he had been watching him for a long time while he plowed his way through the bounty Rose had brought. He felt a rush of guilt, as when, at ten, he'd stuffed his cheeks like a chipmunk at the family table, hoping his father wouldn't notice and give him hell for being greedy. Paul Vasco had cared little for food, despite piles of spaghetti and steaks as big around as phonograph records. He ate swiftly, paying no attention to taste or satiation, and burned it off in his wiry frame.

"Whiskers?" He'd had to chew industriously and swallow in order to get the word out without spitting food. Gluttony was the ugliest of all the deadly sins.

"Uncle Sam." Al stroked a set of billy goat whiskers that didn't exist on his blue chin. "The feds."

"She told me all about it." He made no attempt to keep the admiration from his tone. The thing had been so complicated—water, land, air—and yet so simple, in this age of miraculous means of getting around—that he knew Hoover would have an apoplectic fit when he learned how it had been accomplished. The beehive in the District would be buzzing furiously, and the queen would be awash in resignations before the episode was over. "I could hardly believe it, and yet here you are."

Once again, Capone seemed to have read his mind. "It doesn't take a genius to pull the wool over the eyes of a dumb cluck like Hoover. He's all flap and no guts, like them walleyes when Brownie gets through with 'em. I had a lot of good talks with Al Karpis in Alcatraz. You know how it was Hoover came to arrest him, Alvin Karpis, brains of the Barker Gang?"

He flashed back to a newspaper picture on his bedroom wall in an apartment someone else was living in now: the Director climbing the steps of the federal building in St. Paul with Public Enemy Number One in tow, manacled like a common pickpocket in his sporty straw boater. "It was in all the papers."

"Sure it was. Hoover won't take a shit without an army of reporters and photographers to cover every movement. Some mug in Congress asked him in public if he ever arrested anyone personal. He could've said, 'Congressman, I run the show. I hire guys with experience to do the arresting.' Only he didn't. He had to go out and prove himself. What he did, acting on tips, he sent a mob of G-men to surround Karpis in his car, which they did without no trouble, Karpis being a smart cookie who knew when the jig was up, and when they were sure he wasn't carrying, they said, 'All clear, Chief,' and Hoover came out from behind a tree where he'd been pissing his pants and said, 'You're under arrest.' None of the stupid fuckers even thought to bring along handcuffs. Finally they tied his hands with a necktie and that was it, the end of the manhunt of the century. Say what you like about me—everybody else has—I never took any glory for something I didn't do personal. Just another four-flusher, Hoover, and yellow to boot."

Vasco knew Capone's version for a lie. The incident was chiseled in legend. A career crook like Karpis would say anything to smear the reputation of the man who'd outsmarted him in the end. The story was what kept Vasco going.

Ralph said, "All them independents was dopes. Go around pushing in banks and knocking off cops in broad daylight, stir up the feds and locals, you wind up running in smaller and smaller circles till you got yourself surrounded. You want to get along you need to get into a steady racket."

"Like me?"

"Sure, Al, like you. You showed the rest of us the way."

"So how come Karpis and me ended up in the same yard?"

Ralph paused in the midst of lighting a fresh Egyptian off the butt of the last, then shook his big head and flipped the stub into the bucket. "All the same it's different."

Al laughed, whether at his brother's phraseology or his particular worldview wasn't clear. The laughter had an edge, nasal and unpleasant. He took a stick of gum out of a pocket of his fishing vest and started chewing.

"Enough shop talk," Mae said, rising. "It's bedtime, Snorky."

"Jesus, Mae, he's on vacation. Let him stay up."

Her eyes caught fire, but she didn't point out the profanity. "You should be turning in, too, Ralph. You can't stay up half the night and get up at dawn to fish."

"I can't anyway. I got to be in Milwaukee by tomorrow night."

"What's in Milwaukee?" Al asked.

"Brewery business." Vasco felt Ralph watching him out of the corner of his eye.

"You might've said something before."

"I did, this morning in the boat."

"What about me? I didn't come up here to go fishing all by myself."

The querulous note drove all the tranquility from the scene. It was the prelude to a tantrum, as when Capone had threatened to have the president of the Dade County Realtors Association killed for cheating at cards at the pool. Nothing stirred. Even the bugs had stopped committing suicide.

"Take Brownie." Ralph sounded conciliatory.

"I'd rather take a hunk of driftwood. The conversation's better."

"Don't look at me," Mae said. "I don't like fishing any more than Frankie does."

Vasco sat very quiet. He knew what was coming.

Al's gaze settled on him. That broad grin split his features. "Father, you handle a rod as good as you do a chalice?"

"I've never held one in my hand, but I come from a long line of fishermen."

"I don't give a shit about the fish. They're just an excuse to get out there and float."

"Frankie, you go out with 'em," Ralph said.

Al's grin evaporated. The white of his scars showed against his face. "I don't need Frankie. I'm retired."

"Al—"

"You think the Padre's gonna slip me the shiv, poison my sandwiches like that sonofabitch Aiello?"

"See, Al, that's just what I'm talking—"

Al spat something in Italian, too rapidly for Vasco to follow.

Ralph paled. "Mae, talk to him."

Mae was the peacemaker. "Snorky, you haven't really asked the Father if he wants to go fishing with you."

"Who don't want to go fishing? Why the hell'd he come up here if he don't like to fish?"

Jim Capone was alert now, his single eye glittering in Ralph's direction. "I'll ride along with you to the station. I got to git."

Ralph's big head swung around on a swivel. Here was someone he could unload on. "I bet them C-notes are burning a hole in your britches. Every slot and whorehouse between here and Kansas is saying, 'Where's Jimmy? We ain't seen him around lately.'"

"Nebraska."

"Nebraska, Texas, Mexico. Ain't a bim or a one-arm bandit in any of 'em you ain't hit, and when they strip you down to your long-handles you come crawling back here and hold out that pisspot of a ten-gallon hat and say, 'Fill 'er up.'"

"I got a fambly to support." The drawl climbed to a high-pitched whine.

"We all do, Jimmy. Family's the thing we do best. That's why I'm saying you can ride along, but when we get to the station, stay out of my car. I don't want to see you this side of Milwaukee."

Vasco kept silent, hoping the digression would spare him an invitation and knowing it wouldn't. Whatever answer he gave would bring disaster from one direction or the other. He should have anticipated just such a situation: Ralph did not want to leave his brother alone with a stranger. All Vasco had had to do was let Mae's note go unanswered and stay in Miami. Hoover wouldn't have known he'd ever heard from her, and he wouldn't have risked losing the ground he'd gained.

But then he hadn't known Ralph would be a component. "Mercer, Wisconsin," the letter had said. It might as well have been Sao Paolo for all it had seemed to do with Miami and Chicago.

Rescue came from Frankie Rio, of all people. He was standing next to Ralph's chair now. He leaned over, his pistol sagging through the opening in his mackinaw, and whispered in Ralph's ear.

"Yeah, I forgot he was gonna be there." Ralph spoke in a murmur, more to himself than to anyone present. He inhaled deeply, burning off the rest of the cigarette between his lips, and blew out smoke, like a boiler letting off steam through a valve. "Okay, I can't go in there bare-ass. You better come along."

The air had changed. Mae smiled at Vasco. "What do you think, Father? There isn't much to do around here but fish and chop wood. Forgive me, but I can't picture those hands wrapped around the handle of an axe."

A pile of firewood was stacked against the end of the house almost as high as the roof. That would be Brownie's responsibility; Ralph was too fat and Al hadn't the stamina.

The prison cook who'd taken an inmate's head nearly off his shoulders with a meat cleaver would set up a chunk on the block, grasp the hickory handle with all eight fingers, and swing a long beautiful arc beginning at his heels, striking the dense wood with a report that rang clear across the lake and splitting it like an apple. In the midnight murk when his exposure seemed inevitable, Vasco feared Brownie more than the Outfit, more than Frank Nitti with his eyes like black stones.

"It looks like my mind has been made up for me," he said. "I'd love to go fishing."

Al sat back, chewing his gum and cracking it. "All that fuss over nothing. It's the damn Pineapple Primary all over again."

Ralph's face darkened suddenly. Vasco thought he was preparing to put up another argument, but then he saw Ralph's hands gripping the sides of his chair, the knuckles whitening, and knew he was just making the necessary arrangements to put himself on his feet. When that feat of engineering was completed, he looked at Vasco and jerked his head.

Vasco rose and accompanied him to the edge of the lighted oval, where he laid a big quilted hand on Vasco's shoulder. There was iron beneath all that flesh. Mae was helping Al out of his chair and Frankie Rio stood on his own edge of the light, observing everything and interested in nothing. He'd said a man got tired of sitting around hotel lobbies watching people come and go, but he didn't look tired, just there.

Ralph's wheezy voice dropped to a wheezy whisper. His breath was hot and moist and heavy with garlic. There had been no garlic in the cheese sandwiches. It flowed sluggishly through his circulatory system from years of injections and escaped out the nearest aperture.

"You remember what we talked about in Miami?"

Vasco nodded. "I'm to tell Mrs. Capone everything Mr. Capone and I talk about."

"You remember the rest?"

When he hesitated, choosing his words, Ralph started humming. "Empty Saddles (in the Old Corral)" sounded nothing like Gene Autry coming from that throat filled with phlegm.

"I remember."

The hand relented, only to collide with his back with hurricane force. "I can see you're one Holy Joe has his head on straight. Be sure and spit on the lure before you cast your line. You'll catch your limit in no time."

THE WOODS WERE NOT PEACEFUL. ROBERT FROST GOT IT WRONG. CRICKETS stitched, owls hooted, something made an angry high-pitched gargling noise and jumped out of a tree onto a bass drum. Those sudden unpredictable explosions were what made sleep impossible. In the city, traffic hummed, horns honked at almost regular intervals, trains chuckled, sirens rose and fell and trailed off in a growl. A man could put up with the stitching and the hooting and the wind moaning anguish in the boughs, but there was no telling when something would jump out of a tree onto a bass drum except that it would be just when he was sinking into unconsciousness; then his heart would bump and he would lay there with his eyes wide open and a single mosquito drawing a bow against the strings of a tiny violin right in his ear.

Dawn came blue and cold and much too early. Ralph, Jim, and Rio were still sleeping; the first train wouldn't run for two more hours. Capone, dressed as he had been the previous night, but without the hat and vest, sat at an oilcloth-covered table in a large kitchen that doubled as a dining room, shoveling in fried potatoes and onions and link sausages the size of bottle rockets and washing them down with coffee. Mae, seated across from him in a quilted blue housecoat, her hair in a braid, ate slowly and drank orange juice, wrinkling her nose every time she took a sip. "Concentrated. Florida's spoiled me. How did you sleep, Father?"

"Like a baby," he lied. He'd put on the same shirt and slacks and hadn't shaved. Brownie, as big as the woodstove he was cooking on, wore his chef's toque and long apron. Rose, fresh-looking in another simple blouse and skirt, smiled at Vasco and poured coffee into a thick white mug set in front of his place, between his hosts.

"I'll just keep this coming," she said. "City folk don't sleep like babies up here."

There was a cast-iron sink, a Frigidaire that kicked in with a thump and purred, and a full set of iron skillets hanging behind the stove. A window with plain curtains looked out on the lake, turning coppery as the sun rose.

Conversation was spare, consisting mainly of requests to pass things. Capone, it appeared, was not garrulous at that hour. His silence set the tone. Vasco ate sparingly. Ralph's girth was a cautionary tale.

Suddenly Capone was up and bustling, and Rose was clearing the table. He outfitted Vasco with Rio's mackinaw, which he was leaving behind for his city clothes, and Ralph's vest, which swam on him even with the coat underneath. That, too, was loose, especially under the left arm where the flannel lining had been cut out to make room for his pistol. Ralph's bucket hat would have settled on his shoulders, so he put on his own black snap-brim. Capone, whose tongue was loosening, remarked that he looked like an undertaker who specialized in burying lumberjacks.

"Don't let the father fall overboard," said Mae in parting.

He followed Capone down a path worn between tall wet grass to the lake, where Brownie had stowed tackle, a Thermos, and a picnic basket filled with sandwiches aboard a twelve-foot rowboat with a motor that looked like a chafing-dish mounted on a propeller shaft. His employer was surer on his feet here than on Palm Island. When Vasco was seated in the bow, he pushed off, splashed through water, adding a fresh coat of algae to his high-topped shoes, and clambered aboard like a man half his age and thirty pounds lighter. He used an oar to push them clear of the reeds, then tipped the propeller into the water, grasped the starter rope by its wooden toggle handle, pulled, got a sputter and a gasp the first time, then pulled again. The motor started with a roar. He sat down and steered them away from shore with his hand on the rudder. Vasco turned up his collar against the rush of cold air on the back of his neck.

A little over halfway across, Capone cut the motor. The sudden silence was a relief.

"Drop anchor, Padre. That bucket there; toss 'er over the side."

The rusty paint bucket at Vasco's feet was filled with cement, with an iron ring sunk in it tied with a coil of cotton clothesline to an iron staple attached to the side of the boat. It was heavier than it looked and he used both hands. The bucket splashed when it entered the water and the rope zinged against wood until the weight settled on the bottom. It sent a fresh set of concentric rings overlapping the ripples the boat had made, chasing them toward shore, where the reeds grew straight until they stooped under their own weight like old Jesuits and the pines threw Christmas-cookie reflections onto the lake. A loon started up. A bullfrog gulped. Everything else was the hollow scrape and thump of their feet on the deck when they shifted positions and now and then an inverse splat when something broke the surface from below to sip at the air. Their breath curled in the cold.

Vasco shivered. It was only his first day and he could hardly picture Miami already crawling in heat just an hour ahead of them.

He made himself useful, lifting the battered green metal tackle box from the deck, resting it on the two-by-eight seat that separated them, and unlatching it. Capone stopped him.

"Keep your shirt on, Padre. We got a freezerful of fish on the back porch. I don't even like fish."

Vasco sat back. Capone patted his vest, took a cigar from a deep flap pocket designed for something else, a lure or an olive bottle filled with grubs for bait, bit off the end, and spat it over the side; something struck at it from below, but it was gone before it could be identified. Capone struck a match from a book from another pocket with BILLY'S BAR block-printed on the cover. He sent a brownish-gray plume out over the calm water.

"It ain't Lake Michigan," he said. "That's one of the things I like about it. Too many stiffs cluttering up the bottom there, they make your flesh crawl. They say that sheeny cocksucker Dutch Schultz invented cement overshoes when he dunked Bo Weinberg in New York Harbor, but he got it from Johnny. Of course, that was before the stiffs started falling too fast and too many to stop and clean up after."

Vasco had started to yawn, affected by sleepiness and chill. He broke it off and listened.

THE CONFESSIONS OF AL CAPONE

1920–1925

Compiled from Transcripts
by Special Agent P. Vasco Division 5 FBI File #44/763

TWENTY-FOUR

TIME DON'T COME OFF THE RACK. IT'S MADE TO ORDER FOR EACH OF US. A geezer there in Mercer sits puffing on a corncob pipe all day in front of the hardware store says he's a hundred and three, and last month a five-year-old kid fell into the flowage and drowned. I don't know if the geezer put his time to any better use than getting that pipe going, but it's a sure bet that kid never got the chance to do anything with his.

In November 1920, my old man's heart went flooey watching somebody else shoot pool in the joint next door to the apartment where I grew up in Brooklyn. He was fifty-five. That seemed plenty old to me then, though I could've stood having him around a little longer. Now I'm just ten years short of that and they tell me I'm a long shot to make it. But fifty-five was just past halfway for Old Corncob, and eleven times more than the kid that took the water nap. See what I mean?

Anyway we went back for the funeral, Mae, little Sonny, and me. I let my beard grow for the occasion as was tradition. Deanie O'Banion shipped a blanket of flowers I'd picked out, at cost, which was damn decent of him, and Johnny sent a great big spray of yellow roses, which was Gabriel's favorite color and mine. Father Garofalo prayed him across and sprinkled dirt on him in Calvary Cemetery in Queens. Later I had him exhumed and reburied in Mount Olivet in Chicago under a swell marble monument with his portrait in the base. But before that I shipped in Mama, four of my brothers, and my sister, Mafalda. Ralph was already with me, doing the heavy lifting, and Jimmy was out West, riding cows and punching horses, though we didn't know that then. I put the rest up in the house I built on South Prairie Avenue, with plumbing fixtures imported from Germany and walls of poured concrete; I had an idea even then, when the North and South Sides was shaking hands and slapping each other on the back and swapping cigars, that the shooting wouldn't stop with Diamond Jim. I fixed an escape route from the basement to an alley where I kept a car and driver posted around the clock. I'm just never wrong when it comes to predicting trouble.

The place was big enough for all of us, but not to do business in. Mama didn't have any English, so there was small danger of her ears getting bruised, but Mafalda was studying for the convent—not that you'd guess that now, the mouth she's got on her—so I was sound in my early instincts to hold on to the suite at the Metropole Hotel, which became my answer to Henry Ford's plant in Detroit, where the raw ore came in one end and Model T's out the other. I set up shop in the hotel, and just in time.

Nobody gave Spike O'Donnell a Chinaman's chance at a pardon, except his brothers, who put their faith in Big Bill Thompson and his pull with the governor,

who scribbled his moniker on a sheet absolving Spike of the crime of bank rob-
bery with Bill guiding his hand. Big Bill, I should point out, was a dope who was
always surprising folks with the weight he slung around, which was considerable. He was the duckbill platypus of American politics, with the body of a hip-
popotamus and the head of a horse grafted on by Boris Karloff or one of them
other mad scientists you see at the picture show. Bill made a lot about having
been a cowboy out West, like Jimmy, but like Jimmy it was as real as an injun
trinket you pick up at the five-and-dime. He got into the mayor's office back in
1916 with a gang of blow and steam about making Chicago a wide-open town,
and it didn't matter to him who he wallowed with so long as the town stayed
wide open. It was the thing we all loved about him, even if his main order of business was to keep King George the Third out of Illinois. That was one promise any
politician could keep, because old George had been feeding the worms for a hundred years. He had a hard-on against anything that might put England back in
control of the Loop. So to keep that from happening he returned Spike O'Donnell
to the general population, which put Spike back in business, and his business as
he saw it was to make Johnny Torrio pay for leaving him out of the arrangement
that brought peace to the rackets. I'm not selling this as the McCoy. If you try to
understand how Big Bill thought, you might wind up thinking like him, which is
a one-way ticket to the booby hatch. We was all making it up as we went along, as
I said, and Bill didn't have anything but rotten scrap to begin with.

Well, if you saw a movie in the past ten years you know how Spike operated:
cold-eyed punk swaggers into a South Side speakeasy pledged to Torrio, roughs
up some poor bartender, got nothing on his mind but wiping up wet rings and
twisting out the towel over a pitcher of beer; opens all the taps so the money
spills out ankle deep, flowing out like jizzum going to waste, as the priests say,
only in Latin so's it sounds like it came straight from Rome; signs the barkeep up
for ten barrels of needle beer you wouldn't sell to a yellow dog, then goes on
down to the next speak on the list in the notebook in the pocket of his hundred-
dollar suit, and starts in all over again; I tell you, that Mick Jimmy Cagney had it
all down cold. I'd like to meet him someday, buy him a bottle of Johnny's best. A
couple of dozen stops on this punk's rounds, it starts to cut into the bottom line.

What death does to you, unless of course it's your own, it makes you take
stock of the time you got, and I didn't plan to waste any waiting for Johnny to
come around to what had to be done about the O'Donnells. I kept needling him.
It wasn't as if we didn't have any talent: Willie White could blow out the candles
on a birthday cake with his .38, and Jimmy Belcastro, Bomber we called him,
could mix baking powder with vinegar and a handful of nails and clean out a
roomful of crazy Micks before they finished drinking breakfast. But he didn't
have to go to the pantry, on account of dynamite was cheap and easy to get. Then
there was Frankie McErlane.

"Frankie?" Johnny says. "Frankie's a thug."

"What's Spike O'Donnell? Fight fire with fire."

"But where's it all end?"

"With Spike's head on a pike." See, I'd sucked up all that culture he force-fed me through his fairy professors, they'd lost their tenure diddling the teaching assistants. I read all about Henry the Eighth and Queen Elizabeth and the Tower of London. When it came to bumping each other off, those limeys didn't even stop at family.

"I'm not so sure. Maybe we should have a sit-down."

"There's no sitting down with the Irish. You taught me that."

"Do what you have to do. I don't want to know anything about it till it's done."

Which is what Pontius Pilate said, washing his hands. I had my first small doubts about Johnny in charge. "Leave it to me," I said. It was the second time I'd said that, and it had turned out all right, Diamond Jim underground and piles of jack for the survivors.

Frankie worked fast. This was 1923, and the troubles were just beginning, but none of us could know that. We were putting out a brush fire before we had to call in the ladder trucks.

The operators of all the South Side speaks were put on notice to call Frankie the minute any O'Donnells showed up. One night the call came, and he and three torpedoes trailed them through the broken glass and busted heads till they stopped to wet their whistles in Klepka's on South Lincoln. Three of the brothers skedaddled when the shooting started, but Jerry was slow. Frankie trotted him outside and blew off his head with a sawed-off. That was the shot heard 'round Chicago, the beginning of the beer wars.

Right from the start we were winning. Four or five of the Micks' strong-arms wound up in ditches that year, minus their heads also. Walter O'Donnell went down in Cicero early in '24 after giving a good account of himself in a gunfight; them cabbage-eaters got guts as strong as their livers. On September 25, 1925, a red-letter day in our history, Frankie fired the first tommy gun in town at Spike himself on the corner of Sixty-Third and Western, only he was new to it and Spike ran out from under the spray. I remember the cops scratched their heads over all the bullet holes. They thought they came from a busload of gunmen or else a shotgun with elephant rounds.

That Thompson was the berries, dropping a thousand Micks to the minute. It came out too late to use in France, so the company tried selling it to police departments, only the cops weren't having any, they were stuck on their hip guns and billies. The customers turned out to have names like Murray the Camel and Polack Joe. In Chicago it got so you hung your head if you weren't shot at with one at least once. Jack McGurn took his to bed with him, they said; maybe that's malarkey, but if it wasn't, his girls never complained. Jack and dames, he'd've been called "Machine Gun" even if he never picked one up. It all broke the heart of the inventor, General Thompson his handle was. He sold out his interest and retired to write his memoirs. "On the side of law and order" was the advertising pitch, no shit.

All this time, of course, the O'Donnells are trying to slug it out, but it's tough to lead a charge when you're carrying around a bull's-eye on your back, and they kept losing guys to our side. We already had them bug-ass Gennas, who had Johnny Scalise and Al Anselmi, they rubbed their bullets with garlic and puss so if the lead didn't kill you the blood poisoning would. I can't say it worked, because most of the guys they punctured didn't last more than a day, but the rumor about them bullets was enough to make you piss your pants just hearing their names. But I ducked a couple of slugs from an O'Donnell flivver down the street from the Metropole, and Johnny started keeping irregular hours and never took the same way home twice in a row.

About a month after Frankie whiffed Spike, he got the hang of his weapon and broadsided Spike's car just a block from the same spot. This time he wounded brother Tommy in the passenger's seat.

Spike took the hint then. I was beginning to think he never would. When the reporters came buzzing he said, "Life with me is just one bullet after another. I been shot at and missed so many times I've got a notion to hire out as a professional target." He took the next train east and didn't come back for two years. You don't have to shoot more than three out of four Irish to make your point.

This fight was overlapping other things. Life isn't a Saturday serial, with one chapter followed by the next. It's a jumble of what-you-call unrelated events. When we weren't potting at O'Donnells in the arcade we were building up our truck fleet, acquiring new routes, opening up more joints to handle the inventory. Jake Lingle wrote there were twenty thousand speaks in Chicago proper, counting walk-up flats and potato cellars where they cooked the stuff up on the premises, and Jake would know; he probably went to every one and drank a toast to the Anti-Saloon League. I took the train to Detroit to work out delivery details with the Purple Gang, who were trucking Old Log Cabin over the bridge from Canada. Them Jews was tough, and they didn't enjoy doing business with Italians.

Abe Bernstein told me to stay home next time and send a kike go-between or he'd ship me back in a box. I don't get sore. That hogwash you hear about me busting up furniture and screaming in mugs' faces over some little thing—sure, I made a show now and then, just to keep the crew in line, but that's all it was, good business practice, like any captain of industry puts on so they don't think he's getting soft like Diamond Jim. I even heard where I patted a couple of boys once with a baseball bat, which is newspaper hokum. In the yard in Atlanta I couldn't hit a fat pitch with a tennis racket. What I did in Detroit, I stayed around town a couple of days, making arrangements with some swell designers at General Motors for my armor-plated bus, then bought a round for the house at the bar in the Book-Cadillac Hotel, and sauntered on down to Michigan Central and bought a first-class ticket home. I don't run from Jews or Apache Indians.

The big order of business, so far as I was concerned, was setting up breweries. Beer was bigger money than whiskey, when you figure in all them thirsty day-laborers, slaughterhouse workers, longshoremen, and factory stiffs, and it justified the larger investment. A broke-down whore with a one-room apartment on East Seventy-First could cook up alky on her hot plate, but a brewery needs skilled labor, Germans mostly, a warehouse to hold a vat the size of Comiskey Park, a gangload of barrels, and a hefty layout for protection. You couldn't hide it—we were using army trucks, with green canvas sheets and chain drives, you could hear them flapping and rattling for blocks, and you could smell them long before you heard them, all that bubbling ferment, the brewery too. Somebody tried standing barrels of mothballs around the bay doors to soak up the stink, but it just smelled like a keg party in a closet. There wasn't anything for it but to pay off the harness bull on the beat. Fortunately they came cheap, at least in the beginning. You pay a guardian of the law a salary lower than the Jap you hire to cut your grass, you get what you pay for. I spent more time supervising a brewery setup than I did anything else. Mae made me strip in the laundry room and hang my clothes on the back porch to air out.

I got in a dumb scrape just when we were getting started that could have cocked up our entire operation. I bring that up so you don't get the impression I'm selling myself as a boy genius, never makes a wrong step. It got me my first notice in the press. I was drunk, not that that's any excuse, driving Johnny's brand-new green Locomobile. I ran it into a taxi double-parked on Randolph. I didn't know but that it was a trap set up by the O'Donnells, so I pulled a gun on the cabbie, flashing my honorary sheriff's badge, which Cook County gave out with Cracker Jacks. I got arrested. It didn't come to nothing, I paid a fine, using the Al Brown dodge, but the newspapers dug and still got it wrong. I was "Alfred Caponi" on page three. Johnny gave me blue hell over it: "I told you the first day to get some gorilla to carry your gun for you." He went on about what would have happened if I'd killed a square citizen, what that would do to all the plans we'd made. I earned that chewing out, but the worst thing that came of that dustup was I lost Maggie.

I loved that girl. Not the way I love Mae, mother of my child, the woman who held things together all the time I was in stir, the plot next to mine in Mount Olivet. A man can love two women different ways. Maggie was a pretty blonde, like Mae, and a tough Irish nut, like Mae, but she didn't smile much. She worked the cigar counter in the Metropole lobby. One day I stopped there when I was all set for cigars and asked her out.

"You're married, aren't you?" she asks.

"Yes, ma'am."

"Does your wife know what you're doing?"

"No, ma'am."

"Well, ask me again when she knows."

I didn't take no for an answer. I worked her for six weeks, sent candy, flowers, a mug with a gold bracelet, which she sent back by way of that same mug. I ask her again I don't know how many times. "Ask me when she knows." Did I say she was a tough nut? Ball bearing's more like it. But I wore her down in the end. I could charm the panties off a lamb chop when I set my mind to it. She agreed to go to dinner. We ate. We talked about our families—well, about mine; her parents were dead and she didn't have any brothers or sisters, so she wanted to know all about the Capones from Brooklyn. She knows I'm in the liquor trade, of course, but that was like being a salesman; if we lived in Hollywood and I said I was in pictures, she'd say, "What else?" It's all the same. She wouldn't let me take her home afterwards. I put her in a cab.

Two nights later we went to a movie. Later that week the Four Deuces, only not for dancing because she don't. I took her to more movies. She liked the Gish sisters. I bet we saw everything they were in that year. We went to restaurants, ritzy joints where the waiter clears the crumbs off the tablecloth with a little tin sweeper and they bring you a little bowl of water to dabble your fingers in between courses. We were careful about Mae; I took Maggie to Outfit places and neighborhood theaters clear across town, and there weren't any nosy reporters and photographers hanging around then; I'm Alfred Caponi, remember, just another palooka at harvest time.

I never did see where she lived. When we were alone it was in my hotel suite, and when we said good-bye it was always at a cab stand. I get the idea she's married, but I stop short of having her tailed to find out for sure. What business is it of mine? "Ask me again when she knows." Hell, I think, maybe he knows. Things've loosened up since the Kaiser took it on the ankles. Skirts are short, music's loud, the president's got a chippie right there in the White House. (I got this from Johnny, who got it from Frankie Yale, who had a nodding acquaintance with the commander-in-chief's personal bootlegger.) You can buy a deck of playing cards in the Loop with a different set of titties on every card, right there among the penny whistles and MoonPies. If she can handle it so can I.

But she don't handle my behaving like a mug and getting my name in the papers doing it, even if it is only on page three and it isn't even my name. I made the mistake of telling her about it, laughing, like it's a good joke on me. She didn't join in. We were in bed at the time. She gets right out and starts dressing, saying there's a difference between breaking a numbskull law like Prohibition and threatening to kill a poor hack over a dented fender, and a fender I dented to boot. She left, slamming the door, and the next day there's a different girl behind the cigar counter, milk-faced thing with braces on her teeth. Maggie quit.

Two years later I'm still thinking about her. I'm in a better position to dig up information—the cops are more expensive now, but they're higher up on the ladder—and I find out she's married, though I don't ask how long because it's still none of my business, living in the suburbs, got a kid. She's sickly and the husband's not raking in millions. I start throwing little jobs his way, just to help out; I ain't Santa Claus and a man's got his pride. That's the story on Maggie, the only woman I ever loved outside of Mary Coughlin Capone.

In April 1923, the Outfit went on the ropes when Big Bill lost out for reelection to William Dever, a circuit court judge they said was straight as a horse's dick. It was our own fault for not doing enough to get out the vote, trucking in tramps we paid by the bottle and posting plug-uglies at the polls to send a message to the dopes waiting to cast their ballots—you know, observing the conventions. Well, we didn't, and Dever raided the Four Deuces before his name was even dry on the office door. So we went to Cicero. What the war books call a strategic withdrawal.

Johnny was proud of how he done it. He had a right to be, because we got in our foothold without spilling a drop of blood. The news hawks said I tossed Joe Klenha, the president of the village board, down the city hall steps, but I never laid a hand on him. We were having a difference of political opinions and he slipped, though I will say he was more inclined to see things from the other fellow's point of view on the way back up than he had been going down. That's what a fire or a bad fall will do to a person.

The only gambling sanctioned in town was the slots, so Johnny, not wanting to offend the local franchise, brought in a string of girls. Cicero cops raided the house and locked them up, so he opened another place, but they shut that down too. Then he rang up friends in Cook County and the sheriff came in and busted up all the slots. After that, Johnny came to terms with the locals: they got to keep their one-armed bandits, and Johnny kept his whores, and as a bonus got the exclusive right to sell beer in Cicero. That was his percentage for all the trouble and aggravation. Then he took a holiday.

He earned it. He'd been working nonstop since he left Brooklyn, but till I came along didn't have anybody he could trust to run things in his absence. That was some compliment to a kid who five years ago made his dough roping johns into the Harvard Inn. Johnny drew out a million in cash and securities and letters of credit and booked two first-class cabins for Europe with his wife and mother. I moved my carved elephants into the Hawthorne Hotel on Twenty-Second, took over the top floor, put up steel shutters on the windows. People coming to see me had to walk past guards in the hallway and stand for a frisk if their faces weren't familiar, and in some cases when they were.

But it wasn't all sunshine and two-bit cigars with my feet up on the desk. The O'Donnell business was still going on, and I had to lease some extra muscle from O'Banion, and that cat's smile of his didn't put me any too much at rest about the Irish throwing in with Italians against other Irish. When the other shoe dropped I intended to be ready for it. Also I was in mourning for my brother Frank.

When the fall elections came up in Cicero, we weren't about to repeat earlier mistakes. We set up our candidates with plenty of the folding for megaphones and votes, put the snatch on opposition volunteers and gave them hospitality until after the polls closed, premarked ballots at all the precincts and dropped them in the box so the citizens weren't late reporting back to work. I sent a dozen seven-passenger touring cars to get the boys around. A county judge got wind of all the activity and anted up an army of Chicago police to assist the locals. That was against the state charter, but I never said we had the corner on breaking the law. Nobody's legit, I always say.

Jimmy says Frank was the best of us. I'm inclined to agree, even though he was still in knickerbockers when Jimmy lit out for the territories, so how would he know? Frank was the older brother closest to me in age, and he was always there to pry me out of a jam I got myself into with my hot head, like fights with guys twice my size before I had my growth. He had movie-star good looks, built like a college tackle, never lacked for a dame on New Year's Eve or any other night, and his line of gab—well, he could've been anything he wanted, but he chose to follow me to Chicago and see I didn't fall into a hole he couldn't pull me out of. To that purpose he took command of one of those big touring cars election night.

A squad of plainclothes dicks from Chicago out cruising spotted him with a couple of other guys on the corner of Cicero and Twenty-Second, in front of the precinct building, and pulled over to get out, they said at the inquest, for a look-see. They said Frank started the shooting, and they brought out a pistol they swore was Frank's, with three rounds fired. But my cousin Charley Fischetti was with Frank on that corner, and he said the cops shot first. What are you going to do? You can't even the score with them the way you would a mug. So I swallowed that sour pill. I'm over it now, but they didn't have to pose for pictures holding up Frank like a mackerel they landed. A sergeant named McGlynn drilled him through the heart.

So I laid off the razor again and buried my brother Frank. O'Banion handled twenty grand worth of floral displays, which spilled out of the house on South Prairie onto the porch and even the front yard. I bawled like a baby, and then I did something nobody in the business ever did, before or since: I closed down every saloon in Cicero for two hours until after the funeral. That's something even Eliot Ness couldn't do, for all his press conferences and headlines. The ham.

Mae cried, too. She liked Frank. She said, "Snorky, it isn't your fault." But it was. I thought I was safe in my little sandlot, counted on the gents who made the laws and put teeth in them to obey them. What you have to do, you have to own the gents. Charley Luciano used to say, "If you can't buy 'em, kill 'em. If you can't kill 'em, promote 'em"; which is to say, throw the bastards out of your ballpark. I took it to heart soon as I had the juice. There's a boy in FDR's Brain Trust has me to thank for taking him out of stickball and putting him in tennis shorts. No, no names. Confession only goes so far.

But life goes on, death too. Our slate was in and we were opening joints in Cicero fast as defense plants, which is a good way to put it since we were at war. We were still mopping up O'Donnells and putting out fires, one of which I admit I started myself when Joe Howard, the papers called him Ragtime on account of he could hijack a truckload of Old Log Cabin in the time it took a shine piano player to polish off eight bars, slapped around my pal Jake Guzik just because he could and I braced him at Heinie Jacob's tavern on South Wabash. He called me a pimp.

The cops said I emptied a .38 into his face, but they couldn't find anyone else to say it so they sprung me. I wasn't even heeled when they picked me up. Johnny was back by then, filled with European culture, but he had trouble of his own and didn't chew me out this time.

Mayor Devers' police chief sent a squad to arrest him at the Sieben Brewery on the North Side. Two of his own cops were standing sentry, and they wound up in the wagon with the rest.

Then damn if the chief didn't hand the load over to the feds for violation of the Volstead Act. It was a setup, and it came straight from our pal Deanie O'Banion.

That Mick was slick as an eel. The Gennas wanted him on ice for hijacking a shipment of that government alcohol they'd fixed up a license to distribute, but Johnny counseled peace, which put their backs up against him and also O'Banion's, because he knew Johnny would expect a favor in return, and the Irish hasn't been born who likes owing anybody, especially a wop. But you wouldn't guess it to hear him talk. He offered Johnny a bargain price on the Sieben Brewery. He said he'd made his pile and was ready to pull out for Colorado and raise horses. He set up an inspection tour and was even there to greet Johnny personal. He figured his being on hand to stand the pinch would take the heat off him, and he took the ride to headquarters, cussing out the cops and the reformers along with everyone else, but he overplayed his hand, because when Johnny made bail for himself and his boys he didn't include Deanie. Hymie Weiss was left to cool his heels, too; we knew we'd have him to deal with in time.

"Deanie has to go," I told Johnny. We were alone in the Hawthorne, and he took the drink I offered him, which shows you his state of mind, a teetotaler like him. He was under federal indictment, and you can't fix those birds, not unless you can promise them U.S. Attorney General. (No true bill for Deanie, though; that was his cut for delivering Johnny.) The liquor don't lift his mood. He looked like the widower at a wake.

"It wasn't supposed to be like this," he kept saying. "There was plenty to go around, enough for everybody."

"There's never enough when your name has an O in front of it," I say. "I'll take care of it."

He smiles, but there isn't any gas behind it. I see the spider tracks at the corners of his eyes, gray specks in his chin stubble. He's just forty. "Al, what would I do without you?"

"Snare some other monkey from the Brooklyn Zoo and put him in a boiled shirt." Joshing, you know. Cheer him up.

"He couldn't replace you. A monkey's got only four fists to fight with."

That's not everybody's opinion, despite recent events; it wasn't O'Banion's. I give him rope, send word I'm willing to sit down and work out our differences. I use Frank McErlane, one of his own countrymen. The answer was short and not sweet: "Tell them Sicilians to go to hell." It should be on his headstone.

On November 8, 1924, Mike Merlo, president of the Unione Siciliana, a man of great respect, died of cancer, the first of us to go in bed and the last for a long time. O'Banion sold a hundred grand in flowers for the send-off. What with the turnover among us, I bet Deanie cleared almost as much out in the open as from the rackets. Compared to him I was selling pencils out of a cup in my little antique store. For this occasion, he built a twelve-foot replica of Mike made entirely out of roses and carnations, a masterpiece, and I was tickled to see it. A really first-class chiseler ought to retire at the top of his form. For myself, I do him the honor of bringing in Frankie Yale to show him the door.

Frankie, you remember, is the man who punched Diamond Jim's ticket, and he did it solo, but Deanie wasn't slow and ignorant like Jim, so for backup I borrowed Scalise and Anselmi from the Gennas. You never spoke of one without the other, like Fields and Weber or Leopold and Loeb. They came as a package, the kind Bomber Belcastro sent to certain parties by special messenger, and they never missed. I was so happy with the way things worked out I never got around to returning them to the Gennas, which led to more bad blood, but that situation wasn't likely to improve anyway and I'd rather have that pair on my side than theirs.

Mike was going under on the eleventh, so Deanie was in his shop early on the tenth, rearranging his staff's bouquets and snipping little green sprouts off Mike's statue of posies in the cooler. When the bell tinkles above the front door and his clerk tells him who's calling, he don't leave it to the help. Scalise and Anselmi are two of them Sicilians he told to go to hell, but Frankie Yale, whose great northeastern pipeline keeps the liquor flowing like water, and who's killed more men than Sergeant York, is a man to deal with face-to-face. Out Deanie comes from behind the counter to offer Frankie the rare O'Banion handshake. It's only natural that a muckety from Brooklyn would come to pay his respects to the boss of the Midwestern Mafia.

Frankie's done his homework, about who gets Deanie's hand and who just a nod with his mitts in his pockets, and especially about them pockets; even when he's in his shirtsleeves and a rubber apron, like now, you got to figure him for two rods minimum. So Frankie takes the glad hand and hangs onto it like it's a rescue rope and he's going down for the third time, while Scalise and Anselmi plug away, bammity-bam, so close to him his clothes catch fire, and when Deanie slips his grip and topples, Frankie leans over and gives him one in the brain for the payoff, what we called the *coup de grace*, French, yet; Johnny's Grand Tour is already having its influence on our education. Charles Dion O'Banion cashed in his chips at the ripe old age of thirty-two.

Cardinal Mundelein put the kibosh on a funeral Mass at Holy Name, directly across the street from the flower shop, but what the Church wouldn't do, the boys made up for in spades. It ain't every day a genuine mob celebrity goes to his rest before his time: once every couple of months is occasion enough to pull out all the stops. His casket alone, silver and bronze, ran ten grand, with gold candlesticks all around: it looked like an ocean liner going up Michigan Avenue. Of course, all the flowers came from his own shop. It took two dozen cars just to deliver them to Sbarbaro's Funeral Home, including a big basket I popped for. They said ten thousand people followed the hearse to Mount Carmel Cemetery, tromping all over graves and knocking down headstones just to make sure Deanie didn't pop out of the ground, laying about with a pistol blazing in each hand, the way they said he did back before he could afford mugs to do his furniture moving. The Chicago Symphony Orchestra played "Danny Boy" as he was being lowered into the hole. You had to be made of stone not to cry a little at least.

The North Side belonged to Hymie Weiss now, and he hit back like the Polack welterweight he was. Johnny went away on another vacation, which was becoming his answer to everything, and Weiss's gun punks made themselves conspicuous sweating bullets in their winter hats and overcoats following him through train stations in Hot Springs, New Orleans, Florida, Cuba, and the Bahamas, always a day late and a dollar short; but that was just a feint.

On January 12, 1925, a car carrying Weiss, Schemer Drucci, and Bugs Moran, Hymie's right bower, drove up alongside my car at State and Fifty-Fifth and raked it from end to end with one of General Thompson's trench brooms. I was inside a restaurant at the time, but my driver caught a slug in the back that he was still carrying around last I heard.

First thing I did, I got on the horn to Detroit and promised the head engineer a fat bonus to deliver my bulletproof Cadillac in two weeks. While I was waiting I lined up a two-car escort everywhere I went, one in front and one behind, with plenty of artillery aboard, and set up a perimeter around the Metropole with boys on foot to discourage strangers from parking within four square blocks, which they did by stepping off the curb and sitting on their fenders until the joker behind the wheel got the hint and drove off. I stopped going to restaurants for a while, because I didn't eat in greasy spoons and it meant reserving half a dozen tables for the crew twenty-four hours ahead. Nightclubs, same thing. I was a prisoner in my own town.

But that trick on the corner, that was another feint. Johnny was the one Weiss wanted. The papers were calling him the head of what they tagged "organized crime" in the area, and I was just the hired help. I didn't exactly engage a press agent to claim O'Banion. Johnny suspected what was happening when he read about the attack in the out-of-town papers, and when he came back after a couple of weeks he went before a federal judge and pleaded guilty to the charge of breaking Prohibition. Why waste money on bodyguards when Washington provides them for free, along with three hots and a cot?

The judge gave him five days to settle his affairs before he went away to Waukegan. Johnny and Ann, his wife, spent the next day shopping on Michigan Avenue, which was the thing they liked to do best as a couple and wouldn't be doing for nine months. When they got back to their apartment house on Clyde, Johnny's driver climbed out to help with the packages. Johnny followed, carrying a stack of hatboxes. Weiss and Moran piled out of a Cadillac parked on the corner and opened up with a pistol and shotgun. A slug went right through Johnny and cracked the engine block of his Locomobile. A stray hit his driver, and the glass door of the apartment house fell apart when another went past Ann's head as she was pushing through it with her back because her arms were full of parcels.

Johnny sank down onto the street, still holding the hatboxes so as not to spill Ann's pretties into the dirty gutter; you think you can think straight in that situation, you're just fooling yourself. Wham! A load of buckshot catches him going down, tearing his jaw clean off one hinge. He's lying on his back, the boxes still in his arms, blood snaking his face in every direction, blinking to clear it from his eyes, when Moran leans over him and drops the hammer in his face. It snaps on an empty chamber. He's miscounted his shots. There are sirens now, the bell clanging on a police sedan. Bugs and Weiss pile back into the Caddy and peel out.

We spent the night in a waiting room at Jackson Park Hospital: me, Ann, and what boys I don't have posted at all the entrances and outside the operating room where they're prying lead out of Sonny's uncle Johnny. The buzzards from the papers were circling. They said I had on a "loud checked suit." Hell, I was at the track when I got the word, what do they expect, I stop on the way and change into something appropriate? My friend, my *padrone* is dying.

Well, he pulled through. Nobody gave him any odds, but he was tougher than the whole North Side, as he'd proved. Not that he looked it when I went to see him the day after they took away the tent.

Outside the door was a harness bull and a fed from the Prohibition detail, with a red nose and a flask in his coat pocket, probably filled with our stuff. Johnny's a flight risk, all shot up with more tubes in him than the underground railway.

I thought the bed was empty at first. I realized how little he was then, and pale, you couldn't tell where his neck left off and the sheet began. His jaw's held together with pins, silver wires in his teeth like a kid with his first set of braces. Was this the guy who lit up my head with a short hard jab what, just seven-eight years ago: I took his hand, which felt like a dry empty glove, leaned over him and said, "We'll get 'em, Johnny, don't you worry," which I didn't add might take a while, Weiss and Moran are burrowed in deep with the Gennas and half of Italy out looking for them clear to the Indiana state line.

"Mthrooal," he says, mumbling through all that tin.

"What's that, Johnny?" I lean in tighter.

"Mthrooaltsyrz."

It's like hearing a bee buzzing, caught between screens. I lean in more. I can feel his breath in my ear.

Then he did something nobody would've expected him to have the strength for. He snatches hold of my lapel in one of those dry empty gloves and pulls his shoulders up off the bed. I have to jerk back to keep from biting through my tongue from a head butt. His lip curls back from what looks like a radiator grille and he pushes his words through it one at a time.

"I'm through, Al. It's yours."

"What's mine, Johnny?" Only I know, in my heart of hearts I know. He made the same speech that first day in Colosimo's Cafe right after he said Diamond Jim's got to go, only then he was only offering me half.

"Chicago," he said. "The Pearl of the Midwest, and it's all yours. I'm getting out while the getting's good."

And he fell back.

The getting was good, and he got, the only one of us ever to do it without a long stretch in stir or a liver full of lead. Oh, he kept his hand in; took his percentage from the rackets he invented, and sat in to arbitrate when the killing made it impossible to do business and it was time to talk truce, but there was no more Johnny Torrio, Crime Lord.

Chicago was mine, from the top of the Wrigley Building down to the docks on Lake Michigan, second largest city in the country. I was twenty-six years old.

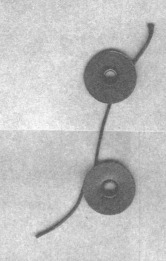

1944

THUGS AND KISSES

TWENTY-FIVE

CAPONE LOOKED AT HIS CIGAR STUB, TOOK ONE LONG LAST REFLECTIVE drag, and flipped it over the side of the boat. It spat when it touched the water and bobbed on its ripples, its wrapper turning dark.

The day was getting on toward noon, and the sun was hot coming off the surface of the lake. Vasco felt the beginnings of a burn on the back of his neck.

"Torrio retired?" Disbelief soured his tone. He still bridled at Hoover's dismissal of the information he'd given him on Capone's mentor. He wanted Torrio to be active still, an operator in the black market.

Capone didn't seem to have noticed his skepticism. "I think his mind was made up before he got shot. Brains and guts are two things you had to have to stay in our business. O'Banion had guts, all right, but framing Johnny was a lunkheaded thing to do, and telling the Sicilians to go to hell was plain crazy. The Gennas wanted to skin him alive, and they didn't deal in figures of speech. I knew they'd have to be dealt with in time; disaster, you know? I always saw a twister coming when everybody else was bitching about rain. Johnny had brains around the block, but he didn't have the stomach for the fight. He was smart to quit when he did. He never did a dumb thing in his life till he crawled in bed with that stinkin' Dutchman in '32."

"Then he didn't retire."

"Sure he did. He just sold his name so Schultz could claim Brooklyn, the way Clark Gable peddles Chesterfields. A man sells his name's got nothing else to sell. They took mine away for seven years. I know what it's worth.

"And look what happened," he went on. "Couple of years later, Schultz declares war on Tom Dewey there in the prosecutor's office and Charley Luciano has the Dutchman popped to avoid the heat. Hit more times than a rigged game of Bingo and he still takes two days to die, jabbering all the time to a police stenographer. I bet Johnny sweated like a horse that whole time, expecting his name to come up instead of a load of crap didn't make any sense."

Vasco didn't care about Dutch Schultz. Capone was wandering off track. Vasco asked an innocuous question to bring him back to the subject of Chicago. He wasn't interested in the answer—tales of adultery wearied him there as they did in the confessional, maudlin self-flagellation or pathetic boasts that they were—but he didn't want to appear too curious about old crimes. "Did you ever hear from Maggie again?"

"I heard she died."

He waited, but nothing more was forthcoming. Capone's face was clouded. It was the first time Vasco had sensed regret for anything in his past; neither his brother Frank's death nor his degrading apprenticeship to Frankie Yale at the Harvard Inn had brought him to this moody silence.

"Did you kill Joe Howard?"

The clouds parted suddenly, split by a grin. "I knew you'd be interested. That was the night I gave your old man a C-note just to drive my piece around the block."

"I was too young to remember when you came to the apartment to get it back. My father never mentioned it unless he was drinking." Too late, he realized that was an admission of indiscretion on Paul Vasco's part. But Capone was thinking along other lines.

"It was a break he was there. Not many hacks would go to that neighborhood that time of night. It didn't matter who dropped the curtain on Ragtime Joe. Some guys are born counting backwards till their number comes up. He roughs around a butterball like Jake who couldn't defend himself, and insults me to my face when I call him on it. No guts and no brains either. He should've been a hotel clerk."

Not exactly a confession, but he had the man's word he'd orchestrated O'Banion's murder. He had to keep reminding himself the Bureau wasn't interested in Capone, only in what he had to say about his accomplices.

"You can't let a man go around beating up your friends and calling you names," Capone said. "Maybe in your line, Padre, but not in mine. You try turning the other cheek, they blow it off with buckshot."

"I don't judge anyone."

"It'd be okay if you did. I'm used to it. Luckily I had an alibi for Pearl Harbor."

"What happened to the detective who killed your brother?"

"He made captain."

Vasco waited again.

"What the hell." A meaty shoulder rolled. "It was war. And I learned enough about the law that night to pass the bar in the State of Illinois."

Vasco probed some more, but the subject—it might have been the word *war*—shifted to what was going on in Europe. The popular opinion that the fighting would be over by Christmas made Capone shake his head. "We're on Jerry's turf now. A punk from another neighborhood don't stand a black ant's chance on a red ant hill, unless the red ants chase him back to his own. Then it's God help the stranger." He blushed, shocking his companion; he wouldn't have thought Capone capable of embarrassment. "Family saying. It sounds better in Italian. Italy didn't always spread her legs for everybody who came along."

They broke out the sandwiches and shared coffee from the Thermos. Cheese on cold toast was delicious out in the open. Vasco was getting used to the hyena laugh of the loons: He saw one when Capone pointed it out, submerged to its neck so that the head on the stalk cleaved through the water like a submarine periscope in a newsreel, then tipped forward suddenly and vanished, to reappear an impossibly long length of time later several hundred yards away, a fish

flapping in its bill. Capone laughed, spitting food. "I don't know what we're doing out here," he said. "The pros got the territory all buttoned up."

After lunch, he handed Vasco a fishing rod and showed him how to attach a
lure he took from his pocket, a masterpiece of wood carving painted to resemble
an arching fish with an iridescent blue top and a white belly, with disturbingly
realistic staring eyes made of glass. Vasco nicked his thumb on one of the razor-
sharp hooks; there must have been an artery involved, because it gushed blood
until he took Capone's advice and submerged his hand in lake water until it
congealed in the cold. The green tackle box delivered up a first-aid kit with
gauze and iodine and adhesive. Capone dressed the wound expertly. "Five
Points," he explained. "You went to the doctor every time you got stuck, sooner
or later it turned into real money."

He learned how to tip the rod back over his shoulder, swing it forward and to
the side in a long graceful loop, and release the catch so that the line whizzed out
in an arc propelled by the lure, which splashed into the water a hundred yards
from the boat. Capone changed seats so that he could embrace Vasco from behind, one arm wrapped around his chest and the other pressed against the arm
manipulating the rod, tipping it back and following through, gripping Vasco's
wrist in his iron grasp. "That's how it's done, son, easy as taking a piss." In the
moment he'd forgotten to call him "Padre," and in the moment, Vasco had forgotten to notice.

He hooked a fish on his third cast. Rather, the fish hooked itself, striking
with an impact he felt through the line all the way to his hand. With Capone
yelling instructions he set the hook with a jerk, released some line for the fish to
run it out, then put the catch back on, bending the rod. With the hook now set
solidly, he released the catch and started reeling in line. The weight on the end
was as heavy as a pipe wrench, and he seemed to have entered into a tug-of-war
with something that wanted the pipe wrench as badly as he did. Then whatever
it was was alongside the boat, writhing and twisting just below the surface, and
Capone leaned over with a net and scooped it up. It flashed silver in the sun, a
sleek torpedo-shaped creature fourteen inches long suited in chain mail. When
the net was safely aboard and he lifted the fish from it at the end of the line, its
body moved convulsively as it worked its parrot-like beak and its eyes rolled.

"Walleye," said Capone. "Your first?"

"My first fish of any kind."

"I'll tell Mae. She'll break out the dago red."

"With *fish*?"

"Hell, no. The fish is dessert. First you got to get drunk on the main course."

When dusk turned the lake purple, Capone started the motor and they
putted toward shore. It took three pulls on the rope; he was visibly tired, and
Vasco thought he saw him shivering. The heat of the day had retreated. Vasco
had caught four fish: two walleye salmon, a trout Capone had persuaded him to
throw back because it was too small, and a bass he said made strong eating but

went well with red wine and to hell with what the snobs said on Lake Shore Drive. He staggered when he climbed out of the boat and Vasco finished beaching it and gathered up the picnic basket and tackle. He stayed close to Capone on the way up the path to the cabin, ready to drop his burden and catch him if he stumbled.

Mae expressed delight with Vasco's success, but saw Capone's condition right away and helped him to an armchair upholstered in an Indian design next to the burning fireplace. She touched his forehead with the back of her hand. "You're burning up. You shouldn't stay out all day."

"Lemme 'lone." His tongue seemed too thick for his mouth. She snatched an Indian blanket off the back of a sofa and spread it on his lap. He dislodged it with a savage kick. "Jesus, I'm roasting."

She used the old-fashioned crank telephone on the wall of the kitchen to call the doctor in town. His wife said he was out on a call, but she'd send him over as soon as he came home.

"He's not Dr. Phillips," she said, hanging up, "but he won't stop to buy a pack of cigarettes. Mercer is one town where the name Capone still means something."

"I'm sure he'll be all right." Vasco was distractedly watching Brownie clean and filet the fish he'd caught, on a slimy cutting board on the counter next to the sink. The hand that was missing two fingers manipulated the wicked curved-blade knife like a scalpel, separating the pinkish meat from bone and entrails swiftly. He repressed a shudder. Rose stood by and wrapped each fish in butcher paper from a big roll that stood on the counter as he finished and put it in the refrigerator.

"He shouldn't have stayed out so long," Mae said.

"I'm sorry."

"Don't be. Al doesn't take orders well. He'd have served all eleven years of his sentence if he hadn't got sick."

The doctor arrived thirty minutes later, driving a Model A pickup that banged and burned oil in choking black clouds. He was a textbook specimen of the country physician, wearing a fishing vest over a blue flannel shirt and bow tie and a weathered fedora with rusty stains on the brim that Vasco hoped was fish blood. He carried a scuffed black leather satchel and smoked a pipe.

Capone was semiconscious. Vasco helped support his weight as he and the doctor got him into a bedroom not much larger than Vasco's and undressed him. He'd sweated through his long gray cotton underwear; they took that off him too. Pale fat quilted a body that seemed built of muscle. It was something to tell his grandchildren when they were old enough; how many people could claim to have seen Al Capone's genitals? They were unspectacular, but engineered in proportion with the rest of him. Counting morgue photos and his father's lack of modesty in semiretirement, Vasco had spent an inordinate amount of time lately inspecting the male sex organs. He covered the sick man to his waist in a buffalo plaid blanket and the doctor shooed him out to begin his work.

He found Mae seated in the chair her husband had vacated, holding a tall water tumbler half-filled with amber liquid. She was wearing a man's hunting shirt with the cuffs turned back to her wrists and the tail out over white duck slacks. They accentuated her somewhat matronly hips and the weary lines in her face made her look her age. "Are you a drinking man, Father?"

"I've begun to develop a taste for Kentucky rye."

"I'm afraid Scotch is all we have. It's in the kitchen; glasses in the cupboard over the sink. Bring the bottle back out with you, please."

Brownie had finished cleaning fish and was outside chopping wood. The blows of the axe sounded like distant mortar fire. Rose, scraping vegetables for supper with a large triangular-bladed knife, smiled encouragingly at Vasco as he joined her at the sink.

"Don't you worry, Reverend," she said. "Mr. Al catches every bug that comes along, but he's strong as a bull."

"I hope so." He excused himself to bring down a tumbler and fill it halfway from the faucet. Rusty water sputtered out.

"Mr. Ralph, he'd be jealous, the fish you caught. He's got a brown thumb when it comes to catching fish."

"Beginner's luck."

"Don't you worry about Mr. Al."

It touched him that she would repeat it. She was concerned more for him than for her employer. He thanked her and went out.

He refilled Mae's glass, which was almost empty, set the bottle on a birch coffee table littered with ashtrays and anglers' publications—big leaping fish on all the covers, hooks in their mouths—and sat on the sofa with his drink. He found he didn't care for the iodiney flavor of Scotch. It reminded him of his throbbing thumb. His face must have shown his distaste, because Mae said, "I don't like it either, but it's all Ralph stocks. It caught on back when everyone thought it must have come from Scotland and not someone's bathtub in Cicero." She drank, wrinkled her nose. "Anyway, it works fast."

"I take it Ralph and Frankie got off all right."

"Jim too, with all his things rolled in a ratty old blanket. Ralph and Frankie will be back tomorrow, starving. Ralph won't eat what they serve in dining cars. I'm considering asking him to raise our household allowance so I can pay Brownie and Rose more for working in a short-order restaurant."

"Ralph's frugal?"

"If you mean is he a cheapskate, no. He doesn't have to give us anything, which is why I hate asking for more. But every time something happens in Europe or the Philippines the cost of living goes up."

The conversation lulled. He was groping for a neutral subject when voices rose down the hall. He started to rise, but she waved him back down with an impatient gesture. "Al's worse than Sonny was when he caught the sniffles at ten. If he's mad it's a good sign."

"I hope so," he said, and was surprised to realize he was being sincere. He'd thoroughly enjoyed the day, more so after Capone finished reminiscing. Catching his first fish had brought a rush of emotion he hadn't anticipated.

Mae was studying him. "I have to ask what you talked about."

He'd been dreading the question, but he'd prepared his answer. He told her what Capone had said, with certain alterations. He employed the same circumspect language Capone had applied to the Joe Howard killing in describing the war with the O'Donnells and the murder of Dion O'Banion, distancing the instigator from the acts, and placed more emphasis on the death of Frank Capone than had actually been the case, to explain away the time. He left out the Maggie episode—not so much, he told himself, to spare Mae's feelings as because telling it would serve no purpose. Capone was unlikely to expose the omission. It wasn't a lie, merely an alternate version of the truth.

Which was, of course, one definition of a lie.

"I got to know Frank when he was living with us on Prairie," she said when he finished. "He was the quietest of the brothers, and he had good manners. He spent a lot of time with women, but he never brought one to the house. He had too much respect for his mother and his sister and me to parade them around in front of us. And he'd have died for Al, as he proved. Mafalda wailed for days. Mama Teresa never shed a tear. Her heart was torn from her body, but she spilled it all out in prayer."

She emptied her glass a second time and lifted the bottle to pour before Vasco could get to it. "When Frank died, that made Ralph the oldest, since no one knew what had become of Jim. Ralph's been doing his best ever since to take Frank's place. That's a full-time job with Al the way he is, but Chicago won't run itself. He's suspicious because he doesn't have time to be anything else."

"I understand."

"Thank you for not telling me about Al's little affairs."

He'd raised his glass to sip and was glad he hadn't gotten farther, or he'd have choked.

Her smile was tight and bitter. "He lived in a hotel. The house was just to visit. Men are weak when it comes to temptation. I suspected right away, and I wasn't so stupid even then. I overlooked the evidence. When he went out to Los Angeles to set up the Hollywood connection, one of those little snips the Coconut Grove hired to take pictures of customers snapped him dancing with that slut Joan Crawford and it got into all the papers. I threw a potted plant at him when he walked in the door. I didn't care so much about Crawford, but I was pretty sure he went to bed with the little snip too. But the only time I came close to killing him was when he ducked out with Sally Rand during a recess in his income tax trial."

"The *fan* dancer?"

"I don't think she was even using the fans then. They came out only when the World's Fair opened in Chicago in 1933. It was under construction at the time of the trial and she was in town to get a look at the pavilion where she'd be dancing. If you were anywhere nearby that month, you went to the courthouse to see the show. Edward G. Robinson sat in the gallery, plugging *Little Caesar,* and Ruth Chatterton sashayed down the aisle wrapped in furs trailing some chorus boys prettier than she was. Rafael Sabatini, who wrote *Captain Blood,* took notes, but I never saw where he wrote a book about it. It was the place to be if you wanted to see celebrities. I took a shot at Al that night with one of his own revolvers."

He set his drink on the table. It wasn't worth the risk.

"I aimed high," she said. "I didn't want to make Sonny an orphan, with his father dead and his mother in prison. I just wanted to make my point clear. I was economizing for the long haul, explaining things to our son, hoping for the best but getting ready for the worst, and he's out showing a striptease artist the wonders of his new suite at the Lexington, with its secret escape hatch leading into the office building next door and down the fire stairs to the alley. If I believed in reincarnation, I'd think Al started out as a gopher. Well, I almost hit him anyway. The bullet ricocheted a half-dozen times and made a ditch in the rug before it came to a stop. I forgot about those damn cement walls."

He wondered if he should be recording the confessions of Mae Capone. He felt like the old family ecclesiastical retainer.

"What happened then?"

"Nothing."

"Nothing?"

"Unless you call Al's turning white and locking himself in the den something. When he came out, he acted as if we'd had a dustup over a burned roast and we made up. He'd been shot at before, you know, so I guess his reaction was bound to be a little off the common."

He liked the way she talked. Capone's FBI file reflected Hoover's dismissal of women—with the exceptions of Ma Barker and Machine Gun Kelly's wife Kathryn—as unimportant in criminal matters, but Mae's slim entry had said she'd spent most of her time reading novels while Al was busy corrupting America. "What about you?"

"I was just happy I didn't hit him, and embarrassed about the whole thing. I'd learned to ignore his little involvements because he was a good father and provider—we never fought about money, which being wed to the Church you may not know how rare such a thing is among married couples—but the timing of this one really stunk. We chalked it up to pressure and never talked about it afterwards. Sally shook her boobies in the pavilion while Al was in Atlanta waiting for transfer to Alcatraz; that made her the problem of every wife whose husband went to the fair, not mine."

"You've a saintly patience, Mrs. Capone."

"Not when it comes to being addressed by my mother-in-law's name. Please call me Mae."

"I will if you'll call me Peter. Sonny does."

"Sonny belongs to your generation. I'm conditioned against it by the life I've lived."

"In that case I'm afraid we're at a stalemate."

She cupped both hands around her glass, lips pursed. "I'm open to compromise. When the collar's off we'll use Christian names."

He smiled and leaned forward to touch his glass to hers. When he sat back, she said, "Anyway, all those women went to bed with Snorky, the human slot machine who paid off in hundred-dollar bills. They didn't have to wake up next to Alphonse. Al knew that. He was too smart to throw me over for the newest thing in a smaller-size girdle, like Colosimo and that North Side crowd. There are all kinds of loyalty, Fath—Peter."

He started to say something, but she set down her drink and rose, smoothing the front of her slacks. He was aware that the doctor had entered the room. Vasco stood and turned to face the rumpled rustic with his satchel.

"Just a bad cold, Mae, but they rock him more than most. Give him plenty of liquids and keep him out of drafts. I'll look in on him tomorrow, and tell Esther to send the boy for me if you call and I'm not in."

"I'm sorry he gave you a bad time." She sounded relieved.

Vasco suspected she'd been putting up a front of confidence for the sake of her guest.

"I've seen much worse. My father was a vet."

"May I see him?"

"He's resting, but I don't see why not."

She excused herself and left. The doctor looked at Vasco. "You're the priest." It wasn't a question. Small-town telegraph worked as rapidly as the neighborhood variety in the city.

"I'm Church of England myself. Up here we talk directly to our Maker without middle management."

"That's an oversimplification." But he resisted being drawn into a theosophical discussion. "Is what you told Mrs. Capone true? You weren't sugarcoating it."

"We generally tell it straight up here, except when it comes to fish. A cold isn't a thing you take lightly. It can be influenza masquerading as a case of the sniffles, or it can turn into pneumonia, which considering the state of Mr. Capone's immune system is more than likely. If you want to call that sugarcoating, I can't stop you. It's a free country, even with Rosenfeld in charge."

He had the doctor pegged then. The white sheet came out Saturday night.

"Ralph's putting you up, so I guess you're okay," the man went on. "I don't mind telling you a lot of us weren't any too pleased when he moved in here a couple of years ago. It was going to be wild parties with half-naked women and the devil's music blasting out over the lake and gorillas chopping leaves off the trees with machine guns all night. We even got up a citizens' vigilance committee with shotguns and baseball bats to meet what we expected would be a convoy of moving vans where it turned off the main highway, but then someone pointed out that the vans might come with carloads of gunmen, the way they moved hooch in the old days, and after that the volunteers just sort of drifted away. The plan then was to give Ralph and his people the silent treatment whenever they were in town, let them know they weren't welcome and freeze them out. We're friendly folk as a rule, but when it comes to getting the cold shoulder you can't beat a place where the winter's six months long.

"Well, there was just one van, filled with the furniture you see, no armed escort, and no loud parties either, just some boys fishing and hunting ducks and deer and sometimes a game of euchre, which can get pretty raucous, but never so much as at the Elks lodge on a Saturday night with just the locals playing. Then some damnfool kids let a campfire get away from them on state land, and Ralph flew in a crew from Milwaukee in a private plane to help the volunteers and took charge of everything with a broom and buckets of water until it was put out. Afterwards he handed out bottles of cold beer for them that drank it and bottled water for them that didn't, all sooty and sweaty as he was. This after he couldn't get so much as a grunt of greeting in the hardware store or on the street."

The doctor put down his satchel, filled his pipe from a foil pouch with the picture of an Indian on it, and got it going with a fistful of matches. He threw them into the big fireplace while the room filled with apple-scented smoke.

"What I'm saying is I don't care if you paint your face and stick pins in dolls," he said. "If you're a guest of Ralph's, you're practically a citizen of Mercer."

Bottles Capone appeared to embrace his nickname as Scarface Al never had his. Vasco had grown up with rumors of vulgar behavior at all the Capone haunts, in Florida, the north woods, and Chicago; Herbert Hoover's campaign in the White House to put Al behind bars was said to have originated when gunfire and drunken laughter had kept him awake while visiting a major donor in Miami. The doctor's testimony was one more example of the mythos surrounding the Capone name. (*Luckily I had an alibi for Pearl Harbor.*) It made one question everything that had been said about the man and his associates. He accepted the doctor's strong grip and double-pump handshake and saw him to the door.

"Make sure he stays covered, even if he's feverish," the doctor said on the threshold. "Give him some soup and maybe now and then a dose of his own medicine." He flipped his fist toward his mouth and dipped one eyelid gravely. Then he went out and ground the Model A to life with a backfire that flushed a huge flock of swallows from the tall cedar where they'd been roosting.

That night Vasco dined on fish with Mae, the walleye coated crisply with breadcrumbs and cornmeal and served by Rose with a pinkish sauce of Brownie's own invention in a gravy boat, a combination of egg whites whipped into a weightless froth and red wine from Ralph's cellar. It came with the inevitable fried potatoes and onions, and Vasco helped himself to seconds, feeling ashamed of his gluttony while Mae picked at her meal and left the table three times to look in on her husband, but not enough so to refrain. Rose seemed to see the emotional conflict and brushed the back of his hand with hers as she filled his glass with cold water from a pitcher.

When Vasco motioned Mae to keep her seat before she could rise a fourth time and made the visit in her place, he found his host fitful, turning his head from side to side and clenching and unclenching a fist, muttering. Vasco leaned down, placing his ear almost against Capone's lips.

"Use Paulie, Frankie. You need a wheel man won't leave you standing in the street with your balls hanging out."

CAPONE RAN A FEVER. MAE WENT IN OFTEN TO REPLACE THE COVERS HE'D thrown off and lay a wet washcloth on his forehead. Vasco spelled her twice. When he removed the cloth to substitute a fresh one it felt as if he'd taken it from a boiling pot. Nearing midnight, Mae moved into a chair beside the bed. She had her own bed in the room, but she remained fully dressed and took Capone's temperature at regular intervals. She'd taken a shot at him once and now she wouldn't leave his side. Her face looked old in the harsh light of a clear bulb in a lamp fashioned from a half-gallon bottle embossed with the name of the Crystal Springs Company in Brookville, Indiana, bottled and distributed by Lake Street Manufacturing of Chicago, Illinois—Ralph's own plant. After the latest reading from the thermometer she asked Vasco to call the doctor. A woman answered, sounding sleepy and irritated, but when she heard Mae's name she woke up her husband.

But before he arrived, with the tail of a nightshirt hanging outside his fishing vest, the fever had broken. Mae helped him change the soaked bedding, rolling the patient first one way, then the other, and they got clean pajamas on him while Vasco watched, feeling useless in the presence of such practiced efficiency. Capone grunted in protest, but didn't fully regain consciousness and was snoring evenly by the time they finished and drew a fresh quilt over him.

"He's tougher than a pine knot," the doctor said. "I've seen lumberjacks half his age just slip away with less temperature than he was running."

"He's in the habit of surviving," Mae said.

Vasco didn't sleep much that night, mulling over Capone's words spoken in his delirium. Paul was a common name among Italians; there were nearly as many Paulies in Cicero and on the South Side as there were Johnnies and Frankies. Some of them were bound to be experts behind the wheel of a car. It didn't have to be Paul Anthony Vasco whom Capone was recommending to take Frankie Rio away from someplace dangerous, and the Frankie might have been some other Frankie also. But such arguments were more convincing by daylight.

Capone sat up in bed the next morning, eating oatmeal from a bowl on a tray and munching toast. He greeted Vasco cheerfully but looked drawn, and the conversation was brief: They shared a distaste for oatmeal, but Mae had been firm regarding its restorative properties and Capone lacked the strength to refuse. If Dion O'Banion had caught him in that condition, the history of American gangland would have gone differently.

Vasco spent the rest of the morning reading. Ralph's birch bark shelves contained a library of westerns by Zane Grey and Clarence E. Mulford, and the hell-for-leather antics of Hopalong Cassidy kept him entertained until lunch, which he ate alone while Mae caught up on her sleep. Rose offered him a second sandwich, salmon salad canned in Mason jars by Brownie himself, but this time he declined. She smiled as she refreshed his coffee. "Told you he's strong as a bull. You should look to your own care."

After lunch he took a walk down to the lake and watched a pair of blue herons take off from a standstill from the surface and fly a wide high loop before landing on the opposite shore. He knew nothing about them but that they mated for life, like the Capones. A loon called. He was growing accustomed to the sound but it would never match the rattle of the el for maintaining his faith in the consistency of things.

When he returned to the cabin, the wood-paneled station wagon was parked in front and Frankie Rio was dragging a pair of leather-bound suitcases from the back. Ralph confronted Vasco in the living room, red-faced and looking rumpled in a two-hundred-dollar suit. "Ain't you got no better sense than to keep a sick man out on the lake all fucking day?"

Mae emerged from the bedroom she shared with Al, looking younger than the night before in pressed gingham but with the circles still apparent under her eyes. "Let him alone, Ralph. You know how it is trying to talk Al out of something. Peter was up most of the night helping look after him."

"So it's Peter now." But that was the end of that conversation.

Ralph was agitated the rest of the day, chain-smoking Melachrinos and never staying seated for long, pacing the floor and walking into and out of his room, barking at Rio when he got in the way, which was difficult not to be with his employer stalking about in unpredictable patterns. Vasco was certain he was disturbed about something other than his brother's health. His business in Milwaukee must not have gone well.

Oblivion came more easily that night; exhaustion was the cause more than any diminishment in Vasco's sense of worry. He dreamed he'd talked to his father and that Paul had provided answers to all his questions that satisfied him he was the son of a onetime beer truck driver and nothing more sinister. When he awoke, the feeling of well-being remained with him until he realized where he was, two thousand miles away from Paul Anthony Vasco and many more times than that beyond hope of such comforting conversation. He was also aware, more from sixth sense than actual evidence of activity, of an unnatural stirring in the household. Long before he became aware of voices murmuring elsewhere in the cabin, he got up and padded to his window. An unfamiliar car was parked outside, its hood pointed toward the road in a position he knew well from the company he'd been keeping.

It was a seven-passenger Lincoln, the Continental model with the spare tire mounted on the back under a sleek doughnut-shaped cover, painted deep aubergine with bottle-green fenders and running boards and more chrome than he'd seen since the auto industry had gone to war. A skin of brown dust covering the bullet-shaped hood and bug splatter on the windshield told him it had traveled a great distance since its last wash and polish. Mud caked the whitewalls and formed clumps inside the wheel wells.

He dressed hurriedly and went into the living room, which was more crowded than he'd seen. Ralph and Rio stood to one side facing four men dressed in three-piece suits cut to accommodate expansive chest and shoulder development and a fifth seated in Al's favorite armchair. This last bent his head to set afire a cigarette in an amber holder from a pigskin lighter held by one of the four. He was slight of build, almost frail in contrast to the others, and wore a double-breasted suit that looked like spun silver, with horn buttons on the cuffs. His black hair was slicked back and parted left of center, and when he turned his head to look at the newcomer his eyes were as dead as if they'd been fashioned from the same material as the buttons. They lifted the hairs on the back of Vasco's neck.

Ralph cleared debris from his throat. "This is the priest I was telling you about. Padre, meet Frank Nitti from Chicago."

He dipped his head to the Enforcer. His jaw trembled. His time was running out, if it hadn't already.

TWENTY-SIX

"A pleasure, Father. I hear you and Al are tight."

"He's an affable man." Nitti's hand felt hot; astonishingly so in contrast to the dry-ice cold of his eyes. Capone had seemed no warmer when he was running a high fever. The Outfit's assassination chief had shaven off the moustache he'd worn in photographs, but looked no less like an Italian store clerk for the absence.

Except, of course, for those eyes.

"Affable, yeah." He bit off his words in the manner familiar to Chicago. "A little heavy on the gun stuff; but times were different then. We try to keep the peace now, no matter what. When we can."

"Mae's in the kitchen," Ralph said.

Recognizing he'd been dismissed, Vasco excused himself and left the room. He found Rose at the stove and Mae seated at the table with her hands wrapped around a steaming cup. She wore a vertical crease of pain between her eyebrows. "Al's theory about avoiding hangovers is to stay drunk," she said by way of greeting. "He may be right, but I decided to go ahead and bite the bullet. Brownie's coffee is strong enough to burn out tuberculosis."

He asked where Brownie was.

"In town, buying groceries. It pays to stock up. You never know when Ralph may take off and leave the car at the train station. When you're stranded out here, brother, you're stranded."

Rose set a cup of coffee and a dish of scrambled eggs and bacon, still sizzling, in front of him. Her face was tight. He asked how Capone was.

"Sleeping like a baby," Mae said. "I don't think he even knows we have company. They woke the rest of the household this morning. I think they drove all night from Milwaukee."

He'd noticed a shadow on Nitti's chin. The meeting in town must have been with him. Breakfast was delicious, no doubt, but he was unable to taste it. He forced himself to eat. "Is anything the matter?"

She set down her cup with a click. "Frank's worried about you. I think if he hadn't had business to finish he'd have come with Ralph and Frankie on the train. Him and his private army. I don't like that man."

Rose let go of the skillet too soon. It landed on a cold burner with a clank. He'd never known her to be tense about anything.

He pressured himself into taking a sip of coffee before he spoke. "I'm nothing to be concerned about."

"I told him that, but he's the most suspicious man I've ever met. He was shot once in his own office and he hasn't trusted anyone since. He has one of his soldiers start his car for him and taste his food. It's the way he is, Peter. Don't let it upset you."

"He hardly even spoke to me just now."

"He's more famous for his actions than for his words. By now he has someone else going around asking the questions. I imagine he wanted to get a look at you for himself."

"I think it's time I went back to Miami."

"I won't have him chasing you away."

"I don't want to be the cause of trouble."

"Al wouldn't have it, and Ralph would never agree to anything Al was against. He knows he wouldn't have anything if it weren't for his brother."

"Still, he runs the organization."

"That's what the newspapers say, and the authorities seem to agree. The steps he took to leave Chicago without tipping them off make what Al and I did look like the Rose Parade. But Ralph just looks after the family interests and owns a few places with Outfit connections. His name sells more papers than Nitti's. Frank runs the show."

It seemed impossible that Hoover hadn't known that. "I'll have to think about it. I didn't come up here to disturb anyone's vacation."

Just then Ralph came in. Vasco had noticed he wasn't in fishing costume. He wore a dress shirt tucked into pleated slacks, without a necktie and with the collar spread. Rio was dressed similarly, only with a suit coat covering his pistol in its harness.

"We got business to talk over," Ralph told Vasco. "Why don't you take Rose out for a walk."

It wasn't a question, but Vasco raised his eyebrows at Rose. "That would be pleasant, if she wants to and if Mae can spare her."

"Go ahead, Rose, if you like. The dishes will keep."

The girl beamed and untied her apron.

TARNISHED CLOUDS HUNG LOW ABOVE THE PINES AND THE AIR SMELLED like rain. Vasco had paused in the mudroom off the kitchen to unhook an old umbrella from a peg, but Rose stopped him. "We won't melt." She tied a white cotton scarf around her head. It softened her features further and made her resemble a little girl.

He helped himself to the old hat Capone had worn fishing, which fit him perfectly.

They walked between columns of trees filled with chirping birds and one angry squirrel, who squeaked at them with its paws wrapped around a pinecone halfway up a tall spruce. Other creatures rustled among fallen needles and last year's maple leaves on the ground. He felt slightly disreputable, unshaven and unshowered, and he was preoccupied with what was being discussed in the cabin in his absence, but Rose looked fresh in a blue cotton blouse printed with pink flowers and her hands in the pockets of a pleated skirt. She wore saddle shoes and white bobby sox.

"That man Nitti scares me," she said. "Did you see his eyes?"

"Yes."

"I wouldn't worry about him, though. That kind lays off reverends."

"I'm leaving, just the same." He couldn't let her know her words weren't a comfort. "I shouldn't be away from Redemption too long."

"I expect we'll be pulling out soon ourselves. Sooner or later those whiskers will figure out where Mr. Al went and Mr. Ralph doesn't want to upset the locals with a lot of strangers hanging around."

It amused him despite himself to hear her using Capone's slang for the agents who served Uncle Sam. "It's so peaceful up here. I've always lived in cities, so all this is new to me."

"Not me. I couldn't wait to get out of that jerkwater town in Alabama. You never see the places we have to live in those small-town pictures, but you can see them when you're sitting on the wrong side of the train."

He had: nine-hundred-square-foot houses with sagging porches and burned-out lawns, wash gathering soot on clotheslines and heaps of rusty oilcans and newspapers blowing about. Black men in undershirts sat on the porches swigging from flat pints and black women worked pump handles, old beyond their years.

"The air here is clean, anyway," she said. "Miami, too. I got dead aunts and uncles never saw the ocean."

"Does it bother you, the man you work for?"

"Well, I told you I was scared at first. But he and the missus treat me better than the banker I used to work for. If I broke something there like Mr. Al's elephant, that missus would've slapped my face."

"Is Mrs. Capone still doing nice things for you?"

"Sure. I thanked you for that."

"I wasn't fishing for gratitude." It seemed very important he kept her good opinion.

"I know, and I'm sorry I thought it. White folks give you their old clothes and think they're doing you some big favor. You get so you expect it."

"Where are we going?" He realized they'd been walking in a straight line, up a hill in the direction opposite the lake.

"Place I found. I don't think even Mr. Ralph knows about it. Fat men ain't in the habit of taking long walks."

He liked the fact she felt relaxed around him so far as to let her grammar lapse. In general she spoke better English than most of the Italians he'd grown up around. She took a hand out of a pocket and it seemed the most natural thing in the world for him to hold it. It felt warm, although not nearly as warm as Nitti's, which seemed to feed on a source of heat he found unhealthy. Hers was a little moist.

In a little while they came to a clearing where stood an old shack, thrown together from packing crates—so much forest around to provide logs, hence the appearance of haste—with half its roof fallen in. A crooked stovepipe stuck out through a hole, with a conical cap on top to keep rain out, cocked like the head-gear of a juvenile tough in a movie exposing the evils of urban blight. Its door was missing and he could see piles of leaves inside, but one window still had all its panes, with gaps showing in the putty, discolored like neglected teeth.

"That's it," she said. "I think some fisherman built it way back before the first war. I found it when I was looking for wildflowers for the table. I'll show you."

He allowed himself to be led inside. It smelled of moss and disintegrating wood. There was an iron bedstead with a mattress whose cover and stuffing had been appropriated by mice and squirrels for nests for their young so that mainly the springs remained, naked and rusted. A barrel stove, rusty also, stood with a pile of shingles holding up the corner where the leg was gone and a stack of magazines moldered in a crate made of staves. The cover of a sportsmen's maga-zine was chewed away except for part of the title and a date: March 1917. For all he knew the place had been deserted since five years before he was born. Had the occupant died or joined the army or grown tired of the isolation and just walked away? Suddenly he was curious about someone he'd never known existed.

There was a pattering sound, accompanied by a plunking, like the music of a washtub band; the rain had started, striking the roof with fat drops and hitting the hollow iron stove through the gap where the shingles had shrunk away from the stovepipe. They made slapping noises on the earthen floor, packed and trod-den as hard as pavement.

"Just in time," Rose said; and then she was in his arms, kissing him hungrily, her tongue working between his teeth. He responded, as famished as she.

They fumbled with buttons, tore shirttails out of waistbands. He found the catch of her bra and it came open almost to the touch, as if he were an accom-plished seducer of women. If she noticed that he seemed more practiced than expected, she was too eager to hesitate. She unbuttoned his fly and then he was in her hand, pulsing hot. He got hold of her skirt and gathered it up in his fist. She was too slim to need a girdle and he slid his other hand into her panties and palmed the warmth of her and his fingers found their way inside her. She was wet.

They lay on the stony earth, he on his back to cushion her, and she straddled him with her panties still on one ankle and he thrust up into her, feeling the electric thrill from the sudden friction, his grunt stifled in her mouth. He ex-ploded after only three thrusts. He tore his mouth away from hers to apologize, but she covered it with a hand and worked herself up and down, now arching her back, now leaning forward with her breasts crushed against his chest, until her panting built to a thin wail and then she slowed down gradually, like a motor sputtering to a stop after the current is cut. She collapsed on him and they lay there while their breathing became more measured and their hearts beat in different rhythms, his heavy and powerful, hers rapid and shallow like the wings of a captured bird.

Her back was wet when he stroked it; the shack gave little shelter from the rain. "You'll catch cold." His voice dragged in his throat as if he hadn't spoken aloud for days.

"Hush, now." She covered his mouth again. "Hush."

After a while she rose and drew up her panties and fumbled in a pocket of her discarded skirt for dry matches. Together they built a fire in the stove, using shredded magazines and dried leaves and twigs blown in and tangled in the corners for kindling and fed it with shards of wood from the fallen-in roof. They dried their clothing piece by piece before the heat, using the stave crate and a broken chair for racks. The rain had stopped by the time they finished drying. Vasco, aroused by the muscular play of Rose's buttocks beneath the lace-trimmed step-ins, seized her again. This time she insisted she be on the bottom. His part of it took longer this time and she cried out before his release.

She smiled, took his head in her hands, and kissed him.

"I do believe you have a confession to make, Reverend."

"Peter."

She shook her head. "I might slip."

"Then don't call me anything. I can stand that better than 'Reverend.'"

"It's a deal, but only if you go easy on me in the booth."

"You've done nothing wrong." If she only knew how true it was.

"Are you sorry?"

"I should be. I don't know why I'm not."

"That's the nicest thing anybody ever said to me."

They dressed and tidied themselves, using each other in place of a mirror. When they went back outside, the air smelled as if it had been scrubbed with wet pine needles. Drops fell off branches in unpredictable patterns that made him jump and her giggle when they landed anywhere on them. Something stung the back of his neck. He slapped at it and rolled off the smashed remains of a mosquito the size of a housefly.

"Told you they's big as B-17s."

He made a tardy admission. "I should have worn something."

"I don't guess you gents go around prepared. I know tricks. My mother didn't want me to have any surprises."

"But you couldn't have known—"

She laughed—not a giggle. She looked around, turned, and went up on the balls of her feet and kissed him again.

He thought, *I've been seduced.*

A loon laughed from the direction of the lake.

Nearing the cabin, she widened the distance between them suddenly. Someone stood on the little covered back porch, smoking a cigarette in a holder.

"You're dry." Frank Nitti had shed his suit coat. He wore a striped silk shirt with black suspenders embroidered with red diamonds. One hand rested in the deep slash pocket of his trousers.

"We found a shack." She spoke matter-of-factly.

"Cozy."

Vasco chose to ignore the remark. He thought it a priestly thing to do. "Have you concluded your business?"

"Not yet."

"Will you be staying the night?"

"I am. You're not. Frankie's driving you to the station."

Rose climbed the steps to the porch, head down and hugging herself with both arms. Excusing herself, she pulled open the screen door and went inside, stepping around Ralph on his way out.

"We thought it'd look better if we didn't all travel together," Ralph said. "I'm closing the place in the morning. Vacation's over, Padre. Sorry it couldn't be longer. When the feds figure out where Al disappeared to, they'll be up here thick as skeeters. I got a reputation to protect in Mercer."

He was making little effort to veil his hostility. What had started out as ordinary suspicion had solidified into something else.

"I'll pack," Vasco said.

"Brownie took care of that. Your bag's in the station wagon."

"May I go in and say good-bye?'"

"Sure," Nitti put in. "You're not being run out on a rail. What we got to talk about you don't want to hear." He turned toward Ralph. "What time's the train tomorrow?"

"Ten-fifteen."

"Swell. The sooner I get away from all these bears and shit the better."

"What about the Lincoln?"

"You and Frankie are going back in it."

"That'll take twice as long!"

"You should've thought of that before you came up here to live with the injuns. I never saw the benefit." Nitti plucked the cigarette from its holder and flicked it off the porch.

Automatically, Vasco crushed it out. Forest fires meant nothing to a Chicago hoodlum. Nitti had already gone back inside. Ralph followed him without another word.

Mae had been right: it was the Enforcer calling the shots.

Vasco knocked on the Capones' door. Mae's voice asked who it was, then invited him in. He found her on one knee beside Capone's bed, tying his shoelaces. He wore scuffed hiking boots, a soft flannel shirt, and the trousers belonging to an old suit, baggy in the knees. He beamed at Vasco. "Valet service. I dumped eight grand a week on the same thing at the Lexington."

"I wish we had it now." Mae stood. "The doctor says a little walk would be good for him. Once around the outside of the house ought to do it."

"I keep telling her I could outrun the dogs at Lawndale." But he looked pale still.

"Maybe when we get back to Miami. I'm sorry about this, Father. I'd hoped we'd have another two weeks."

He noticed it was "Father" once again.

"No apologies necessary. I've had a terrific time."

"How'd you like the fishing?" Capone asked.

"Very much. My father won't believe I had such good luck my first time."

"You're Calabrese. That makes you part pelican."

How could he remember the Vascos were Calabrese?

"Have a safe trip," Vasco said. "I'll see you soon, if I haven't worn out my welcome."

"We'll fish off the pier. You haven't been till you hook onto a marlin."

"Well, good-bye."

Mae took his hand in both of hers, a protective gesture. Her eyes were clearest blue. "Don't be concerned. Once Frank's satisfied you're on the level, you'll never hear from him again."

He thanked her and pulled the door shut in the hallway with a clammy lump in his belly.

There was no opportunity for the conversation he wanted with Rose. She was working at the counter beside the sink with a loaf of sliced bread and a jar of mayonnaise and Brownie was washing his knives. The big Negro manservant always seemed to be occupied with lethal instruments. Over a chipped Bakelite radio a nasal British correspondent was reporting the fall of Saipan to U.S. troops; Emperor Hirohito was encouraging Japanese civilians to commit suicide rather than be taken captive. It was a grim background for parting.

She wrapped something in waxed paper, slid it into a brown paper sack, rolled down the top, and turned away from the counter, holding it out. Her smile was cloudless. "Walleye sandwich," she said. "You don't want that powdered-egg salad they got on the train."

"Thank you."

"You caught it yourself."

"Thank you for everything, I mean." He felt himself flush.

"I wish I could do something as kind for you in return."

"You already did. I enjoyed the walk."

He thought she winked. It was over so fast he couldn't be sure.

RIO SAT BEHIND THE WHEEL OF THE STATION WAGON, LOOKING PREOCCU-pied. Vasco's valise lay on the backseat, presumably placed there by Brownie after he'd packed it. He was sure the man had overlooked nothing, and had not bothered to check to see if anything was left behind. They took off with a spray of gravel. Ralph's bodyguard said nothing the whole way, except to curse when he was forced to brake for a deer bounding across the road. His passenger watched, fascinated, as the golden-brown animal, as much a creature of the air as of the earth, vanished into the brush with its hooves not seeming to touch down. He envied it its power of flight. Then he remembered the heads he'd seen mounted at stops along the way through Wisconsin and knew nothing was immune to fate.

But he was happy for the silence and the opportunity to think. Frank Nitti had his number, he felt certain, or if he hadn't, he wouldn't stop investigating until he had. As authentic as they might appear, the references and credentials arranged by the FBI would not stand up to threats, bribery, and torture. Too many people knew the truth. Surely the Director would see that Vasco's usefulness had come to an end. It only remained to see how far the Outfit would go to make an example to others that its walls could not be breached without bloody consequences. He gripped the sack in his lap and thought he would never have the appetite to open it.

Regret tinged his fear. He would miss Mae and Sonny; he would even miss Al, the ogre of most of his days on earth. He could still feel his embrace, the firm grip of his hand on Vasco's wrist as he led him through the steps of the graceful freedom of casting a fishing lure far out over the calm surface of a lake so far distant from the bloodstained asphalt of Chicago and Cicero as to belong to a planet on the other end of the solar system. He had never known such physical closeness from his father; a quick, self-conscious hug before they'd separated in Fort Lauderdale, unexpected as it was, was unwieldy in comparison, a matter of form only, not genuine.

And he would miss Rose. He did not know what that had been about, only that he'd sensed it coming for a long time without really being aware that he had. Was it attraction on her part, or just a diversion not uncommon among the bitter serving class? The distinction seemed important, although he didn't know why. He could still smell the lemon-scented soap on her skin, mixed with rain and perspiration, the musty air in the cabin. He felt the silkiness of her tongue sliding against his. He felt other things as well, and adjusted the sack to dissemble his physical reaction from the man seated beside him. Dear God, but he was poor material to pose as a priest.

What, he wondered, was expected of him now?

Rio ground to a stop abreast of the train station, dust drifting forward to bread the hood. "Take care, boy." The car was rolling again before Vasco got the back door shut. He had to snatch his valise out of the way to avoid a collision with the rear fender. The back end of the wagon slewed sideways in the dirt and pebbles before righting itself, attracting the attention of a loafer on the platform, who tipped back his straw skimmer to watch it retreat beyond Ralph Capone's clapboard-Tudor hotel, then tipped it back forward to resume his empty ruminations. Was stool-pigeonry (*was* there such a word?) considered contagious in the underworld, like leprosy? Vasco was too fanciful for the work.

The atmosphere in the little pioneer building lacked the electric urgency of Union Station, or even the shuffling hurly-burly of a whistle stop between arrival and departure. He was twenty minutes early for the four o'clock train. A few passengers and well-wishers were seated on benches, chatting and reading newspapers (farm reports, baseball scores, record fish caught, the war) and a pair of old men in overalls played checkers on a board set between them on the polished hickory, making an entire afternoon out of the simplest game invented by man. One was wrinkled and shrunken enough to be the 103-year-old Capone had told him about. What were the thoughts of a man who'd spent most of a century scraping whiskers off the same face in the mirror? At the moment it seemed unlikely Vasco would ever know.

He sought diversion in a small newsstand operated by a woman wearing a perforated aluminum patch taped over one eye, a recent cataract patient. Mac-Arthur scowled resolutely behind dark glasses from *Time,* Superman wound an iron girder around Hitler, Tojo, and Mussolini on the cover of *Action Comics,* pinning their arms to their sides. Retribution drove the world.

Was Nitti the type to torture a confession out of a man before he finished the job, just to be certain, or for the sheer entertainment of the exercise? He'd seemed to enjoy letting a man twist in the breeze of what appeared to be simple conversation. Vasco imagined the Outfit had made subtle refinements on the practice of the homely baseball bat; on the other hand, there was really no need to improve upon perfection. Scalise and Anselmi were no less dead than if they'd been worked on scientifically with electrodes, the tactics Walter Winchell said the Gestapo had employed on American POWs to learn the details of D-Day.

It was a singularly bad moment to turn away from the four-color illustrations and screaming headlines to encounter a man in uniform standing in front of him with his thumbs hooked inside his gun belt.

"Peter Vasco?"

He was dressed in forest green with brown patches on his shoulders, a hard man running to fat around the middle but a hard man just the same, with a toothpick rammed into the corner of his mouth and a dimpled campaign hat strapped under his chin. His middle-aged face was burned red; no amount of suntan oil would render it the burnished brown of advertisements in travel magazines.

"Yes?" He'd conquered a sudden panicky urge to deny his identity.

"Come with me, please."

He followed the man past curious onlookers through a door with STATION-MASTER painted on the frosted glass. A revolver with a saddle ring incongruously attached to the butt rode in a hip holster, secured with a leather strap.

"Vasco, sir."

"I'm aware of that, Deputy. Leave us, please."

The man obeyed, jerking the door shut against a swollen jamb. The small room was decorated by a sepia photograph in a walnut frame of a train pulling logs and steam along a narrow-gauge track. A yellow oak desk and two captain's chairs provided the furnishings. Every cigar that had been smoked and plug that had been chewed there in thirty years haunted the place. The viscous odor permeated the plaster and wainscoting and desk, scalloped as it was with burn canals old and new.

"Special Agent. It seems years since we spoke."

The man seated at the desk wore the uniform of a railroad conductor, too snug for the thick, bulbous body imprisoned within. The band collar fell two inches short of closing, and the flat-topped cap with patent-leather visor upended on the desk had left a ridge in J. Edgar Hoover's coarse black hair.

TWENTY-SEVEN

VASCO SAT IN THE CHAIR FACING THE DESK WITHOUT WAITING FOR AN INVI-tation. The decision was made by a sudden weakness in his knees.

The Director showed no disapproval. "I regret alarming you with the show of local authority. It's no secret who your host is, so routine official interest would not be unexpected. A trim stranger in a business suit would only arouse suspicion. No doubt you're wondering how we found you."

"I wasn't hiding, sir."

"It would be foolish to think you were, if that were your intent. Even so it took an inordinate amount of time to remember that Ralph Capone has a vacation home here. I take some responsibility for that oversight; but I've quite enough to occupy my mind without arrogating unto myself the duties of investigators trained at considerable expense to the taxpayer. It was sheer chance that you were spotted loitering in the waiting room."

He'd seen no evidence of trim strangers in business suits loitering also. It seemed unlikely that even the inexhaustible supply of disguises in the FBI closet would make a convincing old man playing checkers. But Vasco had had no instruction in penetrating the invisible.

Hoover tipped a pink ruthful palm toward the conductor's cap on the desk. "Naturally, I was driven to extreme measures in order to infiltrate such a small community. I wouldn't have risked exposing my already overexposed person if I thought it wasn't important to meet with you face-to-face, assuming you could be found in this wilderness. Clyde Tolson was in favor of issuing an order of detainment in your case. The prevailing theory in Division Five was that you'd gone AWOL."

Vasco suppressed a shudder. Assistant Director Tolson was in the way of being the Bureau's answer to Frank Nitti, the Enforcer. "I never meant to keep you in the dark, sir. The invitation came suddenly, and I thought it unwise to delay. I'd hoped to establish contact with the District once I got here, but—"

"You needn't elaborate. All the telephone subscribers in this county belong to a five-party line. I take it from your presence in the station that your business here is concluded."

"The Capones are returning to Florida in the morning. It was decided I should leave separately."

"Decided by whom?"

He told him, and saw surprise on the bulldog face for the first time. It passed quickly, replaced by annoyance. Hoover sat back, creaking pegs in his chair. "He's here?"

Vasco related the morning's events, leaving out Rose and the shack in the woods. They were not public property. He was aware that he had only minutes before his train arrived. It would stop just long enough to discharge and take on passengers.

"Those fools in Chicago haven't learned a damned thing in ten years." The profanity, together with an acceleration in his already rapid speech, declared the depths of the Director's rage. He had never forgiven Melvin Purvis, the former Special Agent in Charge of the Chicago office, for multiple blunders in the Dillinger investigation, and particularly for his eventual success. Purvis' fame had threatened to eclipse his own, and long after Purvis had been drummed out of the Bureau for a number of widely reported technicalities, his name had not passed Hoover's lips. Their falling-out had permanently contaminated relations between Chicago and the Seat of Government. "These chief rats never travel without an entourage as large as the president's, and still Nitti managed to slip out bag and baggage with no one the wiser. I thought I made my position clear after the Miami exodus, but apparently I was speaking in code where that office was concerned. Have you given Nitti any reason to suspect you?"

"Not that I'm aware of."

"That isn't an answer."

"No. Mae Capone says he's suspicious as a matter of course."

"As well he should be, thanks to that idiot Cermak. But I have confidence in the steps we've taken to protect your cover."

"I don't know how well they'll hold up once he applies pressure."

"He isn't the only one who can apply it."

That seemed vague even for one of Hoover's circumspection regarding the inner workings of his organization. Vasco felt he was being placated.

"Sir, he has a history of rooting out informants and disposing of them without the nicety of a hearing."

"Are you asking to be relieved of this assignment?"

"I thought under the circumstances you might want to suspend it."

The man behind the desk rotated the ball of his thumb against the varnished arm of his chair. "What have you learned up here?"

Vasco produced a thick sheaf of notepaper from his coat pocket. He'd scribbled swiftly in the uneven light of the kerosene lamp in his room and hadn't had the chance to transcribe his notes into legible form. He'd kept them on his person—a prescient precaution, in view of Brownie's having packed his belongings for him—and they'd gotten damp in the leaky shack, but Hoover unfolded the pages and scanned them as quickly as if they'd been typewritten. He refolded them and tucked them inside his tunic.

"Capone's loosening up at last," he said. "It would be disastrous to abort your mission at this time. He won't remain coherent much longer—Dr. Phillips' office keeps us apprised of his deteriorating condition—and we may never be able to regain the momentum. *Will* never, if we're forced to replace you. Let me worry about Nitti."

"Sir—"

An insolent air horn tore the air.

"You need to catch your train. If you miss it and have to go back with the Capones, Nitti will be certain you planned it. He strikes fast when he thinks he's cornered."

"Yes, sir. But—"

"Special Agent, have you been following the reports from the front?"

"They're hard to miss."

"Thousands of young men are hurtling themselves toward certain death even as we speak. Do you hold your life to be of greater value than theirs?"

"With respect, Mr. Hoover, they can see the guns that are pointed at them."

"You'll never catch your train if you insist upon qualifying your responses. I gave you every opportunity at the beginning of this venture to excuse yourself. It's a singularly bad time to show the white feather now that so much time and so many public funds have been spent to bring us this far. I ask you again: Is your life worth more than those that are being tested in the European and Pacific theaters?"

"Certainly not. I'm not a coward."

Hoover appeared clinically interested. "You seem more settled upon that account than you did in Washington."

"I didn't know myself as well then."

"In that case I see no reason to make any changes at this time. You know how to get into contact with me if the situation changes."

"Yes, sir."

"Don't concern yourself any further with Nitti. He's through. He just doesn't realize it yet."

"Yes, sir."

"Go now. If anyone asks why you were detained, it was because the railroad wanted to satisfy itself you weren't carrying contraband in wartime. Given your most recent place of residence, you'd have been more suspect if you were allowed to pass undisturbed."

Vasco rose and picked up his valise.

"Special Agent."

He turned back toward the desk.

"You forgot your lunch."

THE SACK HAD SLIPPED OFF HIS LAP INTO THE SPACE BETWEEN HIS HIP AND the arm of his chair. He retrieved it and left. The station was crowded now with pedestrians streaming toward the platform, where a train stood with its diesel engine idling. He passed a sailor in blues and a jaunty cap carrying his duffel inside, one arm around the waist of a girl whose bones showed under her one-piece cotton dress. When he was in his seat with his valise in the overhead rack,

Vasco kept his eyes on the station through the window, but Hoover didn't appear, in or out of disguise. He wondered what arrangements the Bureau had made for him until he'd determined the Capones and Nitti had returned home.

The old eagle had some surprises left in him. Through newsreels and the wire services his face was as well known as Cary Grant's, but he'd undertaken to enter a rural community where strangers were routinely scrutinized by the natives in the middle of a top-secret operation just to encourage the agent on the scene to stay the course. He was still the man who'd slapped the cuffs on Public Enemy Number One in person.

When the train stopped in Oshkosh, he got out to stretch his legs and buy a Coke from a vendor, which he drank in the shade of the platform roof while he ate his sandwich. He couldn't tell if it was delicious because he'd caught the fish himself or because Rose had made it. He used the empty sack to wipe his hands and dumped it and the bottle in a trash can and gave another vendor a nickel for the *Milwaukee Journal,* which was plastered with details on Saipan.

Heading back toward his car he passed a man browsing among hand-painted neckties displayed on a folding stand belonging to a lanky entrepreneur in a seersucker suit, with the mobile eye of an unlicensed operator. The customer was built from the waist up like a folded napkin, square shoulders tapering toward narrow hips in a three-piece suit with glossy black pumps on his incongruously small feet. His nose was flattened at the bridge, spoiling a collegiate Buster Crabbe profile. The last time Vasco had seen that particular silhouette, the man had been lighting Frank Nitti's cigarette in the living room of Ralph Capone's cabin in Mercer.

By the time Vasco was back in his seat, the man was gone and the vendor had converted his stand into a sample case with a rolled leather handle. The diesel's horn blatted and the train started forward. He wondered if the man had paused long enough to buy a tie.

"HOW WAS THE FISHING?" PAUL ANTHONY VASCO CUT A NOTCH IN A STEAK and turned it over when blood ran out. Yellow flame leapt up from the charcoal grill when grease dripped down.

"The fish were biting."

"Ain't the same as marlin."

"That's what Capone said."

"That all you talked about?"

"That and Chicago." Peter drank from the bottle of ice-cold Altes that Sharon had brought him, watching the muscles tense and relax in his father's naked back as he moved the meat around on the grate. One couldn't tell much about what a man was thinking from his back.

Sharon had made a fuss over Peter at the door, noticed the bandage on the finger he'd hooked, and had him set down his valise while she rebound it with a mother's patient care. Paul had said he might as well throw on another steak seeing as he was there.

"I'll make up the sofa," she'd said.

"So now we're running a restaurant *and* a hotel."

"I'm catching the evening train. I just wanted to say hello."

"I'll never hear the end of it if you don't stay over." But his gruffness had lacked conviction.

While the men stood in her tiny backyard, Sharon busied herself in the kitchen making potato salad.

"German," Paul had said. "You'd think she'd make it some other way."

One could follow the war from the radio waves spilling out of open windows and from portable sets in adjoining yards. The announcers had exhausted the Pacific. Hitler was in Berchtesgaden, making a show of holidaying unconcernedly while the Americans and British pushed across France and Africa and the Russians broke out along the Eastern Front.

"Aren't you afraid of what the neighbors will think when they smell that meat?" Peter had asked.

Paul had pointed his long-handled fork at the board fence separating the patch of grass from the property next door. "Stieglitz there saved up his stamps and boiled a six-pound ham last month. His boy's a rabbi. Nobody said nothing. Them Hebrews mind their own business. Anyway, the show's as good as over. They're taking jitterbug lessons in Berlin."

From there the conversation had shifted to the subject of Wisconsin and the fishing. When Paul replaced the dome-shaped cover on the grill, Chicago was closed. He pulled on his own beaded bottle. "Jesus, it's hot. They're breaking records in Miami. You shoulda stayed up North."

"It wasn't my decision." He was as eager as his father to talk about something else. He couldn't tell if Nitti's man had followed him from the station. There was nothing suspicious about a man visiting all that was left of his family, but he didn't want Paul and Sharon to learn what kind of attention he was attracting and to start asking why. "So this whole neighborhood is Jewish?"

"As Abe's hat. Funny, ain't it?"

"What is?"

"How things change. Back in Cicero, place like this, I dropped my fares off six blocks short and told 'em to walk. After that prick tried to take over that beer hall in Munich, Brown Shirts sprung up all over like toadstools. I didn't want to come home with my windows all smashed."

Sharon opened the screen door and set a huge bowl on the little ice cream table that served as part of a picnic set with three wooden folding chairs. They ate potato salad and day-old bread from a local bakery—it was too hot to fire up the oven and make it fresh—and when the steaks were done they washed them down with beer.

"Tell me all about your stay," Sharon said. "I've never seen a moose even in a zoo."

"Neither did I. I saw loons, and a car I was riding in almost hit a deer."

She asked him about the wildlife and the lake and the cabin. He answered in detail—the subjects were harmless—but he was preoccupied with something his father had said. He didn't know why; he had a sense of two things that didn't quite match, and just what they were eluded him and kept him from devoting all of himself to the conversation.

"It must be nice to know people who go away on vacation. They must be pretty important to get the gas."

He looked at Paul, who was sawing at his steak with what appeared to be total concentration. It was obvious he'd told her nothing of Peter and the Capones.

"They take the train, and stock up on groceries in town a week at a time."

"They were generous to invite you. I guess some people feel they need more spiritual counseling than others."

"Sharon, will you for chrissake leave the boy be? He saw a deer and caught a fish."

"I'm just taking an interest."

"Let's just eat, okay?"

She caught Peter's gaze and crossed her eyes. He choked on his beer.

The sofa was more comfortable than it looked, but he slept fitfully in the heat, with only a table fan to circulate air, an oscillating type that Sharon said tended to wander across the top of the plant stand in front of the screened window without a huge conch shell anchoring the base. Moonlight turned the living room into a black-and-white movie set. He threw on the robe he'd taken from his valise and went out the back door, where his father sat in one of the folding chairs smoking. It was the first time he'd seen him with a cigarette since he'd been in Florida. He wore striped BVDs only with his legs crossed and showing varicose veins.

"Bitch, ain't it?" Paul said when Peter sat opposite him with his forearms resting on the glass-topped table. "Can't catch a breeze on account of all these fucking fences. These kikes sure do like to rope themselves off from each other."

He knew what had been bothering him then. It came to him in a blinding flash, which he managed to dissemble. He was reluctant to break the relative peace. A dog barking in the same monotonous cadence over and over was the only sound on a night without foghorns and the hum of automobile traffic stilled by rationing. It was probably several yards over but seemed like something a long way off, like the crying of loons.

"You're smoking again." He didn't intend for it to sound as accusing as it did in his ears.

"It's this heat. The humidity I mean. It's the only dry you can find when it's like this. You remember when the wind came off the lake in winter? It was cold, sure, but even when there was snow in it they were like ash, the flakes. You never felt like there was mold growing in your crotch. The Chamber of Commerce here don't mention that in the brochures."

"Al likes his cigars."

It was the kind of thing you felt like saying. It didn't have to mean anything. He was putting off the other thing, the thing about the neighborhoods Paul Vasco didn't want to take fares into because of the risk.

"Al." The single syllable sounded strange in that motionless air. "Ten years I worked for him, almost, I never called him anything but Mr. Capone. Three months, he's Al to you. But then I only laid eyes on him twice. I guess to him you're Pete."

"Padre." *Son*, the once. *That's how it's done, son, easy as taking a piss.* Scarface Al, with one arm across Vasco's chest and the other guiding his hand on the rod and reel. He knew he'd never mention it to Paul.

"That's how it's supposed to be. Things've got too chummy since the war."

"Well, Ralph was there. Last names can be confusing in a case like that."

"Nobody ever called Bottles 'Mr. Capone.' I think he liked 'Bottles' because it was the only thing he had he figured he earned himself. That was horseshit, that Crystal Springs thing. He pumped it out of Lake Michigan in tanks. A little fish got into a bottle once and the guy on the valve got all his fingers busted for not checking the screen for holes."

The screen door strained against its spring and Sharon joined them. She wore a flannel housedress over a pale slip with lace peeking out under the hem. "Iced tea for you boys? There's no sleeping tonight."

"Too wet," Paul said.

Peter rose. "Please join us."

"I think I'll go inside and listen to the radio. You can get a repeat broadcast of Wayne King from California if there's no news from overseas." She frowned in the direction of the barking. "That darn dog. Don't people that own dogs have ears? What do you think he's saying?"

"Bark-bark-bark-bark-*bark*." Paul managed to sound just like the terrier or whatever it was.

"I'd call the police, but the last time I did that they put my address in the paper under the complaints column. I keep expecting some mad Cuban to show up on the doorstep."

"This dog ain't Cuban. He's Jewish."

"Now, how can you tell that?"

"Every fifth bark ends in a question."

"Oh, you!" She went back inside and let the door bang shut. A few moments later the tubes warmed up and *The Blue Danube* glided out from inside.

Paul met Peter's stare. "What?" The cigarette bobbed up and down in the corner of his mouth.

"Just wondering why she puts up with you."

"'Cause I'm the only man on God's green earth'd put up with her. You seen what she done to the toilet?"

"Cleaned it?"

"That, yeah; what's the point? It's a toilet, for chrissake. I mean that fuzzy pink thing she put on the lid."

"Women do that."

"Women, that's what I'm talking about. It upsets the balance. You need one hand to hold open your fly and the other to take aim. That means you have to stand along the side and brace the lid with your knee so it don't come down in the middle of the stream. Show me a single man and I'll show you a man don't have to pee sideways the rest of his life." He took the cigarette out of his mouth. "What the hell you laughing about?"

Peter stopped. "I'm thinking there must be compensations."

"What do you know? All the women you have to live with are too busy beating the shit out of boys for jacking off in the cloakroom to put fuzzy pink covers on toilet seats."

"I wasn't born a priest." It was one of those things you had to keep reminding people.

"Well, your mother knew better."

"She couldn't afford fuzzy pink covers."

He bit down on the butt and snapped it into the yard. It made a thin orange arc and splashed brief fireworks where it landed. "I did the best I could with what I had to work with. I'd-a bought her a Packard Eight if it didn't cost so much to keep her breathing."

"I didn't mean that, Dad. What's wrong with peeing sideways if it keeps a woman happy?"

"If I didn't know better, I'd swear you was getting laid."

He felt himself flushing and was glad for the cover of darkness. How did the man know what he seemed to know?

Suddenly, changing the subject didn't seem so bad. "Mr. Capone told me a little about that night in Cicero."

"A little."

"A little is a lot when it involves Capone."

"There was plenty of nights in Cicero, son. We lived there." But Paul's voice was tight. The shadow of the porch roof made a diagonal across his narrow face, leaving only the constricted lips in pale light. They were corrugated, like the packing around bottles of liquor in a smuggled crate.

"The night he emptied a pistol into Ragtime Joe Howard's face at the Four Deuces. The night you happened to come along driving your taxi and he hailed you and threw the murder weapon into the backseat so it wouldn't be found on him."

"I told you all about that. Seems to me I told it the same way a dozen times. I didn't know it was a murder weapon then. There's plenty of more innocent reasons for a man not to want to be arrested with a gun on him."

"The same way, yes. It's important to have all your lines down cold."

Nothing. There would be no help from Peter Anthony Vasco that night or any other.

"Mr. Capone—*Al*—said he was lucky you came along, as it wasn't the kind of neighborhood where cabs cruised because of its reputation. Earlier tonight, you said you avoided bad neighborhoods."

Paul waited. Only the dog, insensitive creature that it was, continued making noise in the gulf of silence.

Peter licked his lips. He couldn't seem to keep them moist even in the sodden air of Fort Lauderdale in late June. "Did you just happen to come along, or did Capone expect you to be in that place at that moment, ready to take away the one piece of evidence that could hang him?"

"What if I said I couldn't remember after all this time?"

"It wouldn't satisfy the prosecutor who wanted to convict you for being an accessory before and after the fact."

"The fact of what?"

"Murder. They execute you for that in the State of Illinois."

TWENTY-EIGHT

"Okay," Paul said.

"What do you mean, 'okay'?"

"It's what regular people say when they mean yeah."

"Yeah, Capone hailed you as you were passing by, or yeah, he arranged for you to be there when he came running out with that gun?"

"Originally he was going to be the passenger, but he didn't figure on the cops having a car in the neighborhood when he started shooting. I'd just let off a fare at the Hawthorne and I was having a beer in the bar when this big guy with a scar climbs onto the next stool and asks is that my hack outside. When I said yeah he gives me fifty bucks to park behind the Four Deuces in an hour and wait. He said he'd give me another fifty after we pulled away."

"Did you know what he had in mind?"

"I figured it was a heist."

"You didn't ask?"

"When you drive a cab in Cicero or anywhere else, you don't ask questions you're better off not knowing the answers to. Anyway it was a joint, who gives a shit if it gets stuck up? A hundred bucks spends the same no matter where you got it."

"Did you know who he was?"

"He said his name was Brown. If he'd said Capone it wouldn't-a meant nothing then." Paul pinched a cigarette out of a pack of Parliaments on the table and lit it from a book of matches with a sailboat on the cover. "I heard the shots, and when that police gong started ringing I about pissed my pants, but I stuck. Brown barreled out with just time to throw that pistol and the second fifty in the backseat before the first cop showed with his gun out. I was rolling then. I bet you can still see my tire marks."

"Why didn't you leave when you heard shooting?"

He blinked at Peter through the smoke. "I made a deal."

"But you didn't know what kind of deal it was when you made it."

"What's that got to do with the price of potatoes? A deal's a deal. I took cash."

"You should've given it back."

"I didn't exactly have time to make the transaction."

"I meant later, when he came for his gun."

"Doctors don't work for free any more than hacks. Anyway, I earned it."

"Blood money."

"Your mother didn't see it that way."

"You told her?"

"I knew Brown would come to collect his property. What was I going to say, I'd gone into the gun business?"

"Did you tell her it was prearranged?"

"No."

Inside the house, a male chorus was singing the praises of Barbasol. Paul took a drag and threw the cigarette after the first. "Women get ideas can mix a fellow up. It worked out okay, because I got a job that kept her in treatments."

"Did it involve more murders?"

"Boy, I don't have to answer to you. If I didn't get drunk once and talked about how I came to work for Mr. Capone, you'd never know what you do. Some things are just between a man and his wife."

"Apparently not everything."

"Goodness, are you boys fighting?" Sharon was standing on the other side of the screen door.

"Sorry," Paul said. "We didn't mean to disturb your shaving cream commercial."

Peter stood. "I think I'll catch that train after all."

"Please don't go. I've got the sofa all made up."

"Let the boy do what he wants."

"I'm sorry, Sharon. I'm very grateful you invited me."

"Well, if you won't change your mind I'll see you out."

"He knows the way. Go back to bed. You got the morning shift."

"I'll see you out," she repeated.

He picked up his valise on the way. At the door he apologized again.

"He's so hard to get along with sometimes," she said. "But I guess I don't have to tell you."

"Sometimes I wonder how two people who are so closely related can be so different."

"Nobody knows anybody else, really. Not even fathers and sons. He's proud of you, but he'd never tell you. You're the first one in the family to enter a profession."

"You're kind to say it, but I don't believe you. He did everything he could to discourage me."

"It didn't work that way, though. All it did was make you more determined."

He looked at her, hugging herself in her housedress and slip. "Dad's never heard of reverse psychology and he'd make fun of it if it were explained to him."

"You can do a thing without knowing what it's called, or believing in it. He's never paid me a compliment straight out. When I take extra time dressing up and putting on makeup, he asks me who I'm trying to impress. It's his way of telling me he noticed."

"I think he'd be happier with me if I drove a beer truck."

"What's wrong with driving a beer truck?"

"To begin with, when he did it, it was against the law."

"He told you why he did it. Peter, I hope you don't mind my saying something, but I'm going to say it even if you do. You expect as much of everybody around you as you expect from yourself."

"Having standards doesn't mean anything if you don't try to live up to them."

"It hasn't made you a very happy person."

"This isn't just about driving a beer truck."

"I know the story about the hundred dollars and the gun. Your father still talks too much when he's drinking. A man in the position he was in, he doesn't spend much time talking himself out of things. He didn't do it to get rich. He was being the head of his household."

"He's a better man than I know. You said that before. Is that what you meant? Because most heads of households find better ways to live up to their responsibilities."

She lifted her chin. Her eyes were hot. "Christians are supposed to be strong in the forgiving department. Didn't they teach you that in the seminary?"

"I can't give absolution to someone who doesn't regret his sin."

"I'm not talking about your job as a priest. I'm talking about your duty as a believer. I think you've held on to this bitterness so long you're afraid to let it go."

"It's hard to do when you keep finding out things."

"What things?"

"I won't burden you with them." The valise was heavy in his hand. He switched it to the other. "I didn't mean to get into another argument. I'm sorry you got pulled into this mess."

"Dear, I pulled myself into it when I told Paul I'd marry him."

He almost dropped the valise. "He proposed?"

" 'I guess if we're going to we might as well get it over with.' His exact words."

"When?"

"Last week. We were walking home from the movies. It was *The Fighting Seabees,* so I don't think he was carried away by the hearts and flowers."

"I meant when is the wedding?"

"Oh, I told him after the war is soon enough. I want a pretty wedding, without drab restrictions, the bride in a quiet tailored suit and Spam at the reception. I think he was relieved, and is rooting for the Nazis now. And, Peter—*Father*—we'd be honored if you presided at the ceremony."

"SORRY, FATHER."

Vasco looked up from the fresh brown puddle at his feet to see Brother Thomas perched atop an aluminum extension ladder, washing Our Lady of Redemption's rose window with a coarse sea sponge. He wore painter's overalls and had a bucket slung across one shoulder from a rope. The sponge dripped again as he was looking down: the water struck the sidewalk with a smack and spotted Vasco's shoes further. He waved a hand in absolution and carried his valise inside.

It was morning. He'd arrived late the night before and rather than arouse the rectory had checked into a seaside hotel, a motor-court type with mock coral walls and two stories of outside entrances under a red tile roof. He'd slept poorly, but the neon sign that buzzed and clicked when it cycled and splashed his room in pink and green had been only part of the reason. His masquerade had cut into his family fabric, what there was of it. Somehow it seemed more blasphemous to have agreed to unite his father and woman friend in matrimony than to guile strangers into believing they'd been forgiven their sins in confession.

He'd lied, concealed information even from the man who had commissioned him to tell the lies, he'd lain with a woman, and a Negro at that. Having grown up among Italians, Jews, Poles, and Irish, each of whom represented a nigger to some brute or other, that last was of less concern to him than it might have been otherwise, but when all was revealed he knew that would prove the worst charge against him in the court of opinion. Florida was filled with establishments requiring separate entrances for coloreds, whites-only restrooms, separate drinking fountains for Negroes and Caucasians; "Only whites need apply" dotted the Help Wanted columns in the *Miami Herald*. A priest sworn to chastity who'd had carnal knowledge of a black woman could be torn limb from limb by an enraged mob; the fact that he wasn't a priest at all would not make it hesitate longer than to draw fresh breath.

But in his hotel bed thinking of Rose, he'd thought nothing of her color except the way the light played off her skin in the green-tinted interior of a tumbledown shack in the Wisconsin wood. He swung between burning shame and the heat of passion, and the gluey, stuffy, motionless atmosphere in a non-air-cooled room in Florida in summer only heaped fuel on the fire. Sex for him had always been an awkward, self-conscious thing, a fumbling in the dark, vaguely unsatisfying and dripping with self-loathing for his poor performance as much as for the violation of decency.

In Rose's arms it was a living, writhing, electrically charged thing, a sensation of sound and sight and touch and taste and smell. She was salty on the tongue and smelled of overripe citrus. His hands hydroplaned on the film of perspiration on her skin, her breath panted in his ear, hot and wet, with a whimper buried deep in the hyperventilation. Without realizing he'd slipped into unconsciousness, he'd awakened with the shock of his discharge, stained.

"How was the weather?" Father Kyril asked. "I'm told it snows as late as May up there."

He'd lingered in the church after Mass, collecting hymnals from the racks behind the pews as Thomas had climbed his ladder for the semiannual removal of soot and grit from the stained glass. Now in his study he removed his stole, kissed it, and hung it on its peg. He looked square and tanned and his pale eyes were searching. When Vasco hesitated, he said, "Mae Capone doesn't regularly attend Redemption, but I know about her brother-in-law's cabin. Where else would they vanish to when you could boil an egg in that huge swimming pool?"

"It was cool and restful. At night you huddle under blankets, if you can believe it."

"I can. God doesn't approve of His creations living in Paradise. That's why He sends palmetto bugs like grasshoppers and hurricanes for floods and heat from the Pit."

"I don't know about grasshoppers, but the mosquitoes are fierce."

"Welcome back. As you can see, nothing's changed. The war is there and I'm still here."

"I'm sorry. I know how much it means to you."

"It borders on envy. Perhaps this is my punishment. Or maybe He has plans for me here. I only wish I had some inkling."

"I hope you won't think I'm being patronizing when I say I know how you feel."

Kyril, in short black shirtsleeves now, was back behind his desk. He met Vasco's gaze and it seemed his search had ended. "I believe you, Father. I take it progress is slow."

"Not really. But toward what end?"

"Do I sense a desire to confess?" But he shook his head before Vasco could think of a reply. "I withdraw that. I promised myself I'd never be one of those priests who attempt to pry a request for forgiveness out of the reluctant. It crooks the system."

"You're a good man, Father." It came out without planning.

Kyril's response was even less anticipated. "What about you, Father? Do you consider yourself a good man? Not a good priest; that judgment belongs to the Lord. The other is personal and altogether a thing much more complicated."

"It must be, because I have my doubts."

"If you didn't, the answer would be obvious, and not the one you'd hoped for."

Vasco considered. "When I was a boy, I thought priests had all the answers. In the beginning that was the appeal."

"You decided that early to be a priest?"

"It seemed the greatest thing a man could aspire to."

"I wanted to be a cowboy."

Vasco laughed.

"It was Tom Mix's fault. Did you ever see any of his pictures?"

"I think I saw all of them. I had a rocking horse with his autograph on it." He'd surprised himself again, letting such a thing slip out. He saw two men wrestling the horse up the last flight of stairs to his parents' apartment, struggling to avoid dislodging the satin bow with their killers' hands.

"Principally," Kyril said, "I think it was because his hat never fell off. He'd get in brawls in saloons and chase bad men on horseback at full gallop and throw his lasso around a rocky outcrop and swing himself up from the bottom of a

canyon and his hat stayed on his head without any kind of strap showing to explain it. I thought it was a miracle."

"Come to think of it, you're right. I never noticed."

"Later I read in a movie magazine he had the wardrobe people glue the rubber ring from the lid of a pressure cooker inside the band so it wouldn't slip. But
by then it was too late because I'd already entered the seminary. The miracle of
Tom Mix's hat had convinced me of the power of faith."

"You weren't disillusioned?"

"Not nearly as much as the first time I tried to ride a horse when I was twelve.
That experience convinced me of the force of gravity."

Vasco laughed again, but only dutifully. He wondered what was the secret of
maintaining faith in the face of overwhelming indications to the contrary. Had
he been weak to dismiss it as a lie without deeper consideration? "Thank you for
that story, Father."

"Don't expect any others. I'm not the avuncular type. Will you be free to
participate in Mass?"

He could think of nothing he wanted to do less. "Yes. Thank you for asking.
And I'll hear confessions this afternoon."

"First, see Brother Thomas about that finger. It appears infected."

He glanced down at it. The skin was reddish around the gauze and the throbbing had contributed to his lack of sleep.

"I snagged it on a fishhook."

"An ideal vacation. I saw the glow the moment you walked in."

THOMAS SCRUBBED THE WOUND WITH DISINFECTANT SOAP, WHICH SET IT
stinging, then painted it with mercurochrome and bound it snugly with fresh
gauze and adhesive tape from a tin first-aid kit with a red cross painted on the
lid. It looked to be of World War I vintage. He had surprisingly gentle hands and
a deft touch. Peter thanked him.

"Try not to bend it, Father. Penicillin's a tough priority. Dying of a cut finger
will never get you martyrdom."

He didn't expect such insight. The brother, he suspected, didn't approve of
him. The man was insular; he couldn't tell if he doubted Vasco's ordination
or thought him a dilettante for his casual approach toward his responsibilities to
the Church. He didn't know the young man well enough to determine if he was
capable of sarcasm. "Are you interested in medicine?"

"I was a hospital orderly when I received the Call."

"Had you planned to become a doctor?"

"My family didn't have the money to send me to medical school. I was going
to become a male nurse and earn the tuition."

"That was a serious commitment. How could you be sure the Call was
genuine?"

"How could you?"

He'd stepped into a trap he'd set himself. "I'm told it comes in many voices."

"I only heard the one. Please remember not to bend your finger, and let me know if it begins to swell." He snapped shut the latch on the kit and left Vasco's room. Vasco walked about the small space. The bed was neatly made. There was no sign that Thomas had slept in the room during his absence. He seemed to move around in a sort of personal vacuum, leaving no trace of his passage. After three months all Vasco knew about him was that he was from Ohio and had worked in a hospital. Such men were more suited to the life that had been forced upon Vasco than he was himself.

He moved aside the muslin curtain that covered his narrow window. Through the bars he saw a gray Plymouth sedan parked on the street on the other side of the spiked iron fence. The window was down on the driver's side and as he watched a hand resting on the sill raised a cigarette and Frank Nitti's man took a puff. Vasco wondered if anyone ever relieved him or if he slept at all.

"FORGIVE ME, FATHER, FOR I HAVE SINNED. IT'S BEEN THREE WEEKS SINCE my last confession."

With a bump of the heart he recognized Sonny Capone's voice on the other side of the partition. He couldn't have summoned any of its qualities to his memory all the time they'd been apart, but there was no doubt who it was the moment he spoke.

"What sins have you committed, my son?" That address never felt comfortable in most company, but in Sonny's it came out naturally. They were practically the same age, yet Al's son seemed less—*developed* was the word that occurred to him. He'd spent his life sheltered by his mother from his father's occupation and by his father's bodyguards from its consequences; a convent sort of existence that had left him ill-prepared for the world of men. He said what was on his mind, without a thought of adjusting content to the character of the listener, and Vasco envied and liked him for it. It was difficult to think of him as a husband and father.

"That's it, actually. Mother made me promise to go to confession while she was away and I didn't get around to it. I guess that means you can add failing to honor her to that side of the ledger. "

"For your penance, say Five Hail Marys."

"That's all?"

"It seems appropriate under the circumstances."

"Gee, I've been fretting. When I told Mother and she read me out I expected an Act of Contrition at least."

"You spoke to her?"

"She called yesterday to tell me she and Dad were coming home. I'm meeting them at the station later. She said you were already on your way back."

"I thought Blessed Sacrament was your usual place of worship."

"It's not on the way to the station. I guess I'm slothful, too."

"Let's call it practical. Our boys need the shoe leather."

"I like the way you think, Pe—Father."

It pleased him that in the formal confines of the booth Sonny had erred toward the familiar. In social discourse it had been the other way around. He realized Sonny had missed him, and he Sonny. Vasco had never had a friend his own age: had never had a friend in the common interpretation of the word. Mentors, companions, but no equals who inspired affection. He pronounced the prayer of absolution in Latin.

Sonny crossed himself behind the screen. "How'd you like Ralph's place?"

"I liked it. I'll be through in a few minutes if you'd care to wait."

"Sure."

There were no more penitents. Vasco excused himself to change out of his vestments and they walked to the Rexall store. No one appeared to follow them, but the entire block was visible from the corner where the gray Plymouth was parked. They sat at the counter and ordered Cokes.

The skeletal druggist set them before them. "Haven't seen you in here in a while, Father."

"I've been away."

"Well, welcome back." He wiped the gleaming chromium of the soda fountain with a white rag and mounted the raised platform behind the prescription counter.

Nothing had changed dramatically about the place: The same magazines occupied the same pockets in the rack, only with different faces on the covers, and the painted couple kissing on *True Romance* might have been the same from last month presented from a slightly altered perspective. The racetrack investor, whom Vasco had begun to suspect lived in the back room among the unclaimed newspapers and empty deposit bottles, had traded his tweed cap for a straw skimmer tipped at an angle that reminded him of the conical cover atop the stovepipe belonging to what Vasco now thought of as Rose's shack, but it might have been the same cigarette bobbing between his lips as he read his picks over the telephone in the booth. Miami was as he'd left it; an odd situation, considering time passed and miles covered, like returning to one's childhood home in the fullness of adult life to find his spinning top just where he'd left it.

Sonny slurped at his straw. He wore a silk shirt of a metallic shade—his hearing aid clipped to the pocket—tucked into white flannels, black-and-white spectators on his feet, no hat. He'd no sooner wear one and spoil the collegiate effect than his father would venture out without his, the brim turned up on one side and down on the other. Apart from that they resembled each other very much, Sonny's inclination toward stockiness promising to broaden into Al's heavy frame quilted with fat. He released his pinky from the bottle to point at Vasco's injury.

"Fishing wound. I got the same one first time Ralph took me out on the boat. Same finger. Did Dad patch it up?"

"The first time, yes." Sharon and Brother Thomas had followed. What a disparate set of nurses for one small laceration.

"He was always the one who took care of my scrapes and bruises, when he was around. Mother said he'd have made a fine doctor if he had the education."

All his life, it seemed, Vasco had heard that Capone would have made a successful businessman, a great general, President of the United States, if things had been different: if he hadn't been Al Capone. A doctor struck Vasco as the diametrical opposite of what he'd become.

"I wish I could've gone. I couldn't get away from the air depot."

"Also you couldn't risk tipping off the FBI by having the whole family disappear at the same time."

"Oh, he told you about that?"

"Your mother did."

Sonny grinned his father's grin. "I guess Dad still has a trick or two up his sleeve."

"He's full of surprises, that's for sure."

"I bet Frankie Rio bitched about the loons the whole time."

"Just once."

"Didn't you enjoy yourself?"

He knew then he had a friend. It took one to interpret his noncommittal answers as something other than casual conversation. He turned to glance at the druggist, busy funneling powder from one container to another with a paper slip, the man in the booth in earnest discussion with his bookie, and turned his stool back toward the counter. He lowered his voice. "I was having a wonderful time until Frank Nitti showed up."

"Nitti."

"You were right about his eyes. They're like stones."

Sonny raised and plunged his straw as if he were trying to impale a fly floating in his bottle. "I can't picture him in that country. If they ever put him in his natural habitat in the zoo, his cage would be made of brick and asphalt."

"He had a meeting with Ralph in Milwaukee and followed him up there by car. Your mother said he wanted to get a look at me."

"She's mistaken. Nitti's got his hands full just staying out of jail without worrying about a priest in the family."

"I'm not in the family, Sonny."

"You're as much family as my Aunt Winifred. She's the main reason Uncle Danny drinks. At least in your case we got to choose."

"I doubt Nitti sees things that way. All he knows is a stranger is suddenly spending a lot of time with your father. I think it would be a good idea if I stopped coming around so often." He was betraying Hoover, he knew. Maybe he was a coward after all. But he couldn't help thinking it was Sonny he was concerned about.

"Bullshit. Drop by Saturday. Danny's sure to be there; we've hardly seen each other since Mother and Dad left. It will be like old times. A family reunion."

"Sonny, Nitti's having me followed. It wouldn't be a good idea."

"Staying away would be worse. You'll look guilty."

The man in the straw hat came out of the booth and left the store, pausing out front to light a fresh cigarette off the butt of the last before he turned left and went down the street with his hands thrust in his pockets. He seemed always to move with jerky urgency. Playing the sport of kings had brought him anything but peace. Vasco didn't understand the gambling impulse. The one he was involved in had given him a chronic lump of hard cold wax in his stomach.

He decided not to argue further with Sonny. Mae, he thought, would be more pragmatic about the situation. "What makes you think Nitti's worried about going to jail?" This was new information to him, and possibly to the Bureau.

"After the government put Dad away they went after Nitti for tax evasion. He got eighteen months, and the word is he didn't do the time well. Now he's facing indictment for some scheme to shake down the movie people in Hollywood for protection; they say one of his gorillas threatened to throw acid in Mae West's face in '33 if the studio didn't pay off. Come to think of it, that may be why he's seeing spies under his bed. He'll do anything to stay out of the clink."

Vasco drew thoughtfully on his straw until it buzzed. *Let me worry about Nitti, Hoover had said. He's through. He just doesn't realize it yet.*

He wasn't comforted. Hoover was in Washington and Nitti was in Chicago and Nitti's man was parked around the corner, well inside pistol range.

TWENTY-NINE

Saturday brunch, 11 A.M. Please come.
Just the family; and Rose, of course.

M.

Mae's tidy turquoise script took up a tiny fraction of the already small square sheet of linen stock in the blue envelope, identical to the one that had contained his summons to Wisconsin. He found it Friday after Mass, which he'd attended purely as a member of the congregation, atop his freshly made bed. It had been placed there presumably by the same hands that had smoothed the sheets. Brother Thomas, in addition to serving as Redemption's majordomo, housekeeper, and cleaning staff, performed the duties of a footman. Vasco's name was block printed on the outside as before, but there was no postmark. Evidently the invitation had been delivered by messenger.

It was inconceivable that so practical a person would ignore the danger in continuing the relationship. Risk, he knew, was nothing new in the Capones' world, but surely Mae knew that he was more in jeopardy than any of them. It wasn't like her to be so cavalier about the safety of one to whom she'd grown close.

Why *Rose, of course*? Would Brownie not be present, or had Mae made special mention of her to persuade him to accept despite his doubts? He could not imagine that Rose had told her what had happened that last day in Mercer. She seemed not the confiding type, and in any case her mistress's devotion would never allow her to encourage romance with a priest. If she was using Rose as a lever to apply pressure, it would be because she'd noted some affection between them and trusted his vows to bind him from committing heresy.

Vows he hadn't taken; and in that moment he feared Mae Capone's reaction to the truth most of all.

He scribbled on several sheets of notepaper, making up excuse after excuse: needed at Mass (but she would know Mass had ended well before the appointed hour), illness (Capone's health was far more tentative, but she made plans anyway), the truth.

The truth.

The thought was so revolutionary it made him sit back against the iron bedstead with the notepad resting in his lap. He'd been lying for so long, the alternative struck him as dangerous in the extreme; the prospect of being caught in a truth stood all his nerves on end. Once begun, where would it lead? But Mae was a creature of logic. He was being watched, and she would understand that he couldn't afford to appear too eager to renew the acquaintanceship.

He had actually begun writing those words, just to see how they looked on paper, when he remembered he'd told Sonny that he was being followed by one of Nitti's men. Sonny would surely have told his mother, and if for some reason he hadn't, she was aware of the situation and would assume that precautions were in place. That knowledge hadn't stopped her from writing him. The woman who had once fired a pistol at her husband for infidelity wouldn't let anything as insignificant as the Enforcer come between her and a friend.

Refusal was no option. He gathered all the crumpled sheets, tore them to bits along with the note and the response he'd started, and mixed them with the trash in the wastebasket, which Brother Thomas would be emptying later. There was nothing new about being under surveillance. Between Hoover and Thomas and Brownie, someone was observing his every move. If they were all to fall into step behind him they'd make a conga line of respectable length, with Nitti's man bringing up the rear.

At Friday Mass, Vasco had performed the Rite of Consecration for the first time, transubstantiating communal wafers and wine into the Body and Blood of Christ—or so thought the faithful; he alone knew that they remained morsels of bread and fermented grapes. It was a sacrilege that would have horrified him at the start of the assignment; but one could only be damned once for all eternity. The men, women, and children who knelt at the rail waiting for him to place what they believed was the Host on their tongues may have noticed that his hands shook a little, but a display of nerves was to be forgiven a young and inexperienced priest on so public an occasion, and in fact expected. He'd withdrawn directly afterward to kneel beside his bed and ask a being he did not trust to overlook a sin he was destined to repeat.

The Model T had been used little if at all while he was away. It refused to start and when he unscrewed the gas cap and sniffed at the contents of the tank, the stale odor told him the gasoline had turned to varnish. He walked ten minutes to the nearest filling station, returning with a can of gas for which he'd paid a two-dollar deposit and a pressurized can containing a fuel additive. The Ford balked, coughed, wheezed, fired a mighty report from its tailpipe, and fell into its jaunty animated-cartoon rhythm. He stopped at the station to return the gas can and retrieve his money. All of this took time, and he was twenty minutes late approaching the causeway.

Henry, the toll guard, smiled and shook his head when Vasco stuck out his quarter. "This one's on me, both ways," he said. "Welcome home present. That ham you gave me near converted my sister."

"Thank you." Vasco returned the coin to his pocket.

"Sure was quiet with everybody gone. We had us a flurry of G-men at the start when they found out Al gave 'em the slip. I waited in the Miami office two hours just to answer the same questions they asked me right here in the booth. After that, things just got dead. The only attraction here in summer is Al. If it wasn't for the spick gardeners and caretakers looking after things, you could sling a bowling ball up and down this thing all day long and wouldn't dent a bumper." He swung up the barricade.

The long straight drive with the bay on either side created an ideal opportunity to learn if anyone was following. There was no sign in his mirror of the gray Plymouth or any other vehicle. Vasco entertained the tenuous hope that Nitti had abandoned him as a lesser evil in order to put all his men to work on keeping him at liberty.

Approaching the Palm Island house, he lifted his foot off the accelerator suddenly and let the Ford coast to a stop. A gray Plymouth was parked across the street from the gate.

The polished wooden hoop of the steering wheel grew slippery in his hands. His shadow had anticipated him. The man's presence could not have been the result of a random guess; even had he expected Vasco to visit the island, he couldn't have known he'd be there that day of all days. *Or could he?* Mae's invitation had arrived by messenger. A stranger bearing an envelope would certainly have attracted attention: there would have been an interception, probably a bribe, and a quick examination of its contents. Opening and resealing a gummed flap in such a way that the intended recipient wouldn't notice signs of tampering was evidently part of the job description of the modern mob henchman.

Nerve, too; *balls,* Capone would have called it. The sedan stood between two of the ever-present commercial vans registered to the FBI. Nitti's man must have known that. Hoover had said Capone's own security force was legally licensed to carry firearms, which meant no felony records were involved. The same must have been true of this fellow, or he wouldn't have risked being pulled out of his car on suspicion and searched.

Vasco reached these conclusions in the space of time required to roll to a stop and then resume moving. The brief hesitation would alert the man that he was aware of him; he doubted it mattered. From Wisconsin to Miami he'd made no attempt to conceal himself. Intimidation was as much a part of his mission as gathering information.

The freckled guard at the gate smiled when he recognized the visitor and waved him up the driveway. For an instant, Vasco thought of telling him of the man in the Plymouth. But he saw no point in sparking an action that would sour the relationship between Capone and his former lieutenant. It would only bring more suspicion upon Vasco, and Nitti would just substitute one bloodhound for another. Vasco raised a hand in appreciation and puttered on up to the house.

When he set the brake and killed the motor, he heard gunshots.

ONCE OUTSIDE THE CAR, HE BECAME AWARE OF A MEASURED CADENCE IN the reports: blam blam blam, with brief pauses in between. He'd visited the FBI firing range only once, to deliver a message, but he'd remembered it and recognized the rhythms of target practice. Capone's bodyguards would be expected to brush up on their skills. The noises seemed to be coming from behind the house, and as the wind freshened from the ocean he saw curls of steel-gray smoke drifting from that direction.

Danny Coughlin opened the door, barefoot in a white sport shirt with epaulets and khaki shorts with square flapped saddle pockets. (Military fashion still dominated department stores.) Despite the lightweight attire he was sweating and his face was red; beads of condensation pebbled the bottle of Pabst Blue Ribbon he held in one hand. Vasco remembered Mae saying that the air conditioner could rarely be used because of Capone's unstable constitution.

To his surprise, her brother threw both arms around him in a terrific bear hug. The bottle made a clammy patch on his back. He'd left his coat behind and wore short sleeves. When at last it was over, Danny gripped him by the shoulders. His breath was hot and beery. "Welcome to Corregidor, Father. Hell's bells, I missed you. It was all surly bartenders and shop stewards till Al and Mae came back, and then Al took to his bed and she turned into Florence Nightingale. He's right as rain now, though." Danny's brogue became pronounced when he drank.

"I'm glad to see you." He extricated himself as delicately as the thing could be done. He liked Danny, but in his cups he was overbearing company. "I'm sorry I'm late."

"Nothing here ever starts on time. Mae's busy with Brownie and Rose in the kitchen."

"What's all the shooting?"

"Come out back and see for yourself. Let's just say it would be a grave mistake for the Japs to pick this spot to land."

Vasco followed him through the house, contemplating the blue pallor of his bare Celtic legs under the fine red hair, like fluorescent tubes. With all the windows open and the sea air crossing through the screens, the interior wasn't as close and stuffy as expected, but there was in it the eye-stinging fumes of chlorine from the pool and the taint of dead fish at low tide. He remembered what Father Kyril had said about God not wanting Man to live in Paradise.

The firing had stopped, but as they stepped out into the pool area it started up again. A small group stood in the grassy area on the other side of a hedge separating the two-story cabana from the bay. The reports were louder now, but flattened by the open air and warped by wind, not at all the powerful explosions one heard in westerns and gangster movies; they might have belonged to a cap pistol. Danny led the way past a table beautifully laid by the pool, with a white linen cloth tied securely at the corners and silver glittering and eggshell china gleaming and crystal sparkling, toward a gap in the hedge.

Capone's striped terry bathrobe stood out among the white shirts and dark poplin slacks worn by the men who patrolled the grounds looking for potential assassins. In the heat, and absent civilian guests who might be disturbed by a show of weaponry, the guards wore no coats. The crossed leather straps holding their underarm holsters in place were bordered by dark patches where they'd sweated through their shirts.

Some ten yards from where the group stood, a trestle bench had been set up with nothing behind it but open ocean, and a row of a dozen or more beer bottles placed upon it: empties, many of them probably supplied by Danny Coughlin. Three exploded in rapid succession as the newcomers drew near, the necks flying straight up and the barrels bursting in shards of brown glass and shreds of paper-and-foil labels. A fourth bullet missed the next target, but a fifth caught it low, detaching the rest of the bottle from the base. The thick circle of glass remained on the bench.

There followed two shocks for Vasco: the first, when the shooter paused briefly to shift the weapon from his right hand to his left and popped the next two bottles in close order (a feat one associated exclusively with Saturday matinee horse operas), and the second, when he realized the man doing the shooting was Capone.

The great bulky figure in the striped robe, hatless and balding, with a stump of cigar stuck in the corner of his mouth, fired one last time, missing the next target and emptying the square black pistol extended at the end of his arm, its slide kicked all the way back exposing most of the barrel. The stench of sulfur stung Vasco's nostrils.

"Shit. Too much soft living. In the old days I'd've hit every goddamn one, and in half the time. Let's see what you can do, Frankie."

"Otis."

"The fuck kind of name's Otis? Load 'er up, *Otis*. Chrissake." He passed the weapon to the man standing nearest him, whose holster was empty. Evidently the gun was his.

In a series of swift movements, Otis ejected the slim magazine from the hollow handle, switched it with another from his pocket, slammed the new magazine into place with the heel of his hand, and released the slide, chambering in a new round. All these operations were conducted with efficiency and an economy of energy, steel on oiled steel, accompanied by metallic eruptions of noise every bit as loud as the shots and nearly as violent. It was like watching a heavy and destructive machine, a pile driver or a wrecking crane, going about its ruinous business heedless of anything but its mission.

Danny and Vasco had stopped twenty feet short of the group. Mae's brother pulled from his bottle and said, "This promises to be educational: diplomacy versus pride of accomplishment."

Vasco had no idea what he was talking about. Otis took aim, standing sideways to the targets with his arm stretched out at shoulder level, all square angles with the muscles of his upper back bunched transparently under his soaked shirt. As Vasco watched, the muscles relaxed, rolling away from one another like a pyramid of cantaloupes after one had been plucked from the bottom. Simultaneously his own shoulders tightened, bracing for the noise.

"Sail!" another bodyguard called out.

The man in firing position lowered his arm as a white shark fin attached to a small skiff glided behind the bench, close enough to shore to appear as if it were crawling along the top of the bench itself. Capone, watching, took his cigar from his mouth, spat out a scrap of slimy brown wrapper, and replaced the stub, tapping a broad square bare-heeled foot in a velvet slipper on the earth.

At length the sailboat cruised out of harm's way, tacking east. ("Bon voyage, you four-f shirking bastard," said the master of Palm Island.) Otis resumed his stance, gathered then loosened his muscles again, and pressed the trigger. The pistol barked six times, the reports so close together they sounded like a string of firecrackers going off, a nib of blue flame coming from the muzzle. Bottles jumped and spun and disintegrated, brass casings twinkled in the sun and vanished in the grass; but as the echo rolled off across the water, one bottle remained standing. A seventh shot cracked and it flew apart.

Capone released a feral snort. "I hope you boys are just shooting lousy to make me look good. I can't use a bodyguard that can't outshoot me."

Otis, crew cut and tanned, with the look of a marine in a recruiting poster— Vasco wondered what his story was regarding enlistment—thrust his jaw forward and popped out the empty magazine. "Set up another dozen."

"On your own time. I ain't running an arcade."

Danny parked his bottle under one arm and applauded.

"You don't need these boys, Al. You're a regular Flying Fortress."

Capone looked up, startled. He spotted Vasco and the sun broke on his face. "Good to see you back, Padre. Scorcher, ain't it? Wasn't for those cocksucking whiskers we'd still be floating out on the lake." He met Vasco at the halfway point and wrung his hand. He smelled of tobacco and brimstone. "Danny, fetch us a couple of cold ones."

Danny strode back toward the house and Capone and Vasco went back through the hedge and sat under the umbrella where they'd played cards and Capone had threatened the life of the president of the realtors' association. It seemed very long ago, but life appeared to have changed little on the island.

Capone's cigar was cold. He patted his pockets, forgetting he hadn't any in the black one-piece bathing suit under the robe. "Got a match, Padre?"

"I don't smoke. I'm sorry."

"You should. A man needs something to give up when he's lost his health. How's your old man?"

"Quite well. He's getting married."

"Peachy. There's no alibi like a wife. Italian girl?"

"Jewish, actually."

Capone frowned, then scratched the graying hairs curling over the top of his swimsuit and shrugged. "Jews are okay, when you find one you can trust. Jake Guzik's dog-loyal. You get to meet him in Mercer?"

"No. I heard he was running Ralph's place in town, but I never made it."

"Swell." He didn't seem to be listening. "I'm not just sure about this brunch business. Mae got the idea from *Good Housekeeping.* I never heard of it. We supposed to starve between now and supper, or we eating four, five meals a day now?"

"I think the idea is to cut down to two some days. Rationing," Vasco added.

"Well, I could eat the asshole out of a skunk. I had a half a grapefruit three hours ago. I'd sooner lap up a bowl of battery acid." He patted himself again. "Got a match?"

Vasco hesitated, then shook his head.

"Too bad. A man needs something to give up when he's lost his health."

It was one of his bad days. Next he'd be asking about Vasco's father.

But his guest was spared the ordeal of conducting conversation on a continuous loop by the appearance of the guard from the gate. As the man out front, he had on his coat, pale blue gabardine with the inevitable room built in for a weapon, and he wore a sheen of sweat over his freckles. He glanced at Vasco, then leaned down and whispered in Capone's ear. His master's reaction was delayed, but unmistakable in its significance. His face darkened until the white scars on his cheek looked like tapeworms. He straightened abruptly and rapped over his shoulder at another guard strolling alongside the hedge.

"Frankie!"

It was the hapless Otis, who corrected him.

"Where the hell's Frankie?"

"We don't have a Frankie, Mr. Capone."

"Well, whatever your name is, take it on the ankles down to the gate with this guy. He'll fill you in on the way."

The guard from the gate looked blank. "What do you want us to do?"

"Bring him back here, what do you think?"

"Yes, sir."

"Jesus."

"Yes, sir," Otis echoed.

"Either of you boys got a light?"

"No, sir." They spoke in unison.

"Well, then get the hell down there. Prove you're good for something."

They left on the trot. Capone said, "Shit," and threw his cigar toward the pool. It fell on the tiles and rolled to the edge. He found a pack of Dentyne in the pocket of his robe and offered a piece to Vasco, who declined with thanks. The foil came off and the great mastiff jaws ground back and forth on the gum. "College boys. Nancies. In the old days I had to knock the bark off 'em before I could bring 'em out in public. This batch I got to throw over my shoulder and burp."

Vasco was aflame with curiosity, but he was struck suddenly by the realization that the only appropriate questions he could ask Capone pertained to events that had taken place many years in the past.

He filled the time with small talk.

"I had no idea you could shoot so well."

The smile returned, and with it some of his normal coloring.

"You should've seen me in the Adonis Social Club basement when I was fourteen. Buffalo Bill was in town, playing the Garden with all his horses and injuns; I think Geronimo was there, but he might've been dead by then. Some big chief anyway. Charley Luciano snuck in to see the show, and he came back and bet me two bits I couldn't bust a bottle aiming back over my shoulder with a mirror in my hand like Annie Oakley. I said, 'I can do anything any dame can do, including pee sitting down.'"

He fell to chuckling, chewing slowly at his gum. Vasco waited thirty seconds, the landward wind stirring the sparse hairs on Capone's crown, then realized he'd lost the thread of his story. "Annie Oakley," he prompted.

Capone shifted his weight in his chair, coming alert. "Two bits, the bet was. I missed the bottle. Charley says, 'Pay up.' I said the mirror had a flaw in it, which it did; when you looked in it your nose bent off to the side like in the funhouse in Coney Island. But we didn't lay down any rules about the quality of the equipment, so I said, 'Double or nothing I get two next time, only I use a different mirror.'

"Charley's game, but the odds of digging up two hand mirrors in a joint like the Adonis weren't great. Ten minutes we're at it, then Charley goes out and comes back with a pocketbook item from a dame of his—they're like subway stations with him, always one handy—a little round gold box that opens up and there's a powder puff in one half and a mirror in the other. It's tiny: Charley's counting that four bits already. But I popped the bottles and we were square. 'Charley,' I said, 'someday them skirts are gonna put you in a mess of shit you won't buy your way out of.' Swear to Christ. And there he is, doing thirty to fifty in Sing Sing for pimping."

Vasco was wondering how much of the story was embroidery when Capone shifted positions again, his jaws going still and his face stiffening into a mask. His companion realized they were no longer alone. He turned in his chair and felt his blood sliding into his feet. Otis and the guard from the gate were approaching from the house with their hands gripping the upper arms of a square-shouldered man with a narrow waist in a suit far too heavy for Miami in summer. It was the driver of the gray Plymouth. His handsome face, spoiled slightly by the flattened bridge of the nose, lacked emotion, but the mouth was drawn tight.

Doubtless all his circulation was cut off above the elbows.

"Mr. Capone—" Vasco began. A heavy palm slashed sideways, silencing him. The gray eyes were fixed on Frank Nitti's man, standing still now between his escorts six feet from the table. His hat was missing, probably knocked off in a struggle; his hair, thick, black, and glossy, had come loose from its careful combing and hung over his forehead. He met Capone's gaze—a courageous feat, Vasco thought; but then he was accustomed to Frank Nitti's ice-water stare.

"What' s your name?" Capone's tone was polished steel. Vasco had heard it in jest, in pleasant conversation, and in rage, but never in controlled fury such as this. He imagined it had sounded that way just before he reached for his base-ball bat.

"Joe Verdi." The man tried to match his tone, with some success.

"What you doing down here, Joe, taking in the beach?"

"Something like that."

"Not following my friends."

Verdi said nothing.

The guard from the gate took something from his side pocket and held it out. "He brought his luggage."

Capone looked at the pistol, square and black and heavy-looking, its butt turned his way. It was identical to the weapon he'd used to shoot bottles earlier. Chicago gangdom, it appeared, subscribed to an unwritten Manual of Arms. Capone took it, and with the same series of movements Vasco had seen previously, popped out the magazine, looked at the brass cartridges stacked inside, snapped it back in, and worked the slide with a jerk and release. "Turn him the other way." He got up, his robe falling open to expose his hard heavy frame in the black swimsuit. His chest was heaving.

"Mr. Capone," Otis said.

"Shut up."

The two men turned with their captive until their backs faced the bay. He struggled, but failed even to slow them down.

"Hang on tight."

Vasco gripped the arms of his chair. He was incapable of moving otherwise.

Capone hefted the pistol in his right hand, as if trying to decide which end to use. Finally he grasped the handle and laid the barrel atop Verdi's left shoulder. The man made a mighty lunge, trying to shrug it off. Capone reached up with his left hand, grasped him brutally by the hair, making him wince, and raised the weapon level with Verdi's left ear. "You boys take measures," he said. "I don't want no deaf men on the payroll."

The two guards stretched their free hands across their faces, sticking their index fingers into the ears nearest the pistol, and craned their necks as far to the side as they could.

Verdi was shaking now, his knees buckled; but the two men held him upright with their bodies braced against his. Capone thumbed back the hammer and squeezed the trigger.

The *blam* was full-throated, a shocking explosion in those close quarters; Vasco's own ears rang, and Verdi's mouth opened wide, but his scream was silent under the report. The spent casing made a glittering arc and landed on the ceramic tiles with a thin, glassy tinkle in the roaring echo.

Capone took a step back, releasing his grasp and dandling the weapon again. Verdi's head fell forward, his chin on his chest. His mouth remained open, his eyes squeezed tight in a kind of pain Vasco could only imagine. Then Capone shifted hands on the gun and snatched the man's hair again, this time in his right hand. Verdi's head snapped back, a sobbing gasp escaping his throat now, the first human sound he'd managed to make since answering Capone's last question. The guards plugged their ears again and craned away. But instead of raising the pistol, Capone leaned close to Verdi's working ear and bellowed: "I'm leaving you one eardrum to take a message back to your boss. Next mug comes inside a thousand feet of one of my friends gets it between the eyes. *Tra gli occhi, capisci?*"

"Yeah." It was a groan.

"*Che?*" He was still bellowing.

"*Capisco!*"

Capone let go of his hair, but not before giving it a final twist that brought another gasp. "Take this piece of shit and dump him back in his can."

The two guards half-carried the man back toward the house.

On the way they passed Mae Capone and Rose, who had stopped halfway to the pool carrying trays of food and drink, and behind them Danny with a bottle of beer in each hand. All were staring at Capone.

He made a backhand swipe with the hand holding the gun, a savage gesture that backed them up as before a hot wind. "Let's you and me take a walk, Padre. I got some trash to throw out." He turned in the direction of the bay.

Vasco rose and trotted to catch up. "Was that necessary?"

"I tried turning the other cheek once. You saw what it got me."

"Did Sonny tell you Nitti was having me followed?"

"Sonny's a good boy. He worries about his friends."

"I can't help thinking you just made a bad situation worse."

"That's what Johnny told me when Deanie got dusted."

"He was right."

"Right or wrong's got nothing to do with staying alive."

They walked around the trestle bench, Capone stepping gingerly to avoid cutting his slippered feet on the carpet of broken glass. When they were a few yards away from the edge of the shore, he swung the pistol back over his shoulder and hurled it far out above the Atlantic. It turned over several times and made a white splash in the relentless blue. A gull swooped at it and wheeled away. "Maybe it'll wash up on Normandy with the rest of the artillery," Capone said.

"Do you think that man will ever get the hearing back in that ear?"

"Who gives a shit? Sonny wears a hearing aid and he does all right." He stuck his hands in his robe pockets, leaving it open to flap in the wind. "Don't waste your prayers on a Sicilian. A cockroach'll keep on crawling with its head cut clean off."

"How do you know Verdi's Sicilian?"

"'Cause he was dumb enough to let himself get spotted by that college boy at the gate. Sicilians." He shook his head, watching a freighter waddling low in the water near the horizon.

"Dumb as turds, tough as horsemeat, do anything for a buck: your buck; my buck, it don't matter. You got to keep outbidding the competition if you want to keep 'em in your pen. Miss one bid and it's *addio, signor,* see you in the obituaries. Take Scalise and Anselmi. Take the fucking Gennas." He worked his gum reflectively, almost ecstatically, as if he were chewing flavor back into it. . . .

THE CONFESSIONS OF AL CAPONE

1925–1929

Compiled from Transcripts
by Special Agent P. Vasco Division 5 FBI File #44/763

THIRTY

I'D BEEN EXPECTING TROUBLE FROM THE GENNAS SO LONG, WHEN I GOT wind of what they were up to I thought it was old news.

The papers called them the Terrible Gennas, and for once they were right. They liked the tag, I guess because the more people were scared of them, the less they had to buy off; they had press on the payroll, and somebody said Angelo himself suggested it. The reporters threw in "Bloody Angelo" as a kind of bonus, and Mike the Devil for one of his brothers. Pete, Sam, and Jim got no nicknames on account of they were run-of-the-mill killers, bullets and razors, no fancy stuff.

Then there was Tony—the Aristocrat he was called, because he had his suits made and put on a fresh shirt every day. He lived apart from the others in a swanky hotel suite downtown, went to the opera, and put up housing for poor immigrants. That's where I got the idea for soup kitchens during the Depression; I always thought the goodwill was why Tony lasted as long as he did.

You remember Frankie Yale put O'Banion on the spot while Deanie was fixing up the floral arrangements for Mike Merlo, who fooled everybody by dying of cancer. Mike was president of the Unione Siciliana—well, the Mafia—and he wasn't cold in the ground before Angelo took his place. That was a poor career decision, because between Bloody Angelo and Tony Lombardo and Patsy Lolordo and that poison-packing *escremento* Joe Aiello, nobody ever held the job long enough to make out his will. In May 1925, Angelo and his new wife, Lucille, found a house they liked in Oak Park, and he went off to the agent's in his swell new Marmon Speedster with eleven grand in his pocket to pay for it. Hymie Weiss, who was running the O'Banion mob then, spotted him on Ogden and took out after him in a seven-passenger Hupmobile with Frank Gusenberg driving. Vinnie Drucci—Schemer was his moniker because of all the big-time operations he always had going but only in his head, like putting the snatch on Man O' War and holding him for ransom—was with them, and that crackjob Bugs Moran. They opened up on the Speedster with shotguns.

Well, Angelo took off like gooseshit, straight into a lamppost on the corner of Hudson. He hit his head on the steering column and was still seeing stars when Gusenberg pulled up alongside and Hymie and Schemer and Bugs let him have it. That was the official version, and whether Hymie or Schemer or Bugs sat it out or it was all three on the triggers or just two, I'm inclined to accept it in principle.

The Gennas spent more on Angelo's sendoff than the Irish did on O'Banion, which was predictable under the circumstances; they even towed that Speedster of his behind the hearse, all hung with crepe and looking like a Swiss cheese with holes in it big as your fist. Marmons were made of aluminum, you see. One of the happiest days in my life was when I took delivery on that armor-plated Cadillac.

It was a North Side job, everybody knew it. O'Banion got his head handed to him for telling the Sicilians to go to hell, so his boys sent the first Sicilian they laid eyes on to keep him company. The Gennas all seemed to go along with that. Three weeks later, Mike the Devil rounded up Scalise and Anselmi and caught Bugs and Schemer in crossfire when they pulled that Hupmobile out of an alley onto Congress, but the car got the worst of it. I think Schemer took some stitches.

Mike wasn't so lucky. As they were driving away, he, Scalise, and Anselmi picked up a police tail, and thinking it was Weiss's boys they floored it. But Mike wasn't any handier behind the wheel than Angelo: A truck shot across Congress on Sixtieth, and he had to stand on the brakes to keep from plowing into it. The truck stopped, too, and then the cops swung their big touring car across both lanes to hem him in. When they got out to make the arrest, Scalise and Anselmi opened fire with the same shotguns they'd used on the Hupmobile. Two cops died, one was wounded, and Mike died in an alley, though not before he kicked an ambulance attendant in the face and said, "Take that, you son of a bitch!" I bet he spit in the devil's eye when he got to hell, fighting over the name.

It was just the kind of mess that happened sometimes, especially in Chicago. The cops were all plainclothes detectives, they were responding to shots fired— that's what they told the papers, the ones that survived—and nobody knew who the hell they were shooting at and who was shooting back. Only Tony the Aristocrat saw it different. Somehow he got it into his head I fixed everything up, starting with Angelo, so I could step in and grab that licensing agreement the Gennas had with Washington to distribute denatured alcohol, which renatured slick as spit if you knew what you were doing. (If you didn't, God help you, because that stuff would strip the skin off a streetcar.) I heard it was Drucci sold Tony that bill of goods, but if so it was the only one of his schemes that ever came to anything. Personally I think it was the cops from the Maxwell Street station put him onto it.

They were into the Gennas for thousands, from the precinct captain on down to the parking detail, and when word got around I was taking over for Johnny Torrio they were afraid I wouldn't be as generous. I lean that way because that part was true. You've got to distribute the grease evenly; too much in one spot just gums up the works.

That joke on Congress cinched it for me. It was Maxwell Street dicks involved, and coincidences like that just don't happen. If it had gone off the way they planned, I'd get the blame for Mike, and there'd be war. The Aristocrat was already predisposed against me for having to borrow back Scalise and Anselmi for the Hupmobile fiasco—I told you I liked their work too much to return them permanent—and he don't stop to consider it was cops all along. Understand, all this came around while we're fighting the O'Donnells and O'Banion's boys. I'm running out of directions to turn where bullets aren't coming from. Meanwhile,

Tony, Pete, Sam, and Jim are undermining the whole South Side: hijacking trucks, pushing our own stuff in our speaks and pocketing the take, kidnapping our people for ransom. You can't make war on three fronts and remain profitable. The Gennas had to go, and high time.

I used one of their own guys, which is what I call street poetry. Joe Nerone started out teaching arithmetic in Sicily, but when he finished adding two and two he decided teaching didn't pay, so he went to sticking up people and when the authorities objected to that he came here and threw in with the brothers. But a man who can tote up a column of numbers can never know satisfaction. He didn't take a lot of persuading; Jake Lingle said I told him you get a lot farther with a kind word and a gun than just a kind word, but he was being dramatic. What I said was a kind word and a C-note. In this case it was a bit more, but when it came to staying alive I never counted pennies.

I had my hands full like I said, so rather than take the time to come up with a new plan I borrowed Frankie Yale's. Joe called the Aristocrat and set up a meet at Cutaia's grocery store at Grand and Curtis. Tony, the dumb cluck, takes his hand just like Deanie took Frankie's, and while they're pumping away saying howjado, hot enough for you, that kind of bullshit, Scalise and Anselmi walked in and aerated him. Five in the back, the easy way, like they say in pool.

So that was it for the Gennas. Tony got forty-two days from the time Angelo went down, which was the same as dying in your bed of old age by Chicago standards. Pete, Sam, and Jim took ship to Sicily right after the funeral. When Jim came back in '30, he went into the import business, cheese and olive oil. I put some money in that concern. What the hell, I never had any complaint with doing business on the legit, and I sort of liked Jim. A man can't help being born into a family of lunatics.

Nineteen twenty-six was a bitch. TURBULENT TWENTY-SIX, the newspapers tagged it; scratch a reporter and you'll find a rotten poet. Thirty died in just the first three months, including Bill McSwiggin, who I liked as much as you can like an assistant state's attorney; he did what he was told and didn't hit me up for any more than he was worth, but he got in with a bad crowd and was gunned. His old man was a police sergeant, so that situation was a long time going away, and of course I had to answer questions, having become a celebrated local character by then. I didn't mind that so much as watching a couple dozen of my joints getting busted up and shut down by cops out for blood. When they can't hit you anywhere else they hit you in the pocketbook.

Say what you like about O'Banion's boys, they went straight for the throat. First they snatched Tommy Ross, my driver, beat him and burned him with cigarettes to get all the dope on me they could, then plugged him in the head and dumped him in a cistern out in the country. Couple of farm boys found him when their horses wouldn't drink from the crock. He was a good boy, Tommy, gave half his pay to his mother every week, and they tied him up with wire and tortured him and shot him like a dog. That was in August. In September, I'm enjoying a cup of coffee and a kaiser roll in the Hawthorne Inn restaurant in Cicero when Hymie Weiss leads a parade of cars down Twenty-Second Street and stitches up the joint with more tommy guns than was ever in one place until our boys hit Omaha Beach.

The guns were new then. I'd seen one or two, but I hadn't heard 'em in action. When the first volley started I thought it was a truck loaded with plumbing fixtures or something barreling past, its brakes went out. I wouldn't be here telling you about it if Frankie Rio didn't pull me down to the floor. That first pass was just to get my attention—they was aiming high—and like a sap I popped up for a better look just before the second came in at waist level. Frankie made his future in that moment. I was trying him out in poor Tommy Ross's place, my mind not yet made up about keeping him around: With that messy lip of his and me all carved up on one side we looked like a bad circus act, and I didn't want to give the newspaper cartoonists any more ammunition than they had already. But hooking up with a new bodyguard is like breaking in a pair of shoes; they might look swell, but if you're hurting at the end of the day the fit's no good. Well, the fit was good.

To this day I don't know how many cars were involved. I heard it was as much as a dozen and as few as three, which plays way low. You don't keep count under those circumstances. It seemed like a hundred. The room was packed—it was the start of the racing season at Hawthorne Park, all the owners and jockeys and trainers and sportsmen and working girls were in town, you couldn't get a room in a hotel or a stool at a bar—and when the real McCoy came along about a half a minute later, busting windows and exploding china and chewing up woodwork, men and women piled every which way to get out of the line of fire, diving under tables, ducking behind the lunch counter, making for the kitchen in back, where the slugs are plinging and planging off pans and pots like tambourines in a hurricane. A bunch of customers and hired help tripped over me and Frankie, or threw themselves down on top of us, I don't know which. For a minute I was sure I'd suffocate. Meanwhile the bullets keep coming, yakity-yak, raking the place right to left, one car coming on the bumper of the one in front of it with another chopper yakity-yaking behind the last. The air's hazy with smoke and plaster dust, you can't breathe, which don't make any difference to me because my face is stuck in a fat waiter's crotch.

They said it was the second to last car in the convoy that stopped first. I don't see why it's important, but this one had plenty of witnesses and everybody wanted to get in his licks. A character in a khaki shirt and farmer's bib overalls gets out, kneels on the sidewalk, hoists a tommy to his shoulder, and brooms the restaurant back and forth. He empties the drum and strolls back to the car, which by now is blasting its horn, let's get the fuck outta here before we wake up the cops. Later I hear it's Pete Gusenberg in the overalls, Frank's brother, and as crazy a Jew as ever came wandering in from the desert. That gang was a hodgepodge affair, all mixed up with Irish and Jews and wops and Polacks, which

Weiss was one, a Polack, Bugs Moran too, despite their names. All the tribes have risen up against me, like it says in the Good Book.

When Frankie gave the all-clear and we got up, I couldn't believe what I saw. The Argonne Woods has come to Cicero. There isn't a pane of glass left in the place, a cup in its saucer. People are slipping and sliding in food spilled on the floor. Coffee's gushing out of holes in a big urn. There's shit floating in the air, feathers and sawdust from upholstered furniture torn to pieces in the vestibule. Customers are patting themselves all over, checking for wounds. You see them cartoons, a talking rabbit—thinks he's all right after getting shot at, then takes a drink of water and it squirts out of him like a watering can, you expect that's going to happen there in the Hawthorne. I mean, what kind of animal would risk pouring lead into a hundred strangers he's got no beef with just to get one guy? You can see what I'm up against.

But the miracle is no one was killed. Weiss's mugs poured a thousand rounds into the place without so much as nicking a major artery. Louie Barko, an old Genna pal who'd seen the light and come over to sit in hotel lobbies and at the next table to see I got to live in peace, caught a slug in the shoulder, and a dame sitting in a car by the curb got a piece of glass in her eye, but apart from those things and some haberdashery and soiled underdrawers, the visiting team batted zero. It cost me five grand to save the dame's eyesight. I'd've billed Hymie, but the collection agencies were so busy I'd've wound up suing his estate as it turned out.

The cops came along finally, to sweep up glass and count bullet holes. They grilled hell out of Louie Barko there in Cook County General with his arm in traction. I got my time downtown, along with Weiss and Schemer Drucci and Moran and whoever else they could scoop up; they already had Scalise and Anselmi in custody for shooting those dicks from Maxwell Street on Congress, though they didn't keep them long because the dicks forgot to identify themselves as officers and the jury agreed they thought they were defending themselves against a rival mob. The law and the gangs both liked Cadillacs and you needed a score card to tell 'em apart. The cops left the file open on the Hawthorne business and went on to other things because out of a hundred witnesses nobody fingered anybody; even the squares who got a good look at Pete Gusenberg wouldn't pick him out of the lineup.

But everybody knew who was behind it. I knew, but I'm a reasonable man. I gave Weiss one last chance. That was a big shitty mess, and anybody in his right mind knew the papers and the Chicago Crime Commission wouldn't put up with a return match.

But Hymie wasn't in his right mind. He was what rackets guys call a twenty-niner: one keg short of a truckload. Tony Lombardo was running the Unione Siciliana then, warming the seat left vacant by Angelo Genna, and I asked him to represent me at a meeting with Weiss in the Morrison Hotel, two weeks after the Hawthorne became temporarily uninhabitable. I knew Hymie wouldn't sit down with me, but everybody knew Tony and trusted him, even Micks. It was a fancy conference suite with a view, good cigars, real Scotch and brandy off the boat. Al wants peace, Tony said. You're both not even thirty yet, you got plenty of time to make your pile and live like Rockefeller, there's cash enough to go around. A solid-gold coffin looks swell, but it's no better to lay in than a pine box; common-sense stuff, you know, same sell Johnny made back before the O'Donnells upset the apple cart. I even threw in an offer to manage all the beer concessions north of Madison Street, which cut straight through the Loop, with more speaks than Weiss had bullets and no interference from me.

Well, he wouldn't listen to money or reason. "Scalise and Anselmi killed O'Banion," he said. "Tell Capone to put 'em on the spot. That's the price of peace."

Well, I wouldn't do that to a yellow dog, and I told Tony to tell him so. And just between you and me and the Atlantic Ocean, once word got out I'd sold two of my own like pieces of meat, my life'd be worth even less than it was with a maniac like Weiss running around. Also he'd never honor the deal, having a hard-on against everybody who had any connection with what happened to his dear old pal Deanie.

So Weiss had to go. I expected it and had already taken steps.

Normally I'd've given the job to Jack McGurn, who always reminded me a little of me when I was at his stage. I started him as a bodyguard at $150 a week, but he took to a tommy like Caruso took to *Pagliacci,* so he was wasted sitting around reading *Happy Hooligan* with a rod under his arm. He practiced out in the country until they said he could put a drumload through the knothole of a tree at thirty paces without touching the sides. I heard he killed twenty-two men, but if so it wasn't for me. I never gave the order for that many. A dozen's a nice round number for anybody. He dressed spiffy and was a devil with dames. Played the ukulele.

But right at the time Tony Lombardo was talking peace to Weiss, Hymie's hotshots Frank and Pete Gusenberg followed Jack to the cigar store of the McCormick Hotel at Chicago Avenue and Rush and opened up on him with a tommy and a pistol in a phone booth.

It took four pints of blood to keep his heart pumping and Machine Gun Jack wouldn't be strumming the ukulele for a while, much less make Hymie the Polack number twenty-three.

I gave it to Frankie Rio. What the hell, a man's got to make his bones sometime, and he proved he was cool under fire. He cased out Hymie, who as it happened had a weakness for religion. He moved around a lot, never took the same route to the crapper twice running, but the one thing you could count on was he'd show up at Holy Name Cathedral, right across from O'Banion's old flower shop on North State. Two days after the talks broke down, Frankie rented a second-story room on the same side as the shop for eight bucks a week and changed the guard often. Far as the landlady knew, it was being used for poker games, which was a cottage industry then; an old bag named Romanian Annie put a celebrated twist on it by training her cat Ginny to snatch dollar bills off the table during games. As dodges go, it was airtight. Johnny always said there's nothing like a crooked front for throwing suspicion off a more serious criminal enterprise.

Right away Frankie showed he had a gift. He committed Scalise and Anselmi right on the courthouse steps after they were sprung on the cop-killing deal, and he hired a first-rate wheel man for the getaway, a beer truck driver who was over-qualified for that position, having outrun a hijacker only a couple of weeks earlier, which considering automotive realities was something rare. It was a ten-year-old Mack against a Packard Eight with a souped-up engine, but he had a downhill run, and with a full load and an operator with *maracas,* that's like putting a rocket on a roller skate. The dough was good and he needed it in a hurry. Frankie posted him at the corner in a Hudson Super Six.

They waited six days. Then on the afternoon of October 11—three weeks to the day after Weiss's army hit the Hawthorne—a Cadillac cruises to a stop across the street from the florist's.

Well, there's nothing much in that, but nobody gets out until a Buick comes around the corner and parks behind the Caddy. That makes it Weiss, whose bodyguards had bodyguards. He was just too cheap to buy top-drawer transportation for the second team.

There's three men in his car besides Sam Peller, his driver, but Hymie's not hard to spot. He was scared of drafts and wore a tan camel's-hair overcoat most seasons and a homburg like Daddy Warbucks', and his ears stuck out like curb feelers; he had to put on earmuffs when the wind blew off the lake or he'd sail right over the Wrigley Building. Peller lets out Pat Murray, his personal security, and behind him Hymie, William O'Brien, his mouthpiece, and Benny Jacobs, who got out the vote for Weiss's man in the Twentieth Ward. Nobody the world would miss.

Hymie was in a hurry to get to church. I guess his sins hung heavy on him. He skips up the steps ahead of the others, and Scalise and Anselmi have to scramble if they're going to get a clear shot. No sweat, though: between John's chopper and Albert's pump gun, Weiss was hit ten times. Murray's liver is shot away, he's a goner, and O'Brien and Peller picked up some slugs. Jacobs didn't get a scratch, which isn't that always the way with politicians; Cermak was the only exception to that rule. Hymie's homburg is still rolling when that Super Six tears off carrying the guys that knocked him out from under it.

So another whiz-bang funeral procession snarls up traffic downtown. Well, that Polack liked his parades, didn't he? He was twenty-eight, a year older than me. Rheumatism's not an issue in our trade.

I sat out the services. I heard John Sbarbaro, the Prince of Undertakers, did a nifty job plugging up the holes, as why wouldn't he, having had plenty of practice on Deanie and the Gennas and O'Donnells? But with Moran and Drucci in attendance and things being what they were, I couldn't count on any of the old truces being in effect. Hymie's ward heeler was sore enough over Benny Jacobs getting scared, and grateful enough for the work Sbarbaro did on Hymie, to run the undertaker for municipal judge. He won, too.

The cops found Scalise's tommy in the street where he ditched it and collected some shells from the rented room and a hat from the bed with a Cicero label in it, but nobody was arrested. That didn't stop the chief of police from tagging me in the press. I threw a shindig for all the reporters in town in my suite at the Metropole—booze, shrimp cocktails, girls—and stated my innocence for the record. I offered to turn myself in for questioning, but nobody took me up on it. And what did they write? "Gangdom literally shot piety to pieces." That line had Jake Lingle all over it. I sent him a case of Scotch in appreciation. Did I get a thank-you? No, but he didn't send back the hooch.

What I felt like saying, what's the city pay for shooting mad dogs? I didn't tell you, I don't like to remember it, I still get nightmares, but I wandered outside the Hawthorne after the dust settled and before the cops arrived, I hear screaming coming from a parked car. Frankie tried to hold me back, but I said, "It's a flivver, for chrissake," meaning a Model T, no rackets guy'd be caught dead riding in one. This is the car I told you about, with the woman inside hurt. I go up to it and the man behind the wheel's talking. Clyde Freeman's the name, this is Anna, the little woman, and that's Clyde, Junior, he's five years old and just started kindergarten. We're in from Louisiana to see the races. He's saying all this like we just met in a bus station. Making chitchat, with a finger sticking through a hole in his hat in his hand, broken glass covering his lap. Junior's in the backseat, face red as a turnip, his nose is running; a slug grazed his knee and his stockings are plastered with blood and he's pissed his knickers. Mrs. Freeman, Jesus. Leaning over on the passenger's side in front with her face in both hands, blood slipping out between her fingers all down the front of her dress. I thought her face was gone. She's got a splinter of glass in her right eye; three inches long, the surgeon said later, it penetrated the brain. Horrible. But the worst part is Clyde, Senior, making casual conversation with his world shot to hell. He's hysterical but calm. I preferred the screaming and blubbering.

Weiss. How much do you have to hate a man to be willing to destroy a hundred people you never met just to get him? He was a dead man from that moment. That peace conference was just a stall while the arrangements were being made.

The heat was on: joints busted up and padlocked, small fry herded into police headquarters and bounced around the basement, editorials demanding martial law. Will Rogers said Chicago wouldn't let a crook in town until he agreed to rub out another crook. It was funny, but it brought pressure from Washington and Springfield. Harness bulls we'd been paying off for years shook their heads, said it was a damn shame, and swung the axe.

In the rackets, cooler heads prevailed. That winter a stray stiff or two turned up, nobodies killing nobodies, and most of them tidily disposed of across the state line. If they ever took a census of the fresh dead in Indiana, they'd outnumber the living. I felt safe enough to plan my first family vacation since I left Brooklyn. But I was never so glad to see a year go out.

The Weiss affair made me a national figure. I'm in headlines and newsreels, Walter Winchell mentions me on the radio. I'm a vice lord, a criminal kingpin, the Sultan of Sin.

Did I say national? When the economy went bust in Germany, von Hindenburg blamed me. I'm a symbol of American gangsterism run amuck, he said, and shot some anarchists. I'm world news. Fame has its advantages. I got tables in reserve at all the best restaurants every night for me and my security, just in case I show up. When the Yankees are in town, Babe Ruth comes up to my box in Comiskey Park to sign a ball for Sonny. When I get back from vacation in Hot Springs, the band at the Hawthorne track strikes up "It's a Lonesome Old Town (When You're Not Around)" on my way to my seat; every soul in the bleachers comes to his feet, clapping. Quite a reception for a guy who less than ten years ago was roping in customers to visit Frankie Yale's girls in the back room of the Harvard Inn.

Well, that's how the world saw it. But I'm a hunted man. Much as I like my new Caddy, it's a jailhouse on wheels, I can't walk down to the corner to buy a paper. You probably saw me up on the silver screen before the feature, loping across sidewalks and up courthouse steps, shoving cameras out of the way; I can't stop to jaw with the boys from the newsroom like I used to, not out in the open where I'm a swell target. When I moved from the Metropole into larger quarters at the Lexington, I had a boilermaker put a two-inch plate in the back of my desk chair, just in case the steel shutters on the windows didn't perform up to advertised standards. I installed a secret door into the office building next door so I could run down the fire stairs away from mad Micks and crazy Polacks. There's a friendly police car parked in front of the house on Prairie Avenue day and night, bodyguards following my eight-year-old kid down the street while he plays kick-the-can. I'd trade the Canada route to be able to take a Sunday picnic with my family.

I announced my retirement.

Johnny was right. The dough ain't worth it if you can't pop into Marshall Field's and spend some of it on a bracelet for your wife or your girl without sending in scouts to pat down all the stock boys. The last straw was when Anton the Greek, who owned the Hawthorne restaurant, left me one night to greet some customers and showed up the next day frozen in a ditch. Troopers had to chip him out with ice picks. That was senseless. The Greek hadn't a thing to do with my business apart from getting a loan to fix up the place after the thing in September. Drucci and Moran couldn't get to me directly, so they set out to hurt me by targeting a friend. The new year's only a week old and already it looks like 1926 all over again. So I brought the press into my home and whipped 'em up a mess of spaghetti and said so long.

"Where you going, Al?"

"Hot Springs, Arkansas. I'm gonna take the waters." Well, that got a laugh, Al Capone mentioning himself and water in the same sentence. They didn't believe me, and I was serious as the clap. But it was too late. I should've gotten out when Weiss had the upper hand, but you can't tell that to a Five Points boy. I had to get my lick in.

Schemer Drucci read the papers. If I thought he ever got past the funnies, I maybe would've considered before answering that last question. He followed me to Hot Springs and made a pass at me with a shotgun. I'd left Mae and Sonny unpacking at the hotel and ducked into a place with Frankie for an Orange Julius, and when we came out I heard a boom and something set the wind chimes rattling under the porch roof two feet from my head.

Drucci scrammed, the yellow bastard, not having fixed the locals to let him plead not guilty on grounds of defending himself against wind chimes.

So it was a short retirement, but at least I got the poisons out of my body.

Big Bill Thompson, that wonderful dope, was back running for mayor against Square Deal Dever, whose reformers had crowded me out into the suburbs, and Bill had history on his side. One term of honest government is as much as any electorate has patience for. Ever since they kept record, far back as the Roman Republic—I did a shitload of reading in Alcatraz, after that first month when they don't let you read or do nothing but sit in your cell, jack off, and think about the mistakes you made in life—no reform ticket ever succeeded itself. To show whose corner I'm in I contributed six hundred grand to the Thompson campaign. He shooed right in, but Schemer never got the benefit. The day before the election he barged into an opposition leader's office, roughed up his secretary, and dumped over filing cabinets and shit, spraying paper the way he liked to spray bullets. A dick named Healy cuffed him, but on the way to the station house Drucci tried to grab his gun and Healy dealt him four slugs off the bottom.

Drucci served in the military, though I think he sat out the war in Kentucky. Still, he got the rifle salute in addition to flowers enough to carpet Flanders Field. Hell, I kicked in a nice bouquet and showed up at graveside in my stubble. I tell you, none of his schemes paid off, right to the end.

Another quiet spell broke out after that, at least locally. In Brooklyn on the first day of July 1928, a carload of mugs chased Frankie Yale's bulletproof Lincoln down Forty-Fourth Street and unloaded a tommy through a window he left open because of the heat. It was the first machine-gun killing in New York, so naturally my name came up. It got out I had Frankie put down for hijacking our shipments from Canada because he wasn't making enough off our agreement. Sure, there was some knickknacking going on, but who am I to set the dogs on a pal when every cop and judge on the payroll is hitting me up for more and more graft? You put up with a certain amount of chiseling to avoid distraction. Consider it a business tax.

Yale was payoff for O'Banion. The North Siders took advantage of the lull in hostilities at home to send personnel out of state and shake his hand the way he shook Deanie's. It broke my heart. He gave me my leg up. It was like losing my old man all over again.

I expected peace then. All the original crowd was dead or satisfied, and not even the square citizens could claim I had a hand in ringing down the curtain on Drucci. We had a friend in office, who'd take any heat and turn it into a nutty debate over King George III, and the reporters got such a boot out of that they forgot all about the issue that started it. But you can figure all the angles and still overlook the human element.

Nobody could allow for George Moran. I read somewhere where I said, "They don't call that guy Bugs for nothing." I don't remember saying it, but I'll take credit just the same. Who'd deny giving voice to a practical sentiment?

Actually it was *Bugger* Moran, on account of rumors about his personal life; but you couldn't get a word like that into a family paper, so they bobbed it.

He was screwy, though, as bad as Weiss, but smarter than Drucci, which is a dangerous combination. He came at me from the side, trying to put his man Joe Aiello in Tony Lombardo's place on top of the Unione Siciliana. I'm starting to come out of my hole, scouting winter property in Florida, when Moran's punks Frank and Pete Gusenberg pushed up behind Tony at the corner of Madison and Dearborn and put three apiece in his head from .45s, square in the middle of the Loop during the afternoon rush hour. They was dum-dums, soft-nosed slugs cut with a cross so they'll fly apart on entry and do maximum damage, messy thing in a crowd like that. The best dry cleaner in town can't sponge blood and brains out of flannel. Joey Lolordo, Tony's bodyguard, told me he picked a piece of To-ny's skull off his lapel. Tony and me was like *that*. I cried big snotty tears next to his coffin.

But I blew my nose and ran Joe Aiello out of town with just a show of guns and a sharp word. You don't waste grand strategy on a shit who'd bribe a waiter to put arsenic in your linguini; which he did, at the Lexington. I had the trots for a week and the waiter left in a hurry to visit his cousins in Sicily.

With Joe out of the picture I moved fast to put in Joey Lolordo's brother Patsy for Unione president. I couldn't serve, being Neapolitan by blood, but Patsy was Sicilian on both sides and had everybody's respect as a cool customer and the voice of reason, but a man you didn't cross: *molto virile.* He owned a tenement on West North Street, a roach house, but his flat was all silver and silk, with Persian rugs and a marble-topped table he swore belonged to one of the Medicis. He spoke five languages, including ancient Greek and Latin. A class act, Patsy. Did all his killings close up with a knife.

He got the votes, and he chaired a conference in Cleveland to air out griev-ances inside the brotherhood; Charley Luciano and Frank Costello attended, along with half the ginzos in the country. Patsy had Johnny Torrio's gift of per-suasion, but his vision was bigger. This Syndicate you're always hearing about was his idea. But he only lasted four months. Aiello, the weasel, waited till I went to Florida again, then slunk back into Chicago and dropped in on him at home; to make peace, he said. He drank his wine, ate his food, smoked one of his cigars, and fed him three pills from a .38 right there in his own parlor. Patsy's wife comes running in from the kitchen in time to see Aiello slipping a velvet pillow under Patsy's head. *Ipocrita.*

I threw a chair through the window of my suite in the Ponce de Leon when I got the call. I got drunk, busted up the joint, cut my hand on a mirror. Frankie Rio had to call down for towels to stop the bleeding. Patsy and I weren't that close, but I was thinking about my own situation, my wife, my little boy. You don't kill a man in his home, where he lives with his family: the Law of Vendetta is clear on that. The Irish, the Polacks, they don't care, they're animals, but Aiello knew the rules. Nobody in town would raise a squawk if I stood that *pustola* in front of city hall and fed him his balls with a fork.

As it happened, though, I had to postpone the satisfaction. That was January 1929, and on St. Valentine's Day something came along that kept me busy for a year and a half.

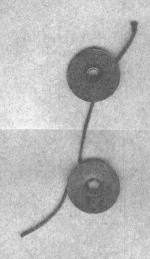

1944

THE ETERNAL GANGSTER

THIRTY-ONE

"ARE YOU TIRED?" VASCO ASKED. CAPONE'S NARRATIVES OFTEN INCLUDED unpredictable silences while he gathered his scrambled thoughts, but this one had stretched more than a minute.

Capone, hands in the pockets of his robe, leaned back, then lunged forward from the waist, spitting his spent wad of gum ten feet out over the bay. Nothing struck at it when it plopped down, but watching its trajectory Vasco saw a torpedo-shaped shadow gliding under the surface nearby. Instinctively he drew back from the waterline, wondering how far a shark would charge onto dry land after prey.

It was an abstract fear, nothing more. He was absorbed in something Capone had said minutes earlier, something about Holy Name Cathedral and a Hudson Super Six, that had struck him like a blow to the heart.

They had wandered down to the beach. Behind them, Mae, Rose, and Sonny had disappeared along with the food and refreshments; clearly, the incident with Nitti's man Verdi had postponed brunch.

"I ain't tired," Capone said. "I'm feeling like I could swim clear to Havana and fuck a tango dancer. There's nothing like a little scrap to put lead in a man's pencil.

"Not that that counts as a scrap. I wouldn't give the sweat off my left nut for a dozen of these punks that came up since Repeal. Either one of the Gusenbergs would've told me to go screw my sister with both eardrums blown out and a bellyful of their own teeth."

He had to ask while Capone was still in a mood to talk about the past; there was no predicting when the clouds of the present would steal across his brain, obscuring the details. At the same time the approach had to be oblique. Ailing or not, the man at his side had spent many years deflecting questions intended to incriminate him. A mistake in timing, a revealing tone, and he would retreat into his shell, perhaps permanently. Vasco decided to start where Capone had stopped and work his way back. "You left St. Valentine's Day hanging."

"I don't like to bore people. You can read up on it in the Sunday section every February. You'd think nothing else ever happened that month. Hell, the *Maine* blew up in February, but you only see it in history books. I got an alibi for that day. I wasn't in my mother's belly yet."

"I'd like to hear your side of the massacre story." ▪

"Worst thing that ever happened."

Vasco held his tongue. He hadn't expected remorse.

"If it wasn't for that fucked-up mess, I'd have sat out my sentence in Atlanta, where they let your friends visit and you get to keep pictures of your family. Where they treat you like a jailbird, sure, but it's better than a hunk of meat. They built that rock in the ocean, they said, to hold the worst of the worst, kidnappers and murderers and rapists: animals. I forgot to pay my taxes. But they didn't lock me up for that. It was for that thing in the garage, where I never set foot."

"Were you upset when you didn't get Bugs Moran?"

Capone had been staring out to sea. Now he turned and fixed his gaze on Vasco. Gray eyes reflected blue sky on a bright day, but his remained wintry. They seemed to draw from ice at the bottom of a shaft where sunlight never reached and blind things swam in black water. "I hate to disappoint you, Padre, but that one came as much of a surprise to me as to everybody else. I'm clean."

Vasco met his eyes. Staring contests didn't intimidate him for some reason, but he lacked the talent to read an experienced liar's features. A patch of skin twitched where the long scar almost met the corner of his mouth, but that was nothing new; Vasco assigned it to nerve damage from that long-ago injury. The face itself was immobile. Al Capone and the St. Valentine's Day Massacre were connected in the public consciousness as surely as Custer and the Little Big Horn, Napoleon and Waterloo. Initial victory that it was, cutting the heart out of the O'Banion/Weiss/Moran gang at a single stroke, it had brought him down in the end as decisively as any battlefield defeat. Seven men slain in a busy commercial block in broad daylight had proven too much for even Chicago's corrupt system to digest; after nearly ten years of mobocracy, the outcry rose at last to the point where Capone had to be sacrificed on the altar of justice. To separate him from the central outrage of that spectacularly lawless era was inconceivable.

He rejected the premise. Capone was playing cat-and-mouse; apparently for his own amusement, because he'd just confessed to a key role in multiple murders, and a man could burn only once. It was the bloodiest chapter yet in his scarlet-soaked memoirs, as well as his most candid. His condition had progressed beyond personal caution. Joe Verdi's ordeal should have prepared his listener for what would follow. He was still shaken and wondering where that confrontation would lead.

"But if you didn't . . ." He left the question unfinished.

"I studied on it for years. It became a personal hobby. See, the cops and the papers can jump to all the conclusions they want, but I never had that luxury. Hit the wrong guy and you just make more enemies on top of the one you should've hit in the first place. They said at first it was cops. Two of the shooters had on Chicago uniforms and their Caddy was fixed to look like a police car. I was inclined that way myself, remembering the dicks from the Maxwell Street station that jumped Devil Mike Genna with the purpose of hanging it on me. When that theory didn't pan out, it was the Detroit Purple Gang. That's still with us, years after it all came winding around to me: I hired 'em from Abe Bernstein because Moran's boys knew all the locals by sight and wouldn't let 'em get within a block. It makes sense, except like I said Abe and me got along about as well as Jiggs and Maggie. I'd never ask, and he'd never deliver.

"It might have been out-of-towners in the blue. On the other hand, who really looks at the face under a policeman's cap? I'm more interested in the guys in plainclothes, who led the shooting. My people on the force told me that when the first officers came to investigate, the stink of garlic was almost as strong as the gun smoke. Everybody knew John Scalise and Albert Anselmi rubbed garlic on their bullets in case lead poisoning didn't finish the job. So that was another nail in my coffin, because they'd been with me so long, and anyway I'm the guy that goosed Mrs. O'Leary's cow."

Capone chuckled, sounding almost jolly, turned, and began walking along the beach. He kept his head down as if he were looking for seashells. Vasco fell into step beside him. The shoreward wind was stiffening, blowing away the summer fug, and he had to strain to catch his companion's words, spoken in a low voice and directed toward the sand at his feet.

"You can look at a thing so long, from all the angles, and get drunk on figuring, and hungover to boot. I did, and people say I had imagination. Cops don't. Reporters don't, or they'd write novels instead of fish wrap. Trouble was, everybody was coming up with suspects, then finding reasons to fit. That's backwards. Reasons come first. Who gained? Well, me, Moran's the pit in my olive, the one I keep biting down on and cracking a molar. But the job was bitched up. The pit's still there. Does that sound like me? If you go by the box scores, I'm way ahead. They miss, I don't. Also I could eliminate myself because I knew it wasn't me. That made two of us, me and the guilty party.

"It wasn't cops," Capone went on. A week after the fireworks, a hook-and-ladder crew put out a garage fire on Wood Street and found a burned-out Cadillac rigged up like a police car. The place happened to belong to John Sbarbaro, who'd laid aside his embalming tools for a gavel; but he'd rented it out through an agency to a man who gave his name as Rogers, so the judge was cleared as an accomplice, though it was an embarrassment to the bench. The fire marshal said it looked like somebody touched off the gas tank while cutting up the car, or maybe a spark from the torch landed on some liquor that was being stored in the garage. I'm satisfied it was the car used in the slaughter job on North Clark. Do you mind switching places, Padre? I'm supposed to avoid chills."

Jerked from his listening attitude, Vasco took Capone's place on the ocean side, becoming his windbreak.

"Thanks. Sen-Sen?"

He stared at the narrow flat box his host had produced from a robe pocket, shook his head. Capone shook some of the buckshot-size bits into his mouth and chewed. He stood with his back to the island, Vasco facing him with the bay behind him. Vasco wasn't fooled; a speedboat flying the Stars and Stripes was razzing fifty yards out, parallel to the beach. He was acting as a human shield in case there was a high-powered rifle aboard. Old habits died hard, but not as hard as Al Capone.

It made his back itch. But he'd have felt even more vulnerable with his back toward Chicago.

"Who gained?" Capone repeated. "Moran, maybe. He's in bed with the sniffles, which some said was an alibi for setting up his own crew. Wasn't he seen big as life, slurping coffee with Willie Marks, his labor guy, and Ted Newberry, who ran his book, in a drugstore up the street when the hammer fell on Valentine's Day? Nuts to that. Even if his boys were double-crossing him, he wouldn't take 'em all out at once and tell the world he was wide open; he'd do it piece by piece and line up replacements first. Anyway, who'd they double-cross him with? I was the only one left, and nobody from the North Side had come to me.

"No. There was only one person in Chicago with the brains to set up a deal that complicated, the guts to go through with it, and a reason to do it in the first place."

"Jack McGurn."

He'd surprised himself as much as Capone, whose breakfront grin shattered the poker face. The name had sprung to his lips without process of thought.

"Now, how'd you come up with *him*?"

"The Gusenbergs were two of the men gunned down in the garage. You said they were the ones who ambushed McGurn in a telephone booth in the McCormick Hotel in 1926. They shot him with a pistol and a machine gun and put him in the hospital."

Capone nodded and chewed Sen-Sen. "I think it was the tommy set him off. He figured he had the market cornered. He was shacked up with a blonde in the Stevens Hotel when the cops pulled 'em in for questioning, but they couldn't shake her story that he hadn't left her side since they checked in at the end of January. I didn't much like him hiding behind a dame, spoiling her reputation; even a slut deserves the benefit of the doubt. But I'm a last-century boy and he was a sheik. The cops let him go because they'd pegged him as a shooter, but I knew from that moment he was the little piggy that stayed home. Jack never spent four weeks with one woman in his life."

"Did you ask him?"

"Why? I was sure, and in my circle you don't let on you're not even when you aren't. Anyway the ketchup was spilt, and the whole town knew he was my right bower, so it reflected on me no matter how it came out. Also I think he was ashamed of what a sloppy job it was. Christ, they killed a nickel-an-hour mechanic and an optometrist; everything but the dog. There was no point rubbing it in. I got to say Jack was no slouch at mopping up after. Cops in Indiana pulled Scalise and Anselmi out of a ditch in Hammond three months later. I got the rap for them, too. They said I used a baseball bat."

Vasco knew this for subterfuge. His father had witnessed the beating. Here in his extremity Capone seemed to have become fastidious about his legacy;

hands-on atrocities were beneath him. He must have taken particular relish in punishing them for such a costly mistake.

"What about Joe Aiello?"

"Joe made good. He got to be president of the Unione Siciliana."

Capone fell silent then, grinning with flecks of black licorice caught in his teeth.

Vasco didn't press him. In October 1930, Aiello had walked out of an apartment house owned by a business associate known as Patsy Presto, straight into the crossfire from two machine-gun nests set up on the street corners. He'd looked anything but surprised in his morgue photos, one eyelid drooping in a solemn wink where a bullet had torn through the socket.

"He had a train ticket to Texas in his pocket when he left office," Capone said. "I was in Philly at the time, serving a year with Frankie Rio in the City of Brotherly Love for carrying concealed weapons. That put me one up on Jack McGurn, who had to marry his blonde alibi so she couldn't be forced to testify against him for Valentine's Day. I was free after ten months."

"You engineered your own arrest." Which was the official theory, never corroborated by its subject.

Nor was it yet. "I went straight in without filing for appeal. I had Johnny's example to thank for that. He asked for time to put his affairs in order before going in on the Volstead violation, and it was during that time Weiss and Moran jumped him with shotguns." He closed his lips, smiling tightly at a sudden memory. "Jake Lingle went berserk when he found out I'd been released and he missed the scoop for the *Tribune*. He threatened Ralph. My brother, Bottles, who couldn't run a bluff past Shirley Temple. It wasn't long after that Jake ran into a bullet in the pedestrian tunnel under Randolph Street. He was into his bookies for a bundle, but they liked me for that, too, and all on account of he showed up on the slab wearing one of my diamond belt buckles. I ask you, who gives a guy a gift with his initials on it in sparklers, then a slug in the skull?"

He was retreating into self-pity, the last querulous refuge of a sick man. Vasco had to step in before the details were lost in the fog of dementia and years gone.

"Who drove the getaway car after Weiss was killed?"

Capone looked surprised; then furtive. It was as much of an answer as was required. With every cell in his body, Vasco wished he could leave it at that. But the God-Devil wasn't satisfied. The last turn in the screw must be made.

"He didn't tell you?" Capone asked.

"He told me about outrunning a Packard Eight in a Mack truck. He left out the rest."

"Well, it ain't my place to horn in on something between a man and his son. I will tell you, you should be proud. A lot of guys with more experience under their belt would've stepped on the gas as soon as the shooting started and went home to rinse out their drawers."

He felt dizzy, and sick to his stomach; there would be no sitting down to brunch that day. A big piece of the puzzle had dropped into place with the slam of a shell going into the chamber of an automatic pistol. Frankie Rio, Paul Vasco, a jug of homemade wine in a homely apartment, a man bleeding out his life on the steps of the Holy Mother Church. No hobby store would carry such a puzzle in its window.

"Snorky?"

Capone turned in the direction of this new voice. Vasco, who was already facing that way, had not seen Mae Capone approaching. She stood hugging her bare freckled arms in a sleeveless printed blouse, ocean wind pulling tendrils of pale hair from the pins struggling to hold them in place. Her blue eyes alone were alive in a face that had encountered thousands of questions from the authorities and the press. She did not wear her emotions on the outside, that was the central tragedy of her allegiance to her husband; the sacrifice of everything granted the feminine race to the volcano of public scrutiny. Of the many who had lost everything in the war against Prohibition, she had suffered the most. She was compelled to go on living after all the others had been lain to rest.

"Snorky, you should come inside. You know what Dr. Phillips said about drafts."

"I was just telling the Padre about how Hymie Weiss was afraid of 'em. He wore flannel nightshirts when everybody else was sleeping in silk."

Vasco felt himself pale. He'd never heard Capone tell another person what had passed between them. If someone who didn't share Mae's respect for secrets happened to be on the receiving end . . .

She twined her arm inside Capone's. "We'll move the meal indoors."

"Jake with me. These Wisconsin skeeters ought to come with navigation lights."

"That was last week, dear. We're in Miami now." Her tone was gentle, unworried. She led him across the sand, whorled like the surface of a clamshell where the tide had advanced and retreated in stages.

Rose had been industrious, Vasco saw as they passed the outdoor table, stripped now of linen and dinnerware.

Inside the house, he blinked until his pupils caught up with the dimmer light. "Take your place," Mae told Capone, steering him in the direction of the dining room. "Don't wait for us. You must be starving."

"You kidding? I could eat Irish."

At a look from her, Vasco remained with her in the living room as the head of the house passed through the arch. She made use of a mirror in a gilded frame hanging opposite the portrait of father and son to restore her hair.

"What was all that about?"

He decided to make a clean breast. Her confidence was one of the few he trusted. "Mostly it was about 1926."

"I didn't mean that. Who was that man the bodyguards took away?"

"They didn't tell you?"

"They report only to Ralph, who I'm sure has the story by now."

"One of Frank Nitti's men. He's been following me ever since I left Mercer."

"I thought he looked familiar, but they all blur together after a while. Did you tell Al about him?"

"I told Sonny, but only because I thought someone in the family should know."

"I wish you'd told me instead. He's never kept a secret from his father, although Lord knows he's kept them from me. We were expecting him today, but there was some sort of emergency at the air depot. If anyone finds out what happened outside, Al could be committed to an institution as a danger to himself and others. I'll take him out of the country before I'll let that happen."

"No one will find out from me, not even Sonny."

She slid the last pin back into place and turned away from the mirror, smiling. "I know that, Father. Let's go see what we can rescue from the menu."

He lied. "I'm sorry, but I'm expected back at Redemption. Father Kyril could only spare me a couple of hours."

"Please? Your company means so much to Al."

"I wish I could stay." He'd never wished less for anything in his life.

She drew in a shallow breath and let it out. "I'm sure he enjoyed your talk. He's never had anyone he could trust to tell things to. Things might have gone differently if he had."

She insisted he join Capone and Danny while she and Rose prepared a package for him. In a room furnished surprisingly simply, with chairs around a table that could extend to serve eight and a sideboard painted country blue, he sipped coffee from a cup with a gold rim and listened to Danny deride the Chicago Cubs with its roster of has-beens and flat-footed rookies while the cream was in the armed forces. Mae's brother ate sparingly and drank beer while Capone helped himself to sausage links from a heaping tray and yellow fluffy scrambled eggs from a huge porcelain bowl and drank tomato juice poured from a pitcher. Vasco had given up trying to keep track of ration points on Palm Island. Capone's cheeks were filling out. It wouldn't be long before the pre-Alcatraz porky Snorky was back in full flesh.

"I wouldn't let Schuster stack cases of Old Milwaukee, let alone play second base," Danny said. "As for Hughes—"

Mae and Rose came in, the girl carrying a wax paper–wrapped package the size and shape of a loaf of bread.

Mae said, "You may need a can opener. Rose should be packing parachutes for the Air Corps."

He stood to accept it just as Mae turned fond eyes on Capone shoveling food into his face. At that moment he felt Rose's hand in his left trousers pocket and heard a tiny rustle of paper. She withdrew her hand quickly, but not before Vasco noticed Danny watching them. He tipped up his bottle, let it gurgle twice, set it back down, and returned to the dismal subject of baseball in wartime; but his eyes sparkled and something tugged at the corners of his long upper lip.

THE NOTE WAS WRITTEN ON RULED NOTEPAPER, COARSE-TEXTURED AND smelling faintly of exhaust from a greasy griddle, overpowering any citrus scent she might have left on it from her skin. The neat schoolgirl script read:

> Black-and-Tan
> 64 SW 3rd
> I'm usually there at midnight

He didn't know if she meant she was there every midnight, or that when she went there, that was the time. He was sure the note meant *that* midnight. No other made sense. The practice of months had him thinking like a coconspirator.

He had no way of refusing. With Danny possibly aware that a communication had changed hands, he didn't dare read it until he was behind the wheel of the Model T, after which going back inside would arouse curiosity in the household, and any reply he sent by messenger might be intercepted; perhaps by whoever Nitti assigned to take Joe Verdi's place.

Then again, he had no intention of refusing. He smelled again the mossy damp of the shack in the woods, the tang of mingled perspiration, and had to shift his weight on the seat in order to drive comfortably.

In a cafe across from the ocean he ordered coffee to justify taking up a booth, transcribed Capone's memoirs from the years 1925 to 1929 into his notebook as legibly as possible, tore out the sheets, and folded them into a pocket. He left out the subsequent conversation involving his father. Paul Anthony Vasco was one former associate who would not be incriminated; not by his son's hand. A Woolworth's on the way to Our Lady of Redemption provided an envelope and a stamp from a machine. He addressed the letter, adding the code number he'd been given that would place it directly in Hoover's hands, and dropped it into the first mailbox he came to.

He caught two hours' sleep early in the evening, having—gratefully—encountered neither Kyril nor Brother Thomas on the way to his room. Less than two hours; he worried a long time about Danny, what he'd guessed, who he might say something to once the beers and whatever else he drank began to work on his caution. If pressed to explain, Vasco would have to say that spiritual counseling was requested and that his oath prevented him from giving details. The Seal was not confined to the booth or restricted to those inside the faith. The lies were coming more easily now, with less bidding.

It only remained to be seen whether Rose would back them up. She was, he had learned, a willful creature who apparently lived without fear. He wondered what that was like. He could no more easily imagine a color he'd never seen.

Rising, he put on lightweight slacks and a sport shirt, no clerical collar. He'd parked around the corner and had hoped to reach the car unobserved, but when he emerged from the rectory Thomas was carrying an industrial canister by its handle along the flagstone path to the church, spraying for palmetto bugs. The novice looked up, seeing him in mufti, and resumed spraying. Vasco would never know the man, how he thought.

He had hours, and he was hungry. When he'd turned down brunch he'd skipped eating at all that day. He'd forgotten all about Mae's food package, spoiled by now in the heat. He dumped it in a city can and stopped at a seafood restaurant he'd passed often, where people were waiting outside under the striped awning for a table; it was Saturday night, and tourists who couldn't afford the winter hotel rates were determined to get the best out of their vacation. He went inside long enough to give his name to the young woman at the reservation desk and went back out. The sun was sliding behind the skyline to the west, taking the temperature down into the low eighties. Suppertime traffic was heavy, but few cars passed that weren't carrying women or children, and lone male drivers seemed more interested in the length of the line on the sidewalk than with anyone standing in it. Steam drifted from overworked radiators, trailing a bitter smell of scorched metal.

The meal was indifferent, ocean perch poached in a lemon sauce patently from the bottle, green beans from a can, and iced tea sweetened with saccharine, all served with a whopping bill in a green leather folder with brass corners. He left a small tip for the service, indifferent also, and went into the warm night, where others were still waiting.

The same pair of blackout headlights turned twice behind him and he was certain he was being followed until he made four right turns, putting him back where he'd started, and the car behind fell away and didn't return in his rearview mirror. It was too much to hope that Capone's treatment of Nitti's man had caused him to abandon Vasco, but the delay in lining up a replacement might give him respite for one night.

His filling-station city map brought him to Southwest Third Street without mishap, but he drove up and down the same three blocks several times looking for number sixty-four. There were no commercial signs and few addresses were posted. The neighborhood was old Miami, predating the boom-and-bust by years, and the few faces he saw on the street were black, belonging to shapeless women in cloche hats carrying shapeless sacks and rangy young men awaiting or avoiding the draft smoking under streetlamps. The third time Vasco passed the same man he saw his eyes following the Ford under the bent bill of his cap, the whites eloquently expressing suspicion. The buildings were blank-faced, residential, with light leaking through cracked or crooked shades and stucco falling off the facades in heaps like tiny rockslides.

At length he selected a block, parked strategically in the light from a lamp, and followed his ear. Music was playing somewhere; working, rather, thumping like a pile driver with a sense of rhythm, growing louder as he approached a squat three-story building with the weathered profile of an Indian's head jutting perpendicular to the sidewalk, identifying it as a former Pontiac dealership. Plywood covered a display window behind which nickel and enamel had gleamed when Coolidge was in the White House.

He raised his fist to knock on the cracked paint of the front door, then noticed a grubby pearl button next to it and pressed it into its socket with his thumb. Something buzzed that reminded him of flying insects sizzling against the bug light under Ralph's porch in Wisconsin and the door swung open, releasing a gusher of noise from inside: people shouting above the general din, glass colliding, a trumpet growling lewdly through a mute, a drummer punishing his snares to a Krupa beat, but as if he were trying to punch holes in the skins; a rendition of "Minnie the Moocher" that would never be allowed within range of a radio microphone. Somewhere in the inky depths of the room a high-pitched nasal laugh rose, peaked for a full second like an air raid siren, and trailed off under the relentless surging of the music.

The man who stood in the opening filled it nearly as effectively as the door had. He was taller than Brownie by at least two inches and heavier by forty pounds, most of it hanging over his belt in a striped jersey, but hard, like dripped limestone that had piled up and petrified. A gold hoop glinted piratically in an earlobe a half-foot above Vasco's head, deep black skin glistened like polished wood in the dusky light escaping from inside. Apart from these impressions, Vasco's picture of the man was of a solid presence, felt rather than seen.

"Uh-uh." The voice rumbled from deep inside that belly, which was evidently hollowed out like a grotto so that the tone reverberated. "Uh-uh." A hand resembling a catcher's mitt rested on something interrupting the smooth curve of the overhang, one end thrust under the belt.

"It's okay, Chester. He's with me."

He recognized her scent before he placed the voice, wafting his way on a gust of music and clatter. The big man turned a little, making room, and Rose craned the top half of her body around him from behind. A rhinestone clip holding a feather to a hat pinned to the side of her head twinkled.

"Maurice won't like it," rumbled the voice from the belly.

"What he don't like won't hurt him." A slender hand gripped Vasco's upper arm and pulled. Big Chester resisted briefly with his bulk, then withdrew far enough to let him past.

The size of the room was impossible to gauge; its perimeters were lost in gloom and the smoke of cheap tobacco and something that didn't smell like tobacco at all, a stench of burning grain he remembered from a rebellious excursion among fellow seminarians into Chicago's South Side. Candle flames flickered pale yellow in jars on tables crowded together. White teeth and an occasional gold incisor reflected their light, also that from a bare bulb under a funnel shade suspended above a bar to one side, where a wide-bodied bartender in a white T-shirt poured beer from a tap and mopped up spills with a rag. On a tiny stage in what may have been a far corner, a trio of musicians brayed and pounded their way through Minnie's fortunes, the bass fiddle thumping under the racket of the drums, working in near total darkness above the candle glow and beyond range of the illumination from the bar. A cigarette burned there, and the orange cyclops eye of a cigar.

His pupils were unequal to the journey. He let Rose guide him through the labyrinth. His hip bumped a table, causing a jingling of glass receptacles and "Motherfuck!" in a voice thin and sharp as copper wire. A pale knee-length dress fitted to the girl's slender form fluttered in the meager light. He prayed his skin was less visible. He was sure it was the whitest in the place, despite its olive Mediterranean tones.

Eternity ended at a table placed where two walls met painted with thick ivory or yellow paint showing coarse brush strokes, an adobe effect. "I went ahead and ordered," she said. "Hope you don't mind hops in your beer. They brew it in the basement."

He drank from a thick glass with a handle. Something that had been floating on the surface lodged between two teeth. He prodded at it with his tongue. The aftertaste was acrid, like harsh medicine.

His expression must have showed in the candlelight. Rose said, "Sometimes they get impatient and serve it green. I can order something else, but you could strip furniture with it."

"I'll get used to it." He sipped at it more gingerly.

"So how you like the Black-and-Tan so far?"

"I'm just glad I found it. There's no sign."

"They don't advertise. It could be someplace else next week. It only opens when all the other joints close on account of the curfew."

"You mean it could be raided?"

"Not if Maurice goes on paying the freight. What he saves on sign painters he spends on cops. He ran rum from Cuba during the dry time and didn't blow any of it on cars or women." She laid her hand on top of his. "Glad you could make it, Reverend."

"I think under the circumstances you should call me Peter."

"Names are for strangers."

The trio had swung into a different tune without pausing, a more guttural melody he couldn't identify. There was no vocalist, but he was certain if there were lyrics they couldn't be sung most places. A few couples found room to dance between the tables; or more precisely, to clutch each other and sway in place.

"Hottest band in Miami," Rose said. "Bass man got kicked out of the Apollo in Harlem when he pulled a razor on Satchmo."

"Everything in here is hot." Salty drops prickled his forehead like cockleburs. Thirty or forty warm-blooded parties crammed into one small space created their own atmosphere.

She smiled broadly. He liked her large even teeth and full lips painted candy-apple red. He hadn't seen her in makeup before. The kohl on her eyelids made her eyes look like polished teak by contrast. "Go ahead and sweat. Don't tell me you took no oath against *that*." Suddenly she leaned forward and kissed him on the lips. Just a peck, like that first time on the cheek; then she sat back and drank from her glass.

He looked around. "Are you sure it's safe?"

"Safer here than downtown. There's Cubans here, Puerto Ricans, Dominicans, all kinds of mixed blood. Anyone don't like what he sees can take it up with Chester. He's got a Purple Heart. VA fixed him up with a steel plate after a Zero fell on his head." She tapped ash from a filtered cigarette into a tray.

"I didn't mean that. You make fun of oaths, but I took one to be chaste." It sounded foolish out loud.

She laughed like a man, full out, without caring who overheard. "You are that. I done chased you down myself."

"It isn't a joke."

"Sure it is. My cousin Roy took fever in basic training in Georgia. The colored doctor was new and didn't know what he was doing. Roy's brains fried. He's out on a medical discharge, but he can't even find work washing dishes. No disability; they said he was ineligible because he wasn't injured in combat. They had a white doctor on staff who specialized in viral infections, but his ethics kept him from interfering with another man's patient. His Hippocratic Oath was how he put it." She didn't look as if she'd laughed in her life.

"I'm sorry."

She drank again and set down her beer. "My friend Charlene has a place near here. She's working the swing shift tonight. It's a short walk. I've got a key."

He opened his mouth to say no. What he said was, "What do they charge for the beers?"

She reached inside a white patent-leather purse and laid a bill on the table. "I asked you out."

He got up to hold her chair. When she was standing, he put a hand on her elbow and turned toward the exit, right into a blow from something solid that filled his world with blinding pain and the bitter taste of blood.

THIRTY-TWO

"No, Brownie, no!" Rose's cries shrilled above the band, which continued to play, more raucously now as if to drown out the distraction. The Black-and-Tan was hell, a country outside mercy.

Great hands with sandpaper palms closed on Vasco's throat. He was leaking fluid out his nostrils, no oxygen was coming in through them, and now his windpipe was shut. He clawed at a pair of forearms made from sheets of burlap wound tight around iron girders. The hands shook him like a rat in a terrier's jaws, banging his head against the floor. His eyes swam with sweat and congested blood in the veins, staring into a face in which showed only the whites of the eyes and bared teeth; the rest was darkness except for red lacquered fingernails dug deep into the flesh. He thought at first this was a monster with two extra hands in reserve, but they were Rose's, groping to gouge out Brownie's eyes from behind. They were stacked three deep on the floor with Vasco on the bottom.

His vision broke into black checks as the blood in his arteries struggled to feed his brain. He felt his tongue sliding out and knew he would make a ghastly corpse in his morgue photo for some Special Agent to study on the train. Pain stabbed his chest, his heart pumping too hard to support the circulatory system. Would it give out before his lungs?

Something struck something solid with the distant sound of a hammer striking the hull of a ship beneath the waterline. The whites of the eyes inches from his face seemed to brighten, then dull as the lids rolled down to cover them. The pressure came off his windpipe and he sucked in air that filled him to bursting, just before a great weight sagged down on top of him, constricting it yet again. It was dragged off him with grunts and curses that rumbled from deep inside a great hard belly, and when it was cast aside with a contemptuous roll of a shoulder he recognized Chester the bouncer in his striped jersey, still clutching the blackjack he'd used on Brownie's head. Vasco had mistaken the object thrust under his belt for a handgun earlier.

He was helped into a sitting position by Rose, wild-faced with her hat still perched at its impossible angle on the side of her head, a comical effect; he started to laugh, but it turned into a cough. She pounded his back, which made it worse. Why did people do that? But he leaned forward, put his head between his knees, and the spasm subsided.

"Rosie, we can't have this, not with no white man. My grease don't spread that far."

When he raised his head, he saw a slight Negro on one knee beside him, facing Rose, on both knees on the other side. The man wore a white dinner jacket over what looked like a pink shirt in the dim light and a black bow tie, factory tied.

His thin face was pockmarked and his hair was black and glossy and as straight as an Indian's. It belonged on the head of a doll.

"He needs a hospital, Maurice. They both do."

"They's a clinic at Nineteenth and Sixth. I don't know as they'll take your boyfriend."

"Drive us, will you?"

"Chester'll help you get 'em into the car, but you'll have to take 'em the rest of the way. What'd I tell 'em, a bus accident? The buses don't run at night."

"I can't drive. I don't even have a car!"

"I'll drive," Vasco said.

Maurice looked at him from under lashes as long as a woman's. "Mister, your nose is done broke."

Vasco heard chuckling and realized it was coming from him. He snuffled up blood and snot. "I don't drive with my nose."

"He's game for ofay."

"Moe, I *know* you got something to stop bleeding." In a little while he felt wet cloth on the back of his neck, and Rose told him to hold it there while she applied another to his face, which was numb now. Her movements were gentle but efficient. "Blow. Not too hard." She was holding the cloth to his nose.

He obeyed. No one else had washed his face or blown his nose since before his mother died.

"Tell Chester to put up that sap and give me a hand."

"I'll do it," Maurice said. "He's the heavy lifter."

Brownie was partially conscious, sitting on the floor with his legs splayed and his elbows resting on his thighs, facing Vasco; they might have been playing spin-the-bottle. He wore a sport shirt printed with tropical fish, open in front, with blood staining his BVD undershirt from a trail that ran to the top of his head. His mouth sagged open and his eyes appeared to lack focus. Vasco doubted he himself looked much better. The front of his own shirt was plastered to his chest by something other than sweat and his breath whistled through his nose. Would he look like an unsuccessful prizefighter, one of those flat-faced lugs who were always appearing in the old apartment in Cicero?

He managed to stand with Maurice's support, while Chester was forced to squat and embrace Brownie under the arms and drag him backward, leaving a wake of bare planks through sawdust and peanut shucks. Incredibly, the trio continued its rapscallious medley uninterrupted; more incredibly still, couples were still dancing. Vasco interpreted this as a sign that impromptu floor shows were not unusual in the Black-and-Tan.

He directed the party to where he'd parked the Model T, Rose with her arm around his waist opposite the club owner, who left him leaning on her while he opened the rear door and helped Chester wrestle Brownie into the backseat. There he sprawled full-length, and they had to bend his knees to push the door shut.

"You don't bring him in here no more," Maurice told Rose.

"He'll be sorry to hear it, the spread you put on."

Vasco grasped the doorpost and hauled himself under the wheel. Rose got in on the passenger's side. "Sure you can drive? I bet I can learn in five blocks."

He remembered something his father had told his mother one night when he was called out after drinking all evening. "I can drive. I just can't walk."

"You're a regular Fred Allen. I guess you'll live."

"I forgot about the crank." He reached for his door handle.

"That I can do. I pull my own weight on dates."

"Keep your thumb on the same side as your fingers."

"You only got to sprain your wrist once to remember that." She got out.

Her first turn was clumsy, but she got the hang of it and the motor started with a noise like coal tumbling down a chute. While she was occupied he stole a glance at his face in the rearview mirror, but the light from the corner lamp came in at an angle that gave him only a ghost reflection. He'd have two black eyes at the least. He was shaking now, and had had to grasp his wrist with his other hand to get the key into the ignition and turn it. Driving, he grasped the wheel tightly to steady himself.

"Turn right up there," Rose said after two blocks. "I can't believe you're driving."

"Do you think my nose is really broken?"

"I'm surprised he didn't push it through the back of your head."

"Is he—"

"Can we have this conversation later?"

"Of course."

The clinic was in a converted storefront, with exposed pipes and old-fashioned light switches that turned, the wires running through conduits on the walls. The staff was colored, as were the patients waiting on folding wooden chairs, men and women with tubercular coughs and a young blade in a purple zoot suit with a torn pocket, grasping a bloodied handkerchief bound around one wrist: another Saturday-night casualty. A hefty nurse in a uniform and starched cap frowned at Vasco, listened to Rose, and dispatched an elderly orderly to bring Brownie in from the car. He rolled an antique wicker wheelchair outside.

Vasco didn't see him return with the patient. The nurse escorted the young man in the zoot suit through a curtained passageway, then came back for Vasco. A storeroom had been partitioned with unpainted drywall into separate examining rooms. He sat on the end of a table upholstered in cracked leather for twenty minutes, then blinked into the bulb of a squat flashlight shone in each eye by a doctor about the age of Zoot Suit, who walked with a rolling limp: clubfoot. He inspected both nostrils with the light, then cleaned away the last trace of blood with cotton soaked in alcohol, clasped Vasco's nose between his palms, and wiggled it. That brought a clicking sound, and tears to his eyes; the numbness was wearing off. The doctor grunted—the impenetrable language of physicians black and white—and packed the nostrils with gauze and pressed a strip of sticking-plaster across the bridge.

"Deviated septum. You can pull out the packing in a couple of days. Married?"

"No." He sounded to himself like a man with a bad cold. If the doctor had spoken to Rose, she'd kept his secret.

"Fix it before your honeymoon. You'll snore till then. I wouldn't bother otherwise."

"What about the other man?"

"The big fellow? I'm keeping him on the cot overnight, in case of fracture. X-ray's broken, no parts in this neighborhood till after the war. You the one hit him?"

"No."

"Okay, then." He turned to leave.

"Doctor? How will I look?"

He turned back. "You in show business?"

"No."

"You'll look fine. Truth to tell, I don't think you were Van Johnson to begin with."

"Thank you." He felt mortified for asking. He chalked up vanity. How many were left? "I want to pay for the other man, too."

"It's a free clinic." The doctor adjusted the stethoscope around his neck, evening the ends; a fastidious man in what must have amounted to a war zone weekends. "You know, if the shoe were on the other foot—your shoe, my foot—I couldn't even sit in the waiting room."

"You don't have to tell me there's something wrong with the world."

"Seems to me I do. No more slumming, y'hear?" He'd slipped into dialect; deliberately, Vasco thought.

"Business is lively enough."

"The Black-and-Tan has seen the last of me."

"I hope the next time they close it down it sticks. I'm getting too much practice sewing up scalp wounds." He left.

Rose was standing in the waiting room, holding her purse in an awkward position at her waist. When she moved, Vasco saw she'd split a seam in her dress. He was appalled that he hadn't thought to ask if she was all right. He asked now.

"I've done worse to myself working in the kitchen," she said. "You look like you were in a fight."

He smiled weakly. "Have you seen Brownie?"

"The doc gave him something to sleep. He's got a knot on his head big as a coconut. They're holding him tonight."

"The doctor told me. I'll take you home."

Passing a house lit up for a party, he glimpsed his reflection in the windshield. His nose was swollen, the nostrils distended from the gauze. He'd been right about the black eyes.

She was watching. "Doc give you anything for the pain?"

"I think he's saving his supplies for more serious cases."

"I've got some Bufferin." She rummaged inside her purse and tore open a foil package. "You need water?" She handed him two tablets.

"They'll work faster if I chew them." His face had begun to throb. He crunched and swallowed. "I'll bring you back to the clinic tomorrow if you like."

"I would, but Brownie wouldn't. I'll tell 'em at the house he was in an accident. They'll believe that. Mr. Al rode with him just the one time and then he gave the job to Mr. Danny. I guess you know by now Brownie's kind of reckless."

"Will he say anything?"

"I don't think so. It ain't something you go around bragging about."

"I'd better stay away from the house for a while."

"Don't you bother about Brownie. I'll talk to him so he'll listen."

"I meant so they don't see me and think we were in the same accident." He drove half a block in silence, then: "He must have followed you tonight and waited for me to show up. I think Danny saw you pass me that note."

"He wouldn't tell Brownie. They don't get along so well. Brownie hates drunks."

"He was suspicious then. I think he's suspected me from the start."

"He thinks he's my Dutch uncle. I tell him I been taking care of myself this long, I can go on doing it, but he's six parts mule. Suspected you of what?" she asked suddenly.

"Rose, I'm not a priest."

They were driving through a blackout neighborhood. He couldn't see her face. They seemed to have been a very long time in the dark before she spoke. "Why tell me?"

"I had to tell someone, and I trust you."

"Why, because we fucked?"

That shocked him. No one except Capone and his father had said a profane word in his presence in months. If he'd expected it at all, he wouldn't have expected it from her. "No. Because you don't have anything to gain by telling my secret. Rose, the reason—"

"Stop!"

He was startled into slamming on the brake. Fortunately there were no cars behind him.

"Not that," she said. "Stop *talking*. If you tell me the reason, I'll have to tell someone."

"How do you know?"

"I just do. Drive and let's talk about something else." They resumed moving. He was deeply ashamed of himself. He'd been about to lie.

* * *

"We had us some fun, didn't we?"

He didn't know how to reply. She sounded as casual as if they'd been talking about something else right along.

"I knew we would," she said, as if he'd agreed. "You were so serious all the time, like you were afraid if you let go you'd knock something over or pass gas. I wanted to snatch that collar off just to see what you'd do. Apologize, probably, for not buttoning it tighter. It buttons, right?"

"It buttons. It's just about the most uncomfortable thing a man can wear."

"A man, maybe. Try putting on a brassiere."

He turned into her street and coasted to a stop before the large Queen Anne house that had been cut up into apartments. The moon was up, shining on the many shades of chalky paint, a peaceful sight. The house had stood since long before wars both recent and forgotten. He wouldn't have been surprised to see a friendly goat grazing the front yard. Air raids and rationing were foreign to such a creature. They sat listening to the chucka-luck of the Ford's motor at idle.

"What now?" she asked.

"We won't be seeing each other for a while."

She smiled in profile. "You sound like a story in *The Saturday Evening Post.* Like we killed someone and have got to lay low."

"The second part is true. It's too dangerous."

"Don't bother about Brownie, I said. He shot his wad."

"I doubt that, but it isn't him I'm worried about so much. Do you remember Frank Nitti? He came to the cabin in Wisconsin that last day."

"I couldn't forget him. Those eyes look right through you."

"He thinks I'm up to something. He sent someone to follow me."

"This have anything to do with that man today?"

"I wish that hadn't happened. Now he'll be sure I have something to hide and ran to Capone for help."

"That man won't be back."

"There are others. If you're seen with me they'll think we're in it together. They won't be as easy to handle as Brownie. Big Chester the bouncer's an amateur in their world. They graduated from blackjacks a long time ago."

"I know. I keep thinking about that colored politician in Chicago. They ran him to ground like a deer and shot him to pieces. He wasn't even a threat. He was black and didn't want to shovel coal."

"You understand, then."

"I don't see any more risk than always. I don't mean about being with a man everyone thinks is a priest. I mean the other thing."

"There is, though. These are professionals. We could deal with the occasional hothead, but these people don't give up until you're dead."

"You think hotheads give up?"

"Well, then, consider that. It doubles the odds against us."

"Doubles the reward, too, don't forget."

"At the track. Not here. Rose, it's suicide."

"Who you afraid for, you or me?"

She was facing him. The moon was behind her, but he could see her eyes by the glisten.

He wet his lips. "Me."

The motor kept running, wasting gas. Suddenly she laughed that loud man's laugh. "Liar." A hand slid inside his thigh.

HE DROVE BACK THROUGH MOONLIGHT, THE BRIGHTEST THING AROUND. His face hurt and now his stomach muscles were sore, although she had done most of the moving. The less traveled streets were unlit to discourage enemy bombers and all the neon signs were extinguished because of the curfew. The ghostly white circle of a flashlight waggled down a side street, followed by a man in a white tin pan Civil Defense helmet, on the prowl for unnecessary illumination.

It had been a very long night, and when he checked his watch while waiting for a signal to change he was surprised to see it was only three o'clock. He'd been expecting dawn any time. He seemed to have most of the city to himself. He passed a police sedan rolling slowly through a residential neighborhood, its search beam poking at bushes and into narrow alleys, and on the third floor of a hotel for permanents and transients the pale orange glow of a radio dial opposite a window, but these things served only to make him feel more isolated. If anyone were following him, he'd have spotted him in a moment. Nitti would need time to put another man into position, but he wouldn't waste any. Vasco fully expected to be back under observation by morning.

Or worse. His first thought, when that blow came out of nowhere in the Black-and-Tan, was that the Outfit had finished deliberating his case and had passed sentence. But his first fear had been for Rose.

Do you consider yourself a man of courage? Hoover had asked.

I like to think so. Then again. I've never been tested.

He'd been tested, and he had passed.

He didn't suppose that he loved Rose. The fact had nothing to do with race. She was beautiful and reckless, brave without having to stop to consider the fact, and she attracted him physically as no woman ever had, but his feelings for her were not deep. His parents were his yardstick. Whatever Paul Vasco's faults, he'd worked a perilous job at all hours to pay his wife's medical bills, and she in turn had waited up for him night after night until he came home safe. Peter Vasco didn't see himself accepting such a responsibility on Rose's behalf, or Rose giving up a night's sleep worrying about him. They were only together because of a set of circumstances that could never be duplicated, against the backdrop of war, which accelerated all things and made the artificial seem real. They were lovers, they could be friends. There was a third ingredient missing that made all the difference.

He was thinking about his father when a stake truck trundled around a corner with THE MIAMI HERALD painted in Olde English letters on the slats, its bed piled high with bound stacks of copies of the early bird edition. It made him think of a man driving an old Mack away from a supercharged Packard; of the same man driving John Scalise and Albert Anselmi away from the scene of Hymie Weiss' murder in a Hudson Super Six. He was so engrossed in these thoughts he failed to take close note of the day's headline on the big sheet of newsprint flapping on the side of the truck as it passed him. In his memory's eye he saw CAPONE. He saw DEAD. He leaned the Model T into a U-turn and gave chase, history repeating itself.

THIRTY-THREE

CAPONE LIEUTENANT FOUND DEAD
SUICIDE SUSPECTED IN NITTI'S DEATH

The name Capone was still magic in Miami, where he was its most celebrated resident; Al Jolson remained a distant second. Perhaps the editor had put the story on the front page to spoil Capone's breakfast. Vasco remembered reading editorials in the file protesting his presence.

He'd parked under a streetlamp to read the article. Details were sparse, as befit a story that had broken only hours before. Frank Nitti, under indictment once again for extorting protection money from key figures in the Hollywood film industry, had been found in a weedy lot near the Illinois Central Railroad tracks in Chicago, shot through the head. Although some thought he'd been executed by Outfit associates for refusing to take the rap quietly and spare a more extensive investigation that might implicate others, the prevailing theory was he'd taken his own life to avoid serving another sentence in Leavenworth.

Vasco had bought the paper at the first newsstand he came to, where a yawning vendor was just cutting the twine on the first bundle of *Herald*s to hit the sidewalk; as he was paying for it another truck, this one from the *Miami Sun*, had rumbled past, slowing down just enough for the man standing in the bed to throw down another bundle. Vasco had bought a copy of that, too. He turned to it now, glanced at a grainy photo of a pathetic-looking figure who resembled an Italian floorwalker, slumped on his back propped up slightly against a board fence with his hat tilted over his eyes as if he were taking a nap, a foreshortened angle with the soles of his hand-lasted shoes looking enormous in the foreground. This account contained late-breaking information not available to the *Herald* at press time. Three slugs had entered the Enforcer's skull.

There were no lights on in the rectory at Our Lady or Redemption. Father Kyril would not rise until dawn to prepare for Sunday Mass, and Brother Thomas was probably taking his rest in whatever quarters he'd arranged for himself while Vasco was sleeping in his bed. Vasco had been exhausted after dropping off Rose, but something more desperate had replaced the need for sleep, and in any case he did not want to be present when the household was stirring. There would be questions then, beginning with his ruined face.

He packed his valise with all the clothes he'd brought from Washington except those he was wearing. He threw in his scant toiletries, the Bible his mother had given him, wrote Kyril a note, and put it on the neatly made bed where he knew Thomas would find it and take it to the pastor. He apologized for leaving without notice, claiming urgent family business and that he did not know when he would return. A lie followed by a half-truth: He doubted he'd be back ever. There would be no questions to answer if Kyril called his father to check his story, but he didn't think he would, and if he did, Paul would not tell him his son never arrived. His first answer to any question was seldom the truth.

Vasco thought of leaving his collar with the note, then changed his mind and put it in the valise. He'd worn it for the last time, but there was nothing to be gained by provoking curiosity, except more suspicion. He crept quietly into Kyril's study and called for a cab, asking to be picked up at the corner. He would not burden the others with the inconvenience of retrieving the Ford from the train station.

A Cuban cabbie with a Rosary swinging from his rearview mirror told the passenger there were no trains running until morning. Vasco said he had a family emergency and that he didn't want to take the chance of missing the first train out.

"Family emergency and how. I'd be in a hurry too if my old lady bust my face like that." He threw down the flag on the meter.

As they got under way, Vasco didn't bother to look out the back window. There would be no one following now.

Let me worry about Nitti, Hoover had said. *He's through.*

At the time, he'd thought the Director was referring to Nitti's legal troubles. For a brief moment he'd suspected Capone. Reading brittle newspaper clippings and hearing other sides of the events from Capone and Hoover had weaned him away from trust in the official accounts, so he'd rejected the suicide theory even before he'd read the details. But Capone was no longer running Chicago. His sphere of influence had shrunken to encompass only Palm Island, where he'd demonstrated the extent of his jurisdiction with Joe Verdi. He was strictly past tense, a magic name in the columns, a wistful memory of bygone days before Poland and Normandy, when seven men slain at a crack still had the power to shock. Capone was through, the Outfit was through. There was a new gang chief in charge.

He managed to sleep on a bench inside the station, but so fitfully he might have paced the floor all night for all the rest it brought. His face throbbed, he snored himself awake, he dreamt in snatches that always ended with him standing in an overgrown lot by the railroad tracks. He saw Nitti from behind, walking to clear his brain, saw him stop and turn at some sound, the expression on his face when he saw the gun, felt the gun pulse in his hand, saw smoke and blood and awoke to the stench of burned powder and the horrible sensation of having killed a man.

FROM CHARLESTON ON HIS CAR WAS CROWDED, PREDOMINATELY WITH women in starched blouses and tailored skirts; government workers filling in for men in the service, but there were men in uniform as well, mostly officers with gold braid on their visors, carrying briefcases. Many of the last were nearing retirement, and looking uncomfortable in their government-issue. These were ranking Pentagon officials who'd been accustomed to wearing business suits to work until the dress code changed to discourage enemy espionage. In Washington he waited for his chance to step out into the aisle, then joined the line waiting to get off. The Russians were advancing toward the west, the Americans and British toward the east, and back home it seemed everyone wanted to be in on the finish. On the platform, boys were waving newspapers and crying the names of foreign cities. In the District, Frank Nitti was strictly second section.

He'd sublet his room to an FBI code clerk who'd been sharing accommodations with a naval courier he didn't get along with, a development approved by his landlord, who still suspected Vasco of giving aid and comfort to the enemy. But he found a vacancy in a residential hotel in a grubby neighborhood not far from where Father Seamus McGonigle was no doubt already drunk at that morning hour and reminiscing about his adventures running guns to Ireland and Scotch to the U.S., about the woman he'd romanced in Belfast after he was ordained. Vasco smiled bitterly at the memory of how much that had shocked him. Less than four months had passed. They might have been years.

The bathroom was down the hall. The shower was running. He waited outside in his robe and slippers with a towel over his shoulders until a stout, Semitic-looking woman came out wearing a raveled housedress and carrying a toothbrush. She shot him a suspicious look and shuffled back to her room in shapeless men's slippers. He showered and shaved, and back in his room put on his priest's suit over a white shirt and black knitted necktie; a secular look and well within Bureau restrictions regarding grooming and dress. He walked two blocks to a streetcar stop and took the car to the Mall. It was July. The air was thick, sopping, but nowhere near the tropical hell of Miami. Collars were wilting all around him but he felt fresh, at least on the outside. Inside he felt old and wrung out.

The Justice Department Building was a beehive as always, clerks and stenographers rustling through air-cooled hallways and watching the needle climb the dial in the elevator. He recognized some faces, but only to nod to. The place was a city unto itself and one could never hope to meet all the neighbors. They registered no reaction to his swollen nose and black eyes. A fellow he'd known well enough to have coffee with in the commissary and discuss the war with entered on the second floor, but the car was crowded and he didn't see Vasco standing in back. Vasco didn't call out to him.

Helen Gandy was on the telephone when he entered her office. She wore a blouse with slightly padded shoulders and one of those scarves women of a certain age adopted when their necks began to show lines. Her hair looked redder, proving either that she did get out in the sun despite the rumors or that she'd been to a hairdresser recently. She looked up at him curiously, but showed no surprise, either at his presence or his bruises. She was listening, a fat fountain pen in her hand moving rapidly across a pad scratching shorthand symbols, making none of the vocalizations people usually made to show they were listening. She filled the page, started another, then thanked the caller and placed the bulbous receiver in its cradle.

"Special Agent Vasco. Your name isn't in the book."

"I need to see the Director. It's urgent."

She glanced at the telephone, where a light glowed. Hoover had been among the first to discard the cumbersome battery of phones in favor of a multiple-line system. "You'll have to wait. He's on the line with the White House."

He chose a seat from where he could see the tiny light. There were magazines scattered on a low blond wood table, *Life* and *Time* with pictures of movie stars and generals on the covers, and city newspapers, but he didn't pick them up. Miss Gandy began typing rapid-fire. In a little while the light went out, but she finished a page and put it on a stack before she flicked the switch on the intercom. "Peter Vasco, sir."

"What line?" Hoover's voice barked from the speaker.

"He's here in person. He says it's urgent."

There was a pause. "Ask him to wait."

"Yes, sir." She broke the connection. "He's very busy. You should have made an appointment."

Vasco didn't reply. He doubted the wait would have been shorter if he'd called ahead.

Forty minutes went by on the twenty-four-hour clock on the wall. Miss Gandy put through five calls and did some more typing; he knew which were outgoing letters and which were interoffice memos by the color of the sheets. Yellow carbons formed a third pile. Nothing about the system seemed to have changed in his absence.

The intercom crackled. "Send him in, please."

She made eye contact. "You remember the way?"

He nodded and went through the connecting door to the dummy office. The scant motherly warmth she'd shown on his first visit was gone, but he'd expected that. He'd breached protocol.

The splendidly furnished office designed for ceremony and public relations—a Bureau term of recent coinage—struck him now as a great empty waste, squandered space that could be used for rolling bandages and holding Red Cross blood drives. He preferred Sergei Kyril's cramped crowded study, the shabby nerve center of a business that traded in hope and salvation and incidentally a place to store hymnals and bundles of paper for recycling to make maps of enemy terrain. He crossed the deep seldom-trod carpet and entered the homely back room without knocking. He thought it a redundancy, like the office itself.

Hoover was sitting at his work table on its raised platform, writing with a buff-and-blue pen wearing the FBI seal. The proportions of the neat stacks of papers and folders may have changed slightly, but they still resembled a desktop model of a modern city. The Director wore a blue suit and a red tie on a white shirt, a subliminal American flag.

"You're away from your post." He continued writing without looking up. "I assume this is important. The word *urgent* is overused these days. It's lost its value."

"I came about Frank Nitti."

"Nitti's dead."

"That's why I came."

"To tell me? The lines of communication between Chicago and Washington are intact. So far the blunderers in that office haven't managed to cut them by accident." Even his attempts at irony were heavy-handed.

"They say he killed himself."

"Who says? I insist upon attribution in this room."

"The newspapers and the radio. Walter Winchell said this morning it was confirmed."

"No doubt they checked their facts. Even Winchell's allowed to get one right now and then."

"He shot himself three times, they said."

"The Associated Press said twice, but I'll surrender the point. The AP reported Churchill's plane shot down last year. It turned out to be a commercial airliner. Leslie Howard, the actor, was aboard. His body was never recovered."

"In the head."

Hoover went on writing, signing letter after letter in the distinctive cerulean blue ink he employed. He was the only person in the Bureau entitled to use the color; blue-signed letters got instant attention in all the regional offices.

"Nitti was a thorough man. There is ample evidence of that in his file."

"How is it possible for a man to sustain two severe head wounds and self-inflict a third?"

"I can cite many similar examples. Records is filled with them. You'd be astonished what a determined suicide is capable of once he's botched the job twice."

"I don't believe you."

Hoover rocked a blotter over the last signature, laid aside his pen, and drummed the sheets together. Only then did he raise his hardboiled-egg eyes to Vasco's.

"Say what's on your mind, Special Agent."

"You told me to let you worry about Nitti, that he was through. At the time I didn't know you meant you were going to order his execution."

"You've let the months you've spent in bad company distort your judgment: an occupational hazard, but in your case the training was insufficient to prepare you against it. There wasn't time. As to your accusation, it's absurd. Murder is Capone's specialty."

"You deny it?"

"Categorically. On your way here, did you take note to see if you were fol-lowed?"

"There was no need, with Nitti out of the way."

"An assumption like that can put your entire mission in jeopardy. Had you gone through channels, I would have decided whether the risk was worth your being summoned. Summoned."

"I don't care about the mission."

"Sit down, please."

"I'll stand."

"*Sit down!*" It was a roar.

He sat, blasted off his feet by a rage he'd seen only in Capone when his mur-derer's instincts flared. He was looking up at Hoover now, but unlike his first time in that seat the Director's stature was unchanged. Vasco had the sensation of gazing at a crude carving of a primitive idol propped on a pedestal. His head was too big for his body, even allowing for the batting his tailor had put in the shoulders of his suit coat.

Hoover ran a pudgy finger down the edge of a pile on the table, slid one out, and spread it open before him. The homely maneuver, so familiar to the born pusher of pencils, drove the high dangerous color from his cheeks, returning them to the indoor pallor. When he spoke his tone was level.

"Our surveillance team outside the Capone estate saw two of his bodyguards forcibly remove a man from his car, disarm him of a semiautomatic pistol, and escort him through the gate. A few minutes later a shot was heard, but the agents took no action because there had been shooting going on for some little while, which they interpreted as routine target practice; they'd heard it before. In any case they're under orders not to try to enter without a federal warrant. The local authorities can be difficult, and they have interfering friends in Congress.

"Moments after that, the same pair of bodyguards came out supporting the man they'd taken by force and dumped him—I don't think 'dumped' is an exag-geration, under the circumstances—back in his car. He sat there five minutes before starting the engine and driving away. He appeared to be disoriented and in considerable pain. You were present on the grounds when whatever happened took place; it's in the report. Enlighten me."

"The man's name was Joe Verdi. He works—worked—for Nitti. Capone had him brought to him and fired Verdi's own pistol close enough to his ear to burst the eardrum. He told Verdi to tell his boss he'd kill the next man he sent to fol-low one of his friends. Meaning me."

"A friend of Capone's."

"His words, sir, not mine." The *sir* slipped out from habit.

"Your identification is accurate. We had him detained by the Miami Police when he came off the causeway. No arrests or convictions, and his permit to carry a concealed weapon was legal, issued by the sheriff's department in Cook

County to one Giuseppe Bartolomo Verdi, born September 1919 in Brooklyn, New York, of immigrant parents. He was held overnight on suspicion of vagrancy and released the next morning. He never got a chance to report back to his boss.

"I see no reason to interfere with an investigation into a local homicide," Hoover continued. "However, in the event the official version is wrong, it might have occurred to you that Capone didn't stop at terrorizing Nitti's man. He has a history of doing nothing by half."

"You said yourself Capone no longer runs the organization. What reason would anyone in Chicago have to do anything he says?"

"They might, if there was a better reason to eliminate Nitti. He was under indictment for extortion, and it would be better for all concerned if the investigation ended along with his life. Better all around. *This* organization has no interest in whether some ape threatened to break Rin-Tin-Tin's legs."

It made sense; everything he said did. But Vasco didn't accept it, as much as he wanted to.

It occurred to him then that he had *always* wanted the Director's explanations to stand up under scrutiny. And now he decided that nothing he had said had been true from the beginning, including his account of how he'd arrested Alvin Karpis, Public Enemy Number One, unassisted by the great machinery he had built single-handed. What was the point of building it, otherwise? Certainly not to let it stand idle while he assumed the role of a lone avenger out of the pages of *Dime Detective*, when the reporters he had planted in key positions would provide the details as he dictated them. Vasco could more readily picture this fat bureaucrat waiting in a position of safety until the prey was tamed and ready to tag. Once a suspect was caught in one lie, everything else he said was to be regarded as less than fact. Official instructions regarding interrogation were clear on the subject; Vasco himself had corrected the misspellings and grammatical errors.

He'd been lied to right down the line: by Capone when he chose to, by everyone who knew his story but thought it could do with embellishing, by Vasco's own father; and it had started right here in this office.

"I resign. If you want it in writing for your precious files, hand me pen and paper and I'll put it on your desk before I leave. Any old pen will do. It doesn't have to be in blue."

"I don't accept."

"You have to. You can't make me go back to Florida. I'll go to one of the eleven recruitment centers within walking distance of this building and join the service under an assumed name. That way there won't be any trouble over my status."

"I assume this has something to do with your beating. I've seen a great deal worse, but in those cases the victims weren't cowards."

"That had nothing to do with Capone." He was unfazed by the insult.

"Didn't it? Well, I'll know soon enough. He wasn't the only one in his household under observation."

He knew that for the truth, and it chilled him. There would be a file in those stacks under her name, whatever her full name was. It surprised him to realize he knew her only as Rose. He'd never thought to ask. Had his actions contributed to that file? Undoubtedly, and it would follow her all her life. From the very start of his—his thing; *mission* was too crisp and clean for what he'd been about—he'd tainted everyone with whom he'd come into contact. Father Kyril would never serve in the Corps of Chaplains. Hoover's friends in the Pentagon could never be sure how much he'd been told—*nothing* was a concept that could not be proved, like innocence itself—or where it would lead. Why Vasco should immediately think of Kyril he couldn't guess, except that he was a good man, and good men were so hard to identify this side of the field of battle, where everything was revealed.

In a week, possibly less, Hoover would know what had happened in the Black-and-Tan. For all Vasco knew, he knew or suspected what had happened in Wisconsin. Vasco had been conducting an investigation for months, unaware that he himself was being investigated just as thoroughly. The whole business was a mirror held up to a mirror.

Someone tapped at the door. Hoover yelped an invitation and Miss Gandy entered. "You've said to bring these in the moment they arrive." She placed a thick envelope Vasco recognized on the table. Hoover thanked her and she withdrew.

He picked up the envelope, glanced at the writing, and balanced it on his palm as if to test its weight. "Since you say this is your final report, perhaps you'd care to summarize it and save me some time on a busy day." He sounded almost jovial.

"I don't see why not." The details of his last interview with Capone were fresh, and he reported them in the order in which they'd been given. He was gifted with a memory like a wire recorder, a fact that had no doubt contributed to his selection for the assignment. It would have come out on his aptitude test and been reported in his file. Hoover listened, staring at him.

"Chicken feed," he said when Vasco finished. "All dead, including Jack Mc-Gurn, ambushed by assailants unknown in a bowling alley on Milwaukee Avenue in 1936. The only exception is Frankie Rio, a mere bodyguard. The Chicago Police could arrest him for conspiracy in the Weiss murder, and under interrogation he might spill some details about Ralph Capone, whom he's working for now, but Ralph is only a figurehead. The fish we wanted is lying on a slab in the Cook County Morgue with a number tattooed on his toe."

"Then there's no point in continuing the investigation."

"There is every point. The Outfit didn't die with Nitti; if it was murder, that's evidence of it. There is Paul Ricca, who will almost certainly succeed him, and Tony Accardo waiting in the wings. Louis Campagna. Those bastards in Congress say I'm soft on organized crime. They have no idea what I'm up against and how little I have to work with."

"Capone never mentioned any of those names."

"Exactly. He's been playing you from the start. He denies any involvement in mutilating Scalise and Anselmi, the murders of Frankie Yale and Jake Lingle, even the St. Valentine's Day Massacre, which every little boy knows is his as much as George Washington and the cherry tree. But he's beginning to slip, as surely you noticed. Six weeks ago he'd never have tied Rio to Weiss, or lain his hand on a disloyal street soldier like Verdi in front of a civilian. Now is the time to go on the offensive, pry as much out of him as you can before he loses all contact with reality. The man is dying. Next month, next week; this *moment* he may be stretched on his deathbed in that pasha's palace of his, pouring his confidences into empty air. Your application to resign is rejected. Go back to Miami." He dropped the envelope inside the folder and slapped it shut.

Vasco realized he'd made a tactical error in attempting to beard Hoover in his own den. Most of the battles he'd lost had taken place on Capitol Hill; here in the queen's chamber in the heart of his hive, he'd launched his counterassaults, arranging press conferences, studying his clandestine files, inflating his successes, and picking at his enemies' flaws until they bled, turning public defeat into private victory and always, always getting what he wanted in the end. Diplomacy was Vasco's best weapon; an appeal for mercy, which however little of that quality Hoover possessed, it made good press when it was revealed.

"He seemed hardy when I left," Vasco said. "He inspires loyalty. His bodyguards take their orders from Ralph, but they do everything he asks, including that business with Verdi."

"That's because they were afraid he'd go berserk if they refused. He told you himself what he did in that hotel suite in Florida when he found out Tony Lolordo had been assassinated in his own home. His assassin, Joe Aiello, paid for that with his life as soon as Capone found it convenient."

"He was on top then," Vasco said. "Any scene he made now would just be a temper tantrum. Mae can bring him to heel with a firm word. They do what he tells them because his old associates take care of him, and they do that because he won their respect a long time ago. He placed loyalty above peace when he refused to turn Scalise and Anselmi over to Hymie Weiss. They remember that. They're returning the favor."

"He spared them then only to beat them half to death personally the first time they failed him. Then he turned them over for execution. They're no less dead than if it were Weiss. Loyalty's not quite the coin you think it is in these rats' world."

"He swore that was McGurn's doing."

"Well, we can't ask McGurn, can we? All the more reason to press Capone."

"You have to go public with his information to indict and convict the men you're after. Once it gets out Capone's been talking—"

"I should not have accused you of cowardice. It's only natural to be afraid." Hoover was only half listening, and had misunderstood the direction of the conversation. "You think you're alone down there, but I assure you you're not. We can protect you, and we will."

"Who'll protect Al?"

The sympathetic expression fled. He flattened his palms on the table, rose to his full height, which was not full at all, and buttoned his coat across the thick roll of fat around his middle. That pig's snout, those flabby jowls, the bug eyes; how could Vasco ever have considered them heroic? "Al, is it? Well, *Al* can take the slug in the belly he's had coming to him for twenty years. After we get from him what we want."

"I won't be party to that."

"You already are." His hand brushed the folder. "Once this is released, your name and Capone's will be linked inextricably."

"You'd never do that. There isn't anything in it you could use."

"CAPONE CONFESSES TO FBI. Our biggest headline since G-MEN KILL DILLINGER, and you know what that did for the Bureau. It would free up allocations currently earmarked for the Office of Strategic Services. I've been waiting twenty-five years to knock Wild Bill Donovan down a peg."

"It would be a death sentence for us both."

"A hypothetical situation, Special Agent. At present."

"That's evil even for you."

"I doubt you know the definition of the term. You've been in the presence of evil for four months and still fail to recognize it. Charming, isn't he? *Colorful*, the newspapers called him. I understand Hitler can still hold an audience spellbound with bombs raining down all around his bunker. Of course, they can't walk out."

"You wouldn't sabotage an investigation that's been going on since last winter just for revenge."

"Are you prepared to put it to the test?"

The silence was so complete he could hear Helen Gandy chugging away at her typewriter with two walls in between.

Hoover broke it. "As it happens, I may not be forced to so drastic a measure. I'd find it personally distasteful to rely upon the underworld to accomplish something I'm capable of bringing about myself. You've been given an assignment vital to national security in wartime; to abandon it now would open you to a charge of obstruction of justice. The article in the U.S. Constitution regarding treason is specific. It's a capital offense. If you were in the armed services you would face a firing squad. The gallows is more common in civilian cases."

His face had ceased to throb. He wondered if his heart had stopped beating. Certainly his face felt cold, as if the blood were no longer circulating.

"It's possible I'm being melodramatic," Hoover said. "Since the last war we've grown shy of extremes. However, after serving one year of a ten-year sentence in a maximum-security facility, you may prefer Nitti's solution. Every man does time in his own way."

"I'd have my day in court. I can't prove murder, but the Bill of Rights has something to say about interfering with the church."

"Your word against mine, as the villain says. A man who would say anything to save his neck versus the man who arrested Public Enemy Number One, the man who sent Lepke to the chair. My face on a motion picture trailer makes Charlie Chan sell like *Gone with the Wind*. We don't exactly belong in the same weight class, you and I."

Vasco felt a tingling, as if a layer of skin had been peeled from his body, exposing the pink tenderness beneath. All his senses were superacute. He could hear his watch ticking, smell the drugstore cologne the Director used, taste the dry bitter aspirin he'd chewed an hour ago. Everything he thought he'd seen clearly before was brilliant now. He was addressing a small man on a hollow stand in a room full of paper.

"You admit you have enemies in Washington," he said. "You're proud of it: a great man has great enemies. They'll be paying close attention during the proceedings. And it's not just my word and yours they'll hear. We aren't the only ones in on this secret. There's the diocese in Chicago—that recreational center you promised had to have left some kind of record—and Father McGonigle. The Vatican doesn't approve of him, but the Church cut its teeth on Ramses the Great. It won't sell out its sacred traditions for a man in a blue suit. Of course there are others, minor cogs in the machine. Your enemies won't give up until someone comes forward. After that, how long do you think it will be before the Nitti investigation is reopened?"

Hoover's flush had returned, like rash on a baby's cheeks; but the tight smile pried its way between them. "A commendable sermon. McGonigle is a better tutor than I'd thought. I'll make note of it in his file."

"The Church is a forgiving institution. I don't intend to shirk my own guilt in the affair."

"I couldn't help noticing you left out your father. After all, the Bureau bought him his boat."

He'd expected an assault on that flank. "My father has his faults, but he wouldn't sell out his son for a fishing boat. In any case he was no part in this. He thinks I'm a priest."

"Your report had holes in it as well. Did you think I didn't know who drove those killers away from Holy Name Cathedral?"

Nothing now, not even the monotonous methodical rhythm of Miss Gandy's relentless writing machine, disturbed the quiet.

"Did you never wonder why Capone even remembered your father, of all the men who delivered beer for him?" Hoover asked. "He went through them like envelopes. But he never forgot a man who'd performed a valuable service. That's only good business practice."

"I told you about the incident with the gun."

"A minor event. Capone was spared an inconvenience: a night in jail, and more likely an hour, followed by a long court date and then a dismissal of charges when no witnesses came forward in a city friendly to the cause. It got your father some money and a job and the debt was discharged. But the wheel man in the murder of an important character like Hymie Weiss was an asset he wouldn't be likely to forget. It took place during business hours on a busy street. The people who saw and described the driver lost their memories when it came time to make a formal statement, but a policeman's notebook is a useful tool, even if it can't be introduced as evidence without corroboration. It's much more reliable than the official record, because the man who wrote in it hasn't had time to reflect upon what the system expects from a man in his position.

"I admit it's difficult to build a case after all this time. I submit, however, that it isn't any more difficult than when city hall was spraining its neck looking the other way. Rio may find it in his best interest to turn state's evidence against a suspect more directly involved in return for the chance to plead guilty and avoid the electric chair. The Outfit hasn't cornered the market on friendly judges. The testimony of a gang flunky may not be sufficient to convict, but the world will be watching. Weiss has friends still."

"My God."

"Not my jurisdiction. I didn't bring up the subject of Paul Anthony Vasco because I thought he might sell out his son. Are you prepared to sell out your father?"

"Never."

"I thought not. It was one of the reasons I insisted you heal the rift." The Director lifted his hands from the table.

"His file isn't here. I've made other arrangements for storing material of a certain sensitivity. No eyes but mine have seen it. I assembled it from loose nuts and bolts and washers supplied by agents who had no idea what the finished product would be. If I took it to the incinerator myself, no one would know it had ever existed. Do I take it to the incinerator, Special Agent?"

One spark of resistance remained.

"I'd rather take it there myself."

"When you complete your assignment. Not before."

"And when is that?"

"When Al Capone is dead. He'll hardly be of any use to us after that."

"That could take years. If you'd seen him in action Saturday you wouldn't guess he's a dying man."

"I'm not going anywhere. The last quarter-century will attest to that."

IN THE LOBBY ON THE GROUND, SOMEONE CALLED VASCO'S NAME. HE TURNED and recognized his friend from the commissary, a portly clerk of about thirty who worked in the attorney general's office.

"Have you been away?" He shook Vasco's hand. "I haven't seen you around."

"I took a leave of absence. I'm still on it, actually. I had some business upstairs I thought was finished."

"Family trouble?"

"Among others."

"What happened to your face?"

"I got beat up pretty bad."

"You ought to pick on guys your own size."

"That's good advice, but I don't think I'll take it."

"What are you, a glutton for punishment?"

"Looks like."

THIRTY-FOUR

"Your last one, sir. I'm responsible to the railroad for the safety of its passengers."

Vasco paid for the glass of Kentucky rye and lifted it off the paper napkin without comment. He'd hardly expected to find the friendly colored bartender who'd served him on his first trip south on duty, but the white, pale-haired man behind the bar in the club car seemed to have no personality at all. He considered telling him this was the first time he'd been drunk in his life, but the man's opinion didn't matter.

He finished the drink and returned to his coach, balancing himself on the backs of the seats and apologizing with a thick tongue to the woman whose foot he'd stepped on. He threw himself into the seat behind her, bruising a hip on the arm.

"What do you expect?" a man's voice said. "All the good ones are overseas."

He thought that was hilarious. Not knowing why struck him as funny too. He chuckled, and then he heard loud snoring, which made him laugh harder. If that fellow could only hear himself.

When he awoke with a snort, the couple had changed seats. Outside the window, the war was everywhere. Clapboard houses rolled past with bronze and silver stars in the windows, dumps from which every scrap of metal had been salvaged, empty lots turned into victory gardens with seed packets staked like sentries at the ends of the rows. He had to pee and his tongue felt as if there were gullies carved in it.

The car was swaying more than seemed right when crawling through a town. He was still a little drunk and his face and his head ached. He'd always heard the hangover came later. He couldn't even get sloshed properly. In the little water closet he addressed the first problem, flushed, and ran water into his cupped hands from the tap and gulped it down. He looked at his face in the stingy mirror and marveled that he hadn't been thrown off the train. He plucked at the gauze in his left nostril and drew out what seemed like a yard and a half of stiff bloodstained material—it seemed to have come from deep inside his brain—unwound an equal length from his right, and dropped both pieces into the trash receptacle. He blew his nose carefully into a wad of toilet paper and examined the pale pink stain. Then he threw that away too and took in air through his nose for the first time in days. It was exquisite, like a bad head cold cured instantly. He'd already removed the bandage from the bridge, but the nose was still swollen and there were yellow streaks in the bruises under his eyes. He winced when he touched the slightly lighter strip of flesh where the bandage had been.

Knuckles brushed the outside of the door. A conductor's noncommittal drawl announced Fort Lauderdale as the next stop. That made up his mind. If he'd slept through it, he'd have stayed on the train even when it stopped. That much he'd left to God. The rest was up to him.

The heat on the platform was terrific, an enormous dog that jumped up on him and lapped at him with its sweaty tongue. The sun looked stale; it had hung too long in one spot. The air smelled fishy and the fish wasn't fresh. There was a streetcar stop, but the car wasn't there and he was afraid if he waited he'd lose his nerve and get back aboard the train. A cab driver parked in the shadow of the station overhang looked up from under a green eyeshade as Vasco approached, stuck a comic book on top of the visor, and got out to take his valise and put it in the trunk. "You okay, buddy?" he asked when his passenger dropped into the backseat. "You look like the bottle hit you back."

He gave the man the name of the marina where Paul Vasco kept his boat and his business.

A SEAGULL PERCHED ON A PILING PAID HIM NO ATTENTION AT ALL AS HE passed within a foot of it; it plucked something edible from between its feathers and tossed back its head to swallow. He figured the bird was new to the neighborhood, and unaware it was risking its life anywhere within pistol range of Sunrise Charters.

The breeze from the ocean never stopped, but today it was barely there. The boat sat motionless beside the pier. His father had made no attempt to paint out the name after taking the boat out before the paint had dried the first time; Peter could read MAUREEN through the streaks. The sight saddened him even more than when it had been blanked out entirely.

He knocked at the door under the name burned into the lintel. When no one answered he tried the knob. It was locked.

"Try prayer. You never know, it might be Catholic. Most doors are Presbyterian, though. Stiff and thick."

He turned to face Paul, coming his way carrying his ice chest by the handles. "I didn't see you aboard the boat."

"That's because I wasn't. You believe they knocked up beer another point? Hirohito's practically sucking MacArthur's dick. What happened to your face, boy? Holy Ghost sucker punch you in the snoot?"

"As a matter of fact it was a very large Negro. You carried that heavy thing all the way from the store?"

"I carried larger loads in my gut, though from the smell of you I'm an amateur. Been into the sacramental wine, my nose tells me. Well, don't just stand there. Key's in my right pocket." He turned his right hip Peter's way.

Peter changed hands on the valise and drew a skeleton key on a fat ring from the pocket of his father's khaki shorts. He pushed open the door and stood aside.

Paul dropped the chest on the floor with a clanking of cans and rattling of ice, opened it, and took out two cans of Pfeiffer's.

"Not for me, thanks."

"Didn't think so, but a man ought to be sociable in his home. You're smart not to mix your drinks. I was joking about wine. I know rye when I smell it. Never liked the stuff myself. Too sweet." He dropped one of the cans back inside the chest, flipped shut the lid, and opened one with the opener attached to a handle. When they were both seated he flung his fishermen's cap at its nail; it landed on an angle, hung there for a split second, and fell. "I raised you better than to pick fights with darkies. The only thing harder'n their fists is their head."

"How many darkies do you know?"

"Well, none, you got me there. I must-a been thinking of Cubans."

"Is it possible for us to have a conversation without saying something ugly?"

"Probably not. I gave up on miracles when I stopped going to Mass." Paul drank. "Where's the choker? Don't say it's too hot. You're supposed to go all the way to hell to save a sinner."

"I never saved a sinner, Dad. I've committed too many of my own to earn the necessary credentials."

"Jesus. If you're gonna be humble you got to take the stick out of your ass first."

Peter said nothing for a moment, listening to the beer gurgling down his father's throat.

"I think I'll take one after all."

"Well, get it. It's the butler's day off."

He got up, opened one, and took a large swallow. His stomach turned over slowly, like a barrel of tar rolling in deep water, and flattened out. His head began to clear. He'd thought that hair-of-the-dog theory was a myth, to justify getting drunk all over again. Lately everything he'd believed had taken a torpedo broadside. Torpedo; the war had entered even the language of his thoughts.

"So what's the squeal?" Paul said. "Catch Father Cyril with his pants down during choir practice?"

"Kyril."

"Commie priest. Fucked-up world since Roosevelt took over. I asked you a question, son."

"Not here." He went over and leaned close to his father's ear. "The place might be bugged."

"You're kidding."

Peter raised his voice a decibel, chuckling. "You'd be surprised the kind of jokes you hear in church. Is the boat taken?"

His father's face smoothed out. "I wouldn't be sitting here this time-a day getting shit-faced if it was. Bring the cooler."

The preparations were a repeat of the last time. Peter put on the cap, Paul the stained and torn fedora. The Chrysler engine cleared its throat and they left the musty mainland behind and throttled forward into the wind. There were some sailboats in the harbor and a pontoon shaped like a barge with people aboard drinking, but out beyond the mouth the ocean seemed deserted. There, Paul switched off the ignition, the sudden silence hurting his son's ears, and directed him to drop anchor. It was a real anchor with barbs and attached to a chain, unlike the paint bucket of cement on a rope in Wisconsin; it entered the water as smoothly as a trained diver and dragged the chain clanking through a brass grommet until it came to the end with a reverberating thump. Water slapped loosely at the hull, the wind carried the cries of gulls and from somewhere behind cloaking clouds the yawing of a single-engine plane.

Peter thought it unlikely a boat could be bugged effectively at sea, but he motioned to Paul to turn on the two-way radio. There was static and unexcited chatter that had nothing to do with them, snatches of music where the nautical air band and the entertainment frequencies collided. ("When you're smiling . . .") Paul climbed out of the pilot house and sat in the fisherman's chair in the stern with a fresh can. Peter, after that inaugural gulp, carried his first unsipped and leaned back against the rail facing him.

"I left the seminary, Dad. You said I'd fail, and you were right. I was never ordained. I'm an impostor."

His father drank, said nothing.

"You weren't the only one I fooled. Father Kyril thinks I'm a priest. I've even taken part in ceremonies."

"Son—"

"Please let me finish. If I don't keep going I won't be able to."

Paul turned his head and stared out at the ocean. Peter was grateful to be spared eye contact. He measured his phrases, not wanting to leave out anything important. He spoke about his job with the FBI, of the assignment Hoover had given him, of its success so far. (Paul's brows rose at that point, but his gaze remained fixed at sea. He lifted the can mechanically to his lips and swallowed.) Frank Nitti's death, Peter's attempt to resign, Hoover's threats, including to try his father for murder, Peter's acquiescence and return to Florida. Once again he made no mention of Rose.

For a full minute after he stopped talking, his father said nothing. Then he crushed the can and threw it over the stern. The wind caught it and sent it slapping across the waves. Peter heard it without turning to look at it.

"What if I told you all I knew was I was picking up Scalise and Anselmi?" Paul said then. "That no one said a thing about Hymie Weiss?"

"Dad, I wasn't asking."

"No, I guess you'd know it was a crock-a shit. What do I care if them bums keep on rubbing each other out till there ain't but one left? And John and Albert never hit no innocents like Weiss's boys did all the time. Frankie Rio came to the apartment, plopped down a roll of cabbage on the kitchen table, and laid it all out. Ten C-notes, it was, and all up front because Mr. Capone trusted me. That was a year of physical therapy for your mother."

"If you'd put it to me that way, I might have understood."

Paul was silent.

Peter shook his head. "No. That's a crock of shit too. I wouldn't have, back when I asked. I understand now. But it's not what I came here to talk about."

"This got anything to do with that busted nose?"

"Not directly. The story's the same, with or without it."

"You're learning. I'll make a first-class liar out of you yet." He scratched his naked stomach. His skin had burned an even deeper shade of cherry, the sparse growth of hair on his chest had bleached white. "Mr. Capone say anything else about me?"

"Is there anything else to tell?"

"I heard he was cuckoo. His memory seems okay. I don't know what I could add."

It was an unsatisfying response, but his father's past had ceased to interest him greatly. "What do I do?"

"If you're asking me how to get you out of Dutch with the pope, that ain't in my league."

"No one can help me with that. How do I get out from under Hoover without landing both of us in jail or the death house?"

"Who says you got to? Do what he says and when it's over forget you ever met him. *He* sure won't bring it up."

"I can't."

"Afraid?"

"Not of the Outfit."

"Hoover neither, long as you play ball. God, maybe."

"It's me I'm afraid of. I convinced myself in the beginning I was helping the war effort, destroying the men who ran the black market. I stopped believing that a long time ago, but I didn't quit. Others would just take their place. I never even heard of the men Hoover said would fill the hole left by Nitti. All he cares about is headlines. Appropriations from Congress. More power. How long can you work for someone like that before you begin to think that's okay?"

"You let that collar go to your head."

"I didn't think you'd understand."

"I mean busting out in a sermon just like that. You ain't thinking nothing I didn't think when Mr. Capone went away. I didn't have the words is all. Bottles, Nitti, McGurn, they was just little Als; dressed like him and acted like him, but they'd throw you to the wolves to save their own hides. Why do you think I got out?"

"Who says you did? You bought a bar with mob money."

"Hoover tell you that? Well, he was right. It was mob money, all right; it belonged to a shylock. He charged me three hundred percent interest and took out his first payment before he handed me the dough. I'd still be paying him if Mr. Capone's cousin Rocco Fischetti didn't come along and buy me out after two years. Selling him the liquor license gave me the folding to come down here and set up shop where the sharks don't eat you more than once. That beer of yours must be warm as piss by now."

Peter had forgotten all about it. He poured what was left overboard and traded the empty for two full ones from the chest; it seemed to him there was more than enough scrap metal cluttering the Atlantic. He opened them, took a long pull from one, and handed the other to Paul. "They say you can't leave the rackets, but you did. How do I get out of the Bureau?"

Paul lifted his can and didn't lower it until it was empty. This time he didn't throw it overboard. He looked down at it. Muscles worked in the corners of his jaw. He looked up at Peter. "It's in your blood, boy. Think. What would Al do?"

He saw clouds reflected in the clear brown eyes. They were moving at terrific speed. "What do you mean, in my blood?"

"You been pulling the wool over a lot of eyes all year long. And not just any eyes. Priests. Guys in the rackets. That takes practice or talent, and you ain't had practice. You sure didn't inherit it from me. You caught me in every lie I ever told you but one. From your mother neither. She never lied in her life."

Out there in the temperate air Peter felt his face grow cold.

"I didn't meet Mr. Capone strictly by accident," Paul said. "That night he killed Ragtime Joe Howard, he came looking for me in that speak, knowing I'd be there. Any hack would've done for what he had in mind, but he wanted to throw the job my way."

"*How* did he know you'd be there?"

"How you think? Your mother told him."

His hand suddenly lost its grip. The can slipped from it and struck the deck. The contents splashed his cuffs and soaked through his shoes. He felt as if he'd lost his hold while climbing and had fallen himself; was still falling.

"Maggie." He whispered it.

"What her friends called her. I told you she never did like Maureen. I guess Mr. Capone told you some of it."

"He remembered her after all these years, and there were so many others, some of them famous. He said she left him the first time he got himself into trouble in Chicago."

"Mr. Capone was a generous man, whatever else you hear about him. You could've grown up in a nice house, had swell clothes, went to the best schools. Your mother loved you more than anything, but she wouldn't have that. She didn't know about that night till Mr. Capone showed up at the apartment to buy back his gun. We had a big fight. You probably heard it."

"There were so many."

"She was a real Irish blowtop. She almost took you and left. The only reason she stayed was she didn't expect to live long. We had a lot of fights before she let me take that job. I told her doctors don't live on air, and a boy needs his mother. Things would-a been a lot different if she was a well woman.

"Everything went to hell after she died," Paul continued. "You was almost grown, and you had her idea of right and wrong. I didn't handle it so good when you told me you wanted to study to be a priest. I guess maybe you know I loved her more than you. You was so different, even as a kid; you had that picture of J. Edgar Hoover up there over your bed. But she loved you more than me, so I thought that was jake. I tried to raise you like you was mine. I didn't marry her to keep her out of a jam, and as bad as things got I never, never threw it up to her that she was in the family way when we tied the knot. Life I lived, I didn't—how'd you say it—have the necessary credentials." His smile was sickly.

Peter took another large swallow. It caught in his throat like something solid, then drained into his stomach, where it soured on contact. "Does he know?"

"I don't know, honest. He sure never brought it up. But he must-a had a hunch or we never would've known each other."

"How much did she know about what you did for him?"

"We never talked about it."

"I don't believe you."

"Pietro, I didn't think she wanted to ask questions she didn't want to know the answers to."

"But you told her about that night Capone beat up Scalise and Anselmi with a baseball bat. I heard you. You were drunk."

"Not so drunk I didn't know what I was saying. She was always after me to quit. After a while even the doctor bills wouldn't change her mind. I told her it was too late for that, that the time to quit was before I took the job. I wasn't at the roadhouse that night. I was loading a truck downtown. I just told her a story I'd heard like I was there. I had to scare her, and I couldn't tell her how deep I was really in. Personally I think it never happened, or if it did it wasn't him on the other end of that bat. It was just one of those stories that kept getting told. That was Jack McGurn's deal, for that fuck-up St. Valentine's Day. Word around town was it was friends of Scalise and Anselmi gunned him down in that bowling alley later. February fourteenth, it was. Seven years to the day."

Peter gritted his teeth in what must have looked like a cynical grin. If Capone hadn't lied about that night, it was possible he'd told the truth about everything else. The only principal in the affair who had.

"He's a better man than you know."

"What?"

"Something Sharon said, about you. I thought she was just sticking up for her boyfriend."

"We got no secrets from each other." Paul shook himself. "Shit. I guess now we'll have to get married by a rabbi. Got to wear that stupid beanie."

Peter said nothing.

"You all right, son?"

"How can you call me that without choking?"

Paul bunched his chin. "I got at least as much right as that man in Miami. He just happened to be in the room at the time."

"Can you turn this boat around? I'm getting sick."

Paul set his can down on the deck and got out of the chair. Peter took his place, leaving him to weigh anchor and start the engine. Sitting in the chair he drank three beers during the trip back and had to be helped onto the pier.

HE WOKE UP HURTING IN SEVERAL PLACES, INCLUDING THE BASE OF HIS spine. The bed he was in was too soft. The cotton blanket covering him was thin, but it took most of his strength to push it off along with the sheet. He was wearing only his undershorts and a skin of perspiration that chilled him when the breeze came in through a screened window. It was light out, but some dim memory prowling the back of his mind told him it was not the same day. Pictures of strangers in homely domestic situations stood in frames on a chest of drawers made of veneered plywood with a straw mat on top: men, women, and children sitting around a dining table, a man in a rumpled double-breasted suit smiling beside a showroom-shiny Studebaker, a man with a vaguely familiar face standing with his arm around a woman's waist. On closer examination he recognized a younger Sharon and the man whose photo he'd seen in uniform on the radio in the parlor the first time he'd visited.

A door opened and Sharon came through it carrying a wicker tray. He hurried to cover himself, setting aflame every ache and pain, especially the pounding in his head.

"No need for modesty," she said. "Who do you think helped undress you?"

"It's only the second time I've gotten drunk. I seem to have a talent for it."

"You got here under your own power, sort of. Paul just did the steering. How much do you remember?"

"It's fuzzy. Then black. Did I behave terribly?"

"You were as docile as a sheep. Cute. Sit up, will you? I'm not a Harvey Girl." She made a motion with the tray. He hoisted himself into a sitting position with his back propped against the maple headboard, drawing the blanket and sheet up over his chest. She placed the tray on its feet straddling his waist. There were two rashers of bacon, scrambled eggs on a blue china plate, coffee in a white mug, and orange juice in a small glass with flowers stenciled on it. "Your father said he thought you liked your eggs sunny side up, but I didn't think you wanted them looking back at you. I hope you like your bacon crisp. Your father does."

"He's not my father."

"Yes, he is."

He looked at her stern face, felt his flush, and drank orange juice. He was parched; the sweet cold liquid was like water in the desert. Coffee next. The real thing took getting used to.

"I brought milk and sugar. For some reason Paul's connections are no good with cream."

"Thank you. If I'm going to be a drunk I might as well start taking it black."

"Stop feeling sorry for yourself. Do you think you're the only one who ever had a shock?"

He thought of the man with her in the photograph, drowned at Midway. "I didn't mean anything. Where is he?"

"Your father?"

He picked up a fork and got interested in the eggs. "Yes."

"Out with a customer. He has one occasionally. He doesn't spend all his time in that shack drinking beer, whatever you may think."

"You don't know what I'm thinking, Sharon."

"Sure I do. I honestly don't understand how you managed to fool so many people for so long."

"He told you." The eggs were bland and a little dry. Butter seemed to present the same challenge as cream.

"Did you think he'd wait till we were standing at the altar?"

She stood with her hands folded in front of her. She wore a crisp blouse under her frilly apron and a dark wool skirt, street clothes. "Am I keeping you from your job?"

"My shift starts at four. Plenty of time. I emptied out the top drawer of the bureau and unpacked your suitcase. You'll find your toothbrush and shaving things in the bathroom down the hall. You're staying with us a few days."

"I don't want to impose. I'll go to a hotel."

"Why don't you finish your breakfast, then plot out the rest of your life?"

After she left, closing the door behind her, he ate greedily. He'd always thought people who drank hard woke up sick to their stomachs, but his seemed to be a special case. He couldn't even get being hungover right. He'd finished and was wiping his mouth on the plain napkin when Sharon returned. The apron was gone. She'd tied on a flimsy scarf and pinned a felt hat to her hair. She picked up the tray. "There are books and magazines, and the radio. It's a good neighborhood to take a walk in, if you don't mind being interrupted by chatty neighbors. Paul will be back around dark. Please don't leave."

"I won't. Sharon?"

She'd turned away. She turned back.

"He—Dad said you don't keep secrets. Did he tell you about the day Hymie Weiss died in Chicago?"

"He did. He said someone like that wasn't worth caring about."

"He told me the same thing."

"He thinks if he says it enough times he'll believe it. Your father's done a lot of things he wished he hadn't. Raising you isn't one of them."

"Thank you."

"I'm not the one you should be thanking." She went out.

* * *

HE FELT SLEEPY—AND HE'D SLEPT AWAY A NIGHT AND MOST OF THE DAY—and slid back down and closed his eyes, but his mind was racing. After an hour of painful tossing and turning he got up wincing, leaned a hand against the wall until he had his balance, and found his way to the bathroom, painted a restful shade of pale pink with chintz curtains on the window. His razor and tube of shaving cream were laid out on the edge of the sink. He thought the swelling had gone down, but his bruises looked darker than ever against his pallor, noticeable even in the rose-tinted mirror.

His hand, he was pleased to note, was steady when he picked up the razor. Shaving for him had never been a tedious chore; the daily pursuit of perfection appealed to his natural sense of order. He wondered if it was the same for Capone. So many things that had baffled him before seemed reasonable now. He had shared none of Paul Vasco's traits. It wasn't uncommon for a son to bear no physical resemblance to his father, but character was altogether more durable in the bloodline.

Shaving represented one of the few moments in the day when a man was completely alone with his thoughts. In the past he'd arranged his schedule as he was rubbing lather into his face, resolved problems that had vexed him nights as he plowed pink furrows through the white and flicked the buildup into the sink and rinsed the blade. His brain slowed to a reliable working rhythm, turning belts and pushing pistons. By the time he toweled off, he had a solution.

It had not come to him in a bolt of inspiration. Good ideas seldom did. It was more like a dirty blossom opening under palest starlight, fertilized by a memory buried deep in the compost of months; an anecdote, enhanced possibly for dramatic effect, and only barely heard in his impatience for information more directly useful, but he was blessed—cursed—with a nearly photographic memory. And he had an insane certainty that it would work, provided he went about it properly. There were a thousand ways to do a thing wrong and there was only one way to do it right.

If only he could. And if the story it was based on wasn't just another lie in a sea of them.

The sun was a long time setting. He dressed, tried to interest himself in a profile of Eisenhower in an old copy of *Newsweek,* cranked the dial on the big Westinghouse radio all the way right and all the way left, never stopping on any one station for longer than a minute. The war news was only slightly more diverting than static, the musical programs were as irritating as the squeal of feedback when he tuned between them, the daytime dramas banal, with overheated dialogue and the organ music played with an elephantine hand. The commercials were aimed at idiots. He switched off the set and thought about going for a walk, but he was afraid he'd miss Paul if he came back early.

When at dusk the front door opened at last and Paul came in, smelling of salt and sweat, fish blood staining his shirt, Peter leapt up from an overstuffed chair, startling him.

"Jesus. You look like you need a drink."

"Dad, we have to talk."

"Jesus," he said again. "I think I need a drink."

But Peter was too impatient to wait. And after they'd talked, both men needed a drink.

THIRTY-FIVE

THE FACE HAD APPEARED—IN PHOTOGRAPHS, NEWSREELS, AND CARICA-ture—in every country in the world. Men with similar features were often mistaken for the original, but when one saw the genuine article there was no doubt. One just knew.

Alcohol use had thickened the skin on his cheeks, and a season of hunting U-boats in the Gulf Stream had burned it the color of hickory, throwing into sharp relief the silver strands in his beard. He wasn't as tall as Vasco had expected—an inch or so below six feet—but his shoulders were broad and his chest deep beneath the faded khaki shirt unbuttoned halfway down the front and his hard belly hung over the wide belt buckled outside the loops on his tea-dyed shorts. He had big feet in dirty white deck shoes wearing through at the toes and a long-billed fisherman's cap like Paul Vasco's tugged down over his left eye. The eyes were oddly vulnerable, watching for the reaction to everything he said, and despite his physical substance and the outdoorsy glow there was something unhealthy about him. He had scales in his beard.

The bar was called Sloppy Joe's, and its cool dim interior, shuttered with wooden blinds against the sun and brutal heat of Key West in July, was parsed into horizontal stripes of light swarming with dust floes. The jukebox was silent; at that early hour of the afternoon the largely male clientele had not gathered there to listen to music. That totem of southernmost Florida, the stuffed marlin plasticized to a blue-and-white sheen, arched on a wall behind the bar with old-time prizefighters in cheap plaster frames and an autographed photo of the man Vasco had come to see standing on a dock beside what may have been the same fish hanging from a winch.

He had keen peripheral vision. Vasco could tell he'd spotted him from among a gaggle of companions at the bar the moment he'd entered—his eyes flicked his way—but it was three or four minutes before he managed to extricate himself—a hand on this back, a likely dirty joke murmured in that ear—from the group and approach the corner table where Vasco waited, carrying a tumbler half-filled with clear liquid and ice cubes. He set it down on the table and took his hand in a hard grasp. His face was broad and his grin seemed broader.

"I'm glad I had a description. You don't look a thing like the skinny old bird."

"No, sir, I don't." The voice surprised him, a flat drone. He'd expected something gruff and booming.

The man swung a leg over a chair like a cowboy mounting up and sat. "Consider it an advantage. My father was a good man, but yellow. My mother's a bitch and I take after her more than anyone in the family."

"Thanks so much for making time to see me."

"It was already made. I'm going to London next month, off to cover the war while there's still time, and you can't start a book with that over your head. I like that old dago. I was pleased as hell when he called. He tell you about our time out on his boat?"

"He said you shot up his beer cooler with a tommy gun."

The dark brows drew together. "I remember it differently. But I'm used to having the facts blown up all around me."

"I know a man who can say the same thing, Mr. Hemingway."

"Ernest. Ernie, if you'll let me buy you a drink. This one's my authorship." The writer tapped his glass. "You mix vodka with water and put it in the freezer in an ice cube tray. The vodka doesn't freeze, so when you float the cubes in more vodka, they break up against your teeth and it's like drinking from a mountain waterfall made of pure grain alcohol."

"A beer would be fine."

"Ballantine's, Joe. And another of these."

A man built along Hemingway's sturdy lines, who didn't look sloppy at all, collected bottles and glasses from a table nearby and returned to the bar. He came back, set another tumbler in front of Hemingway, this one filled almost to the rim, and poured beer into a tall pilsner. When he left, Vasco's host drained his first drink and lifted the second. "To victory. But not till I'm there to supervise it."

He didn't think much of the toast, but he touched glasses and drank.

Hemingway swallowed. "Where's the screed?"

"Screed?"

"The manuscript. Or is that your knitting you're carrying around?"

He opened the moleskin briefcase he'd leaned against a table leg and drew out the bundle of paper tied with a cord. Sharon, who'd worked in a steno pool before the war, had transcribed his hastily handwritten notes into a hundred neatly typewritten pages. Vasco trusted his memory; he doubted the account wandered more than a few sentences from how it had been told to him, and he was sure of the facts.

Hemingway took it and held it out at arm's length to read the title page. "*The Confessions of Al Capone.* Catchy. Is it nonfiction?"

"It's a novel."

"Too short; but they said the same thing about *The Torrents of Spring.* You're in for a legal shitstorm if you get it in print. But being sued by Capone is worth a fortune in free advertising. I was in Paris all the time he was climbing up from the gutter, so most of what I know about him I read in French. The romance languages aren't quite equal to that task. One of the Gennas was gunned down in Oak Park, not six blocks from the house where I grew up. Say what you like about him, his boys hit where they aimed. Did you meet him in Miami?"

"Yes." He was determined to get by with only one lie.

"I'd like to. Franco's already got me down as a gangster." He undid the cord and drew a pair of steel-rimmed glasses from a tortoiseshell case in his shirt pocket. He read five pages while Vasco sipped from his glass, then folded his spectacles and put them away. "You've got an ear for dialogue. I'm supposed to know something about that. He as nuts as they say?"

"His wife says he has good days and bad."

"Don't we all. Hers is the story you should tell. They say I can't write women, but I did a good enough job with Brett Ashley for a real Lady Ashley to take me to court. The press that got sold an extra fifty thousand copies of *Sun*, not that I saw any royalties. Those went to my first wife. How much of this is bullshit?"

"Most of it is public record."

"So it's bullshit. No matter. The only thing that needs to be true is your sentences."

He had no idea what that meant.

Hemingway drummed the sheets even and retied the cord.

"Keep a carbon?"

"No. That's the only copy."

"Dumb. All my early work was stolen in a suitcase at a train station in Paris. I'll keep a close eye on it when I go to New York next week, but I'm not making any guarantees."

"You'll show it to your editor?"

"I promised your father I would if it didn't turn out to be crap. You'd be surprised how much crap is out there, how much I have to paw through for friendship's sake, and how much actually gets into print; although not on my nickle. Don't get your hopes up. Nobody's interested in reading about gangsters since the war. You might as well write about Edwardian tea parties and carriage rides down gaslit lanes. Bootleggers are no less quaint."

"All the same I'm very grateful."

"You shouldn't have to wait long for an answer. Max Perkins is a dithery old fussbudget, but he's my best friend in that goddamn town and anyway he doesn't believe in leaving people hanging." He downed his drink in one motion, doubled the typescript over lengthwise, and stood up with his hand out.

Vasco took it.

"I can't thank you enough, Mr. Hemingway."

"Ernie."

He nodded, but he couldn't see himself calling him that any more than he could address Ralph Capone as Bottles.

"Really, I'd be more comfortable in a hotel. You offered to put me up for a few days and it's been two weeks."

Sharon shook her head. They were all sitting on the front porch of the house in Fort Lauderdale, digesting one of her masterful briskets and watching the twinkling of the fireflies. A boy pedaling a bicycle on the sidewalk slowed to hurl a late edition rolled into a tight tube onto the doorstep. Peter saw WARSAW in bold print in the porch light. "We let you move to the sofa," Sharon said. "That's as far as you get."

Paul belched. He had his legs stretched out from his seat on the glider and his hands folded on the little bulge in his stomach. Every heavy meal he ate passed through his tubular body like a pig in a python. "You need to hang onto your dough. Sooner or later Hoover's gonna figure out you ain't earning your keep."

HE'D CALLED KYRIL AT OUR LADY OF REDEMPTION TO EXPLAIN THAT HE was visiting his father and to ask him to call the house if any calls came in for him. The pastor had agreed without asking questions. He was either the least curious man Peter had ever met, or the most discreet.

But he didn't delude himself that he was hiding out from Hoover. Since what seemed as long as he could remember, he'd sensed he was being watched constantly, and he sensed it now more than ever. Whenever he stepped outdoors he wondered about cars parked on the street he had not seen before. Sharon would know the neighbors' vehicles, but he didn't ask her at the risk of alarming her. She was treating the entire situation as an adventure; or pretending to, for his sake. Paul, after that first conference and his call to Hemingway to set up the interview in Sloppy Joe's, had made no mention of it. He was smoking regularly now. The orange tip of his cigarette glowed fiercely in the assembling darkness.

Sharon rose from her painted wicker chair and announced she was going to bed. Peter got up to say good night. She hesitated, glancing at Paul, then went inside. After the screen door clapped shut behind her, Peter resumed his seat next to Paul on the glider. "I think she wanted you to join her."

"I ain't a machine." The cigarette tip moved. Paul's throat worked, swallowing beer. Then the tip moved back the other way.

"Maybe that isn't what she wanted."

Paul smoked. "I guess you're the big expert on women now."

"What do you mean now?"

"There's only two people worth getting the shit beat out of you for: your mother and your girl. Your mother's been gone a long time."

"It wasn't serious, Dad."

"That's a crock-a-shit."

"That's your answer to everything."

"Only where it fits. It's like a Bible verse that way."

"What would you know about the Bible?"

"Just what you know about women. It's always serious, Pietro. Even if it's for just one night, it's serious at the time."

"What's the point of this conversation?"

"It's like a bad cut. You can't leave it open. You don't stitch it up, it festers. It's a sin to leave a woman in that condition. And don't tell me I don't know nothing about sin. I had practice."

Peter stood. "Good night, Dad. Thanks."

Smoke shot out from the glider and drifted toward the bare bulb glowing above the door, swirling with moths and mosquitoes.

"What the hell for?"

"Whatever you like."

"Well, you're welcome. Get to bed before I start crying in my beer."

Paul Vasco was in the bathroom and Sharon was washing the breakfast dishes when the doorbell rang the next morning. Peter found a white-haired postman waiting with dark circles under the arms of his uniform shirt. "Special Delivery, sir."

He tore open an envelope with a New York City postmark. The letter was typed without error on heavy rag paper; wartime shortages did not appear to apply to business stationery.

CHARLES SCRIBNER'S SONS

Peter Vasco, Esq.
c/o Mrs. Sharon Baumgartner
111 Calle de Nulidad
Fort Lauderdale, Fla.

Dear Mr. Vasco:

Thank you for the opportunity to read and evaluate your novella *The Confessions of Al Capone*, which was delivered to me by Mr. Ernest Hemingway personally and without remark.

Although the story is compelling and competently written, I fear there is not a large enough readership out there for a story that on first glance might seem too familiar. Material restrictions at this time would not justify our taking on such a project.

If I may offer constructive criticism, I find the assertion that Al Capone was innocent of planning and executing the St. Valentine's Day Massacre implausible. Whatever your perceptions, it is always a mistake to swim against the tide of popular opinion.

I am returning the manuscript under separate cover, and am

Yours sincerely,
(signed)
Maxwell E. Perkins,
Editor-in-Chief

He held a conference with Paul and Sharon around the dining room table. When they'd finished discussing details, Peter announced that he was moving out.

"I'd hoped the manuscript would come back with the rejection," he said when they protested. "It's my bargaining chip. But I can't wait for Hoover to find out on his own. I have to strike first and be ahead of him for once. I won't be responsible for putting you both in danger."

"You should write scripts for *The Shadow*," Paul said, "cheesy stuff like that. I got out of Cicero with my skin. I guess I can take care of myself in Lauderdale, Sharon too."

"That popgun you use on seagulls won't protect you. Maybe I *am* being melodramatic, but I can't do what I have to do and worry about you both at the same time."

Sharon asked, "What would you have done if Perkins had accepted?"

"I only thought of that after I met with Hemingway. You're looking at the only aspiring writer who ever prayed for failure."

She asked where he would go. Paul laid a hand on hers.

"Maybe he's better off not saying."

Peter shook his head. "When Hoover's people come around asking, they won't believe you if you say you don't know. If you tell them, they'll go away and leave you alone. I'll check into the Sea Breeze. It's a motor court across the street from the ocean. I stayed there the first time I came down."

"It's a dump," Paul said.

"You're the one who said I need to hang onto my dough."

"Stop trying to talk like me. You sound stupid."

Peter packed quickly. At the door, Sharon handed him leftover brisket wrapped in waxed paper in a paper sack. She hugged him and kissed him on the cheek. She smelled of baking. His mother had smelled the same way when she saw him off to school. He held his hand out to his father, but Paul stepped past it, put his arms around him briefly, and separated himself with two hard slaps on Peter's back. Outside, Peter carried his valise to the streetcar stop without looking back.

In the office of the Sea Breeze, with its odors of nickel, cigarettes, and chewing gum, he registered and asked the woman smoking behind the desk when the mail was picked up.

"Search me. He ain't been in yet today. The geezer on this route belongs in a wheelchair."

He'd put Perkins' letter in an envelope addressed to the Bureau-owned stationery supply store coded for Hoover and stamped it. Standing in front of the brass-faced chute embossed U.S. MAIL he hesitated, then let the letter slide through the slot. He glanced up and down the street before going to his room. He felt like a hunted gangster.

FOUR DAYS LATER HE CAME BACK FROM A WALK ON THE BEACH AND ASKED the clerk again if he had any messages. She finished lighting a fresh Lucky off the

butt of another and took a loose fold of paper out of the only pigeonhole that
held anything. Instead of handing it to him she opened it and read it.

"Some Sharon called ten minutes ago. Said to tell you to come on over."

"Did she say anything else?"

She turned the sheet over and looked at the other side. It was blank. "Nope."

She'd been smart not to mention to a stranger that the package he'd expected
had arrived. He waited a long ten minutes for a streetcar and swung aboard before it stopped rolling. A motorman with a face like a satchel scowled as he
dropped in his nickel. "That's how you lose legs."

At Sharon's house the door opened as he was about to ring. The man holding
the knob was medium-built, with a face that was too young for him. His
summer-weight blue suit fit him well, but there was nothing conspicuous about
the tailoring. He wore a plain black tie on a white shirt. Before Peter could open
his mouth, something hard dug into him low in the back and a narrow heavy-
veined hand slid over his shoulder and under both arms and slid back around to
pat all his pockets and grope inside each thigh. He smelled a sickly sweet odor;
molassesy, only not so pleasant. The point of chewing snuff had always eluded
him. The pressure went away from his back. "Okay, go ahead in and say hello to
Ma and Pa." It was a tight, thin voice that vibrated like a banjo string.

Inside, Peter turned around. The man's gun was out of sight. His gaunt frame
was hung with cheap seersucker and a red bow tie on an elastic band moved up
and down as he worked at the cud in his cheek. He was too old for field duty, with
white stubble sprouting from his brown pleated cheeks and blue eyes faded into
the whites under a straw skimmer worn at an insolent angle. For a brief terrible
moment, Peter thought the Outfit had beat the Bureau to the punch. He didn't
look official, but on the other hand nothing about him said Chicago. He belonged
in westerns, but in different clothes, and the hat he wore would be black. Then
came a voice he had never expected to hear in that house.

"Shut the door. You're letting out all the cool air."

J. Edgar Hoover sat in the overstuffed chair by the big cabinet radio, wearing
gray gabardine and a Panama hat with a black silk band. The chair had a high
back and he looked like a fat little boy in his father's seat with his highly polished
shoes barely touching the floor. Paul and Sharon sat close to each other on the
sofa.

"I came in from the toilet when the bell rang and these two birds was telling
Sharon they was wounded veterans selling magazine subscriptions," Paul said.
"I looked at the skinny jasper and said, 'Who'd you fight for, North or South?'
He put a rod on me and they shoved their way in. No warrant, no nothing."

Peter asked Sharon if she was all right. She looked up at him blankly and
nodded. Her face was colorless.

"Desperate times call for desperate measures." Hoover's tone was unusually
mild. "The local authorities can't be depended on in matters of national security.

Your father neglected to mention he had this stuck down in his shorts. He just wasn't as quick on the draw." He dragged Paul's converted air pistol off the radio.

"He only uses it on vermin. I don't think it would look very impressive in the display case outside your office."

"Shut up, you. Nobody said you could talk." The gaunt man shifted his plug to the opposite cheek.

"I'm considering adding carrying a concealed weapon to the other charges we have against him."

Paul said, "They searched Sharon too. When they was sure she didn't have a bowie knife in her garter, the bashful one went out to fetch the boss."

"Yes. I've heard that's how they handle things when he's in the field."

A light exploded inside his head. Sharon shrieked. He staggered, spread his feet, and caught his balance. The gaunt one had struck him on the temple with the flat of a horned hand.

"Some folks just don't listen."

"Special Agent Vasco, these are Special Agents John Craidlaw and Merle Farmer. Farmer fired the bullet that killed Pretty Boy Floyd."

"I never laid claim to that. We all of us hit him and none to graze."

"I admire your modesty, but I was making a point. Craidlaw broke up a Fifth Column cell in Cincinnati from inside. They are not men to play games with."

Peter knew the story behind the overage man then, and considered him the more dangerous and unpredictable of the two. During the Depression, the freshly armed attorneys and CPAs who populated the FBI had proven no match for marauding bands of Midwestern outlaws. Without fanfare, the Director had recruited a number of former rural lawmen and Texas Rangers who'd been tested against an earlier breed of badman, but one every bit as ruthless. "Hoover's Cowboys" operated outside Justice Department regulations, vigilantes with badges who answered to no one but their employer. They were whispered of throughout the Bureau, but after ten years they had yet to draw a line of notice from the press.

"They made me leave that message," Sharon said. "I'm sorry, Peter."

"It was a request. Were any threats made?"

"You don't need to with that goon on a leash," Paul said.

Merle Farmer's long bony fingers rested on the yellow handle of a revolver stuck under his belt where his suit coat opened. He pursed his lips, caving in his cheeks, found no place to spit, and swallowed his plug. The red bow tie dipped down and up like a bobber.

"It's all right, Sharon." Peter asked Hoover if he could sit.

"I never said you had to stand."

He lowered himself into a platform rocker upholstered in a tropical print. Craidlaw and Farmer remained on their feet.

Hoover reached inside his coat and snapped open a letter Peter recognized. "Forgive me if I don't offer sympathy for your faltering literary career. It's difficult to break into print just now. My own book suffered because paper shortages couldn't keep up with the demand."

He didn't respond to that. His superior in Division Four had grumbled that everyone in a clerical position had been forced to purchase a copy of *Persons in Hiding* in 1938. "I didn't expect you this early. You must have caught an express train."

"Private aircraft. We stopped in Charleston to pick up Agent Farmer. He's police chief in a small town near there. I returned him to active duty."

Paul said, "I guess we're real desperate characters."

Hoover ignored him. He hadn't taken his eyes off Peter. "I warned you about the penalties of treason. This letter is evidence you've been sharing sensitive material with someone outside the Bureau."

"All it says is I submitted a work of fiction for publication."

"Capone's memories aren't fiction."

"The major events of his life are in public domain. I fleshed them out with invented dialogue and description. It's called literary license."

"You're stating for the record that none of the information you shared with this man Perkins is confidential to the FBI."

"I am."

"You're compounding your crime by giving a false statement to federal agents."

"You'll have to prove that."

"It says right here that Capone denies complicity in the St. Valentine's Day Massacre. You got that preposterous notion directly from him."

"Perkins agrees it's preposterous. I should change it before I try another publisher."

"Where is the manuscript?"

"In a safe place."

The red spots showed on the Director's cheeks, as bright as a rash. He fought them back with an effort of will. "Agent Vasco. Peter. You've drawn your father and his lady friend into a mess you made yourself. Even if you don't care what happens to you, have you given them any consideration at all? At the very least they'll lose their American citizenship. The result is deportation, and since we're at war, they will be placed in detention until the sea lanes are clear of enemy activity."

"Deported where?" Sharon asked. "I was born in New Jersey."

"There will be ample time to sort that out while you're in Leavenworth. I'm waiting for an answer to my question."

Peter massaged the spot where Farmer had struck him. It wasn't hurting now, but he was afraid his head would start shaking uncontrollably if he didn't brace it somehow. "The assignment is dead. You said yourself you couldn't convict anyone important based on the material. All it ever meant was some sensational publicity and funding from Congress, but it's not even good for that. Capone isn't even entertainment anymore. His name won't sell books."

"The assignment is dead," Hoover agreed. "You will be, too, if I have to hunt up that manuscript to compare to the version in the classified files. You'd be far better off surrendering it. Surely you know by now there is no place you can hide it, no one you can entrust it to, that I can't find out."

The doorbell rang.

From where Peter sat, he could see the outline of a man in a postman's cap through the curtains on the window in the front door. He was expecting the manuscript back from Perkins any time.

Agent Craidlaw turned his head that direction, then back.

"Just the mail, sir."

Peter spoke up. "I'm not that important, but I will be if you charge me with treason. It will come out that an FBI clerk wrote a novel and you tried to present it as fact just to grab headlines. You'll be a joke and so will the FBI."

The room was a still life. In the silence the mail slot in the front door creaked open and something substantial scraped the edges and thumped to the floor.

"You're absolutely certain of your course? I dislike seeing anyone discharging all his options because of misguided principle. Even a traitor."

"I'm no traitor. You of all people should know one when you see one."

Hoover sat motionless for thirty seconds. Then he rose and looked down at Peter. "This will follow you. Good luck finding employment with a black mark against you in your file."

Peter said nothing. Craidlaw went ahead of the Director to open the door. It bumped against the pile of mail on the floor and Farmer stooped to pick up the bundle. He sorted through letters and circulars and looked at the thick brown envelope big enough to contain a hundred typed pages.

"Sears, Roebuck fall catalogue," he said, placing the pile on the table beside the door. "We're still sweatin' like pigs and they're peddling wool drawers."

The three left without another word. After a moment Peter got up and opened the door to make sure they were gone.

"I'm terribly sorry." He closed the door. "I should've known he'd use you to apply the most pressure."

Paul stayed seated. He got a pack of cigarettes from his shirt pocket. "Everybody makes mistakes. Mr. Capone should-a paid his taxes. But you got off a damn sight easier. They came here measuring you for a rope and left giving you a *F* in deportment and behavior."

Sharon said, "It's much worse than that. What will he do to live?"

"I can use a partner at Sunrise Charters." He struck a match.

"You've barely got business enough for one," Peter said. "I'm enlisting in the army."

She said, "You can't. Your file."

"Pietro Bascana doesn't have one. That's the real family name, right? You didn't lie about that."

Paul lit the cigarette and smiled. "I only lie about the little things."

"But won't you need some sort of proof? A birth certificate or something?"

"A warm body, that's all he needs."

"She might be right." Peter felt a grin coming on. It had just begun to sink in that it was over. "What about it, Dad?"

"I got connections. Don't you worry about that."

When the package arrived from New York the next day, Sharon spoke directly to Peter at the Sea Breeze and he came to get it. Paul was at the marina. She watched his son light the little gas fireplace in the parlor.

"I'm surprised it works," she said. "I haven't used it since I moved in. Are you sure this is what you want to do?"

"I'm not doing anything Hoover hasn't already done. You should see the size of the incinerator behind the Justice Department Building." He opened the envelope and drew out the manuscript. There was no communication inside. "He won't stop looking for the only copy until he finds it. This way he'll stay too busy to focus on me." He burned the envelope first. A bright yellow streamer seized it and closed it into a black fist.

"Do you believe that?"

"No. But I'll enjoy picturing the look on his face every time a promising lead blows up in it." He fed Al Capone's confessions to the flames page by page.

THIRTY-SIX

THE SUMMER OF 1944 WAS ALWAYS THERE, LIKE THE WAR AND RATIONING. The sun was stationary, the sea stale, the merchants who took numbers and sacked groceries moved slowly and doled out pleasantries as if they needed to be conserved, like tires and fresh eggs. Paul and Sharon fought over little things, their tempers in short supply also, and some nights Paul slept at the marina, but neither held a grudge long and they always made up without saying anything about the argument that had led to their separation. Peter had never known a long-term relationship between a man and woman to be any different.

Autumn came without leaves changing, without a snap in the air, without raking or hayrides or apple cider or the smell of burning foliage; without any notice at all, until gradually the heat subsided to an even seventy. Rain came frequently but without the suddenness of summer downpours. The first of the upper-middle-class tourists arrived in late-model Packards and Oldsmobiles (the latest being 1942, before Detroit retooled for defense), launched speedboats, and stretched out on blankets on the beach. The St. Louis Cardinals defeated the St. Louis Browns in what radio announcers called the Streetcar Series, four games to two. Stan Musial hit successfully three times in Game 4, propelling the Cardinals to a 5-0 lead. A Browns rally came smash up against a spectacular double play by Marty Marion, playing shortstop. Paul won forty dollars off the proprietor of a bait-and-tackle shop, disappeared for three days, and showed up at Sharon's house drunk, with a double armload of canned beef. She forgave him over the feast that followed.

Peter signed up for the infantry as Pietro Bascano—the birth certificate looked genuine, yellowed a little and worn in the creases—passed his physical, and was told to expect his call-up anytime. Meanwhile he closed out his account at the Everglade State Bank before the financial division in Washington could do it for him, deposited the remainder of his advance in a competing bank, and drew from it to pay his share of the household expenses. He slept on the couch, cut the grass, and helped with the other chores. Some days he worked as a deckhand aboard Paul's boat, a job that mainly involved keeping the pilot and his customer supplied with beer. Once when they were out together alone, Peter sat in the stern chair with a heavy rod and something struck the lure with a slam that made him think they'd hit something in the water, but by the time Paul buckled the harness securing him to the chair, the fish had thrown the hook.

"Too bad, son. Landing a monster marlin like that could-a put you on the cover of *Fish and Game*."

"Wouldn't Hoover love that."

In the evenings, Paul, Sharon, and Peter went to the movies or stayed home and listened to the radio. The airwaves were filled with war news. Hitler's own officers had tried to assassinate him and failed. U.S. Marines captured the island of Guam. Japan's Premier Hideki Tojo resigned along with his cabinet. Captive Jews mounted an unsuccessful uprising against the Nazis occupying Warsaw. A second Battle of Berlin began with German V-2 rockets raining on London. A French general named DeGaulle liberated Paris. Churchill and Roosevelt met in Quebec to discuss the conduct of the rest of the war, which Lowell Thomas predicted would be a matter of weeks. FDR won a fourth term in November, with Harry S. Truman installed as his vice president.

"You were right, Dad," Peter said. "It'll be finished by Christmas. If I ever get over there they'll take away my rifle and hand me a mop."

Sharon said, "A mop is good. Nobody ever got killed swinging one."

"I ain't so sure about Chicago," Paul said.

"We agreed not to talk about that ever again."

"I forgot."

In December, with the visitors coming in from Fifth Avenue and Lake Shore Drive and steaming down the coast in oceangoing yachts, Peter helped Sharon decorate a fat Douglas fir (and polish a menorah), in shirtsleeves with all the windows open and Bing Crosby singing "Silent Night" on the radio. An announcer broke in. The German Army, under a heavy cloud cover that grounded the Royal Air Force and U.S. aviators, launched a surprise counterassault along a sixty-mile front in the Ardennes Woods and began pushing the Allies back toward the western border. The convex shape of the advancing line of tanks and infantry persuaded Churchill to refer to this new action as the Battle of the Bulge.

The reports were confusing: The British and Americans were holding their position; they were in full rout with the Nazis in hot pursuit; the Russians were slashing at the enemy's flanks; all leaves were canceled as troops from three nations prepared to prevent Hitler from retaking Paris. Peter tried to call the recruitment center, but all lines were jammed. He gave up after a half hour. "They're sure to call now," he said. "They need all the reinforcements they can get."

Paul jiggled the beer in the bottom of his can. "That's six weeks of basic. By then either Jerry'll-a shot his wad or they'll be cooking wiener schnitzel in Buckingham Palace."

Christmas morning, with the crisis still on, the three exchanged presents. Peter gave his father a heavy brass fishing reel he'd ordered from Abercrombie & Fitch.

Paul turned the crank: it went tick-tick-tick. "You could-a bought me a tie. You don't need to be spending so much."

"Consider it a gift from J. Edgar Hoover." He handed Sharon a small package wrapped in tissue. It was a collection of Victorian poetry in a supple leather binding. "I'm afraid it's not very revolutionary, but I thought of you when I saw it in the secondhand shop. I'm sorry it isn't something grand. I know so little about what you like."

"You know more than you think. I adore it. Paul?"

He was still playing with the reel. "That red one there, in back."

"How did I fall for someone so lazy?"

Peter stooped and retrieved the narrow flat packet. He tore away the wrapping and lifted the lid off a box containing a Rosary carved from blond wood, with a crucifix attached fashioned from the same material.

"It was your mother's," Paul said. "I gave it to her as a wedding present. It's cypress. My grandfather whittled it. He had plenty of time. He was a rotten fisherman."

He remembered it. Maureen Vasco had never failed to carry it to Mass. It rattled as it straightened, darkened and lightened in the sun as it dangled from his fingers. It carried a faint scent of sandalwood he associated with his mother.

"Are you sure you want to give it to me? You don't have much to remember her by."

"She wanted you to have it. You and me got in a fight after the funeral so I never got around to it. Anyway, I don't need a string-a beads to remind me."

"Thank you, Dad."

"You ain't gonna start blubbering, are you?"

"Paul."

"Yeah, yeah. Ain't you forgetting something?"

Sharon shook her head, flicking her eyes Peter's way.

"You poked it out-a sight behind the couch. I seen you."

She sighed, drew an oblong package out into the open, and handed it to Peter. "I was embarrassed after what your father said about giving him a tie." He undid the ribbon, spread the paper, and laughed when he saw a blue-and-yellow necktie.

"I had a speech all ready about your neck getting cold without the collar," she said. "The man in the men's store said it's an exact copy of the one FDR wore to his inauguration."

"Which one? He's been around longer'n Andy Hardy."

"I love it." Peter slung it around his neck and kissed her on the cheek.

On the day after Christmas, ten days after it began, the German push collapsed. The sun came out, there was no Luftwaffe left to protect the ground troops from enemy air strikes, and the Panzers were running out of fuel. Whole battalions surrendered. That afternoon, while Paul was at Sunrise, a telegram came to the house ordering PFC Pietro Bascano to report to duty in Miami the following morning. Sharon cried.

He couldn't get away without another emergency food package. The marina was on the way to the station. He got off the streetcar and carried the sack and his valise to the pier where his father stood to his waist in water, painting a new name on the fantail of his boat. When he peeled away the stencil, it read MAGGIE.

"How does Sharon feel about it?" Peter asked.

Paul looked up, saw the suitcase. "It was her idea from the start. Off to town, looks like."

"That's right."

"Got everything you need?"

He nodded. "The army will supply the rest."

"I wouldn't worry about 'em handing you a mop just yet. Them krauts don't know when they're licked." He put his bucket and brush on the pier and hoisted himself up onto it, streaming water from his soaked shorts.

"What happened to your swimsuit?"

"Don't need one. I got a boat."

Father and son stood facing each other on the pier.

Paul spoke first. "You ought-a drop in on him while you're in Miami."

"Kyril?"

"Hell, no. That commie?"

"Dad."

"You know who I was talking about."

"What would I say to him?"

"Try good-bye. I don't know what else there'd be."

"A wise man once told me you can't let a cut stay open. It has to be stitched up."

"I was talking about that girl."

"It still applies."

There was another stretch of not talking. Then they embraced. The moment was better than before, but it would never be less than awkward.

HENRY, THE OLD MAN AT THE TOLL GATE, GRINNED. "HEY, GOING CASUAL. New wheels?"

"It's rented." He'd drawn a five-year-old Chevy that refused to shift into third gear without taking the stick in both hands and swinging for the bleachers. He missed the dependable Model T. He held out a dime.

"Don't insult me. I was starting to think they'd kicked you up to the Vatican."

"I had some family business up north. Have you heard any news about Mr. Capone?"

"He's up, he's down, he's up again. His doc came through about an hour ago."

"Nothing serious, I hope."

"Naw. You kidding? You know anything about germs?"

"Not very much."

"My nephew brought a book home from school. They're too small to see."

"I've heard that."

"Any little bug that hopes to get the Big Fellow better bring along the whole North Side." He raised the barricade.

It was a beautiful day. Whitecaps alone separated the bay from blue sky and there were more boats out than he'd ever seen, more than he suspected had been out of mothballs since before Pearl Harbor. Clouds of seagulls followed them looking for handouts. The wind batted the side of the car and he felt as if he were driving directly across the surface of the ocean. Blasphemous thought: Were He to return to Galilee today, would Jesus walk or drive?

The freckle-faced guard at the gate recognized him after a moment and swung it open. He crunched up the driveway for the first time in six months and coasted to a stop behind a gunmetal-gray Cadillac with medical plates.

At the door he hesitated before knocking. What if Brownie answered? He knocked. Danny Coughlin opened the door. He wore a green silk sports shirt with a square tail outside plaid shorts, sandals on his large bare feet. A tall misty glass beaded in his fist. He narrowed his eyes, then broke out in a leer. Vasco realized at that moment that he had never liked Danny.

"Jesus. How long's it been?"

"Long. I had some personal things to take care of. How is Mr. Capone?"

"He had a stroke."

This wasn't Danny, who turned away to look at Mae Capone standing in the middle of the living room. She had on a blue dress with a knee-length hem and her hair was tied back in a ponytail, a way Vasco had never seen it. Her face was shiny. The air conditioner was off and the ceiling fan seemed to be moving the same old air around in a continuous cycle. Her hands were folded in front of her waist. "Hello, Father. We'd about given up on you."

"Said he had some personal things." Danny leaned a little on the *personal*. Vasco thought anyone would be a fool not to have some inkling of what had been going on even if the man hadn't told what he'd seen.

Mae made a slight gesture. Danny stepped aside to let him in, closed the door, and went outside to the patio, placing his feet carefully. Vasco moved closer to Mae.

"Rose went out to bring him sandwiches and found him floating on his back in the pool," she said. "Al swims like a demon whenever he's in the water; it's the only exercise he gets. He never floats. She called out to him, and when he didn't answer she got Brownie. He dragged him out of the pool and carried him upstairs. He's conscious now, talking. Dr. Phillips said it was lucky he didn't turn over onto his face. He thinks it was a mild stroke, but he's sent for a nurse to stay with him. Until he's out of danger, he says."

"Mr. Capone's a strong man."

"That's what everyone says. If you hear it often enough it gets so it doesn't mean anything."

"It's true, though."

"You're talking about what happened the last time you were here. That's the last anyone will ever see of the old Scarface Al. He'll never be able to manage anything like it again."

"I'm relieved. It was frightening."

"What did you expect?" She was angry suddenly. "Why do you think I attend Mass three times a week? Soup kitchens and a big smile won't save him from hell."

"One thing will."

"He'll never apologize for the life he's lived." The anger was gone. "He asks for you all the time. Where were you?"

"I've been staying with my father in Fort Lauderdale. I'm leaving the priesthood."

"Is it because of Rose?"

"No."

"I won't ask any more questions. In the first place I don't judge people, and in the second I have problems of my own. She hasn't said anything. No one has, and I don't know who knows anything or what they know. It's a house of secrets. But I'm used to that."

"I wasn't meant to be a priest."

"You're too young to know what you were meant for. Al was two years younger than you when he took the path he took. You can see how that turned out."

"In a way, you've made my point," he said. "I want you to know, the Seal of the Confessional is eternal. I can't be released from it no matter what."

"Nothing's eternal in this world. Only in the next." She glanced toward the stairs. "Please don't leave without seeing him. The doctor won't be with him much longer. Rose is in the kitchen if you'd like to talk with her."

"Thank you."

She unfolded her hands and held one out. "I'm glad you came, Fath—Peter. I think you may have added time to his life."

He took it. "If what you said is true, I may have to answer for that."

"We all have to answer for something. God made sin, don't forget." She left him and climbed the stairs.

Rose was wiping and putting away dishes when he went into the kitchen. Brownie was chopping vegetables at the counter. When he saw Vasco his big knife bit into the wooden cutting board with a blow like an axe. After a second's pause he resumed with machine-gun rhythm, his hand a brown blur. Rose wiped her hands and hung the towel on a rod. She looked crisp and efficient in her black-and-white uniform. Her face showed no surprise at his entrance; it might have been twenty-four hours since his last visit.

"You lost weight," she said. "Got yourself some color."

"I've been doing a lot of honest work. You look very nice." She did. He'd forgotten how staggeringly pretty she was.

"Got yourself all healed."

He glanced at Brownie, but the big man seemed engrossed in his chore. He touched the bump on the bridge of his nose. "A little the worse for wear. My father says it adds character."

"Folks never say that when something good happens. You heard about Mr. Al?"

He nodded. "Can we go for a walk?"

"I'm working."

"Mrs. Capone said we could talk. She suggested it."

She thought. Then she untied her lacy apron and hung it beside the dish towel.

They passed Danny sitting at the table with the umbrella on the far side of the pool, smoking a cigarette and drinking from his glass and looking out across the bay. A patrolling bodyguard strolled behind the two-story cabana, his pistol out of sight under a sport coat in the moderate heat of December. Vasco and Rose stepped around the wooden bench, where all the glass shattered during target practice had been swept up, and descended the shallow slope to the beach, Vasco holding her hand in support. Her palm felt warm and a little moist. At the bottom she took off her shoes and carried them as they walked along the shore.

"You still pretending?" she asked.

"Right now I'm pretending I'm a priest who left the Church. It never ends really."

"What are you going to pretend to be next?"

"A soldier. I guess I'll know whether it's real or not the first time I face enemy fire."

She laughed. "Well, you done did *that*."

"Has Brownie given you a hard time?"

"He knows better. I don't need no bodyguards, like Mr. Al."

"What *do* you need, Rose?"

"Not a thing, now I'm engaged."

He stopped and turned to face her. The wind lifted his hair. "Not to Brownie."

"Jesus, no!" She laughed again, the man's laugh now, loud and deep.

"Maurice?" He could think of no one else. He'd seen her with her people one night and had thought he knew everything about her. He knew nothing.

"Maurice is more Chester's type."

"Chester the bouncer?"

"Opposites attract. You've never met my fiancé. I didn't meet him myself till four months ago. He's in the merchant marines. No segregation there, coloreds and whites swab the deck side by side and sleep next to each other in hammocks. A lot of things are going to be different when this war ends. He's in the Bay of Japan now. We'll be married when he gets out."

"You're worried about him, of course."

She nodded, fixed him with her mahogany-colored eyes. "I'll worry about you, too. Write us a V-Mail when you can. Send it to Mrs. Capone."

"I will. I'm happy for you, Rose."

"Me, too, for you. Once you get through pretending to be this and that." She glanced toward the house, up and down the beach, out to sea, where the people under sail were no bigger than gnats. Then she took his face in both hands and kissed him hard enough to bruise.

He said good-bye to her at poolside, where the umbrella table was vacant now. He wasn't ready to go inside yet. He sat in Danny's chair and watched an oil tanker waddling low in the water on the horizon. In a little while a chair leg scraped mosaic tile. He turned to see Sonny Capone seating himself. Sonny wore a white open-necked shirt with an orange scarf tied around his throat, earpiece in place. He looked heavier in the face now and more like his father than ever. More than Vasco did. *My brother.* He knew now why he was drawn to him.

"Long time no see," Sonny said. "Mother told me your plans. When she said you were here, I was afraid it was for Last Rites."

"Did you talk to him?"

He nodded. "He's weak, but you couldn't knock that smile off his face with a naval gun. He said he wasn't born in Brooklyn Harbor to drown in a wading pool in Miami."

"I always admired his sense of humor."

"I wouldn't count him out just yet."

"I'm not. I only spoke in past tense because I'm leaving. I got my orders to-day."

"I wish it was me. Every day I watch those planes taking off from the air depot and I wish I was on one. Or I think I do." He touched the beautiful curve of his upper lip. Vasco hadn't inherited that feature. "I know what it's like," he said. "Not being sure what it is you want."

"I know what I don't want. Maybe that's a start."

"I don't even know that. I know what everybody else doesn't want for me. I've known it all my life, but it isn't the same thing. You're the lucky one."

Vasco watched him closely. The sun was going down fast, as it did at sea level, and Sonny's features were losing their shape. He wondered if he suspected. He was sure Mae didn't, as sharp-eyed as she was; but she didn't share Al's blood, his talent for Machiavellian thought. Sonny couldn't bluff; but poker wasn't life.

"Well, I've managed to bore myself. I can say that, because I'm not as polite as you." He pushed back his chair and got up. "Ruth and the girls are waiting supper. Will I see you again?"

"I don't know when. I'm not sure if I'll get leave before I ship out. If I ship out. With my luck I'll wind up taking dictation at Fort Benning. I test high in stenography." He rose and shook his hand.

"Good luck."

"You, too."

Sonny turned, squared his shoulders, and trotted off toward the house. Vasco watched him go, with an empty feeling of having been part of something that had been handled inadequately on both sides.

He waited a minute before going inside, to give Sonny time to leave. There was nothing more awkward than saying good-bye twice. The lamps were on in the living room. Mae came to the bottom of the stairs as he was closing the French doors.

"The doctor just left. The nurse is up there now. Al won't let her give him a sedative until he's seen you."

He thanked her and started upstairs. She touched his arm.

"I didn't tell him you're leaving the priesthood. Please don't say anything about it. I'll tell him when he's stronger."

"Of course, if that's how you want it."

"I do."

The bedroom was surprisingly spare after Mae's elaborate lace-curtain Irish decor on the ground floor. It was just twice as large as his old cell in the rectory and its furnishings differed from it only by the presence of electric lamps and a second twin bed. Capone sat propped up against pillows in the one by the window, where a horse-faced nurse in a starched uniform sat on a straight chair reading a paperbound book with a pirate on the cover. The air was close, with a sickroom smell of medicine and rubbing alcohol.

"Padre! They tell me I see things sometimes that aren't there. I was beginning to think you was one of them. Beat it, sister. We got business to discuss."

Business?

The nurse drew in breath sharply. Vasco gave her a smile he hoped was kindly. She got up, smoothing her skirt, and left carrying her book. The door closed gently.

"Looks just like Seabiscuit, don't she? I guess all the cute ones are overseas looking after the boys. Take a load off."

He sat in the chair the nurse had vacated. Capone wore yellow silk pajamas with his initials embroidered on the breast pocket. He had a satin quilted bedspread pulled up to his waist and his hands rested on it. They looked bloated, like rubber gloves filled with water. He'd continued to take on flesh and now he was retaining fluid; his face looked fatter than it did in old photographs and the skin was pallid beneath the natural pigmentation. But the lips were still gracefully curved, the smile as broad as the bay doors on a beer warehouse. "Too hot for the collar?"

"I've been on a leave of absence. I just got back to town today."

For the first time he found himself unable to look the man in the eye; and he was telling the truth, so far as he'd gone. He looked at the forest of bottles on the night table that separated the beds, some with eyedroppers; a spoon with brown liquid congealed in the bowl; a heavy volume in a tattered beige jacket with Capone's reading glasses folded on top: Emil Ludwig's *Napoleon*.

The sick man followed his gaze. "Yeah. I read it the first time in the joint, not that I learned anything. Turns out we made entirely different mistakes. The only thing we had in common was we both got fat. That and a fair knowledge of how to use artillery."

"You said something about business."

The thick brows drew together, but not in anger. He appeared troubled. "I wanted you to hear it from me, before my brain gets to where it don't know what my tongue's up to. When the time comes to pray me across, I want somebody who's had a shitload of experience at it. It don't reflect on you, but when I was your age I made some bad decisions I still regret. I'm putting Mae to work on the bishop over at Blessed Sacrament. He's got one foot in the grave himself, so I figure he's got the inside track. I'm a special case, and I need the extra ammunition if I'm not going to wake up with a hot foot every day for the rest of eternity."

It struck him then—for the first time, incredibly, after the medical reports he'd read and the evidence of his own experience during Capone's lapses—that Al Capone would die, and die soon; not by the angry hand of an enemy or of organized justice, but for something he'd done as a lusty sixteen-year-old. It could have happened to anyone. It could not even be called divine retribution, because at the time the poison was planted he was nothing more than a young tough living in a part of the world that bred them like Holland bred tulips.

Capone misinterpreted his silence.

"It ain't you, Padre. Well, it is, but not the way you think. If I was friends with that sour son of a bitch Phillips, I wouldn't let him near me with his needles. You can slip up when you like a guy."

"I'm not offended, Al." It was the first time he'd called him that. That impossibly intimate Christian name sprang to his lips without thought. "It will take more than just experience to spare you the flames."

"Fuck repentance. I'd do some things different, sure, but I ain't sorry for what I am or how I got to be me. I don't expect anybody who wasn't there to understand."

"Times were different."

"Not so's you'd notice. What was Chicago then, it's Washington now. You know, some people say FDR knew about Pearl Harbor before it happened."

"He has powerful enemies."

"Who doesn't? That's one crip I'd like to meet. I think I could've made a deal with him. That sourpuss Herbert Hoover had it in for me ever since a few of my boys kept him awake blowing off steam here in town. I—" He stopped himself, his brow darkening.

"I shouldn't've said nothing about crips. How's your mother?"

He wet his lips. "Al, she died."

His eyes went wide, then shifted. "Yeah. I forgot for a minute. I used to keep whole columns of figures in my head: inventories, who owed who and how much. Now I can't remember when I went to the can last. But you're wrong about whipping the devil. I figure when the time comes I can work out a deal with God. Didn't He shoot craps with Old Nick over who got Job?"

"The holy scriptures don't say anything about craps."

"I could be wrong. Maybe it was solitaire."

He stared at Capone. Who else but his own father could have come to the same conclusion about God and the devil? But Vasco didn't believe it anymore. They were each and separate, pulling in opposite directions with equal strength. In that one area he knew more than the man in the bed.

"Yeah." Capone sounded groggy. "I couldn't get those bastards in Treasury to see eye to eye, but God I can sit down with. He's got a bit of gangster in Him."

The nurse came in without knocking. "You have to leave."

"See how far I slipped, Padre? I can't even win an argument with Seabiscuit in a skirt."

He took Capone's hand. It was limp and clammy. His eyes stung; it must have been the alcohol fumes.

"I may not see you again for a long time."

"Transferred? The hell with that. I'll get the cardinal on the phone."

He had an overwhelming desire to confess. He didn't care if the nurse remained in the room. But Al Capone's face had gone slack, his eyelids were drifting down. His body was producing a sedative fully as strong as the one the nurse was preparing from the bottles on the night table.

NIGHT HAD FALLEN BEHIND OUR LADY OF REDEMPTION. A CICADA MADE A high-pitched noise like an electric drill as he climbed the steps to the front door. He opened it and almost collided with a man coming out. The man stared at him for a full second, then looked away, muttering an apology.

Vasco turned and watched him trotting down the steps. At the end of the short flagstone walk at the bottom he turned right and strode down the street without looking his way. He was out of sight before Vasco placed him. He was the man he'd seen so often in the drugstore in the neighborhood, studying the *Racing Form* at the counter and making calls from the telephone in the booth.

He went inside. Brother Thomas was busy with his carpet sweeper, trundling it over the worn runner between the rows of seats up near the altar end. He looked up, saw Vasco, put his head down quickly, and turned around to chase down lint at the base of the rail.

Vasco had the distinct feeling—the certain knowledge—he'd missed a conference. For months he'd been sure he had eyes on him constantly; until now he hadn't known to whom they belonged. Hoover had assured him he wasn't alone.

It wasn't over. It would never be over. It would not end with Capone's death. As long as he and Hoover lived, there would be eyes on him always.

He didn't bother to confront the novice. He was empty of lies himself, and like a reformed drunk he could no longer tolerate his old weakness in others. He went up the aisle and out the side door and along the barren path worn in the grass to the rectory.

"Father Vasco?" Sergei Kyril rose from behind his desk when Vasco opened the study door without pausing to knock. Nothing about him had changed in six months; in ten. His brush-cut hair might have come straight from the barber's chair and his black soutane hung straight down from his square shoulders like a curtain on a rod. The overhead light was off. The banker's lamp on the desk cast an oval that reflected up onto the planes of his square face.

"I'm barging in uninvited." It didn't sound like an apology even to himself.

"All are welcome here. How is your father?"

"Very ill, I'm afraid."

"I'm sorry to hear that. Have you come to talk about it?"

"I came to confess."

"Very well. Would you prefer the booth?"

"Anywhere is all right."

"Here, then."

"Yes."

Kyril tipped a square palm toward the chair on Vasco's side of the desk. As Vasco shifted a pile of books and rolls of paper to the floor and sat down, the pastor sat down also and pulled the chain switch on the desk lamp. For a moment the room was pitch black. Then ambient light from the streetlamp on the corner sifted between the wooden slats covering the window, casting the room in sepulchral gray. Kyril's voice rumbled smoothly from the darkness on his side of the desk.

"My son, what is your sin?"

ABOUT THE AUTHOR

Loren D. Estleman has won Shamus Awards for detective fiction, Spur Awards for Western fiction, and Western Heritage Awards. The Western Writers of America recently conferred upon Estleman the Owen Wister Award for Lifetime Contribution to Western Literature. He lives with his wife, author Deborah Morgan, in Michigan.

Learn more at www.lorenestleman.com.